"Sara Douglass has the breadth of vision necessary to create sweeping epics and the storyteller's gift that makes readers love her."
—*Locus*

"The dazzling start to a new trilogy . . . Douglass once again combines mythology, fantasy, magic and romance to produce a consistent, well-rounded story full of seriously flawed characters both abhorrently evil and enthrallingly empathetic. Douglass continually surprises, and readers will eagerly await the next books."
—*Publishers Weekly* (starred review) on *Hades' Daughter*

"An Australian treasure comes to America's shores. Sara Douglass makes her mark with this vivid, gritty saga brimming with treachery, action, bravery and dark magic."
—Elizabeth Haydon, author of The Rhapsody Trilogy on *The Wayfarer Redemption*

"With three races, licit and illicit loves, prophecy, fraternal hatred, and enough battles for several campaigns, Douglass has whipped up enough raw material to avoid shortchanging readers throughout her vast undertaking."
—*Booklist* on *Enchanter*

"A stunning tour de force with a full complement of action, mysticism, mystery and magic . . . Sara Douglass is a powerful voice in high fantasy that readers can equate to the likes of Robert Jordan, Marion Zimmer Bradley and Anne McCaffrey." —*Romantic Times,* $4^{1}/_{2}$ stars on *Enchanter*

"Douglass brings to the fore her world-building abilities and storytelling expertise in this satisfying conclusion to a fantasy epic." —*Library Journal* on *Starman*

"A superior adventure fantasy right to the last."
—*Booklist* on *Starman*

"Heartfelt." —*Kirkus Reviews* on *Starman*

TOR BOOKS BY SARA DOUGLASS

The Wayfarer Redemption
Enchanter
Starman
Hades' Daughter
Beyond the Hanging Wall
Threshold

HADES'
DAUGHTER

BOOK ONE OF THE TROY GAME

Sara Douglass

TOR®
fantasy

A TOM DOHERTY ASSOCIATES BOOK
NEW YORK

HADES' DAUGHTER: BOOK ONE OF THE TROY GAME

Maps by Ellisa Mitchell

A Tor Book
Published by Tom Doherty Associates, LLC
175 Fifth Avenue
New York, NY 10010

www.tor.com

Tor® is a registered trademark of Tom Doherty Associates, LLC.

ISBN: 0-765-34442-4

First edition: January 2003
First mass market edition: September 2003

Printed in the United States of America

0 9 8 7 6 5 4 3 2 1

*For Roland C. Greefkes, extraordinary creator
of magical flower gates, with many heartfelt thanks
from Hannah and myself for our own
enchanted protection.*

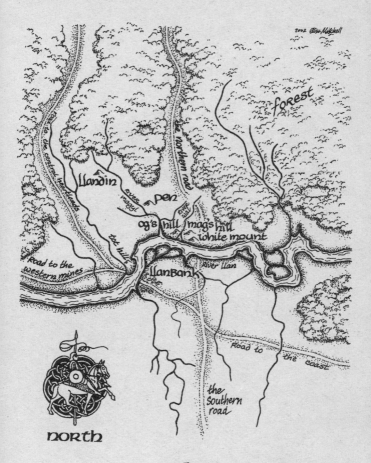

2002 Elisa Mitchell

forest

llandin

river mwg

pen

og's hill mag's hill

track to the central wetlands

the northern road

river llaw

white mount

the hills

road to the
western mines

llanBank

river llan

Road to the coast

the
Southern
road

north

the veiled
hills

Theseus and the Labyrinth

During the late Bronze Age, well over a millennium before the birth of Christ, the Minoan king on Crete held the Athenian king to ransom. Every nine years the Athenian king sent as tribute seven male youths and a like number of female virgins, the cream of Athenian society, to Knossos on Crete. Once on Crete the Athenian youths were fed into the dark heart of the gigantic labyrinth, there to die at the hands of the dreaded Minotaur Asterion, unnatural son of the Minoan king's wife and a bull.

One year the Athenian king sent his own son Theseus as part of the sacrifice. Theseus was determined finally to stop the slaughter, and to this end he was aided by Ariadne, daughter of the Minoan king, half sister to Asterion and Mistress (or High Priestess) of the Labyrinth. Ariadne shared with Theseus the secrets and mysteries of the labyrinth, and taught him the means by which Asterion might be killed. This she did because she loved Theseus.

Theseus entered the labyrinth and, aided by Ariadne's secret magic, bested the tricks of the labyrinth and killed Asterion in combat. Then, accompanied by Ariadne and her younger sister Phaedre, Theseus departed Crete and its shattered labyrinth for his home city of Athens.

THE LATE BRONZE AGE

Prologue: Catastrophe

ONE

THE ISLAND OF NAXOS, EASTERN MEDITERRANEAN

Confused, numbed, her mind refusing to accept what Theseus demanded, Ariadne stumbled in the sand, sinking to her knees with a sound that was half sigh, half sob.

"It is best this way," Theseus said as he had already said a score of times this morning, bending to offer Ariadne his arm. "It is clear to me that you cannot continue with the fleet."

Ariadne managed to gain her feet. She placed one hand on her bulging belly, and stared at her lover with eyes stripped of all the romantic delusion that had consumed her for this past year. "This is your child! How can you abandon it? And *me*?"

Yet even as she asked that question, Ariadne knew the answer. Beyond Theseus lay a stretch of beach, blindingly white in the late morning sun. Where sand met water waited a small boat and its oarsmen. Beyond that small boat, bobbing lazily at anchor in the bay, lay Theseus' flagship, a great oared war vessel.

And in the prow of that ship, her vermilion robes fluttering and pressing against her sweet, lithe body, stood Ariadne's younger sister, Phaedre.

Waiting for *her* lover to return to the ship, and sail her in triumph to Athens.

Theseus carefully masked his face with bland reason.

"Your child is due in but a few days. You cannot give birth at sea—"

"I can! I can!"

"—and thus it is best I leave you here, where the villagers have midwives to assist. It is my decision, Ariadne."

"It is *her* decision!" Ariadne flung a hand toward the moored ship.

"When the baby is born, and you and she recovered, then I will return, and bring you home to Athens."

"You will not," Ariadne whispered. "This is as close to Athens as ever I will achieve. I am the Mistress of the Labyrinth, and we only ever bear daughters—what use have we for sons? But you have no use for daughters. So Phaedre shall be your queen, not I. *She* will give you sons, not I."

He did not reply, lowering his gaze to the sand, and in his discomfort she could read the truth of her words.

"What have I done to deserve this, Theseus?" she asked.

Still he did not reply.

She drew herself up as straight as her pregnancy would allow, squared her shoulders, and tossed her head with some of her old easy arrogance. "What has the *Mistress of the Labyrinth* done to deserve this, my love?"

He lifted his head, and looked her full in the face, and in that movement Ariadne had all the answer she needed.

"Ah," she said softly. "To the betrayer comes the betrayal, eh?" A shadow fell over her face as clouds blew across the sun. "I betrayed my father so you could have your victory. I whispered to you the secrets which allowed you to best the labyrinth and to murder my brother. I betrayed *everything* I stand for as the Mistress. All this I did for you. All this betrayal worked for the blind folly of love."

The clouds suddenly thickened, blanketing the sun, and the beach at Theseus' back turned gray and old.

"The gods told me to abandon you," Theseus said, and Ariadne blanched at the blatant lie. This had nothing to do with the gods, and everything to do with his lusts. "They came to me in a vision, and demanded that I set you here on this island. It is their decision, Ariadne. Not mine."

Ariadne gave a short, bitter laugh. Lie or not, it made no difference to her. "Then I curse the gods along with you, Theseus. If you abandon me at their behest, and that of your new and prettier lover, then they shall share their fate, Theseus. Irrelevance. Decay. Death." Her mouth twisted in hate. *"Catastrophe."*

Above them the clouds roiled, thick and black, and lightning arced down to strike in the low hills of the island.

"What think you, Theseus?" she suddenly yelled, making him flinch. "What think you? *No one can afford to betray the Mistress of the Labyrinth!"*

"No?" he said, meeting her furious eyes evenly. "Are you that sure of your power?"

"Leave me here and you doom your entire world. Throw me aside for my sluttish sister and what you think *her* womb can give you and you and your kind will—"

He hit her cheek, not hard, but enough to snap off the flow of her words. "And who was it showed Phaedre the art of sluttishness, Ariadne?"

Stricken with such cruelty, Ariadne could find no words to answer.

Theseus nodded. "You have served your purpose," he said.

He focused on something behind her, and Ariadne turned her head very slightly.

Villagers were walking slowly down the path to the beach, their eyes cast anxiously at the goddamned skies above them.

"They will care for you and your daughter," Theseus said, and turned to go.

"I have served my purpose, Theseus?" Ariadne said. "You have *no* idea what my purpose is, and whether it is served out . . . or only just beginning. Here. In this sand. In this betrayal."

His shoulders stiffened, and his step hesitated, but then

Theseus was gone, striding down the beach to the waiting boat.

The sky roared, and the clouds opened, drenching Ariadne as she watched her lover desert her.

She turned her face upward, and shook a fist at the sky and the gods laughing merrily behind it.

"*No one* abandons the Mistress of the Labyrinth!" she hissed. "Not you, nor any part of your world!"

She dropped her face. Theseus was in the boat now, standing in its stem, his gaze set toward the ship where awaited Ariadne's sister.

"And not you, nor any part of *your* world, either," she whispered through clenched teeth. "No one abandons me, and thinks that in so doing they can ignore the Game. You think that the Game will protect you."

She hissed, demented with love and betrayal.

"But you forget that it is *I* who controls the Game."

TWO

Death came for Ariadne during the final stages of a labor that had stretched over three grueling, pain-filled days and nights.

She felt the Death Crone's gentle hand on her shoulder as she squatted on her birthing mat, her sweat-drenched face clenched in agony, the village midwives squabbling in a huddle on the far side of the dim, overheated room.

"They have decided to cut the child from you," the Crone said, her voice low and melodious, a comforting counterpoint to her words. "They think that Theseus, not wanting you, will nevertheless be grateful for his child. See, now they hand about knives, trying to decide which would be the sharpest. The fastest."

"No!" Ariadne growled, twisting her head to stare at the Crone who now stood so close to her shoulder. "No. I *will* not."

"You must," said the Crone. "It is your time."

"And I say it is not," Ariadne said, screwing up her face and moaning as another crippling contraction gripped her.

"You must—" the Crone said again, but stopped as Ariadne half turned and gripped the death's claw resting on her shoulder.

"I will make a bargain," Ariadne said. She glanced at the huddle of midwives. They were bent into a close circle, their attention all on the four or five knives they passed between themselves. First this one was held up to catch the flickering light from the single oil lamp in the room, now that, as they assessed each blade's cutting edge for its worth.

Being simple women, untutored in the mysteries, they were unaware that the Death Crone stood so close among them, nor that Ariadne conversed with her.

"A bargain?" said the Crone. "But I want you. You. What could you give me to assuage my grief at leaving you behind?"

"I think we can come to a most singular arrangement," Ariadne said, her words jerking out in her agony. "I can make you the best proposition you've had in aeons."

The Crone was silent a long moment, her bright eyes resting unblinking on Ariadne as the woman twisted and moaned once more.

"I shall want far more than just 'a singular arrangement,' " the Crone said. "Far more. *What* can you give me, Ariadne, Mistress of the Labyrinth?"

The midwives had selected their knife now, and one of them, a woman called Meriam, had drawn out a whetstone and was sharpening the blade with long, deliberate strokes.

The frightful sound of metal against stone grated about the chamber, and Ariadne's eyes glinted.

She spoke, very low and very fast, and the Crone gave

a great gasp and stood back. *"You would go that far?"* she hissed.

"Will you not accept my bargain?" Ariadne said.

"Oh, aye, I accept. But you will destroy yourself, surely, along with—"

"You will have me one day, Crone, but it shall be on my terms, not yours. But, if you want what I offer, then I beg two favors from you."

The Crone laughed shortly. "And I thought you were to be doing all the giving."

"I will need to see Asterion."

"Asterion? The brother you helped murder? You would dare?"

"Aye. I dare. Tell me, is he in Hades' realm?"

"Nay. Hades would not have him. You know this." The Crone paused, her eyes on the midwives who were now slowly rising, their voices murmuring bitterly about the effort this Ariadne put them to. "Very well," said the Crone. "I agree. I can send Asterion to you. And the second favor?"

"Push this child from my body that I may live long enough to play my part in this our arrangement."

"As you wish, Ariadne. But do not fail in your part of our agreement. I would be most disappointed should you—"

"I will not fail. Now, push this child from me . . . ah!"

The midwives stepped close to the straining woman on the birthing mat, Meriam at their fore, a large knife in her hand.

But as Meriam leaned down to push Ariadne to her back, the better to expose her huge belly to the knife, Ariadne screamed, and there was a rush of bloodstained fluid between her legs, and then the baby, hitherto unshiftable, slithered free.

Meriam stopped dead, her mouth hanging open.

Ariadne had sunk to her haunches, and now she looked up from her daughter kicking feebly between her legs to the gaggle of midwives.

"You may be sure that I will repay you well for your aid," she said.

ARIADNE RESTED DURING THAT DAY, AND WHEN the sun settled below the horizon, she dismissed the woman who sat with her, saying that she wished to be alone during the night with her daughter.

Once the woman had gone, Ariadne put her daughter to her breast and fed her, and then rocked her gently and sung to her softly, so that she would sleep through the coming hours.

As soon as the infant slept soundly, Ariadne placed her in a small oval wicker basket, covered her well with blankets, then placed the basket in a dark corner of the room.

She did not want Asterion to notice the child and perhaps to maim or murder her in his ill humor.

Once her daughter was attended to, Ariadne washed herself carefully, wincing at the deep hurt that still assailed her body, then reached into the chest of her clothes that Theseus had caused to be tossed onto the beach. She drew forth a deep red flounced skirt that she bound as tightly as she could about her still-thickened and soft belly, then slipped her arms into a golden jacket that she tied loosely about her waist, leaving it unbuttoned so that her full breasts remained exposed.

Having attended her body, Ariadne now carefully painted her face. She powdered her face to a smooth, rich cream mask, then lined her eyes with black and her mouth with a vivid red that matched her skirt. When that was done, Ariadne dressed her hair. For the finest effect she needed a maid to do it for her, but there was no one to help, and so she did the best she could, finally managing to bind and braid her glossy black tresses into an elaborate design that cascaded from the crown of her head to the nape of her neck.

She was still studying her face and hair in her handheld mirror when she felt the shift in the air behind her.

Ariadne put down the mirror with deliberate slowness, calmly rose from her stool, and turned to face her murdered half brother Asterion.

For an instant she thought him more shadow than substance, but then he took a single step forward, and she saw that his flesh was solid and real . . . as was his anger.

"You betrayed me," he said in his thick, guttural, familiar voice. "See." He waved a hand down his body. "See what your lover did to me."

She looked, for she owed him this at least.

Theseus' sword had cut into Asterion's body in eight or nine places: across his thickly muscled black throat, his shoulder, his chest, both his flanks, laying open his belly. The wounds were now bloodless lips of flesh, opening and closing as Asterion's chest rose and fell in breath (*and why did he need to breathe at all*, thought Ariadne, *now that he is dead?*), revealing a rope of bowel here, a lung there, the yellowed cord of a tendon elsewhere.

Ariadne swallowed, then very slowly lifted her eyes back to Asterion's magnificent head.

It was undamaged, and for that she was profoundly grateful. The beautiful liquid black eyes still regarded her clearly and steadily from the bold countenance of the bull, and his graceful horns still curved unbroken about his broad brow.

Her eyes softened, and at that he snarled, deliberately vicious, spraying her beautiful face with thick spittle.

"You *betrayed* me!"

She had not flinched. "Aye, I did. I did it for Theseus, for I thought he loved me. I was wrong. Deluded with love, I betrayed you, and for that I am most sorry."

He snorted in laughter, and she turned aside her head very slightly. " 'Most sorry'?" He stepped forward, close enough to run prying fingers over her breasts and her belly. She stiffened at his touch, but did not move away. "You have given birth to his child."

Her eyes flew back to his. "You shall not harm her!"

"Why not?"

"Do not harm her, Asterion. I beg this of you."

He merely wrinkled his black brow in that peculiar manner of his that demonstrated mild curiosity. "And why not? Why not? Why should her death not be *my* vengeance for what you did to me?"

"I will give you vengeance enough, Asterion. For you and for me."

He slid his hand in the waistband of her skirt, jerking her toward him, smiling at the wince on her face. "What nonsense. I am capable enough of taking my vengeance here and now."

Their heads were very close now, her aristocratic beauty almost completely overshadowed by his dark and powerful countenance.

"I want you—" she began.

He smiled, horribly, and his hand drew her yet closer.

"—to teach me your darkcraft."

Surprised, his grip loosened a little.

"You are the only one who has ever learned to manipulate the power in the dark heart of the labyrinth. Now I want you to teach *me* that darkcraft. I will use it to destroy Theseus; I will use it to destroy his entire world. Every place that Theseus lays foot, everything he touches, every part of his world, everything will fall to decay, and death. And yet even that is not all. I will combine your darkcraft with my powers as Mistress of the Labyrinth, Asterion, to free you completely." She paused, using her brief silence for emphasis. "I will combine our powers together, beloved brother, to tear apart the Game once and for all. Never again will it ensnare you. That will be my recompense to you for my stupidity in betraying you to Theseus and my payment to you for giving me the power to tear apart Theseus and all he stands for."

He held her eyes steady, looking for deception. "You would destroy the Game? Free me completely so that I may be reborn into life as I will?"

"Yes! This is something that only I can do, you know that . . . but you must also know I need the use of your darkcraft to do it. Teach it to me, I beg you."

"If you lie—"

"I do not!"

"If you do not destroy the Game—"

"I will!"

He gazed at her, unsure, unwilling to believe her. "If I give to you the darkcraft," he said, "and you misuse it in any manner—to trick me or trap me—then *I* will destroy *you*."

She started to speak, but he hushed her. "I will, for there is one thing else that I shall demand of you, Ariadne, Mistress of the Labyrinth."

"Yes?"

"That in return for teaching you the darkcraft, for opening to you completely the dark heart of the labyrinth, you shall not only destroy the Game forever, but you will allow me to become your ruler. Your lord. Call it what you want, but know that if you ever attempt to betray me again, if you do not destroy the Game completely, I demand that you shall fall to the ground before me, and become my creature entirely."

"Of course!"

His expression did not change. " 'Of course!'? With not even a breath to consider? How quickly you agree."

"I will not betray you again, Asterion. Teach me the darkcraft and I swear—on the life of my daughter!—that I will use it to destroy the Game utterly. It shall never entrap you again."

He nodded, very slowly, holding her eyes the entire time. On the life of her daughter? No Mistress of the Labyrinth ever used the name of her daughter lightly. Yes . . . yes, she was being honest with him.

As honest as Ariadne could be.

He smiled, tight and hard. "Your hatred of Theseus must be great indeed to arrange such dark bargains with first the Crone, and then with me."

She inclined her head. "He thought to cast me aside," she said. "No one does that to the Mistress of the Labyrinth."

"Very well," he said. "I accept. The bargain is concluded." His hand tightened once more in the waistband of her skirt, but this time far more cruelly. "You shall have the darkcraft, but I shall take my pleasure in it. Pain, for the pain you inflicted on me. Pain, to seal the bargain made between us."

He buried his other hand in her elaborately braided hair, and with all the strength of the bull that was his, he lifted her up and hurled her down to the bed.

THAT NIGHT WAS AGONIZINGLY LONG, AND SHE emerged from it barely alive, but at the end of it Ariadne had what she wanted.

TWO DAYS LATER, STIFF, SORE, HER BADLY DAM-aged body protesting at every step, Ariadne made her way into the village's herb garden. In her arms she carried the wicker basket, and in that basket rested her sleeping daughter.

Behind Ariadne two of the village midwives who had attended the birth of her daughter watched uneasily from the shadowed doorway of the house Ariadne had left.

Since her daughter's birth, the midwives—indeed, everyone in the village—had become aware that Ariadne was highly dangerous. Yet they could not clearly define the *why* of that awareness. Ariadne had not said or done anything that could have made the villagers so deeply afraid of her, and yet there seemed to hover about the mother and her newborn child a sense of danger so terrible, so *imminent*, that few people could bear to spend more than a moment or two in her company.

The entire community wanted Ariadne gone. Gone from the village. Gone from the island. Gone so completely that all sense of danger vanished with her. Gone, taking her daughter and her hatred (and neither woman knew which one Ariadne loved and nurtured the more) with her.

Ariadne, although aware of the women and their nervous watchfulness behind her, paid them no heed. She moved step by careful step along the graveled path between the raised beds of fragrant herbs and flowers. The basket that contained her daughter she carried with infinite care, and as she walked, she rocked the basket gently to and fro, singing to her child in a slow, rhythmic, almost hypnotic voice.

She sang no lullaby, but the secret whisperings of the exotic darkcraft that she had so recently learned, twisting it together with her own power as Mistress of the Labyrinth.

Most infants would have woken screaming in nightmare at her dark and twisted song, but Ariadne's daughter slept soundly to its meanderings.

Eventually Ariadne's singing drew to a close, and she halted, gazing on her daughter with great tenderness.

"Your father will die," she said, "as all that he touches will die, and as all that declares its love for him will die, and as all that surrounds him will die. Everything. Everything. *Everything*."

Ariadne raised her head, and looked before her. She had come to a halt before a large shrub that delineated the carefully tended herb garden from the wilds beyond it. The shrub's dense gray-green foliage was broken here and there by large white, open-petaled flowers.

Ariadne reached out a hand and touched very gently one of the flowers.

They trembled at her contact.

AROUND THE AEGEAN, IN THEIR HIDDEN, MYSTERIous places, so also trembled the flower gate sorceries that guarded the entrances to the founding labyrinths of several score of cities.

"SUCH DEAR FLOWERS," SAID ARIADNE. THEN, with an abrupt, savage movement, she twisted the flower free from the shrub.

"Thera," she said, "who shall be the first."

She held the flower in the palm of her hand for a moment, smiling at it with almost as much tenderness as she bestowed on her daughter, and then, resuming her strange, low singing, she wound the flower into the wickerwork of her daughter's basket.

So Ariadne continued, her voice growing stronger, the words she sang darker. Flower after flower she snapped, pausing in her singing only long enough to bestow upon each flower the name of a city in which she knew lurked a labyrinth, a city that depended for its well-being on the labyrinth within its foundations. Eventually, as Ariadne plucked flower after flower from the shrub, her child was surrounded by a ribbon of woven flowers about the top of the basket.

Ariadne's thread. The filament that either saves, or destroys.

WHEN SHE HAD FINISHED, AND HER DARKCRAFT was woven, Ariadne cradled the flowered basket in her arms and smiled at her daughter.

"Soon," she whispered. "Soon, my darling."

She looked back to the shrub. It was denuded of all flowers save one, and at the sight of that remaining flower Ariadne's mouth curled in secret delight.

That labyrinth was particularly well hidden in a city extraordinarily undistinguished, and she doubted Asterion knew of its existence. If it survived its influence would be minimal, her brother would never sense its presence, and it would not serve to hold him.

But it would be enough for her purpose, when it was time.

When she was safe.

When she was strong enough to dare.

THREE

Irrelevance. Decay. Death. Catastrophe. Every place that Theseus lay foot, everything he touched, every part of his world. This was Ariadne's curse.

And with it, in gratitude to Asterion for teaching her the darkcraft, Ariadne did what only she had the power to do.

She unwound the Game—that great and ancient sorcery that underpinned and protected the entire Aegean world.

IT BEGAN NINE DAYS AFTER ARIADNE TWINED THE flowers into the basket that cradled her daughter. Meriam, the midwife who had thought to cut Ariadne open to save her child, was standing in the central village open space, the beach where Theseus had abandoned Ariadne a bare two weeks previously some sixty paces distant to the south. It was dawn, the air chill, only the faintest of pink staining the eastern sky, the birds in their trees chirping quietly to start the day.

Meriam had no thought for the beauty of the beach, the dawn light, or even for the sweet melodies of the birds.

Instead, she stared frowning at the empty wicker basket lying at her feet. Flowers, withered and colorless, still wound about its rim.

"Why didn't she take it with her?" Meriam muttered, then bent to pick up the basket.

In the instant before her fingers touched the basket, one of the flowers slid free from the wickerwork and fell to the earth.

The instant it hit, the chorus of the birds turned from melody to a frightful, fractured screaming.

Instinctively Meriam straightened and looked about her, her heart thudding. Birds rose in chaotic clouds from the trees surrounding the village, milled briefly in the air, then turned to fly north.

Their screams sounded like the shriek of a blade on a whetstone.

Meriam put her hands over her ears and half crouched, panicked, but not knowing what to do.

She wanted to run, but she did not know what to run from, or where to run to.

About her, men, women, and children were stumbling from doorways, pulling clothes about them, shouting in confusion.

Something terrible was about to happen, Meriam knew it, just as certainly as she knew that whatever was going to happen was a result of Ariadne.

"Why?" Meriam whispered. "Why hate us this much?"

Then . . . everything went still. The birds had gone, their panic and their screeching gone with them. The villagers who had tumbled from their beds into the village open place now stood, their voices quiet, looking south over the beach to the calm sea.

It was south. Whatever was so very wrong was *south*.

A dog whined, then another, and Meriam had the thought that the cacophony of the birds was about to be replaced by an equally frightful shrieking of the village dogs.

It never happened.

At the very moment that thought crossed Meriam's mind, there was a blinding flash of light far to the south. The light, first white, then a terrible orange, was reflected both in the thin haze of clouds and in the sea, magnifying its effects a hundredfold.

Meriam, as all who stood transfixed with her, barely had time to gasp before they first felt their eardrums swell and burst, and then were lifted far off their feet by a pressure blast of such magnitude and heat that most were dead before they hit the ground.

Those who were not killed in that initial blast died when

the molten rock rained from the sky or when, just as the sun finally crested the flaming horizon, the first of six successive tidal waves washed over the low-lying lands of Naxos.

By the time the sun had reached its noon peak the Aegean world had turned gray and black. Dense clouds of ash, pulverized rock, deadly gases, and steam had mushroomed twenty miles into the sky and spread over the entire eastern Mediterranean region; thick, choking poisonous ash drifted down to layer corpses and ruins alike with, eventually, two hundred feet of death.

The island of Thera, which sat almost halfway between Crete and Naxos and which contained in its harbor the glorious shining city of Atlantis, had exploded with such force that the entire island—save for a thin, sorry rim of smoking rock—vanished beneath the waves.

In its dying, Thera poisoned every land and every city within four days' sailing.

THERA WAS ONLY THE FIRST, BUT ADMITTEDLY THE most spectacular, step in Ariadne's curse. Thera's eruption not only largely destroyed Naxos, but also the northern coastline of Crete. Tidal waves and the murderous rain of molten rock and ash inundated villages, harbors, and the great founding labyrinth that lay partway between the coast and the city of Knossos, which lay almost two miles inland.

Thera, Naxos, and Crete—as well as a score of smaller islands within reach of either the initial cataclysmic blast or the tidal waves—were devastated. Farther distant, to the north and south in the lands of Greece, Anatolia, the Levant, and Egypt, the effects were not so initially devastating, but crept more secretly upon the peoples of the region.

Crops failed for years afterward, and any man or woman who had breathed too deeply of the ash that continued to trickle out of the sky for months after the initial explosion often succumbed to terrible growths in their lungs in later life. Wells were poisoned, and livestock and children alike sickened and died. People rebelled and overthrew governments and societies and abandoned their gods; in Egypt a man called Moses used the death that rained down from Thera to force the pharaoh to set his people free.

In Athens, Theseus watched as his queen, Phaedre, died in an agonizing childbed, calling out her sister's name. In sorrow, he comforted himself with a young virgin called Helen, before he set off on many wandering adventures about the Aegean looking for his own revenge on the woman who had cursed him.

He never found her, but found everywhere the effects of her curse, and, in his very wanderings, spread the effects of Ariadne's curse farther and farther.

It was why she had not killed him outright.

Having survived Thera's massive destruction, the people of those Aegean cities left discovered, to their horror, that the Game that had protected them for countless generations was failing. The Game, a labyrinthine mystery of great power and sorcery, was used to entrap the evil that was always drawn to communities of wealth and contentment. Without it, cities became increasingly vulnerable to the predations of evil, of wrongdoing, of misfortune, of greed and sloth and hubris and all those mischiefs that haunt success and happiness. Cities fell to invaders from the north and west, or were consumed by earth tremors, or by fire.

Evil incarnate itself walked free. Ariadne's destruction of the Game and of its protective sorcery meant that Asterion was reborn into life to work his malevolence and depravity where and as he pleased.

In vain did the Kingmen of the cities, those men who through birth and training worked the magic of the Game alongside their city's Mistress of the Labyrinth, try to arrest the decline. It was pointless, because the mischief that ate at the Games' powers had been generated by the greatest Mistress of them all, Ariadne, who had controlled the founding Game at Knossos on Crete and who had most apparently found the means to undo all the workings of lesser Mistresses about the Aegean.

And Ariadne could not be found. She could not be stopped, and her mischief (as that of her half brother) could not be arrested.

There was worse. As the lands and cities failed, falling to mischief after mischief, so also the gods failed. Whatever Ariadne had tapped into, it was so powerful that it affected even the gods on their heights.

The cataclysmic explosion of Thera had shattered both the equanimity and the confidence of the gods. It had also seriously depleted their power and thus their means to try to undo what Ariadne had wrought. Thera's beautiful circular harbor had contained a great island—the island within the island—upon which rose the majestic citadel of Atlantis. Center of Aegean culture and supremacy, Atlantis had also contained the ancient and mystical God Well . . . the major source of succor and power for the gods.

Without it, the gods were not only ineffective, but they grew ever more so as each day passed. With the destruction of Thera and Atlantis, Ariadne had dealt a killing blow to the gods at the very start of the unwinding of her curse. At the height of their powers the gods could have stopped her; now they could do little but mouth feeble curses themselves . . . and succumb to the evil that stalked every part of Aegean life.

And so, as the seasons passed, and year turned into year, Ariadne's curse wrapped the Aegean world in its malevolent web. There were meager moments of glory, an occasional hour of laughter, but they became increasingly rare, and they passed entirely that day that the Trojan prince called Paris, enamored of the beautiful wife of the Spartan king Menelaus, stole her back to his home city of Troy.

Menelaus' wife was Helen, the girl who had comforted Theseus when Phaedre had died, and who had given him her virginity. Touched by Theseus, Helen was herself a walking curse. In her name all of Greece embarked upon a exhausting ten-year siege of Troy that ensnarled not only the Greeks and the Trojans, but the gods themselves. Weakened by the continuing effects of Thera's eruption as well as by the progressively worsening deterioration of the Game, Troy's collapse dealt the final death blow to the ancient Aegean gods.

Many died amid Troy's smoking ruins, others crept away to agonizing, lonely deaths amid the rocky peaks of Olympus. A few managed to keep drawing breath: Aphrodite, who secured Aeneas' escape from Troy, along with the magical kingship bands of the city; Hera, who, weeping, swore a revenge for Ariadne's destruction of all that was lovely; Poseidon, who crept away to his watery haven and took no further part in the lives of mortals; and Hades, who, alone among the gods, found a measure of strength within all the death.

Within a generation or two of Troy's destruction, Aphrodite had gone, murdered by her sorrow, and Poseidon was nothing more than a faint blue shadow moving slowly within the ocean's depths.

Hades kept to his Underworld, wanting no more to do with the mortal realm.

Only Hera, crippled, dying a little more each day, was left to try to undo what Ariadne had wrought.

PART ONE

Frank Bentley hurried along the railway platform at Waterloo station, scanning the few remaining people standing about. The train from Dover must have come in a half hour ago at least; had he waited? Or grown impatient and decided to seek out a hotel for the night?

He slowed his steps, looking more carefully, wishing he had more than just a casual description to guide him.

His eye suddenly caught sight of a tall man, swathed against the evening chill in a greatcoat over his uniform, the brim of his military cap pulled low over his eyes, the glow of a cigarette in one hand, a suitcase and a bulging satchel huddled by his legs.

It must be him . . . there was no one else. Bentley walked up and smiled a little too brightly.

"Major Skelton?

The man flicked his cigarette to the pavement, grinding it out under his shoe. "Yeah." He held out his hand. "Jack Skelton."

Bentley introduced himself, apologizing for his delay, then picked up the suitcase as Skelton took the satchel. "My motor's parked a couple of streets away. Bit of a walk, I'm afraid."

"I'll be glad of the chance to stretch my legs."

Bentley glanced at Skelton surreptitiously as they walked down the platform; his entire department was abuzz with rumors about this man. *"Enjoyable sea voyage?"*

"It was shorter than some I've taken," Skelton said. He lit another cigarette, holding out the pack to Bentley who shook his head.

"First time in London, is it, sir?"

"No."

"You've been here before?"

Skelton smiled wryly at the surprise in Bentley's voice. *"It wasn't in my file?"*

Bentley flushed. *"I'm sorry, sir. I didn't mean to pry."*

"It was a very long time ago, Bentley."

They were out of Waterloo station now, and Bentley nodded to their left. *"The motor's down this way, sir."*

But Skelton had stopped, and was looking northwest to where the great dome of St. Paul's rose black against the evening sky.

"Sir?" Bentley said, wondering at the bleak look on the major's face.

Skelton turned away from the cathedral, his features settling back into their previous studied neutrality. *"Memories, Bentley. Now, where's this motor of yours?"*

BENTLEY DROVE SLOWLY, CAREFULLY, HUNCHED over the steering wheel as if he was shortsighted. *"Would you like a tour of the city, sir? It's nice at this time of—"*

"No." Skelton had huddled down into his seat, his cap even further down over his eyes, the collar of his coat turned up about his neck and cheeks.

Bentley drove a little further in silence before his natural garrulity reasserted itself. *"Your quarters won't be ready until tomorrow, sir. You'll be staying with me tonight. Hope you don't mind."*

Skelton's head tipped a little in acknowledgment, which could have meant anything.

Bentley shifted in his seat. "Got a nice little place in Highbury with my wife Violet. We've only been married six months. All still a bit of a novelty, sir. Awful lot of fun, though. Are you married?"

"No."

"Well, sir, I have to say that I can heartily recommend the institution. And I can't think that a handsome fellow like yourself wouldn't have had an opportunity or two in the past—"

"My wife died some time ago, Bentley."

"Oh crikey, sir, I'm sorry. Sometimes I do run on a bit. Get myself into some awful scrapes."

There was another silence which Skelton spent smoking, and Bentley peering anxiously over the steering wheel, searching for something else to say.

"Violet's looking forward to meeting you, sir. She's always dreamed of visiting America. I don't doubt that she'll bombard you with questions."

Skelton shot Bentley a dark look from beneath the rim of his cap.

"Ahem. Well then, sir, if you don't feel like talking, perhaps after supper you'd like to listen to the wireless with us? There's a jolly good show on the BBC at eight. Unless you're tired from all your travelling, sir. I'd quite understand if you want to retire early."

"I think I'll go out for a walk after dinner, Bentley. Renew my acquaintance with the city."

"As you wish, sir."

Bentley finally fell into silence.

Chapter One

Cornelia Speaks

TROY FELL WHEN MY SIXTH FOREFATHER was a youth, and thus consequently I had only ever known Trojans as slaves. A defeated, despondent people who I noticed merely as obedient drudges creeping about my father's palace. I paid them little attention; they were but slaves after all, and moreover, they were the sorry remnants of a people who had caused my fellow Greeks much trouble and sorrow. It was not so much that I despised them, for I did not, it was just that they were a people who had caused their own misfortune and who thus needed to have no sorrow, no pity, and certainly no hatred wasted upon them.

So I paid them no regard. I spoke to them only to speak a request (and even that rarely, for my nurse and companion Tavia was the usual intermediary between my wants and those who lived only to attend to them) and I occasionally nodded absentmindedly at one or another of them if they performed me a particular service. That was the entire limit of my involvement with Trojans. They were constantly about me, but they were all but invisible.

I was Cornelia, only legitimate child of the great Pandrasus, king of Mesopotama. Mesopotama was not a particularly notable city, I grant you, but it was important and rich enough, and was one of the very few survivors of the Catastrophe that had rocked our world for the preceding six or seven generations. Other cities may have succumbed to conflagration and earth tremors, or to the swords and hate of the tribes who took advantage of the turmoil in the Aegean world to invade, but Mesopotama continued as if charmed, serene and safe on its tranquil bay on the northwestern coast of mainland Greece.

There was only little contact with the outside world, and I existed virtually unaware of even that small degree of contact. There was my father, who adored me, and there were the joys and pleasures of my father's court from which I rarely strayed.

Why should I have? My father's palace contained everything I could have wanted. Everything was mine for the asking: rare fabrics from the far east, the most tempting of morsels from the kitchens, jewels as I wanted for my neck and arms, the admiration and attendance of all who beheld me.

The last began to amuse me more and more, particularly once I passed my fourteenth birthday and became a woman. I was my father's heir, and whoever bedded and wedded me had not only my undoubted physical charms to enthrall him, but the throne as well.

I taunted my male admirers, naturally. When my father held court in his megaron, every man who had a desire for the throne (and that was most of them) allowed his eyes to stray to me. I would smile, and straighten my shoulders, allowing them a full view of my breasts. We followed the old Minoan fashion here in Mesopotama (one of my foremothers much removed had come from Crete, I believe, bringing the fashion with her), and all noble unmarried girls displayed their breasts above their tight-waisted flounced skirts and between the flaring stiffened lapels of their heavily embroidered jackets. I was glad that we still kept to this custom, for it gave me ample opportunity to tease and tantalize, watching all the while the lust for power (and for me, of course!) flare in the eyes of men.

Sorry creatures that they were! I teased and I flaunted, but it was done only for trivial amusement. I had already secretly chosen my husband—my comely sixteen-year-old cousin Melanthus—and in that winter of my fifteenth year I fully intended to drive him to such distraction that he would not hesitate to take my virginity the instant I offered it to him. Then we could use my swelling belly to persuade my father that Melanthus was a good enough catch for me (it *was* irksome that he was but a third son, for I knew my father would despise that . . . but if I was caught with child, then my father would surely be so delighted he would deny me nothing).

My life was full, it was good, it boded nothing but blessings.

That is, it boded nothing but blessings until Hera spoke to me.

Hera, most lovely of goddesses, and queen to Zeus, had been my personal deity ever since I was old enough to choose one. To be sure, the power of the gods was a faint thing (or even a nonexistent thing if I listened to Tavia, who had said that while the gods were now all but dead, many generations ago they had intervened in most aspects of mortal life, and had even the power to stop the sun and raise the seas) but Hera, at least, was a comforting if distant presence in my life. To her I confided all my secrets in the dark womb of the night when Tavia lay snoring at the foot of my bed; to her I recounted all the happinesses and intrigues of my day; to her I prayed, I *begged*, that Melanthus should be mine, and hopefully without any significant delay.

She did not reply, of course, although occasionally I thought I felt such a soothing presence beside me that I believed her truly with me. She was my friend, and so it was, I presume, that as my friend, and even as weak as she was, Hera made that single stupendous effort to warn me of what approached.

It was a night like any other. Tavia had made sure of my comfort, and had then lain down on her pallet at the foot of my bed.

Snores had soon issued forth from that darkness beyond

my feet. (The snores once had irritated me beyond measure, until I realized that they informed me of when the night was mine to confide either in Hera or in my dreams as intimately as I wanted.)

I lay quietly, a smile on my face, my hands on my breasts as I thought of Melanthus. Tavia—and her snoring—would have to find somewhere else to sleep once he was my husband.

At that thought my smile increased, and I wriggled in my bed, a vague, unknowable wanting deep within my body making me restless. I was about to whisper Melanthus' name as a mantra (the more I spoke it, then surely the sooner he would be mine) when suddenly . . . suddenly . . . I was no longer within my bed, nor even within my home.

Instead I stood on a blasted rock, the sea churning about me, drenching me with its waters. Above me wheeled immense black birds, screaming and shrieking so horribly I put my hands to my ears and cried out in terror.

"Beware!" spoke a voice, and I spun about, almost losing my footing on the treacherous rock.

A woman, wraithlike, so insubstantial the waves cascaded straight through her, stood a pace away at the very edge of the rock.

"Who are you?" I whispered.

The wraith reached out a hand, and as it neared my face her flesh solidified so that warm flesh touched my cheek, and I knew instantly who it was.

"Hera!"

"Beloved child," she said. I saw in her newly fleshed face that her lovely eyes were awash with tears. "Beloved child, beware, for you have a great enemy."

I put my hand over hers, and pressed it more deeply against my cheek. "Hera," I whispered, so overcome with her presence I paid virtually no heed to her words. "Hera . . ."

"A great enemy. The Horned One. Asterion. He will hunt you down one day, Cornelia. Be prepared."

"Asterion?" The name was vaguely familiar, but I forgot anything I might have known about it as the import of Hera's words finally sank into my consciousness. An enemy, and one who sounded so malevolent? My fear, initially comforted by the goddess' presence, now reasserted itself, and I sobbed.

"The Bull. The Horned One. Keep watch for him, Cornelia. He hunts, and he will hunt you."

"What . . . who . . . what do you mean?"

Hera's other hand lifted, and for one blessed moment she held my face cradled between her two hands. "You are so beautiful," she whispered, and I wondered that she, the most lovely of goddesses, could say this. "So beautiful, and you must learn also to be strong, and courageous, for nothing else will stop him."

"You could—"

"No. I am dying, and I am among the very last of my kind. I have not much longer before the waves of the Catastrophe engulf me completely. Cornelia, listen. The Game has been stolen from us, but it will find you again. When it does, my dear, learn it. Learn the Game, child. Learn the Game. It is all that can save you—and through you all of mankind—from Asterion."

I had no idea what she meant. "Hera—"

"You shall meet a distant sister of mine, sad and weary, and damaged by Ariadne's viperish curse as well, but far more cunning than I, and whose well of power has not been destroyed as has ours. She will aid you. She is all that is left, now."

Her hands dropped away from my face, and she stepped back, and her form became insubstantial once more.

"Hera!" I cried, reaching out to her.

"Farewell, beloved," she whispered. "Farewell."

And she was gone.

I WOKE, FULLY CONSCIOUS, INTO THE DARK OF MY bedchamber.

Tavia snored on, unperturbed.

"Asterion?" I whispered. I lay awake a long time, then drowsiness overcame me, and I succumbed to sleep.

I dreamed again, but it was of Melanthus, and its effect was such that when I woke into the bright daylight with Tavia bustling about the chamber, I remembered almost nothing of Hera's visitation.

WITHIN THE MONTH WHAT I WOULD LATER REC-ognize as Ariadne's curse reached out and overwhelmed me, and the Catastrophe finally, calamitously, lay waste to my entire life.

Chapter Two

LLANGARLIA, SOUTHEAST BRITAIN

HE LAND WAS ANCIENT, SCARRED BY THE traverse of glaciers, oceanic inundations, and, most recently, the axes and awls of humankind. Most of the island's forests had fallen victim to needs of men and women; in the past one thousand years 100 million trees had fallen, leaving vast windswept moors where once had been thick forests, and meadowlands where once had flowered dense thickets.

Even if the island had lost its enveloping vast canopy, then there still remained great swaths of green forests that ran through the land like the ancient mystical roads of the gods. In these dark strange woodlands ancient riddles gathered in the twilight shadows, and murderous giant badgers and gray wolves and brown bears roamed paths rarely trod by human feet. Here sprites and imps lived and died, and history itself sank deep beneath the virulent leaf waste that gathered at the base of twisted, prehistoric trees.

Save for those especially marked by the gods, the human population left the forests and woods well enough alone. They worshiped the great stag-god Og who sheltered within the trees' shadows, venerating him with song and dance and sacrifice, but spent their lives amid the sunlit meadows and fields their braver ancestors had carved out of the Neolithic groves. Here, hares and hedgehogs, robins and larks, gamboled, lesser—and far more manageable—creatures than their forest counterparts, and no threat to the herds of domesticated cattle, sheep, and pigs kept to feed the village populations of the land.

In the southeast of the island, a green and verdant land where the forests were fewer and the fields richer than elsewhere, dwelt the people of Llangarlia. The Llangarlians centered their lives, their culture, and their religion about the great River Llan that wound its languid and peaceful way through the southern central parts of the island to its mouth on the eastern coast. As the forests were the home of the stag-god Og, so the Llan and its tributaries, lakes, and springs were the home of the great mother goddess Mag, under whose benefices the Llangarlians grew their crops, bred their livestock, and raised the strong-limbed children that graced their hearts and homes. Llangarlia basked in the union between Og and Mag, and in the marriage of forest and water.

To the south of the Llan lay the fields and villages of the Llangarlians, but on the northern bank of the river spread a series of wild and mystic hills and mounds that the Llangarlians called the Veiled Hills after the mist that often enclosed them. These hills and mounds were the sacred heart of Llangarlia, resting as they did between the dark forest that spread to their north and west and the river to their south.

Here, amid the Veiled Hills, the ordinary people of Llangarlia walked only during holy festivals when their footsteps were directed and protected by the MagaLlan, the

living representative of Mag, and the Gormagog, the living
representative of Og. Between them, the MagaLlan and the
Gormagog guided the spiritual lives of the Llangarlians and
the physical health of the land, personifying as they did the
holy marriage between Mag, the waters, and Og, the forests.

For the past fifteen hundred years, ever since the Llangarlians had replaced those strange, forgotten people who
had built the Stone Dances, this union had been one of great
soundness. The Llangarlians had lived in health and peace,
the men reaping the wealth of field and river while the
women bred children of exquisite beauty and well-being,
the most elderly and respected Mothers among the women
of the land presiding over the Houses, or families, of Llangarlia.

Now, however, a blight had fallen over the land. It had
begun one dreadful night twenty-six years previously when
the Gormagog, Aerne, had lain with his own thirteen-year-
old daughter, Blangan. In itself this was not particularly
unusual, for many Mothers asked the Gormagog to lie with
their daughters and get children of exceptional beauty and
power on them, but on this occasion the sexual act turned
into a cataclysmic disaster. In that instant the Gormagog
spilt his seed into Blangan he felt his Og power torn apart.
Half of it he managed to retain, half vanished into the son
he had planted within Blangan's womb. Divided, the Og
power had become virtually useless. There was no point in
even trying to abort the child; the damage was done.

It was a disaster not only for the Gormagog, as also for
his son, but also for the god Og. As Gormagog was crippled, so also was Og. With every year that passed Og weakened yet further, and as he weakened, so his union with
Mag, which kept the land healthy and productive, also
waned.

There was nothing that could be done about it. No means
existed to reunify the Og power now divided between
Aerne and his son, Loth. If Loth had been a daughter, it
was conceivable that Aerne could then have lain with his

daughter (and granddaughter, as she would have been) when she came of age, and the son thus produced could have reunited the Og power into one body . . . but Gormagog had planted a son into Blangan, a son, a useless son . . .

For all of Mag's power, and the power of the MagaLlan, the land itself began to wither and die. Cattle and sheep birthed thin, deformed offspring. Crops tended more to failure than to bounty, and the winters extended well past their allotted span so that miserable sleet and destructive frosts afflicted the land even in the height of summer.

The daughters of Llangarlia, who traditionally had enjoyed healthy pregnancies and easy labors, now began to miscarry and, worse, die during childbirth. Even if both mother and child survived the perils of childbed, the infants often perished in the first few months of life, and their mothers proved barren of further children.

Older children fell victim to strange fevers, or unexplainable wasting diseases.

The dark creatures of the forests, the wolves and bears and the monstrous badgers, strayed from beneath the trees and into the fields and the sheep runs of the villages, not only destroying crops and hard-bred livestock, but mauling and ravaging adults and children alike.

Llangarlia was dying, and the powerless Gormagog, and his equally powerless and angry shadow, Loth, could do nothing.

Og was sliding toward death, and as he did, he dragged Mag with him. Unaffected as Mag was by the initial splitting of power when Aerne lay with Blangan, as her union with the crippled Og failed, so also did Mag's power wane. Mag could do nothing for the land without a strong mate at her side.

Then, in the twenty-sixth year of the calamity, the MagaLlan, Genvissa (daughter of the MagaLlan who had presided over the disaster, and sister to Blangan), spoke to the Gormagog and to Loth, and said that she thought she could help. She spoke long and gently to them over many weeks, knowing they would resist her plan, knowing it would offend their male pride, but knowing that eventually they would also agree, for in this they had no choice.

Llangarlia must survive before all else.

THEY SAT ATOP THE MOST SACRED OF THE VEILED Hills, the Llandin. It was dawn, the time when minds were the clearest and the power of the land was the nearest.

"Why?" said Loth, leaning forward, his dark green and faintly luminous eyes unblinking and intent. "Why must you do this?"

The MagaLlan, Genvissa, regarded him calmly. Loth's malformed, horrific skull was scratched deeply in places, the blood scabbing into unbecoming lumps in his thin hair, and Genvissa idly wondered which daughter of which House had so marked him.

It must have been a wild night.

As impotent as the Gormagog and Loth might be in the ways of power, their maleness had not suffered when it came to bedding the daughters of Llangarlia. It was almost as if they both somehow hoped to redeem that one malevolent bedding with each subsequent girl they bore down beneath them. It was a useless effort, but Genvissa understood their need.

She was also a recipient of it herself, having borne Aerne three daughters over the past sixteen years.

"There is the why," she said to Loth, waving a hand toward the settlements south of the Llan. "This season over eleven daughters have died in childbirth, barely a half of the livestock born will grow into maturity, and a third of the crops has fallen to the mold blight. Can *you* help, Loth?" It was cruel, she knew, but the need was great, and if she didn't persuade them soon then the chance would pass her by.

Loth's lip curled, and he sat back, wondering if Genvissa hid a sneer behind her beautiful, serene face. His feelings for Genvissa were a mass of conflicting emotions. He resented and desired her, reasonable reactions given her power compared with his relative lack of it, and her beautiful, seductive body that often had him sweating with frustrated desire.

But Loth also deeply distrusted Genvissa, and yet he could not say why.

Unable to hold Genvissa's even gaze, Loth looked at his father, Aerne, sitting hunched over his belly as if his impotency in the face of this crisis might send him to his grave.

"We should take this to an Assembly," said Aerne. His voice was soft, but even if his spiritual and magical powers had diminished into infirmity, his voice still held a vestige of his traditional authority. "The Mothers of Llangarlia's Houses should meet on this." He hesitated, and all remaining remnants of authority evaporated. "Shouldn't they?"

"The Mothers are not due to assemble again until the Slaughter Festival," Genvissa said, remembering how powerful Aerne had been when she'd been a child. Now all that power had seeped away, along with his decisiveness, and Genvissa's respect had vanished with it. He'd fathered three daughters on her, but their beauty and power was all from her, not him. He'd merely planted the seed. "That is almost a full year away. We cannot wait."

"We could call an extraordinary Assembly," said Loth, insistent where his father hesitated and wondering why it was that Genvissa did not call an Assembly. Surely her plan demanded the consultation of the Mothers?

Why didn't she want to call them?

Aerne looked at his son, and something he saw in Loth's face made his back straighten. "We could indeed," he said.

The skin around Genvissa's eyes tightened momentarily, then she smiled, leaned forward, and put a warm hand on Aerne's bare thigh. The movement made the material of her soft linen robe strain against her breasts and hips, accentuating both her sexuality and her success as a mother, and Loth, watching Aerne carefully, was appalled to see his father's eyes actually water with desire.

"Aerne," she said, her voice soft, persuasive, compelling.

"Would it not be best to delay a consultation with the Mothers? Then we can see if my plan works. Why get their hopes up with an Assembly now? We should wait. Wait until we are sure of my plan's success. *Then* we can put it to the Slaughter Festival Assembly. When we are sure." Her hand tightened, gripping Aerne's slack, aged flesh, and Loth looked away, sickened.

"*Strange* magic!" he said, spitting the words out as if they were pig filth. Genvissa's plan repelled him, but only, if he was honest with himself, because its very existence highlighted his own inadequacies. "What need have we of *foreign* magic?"

"Every need, Loth." Genvissa straightened, lifting her hand from Aerne's thigh. She looked at Loth, her demeanor exuding certainty powered with a little impatience, as if Loth himself were the cause of the land's troubles.

Then again, Loth thought, there was every chance that is what Genvissa *did* think. She had ever been impatient with him.

If only Loth didn't exist, if only he hadn't been conceived that fateful night, then Gormagog's power would remain intact and Llangarlia would never have been overcome with blight.

Loth could imagine the words repeating themselves over and over in Genvissa's mind.

Loth had no idea how wrong he was.

"Og is impotent, perhaps even dying," Genvissa continued. "We need a strong male magic to counter his lack, and to combine with my womanly Mag power to weave a web of protection once more over this land. I know where I can find this maleness. This . . . *potency.*"

There, the cruel word was said. Genvissa saw Aerne's face flinch, and Loth's set into mottle-cheeked animosity, but she steeled herself against their hurt. What she did was for her foremothers, from whom she had inherited her strange exotic darkcraft, and even darker ambition.

"Og's power may revive—" Loth began.

"Og's power has failed to revive in these past twenty-six

years, Loth. How can you say, 'Wait a little longer'? We must act *now*, or our land will die! *I* can bring that magic to Llangarlia, no one else." Genvissa looked to Aerne, and he nodded, his face resigned.

"If we must, Genvissa. If we must."

"We must!" she said. "Mag demands it. She needs a mate of potency . . . not what she must endure now." She paused, looking between both men. "The Mag is strong in my womb," she continued, referring to the Mag magic that resided in every Llangarlian woman's womb, but which flowered at its brightest in hers. "I can act. I can save this land. How can you think to prevent me?"

Loth opened his mouth to speak, but his father silenced him with a heavy hand on the younger man's arm.

"Then do it, Genvissa," Aerne said, his voice thick with self-loathing. "Do it. Bring your strange magic here, and use it in a spell-weaving that will save us. *Do it*."

Genvissa smiled, thankful Aerne had summoned enough authority to override his son's suspicions.

Eventually, of course, she would have to do something about Loth.

Chapter Three

AT DUSK OF THAT SAME DAY, GENVISSA walked through a path in the marshlands and water reeds to the northern bank of the Llan.

Behind her, keeping their distance, walked Aerne and Loth, their faces reflecting resignation and obstinacy respectively.

Several paces behind them came a young girl of some ten or eleven years, Genvissa's middle daughter, wearing nothing but a brief hip wrap and a drum hung on a leather band that wound over one shoulder and between her small virgin breasts. On this drum the girl beat out a soft, relentless rhythm that sent the blood coursing through the two men.

Genvissa halted at the water's edge. She was naked, her dark curly hair with its strange russet streak left to flow unbound over her shoulders and back. Unlike her daughter, who had as yet born no children and thus had the thin, unbecoming body of the yet-to-be mother, Genvissa's body was shapely and seductive: her breasts were well muscled and molded by the years she'd spent breast-feeding her daughters; her hips flared invitingly; her waist was narrow between the two sensuous extremes of breast and hip; her legs were long and smooth and graceful. In many ways the MagaLlan's body was like the land itself, deep and inviting, mysterious and strong, secreting within itself that magical spark that, at the touch of a man's body or the caress of the village plow, seeded new life both in womb and in field.

Genvissa was an extraordinarily powerful woman, but her power encompassed far more than the Mag power she held within her womb. She was of a line of five foremothers, singular women all, the first of whom, Ariadne, had brought to this land an exotic dark sorcery.

Ariadne had escaped from Naxos aboard a merchant's vessel six days before Thera exploded, nurturing both her revenge and her newly-won darkcraft. She found a home in Llangarlia that accepted her (and, more importantly, added to her power), and she settled, waiting. Waiting for the right moment, the moment when Asterion, now wandering the earth reborn, was far enough away that Ariadne could risk working the final part of her revenge.

That moment had not come in Ariadne's lifetime, and such was the strength of her hatred and ambition, she had not truly minded. The time would eventually be right, Asterion would be far enough away and, hopefully weak enough that he could not interfere, and one among her daughter-heirs would be the one.

So Ariadne had nurtured her darkcraft, and then handed

it down to her daughter-heir, who nurtured and fed it in her own right before handing it, in turn, to her daughter-heir. For well over a hundred years the women had passed it down their line, mother to daughter, each adding to the store of the power that by the time Genvissa's mother, Herron, had come to her full power had grown into a dark, twisting thing indeed.

It was Herron who laid the foundations for the final part of Ariadne's plan: the eventual reactivation of the Game far, far from the Aegean world and its gods. First, she had engineered the splitting of Aerne's Og power so that Og, and through him Mag, would be too weak to interfere. Well might the Gormagog despise himself for his weakness in losing half of his power to his newly conceived son, and thus crippling Og (and, by association, Mag), but in actuality he'd been the victim of Herron's spell-weaving rather than his own unwitting error. Aerne and Loth blamed the pitiful Blangan for the catastrophic event—they still lusted for her blood—but Blangan had simply been a means, a vessel to be used.

Blangan had been Herron's eldest daughter, and thus expendable in a world where it was the youngest daughter who inherited.

Finally, in a final act of darkcraft so powerful it had ended her life, Herron had caused Asterion—at that moment moving from one life to the next—to be reborn into a body calamitously weak *and* so far distant that he, like Og and Mag, would be able to do nothing to prevent Herron's daughter-heir Genvissa in the final fulfillment of Ariadne's design.

Even though all these women had held the office of MagaLlan, none of them had much regard for Mag herself, although they were content to mouth their respects while all the time drawing on the goddess' power. They loved this land that sheltered them, but they secretly despised the gods who had protected it and, as generation succeeded generation, plotted to overthrow them.

After all, they had something far better than Mag or Og planned for this land.

Standing at the edge of the Llan, shivering as the cold water lapped at her ankles, Genvissa sent a prayer of thankfulness and honor her mother's way. Now it was Genvissa's turn to build upon her five foremothers' work and execute the final turn of the labyrinth, place the final piece of the puzzle, work that magic that would allow power once more to rise from the ashes of her fifth foremother's betrayal.

The time was finally here. Asterion was far, far away and currently trapped in his weakest incarnation ever, and the man Genvissa *did* need was in place—and far closer than Asterion.

Genvissa shivered again, but this time with desire rather than cold. She'd had many lovers in her lifetime, but they were as nothing when compared to the man who by blood and by shared knowledge, power, and training was destined to be her mate.

The man she needed to bring to Llangarlia.

The man she (as her five dead foremothers) needed to bring all their plans to fruition.

The one man, that single man remaining, who could aid Genvissa in her quest.

A Kingman. The last one left out of the catastrophes that had wracked the Aegean world over the past five or six generations. The one man who had the power to match her step by step in the twin dances of power. The one man who could earn Genvissa's respect and match her strength and wit. A Kingman, the only one who could weave with her that enchantment that would raise this land to everlasting greatness.

A fitting mate.

A Kingman. Genvissa, still hesitating at the Llan's edge, placed a hand on her belly. She had two years' life left in her womb, two years remaining in which to conceive and bear her heir . . . and she'd be damned if she'd allow Aerne to get this one on her.

Genvissa took a deep breath, then dived headfirst into

the river, sliding smoothly beneath its waters and into the power reservoir of the ancient goddess Mag.

DEEP IN HER WATERY CAVE-WOMB, MAG WAILED. The darkwitch was with her again, draining yet more of her life force, and there was little Mag could do to prevent it. Once Og could have protected her, but now he was impotent, reduced to helpless whimpering as he crawled on his belly through the forests.

For six generations the Darkwitches had held the office of MagaLlan, and for six generations they'd been binding Mag tighter and tighter in their spell-weavings. At first Mag had been able to resist them; now her resistance was a tame thing, and she was all but the MagaLlan's pet. She still retained some of her power, but it had become a mere servant to the MagaLlan's wishes.

The MagaLlan before this, Herron, had even used it to cripple her mate, Og.

Now Genvissa was absorbing the last remaining vestiges of Mag's power, using it to further Genvissa's own plan for this land. Mag knew that if she couldn't find the means to counter Genvissa soon, she would fade away as Og had done. Mag's name might still be invoked, and her power used, but Mag herself would be dead, and Genvissa, and those who succeeded her, would wield Mag's magic.

But what could she do? *What?* Mag needed somewhere to hide, somewhere to lick her wounds and regain her strength. But there was no place in this land, no womanly harbor, in which she *could* conceal herself. Genvissa knew all the dark spaces of every hill and every woman's body; there was no escape into any of them for Mag.

Nowhere to go, once Genvissa had drawn away from Mag every last iota of her ancient power, save into extinction.

Mag twisted and wept, and felt yet more of her power drain away.

Her life, once measured in aeons, was now measured in weeks at the most.

Chapter Four

NORTHERN EPIRUS,
ON THE WEST COAST OF GREECE

THE BEACH LAY IN A GLIMMERING WHITE crescent, semicircled by the steep slopes of a forested mountain, drenched in heavy moonlight. Several hundred men lay wrapped in blankets on the sand, deeply asleep, enslaved to dream, incapable of movement. Five fires had been lit along the line of beach and the ranks of sleeping warriors, but now they were all but dead, cooled into mounds of graying coals. At each fire stood a sentry, leaning on a spear; all five slept, their chins resting on their chests, soft snores rattling through their slack lips.

Beyond the beach three low-slung warships bobbed gently in the ocean swells of the bay, uncaring witnesses to the enchantment settling upon the sleepers.

The waters at tide's edge were calm one moment, bubbling silently the next. A woman rose from the shallows, strangely dry for the manner of her arrival.

For a heartbeat she shimmered, as if she were a mere apparition . . . then her figure hardened, and became as if real.

She was tall, and sturdily built, her dark auburn hair bundled carelessly into a knot on the top of her head, her small, high breasts left bare, her hips clad with a short green kirtle bound about her waist with a few twists of a leather thong.

Across her back rested a quiver of golden arrows, and over her left shoulder lay a silver hunting bow of exquisite workmanship.

The woman strode across the beach and paused at the

edge of the first wave of sleepers. Her lip curled, as if she found them not to her taste.

She stepped over them and walked loose-hipped and confident between the ranks of sleepers to the very far end of the beach.

Here, slightly apart from the others, lay a single warrior. To one side lay his clothes, a waistband of twisted leather wound about with scarlet and gold cords. His scarlet waistcloth, fresh-washed from the sea, lay folded neatly beside it.

He had thrown off his blanket, as if it constrained him, even in sleep, and his body lay naked save for the bands of gold he wore about his biceps, upper forearms, and just below his knees.

Fine craftsmen had wrought these golden bands, and on each of them they had embossed the same repeating symbol: a spinning crown over a stylized unicursal labyrinth.

They were the bands of kingship, yet this man ruled over no kingdom.

They were the bands of the Kingman, the only set left surviving from the catastrophes that had enveloped the Aegean world, yet this man had no partner with which to dance through the sorcerous twistings of the labyrinth.

The woman stood, her face expressionless, staring down at him.

He was not a handsome man, being too blunt of feature and his black eyebrows too straight, but he was well made with wide shoulders, flat belly, slim hips, and long, tightly muscled limbs, and she knew that when his eyes opened they would be of that liquid blackness she had always craved in her lovers.

And his hair. She smiled. His hair was long and black and tightly curled, jouncing out of the thong that held it at the back of his neck into a riot of wildness across the backs of his shoulders. She longed to free it, to perfume it with scented oils, to run her fingers through it and bring it to her lips, and to sink her fists into it so tightly that he could never escape her.

She could see Aphrodite's blood in that hair, and it excited her.

Her body trembled, and suddenly sick of her silent watching, she bent down, grabbed the man's beautiful hair, and gave his head a hard yank.

He jerked instantly out of dream and, as instantly, knew by the bow and arrows who it was bending down over him, staring at him intently.

"Artemis?" he whispered. He rose on his elbows, his face showing both confusion and awe. "I thought you dead!"

She smiled, pleased with her deception. "Me? Dead? How so when I am so fully fleshed?" She pulled her hand from his hair. "Rise, and walk with me."

He did so, not once taking his eyes off the Goddess of the Hunt, his movements fluid and graceful, warrior-trained and battle-honed.

He did not reach for his waistcloth, treating the goddess with the same respect he would one of his warriors.

Once he was standing Artemis turned and walked a few paces away, and the man followed, tense with excitement. They walked in silence, Artemis a pace or two ahead of the man, until they had reached the very end of the beach where rocks rose in a sheer face to the first of the forested slopes of the mountain.

"You have been wandering now . . . for how long?" she asked as she turned to face him. She leaned back, resting her buttocks on a rock and folding her arms. She considered him carefully, not bothering to disguise the admiration with which she ran her eyes down his body.

It was, after all, what she and hers had been waiting for for so long.

"Fifteen years." He regarded her evenly. There was still awe in his eyes, but caution and speculation also, and that pleased Artemis.

This man was no fool.

"Fifteen years. And what have you learned in those fifteen years?"

"Hunger."

She smiled, the expression predatory. "Hunger for what?"

He took a deep breath, his wonderful black eyes losing some focus, and she needed no more answer.

She laid a finger on one of the golden bands about his right arm. "You hunger for your heritage. You hunger for power. You hunger for Troy."

"Aye." His voice was tight, almost breathless.

"Yet how can this be? Troy has been ashes for over ninety years."

"Troy is in my blood." He placed his left hand over her finger where it still lay on the golden band. It was a bold move, touching a goddess. "And I wear it about my arm. I cannot forget."

"No, of course you cannot." She pulled her finger out from under his hand—slowly, teasingly—and rested her hand on the warm skin of his chest. "Brutus," she said, rolling about her mouth the Latin name his dying mother had given him, "if I offered you power, would you take it?"

He hesitated, but she knew it was only because he was considering her, not because he was afraid. "Yes."

"And if the path I showed you to this power was strange, but resulted in you reaching this power stronger than you have ever been before, would you nevertheless take it?"

This time no hesitation. "Oh, yes."

"If I tested your resolve and your courage and your training along this path, would you resent me for it?"

Her hand was still on his chest, and he leaned very slightly into it. "And what," he said, "would be my prize at the end of all this travail?"

She moved closer to him, her face barely an inch or two from his, their breath intermingling, their bodies touching at a half-dozen different places, their mouths a single dangerous moment away from a kiss.

Me. The word hung between them, and Artemis actually put her mouth against his to verbalize the word.

"Troy," she whispered.

He drew in a sharp, shocked breath, and his muscles jumped under her hand.

She moved away from him, just slightly, the better to see the incredulity, the *lust*, in his face.

Oh, yes, this was the man she wanted.

"Troy?" he said, his voice barely above a whisper.

"Do you not wear the kingship bands of Troy?" Her hand was moving in warm, slow circles over his chest.

"Troy is gone. Ashes. Crumbled stone. It would take me a thousand years to rebuild it."

"And what if I offered you that thousand years?"

Now the look on his face made her laugh, and she relented. "Not the old Troy, Brutus, for this world is diseased and could no longer support the power and glory of"—*you*—"such a magnificent and glorious city. No, I shall send you to a new land, a strong land, a bright land. Build me a new Troy, Brutus, and I can give you *everything* you could possibly want."

Her tone, her wandering hand, the tip of her tongue between her teeth, left Brutus in no doubt whatsoever that the "everything" included Artemis.

"Troia Nova," he said. "And you." All his life he'd felt that there was *something* toward which he should be moving, something that awaited him. His father had smiled at him, the companions of his childhood had jeered. Others had been indifferent. No one had believed him save these men who currently slept at his back.

Now . . . he swallowed, almost overcome both by the presence of the goddess and by what she offered him.

Artemis watched his reaction, and knew the thoughts that jumbled through his mind. She turned her hand so that its back was against his skin, and she let it drift lower, down to his belly where she could feel his muscles quivering in excitement.

"Where?" he said, his voice almost breathless now in his excitement. "Where is this strong and bright land?"

"You will reach it in time, Brutus. First, however, you must sail south for two days to a city called Mesopotama."

"My long and dangerous travail."

"Aye." Her hand was moving more deliberately now, and she could feel how much her touch excited him; their eventual matching would be all she had hoped for. "Mesopotama is ruled by a king called Pandrasus. There is a great test for you in this city of Mesopotama, one you will pass *only* if you have the strength and ability to rebuild Troy." *And win me.* "When—if—you have won through, and have set your fleet to sea once more, sail a further day's journey south, and you will find an island. Seek me out there, and I will show you the path to your Troia Nova." She pressed her hand deeply into his flesh, then withdrew it and stood away from him. She smiled, holding his eyes, then stepped forward and brushed past him.

He turned as if to follow, but she held out her hand, halting him. "Do as I say, Brutus," she said, and then, suddenly, Artemis was gone, as if she had never been.

IN A LAND FAR DISTANT, SO DISTANT IT WAS ALMOST incomprehensible to either Trojan or Llangarlian, a naked youth of particular dark beauty sat in a barren dry plain in the valley of an alpine landscape. Above him reared snow and ice-capped mountains, about him whistled frigid winds, but none of this did he notice.

He sat cradled within the dark heart of the unicursal labyrinth that he had scrawled in the dry earth with a knife. The knife lay on the soil before his crossed legs, its blade pointed outwards towards the entrance of—the escape from—the labyrinth, its curious twisted bone haft pointing towards the youth.

Asterion sat, his black eyes riveted on the knife, drawing strength from its curious dark power, thinking on what he had just learned: one of Ariadne's daughter-heirs had made her initial move in resurrecting the Game.

And here he sat, "trapped" in this calamitously weak body. He smiled, as cold and malicious as the landscape about him. Asterion had known exactly what Herron was doing when she interfered in his rebirth, forcing him into this body and this distant land. He had expected it, had known that either Ariadne or one of her daughter-heirs would try to negate his power so they could restart the Game. Having anticipated the betrayal, Asterion could very well have stopped it, and escaped Herron's darkcraft.

But that was the very last thing Asterion wanted to do. Above all else he wanted Herron and whoever followed her to believe he was incapacitated, that he was trapped and impotent. Asterion's smile grew colder, his eyes darker. Weak his body might be, but his power was stronger than ever.

He reached out a hand, and touched the knife gently, loving it. This knife was very precious to him, for it was of him. In his first rebirth after Ariadne had enacted her Catastrophe, ruining the Game in the Aegean world, Asterion had journeyed back to the devastated island of Crete. There he searched out the remains of his former body—the body that Theseus had murdered with Ariadne's aid—and cut from its skull the two great curved horns. These Asterion had then worked, with the skills both of power and of craftsmanship, into the twisted bone handle that now adorned the blade of the knife.

In the months and years ahead this knife was going to be his friend and his ally, his voice, and the weapon that he would use against Herron's daughter-heir Genvissa and this man she had picked as her partner in the Game.

Weak? No, Asterion was stronger than ever.

His smile died, and his eyes glittered.

BRUTUS STOOD FOR A VERY LONG TIME, WATCH-ing the moonlight play out over the crescent of sleepers and the waters wash in gently, gently, gently to the sand.

Troy. He was to rebuild Troy.

He could feel the excitement deep in his belly, as powerful an urge as the sexual longing Artemis had roused in him, and he lifted his arms and placed his hands on each of the golden bands that encircled his biceps.

Troy. Home regained.

It was ninety-eight years since Troy had fallen to trickery and betrayal, ninety-eight years since the Trojans who'd survived that betrayal had wandered homeless about the lands of the Mediterranean. Ninety-eight years during which thousands had died, more thousands had been enslaved, and others, like himself and his comrades, had journeyed purposeless, fighting as mercenaries when asked, sometimes fighting when not asked for the sheer relief of it, sometimes settling for a season or two to aid some tiny community sow and harvest crops, always constantly searching, searching, searching.

Now, the searching might not completely be done, but the waiting was over. Brutus was to regain his heritage: Troy.

He took a deep breath, tipped back his head, and opened his arms to the moonlight, as if in silent exultation.

The next moment he was crouching in the sand, eyes moving warily about the beach, as a shout of sheer terror swept over the sleepers.

Men rolled out of their blankets, hands grabbing at weapons, and Brutus, vulnerable in his nakedness, ran back to where his sword lay.

But by the time he had reached his tangle of blankets, both he and the other men were relaxing back from their alert. The shout had come from one of the sleeping men.

A dream, no doubt.

There were a few murmured words, and a snort of laughter, then men lay back down to their sleep once more, but Brutus now could see which sleeper it was who had shouted in dream terror, and his shoulders were again tense.

Membricus, tutor, friend, onetime lover, and, Brutus knew only too well, a powerful seer.

"Membricus?" Brutus said, kneeling where his friend sat wide-eyed in his blanket. "What have you seen?"

Membricus—a lean, older man with wide, thick lips, even but yellowing teeth, and a shock of gray curls twisting around the sides of his balding pate—turned to look at Brutus. His gray eyes, normally cool and distant, now had retreated to the color and warmth of ice.

"The Game has begun," he said, low and hoarse.

"The Game is dead," Brutus said, perhaps too sharply. "It died with Ariadne's betrayal."

Membricus shook his head, then looked at where his hands clutched into his blankets. Brutus could see that their fingers trembled. "The Game has only been waiting. Now it has woken."

"It was a dream, Membricus. A dream."

Membricus raised his eyes back to Brutus; they were once again clear and part of this world. "The Game is stirring," he said, then he sighed, turned away from Brutus, and rolled himself back into his blanket.

The Game is stirring? Brutus slowly stood, staring at Membricus' form.

Power, the goddess had offered him. His heritage.

Again Brutus' hands strayed to the golden bands about his biceps: "Of course," he whispered, and he shuddered at the thought of the degree of power that would be his if the Game was indeed stirring.

A thousand years, she had teased him.

And perhaps that was no tease at all.

Brutus did not sleep the rest of the night. Instead he paced up and down the beach, staring out to sea, watching the light catch on the crescents of the breaking waves, waiting impatiently for the dawn and the start he could make toward his heritage.

Chapter Five

T HE NEXT MORNING, WHEN THE MEN ROSE and set to break their fast, Brutus called them to stand before him, and announced that they were to sail two days' south to a city called Mesopotama.

"And from where has this idea sprung, Brutus?" asked Membricus, laying down the bowl of maza one of the other men had handed him. The older man looked tired and drawn, as if the fear of his dream still lingered within him.

"Last night, as we slept, the goddess Artemis came to me," Brutus said, addressing the crowd of warriors rather than answering Membricus solely. "She announced to me that it was time for me to resume my great-grandfather's inheritance." He drew in a deep breath, his face joyous. "We are to rebuild Troy in a land untouched by troubles! Troia Nova! A city, not of ill luck and trickery, but of strength and nobleness, blessing and peace."

Instantly men shouted questions at Brutus, but he held up his hands, and hushed them back to silence. He still had not dressed, and standing naked under the clear morning sun, the golden bands gleaming against his deeply tanned skin, his wild black hair flowing about his shoulders, Brutus looked like a god himself.

"For years you have followed me, giving me your loyalty and your swords," he continued. "I could have asked for no better. And neither could the gods! We are to be blessed again, my friends. Handed back the favor of the gods!"

One of the warriors stepped forth. He was of an age with Membricus, but tightly muscled and barrel-chested and completely bald above his hook-nosed face.

He strode up to Brutus, leaned close, and touched his

mouth to the band that encircled Brutus' right biceps. "I am always proud to serve you, Brutus. But today my joy transcends my pride. Troy. Oh, gods! That we shall rebuild Troy!"

His voice trembled, but he controlled himself. He was one of Brutus' most respected officers, and had traveled widely before joining Brutus' band some eight years previously.

Brutus smiled, and laid his hand on the man's shoulder. "Hicetaon? I can see by your eyes that there is something more you want to tell me."

"I know of this Mesopotama," Hicetaon said.

"It is ruled by a man called Pandrasus," Brutus said. "This the goddess told me."

"Oh, aye," Hicetaon said. "And did she say more?"

"That it contains a test I must endure before we travel farther."

"Ah." Hicetaon nodded. "I think I may know to what she refers. My mother came from Mesopotama. She and her mother escaped when she was but a babe in arms—"

"Escaped?" Brutus said, and his hand tightened on Hicetaon's shoulder.

"Escaped. If the goddess has commanded you to rebuild Troy, then I wonder not that she directed you to Mesopotama, Brutus. When Troy fell, the cursed Pyrrhus, son of the even more accursed Achilles, herded several thousand Trojan men and women and children into deep-bellied merchant ships, and brought them to this city of Mesopotama, where he sold them for good coin as slaves to the Dorians who live there. The Dorians kept—and still keep, for all I know—the Trojans in vile confinement within the city walls, and made them haul timber and stir pots and wipe the shit from the arses of their Dorian masters. This must be your test—to free the Trojans held in captivity, and to lead them to Troia Nova."

A murmuring rose from among the ranks of the Trojan warriors. The fate of all Trojans since the fall of Troy had been poor, but this slavery . . . this was obscene!

"This king, Pandrasus," Brutus said. "Tell me of him."

Hicetaon shrugged. "If he is like the king of my mother's time, and the ones before that, then he will be cruel and arrogant, and think of his Trojan slaves as little more than despicable beasts, fit only to be worked to death and then discarded. *I* say, that if the goddess has directed you south to Mesopotama, then I am glad, for I have a great longing to free my mother's people."

"*Our* people," Brutus said softly. "Trojans, all."

"And when we have freed our fellow Trojans," Membricus asked, startling Brutus a little, for he had forgotten Membricus sitting so silent to one side, "where then do we sail?"

"Artemis will show me once we have taken our people from Mesopotama, and sailed one day south to an island where she has promised to meet me."

LATER, WHEN THE MEN WERE BREAKING CAMP and wading out to their low-slung warships, Membricus pulled Brutus to one side.

"My beloved companion," he said, low, so that no one else would hear them. "I feel a great wariness in my gut."

Membricus moved very close to Brutus, so close their shoulders touched, and Membricus shivered. "Artemis?" he said. "How can this be so? None of the priests or seers have felt, let alone spoken to, any of the gods in at least three generations. But, lo! Suddenly Artemis appears strong and powerful and full of promises of future glory and Troy reborn. Have you no wit, Brutus? No caution?"

Brutus' face went dangerously expressionless. "Jealous, Membricus? Jealous that she should approach me rather than you?" He grabbed Membricus' hand and held it hard against one of his golden bands. "*I* wear these, my old foolish friend. Not you."

"But—"

Brutus sighed, relenting. The fact that he and Membricus had once been lovers constantly disturbed their current relationship, and Membricus, as Brutus' adviser, was right to question. His hand softened on Membricus', patted it, then allowed it to drop.

"Do you think I was not dubious, my friend? That I did not narrow my eyes and think, *Who is this?* Was it truly Artemis?" Brutus gave a half shrug, then an ironic smile. "For a virgin goddess she was remarkably . . . forthright, but, well, for now I listen to her. These"—again he touched one of his bands—"responded to her. The power that are in these and which was in her was sympathetic, not antagonistic. I did not feel evil or darkness or ill will from her. Only . . ."

"Oh, I can see well enough what you felt from her, Brutus. Let not this"—one of his hands brushed gently against Brutus' groin—"direct your thoughts, and thus our lives."

Brutus stepped back a half space, his eyes flinty. "I let power direct my thoughts, Membricus. That is, after all, what I was bred for."

Chapter Six

BRUTUS' SANDALED FEET SLIPPED ACROSS the loose rock and gravel, and he had to bend down a hand momentarily to steady himself. He took a deep breath, forced himself to ignore the pain in his calves and chest, then scrabbled to the top of the rocky ridge, laughing breathlessly as he gained its summit.

"Come on, my friends!" he shouted to his still-climbing companions. "What ails you both? Age? Infirmity? A girlish fear of falling?"

Membricus and Hicetaon, both breathless and flushed of face, nevertheless managed a laugh, although Hicetaon's ended on a soft curse as he jammed his fingers between two rocks.

Brutus, still smiling, reached down an arm and aided first Membricus and then Hicetaon to the summit of the ridge that they'd been climbing since dawn.

"Ah," Membricus grunted, staggering a few paces away before sinking down to rest against a stubby pine tree that had somehow managed to survive the winds atop the ridge. "Are you *sure* you need my old eyes on this excursion, Brutus?"

"Ever since you confessed your fears to me, then aye," Brutus said, looking meaningfully at Membricus, "I do."

Hicetaon stood a few paces away, hands in the small of his back, stretching out abused muscles. Something cracked in his spine, and he sighed in relief and relaxed.

"I am not sure this is an excursion at all, Membricus," he said, grinning over to the gray-haired man, "but a punishment for whatever sins Brutus has catalogued against us these past few years."

They all laughed, then Brutus helped Membricus to rise.

"You know well enough why we are here," he said, and both his companions grunted their agreement. Late on the morning that Brutus had announced that Artemis meant them to rebuild Troy, they'd boarded their warships and sailed south. Now the warships lay at anchor in a shallow inlet that Hicetaon said was less than a half day's walk above Mesopotama, and Brutus had brought his two companions climbing to this vantage point.

"Where is it?" Brutus asked softly, shading his eyes with a hand. Of the three men, he was the only one not sweating heavily.

Hicetaon scanned the coastline that stretched south, then pointed. "There," he said. "Follow the line of the coast to that bay, then look to the southern shore of the bay. There is a hill, and—"

"Atop that hills sits Mesopotama," said Brutus. "Aye, I see it."

Membricus, who had the oldest eyes, was squinting painfully under the shade of his hand. "It is well fortified," he said, noting the high wall that encircled the entire city and the single gated entrance.

"And rich," added Brutus. "See the roof of the palace at the very pinnacle of the hill? It gleams with gold."

"Trojan gold, no doubt," said Hicetaon bitterly.

"It will be soon," said Brutus, and all three men laughed again, relaxing in the shared warmth of their companionship.

"There are some workshops but very few dwellings outside the walls," said Hicetaon.

"Aye," said Brutus. "The Trojan slaves, however many are left, must be sequestered behind the walls. To free them, we shall have to take the city."

Hicetaon turned and looked at Brutus, raising his eyebrows.

Brutus shrugged. "That is a city full of Dorian Greeks, my friends," he said. "When have *they* ever won a battle against true warriors?"

"You want to storm the walls?" Hicetaon said.

Brutus shook his head. "I think not. At least, not with warriors. With a little cunning, I think, to draw out this arrogant Pandrasus. This is a sheltered city—I can think of no other reason it has survived so long the Catastrophe— and I am thinking that maybe the Dorians of Mesopotama have grown a little soft in that isolation."

"Is that a river I see emptying into the bay?"

Startled, Brutus and Hicetaon looked at Membricus. He'd been so quiet they'd almost forgot his presence.

"Aye," said Hicetaon, and something in his tone made both the other men stare at him in turn.

"It is the River Acheron," Hicetaon said. He should have mentioned it sooner. He really should, but how does one ever break bad news?

There was a momentary silence, then . . .

"The Acheron?" Brutus said. "One of the rivers that leads to Hades' Underworld?"

"Aye," Hicetaon said unhappily.

Membricus stared at Hicetaon, then looked back to the view of the city. For some reason the distant city seemed clearer now, more in focus, and Membricus could easily make out the river winding its sinuous way from a distant gorge, through the valley system bounded by steep wooded hills, past the fortified city atop its hill, and then emptying into the bay.

Something thick and corrupt coiled about his belly, and he moaned.

Hicetaon made as if to reach out to him, but Brutus, sharp-eyed, held him back.

Wait, he mouthed at Hicetaon.

Membricus drew in a deep, horrified breath. There was something dark crawling down the river, a great cloud that, as it reached the city, settled over it like a heavy, angry hand over the delicate crown of a baby's head.

"There is darkness there!" he gasped.

"What do you see?" Brutus said.

Membricus cried out, but Brutus' voice had broken his vision, and as he sucked in several lungfuls of air, his face cleared of horror, although it remained grim.

"There is darkness—an evil—crawling down the Acheron toward Mesopotama," he said. "But I cannot . . . I cannot see what."

Hicetaon muttered something about the uselessness of seers whose eyes had clouded with age, but Brutus ignored him.

"Membricus?" he said, very gently, moving to stand close to the man.

"Brutus," Membricus said, "Brutus . . . are you sure that you can handle the Game, if it does stir?"

Brutus took a deep breath. "Are you still so caught in the grip of your vision? Membricus, it is pointless to talk of the Game. Ariadne destroyed it, along with most of our world, and *all* of our hopes."

Membricus' eyes moved deliberately to Brutus' golden bands.

"Damn it, Membricus. There is not a single Mistress of

the Labyrinth left. These bands mean nothing without a Mistress."

"And yet you said that those bands were sympathetic to—"

"Enough!" Brutus snapped. He found himself curiously annoyed with Membricus and his continual prattle about the Game. It was somehow . . . intrusive. Almost sacrilegious.

"And if you are going to rebuild Troy to even half its former glory," Membricus went on, "you will need the Game to—"

"Enough!"

Membricus shrugged, and looked away, and for a long minute no one spoke.

Hicetaon, whose eyes had been flitting between Brutus and Membricus during this exchange, finally broke the silence. "Brutus, are you trained in the Game? *Are you a Kingman?*"

Brutus sighed, and looked away.

Hicetaon raised his eyebrows at Membricus.

"Brutus is the son of Silvius, son of Ascanius, son of Aeneas, who was the son of Aphrodite," Membricus finally said softly. "Brutus is of the line of gods and of kings, and he wears the kingship bands of Troy. Yes, Hicetaon, Brutus is trained in the Game. He is a trained Kingman. How could he not be?"

Hicetaon looked back to Brutus, and he inclined his head in a gesture of the deepest respect. "Then I fear not, whatever shadows lurk above Mesopotama," he said. "Do you, Membricus?"

Brutus, who had been looking at the city in the distance, now turned his head very deliberately toward Membricus.

"I always fear," the old man snarled. "That's what seers do best."

Brutus grunted, half in laughter, half in derision. "Enough talk of this Game. It only distracts me. Beyond lies Mesopotama, and in it lie the people who will populate

Troia Nova. Come, we need to talk of their rescue before we lose ourselves in talk of legend."

"The Game is not legend," Membricus whispered, but Brutus ignored him.

"Now, old men," he said, "are you up for the journey down?"

ONCE RETURNED TO HIS THREE WARSHIPS moored in the shallow inlet some twelve miles north of the Acheron and Mesopotama, Brutus hesitated just long enough before sitting down to his evening meal to send two of his warriors, disguised as laborers, to Mesopotama.

"Find the man who speaks for the slaves and tell him, whosoever he might be, of who I am. Tell him that I would speak with him. Tell him that I have come to lead his and mine into Troy."

Chapter Seven

THE RESPONSE TOOK JUST OVER ONE DAY, the two soldiers finally returning in the hour after the sun had fully risen to where Brutus' three warships lay at anchor. Both were still dressed in the dusty garbs of laborers, but looked well rested and fed; patently they had met with good hospitality. "Well?" said Brutus, who sat with Membricus and two other of his senior officers, Idaeus and Hicetaon, on the aft deck of his lead ship. Below them, in the belly of the open ship, men sat on the rowing benches, cleaning and oiling weapons against the constant depravations of the sea.

"We have a return message, my lord. You are to travel this evening to Mesopotama itself, where you will meet in the residence of Assaracus, who dwells in the highest house against the northern wall."

" 'The *highest* house'?" Brutus said, raising his eyebrows. Obviously, this was no slave dwelling—not where it could catch the cooling breezes and offer its occupants a fine view.

"Aye, my lord."

"This is a trap," said Idaeus, whose manner was always one of caution when others advised action. Brutus sometimes wondered if his innate caution extended to his eating habits as well, for Idaeus was an unnaturally thin man for his height, but for all that Brutus valued such circumspection in a world where so often men thought that wisdom equated with action.

"Too obvious," said Hicetaon, who was a man more disposed to think of prohibitive caution as a greater risk than unthinking daring. His face, chest, and flanks had the scars to attest to his philosophy.

Brutus had many years' association with both men, and understood the extent of the arguments that lay behind their terse statements. He nodded once, slowly, acknowledging their advice, then looked back to the soldier who had returned with the response. "Tell me in what manner you received this message."

"We found our way to a man called Deimas in the slave quarter," the soldier said. "He speaks for all the Trojans. This man Deimas considered your message, and then asked us to return in the evening. When we did so, he asked us to relay to you the request to go to the house of Assaracus in the city tomorrow night after dusk, just before the gates close."

Idaeus hissed softly at this last.

"What do you know of this Assaracus?" Brutus said to the soldier.

"Deimas said only that he was allied with the Trojan cause. However, he said further, to his request that only you attend Assaracus, that too many strange faces within the city walls would cause comment. One man will attract no comment, especially should you dress as a lowly laborer or farmer. He has given us words for you to say, so that Assaracus' doorkeeper may know you."

"And Deimas' manner? How would you describe it?"

"He was not overly impressed at your message, my lord," said the soldier. "He merely grunted, then laughed shortly."

"I *still* say 'trap,' " said Idaeus. "Enter the city 'just before the gates close'? You *will* be trapped!"

"Deimas is being prudent," observed Hicetaon, folding his arms and staring at Idaeus.

"I agree," Brutus said. "Deimas must be asking himself who is this man who arrives unannounced and says, 'I am here to lead you into Troy'? I also would first make certain of my own safety." He paused, dismissed the soldier, then studied each of his advisers' faces in turn. "Membricus? Tell me your thoughts. Does this response cast a shadow over your soul? Do the gods whisper 'Caution!' in your heart?"

"No, Brutus. This message causes me no disquiet. Do what you will."

Idaeus' mouth folded in a tight line, and Brutus had to suppress a smile.

"Then I will go," he said. "It can do our cause no harm that I should study the defenses of both wall and gates from inside the city . . . and perhaps that was Deimas' part intention."

IN MIDAFTERNOON BRUTUS DRESSED HIMSELF IN the garb of a simple farmer: a well-worn tunic of coarse weave belted at the waist with a leather strap, a woolen half cloak against the evening coolness, and leather sandals on his feet. He removed the gold and bronze rings from his fingers and ears, but left the golden bands of kingship on his limbs, blackening them with a liquid made of oil and ash so that they appeared as if they were made of worthless, stiffened leather. He rubbed a little dust into the otherwise clean and well-oiled black curls of his head, and some more over his hands and arms. He shaved, but only roughly, as would any farmer who had little time for the niceties of ablutions; his shadowy beard also helped to disguise his Trojan features (and for the first time in his life Brutus thanked the gods for his Latin mother, whose blood had diluted his Trojan appearance). At his belt he hung a pouch into which he placed some small vials of herbed oils, to present as gifts to his host, and over his shoulder he slung a larger rope sack containing wild onions, garlic, and a measure of dried figs, as if he intended to sell them within the city.

"Do I look like a hero?" he asked Membricus, ready finally to make the journey to Mesopotama through the afternoon heat.

"No," Membricus replied with a half smile to take away any sting that might be construed in his words. "You look like a forest brigand. I hope this Assaracus has the nerve to admit you to his house."

BRUTUS APPROACHED MESOPOTAMA JUST BEFORE dusk. The two-hour walk through forest and rocky slopes from his ships' anchorage point had been hot, but not as tiring as Brutus had feared it might be.

But perhaps Brutus' own sense of excitement and purpose had rid his body of any tiredness it might have felt. For fifteen empty years, ever since his exile from Alba on the Tiber, Brutus had been wandering the central Mediterranean, seeking some sense of "home." He'd met up with small bands of exiled Trojans, many of whom had joined his band of warriors, and he and his band had fought as mercenaries in the constant intercity struggles and feuds that gripped the disintegrating Mediterranean world.

But he'd never found a home. Never found a place where he felt any sense of belonging. Never found a true sense of purpose.

Now, since Artemis' visit, all had changed. Now he had purpose, a home to aspire to, and power beyond anything he'd dared hope for, if the goddess was to be believed.

And it was he, not his father, nor his grandfather, nor even his noble but ultimately luckless great-grandfather Aeneas, but *he* who was given the task of rebuilding Troy.

For fifteen years Brutus had wandered, fifteen years since that terrible (*wonderful*) day when he had taken the kingship bands from his dead father's limbs. He'd taken a great risk that day—and had been exiled for it—but now that risk had been justified and rewarded.

He looked at Mesopotama as it rose before him. Membricus might mutter about shadows, but all Brutus saw was the opportunity to prove conclusively to Artemis that he was fit for her trust and belief.

Fit to rule over Troy.

MESOPOTAMA SAT ON A HIGH HILL SOME ONE hundred paces south of the River Acheron and some eight hundred paces north of where the river emptied into the bay. The walled city encompassed the entire hill, although a scattering of hovels, workshops, and tanneries sprawled unprotected beyond the walls. Brutus looked closely at the hovels, and saw that the women wandering in and out of doorways, and the children who played in the dust, were Dorians rather than Trojans, confirming his earlier belief that the Trojan slaves lived inside the city.

The Trojan slaves likely lived in the houses of their masters (most probably crowded into windowless, cramped rooms in basements) or in hovels set against the interior of the city's walls where space and light were at a premium.

He adjusted the sack over his shoulder as he paused to rest, leaning from one foot to the other so that any observer would think him merely tired, and studied the city as best he could. Most of the houses inside the walls, leading up to the civic buildings and the king's palace at the very top of the hill, were well constructed in pale dressed stone with guttered roofs of red tile. The city walls themselves were solid stone, the height of five men and, from what Brutus could see, almost as thick.

His eyes watchful now, Brutus resumed his walk toward the city gates, marking their construction and defenses as he neared.

The gates, still open, were of reinforced thick planks of cypress, barred with bronze and hung so that when closed they would give little purchase to attackers.

The outer gates opened into a narrow, dark roadway that broached the ten-pace-thick walls: anyone who managed to penetrate the outer gates would suffer heavily from the missiles of defenders positioned high above.

Beyond this, on the inner face of the wall, were another pair of gates, almost as solidly built as the outer pair.

Once at the outer gates, Brutus was stopped by a guard who seemed more than half asleep with boredom: Brutus smiled to himself—if his ships *had* been noticed and reported, the guard would have been far more alert. The guard spoke to him, asking his business, and Brutus, hanging his head so that his features remained largely hidden in the shadow of the wall, replied in his best rustic Greek, saying that he had some dried figs and wild onions to trade for some town-made pots for his wife.

The guard, uncaring of either figs or pots or any other doings of peasants, nodded Brutus through, observing as he passed that at this late hour he'd need to find himself a bed for the night until the gates reopened in the morning.

Brutus acknowledged him with a wave as he trudged through the initial defensive alley, then glanced to either side as he passed through the inner gates.

As he'd theorized, the narrow spaces between wall and the lower blocks of Dorian houses and tenement buildings were packed with poorly built and thinly thatched hovels. And even with that brief glance, Brutus could see several women and children moving in the shadows between wall and tenement buildings . . . women and children with the distinctive features of Troy.

His people.

Dampening down his excitement—time enough for that once he'd managed to secure their freedom—Brutus walked farther into the city, moving higher through the streets to where he supposed Assaracus' house stood.

The city was clearly wealthy, and this pleased Brutus; the pickings would be good. The streets were paved and guttered in stone—a rare luxury. The city's Dorian citizens, now engaged in their final few tasks for the day before the evening set in, were well garbed in clothes that made use of fine materials; Brutus even saw two women wearing robes made of rare wild silks. The houses were indeed well built and maintained, and the glimpses inside that Brutus gained through several open doors showed fine interiors, decorated with vivid paints and tiles and even, in one instance, gilding.

"A rich city, indeed," Brutus murmured to himself, pausing at a street corner to stare about with what he hoped would be taken for the wide-eyed wonder of a countryman.

All well for his purpose.

He turned left at the street corner, walking up the center of an emptying street that led toward the northern quarter of the city. As he climbed, the houses became larger and grander, clearly the abodes of wealthy and important citizens. Many of them were gated and walled, mini-fortresses within the larger city fortress.

Palaces, almost, rather than houses.

Brutus' curiosity about Assaracus grew even stronger. Who was this man, clearly wealthy and influential, and even more clearly Greek, to be so allied with the Trojan slaves?

Chapter Eight

*B*RUTUS CLIMBED THE STREET FOR A FEW more minutes, the way becoming ever steeper and the houses on either side more palatial, until he came to what was clearly the northernmost point of the walls. Here the street ended in a wide court. High walls surrounded the semicircular court, behind which rose grand houses.

All gates but one were tightly bolted against the coming night.

To this gate Brutus turned, noting without surprise that it belonged to the house at the northernmost point of the walls. He approached, wondering what awaited him behind the darkened angle of the partly open solid wood gate.

As he stepped up to the gate, there was a movement inside, and a servant emerged, his head bowed. "Have you figs for the master?" he asked, his voice low. He spoke in Dorian Greek, a rough but easily understandable dialect of the sweeter southern language of the Peloponnese.

"Aye," replied Brutus, using the code that had been passed to him. "But they are of unusual taste, having come from far away."

The servant bowed, accepting his answer, then opened the door fully.

Behind it waited a short man of solid build. He was in early old age, his face lined, and his nose prominent amid his sunken cheeks. He was dressed plainly—his tunic of poor quality linen but of a good cut—yet stood with the bearing of a man in authority. His gray hair was still thick but was cut in an unusual fashion—the left side hung free but only to his cheek whereas the right side was braided and hung almost to his shoulder.

Brutus, frowning over the hair, nevertheless knew immediately who he must be . . . and, knowing that, knew what the hairstyle signified. "Deimas," he said, and inclined his head.

"You are Brutus," Deimas said, inclining his own head, although with noticeably less respect than Brutus had given him. "A Trojan . . . apparently. I welcome you to Mesopotama, and to the house of Assaracus who waits inside to greet you. You have intrigued us greatly, with your arrival and the"—he paused, a small derisive smile playing about his mouth—"tone of the greeting you sent to me. It is a long time since I have heard such arrogance."

"Then perhaps my arrival is most timely, indeed, Deimas, if you so forget your heritage. Now, I have walked far, and my feet and face are dusty. May I take advantage of the hospitality of this house?"

In answer Deimas stepped aside, indicating that Brutus should enter before him.

THE ATRIUM OF THE HOUSE WAS WELCOMING, cool, and well lit with oil lamps against the encroaching dusk. Rush mats, woven into intricate designs, had been spread across the stone floor, and the walls were painted with vivid blues, reds, and golds into scenes of rustic idylls. Just inside the entrance and to one side there was a small but finely built altar, and Brutus paused to make brief obeisance to the gods before he walked into the atrium proper.

Deimas, having made his own respects to the deities, waved Brutus to a chair, where a young woman wearing a similar haircut to Deimas' waited with two bowls of scented water, several vials of oils, and some thick towels. Brutus sat, and allowed the woman to take off his sandals and place his feet into the first bowl of pleasantly warmed water.

"This is a Dorian house," Brutus said to Deimas as the woman carefully dried his feet before using her gentle hands to rub them with scented oils. "Why have you brought me here?"

Deimas looked at him oddly, then looked pointedly at the woman, now washing Brutus' face and hands with water from the second bowl.

Brutus looked at her, then back to Deimas. "I would trust a fellow Trojan with my life, even though she be a stranger to me."

The woman paused, staring at Brutus in surprise.

He smiled at her. "I know my fellow brothers and sisters by their blood," he said. "By the arcs of their brows and the planes of their faces and the sweet curls of their hair. I am glad to see you in good health, sister, although saddened by the cut"—he touched the line of her short brown hair where it swung against her left cheek—"of slavery."

"Then perchance you will recognize *me* as a brother and not as a stranger of whom to be wary," said a new voice, and Brutus turned his eyes to the man who had emerged from one of the interior doorways. He was much younger than Deimas, but carried himself with even more authority—and why not? thought Brutus, for unlike Deimas and the young woman he carried no mark of slavery.

The female slave, her cheeks now prettily stained with a little color, hurriedly finished drying Brutus' hands and face, before backing away and exiting the room.

"You are Assaracus," Brutus said.

Assaracus inclined his head. "Aye," he said, "I am he. Will you attend me, and the dinner I have had caused to be made, in the andron of my house?"

"Gladly," said Brutus, rising from his chair.

The andron, or dining chamber, of Assaracus' house was truly magnificent. Its roofline rose fully the height of three men, supported by well-spaced and proportioned columns, and covered a large chamber whose walls had been painted with exquisite scenes of the gods' frolics and, Brutus was somewhat aggrieved to see, of some of the Greeks' most devastating victories.

"A poor view," Assaracus said, waving nonchalantly at the eastern wall that held an unmistakable depiction of Greeks ravaging the streets of Troy, "but I hold as my excuse only that this was my father's house before mine, and he enjoyed that view, while I do not. Please"—now he waved at one of the several couches laid about the laden low table—"take your ease.

"Now," he continued as all three men each reclined upon a couch, "you say that you are Brutus. Of Aeneas' lineage?"

"Aye," said Brutus, accepting the cup of watered wine that Assaracus handed him, but declining to sip from it. "He is my father twice removed. I am his heir." He paused. "To *all* that Aeneas could claim."

Now Brutus did sip from his cup of wine. "And now you know of my lineage, might I ask yours? Your features bear the unmistakable stamp of Troy, you associate with Deimas, who I understand to speak for all Trojan slaves here in Mesopotama, and yet you live in a Greek house painted with gaudy representations of Troy's ill fate, and you wear your hair in the Greek style . . . not in the style of slavery. I am curious."

"As you should be. Deimas, perhaps you might answer for me?"

"Assaracus is the son of my sister," Deimas said, his eyes cast down. "Lavinia was most beautiful, and was thus taken as concubine to Assaracus' father, Thymbraeceus. He so honored her that when she bore him a son"—Deimas nodded at Assaracus—"Thymbraeceus caused the boy to be named as his heir, above the sons of his Dorian wife."

"And thus my allegiance to Deimas, and my mother's people," Assaracus said. "I am well hated within Mesopotama for my Trojan blood, and only my inherited wealth, and the swords I can buy with that, keeps my person and home safe from harm."

Assaracus saw the interest on Brutus' face at the mention of swords, and though he half smiled, preferred to ignore it for the moment. "My true friends remain among my mother's people, Brutus. Not with the Dorian Greeks of my father's lineage."

"Assaracus is our friend and our ally," said Deimas, now helping himself to several spoonfuls of maza and some of the raw vegetables, "in a world where we have few friends or allies."

He paused, crunched on some celery, then said, "As you must well know."

"Does any Trojan have a friend or ally save among his own people?" Brutus replied.

"I have heard," Deimas said slowly and very deliberately, "that even your own people, your own *family*, turned against you after your father's untimely death."

"I—" Brutus began.

"For which you were undoubtedly responsible," Deimas finished.

"My father's death was an accident," Brutus said. His voice remained even, but there was no doubt in either Deimas' or Assaracus' mind that he was angry at the mention of his father's death.

"With your arrow through his eye?" Assaracus said. He drained his wine cup, and refilled it.

"But then you did think he was a—what was it? Ah yes—a stag," Deimas said.

Brutus said nothing, gazing back at the two men with a calm regard. The manner of his father's death was, in the end, nothing to do with them.

"And now," Assaracus interrupted, placing his wine cup down on the table so hard that red wine spilled across its surface, "having killed your father, accidentally or otherwise, then having been exiled from your home community for the act, and *then* having wandered only the gods know where for the next fifteen years, you arrive off the coast of Epirus and say to your fellow Trojans, 'I am your savior, I will lead you from bondage into Troy.' You are lucky, Brutus, that you even received the courtesy of an invitation to meet with Deimas and myself."

"I am my father's heir, and through him my great-grandfather's heir," Brutus said, his demeanor remaining cool. "I am the heir to all that was lost at Troy. If you had not recognized that then you would not have responded to my message."

"We could just have been curious," Deimas murmured, staring at the wine as he swirled it about his cup.

"Troy is dead and gone," Assaracus said, ignoring Deimas' remark. "It is nothing but a rubble of smoking ash and broken dreams. There is nothing to be heir to. Claim what you want, Brutus, it means nothing to us."

"And do you say the same to these?" Brutus said, and reaching for an ewer of water that stood to one side, wet a piece of linen and rubbed away the oil and ash that obscured the golden band on his left biceps.

"Very pretty," Assaracus muttered, but Deimas' eyes widened at the sight, and Brutus did not miss it.

"I say to you," Brutus said to the two men, "that while there are still men who call themselves Trojans, then there *is* a Troy to be heir to! Not the old Troy"—now he included both men in his gaze—"but a new Troy. When I said that I would lead you into Troy I meant not the ancient Troy, but a new one, alive with the hopes and dreams and the heritage of all those who still call themselves Trojans."

"And where might this new Troy be?" Deimas said. His tone was aggressive, his manner confrontational, but Brutus thought he saw a gleam of desperate hope in the man's eye.

Deimas wanted to believe, but could not yet find the means to do so.

"Not in this world," Brutus said. "All the great cities of the Minoans, the Mycenaeans, and the Trojans—and the Egyptians as well for all I know—are now rubble. Troy, Atlantis, Knossos, Tarsus, Pylos, Iolkos, Thebes, Midea, and a score more that I could name. They have been destroyed by invasion, by upheavals of the earth, and by fiery mountainous eruptions. What further can the gods do to voice their displeasure? It is time for a new beginning, and a new Troy, but one very, very far from here."

"Where?" said Deimas softly. *"Where?"*

"The gods will show me."

Deimas threw up his hands, disbelief winning out, and Assaracus grunted derisively. "I say to you again, Brutus," Assaracus said, "what do you here, saying you wish to lead your brethren to a new beginning? Why should anyone follow *you*?"

"*Because* of my lineage! I was born to lead, and I have the *right* to claim my heritage. I am born of the god-favored . . . my own great-great-grandmother was Aphrodite, and my line is favored by the gods!"

"Not your father, most apparently," Assaracus murmured, but Brutus took no notice.

"And because of my fifteen years spent 'wandering.' Do you think those years were spent in vain? I have three shiploads of seasoned warriors at my back and these fifteen years have made me a seasoned leader of men! And yet further, because my people, my fellow Trojans, are kept here in slavery—I cannot believe they wish to remain so! And, finally, do either of you believe that Mesopotama will escape the fate of so many other cities of our once-proud region? Sooner or later Ariadne's revenge will envelop this city as well. It is time to leave now."

"How?" Deimas said. "This talk of freedom is all very well, but how shall it be accomplished? Will you ask Pandrasus for our freedom?"

"Aye," Brutus said. "That is what I will do."

"Bah!" Assaracus said. "I know Pandrasus, and a prouder man I have never met. He will not let his enslaved work force just 'leave.' And leave *how*? Would you have your fellow Trojans walk to wherever you decide to build a new Troy? The land about here is mountainous and treacherous . . . and you have only three ships. Deimas, how many Trojans are there?"

"Seven thousand."

"Seven thousand. I ask you, Brutus, how will you shift seven thousand, including women and children, ancients and infants, and all their worldly goods, to a 'new Troy' in some far distant land?"

"I intend to ask Pandrasus for the ships," Brutus said, and grinned at the expressions on the faces of his companions. "Listen to me, if I can get Pandrasus to not only agree to allow the Trojans their freedom, but also to provide the ships and provisions for our journey far distant, will you then agree to sail with me? Will you agree that if I accomplish that much then I have the *right* to claim my heritage?"

Assaracus and Deimas looked at each other, and Brutus could see the misgivings in their faces.

"I am sorry," Deimas said. "But none of this has convinced us you are the heir of anything but hopes and words. You cannot seriously mean us to believe that you can somehow manage to persuade Pandrasus to grant freedom to his slave force, then manage to get him to donate several score ships so that we may sail to 'somewhere'—a somewhere that the gods will reveal to you in their own sweet time—so that you can build a 'new Troy.' Brutus, I can't possibly—"

"I am the man," Brutus said, his tone very low, "and I have the means to accomplish this. The way will be hard, yes, but I *can* lead the Trojans back into their pride and their heritage."

"Then prove it!" Deimas snapped. "And with something other than words!"

Brutus stared at him, then abruptly he again reached for the water and linen cloth and rubbed away at the other kingship bands, revealing their golden splendor.

Then he briefly closed his eyes, praying to Artemis for strength.

He thought he heard a soft laugh, and knew that she was with him. *Let me tell you a secret*, she whispered into his mind. *Ariadne left the Game alive, weak and insignificant, in one place only. This is it. If you wish to impress these two fools, then draw on the power of the Game as you were trained.*

Brutus almost stopped breathing. Draw on the power of the Game? Here and now?

I believe in you, she whispered. *Do it.*

Brutus opened his eyes, then made a strange gesture with his right hand that had Deimas suddenly leaning forward in his chair, his eyes sharp with puzzlement.

"See," Brutus whispered, and with his right hand still open from the gesture it had made, he pointed to the eastern wall of the andron where spread the scene of Troy's fall.

Save that now the scene had shifted, and the mural did not depict Troy's death at all. Instead, it showed a city rising on the far bank of a mighty river. As yet the city contained little in the way of buildings, save for a magnificent palace atop a mound in one corner, but the walls had been completed in pale dressed stone. They were thick, and high, with well-fortified semicircular bastions every twenty score of paces.

At one end of the city there sat the main gateway, and before this gateway danced two long lines of maidens and warriors, holding in their hands flowers and torches.

A beautiful, black-haired woman led one line, while at the head of the other danced Brutus.

"I am heir to *all* that Troy implies," Brutus said softly. "*All of it!*"

He dropped his hand, and the mural reverted to the old aspect of Troy destroyed.

Assaracus and Deimas stared a moment longer at the wall, then, very slowly, turned back to face Brutus.

It was Deimas who finally spoke. "I will speak to my people," he said, his voice a little hoarse, "but already I know that they will say: we are with you."

"Good," said Brutus. He looked at Assaracus. "And you?"

"I am yours, too," Assaracus said.

Brutus nodded, and smiled. "Now, these 'swords' that you mentioned, Assaracus. Of what exactly do they comprise?"

TWO NIGHTS LATER—AS THE GUARDS AT THE gates lay insensible, well drugged with the wine Assaracus had sent down earlier—a group of some three hundred men, well armed and armored, slipped out of the city.

Assaracus was at their head, and Deimas, leader of the enslaved Trojans, as well as several score of Trojan men, their hair cropped close to their skulls to lose their hated mark of slavery, ran among Assaracus' mercenaries. They exited the city, then turned onto the road that led east to the steep, forested Acheron gorges.

There, silently and patiently, awaited the bulk of Brutus' warriors.

Behind him, Assaracus left a Trojan population holding their collective breath in hope, and a small but courageous boy on his way to Pandrasus' palace to deliver a modest roll of parchment wrapped in pristine linen.

Chapter Nine

LLANGARLIA

LOTH SAT CLOSE BY HIS FATHER, HIS HEAD bowed in respect.

They were alone in the strange stone house that Genvissa's third foremother had caused to be built. Unlike most Llangarlian houses, which were round with conical thatched roofs, this was a rectangular structure with a heavy (but admittedly completely weatherproof) slate roof. It made Loth uncomfortable, as if the strangeness of the structure kept him a prisoner from the land he loved so much, and he rarely came in here. He couldn't understand why his father wanted to live here with Genvissa . . . but then, Aerne was all too clearly approaching his ancient addleness; Genvissa had him where she wanted, in her house, in her bed, and, like any defenseless infant, dependent on her breast for comfort, nurture, and safety.

Tonight, however, Loth had ventured into the hated structure because he wanted to speak with his father alone, and he knew Genvissa was meeting with Mother Mais at her house some way distant.

Loth almost grinned at the thought. Mother Mais was one of his, and he doubted she'd be giving Genvissa much more than the merest courtesies demanded of any host.

Aerne patted his son's knee, happy to have him near for a change.

"I am pleased you came, my son."

Loth successfully fought the urge to roll his eyes, and merely nodded, as if this domestic harmony was what he, too, had craved all this time.

"I needed to speak with you, Father. Genvissa—"

"I know what you want to say, Loth. No reason to speak it aloud."

"But I *need* to. Father, I have strange doubts regarding Genvissa. I distrust her, and yet cannot form that distrust into words. What she proposes, to bring a strange magic into Llangarlia to counter Og's weakness, is . . . is . . ."

"Is *necessary*, Loth. You know that. What can you and I do, weak as we are?"

"We still have some power left, some of Og's benefice! Surely—"

"What we have is a mere shadow of what once existed, Loth. I should know. I once commanded all of Og's power. Tell me, how long has it been since anyone has seen the stag run wild through the forests?"

"Only last week Coel brought down a magnificent red stag."

Aerne smiled sadly. "You know that is not what I meant. How long has it been since anyone has seen *the* stag? The white stag with the bloodred antlers? Og himself, running free?"

Aerne gave Loth a long moment of silence, then spoke again, infinitely gently. "The last time was the night of your conception, Loth. Running as if panicked through the forests in which I lay with the witch, Blangan. And he had good enough reason to fear . . . didn't he?"

Loth hung his head, hating himself for his own conception, hating his mother for what she had done.

"You have been the best of sons," Aerne said. "I wish I was able to hand over to you Og's full power on my deathbed."

"Perhaps, when you die, the power *will* be reunited in me . . ."

"No. *No*, Loth. When I die what I have will die with me. Og will be even more lessened. Genvissa *needs* to bring in this male magic, Loth, for this land . . . if not for our peace of mind and pride. She needs to act *now*, for if we are both dead before she has completed her task, then this land will lie defenseless."

Loth shook his head, desperate not to accept what his father was saying. "I know what Genvissa proposes makes sense. I know it in here"—he tapped his deformed skull—"but not in here." He tapped his chest. "Every part of me hates it."

"That is your pride speaking, Loth."

Loth raised his head and stared at his father with his beautiful green eyes. "What if it is not my pride, Father? What if it is the remaining part of Og within me that speaks?"

"Oh, *Loth!*"

Both men jumped slightly, as if they were boys caught out in some mischief, then looked behind them.

Genvissa had come through the door, and had now paused just inside it, one hand resting on the door frame.

She looked breathless, as if she'd run all the way from Mother Mais' house, and also fearful, as if she'd come back to her home to discover the worst of the night's monsters cheerily settled within.

Then she smiled, and dropped her hand from the door frame, and walked slowly into the single large chamber of the house. The firelight from the central hearth reflected over her face and body, shadowing her eyes and shrouding her in a mysterious allure that had both men holding their breath.

"Aerne," she said, dropping gracefully down beside him, "will you give me some space to speak with your son alone? Perhaps I can soothe his fears."

Aerne returned her smile, and nodded. "I need to make obeisance to Og anyway. That is always best done outside, beneath the trees."

"Take a cloak," Genvissa said, patting him on the hand as he rose, and ignoring Loth's grimace at the somewhat patronizing action. "The night has grown cold."

She waited until Aerne had left, then she moved her stool about the hearth a little so that she sat close to Loth.

"You do not trust me," she said.

"No."

"Then perhaps I can give you a reason to trust me."

He was silent, studying her face.

"I have a twin purpose in bringing to Llangarlia this strange male"—she paused fractionally, giving her next word added weight—"potency. This man who can replace with his magic what Llangarlia has lost with Og's failing. True, he will bring with him a new magic, something which can be used to combine with Mag's power to revive this land . . . but he can also bring with him something else."

She paused again, a smile playing about her mouth, the firelight sparking brilliantly in her eyes.

"He will also bring with him . . . Blangan. Your mother."

"The Darkwitch?" Loth was stunned. His mother Blangan had fled a few days after she'd given him birth. No one had ever seen her again. "My *mother*." He said the word with hatred.

Now Genvissa did smile, pleased with his reaction. "Aye. He will return Blangan to Llangarlia."

Loth was silent, his face introspective, thinking over the myriad implications of his Darkwitch mother's return.

"Loth," Genvissa said softly, leaning forward and placing a hand lightly on his leg, "there is a possibility, a faint possibility, that if Blangan is destroyed, then so also may be destroyed the darkcraft that she cast over your father. If she dies, then perhaps Og will revive, and we will not need the magic of this stranger."

"What are you saying?" Loth was very aware of Genvissa's hand on his thigh, the warmth of it, the very slight weight of it, and he was dismayed at how easily his body responded to her.

Her hand moved much closer to his groin, one of her fingers straying tantalizingly under the edge of his hip wrap, stroking, its nail teasing. Loth knew very well what Genvissa was doing—with both her words and her hand— but he was almost powerless to resist it. What she was offering was—he drew in a ragged breath—was what he had always wanted. Power.

"If you take revenge on the Darkwitch your mother," Genvissa said very softly, her eyes holding Loth's, her hand now sliding completely beneath his wrap, "then perhaps Og's power be revived . . . in *you*, his avenger."

He couldn't look away from her, and while one part of his mind screamed at him to brush aside her hand, stand, and leave, the rest of his mind was utterly seduced by the possibilities suggested by word and hand.

"And if that is the case," Genvissa continued, her voice still very low, her hand stroking very gently, her face, her mouth, very close to his, "then what need will I—and this land—have of this strange man and his strange magic? Og will be resurgent again, in *you*, and then you and I . . . you and I . . ."

There was barely a coherent thought left in Loth's mind at this point, but he clung to it grimly. "Then if you have no need for this strange man, if all you need is for me to take revenge on Blangan to break the darkcraft which binds Og, why bring him here in the first instance?"

"Because I need him to bring to us Blangan . . . and because you might fail. Blangan may be too strong for you. If you fail, then I will need him to—"

"I will not fail!"

She only smiled, and increased the pressure of her hand.

Loth closed his eyes, fought for some control, and managed to find it. "Why not my father? Why not tell Aerne this? Why not send him to—"

"Aerne is an old man. Weak. Blangan bested him once before. Neither you nor I nor this land can afford it to happen again. *You* must do this, Loth. I need a strong man, Loth." There was infinite promise in the manner she said "need." "Not your father. Never your father."

She leaned forward and kissed him, and that was the final weapon that shattered the resistance both of Loth's mind and of his body.

He shuddered under her hand, and sighed, then nodded.

"YOU SPOKE WITH LOTH?"

They were in her bed now, sweaty and relaxed from sex.

"Aye." Genvissa pushed her body even tighter against Aerne's. "He has come about to my plan."

"My dear"—Aerne's hand stroked her shoulder, as if apologizing for what he was about to say—"I accept that you need this man to counter Og's weakness . . . but will you perhaps confide in me what he will do? How it is that his magic will protect this land?"

Genvissa lay silent for a while, thinking over what she should tell Aerne. Eventually, as Aerne waited patiently, she decided that a little of the truth might not hurt too much.

"This man, Brutus, controls part of what is called the Game."

"The Game?"

"Aye . . . you know that my fifth foremother was not of this land?"

"Aye." Aerne smiled and moved his hand to Genvissa's luxuriant black hair. "Thus these dark curls of yours."

"She came from a land in the southern waters of a sea called the Aegean, Aerne. In her world, in this Aegean world, the great men of power used something called the

Game to protect their lands. When my fifth foremother came to this land, she truly became as all Llangarlians . . . but she remembered what she knew of the Game, and taught it to her daughter, as her daughter passed it on to her daughter, and thus to me."

Aerne felt a flicker of unease. "Do you mean that all the MagaLlans, from the time of your fifth foremother to you, have secret knowledge of power other than that of Mag and Og?"

Displeased, Genvissa propped herself up on an elbow. "Indeed!" she said. "And what a good thing, too, otherwise this land would face certain ruin!"

Aerne laughed softly, apologetically. "Of course, Genvissa, forgive me."

She lay down again, nestling her breasts against his chest.

"Please," Aerne said, fighting down his arousal, "tell me more of this Game."

Genvissa shrugged, as if the subject was now of disinterest to her. "It is a powerful spell-weaving which uses both male and female power to protect a land against all evil set against it. There are very few left who know how to manipulate the Game, who know how to use it . . . two people, in fact, myself and this man I have summoned to us, this Kingman."

And one who will want to destroy it, she thought, *but Asterion is far away, and no threat.*

"Once many people within the Aegean world knew how to play the Game," Genvissa continued, "but over past generations the knowledge has died, as have the people who had access to the Game's secrets. This man, this Brutus, is the only Kingman left . . . and thus his usefulness to us, my love, for if we use him to build the spell-weaving here, then there will be no one who can subsequently undo it. Our land will remain forever protected while all others about it will fall victim to plagues and disasters."

"And where is this Brutus from? What manner of man is he?"

"He is a proud man, and a courageous and skillful warrior, both requisites for a truly great Kingman. His bloodline comes from a city called Troy, now destroyed . . . and so thus the Game that he knows is the Troy Game. In that we are lucky, for the Troy Game was one of the most powerful of all the Games about the Aegean. So we shall use the Troy Game to protect this land, my love."

Aerne shrank away from her wandering hand, concerned. "I have heard of this Troy from the traders who come to buy our copper and tin. Troy was attacked and ravaged, as you say. What manner of protection is this Troy Game then, if Troy itself lies destroyed?"

Genvissa sighed. "Have you not been listening to me, old man? Troy was destroyed many generations ago—Brutus' line has been wandering seeking a home ever since. Then there were many Kingmen, many men who knew how to manipulate the Game and who knew how to unravel the spell-weaving that protected any given land or city. Troy's Game was unraveled by a man called Achilles, who knew the means by which to dispel the magical protection that hung about Troy. But Achilles is long dead, as is his line. Every other Aegean Kingman and their lines are dead, save for the Trojan kingline. This Brutus is the only man left who can weave the enchantments needed to resurrect the Game. The only one. There is no one who can unravel the Game this Brutus and I will build to protect Llangarlia, Aerne. *No one.*"

No one, she repeated in her mind, and smiled at the thought of useless, feeble Asterion raging far beyond the peaks of the great Himalayas.

The instant I close the Game with Brutus, Asterion will be trapped. There is no need to worry about Asterion. No need at all.

IN HIS DISTANT ALPINE VALLEY, DEEP WITHIN THE *dark heart of his roughly-drawn labyrinth, Asterion lowered his head, and smiled.*

Power throbbed about him, so virulent it had devastated the entire valley of all life. One day . . .

"One day!" whispered Asterion.

. . . he would fling that power at Genvissa and all her hopes and plans and ambitions.

Meanwhile, all he had to do was sit, and observe.

Chapter Ten

MESOPOTAMA

Cornelia Speaks

I SHIFTED SLIGHTLY, TURNING MY SHOULDER just so, knowing that the movement caused my breasts to catch the morning light as it flooded through the windows of the megaron. I had dressed carefully that morning, donning the stiffest and thickest of my flounced ankle-length skirts, knowing that their swaying as I moved drew the eye to my hips. I had begged my nurse, Tavia, to tighten my wide embroidered girdle that extra notch so that my waist narrowed to the span of a man's hands. And above my narrow waist and my sweeping flounced skirts I donned the very best of my jackets; its stiffened emerald linen fitting tightly to my form. I had tied only its bottom two laces, leaving the rest of the jacket open to frame my breasts, as I was allowed to do as an unmarried woman. My dark hair, although not as glorious as that of some women's, was nonetheless left to curl and drape over my shoulders most becomingly. I looked my absolute best that morning and, from the admiring glances that fell my way, I knew I was not the only one to think so.

Every man in the megaron who saw me lusted for me. Even my own father, I think, for I saw the tip of his tongue moisten his lips as his eyes lingered on my breasts. It was not unknown for a king to take his own daughter to wife, especially when she was his only heir, but if my father had thoughts in that direction, then I should shortly have to disabuse him of them. There was only one man I wanted, and that was my cousin Melanthus.

Eight paces away, Melanthus' mouth lifted in a knowing smile as he beheld me, and he shifted, aroused.

He would be mine within the week. I knew it.

Suddenly happy, I relaxed, slipping away from my provocative pose. My mind slipped into one of my frequent fantasies about my life with Melanthus: the long hot nights spent in wild abandon in our bed; the children I would bear him (many strong and courageous sons ... I would not waste his time nor my strength on mere daughters); the extravagant feasts and celebrations we would preside over when he was my consort; the epic poems Melanthus would compose in my honor; the ...

"What is this?"

So startled I could not repress a small jump, I looked to my father Pandrasus. He stood before his throne on the raised dais of the megaron, one of his legs thrust back as if to retain contact with his golden throne, a piece of somewhat tatty parchment in his hand.

His shoulders were back, and stiff, as if in affront. His belly was thrust forward, as if in challenge, and his face was flushed, his eyes bright, as if in outraged anger. On the wrist of the hand that held the offending parchment gleamed the thick gold and ruby bracelet of his office, a larger and only slightly richer version of the similar bracelet that encircled my wrist.

He looked magnificent—all the women in the chamber must have been set a-trembling, and even I felt my tongue circle about my lips in appreciation, but I managed to turn my mind away from my father's undoubted sexual appeal (besides, what was it when compared to Melanthus' youthful beauty and prowess?). When I was young, a mere four or five, a prophetess had said I would marry a great king and bear him many children, but that great king was surely not my father. She must have seen Melanthus . . . perhaps in our bed, getting one of those many children on my body.

Again my mind threatened to drift off toward yet another fantasy about my cousin, but then my father shouted again, and I forced my mind back to the matter at hand.

"What is this?"

Several servants cowered before my father, falling to their knees, and the soldiers about the walls of the megaron had stiffened, hands to their swords.

My father waved the parchment about, still shouting. I had no idea what it contained, but it was undoubtedly the reason my father had summoned his court early this day. I hoped it would not detain us long, so that I could draw Melanthus into a private corner, and test just how deep his desire ran.

I glanced again at Melanthus, and I saw that he had eyes for no one else but me, and the linen of his waistcloth bulged most promisingly.

Perhaps he would be mine before the morning was out.

"Listen!" my father said, and began to read.

"ı, ƌrutus, leader of all those who survived the fall of troy, send greetings to pandrasus, king of the dorian greeks in mesopotama. ı am come to demand that you immediately free all trojans from your slavery, for ı find it intolerable that you should treat them in any way other than that which their nobility demands. ƌe moved to pity them, and bestow upon them their former liberty and grant them permission to live wheresoever they please. furthermore, as example of your grand benefice, ı demand that you shall also grant your former slaves the means to remove themselves from mesopotama . . . five score of ships, well stocked with food, water, wine, and cattle, that they might begin their new lives far away from here in grand manner. ı await your decision in the forests to the east of mesopotama, knowing that you will do what is best for your people, and your own greatness."

I paid all this little attention. It had nothing to do with me . . . Melanthus was all that mattered.

My father finished with the detestable letter, then threw back his head and roared with laughter.

"I have heard of this Brutus!" he said. "Cornelia, shall I tell the court of what I know?"

Startled by the direct question, I gathered my thoughts. "Of course," I said. "Unless what you know is unseemly."

"Oh, it is unseemly enough, but I think you should hear it."

Somewhat interested now (scandal was always delicious), I lifted my eyebrows—newly plucked and darkened to just the right shade to complement the rich blueness of my eyes—and hoped that Melanthus was close enough to see their full effect.

"A Trojan," my father continued, and I would have dismissed Brutus from my care instantly save that he had so impudently demanded such nonsense from my father. From the tone of his communication, one could almost have believed that Brutus thought himself an equal of my father. It was laughable. Ridiculous! I found it difficult to believe that a Trojan had found the temerity to write thus to my father. He must suffer from a malaise of the mind. I shivered at the thought of how my father would deal with him.

"A Trojan," my father said again, his voice venomous, and spat on the gleaming floor of the megaron.

The phlegm sat there, glistening in the sun as it streamed through the windows, a fitting response to this man Brutus' slur.

"He is an exile, even from his own people," my father continued. "He tore his mother apart in childbirth and then, when he was a youth of fifteen, slew his father with a 'misplaced' arrow. He is a man who has murdered his parents, who is condemned, even by the Trojans"—he spoke the word as an insult—"and now, having come to disturb *my* peace, he thinks to demand I set my slaves free! Ah!"

One of my father's advisers, a man by the name of Sarpedon who was known for the prudence of his advice, stepped forward and raised his head as if seeking permission to speak, but my father waved him back to his place. This was no time for *prudence*, surely!

"Cornelia, beloved," my father said, holding out the parchment to me. "You are my daughter and my heir. What would *your* answer be to this man?"

I tossed my head, enjoying the moment. My father, the mighty Pandrasus, asked me for advice when he had waved Sarpedon back. How everyone must admire me at this moment! I walked forward, my step springing, knowing how pleasingly such movement would make my loosely bound dark curls and my ivory breasts sway and catch the sun.

I took the parchment from my father. "He is ridiculous," I said, and tore the parchment into two, then two again, and then even again, until the thing lay scattered about the floor in tiny pieces. "He cannot know of your greatness to send such a thing. Do not our laws state"—I was showing off my learning before Melanthus at this point—"that such disrespect should be rewarded only with death?"

My father laughed, proud of me. "Well said, daughter. Shall I kill him for his impudence then?"

It was a game to me. I thought nothing of it. All I wanted was to make Melanthus smile. "Indeed, Father. You are too mighty to let such impudence pass unheeded." And, oh, Hera, how I wished in the weeks and months to come that I had never spoken such thoughtlessness. Was I to blame for what ensued?

"As my daughter wishes! There shall be a slaughter so great that when next you bathe it may be in Trojan blood!" My father laughed again, hearty and confident. "Antigonus!" he called to his younger brother (and sire of the most adorable Melanthus). "Set the trumpets a-blowing and the archers a-racing to their chariots! We shall go a-hunting this morning!"

A movement from the corner of my eye distracted me from the excitement, and I saw Melanthus approach his father, and lay a hand to his arm.

His waistcloth now lay smooth against his thighs.

Suddenly worried, I hastened over.

"Father," I heard Melanthus say in his honeyed voice, "allow me to ride with you, I pray! I am old enough now to play at war!"

Antigonus roughed the black curls of his son's head, considering. "Your mother treasures you, the last of her sons to remain at her side. Should I so distress her to allow this?"

"I am a *man*!" Melanthus growled in as deep a voice as he could manage. I would have laughed were not the situation so serious.

Antigonus leaned forward and kissed his son's brow with soft lips. "Ah, my best beloved son, I forget that last summer you passed your sixteenth year. Very well then, this will be no more than a skirmish in any case. You may ride with me."

Melanthus was too excited to do anything but glow at his father, but I was not so lost for words.

"Uncle! How could you risk your best beloved son this way! Surely he needs a year or so yet before he must ride to war?"

"He is a man, Cornelia," my uncle said. "Have you not realized?"

I blushed, as I was meant to, and Melanthus laughed, and spoke to his father. "I will go to Mother, and tell her that finally you have allowed me to stray beyond her skirts. Cornelia, will you walk with me? Knowing Mother, she will have need of a woman's comfort at the news that her youngest son has now stepped into his manhood."

Antigonus grinned at both of us, then walked away with a quick step to organize the raiding party needed to subdue this absurd Brutus.

"Come with me," Melanthus breathed into my ear. "We can have a moment in peace before Tavia seeks you out for your morning milk."

My flush deepened, but with indignation now. "I am a woman grown—my nurse does not rule *me*!"

"Come," Melanthus said again, and he pulled me down the corridor toward his mother's apartment.

We never reached it. The corridor was bustling with people hastening to and from the courtyard where the soldiers were gathering, and when Melanthus pulled me into a small storeroom no one noticed.

Melanthus closed the door, and, presumably hot both with his lust for me and his pride at going to war, thrust me against a wall and grabbed my breasts in his hands. I gasped at his daring, but then leaned in against him, pushing my breasts the more firmly into his hands and, for the first time, laid my mouth to his.

It was our first kiss, and—I must admit—it was a little more brutal and uncomfortable than I'd dreamed. His mouth crushed mine, our teeth clinked, and then his tongue was thrusting deep into my mouth. His hands about my breasts squeezed, painfully, and I felt his hips shove against mine.

I was startled at his ardor, but it was what I had wanted for so long, and so, in a spirit of great adventure, my eyes staring into his, I pushed my tongue against his.

Suddenly his hands had left my breasts and were tugging at my skirts, bruising their silk in his desperation to pull them above my waist.

I was about to lose my virginity. I was both scared and excited; this wasn't the gentle, romantic procedure I'd always imagined, and I was beginning to think that Melanthus was a little too knowledgeable for my peace of mind, but at the same time my spine felt as if it were on fire, and I had an ache deep in my belly that I knew only Melanthus could relieve.

He grabbed at my thighs, then my buttocks, and half lifted me up so that I sat against his hips.

"Wrap your legs around me," he said, his voice breathless and hoarse, and hesitating only momentarily, I did as he asked. I was trembling now and, to be honest, a little more scared than excited.

His mouth was back on mine, his tongue thrusting deep, and I felt the first determined thrusts of his erection bruising the delicate skin between my thighs. He pushed against me, and I screwed my eyes shut, knowing that there would be a momentary pain when he finally managed to pierce me. I sent a quick prayer to Hera, begging that the pain *was* only brief and more than compensated for by the wondrous sweet feel of Melanthus deep inside me.

And then, suddenly, it was all over: for him, at least. Melanthus gave a ridiculous hiccupy gasp, and I felt a warm sticky wetness flood over my inner thigh.

He sighed, and closed his eyes as I opened mine in bewilderment and a horrible sense of failure. I might be an innocent when it came to what happened between a man and a woman, but I knew that this was not all that there should be.

I was still a virgin, to start with.

My cheeks flooded with warmth (had I done something wrong? Had Melanthus not found me desirable enough?) and I placed my hands on his shoulders to push him away (all I wanted to do at this point was to pull down my skirts and find somewhere private to clean myself) but before either he or I could move the door to the storeroom flew open, and there stood my nurse Tavia in a narrow rectangle of bright light.

"Princess!" she wailed, and Melanthus dropped me so quickly my bare buttocks hit the stone floor with a bruising force. He fumbled with his clothing, but Tavia paid him no more mind as she ran over to me, patting incoherently at my face and hands and sobbing something unintelligible.

I managed to rise to my feet, surreptitiously trying to wipe the mess off my thigh with a corner of my skirts as I did so. But Tavia was fussing too much, so I gave up the effort, and let my skirts drop down to cover my nakedness.

His clothes now in some order, Melanthus looked at me, his mouth opening and closing as he fought to find something to say. He gave up, gave me a lopsided grin, and fled out the door.

By this time I was so embarrassed I succumbed to a shameful display of waspishness. "Be quiet, Tavia! Do you want to attract the entire household with your fuss?"

She did quieten, although it took her several gulping breaths to do so. She looked at me, noting well the stain on my robe. "Princess, did he . . . did he . . ."

"Yes," I said, wishing it were so, then decided to tell the truth. "But not in me. You may rest assured, Tavia, that I am as yet still intact. It was but play."

There. Let her think what she would. I brushed past her and marched back to my chamber, trying to ignore the increasingly uncomfortable stickiness between my thighs and Tavia's fussing at my back. But by the time I'd washed and changed, my good humor had returned. Melanthus *did* desire me. It was only my inexperience that had thwarted him.

Tonight, when he had returned victorious from battle, I would ensure that I was better prepared and that we would have the time, the privacy, and the comfort to more fully consummate our passion.

Tavia, unfortunately, would have to take her snores elsewhere.

I smiled, happy once more, and slipped back into my fantasies.

Chapter Eleven

BRUTUS MOVED CAUTIOUSLY ACROSS THE slope of the hill, ducking behind the trunks of the thick beech, elm, and oak trees and the occasional outcrop of limestone rock that had erupted forth from the earth.

All about him, hidden within shadows and behind trees, stood still, silent men armed with swords, daggers, and lances, their bodies protected with hardened leather corsets, greaves, and helmets. Small circular shields were slung across their backs, ready to be pulled about and used at a moment's notice. Their faces, as any reflective surface on their bodies or armor, were dulled with dirt.

Warriors similarly lined the shadowy spaces of the forest on the other side of the gorge. There were almost eight hundred all told, Assaracus' men as well as Brutus'.

Between the two slopes of the gorge gurgled the shallow River Acheron. Its clear waters slipped over the sand and gravel of its bed as if it had not a care in creation, and yet, watching, some of the waiting warriors wondered how that could be, given that surely the Acheron's waters carried within them the moans of warriors long dead and trapped by Hades.

Even if not contemplating the waters that flowed from Hades' realm, every one of the silent warriors was tense with the waiting.

Surely Pandrasus would not ignore Brutus' taunting letter? Surely he must soon issue forth from his citadel?

"He will not ride up this gorge." Assaracus slid on his haunches down the slope to join Brutus. "He will know it is a trap. Pandrasus may be many things, but he is not stupid; he will have his brother Antigonus with him, a tried and true general."

"He will come," Brutus said, knowing the doubts that riddled Assaracus. The man had chanced everything on Brutus' plan. "They both will. And they will *both* slip into the trap."

What trap? Assaracus wondered. We have the advantage of height, to be sure, but the floor of the gorge is flat, and wide, and Pandrasus and Antigonus will have their chariots filled with archers. Moreover, *who* is trapped? Not a hundred paces farther into the gorge the river sank into a sheer face of rock, descending into Hades' realm, and if Pandrasus blocked the entry to the gorge, then Brutus' and Assaracus' men were dead, trapped here for Pandrasus' army to pick off at their leisure.

"Brutus—" Assaracus began, his nerve finally failing as he realized he wanted to be anywhere but here, and then stopped as one of the forward scouts waved a coded message.

"They're coming," Brutus said and signaled the men on both sides of the gorge to move slowly down the slopes to prearranged locations. He moved his head so he could stare Assaracus full in the face. "It is too late to change our plan now, my friend."

ANTIGONUS RODE IN THE LEAD SIXTY-FIVE CHAR-iots. He clung to the handrail, his feet firm against the stiffened leather-and-wood deck, bracing his body against the lurching, jolting movement of the chariot. Beside him the charioteer hung on to the reins of the team of three horses, his shoulders bunched against the strain, his eyes narrowed in concentration, keeping the horses to a slow trot, even though they wanted to race.

On either side of Antigonus chariots fanned out, archers braced beside the charioteers, their quivers of arrows tied firmly before them to the front walls of the chariots.

Behind this forward wave came Pandrasus, leading the second wave of some fifty chariots. And behind this came almost a thousand men, jogging easily, their shields across their backs, swords sheathed, helmets firmly placed, minds and hearts set on proving their own glory against the descendants of the Trojans their forefathers had defeated.

Among them jogged Melanthus, desperately trying to keep the grin from his face, his two elder brothers on either side of him.

From the gates of Mesopotama they had turned to the wide road that led east along the banks of the Acheron. Two thousand paces from the city the road began to narrow and then climb, slowly at first, but then more steadily, and Antigonus waved the forward movement of the army back to a more sedate walk: no point in having his fighters arrive breathless. The ground rose to either side of the river, thickly wooded, and Antigonus peered closely at it, not wanting to be surprised by a sudden attack from the trees.

Nothing. The day was as still as a grave.

Antigonus put up his hand, halting the column. Before him the Acheron issued forth from a gorge, the floor wide and easy to maneuver in to be sure, but still a good place for a trap. If he were Brutus, this would be where he would set it.

There was movement behind him, and Antigonus turned.

Pandrasus, directing his chariot forward to view for himself.

"They must be in there," Antigonus said to his brother. "The fool said he'd wait in the eastern forests. But where? Would we be better riding in, or sending the infantry?"

Pandrasus grinned. "They think themselves cunning, but perhaps they have outmaneuvered themselves. We leave a squad of chariot here, should they think to come running out toward us, and the other chariots, and all the infantry, we divide into two forces and take the back tracks behind the hills. They surely have not the numbers to cover both the gorge *and* the back paths—even if they know they're there. Then we come on them from above with both arrows and swords."

"They are trapped. They cannot escape this gorge from the other end, for the mountains are too steep, and we have this single escape plugged."

"They are truly a worthless foe," Pandrasus said, swiveling where he stood in the chariot to give the signal for the men to break into two groups and climb the paths behind the Trojans.

"Wait!" said Antigonus in a most peculiar voice.

"THEY WILL NOT COME IN," ASSARACUS SAID TO Brutus, staring with squinted eyes down the distance of the gorge to where the Dorian army stood. "They are not that foolish. Look! Even now Pandrasus turns to give the signal that will see us dead!"

But Brutus did not respond.

Assaracus turned to him, and gasped.

There was a woman now standing beside the crouched Brutus, a bow and a quiver of arrows across her back, her hand on his shoulder, and she was surely no mortal woman.

She turned her head toward Assaracus, and bared her teeth, and her face was as Death.

"WAIT," ANTIGONUS SAID AGAIN, HIS VOICE SLOW, lazy, seeming almost drugged. "I think we have been mistaken, brother. See? This is no gorge, not at all, but a flat field, newly harvested of barley. Even a mouse cannot hide among that stubble."

Pandrasus looked, not understanding, then blinked. How could they have been so mistaken as to have seen a gorge before them? There were no mountains, no forests, no river. Instead there lay before them a flat stubbled field, and see! There lay the Trojans, unprepared, sitting about campfires drinking cups of unwatered wine!

These fools could be overcome with a squad of toddlers wielding nothing but their bone teething rings.

"Ride!" whispered Pandrasus. Then, screaming, "Ride! Run! Mow them down!"

THERE WAS A SUDDEN THUNDER OF HOOVES, THEN a roar of voices, and Assaracus jerked his head back to where the Dorian army now rode and ran unheedingly into the gorge. They splashed through the shallows of the Acheron, some tripping over in their haste, their comrades behind them treading in their backs in their haste to propel themselves forward.

The chariots came first, leading the charge, then hardly a breath behind them came the infantry, swords and lances raised to shoulder height, faces screwed up in battle lust.

"Pandrasus! Pandrasus!" they screamed.

"Brutus," Assaracus whispered, overcome.

"Wait," Brutus said, and beside him the strange goddess tightened her hold on his shoulder.

*   *   *

ANTIGONUS FOUND HIMSELF SCREAMING WITH
the men, screaming in bloodlust and triumph. He pounded
the back of his charioteer, urging him forward, forward,
forward, while to his right Pandrasus did likewise.

None of the men saw anything save what the Darkwitch
put before their eyes.

"WAIT," BRUTUS WHISPERED AGAIN.

Assaracus could not tear his eyes away from the Dorians.
They were well into the gorge now, charging as if they had
no care in the world, as if all that lay before them was a
family of mice who had given themselves to the slaughter.

As the road narrowed deeper into the gorge, most of the
men and chariots had been forced into the shallow river
where, given the firm surface of the river bottom, they still
managed good headway.

But headway toward what? Assaracus wondered.

Then he gasped, horrified even though what was happening would win them an almost bloodless victory.

SUDDENLY ANTIGONUS SCREAMED. THERE WAS
no stubbled field! No Trojan army sitting heedless and
drunk about campfires!

There was only the steep and densely wooded gorge
walls rising to either side of him, and a river underfoot . . .

. . . a river underfoot that had abruptly risen to thigh
height . . . no! Waist height!

*Or was it that the river bottom had given way to the
treacherous quicksand of the marshes? Were the men, the
chariots, sinking into the very heart of Hades' realm itself?*

"Brother!" he screamed to Pandrasus who was riding in
one of the few chariots still on the solid banks of the river.
"Save yourself! Get yourself and as many as you can back
to Mesopotama!"

*   *   *

"WE MOVE," BRUTUS SAID, AND STOOD, WAVING his left hand in signal.

Assaracus glanced at him. The goddess was gone now, and Brutus was grinning at him with a strange light in his eyes. "Will you join the killing, comrade?"

IT WAS A SLAUGHTER. ANTIGONUS' ARCHERS MANaged to get off some arrows but they were soon overwhelmed by the Trojans—who, graced by the gods—walked across the river as if its waters were solid rock! What men of his that had not succumbed completely to the ensorcelled riverbed were all but trapped to their hips, unable to do more than parry a few blows with their swords, or jab uselessly with their lances.

"Father!" came the desperate cry, and Antigonus turned in horror.

There, only a few paces away, were his three sons. One, his eldest, had gained purchase on a sinking chariot, and had dragged the two younger boys to a momentary safety. All were covered in the slime of the river, their weapons gone, their faces crumpled in horror, their eyes shining at their father in a frightful hope that somehow he would save them.

Antigonus gave a wordless cry and stretched out a useless hand even as his own chariot lurched, its horses shrieking, and began to sink.

THE TROJANS, AUGMENTED BY ASSARACUS' MEN, surged into and among the trapped Dorian army.

It was as if they were once again in their youth and on the practice field, sticking their swords into straw dummies. Some of the Dorians screamed, some pleaded, some swung weapons uselessly.

All died.

Assaracus fought—if fighting it could be called, slaughtered, more like—at Brutus' side, when he suddenly realized that Pandrasus, together with perhaps five or six chariots and a hundred men, were escaping out of the gorge.

"Brutus!" he cried, grabbing at Brutus' left arm to gain his attention.

Brutus stilled instantly, his sword almost fully through the neck of a Dorian charioteer. "What is it?" he asked, his voice still strangely calm.

The stricken charioteer grabbed uselessly at the blade in his neck, his mouth open, gurgling as blood bubbled forth.

"Pandrasus escapes," Assaracus said, staring in horror at the charioteer. "He—"

Brutus leaned back, pulling his sword free, and the charioteer collapsed, his hands still trying to plug the gaping wounds in his neck.

The man's head rocked, and Assaracus realized, sickenly, that the charioteer's hands were the only thing holding his head on.

Then the hands collapsed nerveless, and the head dropped, splashing into the river. For an instant the body still stood up to its waist in water, and then, gently, almost apologetically, it too sank beneath the waters of the Acheron.

"It is of no matter," Brutus said, and it took Assaracus a moment to realize he talked of Pandrasus, not of the dead charioteer.

"We must send men after him! If he manages to lock himself into the city he can hold out for a year, maybe more! The city is well stocked for a siege, and we hardly manned to conduct one! Brutus, you said we *need* Pandrasus to supply us with ships, and provisions, and . . ."

Assaracus slid to a halt, wondering why he was giving this speech when Brutus was grinning at him as if Pandrasus' escape was of no consequence.

"I do not think we shall have much trouble gaining an entry to the city ourselves," Brutus said, then extended his sword to a group of sinking chariots some ten paces away. "Look."

*   *   *

ANTIGONUS CALLED OUT TO HIS SONS, TEARS IN his eyes as he considered their bravery.

"Peleus! Andronus! Melanthus! Oh, gods, I am cursed to have led you to such an inglorious death! Peleus, hold Melanthus' chin higher, for the gods' sake! I cannot lose him! Oh, I cannot!"

"And there is no need for you to do so," said a voice behind Antigonus, and he whipped about.

A man stood in the river, as if on solid ground, his sword sheathed, holding out his hand for Antigonus to grasp. He was tall, and solidly built, and beneath his boar's tusk helmet his eyes burned black and fierce amid features clearly Trojan.

"There is no need for either you or your sons to die," the man said, and waggled his hand a little in his impatience.

"Brutus," Antigonus said, his voice flat. "Are you to walk through life as god-favored as your ancestor Aeneas?"

And then, as he heard the sound of sucking mud behind him, and Melanthus called out in horror, Antigonus dropped his sword into the river and grasped Brutus' hand.

Chapter Twelve

LLANGARLIA

TIRED FROM HER EFFORTS ON BRUTUS' BE-half, Genvissa strode through the meadowland that led from the northern bank of the Llan to the Llandin, the most sacred of Llangarlia's Veiled Hills.

She was pale-faced with fury.

Not at Brutus, nor at anything that had happened during

the battle—all had gone well, and Brutus had acted with as much decisiveness as she had expected—but at what she had felt from *here* during that battle.

Mag, trying her pathetic best to wriggle away.

That had shocked Genvissa. She didn't think Mag had that much spirit (let alone energy) left. Indeed, Genvissa thought she'd cowed the ancient mother goddess completely.

"Well," Genvissa muttered, "perhaps it's time I made sure of it now." She didn't need Mag anymore. The power she commanded from her darkcraft and as Mistress of the Labyrinth would be enough for what she needed.

Genvissa slowed her pace as she neared the base of the Llandin, coming to a final halt by a pretty spring that gurgled out of a nest of stones shaped like a woman's vulva. Above it, shading the waters from the hot sun and the cold starlight, spread a massive oak tree, almost as old as the hill itself.

Genvissa stared at the waters as they emptied into a small rock pool before finally spilling over and running down in a small rivulet to join with the Magyl River. This was Mag's home, her blessed waters. She would be inside, somewhere, cowering, terrified, knowing Genvissa stood outside.

Genvissa felt a small twinge of sympathy (it was, after all, Mag who had welcomed Ariadne into the land, and given her succor) but she suppressed it quickly. "I'm sorry, Mag," she murmured, "but it is truly more than time you joined your lover Og in perpetual obscurity."

Her eyes still on the pool, Genvissa slipped out of her robe. Naked, she stepped to the edge of the pool and stared intently into its shallow depths. Many Llangarlian women came here when they wanted to conceive and wished to ask Mag's blessing for a healthy child and an easy childbed . . . but today conception and the pangs of labor were the very last things on Genvissa's mind.

She stepped into the pool and, despite its apparent shallowness, sank from sight.

*   *   *

MAG'S REALM WAS ONE OF EMERALD LIGHT AND eternal space. As Genvissa sank deeper and deeper, she caught sight of strange ethereal creatures at the very edge of her vision, sprites from the Far World, Mag's familiars.

Where is she? Where is she? Genvissa hissed at them. *Where is the ancient hag?*

There was no answer, save a scattering as the sprites withdrew, and Genvissa hissed once more. *Where is she? Where is she?*

But Mag, stunningly, had gone.

AS GENVISSA HAD STEPPED INTO THE WATERS SO Mag had summoned every remaining scrap of power she'd still commanded and did what Genvissa would never have expected her to do—flee into the darkness of the unknown beyond Llangarlia.

She risked annihilation, for this was alien to her, and she could do little to protect herself were she to be attacked.

Leaving herself vulnerable to Genvissa, however, was a far worse fate. Better the unknown than the Darkwitch.

Almost as soon as she had left the boundaries of Llangarlia's magical protection, Mag felt something reach out for her. At first wary, she resisted, then realized that this presence was comforting, reassuring, *sisterly*, rather than aggressive or destructive.

It most certainly was not Genvissa.

Sister? whispered a voice at the very limits of its reach.

Who are you? Mag responded, not yet ready to trust entirely.

My name is Hera, said the voice, *and I have somewhere for you to hide. I have someone who can aid you. Will you come with me?*

Mag allowed herself to follow the voice, and in the blink of an eye she found herself standing in something so abhorrent she gagged instinctively, managing to stop herself retching only by the most extreme effort.

She brought her stomach under control and stood straight, looking about her. She stood in the center of a stone hall so vast there appeared to be no end to it. It stretched east to west—Mag felt, if not saw, the presence of the rising sun toward the very top of the hall—and above her a golden dome soared into the heavens. Beneath her feet lay a beautifully patterned marbled floor; to her sides soared stone arches protecting shadowy, mysterious spaces.

Mag relaxed a little. It was not as bad as she had first thought. As a creature of the fey, the womb and the water, she usually hated beyond measure any enclosure of stone, but this hall had a warmth about it, a comfort, as if . . . as if . . .

"You stand in a womb," said a woman's voice, and Mag recognized it as the voice of she who had called out to her. Hera.

She turned toward it, and saw a woman approach her from beneath one of the side arches. She was tall, graceful, and had about her the faint aura of power, but Mag could see that she was dying.

Streaks of decay stretched up and down the woman's arms, and marred her smooth cheeks.

"Hera," Mag said.

Hera nodded, and smiled, then held out her arms to her sides, displaying them. "See what the Darkwitch Ariadne has done to me."

"Ariadne was the first of the Darkwitches to come to Llangarlia's shores," Mag said. "I trusted her."

"As did we," said Hera. "Once I was one among many; now I am the only one left, and I am close to death. Soon what once was many will be none. Mother Mag, Ariadne's daughter-heir will do this to you as well—"

"She already has! She has broken the power of Og, and drained me to—"

"Hush, Mag. I know. Listen to me. If I say to you that I can give you the power, the *key*, to undoing Ariadne and her daughter-heirs' darkcraft, will you take it?"

Mag did not even have to think about it. "Yes."

"It will be a strange power to you. Can you accept that?"

"Yes."

"And in order to wield it, to build the circumstances in which you *can* wield it, you shall need to make the most loathsome of alliances. Can you do *that*?"

"Yes. If it will restore my land, then yes. *Yes*."

"Then look below you," Hera whispered, "and see what the Darkwitches used to destroy me and mine, and are using to destroy you."

Mag looked down, and to her surprise saw that she no longer stood on a marble floor, but on a plain sandstone floor into which had been carved the outlines of a unicursal labyrinth. She and Hera stood in its very heart, on a flat gray rectangular stone that had carved in it a most strange set of symbols:

Resurgam

"It is a prophecy," said Hera. "I cannot read it, for it is a strange language, but I *know* what it means."

She hesitated.

"Yes?" said Mag.

"It means," said Hera, not lifting her eyes from the stone slab, *"I will rise again."*

"You?" said Mag.

Hera shook her head. "I will never rise again. It is hope and darkness which will be reborn, and you must be the one to manipulate them both so that it is hope which prevails. Only you, and I pray you have the cunning."

She sighed, and the sound shuddered through her. "Mag, we stand in the heart of the labyrinth, and it is this which Ariadne used to destroy me and mine, and which her daughter-heir Darkwitch—Genvissa?—now deploys against you and against your land. It is called the Game, and I am going to teach it to you, Mag, that you know what you face, and so that one day you can teach it to she who can—perhaps—use it for its true purpose rather than the dark one that Genvissa turns it to. Used well, Mag, the Game is a great and glorious thing. Used darkly . . ."

"I will teach it to . . . who? Hera, I don't understand."

Hera nodded toward the eastern end of the great hall.

There walked a girl on the verge of womanhood. She paced slowly, her eyes looking up and about her, clearly overawed by the surroundings.

She did not see the two goddesses standing in the heart of the labyrinth under the dome.

"Her name is Cornelia," said Hera, "and she is your last remaining weapon."

Just then the girl looked up, and started, as if she had finally seen Mag and Hera.

"This"—now Hera cast her eyes upward—"is *her* womb, Mag, and in it is not only your succour, but the only hope that you have."

"And this most loathsome of alliances?"

Hera actually laughed. "Oh, I have so much to tell you, Mother Mag. Bend close now, and listen . . ."

FAR, FAR AWAY, A YOUTH OF HAUNTING DARK BEAUTY sat within his scrawled labyrinth in the dirt of the high Himalayan pass. Before him lay the knife, but Asterion no longer looked at it. Instead, he stared into the middle distance, his eyes glazed and unseeing as he contemplated the strange alliance he had just witnessed.

Resurgam . . . it is hope and darkness which will be reborn, and you must be the one to manipulate them to ensure only hope prevails.

Asterion was astounded. Did they think they could manipulate him? Gods, did they also think he was as weak and helpless as a baby?

Had the entire world gone to fools? It was of no matter, of course, all this only worked to Asterion's advantage, but he was beginning to wonder if there would be any pleasure in his eventual victory at all.

"Resurgam indeed, my fine ladies," he said, "but there will be no hope in that black, bubbling day. Not for you, not for anyone."

Chapter Thirteen

MESOPOTAMA

WITHIN THE HOUR, NO CASUAL PASSERBY could have believed that a battle had recently been fought in the gorge, and that scores of chariots and horses and hundreds of men had been consumed by the river.

The Acheron burbled peacefully over its shallow bed, the cool shadows of trees quivered to and fro at the edges of great pools of sunlight, and birds and small animals rustled within the forests that lined the gorge walls.

The only thing that might have indicated a battle were the groups of men who sat cleaning their swords and armor in the patches of sunlight. But, then none of them were wounded, or even out of breath, and they were calm and cheerful, and if they were cleaning swords then that might have been merely because of the damp of the morning dew.

But if that passerby had stopped, and peered closer, he might have seen that the swords and armor plate being so carefully cleaned were stained with the blood of men, and that, under one tree sat an older man and three younger ones, all dejected, and all carefully guarded.

DEIMAS, WHO'D WATCHED FROM HIGH IN THE gorge, had drifted down to join Brutus, Membricus, and Assaracus. Now the group of four men sat under a tree some little distance from Antigonus and his three sons. During the brief battle of the Acheron, Brutus had realized quickly Antigonus' value—his insignia were clearly those of an important man, and the three younger men he'd been calling out to were just as clearly very dear to him—but it was only in the past minutes that Assaracus had told him exactly *who* he'd captured.

"Pandrasus' brother? And his sons? Far better than I'd hoped," Brutus said, noting how the youngest of the sons sat close to his father, and how Antigonus kept a hand on the boy's shoulder, as if trying to offer him both comfort and protection.

"The youngest boy," Brutus said. "What do you know of him?"

"His name is Melanthus," Assaracus replied. "Antigonus' youngest son, and most dearly beloved because of that."

"Is he a father before he is a general?" Brutus asked.

Assaracus hesitated before replying. "Aye, I think so. If you'd asked me that fifteen years ago, I would have said he was the general first, but as his family has grown, so Antigonus has grown more devoted to them."

"Would he put them before his people? His city? His *brother*?"

"Brutus, be careful what you scheme," Membricus said, his brow furrowing as he realized what Brutus considered.

"I only do what I must," Brutus said, rising and walking toward Antigonus and his sons.

"Antigonus!" he said as Antigonus and his sons stood, wary-eyed. "Have my men treated you well? Do you have need for anything I might provide?"

"What do you want of us?" Antigonus said. His posture was tall and erect, his manner dignified. He'd moved very slightly, placing himself between Brutus and his sons.

Brutus nodded at Antigonus to acknowledge his words, but spent some moments studying the three sons. All were tall, handsome young men, and all three very obviously well nourished both with food and with love.

And all three, all still very young men, were in various stages of terror, which they could not quite hide behind their cloaks of assumed bravado and defiance.

They were too proud, Brutus realized. Too well nourished by their father and their society in the belief of their own nobility and invulnerability. This day's debacle must have come as a considerable shock to them.

Brutus' face remained impassive, but inwardly he regarded the three boys with not a little contempt: they were soft and callow youths, ill-served by their father's love—by the gods, had he not seized his heritage by the time he was fifteen? *He* had not wasted his youth sniveling about his father's skirts! Antigonus had made a critical error in allowing these boy-women to ride with Pandrasus' army. Now, both Antigonus and his sons—and Pandrasus, come to that—were going to have to pay the price of that error.

Brutus' eyes flickered back to Antigonus, whose stance had stiffened noticeably in that time Brutus had spent studying his sons.

"What do I want?" Brutus said. "I want to offer you your lives."

"For what payment?" Antigonus said. "I am no traitor to my king and my city like Assaracus here." He looked like he wanted to spit, but then thought better of it.

"If I had not been so reviled throughout my life for the blood of my mother, then I might not have turned traitor," Assaracus said, not overly perturbed by Antigonus' scorn.

Antigonus gave Assaracus one more particularly baleful glare, then addressed Brutus once more.

"I say again, what payment do you demand for our lives?"

"Only that, in the dead of the night that is to come, you approach the gates of Mesopotama and call out to the sentries. You shall tell them that you, and the companions who shall be with you, are fellow Dorians who escaped the slaughter in this gorge and who have now only just managed to make their way safely back to the city. You shall ask for entry, and, I have no doubt, you shall be granted it. Pandrasus will be glad to see his brother once more."

"No," Antigonus said. "There is nothing you can do to make me agree."

"No?" Brutus whispered, and then, in a move so fast that neither Antigonus nor his sons could thwart him, he seized Melanthus by the black curls of his head and dragged him away from his father and brothers and to the ground at Brutus' feet.

Antigonus and his two remaining sons started forward, their faces appalled and angry all in one, but a score of Brutus' soldiers moved to halt them.

"Father!" Melanthus cried out in a pitifully—and shamefully, to Brutus' mind—terrified voice. Brutus tightened his already painful grip in the boy's hair, and twisted his head so cruelly that Melanthus could barely move.

Antigonus drew in a deep, horrified breath, his eyes riveted on his youngest son.

"Father!" Melanthus cried out again, his voice now shrill with his terror. *"Father!"*

Antigonus groaned at the intensity of his son's plea, and dragged his eyes back to Brutus.

"Will you do as I ask?" Brutus said, very calm, his own gaze steady on Antigonus.

"I . . ."

Brutus' hand drew out the sword at his hip, placing the blade hard against Melanthus' throat.

The boy squealed and tried to twist away, succeeding only in opening a shallow cut across his throat.

His entire body trembled, jerked, and then, horribly, he voided himself, the front of his tunic staining warm and wet.

"Melanthus!" Antigonus cried, his eyes starting from his head.

"You *will* do as I say," Brutus said, and in one single appalling movement, jerked Melanthus' head far back with one hand and with the other sliced the razor-sharp blade hard across the boy's throat.

Bright blood fountained across the gap between Melanthus and his father.

Antigonus started forward with a horrified cry, but the Trojan soldiers grabbed him, as Melanthus' two brothers, and held them firm as Brutus let go of Melanthus' head.

The boy grabbed at his throat, his staring eyes desperate on his father, his mouth in a surprised "O," then collapsed to the ground. He curled up into a fetal position, his hands frantically scrabbling at his throat, his eyes desperate, terrified. Then, as the blood continued to spurt with the strength of his heart's beat, his body fell slowly still.

Brutus, hefting the bloodied sword in his hand, looked to Antigonus. "You *will* do as I say, or I will take one of your other sons—you may choose which one this time—and if you make me kill all three, then I will, and I will lay their blood- and urine-soaked bodies in the dirt before Mesopotama's gates so that their mother may see them, and may know that you moved not to save them from the terror of their deaths."

At his feet Melanthus gave one soft, wet sigh, and died.

"Is that what you want?" said Brutus softly.

He had not once glanced at Melanthus dying.

Chapter Fourteen

T HE THREE SENTRIES ON DUTY ATOP Mesopotama's gates had watched the straggling group of twenty-five or thirty limping, bloodied men approach the gate for some minutes before one of them threw out the verbal challenge.

"Hold! Name yourselves, and your business!"

The group, some ten paces from the gates, came to a

stumbling halt, the stragglers at the back taking the opportunity to catch up with the main group.

One of the men stepped forward so that the sentries could see his face clearly. "I am Antigonus, brother of Pandrasus, escaped finally from the nightmare of the gorge. Can you not see me, and know my face?"

Several paces behind Antigonus, Brutus dug the blade of his dagger a little deeper against the neck of Peleus, Antigonus' eldest son. "Be careful what you say!" Brutus hissed at Antigonus. "And remember, that should you betray me once we gain the city, you also betray the life of your sons!"

Antigonus' back stiffened, but he gave no other sign that he'd heard Brutus.

"General!" the sentry called back, the relief in his voice obvious to all who heard it. "General! We thought you dead!"

Antigonus made a depreciatory movement with his hand, earning another hiss from Brutus. "And I thought myself dead, too, but I, with these my comrades"—he indicated the group behind him—"managed to fight our way clear. We hid in the forests for the day, and have only finally found our way back here at this dark hour."

"And the Trojan warriors?" the sentry asked.

"Gone, we think," Antigonus replied. "We saw no sign of them in the gorge as we made our way back to the city."

"Wait, Lord," called the sentry, "and we shall open the gates for you."

THE SENTRIES, UNSUSPECTING, UNBOLTED THE INner gates, leaving them standing open, then drew back one of the two massive cypress and bronze-bound outer gates, allowing the small group of men through.

But when the two sentries who held the door made to close it, five or six of the stragglers at the rear of the group suddenly lunged at them, planting silent daggers in the sentries' throats, and the men slid to the ground making no more noise than a whispered sigh.

Several of the Trojans pushed the gate to, but did not bolt it.

Others pulled Antigonus and his two sons back toward the gate, keeping knives at their throats as they gagged them with linens torn from the men's own tunics.

"Assaracus!" Brutus hissed, and Assaracus nodded, threw aside his disguise, and took some twelve men to secure the immediate area and silence any guards on the walls.

When his soft whistle told Brutus the guards had been dealt with, Brutus signaled one of the Trojans waiting at the gates.

The man opened the gate, slipped outside, and mimicked the soft call of a rock partridge.

Instantly, scores of shapes rose silently from their hiding places behind the vines in the fields to either side of the road leading to the gate, and moved forward.

PANDRASUS SLEPT BADLY. HE TOSSED AND turned, twisting the fine linen of his sheets into sweat-matted ropes, and causing his concubine, already wearied by the king's temper during his earlier waking hours, to slip from the bed and sit wakeful in a chair by the window.

When the door opened, and the shapes of strange men slipped into the chamber, she gave a small squeak of terror and drew her hands to her mouth, but already cowed into a total subjection by years of Pandrasus' mistreatment, made no other movement or sound.

The men hesitated an instant at the sight of her, but realized that she would pose no threat.

The next moment they had dragged the naked, sleep-confused king from his bed. Pandrasus fell to the floor, shouting with anger.

"Silence him as best you can," Brutus said, "although not permanently, then bring him to the megaron once I send word that the palace is secured."

Chapter Fifteen

Cornelia Speaks

I HAD WAITED ATOP THE WALLS BY THE GATES, wanting to be the first to welcome home my victorious father and, of course, my soon-to-be-lover-and-husband, Melanthus. If I had not lost my virginity in the morning, then I was certain I would lose it during the coming night.

While I waited I lost myself to daydreams of Melanthus, of his sweet wondrous face, his strong, lithe, exciting body. I remembered how I had felt when he had seized me and caressed my breasts—the sensual flare in my belly, the weakness in my thighs—and as I remembered the sensations flared all over again, and I had to lean against the wall, weak and trembling at the thought of finally bedding my hero.

As hero he surely would be! I had no doubt that Melanthus would have killed ten thousand Trojans—for how could they stand against such as he! My love would return, drenched in the blood of his despicable enemies, and I would wash it from him, slowly, and with many a lingering caress.

At the thought, my face must have grown even more dreamy, for the two sentries standing guard a few paces away grinned at me in a most unseemly manner.

I brought myself under control, wondering if I should remark on their insolence, or if that might only serve to embarrass me further, when the taller of them suddenly looked at something beyond the wall.

He swore—quite foully—and grabbed at his companion.

The next instant both were gone, clambering down the ladders leading to the gate.

I looked over the wall, and gasped.

Four or five chariots were hurtling down the road. The charioteers and archers were huddled deep within the body of the chariots, almost as if they were desperate to hide from something, and the horses ran as if possessed, their training and war dignity entirely forgotten.

The sight was so astounding I merely frowned, unable to comprehend what was happening.

Had the horses panicked, and bolted for their stables?

But how could that be? All the warhorses had been trained for years, and were experienced in battle. Well . . . in the mock battles my father had arranged . . . and surely they were more warlike than the real thing?

If the fault lay not with the horses, then had the men controlling them panicked, and caused their horses to dash for home?

But that was even more incomprehensible, for all my father's warriors were brave beyond belief, and the best warriors in all of Greece.

Had not my father told me thus on countless occasions?

There was movement below me, at the gates, and I realized they were being opened. I returned my gaze to the chariots, now very close, and I realized with a horrifying lurch in the pit of my belly that one of them contained my father.

His face wore an expression I had never seen before, and which I had never thought would fit my father's features—fear.

"SHUT THE GATES!" MY FATHER SCREAMED, EVEN as I was still making my way down the ladders to the court just inside the gates. *Shut the cursed gates!*

If his face had showed fear, then his voice revealed defeat, and that was so incomprehensible to me that as I reached the ground and walked toward where my father stood by the heaving horses of his chariot, my legs gave way beneath me, and I crumpled to the ground.

"Cornelia!" my father cried as he caught sight of me. "Daughter! What do you here? Get back to the palace! Go! Go!"

"Father." I reached for the hand he extended to me, and managed to regain my feet. "What is wrong? Why . . ." I stumbled to a halt, not knowing what should follow that "Why?"

"Trickery! Magic! Foulness!" my father spat, and I frowned all the more, for I could understand none of this.

"Where is Melanthus?" I asked.

"Dead, most like," my father said, shoving me into the hands of one of the guards. "Get her to the palace, and keep her under close care, or I will take your life for your negligence. *Now!*"

And so I was dragged off without a chance to further question my father.

Melanthus? Dead? How could that be?

"Melanthus?" I whispered, in shock, I think, as the guard eventually handed me into the care of Tavia. "How can that be?"

My father must be wrong . . . and that thought was almost as unintelligible as the one that proposed my beloved hero might be dead.

TAVIA EVENTUALLY DISCOVERED WHAT NEWS there was. The Trojans had tricked my father into a trap, and then used the black arts—as would cowards—to ensnare my father's army in a slaughter. My father escaped, but only because of his heroism and skill, while most others had died.

Melanthus? Dead? My mind could not grasp that concept, and could not pass beyond that concept. I thought nothing of the greater implications of this defeat, had no thought of the other men I knew that must have died, but only tried without success to grasp the concept that Melanthus might be dead.

This could not happen. Not to me. Not to my beloved Melanthus. No. No . . .

For hours, all through the afternoon and into the night, Tavia held me as we lay on my bed. She whispered nothingnesses to me, and stroked my brow with soft hands, and begged me to eat and drink to maintain my strength.

And when I responded to none of that, she tried to shame me into responding by suggesting that I behaved in a manner most unbecoming to a woman of my nobility and station.

At that I wrenched myself away from her. All I wanted to do was think about Melanthus, to find some means of explaining away my father's news.

"My dear," said Tavia, "he must be dead. So few returned . . . and he is not among them . . . I know you adored him, but he was but a boy, and—"

"Get out!" I yelled, bursting into tears. "Go! *I don't want to hear that!*"

She went, and I fell back to the bed and succumbed to such a fit of sobbing that I thought my heart would burst. He was not dead! He could not be! I remembered how we had caressed earlier in the day, I remembered the crushing of his mouth against mine, and I vowed that if Melanthus was dead, then I would allow no man to kiss me again.

There was no one who could ever take Melanthus' place. No one who could match him in nobility and bravery and prowess.

"If not you," I eventually sniveled, blowing my nose on the hem of my skirt, "then no one. No one save you, beloved Melanthus, shall ever lay his mouth to mine!"

Slightly hysterical that vow may have been, but it made me feel better. After all, as a vow it was assuredly quite useless. Melanthus could not be dead. I would wake in the morning and he would be here, and he would fall to the bed beside me, and . . .

I drifted off to sleep, content that I should pass the night in dreams of Melanthus.

Instead, I dreamed most peculiarly. I found myself standing in a stone hall, of such construction and such overwhelming beauty that I am sure it was of the gods' making. Above me glowed a golden vaulted roof, to either side of me soared great stone arches that lined the shadowy side aisles of the hall. Although the outer walls of the hall were solid stone, I could somehow still see through them to the countryside beyond where a majestic silver river wound its way through gentle verdant hills and fertile pastures. It was an ancient and deeply mysterious land, such as I had never seen nor even imagined.

Oddly, it felt like my homeland, and yet this was nothing like the hills surrounding Mesopotama.

I looked back to the hall. There was a sound of laughter, and from the very corner of my eye I saw the figure of a small girl dashing between the stone arches. It was my future daughter, I knew this, and my joy deepened, for this must be Melanthus' child, too. I was sure of it.

Then a great joy swept over me. There was a man here, a man I loved beyond any other, and he me. Melanthus! I turned full circle, but I could not see him.

Melanthus?

I frowned, and looked more carefully, and saw instead two women standing at some distance from me. One was . . . one was Hera, while the other was a much smaller and darker woman, mysterious like the land I had glimpsed beyond the arches.

Hera put her hand on this dark woman's shoulder and bent to her, and spoke in her ear.

Although I could not hear, and certainly not comprehend, I had a sense of a great many words being spoken and, also, most remarkably, a sense of a vast amount of time passing.

And then, just as I walked closer, and opened my mouth to speak to Hera, the smaller dark woman took a step toward me, then another, and then she was rushing at me as if she were not a woman but a pinprick of brilliant light.

I tired to take a step backward, to evade this light, but there was nowhere to go, and suddenly the light was upon

me—it was so hot!—and then it was gone. Vanished as if
it had never been, although there was a horrible burning
sensation in my lower belly.

"Hera!" I whispered, thinking to ask her of Melanthus,
but I was alone. The hall was empty save for me, and suddenly it seemed a very forsaken place indeed.

THE DREAM WAS SO NASTY I WOKE WITH A START. I
lay a hand on my belly, feeling a warm heaviness in its
lower extremity. For a moment, still befuddled by sleep, I
wondered if my monthly courses were about to flow, then
realized it could not be as they'd only completed themselves a mere week previous.

I frowned, and thought to rise and pour myself some
wine so that I might put the dream from my mind, but just
then the door opened and a shape approached my bed. I
thought it must be Tavia, and I was glad, for I had need of
her comfort. I opened my mouth to apologize to her for my
earlier spitefulness, then closed it with a snap.

This wasn't Tavia.

It wasn't even the strange dark woman of my dream.

Nor even Hera.

Instead, it was horror most foul come to snatch me.

"GET UP!" THE SHAPE SAID, AND I REALIZED—TO
my total stupefaction—that it was a man. In the instant
between when he spoke and when he strode to my bed and
grabbed me by my hair I wondered consecutively whether
this was somehow, wonderfully, Melanthus come to me, or
my father returned to explain it was all a bad dream, or
perhaps a god come to take me as his own.

But then the man, this *intruder*, grabbed the hair at the
crown of my head and dragged me naked and crying from
the bed, "I said to get up, girl!" and I knew then that this
was neither Melanthus, nor my father, nor even a god.

He dragged me several paces away before I managed to

regain either my feet or my voice. "Let me go! How dare you touch me!"

And I kicked at him with a foot.

He evaded me easily, and in the next moment delivered a stinging blow to my breasts.

I gasped in twin shock and pain, and he gave my hair a vicious twist for added measure. "I have no time for kicking, squealing girls," he said, his voice harsh. "Now keep quiet and *do as I say*!"

Now terror had overwhelmed my shock, and I tried— difficult with someone's hand twisted tight into the hair of one's head—to nod. He seemed to understand my efforts, for he gave a curt jerk of his own head.

"Good. I have not come to rape you, but to take you to the megaron. If you remain quiet, and amenable, you will come to no harm."

I managed an almost nod again, and he grunted and, hand still in my hair so that I had to walk with my head cruelly twisted, pulled me out the door and down the palace corridors toward the megaron.

I could not see his face, but somehow I had no doubt this man was a Trojan.

And not one of the tame slaves I had known all my life.

Chapter Sixteen

SINGLY, OR IN THEIR TWOS AND THREES, BRUtus' men dragged variously shocked and compliant, still sleepy and murmuring, or angry and struggling people into the megaron.

Every single one of them, as soon as they entered the megaron, fell still and silent as they saw Pandrasus' burly figure kneeling, head bowed in his utter humiliation, several paces before the dais on which stood the throne. He was completely naked save for minor gold jewelry at his wrist and neck and ears. Then, as if they'd been instructed, every one of them in turn shifted their eyes from Pandrasus to the warrior slouched in the throne. He was of some thirty years, wore nothing but his boots, a golden and scarlet waistcloth, and six magnificent golden bands about his limbs. His long black curly hair was left unbound to course down his back and about his blunt-faced and dark-eyed visage. A sword rested across his knees, and Pandrasus' gold and ruby bracelet lay on the floor between his feet.

Brutus, staring unblinking at Pandrasus.

Finally, as a guard signaled that all the palace Dorians had been brought to this chamber, Membricus walked across the megaron, paused momentarily to stare at Pandrasus, then moved to Brutus' side to murmur something in his ear. Brutus nodded, gave Membricus a brief smile, then stood.

Membricus stepped back to stand just to the left of the throne.

Brutus walked very slowly to the edge of the dais where he stopped, his sword swinging idly in his hand, staring about the assembled peoples.

With only the exception of Pandrasus, who kept his eyes on the floor, they were all staring at him.

"My name is Brutus," he said slowly, but very clearly, his eyes moving with deliberate precision from person to person within the megaron, "born of Silvius, born of Ascanius, born of Aeneas, hero of Troy and son of Aphrodite herself. I am of the blood of gods and princes, and I am heir to Troy, and to all that Troy claims. This man"—he lifted his sword and pointed it at Pandrasus—"has denied the rights of freedom of body and dignity to my people, whom he keeps as slaves. I have come to rectify this matter."

Brutus stepped off the dais, his booted footsteps ringing about the megaron.

"I offered to Pandrasus the means to free his people without harm to him or his, but he refused." Brutus was now circling the megaron, staring at each of the Dorians in turn, as if assessing their worth. "He thought to deny my people their freedom, and the gods, in their anger, have humiliated him."

Brutus paused before a girl of some fourteen or fifteen years. She had a round, somewhat plump face—typical of so many girls her age—above a body that was also still caught in a remnant of its childish plumpness. While her features were unremarkable, the long shining brown hair that tangled over her shoulders and her startlingly deep blue eyes showed that she would one day grow to an attractive woman.

She was naked, although apparently unconcerned about the matter, and Brutus was surprised by the shudder of need that ran through him as he studied her flesh. She did not have a particularly seductive body—Brutus would certainly not have looked twice under normal circumstances—but there was something about her . . . something compelling . . .

Brutus looked back to her eyes, trying to see past the anger within them, trying to see what it was about her . . . then she moved her arm slightly, and a gleam caught Brutus' eye, and he saw the gold and ruby bracelet that encircled her right wrist.

Apart from its size and weight, it was a mirror image of the one that Pandrasus had worn.

Brutus smiled, certain now of what it was that must have made him study her so closely. She would prove as useful as Melanthus.

"I am Brutus," he repeated, his voice soft, his eyes holding the girl's, "and I am god-favored. It is not wise to deny me."

He began to move once more about the megaron. "I control Mesopotama. I control this palace. I control *you*. Be wise. Do not deny me."

Abruptly Brutus turned on his heel and walked back to stand before Pandrasus.

"My price for your freedom, and the freedom of your people, is but a small one," Brutus said, and Pandrasus finally lifted his face to Brutus. "Give the Trojans their freedom from slavery, as graciously as you may. And"— his mouth twitched—"as a mark of your sincerity, I ask that you give to them the *means* of their freedom." He paused, his grin growing wider, more substantial, as he saw the hatred in Pandrasus' face.

"The *means* to their freedom, being one hundred ships, and provisions and livestock for their sustenance for one year, as well as seven hundred talents in gold, silver, and other jewelry."

Pandrasus laughed, a big belly laugh, his body shaking with the strength of its merriment. "Who do you think you are? A god yourself, to demand such things of *me*? Ah!" He spat on the floor before him. "You are nothing but a dung merchant who has let the stink of the shit he peddles addle his wits."

Brutus gave a small nod in the direction of a guard, and Pandrasus suddenly stiffened, his laughter vanished, as he heard his daughter shriek in protest.

The guard dragged Cornelia over, his hand once more in her hair, and Brutus grabbed her from the guard's grip.

Before Cornelia could react, Brutus twisted her neck with a vicious force, subduing all her fight, then forced her to her knees.

Then, one hand in her hair as it had once been in Melanthus', with the other Brutus put his sword to Cornelia's rib cage, just under her breast.

She reflexively jerked away from its cold touch, but Brutus easily managed to keep it pressed against her.

"With one movement," he said, noting Pandrasus' frantic eyes, "I can slide this blade deep into her heart. And if you doubt me, for one instant . . ."

"He will do it." Antigonus, heretofore kept in the shadows at the back of the megaron, now stepped forward.

Pandrasus looked over his shoulder, shocked, and Cornelia stiffened in Brutus' grasp, her eyes, impossibly, growing even wider than they had been.

Antigonus walked forward, each step a shuffling testament to his own sense of shame, his face haggard.

"He *will* do it," Antigonus repeated softly as he finally halted a few paces away from Brutus, Cornelia, and Pandrasus. "He took my beloved Melanthus from me, and taunted me, and put his sword to Melanthus' throat . . . and then he tore it out. He killed him." Antigonus' voice broke. "He killed him," he whispered.

"And he died badly," Brutus said, giving Cornelia's head another twist as she let out an appalled sob. "He was so terrified he pissed himself. Do you want that for your daughter? In front of all these people?"

Silence, save for Cornelia, who was moaning.

"Freedom for my people," Brutus said, his voice dangerously quiet. "One hundred ships. Provisions for a year. Gold and jewelry . . . and . . ."

He had not meant to add that "and" but suddenly, stunningly, he was overwhelmed by a staggering desire and need.

It was almost as if he had been god-struck.

". . . and your daughter as my wife, for I find in these past few minutes that I have grown accustomed to her flesh."

"No!" Cornelia screamed, struggling, heedless of the blade. "No!"

Standing forgotten behind the throne, Membricus was again overwhelmed with the vision he'd had when first he'd cast his eyes on the distant city of Mesopotama. Shadows. Death. Bewilderment. "No," he whispered, his eyes blank, but no one heard him.

"No!" Cornelia shrieked yet again, writhing desperately.

"*All of this!*" Brutus hissed, his hand tightening in Cornelia's hair in the struggle to hold her, and his other hand tightened as well, and the sword shifted, and Cornelia screamed as it bit across the flesh of her rib cage. "*All of this!*"

"All is yours," whispered Pandrasus, his eyes on Cornelia.

"Say it! Stand and say it to these people, who shall bear witness!"

Pandrasus stood, almost slipping, his eyes unable to tear themselves from the sight of his daughter unsuccessfully trying to pull away from the blade, her pathetic efforts only serving to add more cuts to the one already marring her flesh.

"All is his!" he shouted. "Freedom for the Trojan slaves, one hundred ships and provisions for a year. Gold and precious gems. And . . . and, oh gods, oh gods . . . and my daughter, whom I hereby give to him as wife." And with those words, Pandrasus knew that he had, surely, killed his daughter.

Brutus nodded, satisfied, and lifted the sword away from his wife's body as he had failed to lift it from that of the boy she'd loved.

Chapter Seventeen

Cornelia Speaks

ONCE MY FATHER HAD DECLARED BRUTUS my husband (and what choice had he? Hold his tongue, and watch me die?), Brutus had taken the sword from my breast, dropped my head so suddenly I fell to the floor, and wiped my blood from his blade in my hair before sheathing it.

Tavia, who'd been watching distraught from the walls of the megaron, rushed to my side and aided me to my feet. She carried a light cloak, which she'd snatched from someone else, and she threw it about my shoulders before hastening me from the chamber (Brutus sent guards after us, as would come naturally to such a savage), taking me to my chamber, where she cleansed and dressed the wounds underneath my breast. They were stingingly painful, but they were not deep enough to require stitches, and so once she had cleaned them Tavia gently rubbed an unguent over them, and kissed my brow, as if I were a child, and as if that single kiss would make better all the grief and shock and humiliation of the past day.

Having attended my wounds and my heart as best she could, Tavia then sat with me in my chamber. We waited together all day, waiting for . . . well, I am not sure for what we waited. We merely sat, holding hands tightly, jumping at every sudden noise. Every so often there would be the sound of running feet in the corridors, and shouts, and once a scream—no doubt of some hapless woman being raped. The streets were similarly frenzied, filled from time to time with screams and shouts and noises that I did not care to clearly identify. By the evening, however, both the palace and the city streets beyond had quietened.

Eventually, of course, Brutus remembered me.

As night fell he came to this chamber, and ordered Tavia to begone. Servants fell to his bidding (I could not begrudge them their terrified willingness) and arrayed the low table by the window with food and fine wines.

He asked me to sit with him (I was by this time standing in the farthest corner of my chamber), and when I refused with a mute shake of my head, dragged me with a hard, repulsive hand to the chair by the table of food.

So we sat, watching each other wordlessly, the table standing between us.

Of course, so much more stood between us.

He watched me with an air of slight puzzlement combined with amused speculation. He wore nothing but a somewhat sweat-stained gold and scarlet waistcloth and what even at this moment I recognized as exquisitely worked golden bands about his tightly muscled limbs. Used only to the soft, slim bodies of courtiers—and the beautiful fineness of my beloved Melanthus—I found his warrior musculature and sun-browned skin displeasing, almost ostentatious. He was physically suited to guard duty, perhaps, to the receiving of orders, not to sitting here before me, so relaxed and confident, as if he had . . . as if he had the *right*.

He continued to watch me with measured deliberation, and I stared at him, refusing to give him the satisfaction of looking away, my apparent calmness hiding a tumultuous cauldron of emotion. I was humiliated, angry, terrified, shocked, grief-stricken, and guilty, and of all these, the guilt was the worst.

If only I had not so thoughtlessly sent my father "a-hunting" after this Brutus. If I had thought, and been more circumspect, if I had begged my father to listen to the prudent wisdom of Sarpedon, would then Melanthus still be alive? Would my father still be laughing, proud and strong, in his megaron? Would my fellow Mesopotamians not be subject to the brutality and rape I was sure was being enacted in every house within the city as this man, this Brutus, and I sat in silence, staring at each other?

My guilt was too terrible to bear, and so I used it to fan my outrage and anger. Who was this man, this piece of filth, to so humiliate myself and my father? Who was he to so carelessly murder Melanthus?

Who was he who had so completely destroyed my life?

In a moment of horror I remembered my vision of Hera. She had tried to warn me, and I had forgotten it.

I swallowed, almost totally consumed with guilt now, and, horribly, he saw it.

"Eat," he said, and I shook my head in a single jerky motion.

He bent forward, picked up an apple, then leaned back in his chair and considered me as he bit into the fruit. The sound of his teeth biting into the crispness of the apple was shocking in the otherwise silent chamber, the steadiness of his eyes as they regarded me alarming, and the juice of the apple as it trickled down his stubbled chin made my mouth and throat dry out in sheer terror.

For some reason, it reminded me that this man had declared himself my husband, and if now he was here in my chamber, then there was a good reason for that.

My hands clenched together in my lap, and I concentrated on my anger. If he knew of my terror, then he had surely won.

As he finished the apple, he signaled a servant standing by the door, and the man came running.

"I would bathe," Brutus said. "Fill the tub, if you please."

The servant scurried away, and Brutus slurped the last of his wine, banging the empty cup on the table.

Oh, Hera, I hated him! *Everything* about him repulsed me. His barely clothed body, his sweat, his blunt, unattractive Trojan features, his stableyard manners, his sheer, damned confidence.

"What is your name?"

My mouth dropped open. He didn't know my name? He had taken me as wife, he had murdered my lover, he had humiliated my entire world, *and he didn't know my name?* It was, I think, the ultimate insult, and at that moment my anger won out over all my other emotions.

He raised his eyebrows, no doubt thinking he was being patient.

I compressed my lips, refusing to speak.

He sighed. "I have a wife, but I do not know her name." He shrugged, his dark eyes very still. "What shall I call her, then, when I cry out in my passion?"

Furious, my entire face flaming, I refused to answer. I could not believe this brute thought he was going to bed me. He was a *Trojan*, for Hera's sake. He could not possibly think that he could . . . that he could . . .

He smiled. It gentled his face, and I turned my eyes from him, not wanting to fall for such trickery.

"I am sorry for what has happened," he said. "You must be scared."

"I am not!" I said, stung finally to speech. "I am a princess, a daughter of Mesopotama, and a Dorian of proud lineage. I do not 'scare.' "

He managed to dampen his smile. "Please, tell me your name."

I hesitated, then, because he might construe my continued refusal to tell him as childish, I finally relented. "I am Cornelia."

"Cornelia." He tried it out in his mouth. "It is a strange name, and not beautiful enough for you."

"It is a *proud* name!"

"For a proud and most indignant girl," he said, the laughter escaping now, and I was so enraged I would have leaned the distance between us and slapped him had not a bevy of servants filled the room with their scurrying and pails of hot water to fill the bath.

Once they had done, and scented the water and laid out the best of our towels, he nodded a dismissal, and they left us.

I, too, rose to my feet, meaning to follow them, but he rose as swiftly as a striking snake and caught at my wrist.

He was a head taller than I, and I found myself hating him for that.

He twisted my wrist, just very slightly, enough to make me take a step closer to him. "Stay," he said, "and aid your husband in his bath."

"You are not my husband!" I spat. "I refuse you! Melanthus will be my—"

I stopped, suddenly remembering that Melanthus was dead, and that he would never be my husband. Unbidden, childish tears sprang to my eyes, and I hated it that this man standing so close to me would see them, and would know the reason for them.

"Melanthus," he said slowly. "Melanthus . . . that was the name of the boy whose throat I slit. Antigonus' young son."

I sobbed, and tried to twist my wrist free from his grasp. It did not budge.

"You loved him?" he said.

"He was honorable, and beautiful, and noble. All the things you are not! *He*"—I allowed my eyes to sweep down Brutus' form contemptuously—"did not stink."

"And *I* do not whimper and piss myself in childish terror," he said very softly, and I knew I had at last nettled him. "Do you think that he would be a more deserving husband for you than I?"

"Always!" I hissed.

"I am the only one you have," he said. "Stink or not, I am the only husband you have."

And with that he grabbed me to him, and made as if he would kiss me.

I hit his face as hard as I could with my free hand. "No!" I hissed. "I have vowed my mouth to Melanthus alone. If he can no longer kiss me, then no man shall! Let me go. Let me *go*, you . . . you . . ." I struggled against him, even more furious because I could find no word vile enough for him. "You *goat*!"

"Then I never will lay my mouth to yours," he said, in a voice so low and vibrating with fury that I could not help but tremble. "Never! So long as we live, no matter how much you beg me! But see what I can do to you, what rights I shall take for myself!"

He lifted me, even though I beat at his shoulders with my fist, and carried me to the bed.

As he bore me down against the mattress, I kicked and scratched at him, shrieking, hoping that the sound would bring the servants scurrying.

None came.

He bore me down to the bed, then stood back. He shook out his wild hair down his back, then reached his hands to his waist to divest himself of his waistband and waistcloth.

I rolled away, thinking to escape from the other side of the bed, then cried out as the wounds in my rib cage bit deep.

"Hera!" I cried, but there was no answer. It were as if she had never been.

I heard the rustle as Brutus dropped his waistcloth and band to one side, then a surprisingly gentle hand touched my shoulder as I lay, curled about my wounds and weeping in pain and humiliation.

He rolled me back to face him—I turned my face away

from his nakedness—and he touched the newly blood-stained cuts beneath my breast.

"I am sorry I had to do that to you," he said softly, climbing in beside me. "Cornelia, I—"

"I find you loathsome," I sobbed. "Horrid. You killed Melanthus!" Then, to my everlasting shame, I burst into childish sobs, hiccuping and snuffling as if half the Acheron had flooded my nose.

He rolled himself close to me, and I drew away from his hateful, coarse flesh. He pulled me yet closer, his unkempt hair surrounding me—a torment of ten thousand fingers dragging slowly across my skin. His arms tightened, brooking no resistance, and he began to caress my breasts, my belly, and those parts that hitherto had felt only Melanthus' probing.

It was repulsive. I cringed under his hand and I tightened my legs against the intrusion of his fingers. I twisted my face away from his and I tried to tear his hands from my body.

All to no avail.

He never did manage to lay his mouth to mine . . . but he did far, far worse.

I swore, as he knelt over me, both my wrists held tight above my head in one of his great hands and the other forcing my legs apart, that I would not cry out, that I would not give him that satisfaction. I screwed my eyes tight shut, that at least I might not see, and I bucked beneath him all I might, but he was too strong and too determined in his aim to humiliate and subjugate me.

"If you did not fight me," he said, "then I would not have to hurt you so badly."

But I continued to fight, of course I did, and he hurt me so horribly that I swore as the burning, brutal agony coursed through my body that I would hate him forever, that he would spend his life regretting that ever he thought to do this to me. The feel of him forcing his way inside me, thrusting unbelievably deep, was so vile, so obscene, that at one point I held my breath, hoping that somehow I could escape him through death.

But I had to breathe, I couldn't stop myself, and my entire world collapsed into nothing but the wild thrusting of his body, the wretched stink of his sweaty flesh rubbing and pressing against mine, the harsh sound of his gasping lust, and—finally, despicably, the ultimate humiliation—the spurting wetness of his seed inside me.

"Melanthus!" I sobbed, holding on to his name as a charm. "Melanthus!"

Finally, thankfully, I had hurt him.

He cursed, and pulled himself free of my body, bruising me even in that action.

"I am going to bathe," he said, and he rolled away, and rose from my bed.

I lay there, weeping softly, my mind scattering in a thousand different directions. Everything had gone so wrong, everything that had kept me safe was destroyed, every dream and hope of mine lay ruined.

Was this what Hera had tried to warn me against? What was that name she had called my enemy? The Horned One?

"Asterion?" I whispered. Was this the creature that had raped me?

Chapter Eighteen

BRUTUS SAT IN THE NOW-COOLED WATER OF the tub, washing away the battle and sex sweat from his body.

He regretted what he had done—not so much the bedding of Cornelia, it happened to every girl sooner or later, but the marrying of her in the first place. Artemis, what had come over him? He'd taken everything he'd needed from Pandrasus, he most certainly could have had his bedding of his daughter without marrying her . . . so . . . *why had he done it?*

It was as if someone else had spoken those words for him, or had forced them out of his mouth. They'd been a deep compulsion, shot through his mouth before he'd been able to swallow them.

Well, no matter. He was well past the age when most men married, and a Dorian princess was not the worst contract he could have made. If she bred him sons—and if he could manage to teach her to keep her mouth shut—she would do well enough.

Brutus moved slightly, suddenly uncomfortable as he remembered how Artemis had all but promised herself to him as a reward should he win through the test within Mesopotama. How would *she* react to this girl? He fretted over it for a few minutes, then relaxed, smiling at himself. How could *Artemis* be jealous of *Cornelia*?

Brutus raised his head and looked to the bed. Cornelia lay curled up tight, her back to him, the slight shaking of her shoulders betraying her weeping. She was not a beautiful girl, but she was comely enough, and had pleasantly rounded limbs that were they ever to wrap themselves about a man in pleasure, would be as sweet as honey.

He could have done worse in a wife.

Refreshed, even though the bathwater had been cool, Brutus rose, dried himself, and walked slowly back to the bed. His body was very dark in the night, his hair, still unbound, drifted cloudlike about his shoulders and back.

Only the gold banding his arms and legs glistened bright as he moved.

He reached the bed, stood a moment, then sat down and laid a hand on Cornelia's shoulder.

"You will get used to me," he said. "I will not be a bad husband to you."

She stiffened, and Brutus sighed, and his hand tightened on her shoulder, then slid about to her breast.

Surprisingly, she rolled over and looked him in the face.

"Are you Asterion?" she said. "Are you he?"

Brutus was momentarily stunned—he could not think of anything further from what she might have said—then laughed, half in genuine amusement, half to cover his surprise.

"Asterion? I? You flatter me, child, if you think me that malevolent."

Then his smile died. "Did I hurt you so badly," he asked, "that you would name me Asterion?" His eyes moved down to the red, angry wounds beneath her breasts, and his fingers traced gently over them, then he lifted his hand to her face and wiped the tears from her cheeks.

Then, very slowly, very carefully, he began to make love to her again, and this time she did not fight him, but only turned her head and closed her eyes so she did not have to see him.

Chapter Nineteen

LLANGARLIA

ENVISSA STILL HADN'T COMPLETELY calmed down after Mag had managed to escape her, so that when she gleaned the knowledge that Brutus had taken a *wife*—of all things!—in the full flush of triumphant victory Genvissa descended into a truly black humor.

She was grateful that her ill temper had caused Aerne to seek a bed elsewhere this night; at least her grumblings and mutterings would not disturb him—or cause him to ask questions. So Genvissa lay there, sensing the pain and force of Brutus' nuptial conquest, and finally managed to calm herself down. She was surely too old and mature to allow herself to be waylaid by a little petty jealousy.

A wife was, in the end, not too much of a trouble. It certainly wouldn't keep Brutus from her side, nor from his duties to the Game. And what a petty, pudgy-faced, plump-thighed, self-obsessed child his runaway mouth had caught for him!

Genvissa lay very still, trying to glean what she could about the girl. She was a child, and silly, and unlikely to hold any man's attention for longer than it took to bed her . . . but the more Genvissa tried to scry the child's true nature out, the more she came to realize that there was something *else* about her.

Something shadowy. Something unknowable.

Genvissa did not like that. She did not like it that this child-bride of Brutus' *hid* something about her that Genvissa could not discern.

For hours Genvissa lay there, growing more frustrated and ill-tempered until, in the end, as dawn was finally pushing back the darkness, Genvissa managed to put aside her concerns. There was nothing about Cornelia apart from her actual existence. If Genvissa thought there was something shadowy about the girl, then that was only because she had been shocked by Brutus' sudden action in taking the girl to wife. That was all.

Cornelia was no threat, and surely the girl's childish silliness would surely drive Brutus into her own arms with more speed than possibly might be seemly.

As the house grew lighter, Genvissa smiled even more and stretched lazily under the bed-furs, enjoying their soft caress against her naked flesh.

Cornelia might even come in useful.

Genvissa wondered if Brutus had truly allowed himself to believe that "Artemis' " test was merely to free the Trojan slaves. If so, then he was in for a massive shock . . . Mesopotama held a much more dangerous and critical test . . . and Genvissa, thinking, came to realize that Cornelia might be just the one to propel him into it.

With luck, Brutus might be angry enough to take the foolish child's head off after the event.

After all, what plump shrieking virgin could hold a man such as Brutus for long?

So delighted at her visions of plump shrieking virgin deaths that all thought of Cornelia's strange hidden shadows vanished, Genvissa rose from her bed and walked over to where her three daughters slept cuddled together in the one bed. She gazed at them lovingly for several moments, then leaned forward and patted each one lightly on the cheek, raising them to wakefulness and the new day.

PART TWO

LONDON, MARCH 1939

M ajor Jack Skelton walked slowly out of Monument Underground station, a newspaper tucked under his arm, relieved to have escaped the hearty joviality of the Bentley household but apprehensive about what waited for him on London's streets.

The night was bitterly cold, frosting his breath around his face. There were few other people about: a couple, laughing softly, walking hand in hand towards a brightly lit tea house; a soldier who glanced curiously at Skelton before moving briskly down a side street; an old man, sitting hunched and broken in a doorway.

None of them were who Skelton had come to see. None of them were part of Asterion's Gathering, although all would be affected by it, one way or another. Eventually.

He turned east down Fish Street, drawn despite himself to the site where Asterion had engineered his last horror.

There it was, the great fluted Doric column that Sir Christopher Wren had built to commemorate the Great Fire of 1666.

Skelton stopped, shivering, thrusting his hands deep into the pockets of his coat. He hated it that Wren had chosen *to raise a monument to Asterion's overwhelming evil—but then, what was it to Wren but a fire?*

Oh God, the fire! *He could feel it rage about him again, taking everything from him, destroying his life yet one more time.*

He could hear Asterion's laughter above even the maddened cackle of the flames.

Skelton shivered once more, cold from memory rather than the night-time frost, and left Fish Street for King William Street. He crossed over it quickly; not looking at London Bridge to his left, and strode briskly down Upper Thames Street towards Blackfriars Bridge and Victoria Embankment. He stopped once or twice, peering into darkened laneways, adjusting the newspaper under his arm.

Asterion was here, somewhere, smiling, not revealing himself, lurking within the darkness of the night. Pulling them all together, one more time.

For one last time. Twice before Asterion had gathered them, each time garnering more and more control, both over them and over the Game. Skelton had no doubts that this Gathering would be the final one; this time Asterion meant to wrest from Skelton what little control of the Game he still commanded.

As he approached Blackfriars Bridge, Skelton looked up to his right to the dome of St. Paul's. God, how many years had it stood there, guarding its secret? How many years had it waited?

His steps slowed, and he stopped, his gaze riveted on the cathedral. He could feel the pull of the Game, feel the call of the labyrinth, feel . . .

He jumped, his eyes jerking to the shadows beyond the circle of light cast by a lamp.

Asterion stood there. Skelton could just distinguish his dark shape, but could make out no features.

Skelton kept his own face neutral, aware that he was spotlighted under the lamp. He nodded, acknowledging the Minotaur's presence, then moved on.

Once past Blackfriars, Skelton moved down to the Embankment, and there she was, standing in her own pool of lamplight, waiting for him.

Genvissa.

Chapter One

MESOPOTAMA, THREE MONTHS LATER

MEMBRICUS WALKED THROUGH THE dimly lit predawn corridors of the palace in Mesopotama. Warriors stood about at various guard points, alert but not overly so; the Dorians had been subdued many weeks ago, and now no one expected much more from them save the odd resentful glance.

Membricus nodded at the guards, knowing each man from the many years he had traveled with Brutus. In the palace, Brutus used only his own men for sentry duty; in the city Assaracus' men stood watch.

He murmured a greeting to the warrior standing at the entrance to Brutus' chamber, then slipped silently through.

The chamber was large, and even though no oil lamps burned it was dimly lit by the quarter moon whose light slipped in through the large unshuttered windows. It was enough that Membricus could see well enough for his purpose. He moved silently to the bed, and stopped at its side, looking down at its two naked occupants.

Brutus lay on his stomach half covering Cornelia, as if even in sleep he needed to subdue her. She slept on her back, the moonlight glistening off her pale skin. Membricus could see dark shadows circling her eyes, and he wondered how many nights she actually slept, and how many she lay, wakeful but inert under the heavy weight of Brutus' body.

Membricus' eyes left Cornelia to trail over Brutus. He did not think he had ever seen a more beautiful man, and the sight made him draw in a deep breath . . . which he instantly regretted.

The warm night air was rank with the stale odor of sex.

Membricus' nostrils flared in distaste, and his belly tensed in sudden jealousy. Many years ago it was he who would have been lying under Brutus' weight . . . but as Brutus had aged into mature manhood his tastes had veered from his boyhood tutor toward women, and Membricus had been left with only memories. He'd long ago realized that Brutus would one day take a wife, and had long ago resigned himself to it.

But to marry *this* bitch! Every time he saw her Membricus was reminded of the malignant evil he'd seen crawling down the Acheron toward Mesopotama. What was the connection, he wondered, between this Cornelia and the evil that had crawled from Hades' Underworld?

Membricus looked back to Cornelia, and started.

She was awake, her heavy-lidded eyes staring at him with flat hatred.

"Brutus," Membricus said, not dropping his eyes from Cornelia's stare.

Brutus woke, instantly and completely. "Membricus!" he said, half rising. "Is there—"

"Nothing is wrong," Membricus said, "but the first of the ships has arrived, and are at anchor beyond the bay. I thought you should know."

"Ah," Brutus sighed in relief, and relaxed back to the bed. Over the past three months he'd forced Pandrasus to purchase or lease (with Dorian gold, naturally) every available ship from those eastern Mediterranean ports still operating. Now the first of them had arrived.

"How many?" he said.

"Eight," Membricus said, then, as he was about to elaborate, he drew in a sharp breath, and sat down on the edge of the bed by Cornelia's side.

She shrank away from him, and Membricus' mouth curled in amusement.

"What is it?" Brutus said, staring at Membricus' face.

In reply Membricus laid his hand on Cornelia's breast. She hissed, and made as if to strike him, but Brutus held her arms. "What is it?" he said again, with more concern this time.

"Her breasts are no longer those of the virgin girl," said Membricus. "See how they have swollen, and their veins have become engorged. And see here, her nipple." His finger brushed over it, and Cornelia's entire body twisted as she unsuccessfully tried to dislodge his hand. "It has darkened, and become more prominent."

Membricus glanced at Cornelia's face, then slid his hand to her belly. "And feel how her belly's roundness has firmed from its girlish plumpness. Has she had her monthly courses since you have been sharing her bed, Brutus?"

"No, I think not . . . or perhaps it is that I have just not noticed."

"She is with child, Brutus."

Brutus' eyes flew to Cornelia's face. If she had known, and there was every reason to suppose she had, then frankly Brutus was not surprised she had neglected to tell him; they had not become the closest and most trusting of companions. He looked back to Membricus. "What do you see? *Tell me, Membricus!*"

Membricus drew in another deep breath, firmed the pressure of his hand on Cornelia's quivering belly, and closed his eyes, searching for the vision.

It came to him quickly:

CORNELIA, GREAT BELLIED WITH CHILD, WRITHING on a bed in the agony of birth. Her face was twisted, but with terror as well as with pain.

MEMBRICUS FROWNED, AND PRESSED HIS HAND more firmly into Cornelia's belly.

SHE LAY ON A BED MADE OF ROUGH WOOD AND coarse blankets. It was dark night, but in the flickering torchlight Membricus could make out that this was no palace, but the sorry tumbledown hut of a peasant.

A midwife was crouched at the foot of the bed, her hands extended to the baby's head as it emerged from Cornelia's body. Her face was stretched in terror as well, and Membricus wondered why, what it was about this birth that so—

Swords flashed, glinting in the lamplight, and there came the sound of close combat.

Both women screamed.

The baby slithered forth, and Membricus looked at it.

It was a boy, and on his arms and legs he wore the gleaming golden bands of kingship.

Then the visionary Cornelia screamed again, and Membricus' eyes jerked toward her. A sword flashed down, and buried itself in Cornelia's now flaccid belly.

Blood spewed from the wound, smothering both Cornelia and the baby that lay crying between her legs.

Cornelia jerked and twisted in her death agony, but the baby remained unharmed, warmed by the blood that bathed him.

He stopped crying, and as his mother died, waved his gold-banded arms and legs as if in celebration.

Or victory.

MEMBRICUS LIFTED HIS HAND FROM CORNELIA, and looked at Brutus. "It is a boy, and he will be a king. All is well."

Brutus smiled, first at Membricus, then, to Membricus' horror, at Cornelia.

At that moment Membricus had never hated Cornelia so much, and even the knowledge that she harbored within her the manner of her own death did not assuage his jealousy.

SAFE WITHIN HER STONE HALL, FEELING BETTER than she had for many scores of years, Mag smiled at the small boy that sat under the arches framing the side aisles.

he was regarding his toes as if they were the most fascinating things in creation.

She walked over to him, softly so as not to frighten him, and held out to him a red ball made of finely combed sheep's wool.

He lifted his eyes from his toes and regarded her with solemn dark eyes—his father's eyes.

Mag waggled the ball at him, and the boy smiled, and reached out his hands.

"Silly, spiteful Membricus," Mag said. "We can't have your darling mother dying in your birth, can we?"

Now the boy laughed, and grabbed the ball.

"What a dark ugly vision," Mag continued, then paused to laugh herself at the boy's joy. "I can't think who could have put it into his dark ugly mind."

Chapter Two

Cornelia Speaks

I HAD KNOWN FOR MANY WEEKS ABOUT THE child but, naturally, had not told Brutus. It was one more reason to hate him. Hating Brutus had become the focus of my entire existence. If I didn't hate him, if I didn't concentrate on that hatred and nurture it with everything I had, then I was sure I would lose my mind.

Since that first night when he had raped me with such violence, and then wiped away my tears and was gentle with me (had he thought that would somehow appease me?), the daily ritual of my life was centered about him. Apart from Tavia, who came to me every morning and stayed with me until noon (when she was sent away to her new lodgings beyond the palace until the next day), Brutus was one of the few constants in my life in the first weeks since that disastrous day when Melanthus had been so abominably slain and my father and I had been so horribly humiliated. For weeks Brutus kept me relatively isolated; everyone I knew save Tavia was gone. The servants in the palace were replaced with Trojans, the courtiers were either dead or dismissed, my father imprisoned.

Brutus usually ate alone with me in the evenings in my chamber (I could not yet think of it as *our* chamber), but sometimes he caused me to sit with him and his fellows in the megaron for the evening meal. That was true torture, to be forced to sit among his companions, and listen to their laughter and jests, and to feel their eyes slide over me, considering, perhaps enjoying my humiliation.

Deimas, who my father had treated so well, who had been given so many privileges, was generally among Brutus' companions, as was Assaracus, the ill-bred renegade. I considered the both of them traitors. They'd been dealt with well, they'd had good lives—why then betray my father and myself to this degree?

Of Brutus' own warrior companions, Hicetaon and Idaeus were always present, as was Membricus. Hicetaon and Idaeus were pleasant enough to me, but Membricus always looked at me with eyes dark with hatred and, I eventually realized, jealousy. He was a vile man, a snake in man's skin and a man who lusted for Brutus. I had not realized that until that wretched morning when he had touched me as Brutus lay beside me in my bed. I had not realized before then that Membricus resented me, but I saw it clearly that morning—as I also saw that Membricus was one of those men who preferred a man's touch before a woman's.

If I could have given him Brutus, I would have done so, but if there had ever been anything between Brutus and Membricus, Brutus showed so sign of wanting to resume it now.

Not when he had me to torment.

For weeks all I heard was Trojan laughter, all I saw were Trojan faces, all I had was my own despair and fright and pain. Tavia did her best for me, but her efforts did not, *could* not, counter the weight of sheer "difference" in my life. Everything I had known had been swept away in the most brutal fashion possible; everything that had been familiar and which I had loved had been replaced with Brutus.

All I wanted to do was destroy him as repayment for the destruction he had wrought in my life.

I ceased to fight him in bed after his first horrific assault on my body. There seemed to be no point in hurting myself and, besides, after that first night, I'd decided that my revenge would be the easier if he thought he'd completely cowed me. So I lay there, night after night, my eyes closed, my head turned aside, and let him do what he wanted.

Eventually, and perhaps naturally, this merely gave me one more reason to loathe him. The first time had been painful, frightening beyond belief, humiliating. It was never so again. Having conquered me, Brutus had become much gentler. He took care, he took his time, he tried to make me respond in the way that he wanted. Infuriatingly, he sometimes succeeded. It was all very well for me to decide not to resist, and to merely turn aside my head, but once my fear of his lovemaking had gone it was difficult to completely ignore what his teeth and tongue and hands were doing to my body.

I *hated* him for that. I lay there and tried to remember Melanthus' face, tried to remember the feel of his hands on me, but all I could feel was Brutus. One night, one terrible night, he made me moan involuntarily and arc my body hard against his. He paused, and stared at me, his eyes laughing, and said, "So Cornelia *is* a woman, after all!" and then resumed tormenting my flesh into a state of arousal I did not want it to experience. Not with *him*.

I swore silently that I would see him dead. This was the ultimate degradation: that he should have so destroyed my life, that I should hate him so greatly, and that even so my traitor body should respond so eagerly to his touch.

Worse was the day I realized I was pregnant. He put that child in me, I think, that first horrible night. Now I was going to swell with the child of Melanthus' murderer. I begged Tavia to find me the means by which to abort the child—I was sure she would know the herbs to use—but she refused. She said it would be too dangerous to anger Brutus that much; he was around me day and night, he would hardly be likely to overlook a miscarriage and would certainly suspect the reason for it. I argued vehemently with her: Brutus had not noticed the absence of my monthly courses . . . and surely I could pass off a miscarriage as merely a heavier than normal flow.

But no, she would not do it. *It is your child,* she said, *how could you want to murder it?*

I loved Tavia, she was the mother I had never known, but when she said that to me I could cheerfully have slapped her. This was not *my* child within me—I could not even conceptualize the fact that it was as much my flesh and blood as Brutus'—it was an alien creature that fed off my body in order to grow, a horrible hateful thing that with the changes it increasingly wrought in my body reminded me every waking moment of Brutus' power over me and my father and of his murder of Melanthus.

It was a daily reminder of Brutus' virulent success as measured against Melanthus' pitiful failure in the battle-fields of war and sex.

Hate Brutus I might, but I think I disguised the depth of that hatred reasonably well. I was compliant, I did not hiss and spit, and while I was not the most pleasant of companions (that would have surely roused his suspicions), I did enough to make Brutus think my spirit was truly vanquished. I certainly did a good enough impression of the compliant wife for Brutus to allow me, after a few weeks, to move freely about the palace and to visit my father once or twice a week.

I was sure that eventually that would prove his fatal mistake. Once I could move freely and widely, then the possibilities for revenge increased exponentially.

Especially after the vision that came to me the night after the repulsive Membricus had revealed my pregnancy.

Brutus had made love to me, as usual, and had then fallen into a deep stupor. As usual. I lay awake for some time, unable to get comfortable—partly because Brutus had fallen asleep across my body and his muscular frame was an uncomfortable weight to bear, and partly because his child was making me feel a little nauseous. I moved slightly, trying to ease Brutus' weight away from me, but he grunted in his sleep and moved even more heavily across my body.

Frustrated, irritable, exhausted, sick to my stomach, close to tears, I was just about to put my hands on his shoulders and give him an almighty heave—I cared not if I disturbed his sleep—when a voice spoke.

"Cornelia."

It was barely a whisper, but I was so surprised I jumped as if I'd been slapped.

"Shush, Cornelia, do not wake your husband. This is not for his ears."

I looked about the room, and finally saw a figure silhouetted against the open windows.

"Hera?" I whispered.

The figure walked forward, and I saw by its movement and form that it was indeed a woman.

"Hera?" I said again, although now that she was closer I saw that she did not look much like the goddess who had come to me on the blasted rock to warn me of the impending catastrophe in my life, but someone slightly younger and of a more rounded build. I thought for a brief moment it might be that smaller, darker woman I'd seen with Hera in the great stone hall, but, no, this woman was far taller than she had been.

"Shush, Cornelia, and listen. Tell me, do you want a revenge on that man who lies beside you?"

"Yes!"

"Then listen closely to what I say," the visionary woman said, "and you shall have what you want."

She stepped yet closer, and now I saw that she had glorious black hair with a curious russet streak through it.

I wondered if she was the distant sister Hera had talked of, but in truth, I did not care who she was. If she could give me the means to destroy Brutus, then she was *all* that I wanted.

"Listen, Cornelia," the goddess said, and bending gracefully beside the bed, began to whisper in my ear.

Chapter Three

LATER THAT MORNING CORNELIA WALKED the corridors of the palace to her father's closely guarded chamber.

She walked gracefully, unhurriedly, her head high and her shoulders back, as if she still ruled this place as the beloved only heir of its king. Her dress was meticulous: the heavy, flounced embroidered skirts that flowed to either side of her as she walked; the wide tight girdle that flattered her still narrow waist; the tightly fitted emerald jacket with its stiffened high neck and lapels that flared to either side of her breasts.

But now she wore a filmy linen blouse under the jacket that while it revealed the bounce and shape of her breasts, hid their more intimate features. It was a wife's dress, and those that passed her in the corridor assumed Cornelia had accepted her place by Brutus' side.

The two warriors stationed outside Pandrasus' door nodded her through, used to Cornelia's visits.

She ignored them, brushing past without a glance.

Pandrasus sat on a stool by the solitary small, narrow window. It was open, revealing the bustle of the city below.

He was staring out, his face expressionless, his eyes blank.

She found him thus on every morning that she came to visit.

In the past few months Pandrasus seemed to have shrunk. He was clothed in a simple waistband and short linen waist-cloth, his belly folding over the waistband in flabby folds where once it had rounded firm and proud. His arms and legs had thinned as if, having no longer the duties of king-ship to support, their muscles had lost their strength and dwindled into uselessness.

His hands, dangling between his legs, quavered with slight tremor.

"Father?" Cornelia said, drawing up a stool to sit next to him.

He turned his head listlessly. "Daughter."

"Ships have arrived," she said. "Two nights since. Eight of them."

Pandrasus grimaced, the only sign that he'd heard.

"Your fellow kings betray you," she said.

"They have been paid well with Dorian jewels," Pandrasus said. "Riches buy any loyalty."

"Then use those riches to purchase your own loyalty," Cornelia said, keeping her voice low lest the guards at the door heard her.

Pandrasus shrugged, turning his eyes to gaze blankly out the window once more.

"*You* do not have to lie each night under the weight of his body!" Cornelia whispered harshly. "*You* do not have Trojan sweat ground into your pores! How can you just sit there and *shrug* when it is *I* who must endure him?"

Pandrasus turned his face back to her, his eyes a little less dull than they had been. For the first time he noticed the filmy linen she wore under her jacket, and he frowned.

His daughter was proud of her breasts, and enjoyed dis-playing them.

Lifting one trembly hand he tugged at the linen where it was tucked into her girdle, finally managing to free it so he could pull the material toward her neck.

The material caught on one of Cornelia's breasts, and she flinched.

Pandrasus saw her movement, paused, then raised the material more carefully.

His face, if possible, became even more expressionless than previously.

Cornelia might be his only heir, his only legitimate child, but Pandrasus had impregnated so many of his concubines that he was well used to the early changes pregnancy wrought in a woman's body.

He lifted a finger to one of her breasts, and traced the engorged blue veins as they marred her ivory flesh.

"You are breeding to him," he said, now cupping her breast in his hand, as if to gauge its weight and value.

"You think to blame *me*?" she said. "You think this my fault?" She brushed his hand away and jerked the material back over her breasts. "Save *me*, Father, if not yourself."

"How? How?" Pandrasus was finally roused. "Here I sit day and night cosseted about with Trojan spears! How am *I* to save you? Would you like me to beat that child from your belly? Throw you from this window to a final release? Is that what you want?"

Cornelia drew back from her father, her expression hard. "I need a father. I need a man who can protect me." She tossed her head. "That is not what sits before me now."

Color mottled Pandrasus' cheeks, and his mouth clamped into a thin line.

She held his stare, where once she would have looked away. "Nichoria," she said. "If you ask Podarces of Nichoria then he will help. Remind him of the debt he owes you."

Pandrasus looked at Cornelia carefully, both surprised and a little disconcerted at her knowledge. "The 'debt'?" he said.

"You knew Podarces well when you were young together. You found him one day, burying his youthful manhood between his mother's legs even as he tightened his hands about her throat. You kept your silence, even though matricide—and maternal rape—is a most unnatural offense. Podarces owes you his throne. Call in the debt."

"How do you know this?"

"A woman came to me," Cornelia said, her very calmness unnerving. "She said she was a goddess, and showed me the manner of Podarces' mother's death. She said you knew, and it was a knowledge that you should now use to throw off this Trojan insult to your kingdom *and* your daughter."

Pandrasus stared, then relaxed, nodding a little. "The gods came to you, and have shown you—and thus me—the means to our freedom." He smiled, proud of his daughter, and patted her cheek. "I will need you to send him a message, demanding his aid. Can you do that?"

"Yes!" Cornelia leaned forward, taking her father's hands and, not even flinching at the discomfort, pressing them to her breasts in the traditional Dorian woman's gesture of gratitude. "Yes, I can arrange that!"

Chapter Four

MEMBRICUS? ASSARACUS? HOW STAND our preparations?"

Brutus and his two companions stood on the beach of the bay just west of Mesopotama. It had been three months since the first ships had arrived. Now almost one hundred black-hulled ships bobbed at anchor in the waters before them, crowded so closely together there was scarcely an arm's breath between their sides. Brutus called the flotilla his "kingdom," for a man could step onto one of the outside ships and jump easily from ship to ship, traversing a territory of undulating wooden decks and platforms.

"The last of the ships arrived last night," Membricus said.

"Pandrasus said he could get no more," Assaracus put in.

"Hmmm," Brutus said, not unduly upset. In the past six months Pandrasus had purchased, leased, begged, stolen, and commandeered virtually all the ships along the west coast of Greece, and some from even farther afield. Brutus could see, even from this distance, the distinctive lines of several Egyptian merchant vessels. "What ratio war vessels to merchant?"

"Seventeen war vessels," Assaracus said. "The rest are merchantcraft. We shall be at risk from pirates, if we sail very far south."

His last sentence was both statement and question. Brutus had, as yet, confided none of his plans to any of his lieutenants. Seven thousand Trojans were about to sail into the unknown, and to an as yet unknown destination, and Brutus wanted them to do so without question.

"The gods shall watch over us," Brutus said, then turned so he could look at Assaracus. "Remember what happened to Pandrasus and his army."

Assaracus grunted. What had happened to Pandrasus was a fading memory, both for the Trojans and the Dorians. Brutus had established his authority quickly and cruelly within days of taking Mesopotama, and for months the Dorians had been so cowed, and so shocked, by the turn of events that there had been no resistance or questioning of anything Brutus ordered.

But now there was a growing undertow of resentment and loathing within the Dorian community. Brutus' preparations for the outfitting of his fleet had stripped the city and its surrounding farming land of all its wealth, both of food and of gold. Everything Mesopotama had was being poured, both literally and metaphorically, into Brutus' fleet. Pandrasus himself had overcome the sloth and depression that had at first gripped him and was growing more confident, more ready to express openly his contempt of Brutus and the Trojans where before he had taken the effort to veil it.

And more Dorians were following his example. Assaracus had no doubt that sooner or later their resentment would explode into violence, and an attempt to wrest back from the Trojans everything they had won.

Their departure could not be too soon for him.

"The oar crews are training well," Membricus said.

"Good," Brutus said, and both the men with him could hear the relief in his voice. All the ships would require oar crews to augment their sails, some forty to sixty men per ship, and much of the past months had been spent training sufficient crews from among the Trojans.

It had been difficult. Oar crews took years to train well, and generally only voyaging experience hardened them into mature crews, but the Mesopotamian Trojans had little practice at sea. Instead, the men and youths pressed into service generally spent hours per day on practice platforms that had been built along the shoreline. Experienced orderers, the men who beat the time for the oars, shouted and cursed in their efforts to get the trainees to stroke together, or to learn to back water, or to dip and hold, all maneuvers oar crews needed to learn in order to control a ship. Sails were all very well, but too often the waters of the Mediterranean lay becalmed . . . and Brutus did not have enough provisions to feed the entire fleet while they drifted about aimlessly.

"We must leave soon," Membricus said, unable to stop himself glancing at the waters of the shadowy Acheron River as it emptied itself into the bay. "It is midsummer now, and we will not have many months left before the autumn storms begin to bite. No matter how enthusiastic, our oar crews are not good enough to deal with the anger of the autumn storms. When, Brutus, *when?*"

"Within the week," Brutus said. "We will leave within the week."

"Where?" Assaracus said softly.

"Artemis will guide us," Brutus said, then he smiled, as

if he had suddenly realized the concern of the two men. "A day's sail south of this bay is an island. There Artemis is waiting for me. There she will show me the path toward Troia Nova."

He turned, as if to go, then stopped as he caught sight of a figure standing atop the walls of Mesopotama.

Even at this distance he knew who it was.

Cornelia.

Beside Brutus, Membricus hissed as he, too, recognized the figure.

Cornelia moved a little, perhaps uncomfortable under the regard of the two men, and as she did so a shadow suddenly poured from her, as wine pours forth from a ewer, and slithered down the city walls and across the ground to where the three men stood.

It touched Brutus, enveloped him in its gloom, and traveled no farther.

"Sorcery!" Membricus said, grabbing Brutus and pulling him to one side.

But as Brutus moved, so the shadow moved, and Brutus could not escape its touch.

Membricus hissed again. "She is a witch, Brutus! Beware!"

"Witch?" said Brutus. "Surely not, unless hatred and scheming can brew sorcery of its own accord." He paused, not taking his eyes from Cornelia's distant figure. "But I do not trust her." Again he stopped. "I have only just discovered that Cornelia has been sending and receiving secret communications from . . . I know not who. She uses her nurse Tavia as her messenger."

Both Assaracus and Membricus exclaimed, and would have spoken save that Brutus continued.

"No, you do not need to say it. I now watch her like a hawk."

"Kill her," said Assaracus flatly.

"She carries my son."

"Then kill her once she bears him."

Brutus gave a small smile. "There shall be no need, I

think." He glanced at Membricus, who had long ago told him of the full extent of his vision concerning Cornelia's death. "Tell Assaracus what you saw."

Membricus grinned. The retelling of Cornelia's forthcoming death was always an enjoyable experience. "She will die with a sword in her belly in the dank harbor of a peasant's shelter the instant Brutus' son has slithered from her body," he said. "I have seen this." He looked back to Brutus. "But I agree with Assaracus. Kill her now."

"No. She carries my—"

"Brutus, *listen* to me! *See* this shadow! Do you remember, when we stood atop that hill overlooking Mesopotama, that I said I could see a darkness crawling down the river toward the city? It came from Hades' Underworld. Look at this shadowy darkness crawling toward you now. Brutus, can you not understand what I am saying?"

Brutus glanced at his wife—she still stood, watching them, and it seemed that in that moment the shadow deepened about them—then looked back to Membricus. "No. I can't. What do you mean?"

"Cornelia was born and raised and fed by the evil that crawled out of Hades' Underworld down the river to Mesopotama," Membricus said. "She is *Hades'* daughter, not Pandrasus', even though he might have given her flesh. Thank the gods we have to endure only a few more months of her." He paused. "For otherwise, my friend, if she continued to draw breath, then I think—I *know*—she has the power to destroy your entire world."

Chapter Five

DEIMAS STOOD IN THE DOORWAY OF THE bakery, watching his people bustle up and down the streets. He thought that a casual observer would believe that Mesopotama was, and had always been, a Trojan city, for it was the people of his blood who filled the streets, hastening between market and home, baths and city square, their hair now recut and partly regrown to blot out forever the signs of their slavery. In contrast to the Trojan presence, there was hardly a Dorian to be seen. Ever since Brutus had subjected the city the Dorians had kept to their homes: silent and watching. Deimas grinned, folding his arms and leaning his shoulders against the warm stone wall of the building. Doubtless the Dorians stayed at home because they now had so many chores to occupy them. Where once despised Trojan slaves had dusted the hearth, folded the linens, and cooked the Dorian's daily meat, now the Dorians had to do these onerous tasks for themselves.

The Trojans were free, and none had any taste for aiding their former masters in their daily grind.

Deimas suddenly caught sight of Cornelia, walking slow and heavy through the streets. Her face was lowered, one hand was resting on her belly, her body constantly twisting and turning to avoid the Trojans who pushed heedless past her. Deimas' smile died. Few among the Trojans liked Cornelia. Not only was she a Dorian, but she was the daughter of the hated Pandrasus. Deimas didn't blame Brutus for taking her to his bed—she was legitimate spoil of war, after all—but to name her his wife? Deimas shook his head. Cornelia barely spoke to anyone save her nurse, Tavia; Deimas hadn't seen her pass more than a few words with Brutus in all the months they'd been together.

He shuddered, then grinned. Brutus no doubt didn't require her to be particularly articulate in bed.

Then Cornelia was upon him, and Deimas inclined his head politely in greeting. Her face was red and sweating from the climb and the weight she carried in her belly, and her arms, Deimas noted, were much thinner than once they had been. Brutus' son was draining her of all her plumpness.

Poor Cornelia, Deimas thought. Only some seven months ago she would have had a litter borne by sweating Trojan slaves to carry her to her palace in comfort. Now she was nothing but the sweating, exhausted litter for Brutus' son.

"I am glad to see Brutus' son grow so well," Deimas said.

"Or daughter!" Cornelia said, stopping to catch her breath. "Who knows? Brutus may be capable of siring only girls."

"Membricus says a son," Deimas said mildly, watching her face and thinking that Cornelia must truly despise her husband. "All know he is a potent seer."

She opened her mouth, but could patently think of no response. Instead, she wiped a straggle of her hair from her forehead, gathered her skirt in her other hand, and stepped back into the climb.

Deimas watched her as she stepped out of view around a corner, then his eyes flickered upward to an opened window in one of the houses lining the street.

A Dorian man was leaning out slightly, his eyes tracking Cornelia. As she disappeared, the man turned, and saw Deimas staring at him.

He grinned, insolent, then leaned out for the wooden shutter and banged it closed as he stepped back into the room.

Deimas' face went expressionless. That had not been the face of a cowed and humiliated man.

PANDRASUS SAT IN HIS SMALL CHAMBER IN THE palace he had once called his own, and waited for his daughter to join him. His Trojan captors constantly moved him from chamber to chamber, as if they wanted him to experience the discomforts of every pitiful cramped room they could find, and this chamber was particularly bad. It was bare of all ornamentation—there was not even any plaster on the walls, let alone painted murals—had nothing but a rush matting floor, and its window was small and all but useless as it opened onto a back courtyard that the butchers used for their slaughtering.

His chamber was constantly filled with the stink of blood and burst entrails and, even worse, the sound of cheerful Trojan voices as they discussed their impending departure.

Pandrasus' face twisted in a grim smile. Once he had found that talk disagreeable beyond measure. Now he found it amusing.

If only they knew.

He stood, impatient for Cornelia's arrival, and brushed down his waistcloth. It was creased and stained. No one now came to robe him, and none to wash and brush his linens. Pandrasus the king was served no longer, save by his vengeful thoughts, and by his daughter, who brought to him what she could beg or steal from the Trojans who now cavorted about the palace.

When all was done, and the Trojans dead, Pandrasus knew he would need to spend months repairing the palace from their carelessness, and airing it from their stink.

There was a step in the door, and Pandrasus looked to it eagerly.

"Cornelia! Beloved daughter!"

She walked to meet him, limping slightly from what Pandrasus thought was likely a sprain caused by being forced to walk so far in her condition, and embraced him.

Both she and Pandrasus leaned away from her bulging belly, both hating it equally.

"Sit," Pandrasus said, taking her arm and guiding her to the single bench his captors had allowed him, abhorring the grateful sigh she made as she finally relieved her legs of her weight.

If Pandrasus thought he could wrench that child from Cornelia's belly without causing her any harm in the doing he would have torn her apart in a moment. Every time he saw her, that belly had grown just that bit more. And every time Pandrasus saw that belly, he was reminded of how it had been made, and his mind's eye saw his beautiful daughter pinned beneath Brutus' body, and every time he thought of that, he vowed revenge.

And how strange, he now thought, sitting by Cornelia

and taking her hand, that the revenge should have come from this girl.

No, girl no longer. These past seven months had turned Cornelia into a woman, and her humiliation at Brutus' hands had turned her mind from girlish things to schemes of revenge.

"You are tired," Pandrasus said. "I have some wine. Would you—"

"No, Father. I paused to drink on my way to you. Save it for yourself." She heaved a sigh, and patted her belly. "It grows larger each day." Her mouth twisted. "And each time it moves within me I am reminded of my purpose. And yours."

"Aye. Did you . . . ?"

Her eyes flitted to the door, knowing she must watch every word spoken. "Yes. All is well."

"And ready?" His voice was soft, and both fearful and hopeful. So much rested on her reply.

She nodded, her eyes shining, and the hand on her belly clenched into a fist. "Yes. The final ships have arrived." She raised her eyebrows significantly at her father.

Pandrasus drew in a deep breath, keeping his excitement under control. The final ships had arrived . . .

"From Nichoria?"

"Yes."

"And their cargo?"

"Undamaged," she said, very low. "And undiscovered. The ships arrived at night, and disgorged their payload on the coast some two hours' sail south of the Mesopotamian bay. Needless to say"—her eyes flickered once more toward the door—"I am sure that payload is now much, much closer."

Pandrasus' tongue crept over his lips, tasting the revenge that was now so close. Cornelia had worked tirelessly these past few months, using Tavia to conduct the secret negotiations (and the necessary threats) between himself and Podarces, ensuring that all was in its set place, using her quick mind to solve any potential hurdle. Their revenge was brilliant not only in its audacity and potential, but in its ability both to defeat *and* humiliate the Trojans. It was Troy all over again. The ships that Brutus had forced Pandrasus to requisition carried not only Brutus' hopes, but also his doom.

Chapter Six

IVE DAYS AFTER CORNELIA'S SHADOW HAD fallen across him, Brutus gave the order to load the fleet for sailing. The ships were already stocked with nonperishables: thousands of amphora filled with water, wine, oil, honey, grains, herbs, nuts, preserved eggs, dried vegetables and fruits and stoppered tight against the sea; spare linen sails and fiber ropes, enough to refit half the fleet if need be; woolen wraps and blankets against the night cold; vials of medicines and unguents; and those most useful household items that could not be left behind—utensils, pots, tools, looms, spindles, and baskets.

Tucked into the holds of the deepest merchant ships were stacks of gold and silver and baskets of gems; Pandrasus' wealth, given into the keeping of the Trojan fleet.

Now the rafts floating goods out to the ships were filled with more perishable items: three score of milking goats and ewes, as well as a few billy goats and rams; cheeses, meats, and fresh fruits; broths of beans and pulses; fresh cakes of maza and turon.

Brutus did not know how long they would need to sail, nor what they could garner along the way, and he fretted night and day as to whether or not they would have enough to sustain seven thousand mouths during this unknowable voyage.

At night, when the palace was quiet, he knelt before an

altar to Artemis he'd found tucked away in a chamber just off the megaron and prayed to her for guidance and the wisdom to direct his orders. He could barely wait until the fleet had sailed and he could reach the island where Artemis had promised to meet him. He'd included a pure white goat in the cargo of his own ship, meaning to take it to the island and sacrifice it to the goddess in thanks for her aid and blessing.

Then, much later at night, when he had returned to the chamber he shared with Cornelia and lay by her side, he wondered at Membricus' words. Hades' daughter, he'd called this girl. Sometimes he rolled over to face her, and placed a gentle hand on her belly, feeling his child move within her.

At those times he would also feel her muscles tense with her hatred, and he would sigh. Again and again he regretted taking her in marriage, and taking her with such pain and violence that first night, but every time he felt the movement of his child his regrets would fade, and he felt only the wonder of the new growing life.

THE NIGHT BEFORE THE TROJANS WOULD SAIL, Brutus came to his and Cornelia's chamber very late. He had spent most of the evening on the beach supervising the loading of the last of the livestock, then the earlier part of the night praying to Artemis. Now, although he was tired, he knew his anxiety about the coming day would keep him wakeful, and when he lay down beside Cornelia, he placed his hand again on her belly, and spoke.

"Have you said your good-byes to your father, Cornelia? Tomorrow will be a crowded and busy day, and it is possible you will be so hurried onto our ship that you will lose your chance to kiss him farewell."

For a moment he thought she would continue her pretense at sleep, but then she sighed, and opened her eyes. "My father and I have nothing more to say to each other. All that could be said, has been said."

"Are you angry, Cornelia, that I drag you away from your childhood home?"

"What do you think? Am I happy that my father was humiliated and destroyed by Trojans? No! Am I joyful that you murdered the man I loved? No! Am I happy that you then seized me and put this child in me? No! Leave me here, I pray you, Brutus, and I swear before the gods that I will remember you kindly."

He laughed softly, his hand caressing her belly, then her thigh. "Everyone begs me to leave you behind, but I cannot. Perhaps we should put our hatred away, Cornelia, and play at being a true husband and wife together. Make the best of what is."

"Why? You have destroyed everything I loved."

Brutus bit down a sudden flare of temper. By the gods, would she never get over her resentment? It was a poor dowry indeed to bring to a marriage. "We go to rebuild Troy, sweet. Does that not excite you? I will make you a queen, and burden you with jewels, and you shall be the envy of every woman and the lust of every man in Troia Nova."

"I want to stay *here*. I want to stay with my *father*, and I want you *gone*!" One of her small hands had clenched into a fist, and she beat it gently against her taut belly as she spoke.

"I cannot turn back time, Cornelia. For the love of the gods, girl, stop this whining about what once was, and learn to live with what is! You are carrying my child. I am *not* going to leave you behind!"

"I wanted Melanthus," she said. "I loved Melanthus! I did not want *you*. I will never love *you*!"

Brutus moved closer to her, her mention of Melanthus stirring him to jealousy and resentment as it always did. She might have loved Melanthus, and still love his memory, but Melanthus was not the one who she lay with at night, nor the one to get her so large with child. Why did she not forget the boy? "I do not want your love. I do not even require it. But I *am* your husband, and that bond allows me to demand your loyalty and your service, as it binds me to your protection and care."

He began to make love to her, gently as he always did, and she averted her face and pretended indifference, as she always did. And, as so often, he felt her body respond to his; Cornelia could pretend many things, but she could not hide from him the involuntary responses of her muscles nor the raggedness of her breath.

Much later, when he had done and had felt her own body shudder in its own release, he moved back from her, intending to withdraw and lie by her side, holding her until she slept.

But as he moved, she turned her face back to him and opened her deep blue eyes, and said, "Did you know that whenever you lie with me I imagine that you are Melanthus? That the reason I respond as I do to you is by repeating Melanthus' name as a mantra over and over and over in my mind?"

He froze, shocked and angry, and furious at himself for allowing her words to sting so deeply. She was lying, he knew it . . . surely? No woman could have one man make love to her and yet keep another man's face and name at the forefront of her mind . . . could she?

Cornelia watched him carefully, and as she saw his reaction her mouth curved in a cold smile. "Of course, Melanthus would have had more stamina than you," she said. "He was so much younger. So much more athletic."

He pulled away from her, swinging his legs over the side of the bed and sitting, head in hands, trying to bring his temper under control. *Witch!*

"Far more desirable," she whispered, and he heard her shift on the bed, as if in an agony of wanting.

It was too much. He swung back to her, grabbing one of her wrists in his hand, and jerked her across the bed to him.

"You wouldn't dare!" she hissed. "I carry your son. You wouldn't dare."

"Then beware of the day you no longer carry that child, Cornelia. Beware the day."

"On the contrary, beloved," she said, the word an insult, "I look forward to it greatly."

Then she rolled away from him, made herself comfortable with some ostentatious fuss, and pretended to fall into sleep.

Chapter Seven

Cornelia Speaks

O H, HIS EXPRESSION! I HAD WANTED TO SAY that to him for months, to taunt him, to *insult* him. And to watch his face redden as my barbs hit home, to watch the hurt in his eyes. It partly repaid him for all the humiliation he'd put me through in the past months.

Another day, and he would be dead.

Brutus took some time to lay back down to sleep, and I wondered if I'd been as clever as I'd initially thought. I couldn't afford to have him awake *all* the night through. Should I have to turn, and say something sweet to placate him? The thought made my stomach turn, but if I had to ... No, praise Hera. Eventually I heard the deep regular breathing of sleep.

To be sure, I lay awake for many hours, enjoying the sense of happiness and anticipation that flooded through me. Tomorrow night Brutus would be gone, and all the other Trojans either dead with him or reenslaved into such bondage it would be the ruination of all their hopes.

Tomorrow night I and my father would again be supreme within Mesopotama, laughing together as we surveyed the destruction we had wrought.

Tomorrow night I could prevail upon Tavia to feed me those herbs that would cause me to birth this hateful baby before its time. Then neither of us would need fear Brutus' wrath at the murder of his son.

Tomorrow night I would sit and watch the horrid thing between my legs, bathed in its birth blood, gasping for— yet never gaining—air, and I would laugh with delight as it died, as Brutus' hopes would die during this coming day.

Within the week my belly would be flat again, and I could forget all the horror of these past few months. My father would again rule from his megaron, and I would again stand beside him, clad in the most wondrous of linens and the rarest of silks . . . and no one would ever dare to think of that time that Brutus and the Trojans had humiliated us.

These past months would vanish as if they had never been . . . and perhaps the gods would even be generous enough to allow Melanthus to rise from the dead, and take his rightful place beside me and in my bed.

Tomorrow night . . . tomorrow night . . . tomorrow night all these things would come to pass.

But first, as Brutus slept in sleep, I needed to spend the darkest hour on one last task to ensure that tomorrow night was indeed all that I could hope.

Silently sending my nightly prayer of thanks to that strange goddess with the black curly hair with its peculiar russet streak who had come to me in dream and told me what to do (Hera might be weak beyond telling, but her distant sister was proving more than beneficial), I sat up carefully and looked at Brutus' face.

He was deeply asleep, his face slack, his chest moving in slow, lumberous breaths.

I slid from the bed and reached for a loose gown to pull about my bulky nakedness.

Chapter Eight

THE INSTANT CORNELIA SLIPPED FROM THE room, Brutus' eyes flew open. He rose, snatching at his waistband and cloth, then trod silently to the door.

What was she doing?

He had not slept. Instead, Brutus had lain seething beside Cornelia, controlling his breathing and muscles so she would not know he was awake, wondering how he could rid himself of her once she'd borne his son.

Her vicious words had upset him beyond knowing—and he was angry that he was so upset. He had gone out of his way to be kind to her over these past months . . . and to repay him with such vituperation . . . Membricus was right. Deimas was right. *Everyone* who had spoken to him wary words about the bitch he'd taken to wife was right.

The instant she'd birthed his son he would rid himself of her. The very instant . . .

Brutus had been lost in a fantasy of tipping Cornelia over the side of a ship for the giant marine worms to consume— he standing watching as he cradled his newly-born son— when he felt her rise.

At first Brutus thought she was just using the chamber pot, or perhaps washing away the traces of their sex, as she usually did. But instead she slipped from the chamber, and his mind instantly flared with suspicion.

There was no need for her to leave the chamber at this hour of the night.

At the door Brutus peered carefully up and down the corridor's length. It was the main thoroughfare of the royal chambers of the palace, and silent and still at this hour of the deep night.

Save for the soft tread of Cornelia's feet.

Brutus slipped silently into the corridor, following the sound of Cornelia's footsteps, and thanking Artemis that she was so awkwardly pregnant now that graceful, silent movements were long since unachievable and that the small oil lamp she carried threw flickering shadows that he could follow at a safe distance.

Still, she moved quickly enough for her bulk, and Brutus had some trouble keeping her in view, yet staying hidden himself. She left the main corridor for a narrower passage used for servant access, then leaving that in turn for a staircase that wound down through several levels into the basements of the palace.

Brutus was sweating now, not from any effort required to keep up with Cornelia, but because of the increased risk of discovery in this narrow, winding stairwell. He could keep out of sight of his wife, for the glow of her lamp guided him, but of necessity he had to climb down in the dark, and Brutus was concerned that he should trip, and so alert Cornelia to his presence.

But the gods were with him, and he reached the bottom of the stairwell without mishap.

He looked slowly, infinitely carefully, about the corner of the stairwell.

There was a flash of blue linen—Cornelia's gown—in a doorway that had been so cunningly concealed within racks holding a legion of dusty and cracked amphora that Brutus would otherwise have walked straight by it. Even so, by the time he'd worked out exactly where it was, several minutes had passed, and Brutus was worried Cornelia would have slipped away completely in that time.

Again the gods were with him. When Brutus stepped carefully through the door, he saw that Cornelia's lamp glowed not far distant, around one turning of a short corridor.

There was a soft murmur of voices, and Brutus' heart beat harder.

With the utmost care, tense and ready to flee the instant the lamp glow moved back toward him or the voices drew closer, Brutus crept down to the turning. He thought of peering about, but his innate caution won out, and so he pressed himself against the stone wall, and listened.

"You came safe?" he heard Cornelia say.

"Aye." A man's voice, deep and confident. "Although the tunnel to this place was damp and running with filth. You could have told us it was a sewer."

If Brutus was not so consumed with anger, he might have smiled at that.

"How many?" Cornelia said.

"All you requested."

"And you have arms?"

"Aye, more than enough to equip three times our number."

"Good." Brutus could hear the satisfaction in Cornelia's voice, and it was all he could do to keep his rage under control. A daughter of Hades, indeed!

"You will follow me up these corridors," Cornelia said, and Brutus tensed, ready to move, "and I will show you the way to the streets outside. Hide yourself until it is time. Now, be quiet, for the palace sleeps about us!"

BY THE TIME CORNELIA ARRIVED BACK IN HER chamber, no doubt tired and anxious lest her husband had awoken during her absence, Brutus was back in bed, his face slack, his chest drawing in the long, slow breaths of deepest sleep.

Chapter Nine

*Y*OU WERE RIGHT TO WARN ME OF CORNELIA," Brutus said, his voice dangerously expressionless, "and right to think that some Dorian mischief is planned." Treachery aside, her vicious words regarding Melanthus were still what played over and over in his mind.

He took a deep breath, and looked about at the men in Deimas' house: Deimas himself, Assaracus, Membricus, Hicetaon, Idaeus, and several other of his senior officers and Trojan men from Pandrasus' former slave community. Brutus had risen just before dawn, murmured to Cornelia as she mumbled a query that he wanted to check the final preparations for the boarding and that he would send for her later, and come to Deimas' house, shouting that he wanted his senior commanders and leaders of the Trojan community here within the half hour.

"What has she done?" Membricus asked.

Brutus briefly told them of what he had seen and heard during the night.

"How many?" Hicetaon said.

"I do not know. Many, I am sure. And with enough weapons to further equip Dorian men."

"Where are they now?" Assaracus asked.

Brutus shrugged. "Hidden in small groups deep within the city, Assaracus, but I do not know the exact 'where.' If they are experienced enough, and we must assume they are, they would not take the risk of hiding in one single large group."

"They could have disguised themselves as laborers or

carriers by now," Deimas said, "their weapons hid within sacks of barley or beneath cloaks."

"You would not recognize strangers?" Brutus asked.

"Maybe one or two, here and there," Deimas said. "But not only do these armed men need to be out on the street for I, or any other, to recognize them as strangers, finding them in ones and twos is going to take several weeks . . ."

"And they will strike today," Brutus said, wiping a hand across his stubbly chin, wishing he'd had the time to shave this morning. "But *how* and *when* will they strike? Hicetaon, Idaeus? If you were commanding this group, and you needed to stop a crowd of seven thousand leaving this city, how would you do it?"

Hicetaon and Idaeus glanced at each other, each knowing they thought the same thing.

"It would be easier than you perhaps imagine," Hicetaon said. "In order to move the Trojans down to the beaches to board the ships, they will first need to leave their houses and walk down through the streets. Seven thousand people, through narrow and confining streets, the greater majority of whom will be women and children and grandparents who will panic and mill in confusion the instant an attack is started . . . it will be a slaughter, Brutus. Especially if they have twenty or thirty men at the gates to slam them shut at the critical moment. Even with the gates open, people will not be able to move through quick enough."

"These armed men need not number more than two hundred," Idaeus put in, "to create havoc and death. And remember, you said they had arms to equip three times their number of Dorians."

"But if I move my men onto the streets," Brutus began.

"Where, Brutus?" Hicetaon said. "We do not know from which point these men will strike . . . and our men, to cover the entire length of the streets, will be spread too thin to be of much use."

Brutus bit his lip, thinking. "Can we send our men through the city to find them?"

"The Dorians will have hid them well," Deimas said.

"And it would take too long. We *must* leave today, Brutus. The ship captains say the winds and tides will turn by tomorrow morning, and we shall have to wait many more weeks for another suitable sailing. But by then it will be too late anyway, as the autumn storms will have set in and sailing with so many heavily loaded craft will be too dangerous."

"So," Brutus said, looking about the group, "we must leave today, yet if we move our people out into the streets there is likely to be a slaughter."

Assaracus remembered how Artemis had aided Brutus against Pandrasus' army. "Artemis?" he said.

Brutus shook his head. "I do not think Artemis will aid us here, my friend." He grinned wryly. "She may even have sent these soldiers to test us, to see if we are worthy. We must make use of our own cunning in this instance. Tell me, how will these armed men—strangers to this city—recognize Trojans from Dorians? Presumably Cornelia and her father do not want a wholesale slaughter of their own people."

"But there will be only Trojans on the streets," Deimas put in. "No Dorian will venture out, not if they know an attack is planned."

"But *if* the streets were crowded with both Dorians and Trojans," Brutus continued, apparently not the least bit put out by Deimas' response, "how will the strangers recognize Trojan from Dorian?" His eyes were still amused, as if he well knew the answer.

"By the difference in our hair," Deimas said, waving his hand at his hairline as proof. "Every one of us have shorn our hair short to even up our hairlines from the mark of slavery. The Dorians, men and women both, have long, luxurious hair. Months have passed, yes, but not long enough for our hair to reach our shoulders. There is nothing, surely, we can do about that."

Assaracus suddenly laughed. "Unless the Dorians have short hair as well!"

"What?" said Deimas. "You think to shear every Dorian's hair within the space of a few hours?"

"Not every one," said Brutus, grinning at Assaracus, "but many, to be sure."

"Children," said Hicetaon.

"Aye," said Brutus. "As many children as we can, and after that as many adults. Shear their hair to the same length as your growing tresses, Deimas."

"Yes," said Deimas slowly, as he thought, and then he, too, was grinning with the other men in the room. "If you lend us some of your men, Brutus, Assaracus, we can force our way into enough homes, and shear enough of their curly locks to make a difference." He looked about. "And if Trojans took Dorian clothes, and spoke in the Dorian manner, then their Trojan features would fade into obscurity, and in the heat and haste of crowded streets strangers would find it all but impossible to tell them apart."

Brutus nodded, smiling, well pleased. "Then send out your men," he said to Hicetaon, Assaracus, and Idaeus. "And arm them well with sharpened shears."

"But this will only work to our advantage if the streets are crowded with Dorians as well," said Idaeus. "How do you intend to manage that?"

Brutus' smile stretched into a mischievous grin and he nodded at Deimas and the three other Mesopotamian Trojans in the room. "Tell the bakers to stoke their ovens, and to leave the doors ajar. With straw and spare lumber laid out before them. When Mesopotama catches fire, the Dorians will flee into the streets in as great a number as we could wish."

"This will take time to organize," Membricus observed.

"Aye," Brutus said. "We will delay our departure until the early afternoon—that should give people enough time to prepare. I'll tell Cornelia that there's been some problem with the ships."

"And what *are* you going to do with Cornelia and Pandrasus?" Deimas said.

Brutus' face lost its smile. "Ensure neither lays an obstacle in our path again," he said.

As the group broke up, Brutus drew Membricus aside. "My friend, can we talk alone a moment?"

Chapter Ten

"THERE IS SOMETHING I NEED TO TELL YOU. Something we can use to our advantage," Brutus said.

"Yes?"

"The Game lives on in this city, my friend."

"*What?* How do you know this?"

"Artemis told me. She said that Ariadne left the Game alive in one insignificant city. This is it."

"When did she tell you this?"

"On that night I journeyed alone to Mesopotama to speak with Assaracus and Deimas. I needed power to persuade them, and I drew on the power of the Game. It *is* here."

"And you now, only *now*, think to tell me? By the gods, Brutus, how many months has it been?"

Brutus' voice was very cold. "I have told you as and when you needed to know. There was no point beforehand. Do not assume too much from what was once between us, Membricus."

Membricus drew in a deep breath, visibly relaxing the muscles of his face. "Very well. The Game lives on in this one insignificant city. Surely that will work against us. It will protect the *city*, Brutus, not us."

"Do you remember Achilles?"

"What?" Membricus wondered if he was ever going to find a safe harbor in this conversation; Brutus kept knocking him sideways every time he drew breath.

"Even though Ariadne had undermined the power of the Game in Troy," Brutus said, "there was still a little left, protecting the city against its Greek invaders. Otherwise Troy could not have held out so long. Correct?"

Membricus considered the question for traps, then decided there were none. "Correct."

"And what did Achilles do?"

"He turned the power of the Game, whatever was left of it, against Troy."

"Yes. Achilles drove his chariot about Troy seven times, countersunwise," Brutus said, "dragging poor dead Hector with him. He unwound the Game, Membricus, he undermined the magical 'walls' of Troy."

"He unwound the thread," Membricus said, very softly, "as Jericho's enemies did also long ago. What do you suggest, that we unwind Mesopotama's luck as Achilles unwound Troy's?"

Brutus shook his head. "Achilles only employed that tactic because he had no access inside Troy's walls. Somewhere in this city, Membricus, lies the labyrinth that was used to construct the Game. If we can destroy that, if we can unwind it, you *know* what will happen." He paused, as if wary of even speaking the words. "If we do that, then we let loose the black heart of the labyrinth."

"And then Mesopotama will fall," said Membricus, "*more* easily than did Troy." His voice deepened, became thick with bitterness. "And the Dorians will die more easily than did so many Trojans."

"Aye," Brutus said. "The others can manage the disguising of our people well enough." His mouth twisted, the movement devoid of all amusement. "Would you like to join me in the hunt, my friend?"

"We should start at the gates," Membricus said. "It is where the labyrinth most likely lurks."

THE CITY WAS QUIET BUT TENSE AS THE TWO MEN strode down the virtually empty streets toward the gates.

The Trojans were still ensconced in their homes, now hopefully following directions to disguise their persons into the most complete imitation of the Dorian demeanor possible. The Dorians, doubtless warned about the planned attack (although from a different source), were also tight within their homes, not daring to venture out (doubtless, many were now regretting that decision as bands of armed haircutters burst through their front doors).

Brutus and Membricus, eyes moving warily from side to side as they walked, approached the gates that were still closed and tightly guarded by Trojan warriors; Hicetaon's warning of a possible surprise attack had patently already reached them.

"Where, do you think?" said Brutus, standing looking about.

Membricus looked at the stone-flagged road immediately inside the gate. "Under these stones?"

Brutus shook his head. "No. If the labyrinth was stationed immediately inside the gate it would have been in full view. It would have been pointless placing it beneath paving stones."

"But full view is also dangerous . . . too easily accessible, so . . ."

"So," Brutus said, turning around and looking at the buildings in the immediate vicinity. "So . . . it would have been placed somewhere where it could be accessed, but only by those who needed to." He turned about slowly, his eyes tracing the contours of rooflines and alleyways. Suddenly he stopped, and pointed. "There."

Just to the right of the inner set of gates was a solidly built guardhouse, set almost directly against the city walls.

"There will be a cellar," said Membricus.

"Oh, aye. What better place than a guardhouse to hide something of immense value?" Brutus grinned, and clapped Membricus on the shoulder. "Come, let's make some uses of these strong warriors of ours. I think I can see a heavy slab floor through that door."

* * *

THE FLOOR WAS INDEED HEAVY SLAB, AND IT TOOK four of Brutus' strongest warriors to clear the room of various benches and weapons racks, then lift corners of sundry slabs to see if there were steps underneath any of them.

Brutus was heartily relieved when the eighth slab the men lifted in the northern corner of the room did indeed reveal steps: he wasn't sure what he feared more, being wrong about the existence of the labyrinth, or about its location. He didn't think the men would willingly follow him from one building to the next in the vague hope they might find hidden steps underneath the next lot of heavy slabs.

One of the men silently handed Brutus an oil lamp. He nodded his thanks, drew a deep breath of reverence—how long had it been since a living man had set eyes on the labyrinthine enchantment of the Game?—then motioned Membricus to follow him down the steps.

THE CHAMBER BELOW WAS MUCH LARGER THAN the floor area of the guardhouse would have suggested. Its northern wall was formed by the lower masonry courses of the city wall itself, while the other three walls were of pale plastered brick.

The construction was simple, the walls unadorned, for nothing mattered save the sign of the Game carved into the entire floor space.

It was a unicursal labyrinth, its lines chiseled into the stone slabs. The initial opening of the labyrinth lay directly before the base of the steps, marked at the entrance by a beautiful carving of intertwined flowers, its path winding through seven circles and four quadrants, ending in a rounded center that had been entirely swabbed in pitch: the black heart of the labyrinth, the mirror of the unknown darkness within the soul of a man.

Membricus stepped down to join Brutus on the final step. They stood, arms touching, staring at the labyrinth in utter silence.

"Dare I the labyrinth?" Brutus whispered. This was Artemis' test, he knew it as certainly as he knew he still breathed.

And he also knew what this test implied. If Artemis wanted him to rebuild Troy, then she also wanted him to employ the Game to do so.

"Who else?" said Membricus, not surprised to find his voice hoarse.

"Aye. Who else." Brutus continued to stare at the labyrinth for long minutes, then he motioned to Membricus to stay where he was before briskly climbing up to the ground floor of the guardhouse.

Membricus could hear him as he walked out to the street, asking for a pail brimming with hot wet pitch and giving orders that the Trojans begin to leave their homes at noon.

He swallowed, suddenly nervous at what Brutus was going to do.

Who else would dare the black heart of the labyrinth? And then let it walk at his back into the daylight?

Chapter Eleven

T NOON, AS TROJAN MEN, WOMEN, AND children began to file from their homes, a shout rose from a market street that abutted one of the most densely built and overcrowded sections of Mesopotama.

"Fire! Fire!"

At first the shout was muted, as if it thought no one would pay heed, but then someone else noticed the smoke drifting from the rooflines of the houses, and he, too, screamed.

"Fire! Fire!"

To these shouts were added those of Trojan men, who,

dressed in the fine patterned tunics of Dorian citizens, ran through the streets, their voices panicked. "Fire! Fire! Fire!"

Then, as Dorians cautiously opened shutters and peered into the streets, the sound of the fire itself trickled along the streets—a snapping, a hissing, and then a twisting and a shattering, as if beams and tiles cracked and fell to stone floors in the heat of the conflagration.

The fire could not yet be clearly seen, and it had not spread much beyond the half-dozen bake houses, but already it had done its worse damage—igniting panic among a citizenry who well knew that a fire within the tightly packed dense housing of a walled city was death incarnate.

BRUTUS TOOK THE BRUSH AND THEN THE PAIL brimful of hot pitch from the soldier—who stood a long moment staring at the labyrinth on the floor of the sub-chamber before remembering to let go of the pail's handle—and turned back to the chamber.

"I was only taught a memory," he said. "I did not think I would ever encounter the Game itself."

Membricus didn't know what to say. As one of the few surviving remnants of Trojan nobility and heir to Aeneas' line, Brutus had been taught the intricacies of the Game from a young age—but he would have been taught it as something long dead. A tradition, a memory, a slice of his princely past—not as something he would ever be likely to perform or have to manipulate.

"It is weak," he said, laying a reassuring hand on Brutus' shoulder. "Barely alive. It still casts some protective enchantment over Mesopotama, but if I am right, it does not hold enough power to truly hurt you."

Brutus gave a very small, wry grin. "I wonder why your phrases 'if I am right' and 'not hold enough power to truly hurt you' do not reassure me as greatly as they were intended to?"

Membricus gave a soft laugh. "I will be here. Remember that."

Brutus put the pail of pitch down on the stairs, then stepped down to the paving slab just before the carving of the intertwined flowers that marked the entrance to the labyrinth. He stared at them, knowing that if he failed the flowers, then everything else was lost.

As Membricus watched Brutus step up to the intertwined carving of flowers he unaccountably thought of Cornelia, and for the briefest of moments thought he saw the blade of a dagger, its handle curiously carved from twisted bone and its blade thick with blood, slice through the air.

He shuddered with foreboding.

THE TROJAN EXODUS WAS GOING WELL, IF SLOWLY. Forewarned of the fires—and that they had been set to panic rather than to incinerate—the Trojans moved as quickly as they could through the streets toward the gates and the eight-hundred-pace walk to the edge of the bay. They were anxious, constantly looking over their shoulders for the swordsmen they'd been warned about, and just as constantly hoping that Brutus had been mistaken, and that there were no swordsmen at all. Men and women, wearing Dorian clothes, walked with as much arrogance as they could, aping the habitual movements of the Dorians. Their children were silent, clinging to their mothers' shawls and skirts, chastened by their parents' strict warnings to be quiet once they'd left their homes.

Brutus' warriors, together with Assaracus' swordsmen, moved among the crowds, reassuring and hustling, their eyes lifting above the crowds for any sign of strangers or the glitter of swords.

A man shouted at the sound of running feet, causing everyone to tense, but the cause of his cry was soon apparent: not swordsmen, but panicked—and strangely short-haired—Dorians, running from their homes to intermingle with the Trojans.

Hicetaon caught the eye of Deimas, standing three or

four steps up in the entranceway to a house, and nodded in satisfaction.

All was going well.

BRUTUS STOOD BEFORE THE ENTRANCE TO THE labyrinth, his head bowed, then slowly he looked up and made a sign with his left hand.

Membricus gasped, awed by the ease with which Brutus had raised the gateway.

Hanging before the entrance, where before there had been mere air, was a gateway of entwined flowers—the same flowers that moments before had rested as a lifeless carving in the stone floor.

It was the magical protection of the labyrinth: it guarded against entry . . . *and* against escape. It was, to be blunt, a plug, and what it dammed was evil.

Brutus spent another few moments studying the gateway hovering before him, then, without any hesitation, reached into it and pulled forth one of the flowers.

"For the Mistress of the Labyrinth," he said, then kissed the flower and threw it gently back against the rest of the gateway.

Instantly the entire gate collapsed, and as each flower hit the stone floor, it vanished.

The Dance of the Flowers, negated.

The death of a city.

FAR, FAR DISTANT, ATOP THE LLANDIN WHERE SHE sat alone and undisturbed in the summer sunlight, Genvissa breathed one wonder-filled word. "Brutus!"

Then she lifted out her arms, and tipped back her head, and laughed with delight and love.

Before her, on the ground, lay the flower that Brutus had kissed and tossed back against the flower gate.

*   *   *

BRUTUS HEFTED THE PAIL OF PITCH IN HIS HAND and stepped into the labyrinth. He turned to his left first, walking a track that led through the midsection of the labyrinth, then around its top, before the path wound back upon itself to take him to the second-most outer right track of the design.

In this first section of the labyrinth it seemed as if nothing had changed, as if he would do nothing more than walk in ever-varying degrees of semicircles and about turns until he reached the black heart of the labyrinth. But as he turned once more, this time onto the extreme left-hand outer path, it seemed to him that the cellar chamber about him faded, and he walked not a stone floor, but a field of waving wheat.

Then, as he turned yet again, the field vanished, and Brutus found himself in a forest surrounded by the horns of the hunt and the pounding hooves of horses.

He began to sweat, knowing what the black heart had waiting for him.

THE PRESS OF TROJAN AND DORIAN BODIES, ALL heading for the gates, worsened immeasurably, and Hicetaon fought down panic. If they were attacked by Cornelia's hired swordsmen, then the press would work in their favor . . . but such a tightly packed and half-panicked crowd might just as easily turn on itself, crushing people underfoot and against enclosing walls.

There came another shout, far above the crowd, and Hicetaon looked up in its direction.

There, high above the crowd on the flat roof of house, stood Cornelia and her father . . . and Pandrasus had a sword, and he was waving it at the crowd.

BRUTUS GRIPPED THE PAIL TIGHTER, AND SOME of the pitch slopped out, making him jump aside to avoid splashing his booted foot. The labyrinthine path led through tall trees and thick shrubbery, rustling with the stiff breeze. Overhead the canopy of the trees swayed and shifted, allowing occasional shafts of hot sunlight to illuminate the path.

On all sides came the sound of the hunt: the thud of horses' hooves and the snort of their breath; the shouts of the hunters, alive with excitement; the angry shrieks of wild birds, disturbed from their roosts; the gasping terror of the quarry.

Brutus hefted the pail of pitch once more, trying to maintain his grip in his sweaty palm, and was unsurprised when he felt in his hand not the wooden handle of the pail, but the sweet soft feel of a beloved bow.

He lifted it, and knew it at once. It was the bow of his youth, the one his father Silvius had gifted him for his fifteenth birthday . . . and this day *was* his fifteenth birthday, and he was in no labyrinth, but in the forest, out to shoot the stag that would signal his ascent into manhood.

"THEY ATTACK!" CRIED HICETAON, AND THE CRY was passed over the crowd so that soon all heard.

Within the crowd, in groups of four or five, men dropped sacks or the folds of the thick blankets they had over their arms, and drew forth swords.

They lifted them, and looked for Trojans to attack.

"They have disguised themselves!" Cornelia cried from her perch on the roof, her voice angry.

BRUTUS FITTED AN ARROW TO THE BOW, AND lifted it to his shoulder. He could hear the crashing of hooves in the shrubs just to his left, could see the flash of the stag's antlers above the greenery, could hear the beast's terrified exhalations.

Excitement flared in his chest, and he let fly the arrow.

There was a silence, then a shout of horror from beyond the path.

"Our king! Our king! He has been struck!"

And the excitement in Brutus' chest collapsed into dread, and he knew what he had done.

FRUSTRATED, AND ANXIOUS THAT THEY WERE themselves trapped, the hired swordsmen struck out in all directions. Dorian and Trojan alike were struck down, and in the press and the heat and the panic, more people were injured or killed as the crowds surged, trying to escape the death being dealt among them.

Hicetaon, Idaeus, Assaracus, and Deimas called for calm, and urged on their own swordsmen to fight their way through the crowds to those who were inflicting such injury among the throngs, but it was nigh impossible to get through.

High above, Cornelia shouted, but it was a cry of fear rather than triumph.

SUDDENLY THE FOREST WAS GONE, AS ALSO THE bow in his hand. Again Brutus walked the labyrinthine path in the subchamber beneath the guardhouse, and again he held the pail of hot pitch in his hand.

But there was one difference. In the black heart of the labyrinth, and Brutus was almost there now, sat his father Silvius.

He was contorted in agony, both his hands wrapped about the shaft of the arrow that had pierced his eye.

AT CORNELIA'S SIDE, PANDRASUS CURSED, AND leapt down the stairs that led to the street.

Sobbing, her senses swamped both by the horror enacted in the streets below and by the growing fires that had by now cast a great pall of smoke over Mesopotama, Cornelia grabbed at her skirts and followed him.

She stumbled often, her bulk and awkwardness combining with fear to trip her feet, but there was no one there to aid her. Pandrasus had long gone, vanished into the swirling guards, and Tavia Cornelia had left back at the palace, and was now either caught in the fires or in the desperate struggle through the streets.

BRUTUS STEPPED INTO THE DARK HEART OF THE labyrinth, and looked at his father.

Silvius, blood streaming in a thick rich river down his cheek and neck, gradually became aware of him. He dropped his hands from the shaft of the arrow, and held them out in appeal to Brutus.

"What have you done?" he said, his voice a groan. "What have you done?"

Brutus looked at his father for a long moment. There was no pity on his face.

"I have taken my heritage," he said, and placing the pail on the floor, he leaned down and took the arrow in one hand and a handful of his father's hair in the other.

Steadying himself, and firming his grip on his father's head, Brutus said, "This I do for all Trojans, but I leave the Dorians—and all kin who ally with them—to their fate."

And then he thrust the arrow brutally deep into his father's brain.

HIGH ON HER SACRED HILLTOP, GENVISSA BOWED her head, and smiled secretly, and kissed the flower that Brutus had sent to her.

He was the man she needed.

CORNELIA REACHED THE DOOR OF THE HOUSE ON which she had stood, and stopped, staring at the chaos before her.

Suddenly Deimas materialized out of the crowd, blood

streaming from a cut in his scalp, his face both pale and furious.

"Witch!" he spat. "Look at what you have done."

More angry than he could ever have thought possible, Deimas seized Cornelia by the arm and shoved her back inside the house.

"Know that I save Brutus' son, not *you*," he hissed.

HIS FATHER'S CORPSE VANISHED, LEAVING BRUtus breathing heavily, staring at the now-empty blackened floor of the heart of the labyrinth.

"Quick!" Membricus called. "People die!"

Without acknowledging him, Brutus picked up the pail and the bristle brush, and turned to the path that led back out of the labyrinth. He began to tread it slowly and most awkwardly, for as he went he bent down between his legs and drew a long line of pitch from the black heart of the labyrinth out along the path that led to the steps leading upward.

As Brutus walked, a growing line of black trailed behind him, leading the darkness from where it had been trapped in the labyrinthine heart to its escape at the foot of the steps.

And as he walked, Brutus was very careful never to look behind him, never to look at that trail of pitch.

He could not afford to see what it was that followed him along that black path from the heart of the labyrinth. If he saw it, if it knew he had seen it, it was close enough to snatch him.

Membricus, who could see, moaned, and turned aside his head.

Brutus was leading forth the evil that for centuries the labyrinth had trapped. It was the heart of the Game, the seduction and then the entrapment of evil, and Brutus was leading it directly into the streets of Mesopotama.

DEIMAS SHOVED HIS FACE CLOSE TO CORNELIA'S.
"Call them back!" he shouted, trying to make himself heard

above the shrieking and crying of the crowds. "Call your hired swords back!"

She stared at him, as if wondering who he was, then managed to collect herself. "I cannot," she said. "Who could make themselves heard above this din? Besides, I doubt they would listen to me. Not now."

She was right—no one person could now make their voices heard above the horrific din of the crowds and the fighting and the roaring fires—but that did not stop Deimas giving her a sharp, frustrated shake.

Then he looked back out at the death flowing down the streets, his face despairing.

BRUTUS WORKED QUICKLY AND METHODICALLY, the sounds of the chaos outside sifting through the guard-house and down to its subchamber.

He had almost reached the path's final curve when Membricus, against all his better judgment, looked once again at what followed Brutus along the line of black pitch.

DEIMAS, ONE HAND BURIED IN THE SHOULDER OF Cornelia's robe, studied the crowds, then abruptly lunged into them, dragging Cornelia behind him.

She cried and beat at his hand and arm, but Deimas ignored her as best he could, and dragged her deeper and deeper into the press.

He prayed to whichever gods that were listening that the Trojan swordsmen would soon put a stop to the slaughter.

MEMBRICUS SAW A DARK, SWIRLING CLOUD OF darkness, evil incarnate—all the evil that had been trapped in the labyrinth since the day the city had been founded and the Game called into being.

He groaned again, then sobbed, and turned his face aside once more, a hand over his eyes, wishing he'd not been so foolhardy to look at what he *knew* would be there.

"Courage, Membricus," Brutus muttered as, finally, his back aching with having to walk doubled over, he reached the foot of the steps. He painted the pitch up to the foot of the first step, then stood up, wincing as he straightened his back.

"We must get out of here," he said. "*Now!*"

Chapter Twelve

BRUTUS AND MEMBRICUS SHOUTED AT THE single warrior remaining in the guardhouse to flee, then they burst into the street.

And instantly stopped, unable to move for the press of the crowds that fought to pass through the narrow gate opening in the walls.

"Gods!" Membricus muttered. "I had not thought it would get this injurious!"

Brutus didn't even bother to reply. He placed one hand on Membricus' shoulder, then gave a great heave, pushing him along the wall of the guardhouse and away from its door. With his other hand, Brutus grabbed at the warrior who'd followed them out, pulling him to safety as well.

There had not been an instant to spare. Blackness seethed out the doorway and instantly poured upward, as if seeking the light. It combined with the smoke of the fires, acting upon it as would cold water poured on red-hot metal.

There was a crack, followed almost immediately by a hissing and spitting so violent that the crowds forgot their desperate need to push and shove, and instead crouched down, hands over their heads.

Then, stunningly, the blackness and smoke overhead disappeared, leaving nothing but uncorrupted blue sky above them.

There was a stillness as, for a time, no one dared to move, then, from far away, came a faint shout.

"The fires have gone out! The fires have gone out!"

Membricus, lowering his hands from his head, looked at Brutus, and frowned.

"There is great danger," said Brutus, standing. "We must get our people out. *Now!* There is no time to waste." He shouldered his way into the now rising and murmuring people in the streets.

"Trojans, hear me," he shouted, his voice carrying far back into the city. "This city is doomed. Run, run, run for the bay and the ships!"

There was another long, still moment, then a sudden surge of movement as people once again grabbed at the hands of children, and at the baskets and packs tied to their backs, and hurried toward the gate.

"Quick, but calm," Brutus shouted, and amazingly, people seemed to heed him, for there was no more pushing and shoving, nor was there undue panic, although faces were tight with anxiety. "Quick, but calm. If we hurry we will be safe, *we will be safe!*"

And the Trojans, composed but hurried, poured in an ever-increasing stream through the gates of the city and ran down the road toward the beach.

Brutus strode into the street, moving several paces away from Membricus, shouting encouragement and urging people ever forward. Membricus was about to follow him, when he stopped, stunned.

While people were now more relaxed, and moving quickly and far more efficiently through the streets toward the gate than they had previously been, not *all* people were moving.

Stranded here and there were still islands of people, sometimes composed of a single person, sometimes of a group of three or four or more. About them parted and flowed the stream of Trojans on their way to the gates and escape.

"Who . . . ?" Membricus murmured, then stopped, knowing the answer.

This I do for all Trojans, but I leave the Dorians—and all kin who ally with them—to their fate, Brutus had said as he murdered (once again) his father, and now Membricus knew what it meant. The Trojans were free to go, free of the long-trapped evil that Brutus had released to settle on Mesopotama, but the Dorians, and presumably the swordsmen that Cornelia had hired to kill the Trojans (*kin allied with the Dorians*), seemed as if they were stuck, their feet mired into the street paving.

Their faces were frantic, wreathed in horror, yet their gaping mouths gave forth no sound.

"Membricus!" Brutus shouted. "I could use your aid!"

And Membricus blinked, gathered himself, and pushed into the flowing throng to help as best he could.

DEIMAS YANKED CORNELIA ALONG AS FAST AS possible, but the girl was proving more than difficult. For every pace he managed to force her down the street toward the gates, she dragged him several paces sideways.

She kept calling out for her father, her voice frantic, and nothing Deimas could do would deflect her from her purpose.

"Stupid girl!" he shouted at her. "Can you not see you will die if you linger? Your father, wheresoever he be, is doomed, along with all your kin! Look! Look! See their feet sink deeper into the stone?"

Deimas was not sure what kind of magic Brutus had worked, but it was proving cruelly effective. All about him Dorians swayed in hopeless efforts to free their feet from the stone paving that held them fast. Deimas even saw one man, one of Cornelia's hired swords by the look of him, so desperate that he held his sword up high, then swung it down in a frightful arc, cutting through both his legs at the ankles.

He roared in agony, falling over and dropping his sword, but almost immediately tried to struggle forward, dragging himself by his hands.

His efforts were useless. As soon as he had fallen over, his hip had sunk into the stone paving, and he was stuck as fast as previously.

The man's roar turned into a horrific, high-pitched squeal as he struggled desperately against the grip of the stone, his lower legs spraying blood over whoever came within three paces of him.

As Deimas watched, one hand still buried in the shoulder of Cornelia's gown, the man thankfully fell senseless to the ground, and Trojans, seeking whichever was the quickest way forward, stepped uncaring over him.

Then a woman cried out, and pointed, and Deimas jerked his eyes in the direction the woman indicated.

To his right, and perhaps some eight or nine paces before him, stood the wall of a substantial house. It rose window-less and smooth some twelve paces into the air. Yet now its smoothness had been adulterated, for cracks spread from the ground upward, like fast-flowing rivulets of water.

The cracks were as wide as the palm of a man's hand, and they were filled with gray, as if all the smoke that had disappeared from the sky had been drawn into their depths.

There were several more shouts, and Deimas jerked his gaze about. Cracks were spreading up every wall he could see.

The city was disintegrating.

To his left, Cornelia gave another lurch, trying to escape him, still crying for her father.

"Curse you, Cornelia!" Deimas cried out, his fear and frustration combining into a fury that gave him enough strength to pull her struggling body close and to deliver her a stinging slap across her cheek.

She reeled away from him, and would have fallen save

that Deimas still had tight hold of her gown, one of her hands to her reddened cheek.

"Come!" Deimas said, and pulled her forward at a stumbling and, thankfully for the moment, unresisting trot down the street.

Every few paces they had to dodge another Dorian man or woman or even, horribly, a child, mired in the stone. Without exception the trapped Dorians twisted and turned, tried frantically to escape, their faces ravaged with despair, their hands held out for aid from those streaming past them.

None helped them.

Every so often Deimas glanced at Cornelia, and saw that her face was white (save for that cheek), and her eyes wide and appalled at the scene about her.

He hoped she felt some measure of guilt.

They managed to travel relatively unimpeded through the city to a point only some hundred paces from the gates. Around them the buildings were crisscrossed with wide cracks that seethed with gray; the buildings groaned, and some of them trembled, as if they knew their doom was upon them.

Deimas, although still anxious, was beginning to foster some small hope that he and Cornelia, and all other Trojans about them, were close to escape when, suddenly, Cornelia once more lunged to the side, managing to finally pull herself from Deimas' grasp.

Cursing, he managed to push through the crowds of escaping Trojans about them to see her standing by what at first he thought was a statue attached to one of the buildings.

Then he realized Cornelia's hands were twisted in her hair, and she was screaming, and that the statue was no statue at all, but Pandrasus, more than half fused into the wall of a building.

Cornelia cried out, and reached for her father, but just before she touched him, Deimas lunged forward and grabbed her, managing to pull her back from him.

"You witless girl!" he cried. "Touch him and you risk being dragged into that wall as well!"

Pandrasus, his eyes wide and staring, was straining one of his arms toward his daughter writhing and sobbing within the circle of Deimas' arms, but his arm was caught fast from elbow to shoulder, and all Pandrasus could do was waggle his hand helplessly at his daughter.

He tried to speak, but all that issued from his mouth was a moan . . .

. . . and dust, as if the mortar from the wall embedded in his back had been forced out his throat in his desperate efforts to speak.

"He is dead, Cornelia. Leave him," Deimas said.

"Father!" she sobbed, reaching out to him again, and Deimas had to wrap both his arms tightly about her and physically wrench her away.

"Deimas!"

He swiveled his eyes in the direction of the shout and felt a surge of relief.

Brutus and Membricus were pushing through the crowd toward them.

"I can't get her away from her father!" he said as the two men reached him.

Both Brutus and Membricus stared at Pandrasus, still straining hopelessly toward his daughter, then at Cornelia, who gave no sign that she realized her husband was at her side.

Membricus' gaze went from father to daughter. "How is it she can still walk?" he said.

"Her child is Trojan," Brutus said, "and her legs are needed to carry it from this tomb. That is all that has saved her. Deimas, give her to Membricus and myself. We can drag her away, and you look exhausted."

Deimas exhaled gratefully as Brutus managed to take Cornelia from him.

She struggled, still weeping, her arms still outstretched toward her father.

Brutus tightened his hold on his wife, and Membricus

grabbed her wrists, but she struggled violently against them, kicking out with her feet, and started a high-pitched keening, as if that could break their hold even if her physical efforts were in vain.

She managed to free one of her hands, and hit Membricus a heavy blow on his head.

"Foolish child!" Brutus seethed, and tightened his hold so much she gave a shriek of pain. "Do you see your father there, mired in the stone? Do you see your fellow Dorians, dying in the streets? Do you understand, *can* you understand, that their deaths are on your conscience? *Can you?* If you had let all be, if you had merely allowed my people to walk out those gates and sail away, *none of this would have been necessary!* You are death incarnate, Cornelia. Hades' daughter indeed."

HIGH ATOP HER SACRED HILL, GENVISSA BARED her breasts to the sun, tipped back her head, and ran the flower lightly across her nipples.

She shuddered, then sighed, content, even though Brutus had not allowed that damned bloated wife of his to die within the crumbling mausoleum that was her home.

Never mind; Cornelia would always wait for another time (definitely before she had time to bear that ugly little son she was brewing) and the most important thing had come to pass. Brutus had passed the test. He was strong enough to manage the Game. What he could destroy, he could also build.

All was well.

All was very, very well indeed.

Genvissa closed her eyes against the sun's warmth, and once more traced the flower over her nipples.

A WORLD AWAY TO THE EAST, ASTERION SAT WITHIN the dark heart he had constructed for himself. The bone-

handled knife was in his hands now, and he turned it slowly over and over as he thought.

Perhaps there would be an enjoyment in his eventual triumph. The world had not gone entirely to fools after all. Despite himself, Asterion was as impressed as Genvissa by Brutus' skill: he would make a fine adversary.

But, as with everyone else Asterion faced, the man had a weakness—a weakness that would eventually prove Asterion's strength. The man's power derived largely from his kingship bands—Asterion was sure of it—and the kingship bands of Troy were very powerful. Possibly the most powerful ever constructed.

Power that Asterion could use.

"But only once you are dead, my friend," Asterion said. "Then I shall take great pleasure in tearing those bands from your cold, gray limbs and . . ."

And?

"And placing them about my own," Asterion whispered, his mind racing as it encountered a possibility he'd never thought of previously. He had been planning to use the Game's one fatal weakness to destroy it completely . . . but why should he?

Asterion's belly contracted in sudden, almost sexual, flare of excitement. The Game was powerful beyond belief. Better he control and wield that power than destroy it.

Once Genvissa was brought under control . . . and once he had those kingship bands.

Asterion's eyes narrowed and the knife fell still in his hands as cunning consumed his mind.

PART THREE

LONDON, MARCH 1939

Skelton walked very slowly towards Genvissa, unable to sort out the confusion of emotions within him at the sight of her.

"My," she said as he stopped a pace away, "that uniform suits you well, Brutus. What are we now? A captain? A lieutenant?"

"A major," he said. "Jack Skelton."

She smiled. "A major. And an American. Always the foreigner, eh?"

He studied her, taking his time about it. She was, as always, a few years older than himself, but she looked tired now, worn out. Desperate. Yet still that magnificent black hair curled about her face, barely restrained by the clip at the base of her neck. Still her seductiveness shone forth, even cloaked as it was by her heavy green woollen coat. Still her beauty radiated, touching him deep within.

"Look," she said, pointing with a gloved hand to where the Thames curved away south before them. "Does this Embankment not remind you of that beach where first I came to you?"

"I have not come to lose myself in memories, Genvissa . . . ah, dear God, what name do you go by this time?"

"Stella," she said. *"Stella Wentworth."*

"And the others?"

She raised an eyebrow.

"Don't play your games with me; I'm tired of them. Where are the others?"

She looked to the dome of St. Paul's. *"You can find Loth in there."* Her mouth twisted cynically. *"Wearing the cloth. I find that quite amusing."*

"And . . . ?"

"And . . . ? Oh, do you mean Cornelia?*"*

"Where is she?"

Stella shrugged. *"I have no idea."*

"Dammit, Genvissa . . . Stella. You must *know—"*

"I do not! If she is here, then I have not yet discovered her."

Skelton stared at her, wanting to shake the truth out of her, but knowing it would do no good. *"Does Asterion have her, Stella? Does he have* her, *as well?"*

Chapter One

Cornelia Speaks

*F YOU HAD LET ALL BE, IF YOU HAD MERELY AL-
lowed my people to walk out those gates and sail
away, none of this would have been necessary! You
are death incarnate, Cornelia. It stains your soul."*

I knew it, I knew it, and hearing it said so baldly and
cruelly added no more pain to the guilt that was already
coursing through me.

Oh, Hera, if only I had let be, if only I had not pestered
my father into asking the king of Nichoria for aid, if
only . . .

All I had wanted was a revenge for myself, my father,
and Melanthus, and a return to the life I'd had.

What I had *accomplished* was the murder of my entire
people.

*Why had it all gone so badly, when the unknown goddess
had said it would all work so well?*

Brutus' arm tightened even more painfully about my
midriff and he dragged me through the streets of my home.
I did not resist, nor protest, and made all the proper movements with my legs that were needed to propel me forward.
But my mind was back with my father, mired in the stone
with him, enduring his agony.

Ah, that is foolish! A girlish stupidity. How could I "endure," even *imagine*, the agony my father must have gone
through in his dying? How can I know what it feels like to
have my back and legs and arm swallowed by stone? To
have my bowels and lungs and brain surrender to rock?
To take a breath and then to have it caught, unable to draw
more . . . and yet all the while remain aware of my suffering
and dying?

No, I cannot imagine that, even though it was all that consumed my mind as Brutus hauled me along streets choked with my people's struggling bodies, and littered with the debris of collapsing buildings. Fleeing Trojans buffeted us from all directions as they fled alongside us, but I felt not their bruises, nor heard their cries to hurry, hurry!

All I saw was my father, his hand held out to me in mute appeal, his eyes agonized.

I wish I had suffered with him. I wish the stone had swallowed me, too, but it did not, it did not because of this burden I carried in my belly, this Trojan child.

Isn't that what Brutus had said?

I did not understand it, and for the moment I did not want to even try. All I wanted to do was die to escape my overwhelming guilt, and yet I knew that Brutus would not allow that . . . all for the sake of this child.

I HEARD HIM, EVENTUALLY, GASP SOMETHING TO his friend Membricus. His voice held immeasurable relief, and it stirred me enough to look about. We were beyond the gates now, on the road that led between the rows of vines toward the bay. Fleeing Trojans still crowded us, but their efforts was less now that they were free of the city.

Brutus stopped, again spoke to Membricus, and then turned about—me with him, still clasped tight in his arms— to stare back at Mesopotama.

"Look," he said, and then again, more forcefully. "Look!"

I raised my head, and I moaned and would have fallen, had not Brutus still held me so tight.

Mesopotama was crumbling. It appeared as if an indistinct gray cloud hung over it—it might have been the dust from the collapsing masonry, but somehow I knew it was something far more vile and evil—and under the weight of that noxious cloud the city was collapsing into itself. Towers imploded, tenement buildings tumbled, palaces slid ignominiously into gutters, and the city walls turned into the consistency of sodden pastry and merely folded in upon themselves in resignation.

"The evil swallows it," Membricus said.

What evil? I thought, but did not dare ask.

What evil had my husband conjured?

All of my initial terror of Brutus, which had faded away over the past months, now returned to me a hundredfold. I had once feared Brutus as a murderer and a rapist, now I feared him as a sorcerer. Oh, Hera, Hera, had he known all along what I planned, and let me continue, just so I could damn myself?

How could I have been so foolish? How could I ever have thought to best him?

How could I so callously have gambled with the lives of everyone I loved?

And lost?

"Did all our people escape?" Brutus asked Membricus, and I shuddered in his arms.

"Aye," Membricus replied. "All those who escaped the swordsmen's blades. The last groups ran out the gate well before the final destruction."

Brutus breathed deeply in some consuming emotion—I could feel it course through his body where it pressed against mine.

"And now," he said. "Troy."

I closed my eyes. His dreams lived, mine were dead. As we stood there, his strong arms holding me tight against his body, I watched Mesopotama fall into ruin, knowing that somewhere in there my father—perhaps still aware and screaming with his mind—was being finally entombed by the stone.

Melanthus . . . my father . . . Antigonus . . . all my people. All gone. *Everything* I had loved was gone.

The child stirred within me, and I began to cry with deep wracking sobs.

TROJANS THRONGED THE SHORELINE OF THE BAY as they waited to board the ships lying at anchor some fifty paces out to water. A score of rafts ferried them out in groups of thirty or more.

The mood was calm, some people even managed to laugh, while the sun shone overhead, its heat alleviated by a cooling northerly breeze.

I found it strange that the world continued as if little of consequence had passed.

Undoubtedly sick of my weeping, Brutus handed me into the care of a broad-faced woman with a child slung in a blanket over her back. He told me her name was Aethylla, and that she would watch over me for the time being. It was, I think, the final humiliation: he thought so little of me—whether as a wife or as an enemy—that this simple peasant woman sufficed to either comfort me or guard me.

At that moment I suddenly remembered Tavia. Tavia! Oh, Hera, Tavia was entombed in Mesopotama's destruction!

Ignoring Aethylla, who was watching me with ill-concealed disdain, I sank to the sandy ground and buried my face in my hands, my shoulders heaving with the renewed strength of my wretchedness. Tavia was gone, consumed with everything else I loved, and never again would she curl up with me in my bed, and sing me to sleep.

Aethylla sighed, stroked my brow, and said numerous things that I suppose she thought might be comforting.

Her efforts made me sob all the harder. *Stop it!* I wanted to tell her. *Go away!* I wanted to shout at her, but none of these phrases came to my lips. Instead I sat there in the sand, my legs sprawled most ungracefully, my belly bulging between them, my robe half ruined, its hem rumpled somewhere about my thighs, and I cried like a child.

Aethylla eventually sat beside me, and held me, and soothed me and, eventually, when I had calmed down somewhat, wiped my nose with the hem of my robe, sat back a little, and lifted the child from her back.

I was vaguely aware that it had been crying itself for a little while.

Aethylla smiled at me conspiratorially as if we were

somehow made sisters by the shared fact of our maternity, and cuddled the child to her. She pulled aside the bodice of her robe, and offered her breast to the baby.

Its mouth latched on to Aethylla's nipple like a starving dog snatches at meat, and I winced, instantly vowing to find a wet nurse for this load within me.

She saw me frowning.

"Do not think the feeding of a child is a burden," she said. "There is no sensation a woman loves more than the feel of her child at her breast."

I looked away. I didn't want this child at all, let alone to have it grub for sustenance at my breast.

"When you birth your baby," she continued, her eyes watching me with a faint and highly irritating degree of condescension, "you will want to snatch it up and place it at your breast. All women do."

"I don't want this child!" I said, balling up a fist and striking it against my belly. "I don't want it! I don't want it! I don't—"

To my shame, I began to sob again, and Aethylla sighed—again—and looked away.

AETHYLLA, HER BABY, AND HER HUSBAND, PELO-pan, were to accompany myself, Brutus, Membricus, and Deimas (who showed not a single sign of grief at the destruction of the city that had sheltered and nurtured him) on a raft to Brutus' lead ship.

Apparently Brutus had decided that Aethylla would make good company for me.

I didn't care one way or the other. I was weary beyond belief, both my sadness and the physical effort I had been forced to undertake in order to escape the destruction had taken their toll on me. I just wanted to sleep, and some small part of me hoped that when I woke it would be to find that this entire day had been a nightmare—that this last seven months had been a nightmare!—and I was once more home with my father and a life to look forward to with Melanthus.

Membricus aided me to the center of the raft—I hated the feel of his hands on my flesh, but I did not complain— while some twenty or twenty-five other people crowded about me.

Brutus was the last to leap on the raft—his energetic leap causing the craft to rock alarmingly in the water—and he shouted to the men with the poles to take us out to the ship.

At this I raised my head, and looked ahead. All of the ships bar one had raised anchor and were under oar toward the mouth of the bay. The ship remaining was a sleek warship, its black hull sitting low in the water, its prow and stern curving gracefully in arcs at either end. I could see the heads of the men who sat on their oar benches, waiting for us.

I looked behind.

There was no one left on the beach. Somehow I had been so absorbed in my grief that I'd not noticed we were the very last to leave.

Something went cold and hard within me.

I was leaving. *Leaving*.

I cast one more glance at what was left of Mesopotama— nothing but a small hump of rubble that even still was collapsing into itself; in a week's time there would be nothing remaining to tell anyone that once a proud and glorious city had stood on that hill by the Acheron.

Brutus had apparently seen where I looked, for I heard him say to Membricus, "Mesopotama no longer. Necropolis now, I think."

"A fitting city for the river of Hades, my friend," Membricus replied.

Oh, Hera! How I despised them both. I might berate myself for my part in Mesopotama's destruction, but that did not stop me loathing those men who had pushed me to it.

The raft journey was brief, and soon we were at the ship. Most of the others boarded first, and then I had to suffer the indignity of having Brutus and Aethylla's husband, Pelopan, lift me into the ship as if I were a loosely tied pile of goatskins.

What am I thinking? Brutus would have handled even those goatskins with more care than he did me.

I had never before been aboard one of these warships, even though many had docked in the bay at Mesopotama before, and so once aboard I forgot my exhaustion for a moment to stare curiously about me.

The body of the ship was open-hulled, a row of benches for the oarsmen on either side of a great gaping chasm that went down to the keel. This space was now filled with people, all turning themselves around and around like dogs as they arranged their blankets in the limited room available to them. Here and there chickens squawked, dogs barked, and—I could not believe it—several goats farted happily.

For one appalling moment I thought Brutus expected me to bed down in this chaos, but he put a hand to my elbow and nodded toward the back of the ship.

"There is a small cabin on the aft deck," he said, "where I have arranged a sleeping space for you."

I wrenched my elbow away from his hand and looked. There was indeed a small raised deck across the stern section of the ship. On this was a timber construction that may, with imagination, have been called a cabin.

There was also a rickety enclosed affair suspended over the very stern of the ship, which I instantly realized was a means of some privacy to allow one to void one's bodily wastes.

I suddenly realized how full my bladder was and, *again*, my eyes filled with tears.

Embarrassingly, Brutus had seen the direction in which my eyes had traveled, and he turned to Aethylla. "Perhaps you could assist Cornelia? The deck of a ship can be treacherous for one unused to it."

Thus it was that I found myself being aided aft by Aethylla, chatting all the way about how carrying a child made a woman apt to the most embarrassing urinary accidents, and while I wanted to hate her as much as I hated Brutus, all I could feel was grateful, because I do not think I could have managed unaided on this constantly tilting footing, and with my triple burdens of child, exhaustion, and sorrow.

"Thank you," I muttered as Aethylla aided me into the privy, and the woman nodded at me, as if I were a child who had suddenly decided to be good.

Later, when she accompanied me into the cramped and stifling cabin and to the straw mattress atop the sleeping pallet, she said to me, "How many months to go?"

"Two or three," I said, lowering myself to the mattress, and sighing with relief.

And then the relief caught like stone in my throat, and dread overcame me.

I LAY ON THE MATTRESS ALL THE LONE HOURS IT took us to row to the open ocean and to get under way— south, from what I heard someone shout from the open hull of the ship as the crew raised the great linen sails.

I lay there as afternoon slid into night, and Aethylla brought some bread and wine for me to eat.

I lay there for hours, terrified for my life, and not knowing what to do about it.

Two or three months to go. Two or three months before I gave birth to this baby.

Two or three months to live.

I had no illusions about how Brutus felt about me. I think he hated me almost as much as I him. If he initially hadn't, then he most certainly did now after those viciously spiteful words I said to him the previous night. Oh, Hera, if only I could take back those words now!

If I was alive and on this ship now, then the only reason was because of this child.

I placed my hands on my belly, feeling the shape of the child within, and for the first time realized just how precious it was to me.

This child was the only thing keeping me alive . . . and when it no longer depended on me for survival, then Brutus could well hand it over to a wet nurse and decide I was eminently disposable.

Maybe Brutus would not actually kill me—although, frankly, I thought he would have no hesitation in doing so—but at best I would be abandoned on some tiny atoll or barren stretch of coastline.

I remembered again, with growing horror, the words I had thrown at Brutus last night. How I'd taunted him. How when he snatched at me as if to strike me, I'd said, "You wouldn't dare! I carry your son. You wouldn't dare."

And how he had then said, "Then beware of the day you no longer carry that child, Cornelia. Beware the day."

Beware of the day you no longer carry that child, Cornelia. Beware the day.

I swallowed, my throat dry, and reached for the flask of wine that Aethylla had brought me.

She, lying by my side, her baby at her breast again, thoughtfully handed it to me, and I murmured a thank you.

I drank, then gave the flask back to Aethylla, and lay down again, my thoughts racing. I had two or three months to make Brutus decide he might like to keep me, after all. I had two or three months to change the minds of most Trojans about me, for I was aware that most people would realize my involvement in the debacle in the streets, and not thank me for it.

I tried to remember if I had ever been disparaging to the Trojan slaves in my father's palace. I'd ignored them mostly . . . I don't *think* I'd ever purposefully humiliated or rebuked one of them . . . but who knew what I may have said and done inadvertently that would now be used against me?

Here I was, surrounded by people who had every reason to hate me, without a single friend, and I had two or three months to make myself *wanted*.

I closed my eyes briefly and offered up prayers to Hera for what might well appear a deceit to the memory of my father and Melanthus, and then I sat up, laying a hand on Aethylla's shoulder to stop her rising as well.

"No, stay here, Aethylla. I have a mind to talk to my husband. There is no need for you to disturb yourself. Besides, see how peacefully your child now sleeps in your arms."

"Be careful," she said.

"I will be," I replied, my voice light and, I hoped, sweet. "Thank you for your concern—for this matter, and for all you have done for me in this past day, Aethylla."

She looked at me slyly, and then grinned, as she knew the direction of my thoughts. I gave her an embarrassed half smile, then heaved myself most ungracefully to my feet and made my way out the cabin and down the narrow walkway to where my husband sat with his friends and the ship's captain at the edge of the deck.

THE NIGHT WAS BEAUTIFUL, EVEN I HAD TO ADMIT that. Moonlight dappled over the calm waters, and the northerly wind brought with it the scents of cypress and pine.

I gathered myself, wishing I had a robe other than this torn, stained thing I wore, and stopped hesitantly at the edge of the group.

"Cornelia?" my husband said, looking up at me.

The others—Membricus, Deimas, the captain, whose name I did not know, and several other of Brutus' officers—all looked at me likewise, their faces devoid of emotion, their eyes carefully blank.

They must truly loathe me, I thought, and fought down an unwanted flare of panic.

"Brutus," I said, then stopped, scared and unsure of how to go on.

"Is there something I can do for you?"

"I . . . I wanted to say to you . . . to all of you . . . that I regret my actions that resulted in . . . in so many people's deaths this past day. I . . . I was stupid. Naive."

"You were treacherous. Not 'naive,' " said Membricus, his voice hard.

"Yes," I said hastily, willing to agree with anything and everything if it would make Brutus think the better of me. "Treacherous. I . . . I wanted to assure you—" No, that was stupid, the wrong thing to say. "Brutus, I will not blame you for disbelieving me, but at that moment when I saw my father, and realized his death was caused from my actions . . ."

I stopped, lowering my eyes, feeling the terrible weight of their judgment.

"I will never be so foolish again," I whispered. "Never."

And with that I mustered all my dignity, and whatever balance remained to me on this rocking ship, and made my way back to the cabin.

It was not much, but it was a start.

Chapter Two

THEY WATCHED HER WALK AWAY IN SIlence, and remained in silence some time after Cornelia had retreated inside her cabin.

Then Membricus spoke. "She is death incarnate," he said. "No one can trust her. Her words are those of the viper."

"She is a stupid young girl," Brutus said eventually, "and perhaps her father's death *has* taught her a lesson. She is without friends here, and harmless enough, surely."

And *doomed to die*, thought Brutus, *if Membricus saw aright.* He dropped his eyes and studied his hands, suddenly sick of death.

Most of the others shrugged, the matter of little concern

to them now that they had escaped Mesopotama, but Membricus looked at Brutus, and wondered.

About them, as far as the eye could see, ships sailed through the gentle waters of the Ionian Sea.

All was calm.

In the cabin, Cornelia finally slept. She dreamed, but not of the destruction and death she'd witnessed that day. Instead she dreamed of that strange stone hall where she'd seen Hera and the small dark fey goddess, and where she'd heard the laughter of her daughter.

In her grief and guilt, the dream gave her some measure of comfort, and she clung to it all the night through.

MIDWAY THROUGH THE NEXT DAY THE FORE-looker standing on the stem platform of the lead ship gave a great shout, and pointed to the hazy outline of an island on the horizon.

"Artemis waits," Brutus said, his voice trembling with emotion.

"Are you prepared?" Membricus said.

"Aye." Brutus turned aside, and signaled first to the captain who steered the ship to turn the ship direct for the island, then to the fore-looker to signal the other ships of his intent.

All the other captains had been forewarned of this break in their journey, and all would turn their ships after Brutus' and anchor off the coast while he went ashore.

THE CAPTAIN SHOUTED SOME ORDERS, AND FOUR of his men dropped overboard a small rowboat made of pitch-blackened pine.

Into this they placed carefully a beautifully crafted pottery flask of the best wine, a cache of the finest herbs, and a pitifully bleating pure white billy goat, its legs tied together and a halter on its head.

While they readied the craft, Brutus stripped himself of

his waistband and cloth and washed himself in some pail-fuls of seawater. As he soaped his long, curly hair, Cornelia wandered up, and sat on a barrel close by.

She eyed his naked, glistening body, but he could see no derision in her eyes. "Where go you, husband?" she said, watching as Brutus sluiced a pailful of water over his head to rinse out his hair.

Some of the soapy water splashed Cornelia's robe, but her face did not twist in distaste as he would have predicted, and she merely lifted the sodden piece of material away from her body and flapped it a little in the air to dry it. Her eyebrows lifted inquiringly as she saw him watching her.

"The island," he said, nodding toward it, "is a most sacred place. Artemis awaits me there. She will show me where to direct these ships."

Cornelia's eyes flared, perhaps in awe at his mention of Artemis' name in so casual a manner. "You are favored by Artemis?" she said.

"Aye."

She smiled, a poor girlish imitation of coquetry. "But Artemis is an eternal virgin. She can satisfy no man."

"It is not why I go to see her," Brutus said flatly, and Cornelia's smile vanished.

"I meant no disrespect, husband."

He looked at her steadily. "I thought disrespect was the creed you prayed to, Cornelia. I have never had much else from you."

She flushed, whether in anger or consternation he could not tell.

Brutus picked up a fresh waistband and waistcloth; they were of fine ivory linen threaded through with gold, and Cornelia—awkwardly—leaned down to pick up his discarded and sweat-stained waistcloth.

"I will wash this for you," she said.

Now it was Brutus' eyebrows that raised. "And you know *how*?"

When she flushed again he was almost certain it was that of embarrassment. "I shall ask Aethylla," she said. "To show me the means, not to wash it herself," she added hastily, seeing his expression.

Brutus tied the waistband about his waist, then threaded the waistcloth through from the back, between his legs, and folded it over the waistband at the front. He adjusted its folds, then slid his feet into some sandals.

"Aethylla can teach you a great deal," he said, twisting the golden band above his left elbow into a more comfortable position.

"I know she can," Cornelia said, dropping her eyes.

He laughed, although it was difficult to tell if there was any humor behind it. "The first lesson in the art of deception, my dear, is not to take the act too far."

Her eyes flew up, but he had already turned away, and was talking quietly with Membricus.

BRUTUS DIPPED THE PADDLE GENTLY INTO THE water, guiding the boat toward the small beach. His eyes were fixed on the island, his body rigid, and he ignored the evermore frantic bleating of the goat.

As the bottom of the boat scraped the sandy bottom of the small bay, Brutus climbed out, careful not to splash his clean waistcloth. He grabbed the rope in the stem of the boat and tugged it closer to the beach, grunting as he eventually hauled it above the high tide mark in the sand.

Once he'd secured the boat, Brutus glanced one last time at the forest of black-hulled ships standing out to sea, then turned and studied the landscape beyond the beach.

The sand rose gently some twenty-five paces toward some rocky ground sparsely foliated with gray-green spiky-leaved shrubs that after another thirty paces, gave way to a dark forest of pine.

Even through the thickness of the trees Brutus could see that the ground rose steeply toward the island's central peak he'd seen from the ship.

He'd have a climb ahead of him.

It didn't matter.

Brutus carefully lifted the struggling goat from the boat, untied its legs, and set it on its feet, keeping tight hold of the rope attached to its halter. Then he leaned back into the boat, took the flask of wine and the bag of herbs, and carefully slung them over a shoulder.

Once he was set, Brutus gave a tug on the goat's rope, and led it up the beach toward the forest.

THEY CLIMBED UPWARD FOR WHAT FELT LIKE hours but which, Brutus realized from the occasional glimpses he could see of the sun through the pines, was probably not much longer than the morning. The going was steep, but not otherwise difficult. No vegetation grew beneath the pines, and the forest floor was soft and thick with millennia of discarded pine needles. Apart from the occasional movements of birds overhead, there was little evidence of life. No smoke from village fires, no soft whistles from wandering shepherds, no sound of domesticated animals, not even any sound of the wildlife he might have expected in the forest—squirrels, foxes, hares.

This was a forest of the gods.

In the hour before noon Brutus led the goat into an almost perfectly circular sunlit glade close to the summit of the peak. Here gray, weather-worn rock had pushed its way through the ground, creating a smooth hard surface covered in part by irregular patches of soft, emerald-green moss. The rock sloped gently toward the center of the clearing where stood an altar pedestal made of the same gray, weather-pitted rock. Before it a shallow basin had been smoothed out of the rock.

To one side of the glade Brutus could hear the soft murmur of a natural spring.

He drew in a deep breath, then he tied the goat to a tree at the edge of the glade, carefully placed the bag of herbs and flask of wine to one side, and walked about the edge of the clearing to reach the spring under the trees of its far side.

He crouched down by the small pool of clear water and carefully washed his face and hands, murmuring a prayer as he did so.

Then he walked back to where the goat stood waiting, very still, its ears pricked and its dark eyes following Brutus' every movement. Brutus picked up the bag and flask, untied the goat, then led it toward the depression before the altar.

There, placing the bag and flask again to one side, Brutus quickly and cleanly slit the goat's throat, angling its neck so that the blood flowed into the depression.

The goat collapsed, kicking, and Brutus held it tight until its struggles ceased and its eyes glazed in death, then he arranged its corpse so that its blood would continue to dribble into the depression, and walked back into the woods.

There he spent some time collecting fallen pieces of wood and handfuls of pine needles and cones, returning every so often to pile them beside the goat's carcass. Once he had a good-sized pile of fuel, Brutus set about building a fire before the depression filled with congealing blood.

When he had laid the fire to his satisfaction, Brutus said a word, and flame sprang to life within the depths of the stack.

Soon a fire roared.

As it burned itself down into coals, Brutus butchered the goat, taking great care not to mark or to stain with blood its beautiful white pelt. Once he had freed the skin entirely from the carcass, he spread it pelt-side up to one side of the blood-filled depression, then went back to butchering the goat.

Once the meat lay neatly in joints, Brutus took his bag and, again murmuring prayers, rubbed the meat with herbs and oil from a small flask kept in with the herbs.

Then, very carefully, he spitted the joints, and laid them across the coals of the fire.

As they cooked, Brutus sat back on his haunches, waiting silently, his gaze never leaving the meat.

Finally, as the sun dropped from its noon position toward

the western edge of the glade, Brutus lifted the cooked meat from the fire, and laid it before the depression of blood.

Then he took the flask of wine, unstoppered it, and sprinkled both meat and blood with a small portion of its contents.

"Goddess of the woods!" he cried, standing now, and holding out the flask of wine as offering in one hand while with the other he gestured toward the meat and blood. "Goddess of the hunt! Thou who art privileged to range over the celestial and infernal mansions, come to me, accept these my poor offerings. Speak to me, I pray, and say to me in what land I will build new Troy. Blessed Artemis, accept my homage. I am your man, and all I have and command is yours."

He finished, and stood motionless, arms still outstretched, head thrown back slightly, eyes closed, waiting.

The wind rippled about him, lifting the flap of his waistcloth and pulling at his long black hair caught in its thong at the nape of his neck.

He waited, confident both in himself and in her.

"Brutus," she said, and his mouth twitched in a smile. He did not otherwise move, and did not open his eyes.

"Brutus." He could feel her now, moving about him, inspecting the offerings he had made, judging the quality not only of the meat and blood and wine he had brought her, but of the man who stood before her.

"This is a fine goat," she said eventually, "and you have slaughtered it well and with honor."

He opened his eyes.

Artemis stood slightly to the side of the altar, looking at the blood-filled depression, the meat, and the white pelt that lay beyond it. Her hunting garb was gone, and she had gowned herself in an ankle-length ivory linen robe, cinched at her waist with a twisted piece of wild silk the color of the sky at dawn. Her deep auburn hair, worn coiled atop the crown of her head on her previous visit, was now loose over her shoulders and back in a mass of shining curls and waves.

Her face was pale, and very still, and when she raised her dark blue eyes to Brutus his breath caught in his throat.

He had never seen a woman so beautiful, so desirable, and so untouchable.

"Will you drink of the wine I have brought you?" Brutus said. "It is of grapes grown in virgin soil, and trod with the unstained feet of virgin boys."

"I thank you," she said, and took from him the flask. She raised it to her lips, and drank of it deeply, wiping her mouth with the back of a hand when she was done.

"It *is* good," she said, and handed the flask back to Brutus.

He too drank, his eyes never leaving hers, and when he'd done, and had wiped away the red stain from his own mouth, she smiled, her teeth startlingly white against her crimson lips.

"We shall eat of the meat you have prepared," she said, and gestured to Brutus that he should sit beside her on the white pelt that, despite Brutus' careful cleaning, still stank of recent death.

She picked up a haunch of meat, took from it a small bite, her eyes steady on Brutus, then offered it to him.

He bit into it, his eyes likewise on hers, and when he handed it back to her, he laughed.

"And this meat is good also," he said. "As it should be, since I dragged that beast protesting all the way from the beach to this mountain glade."

She smiled, and lay the meat aside. She drank deeply of the flask once more, handing it to Brutus so he could also wash the meat from his mouth, then took it once more from his hands and laid it aside also.

"You have done well," she said. "You have pleased me. You took what you needed from Mesopotama."

"My people," he said.

"Yes," she said, "your people are important, but the real importance of Mesopotama was the test."

"Of course," he said, his mouth curving at the manner in which she toyed with words. "The Game."

"You played the Game with skill in Mesopotama. That was important to me. You needed to have passed."

"And if I did not?"

Artemis showed her teeth, but it was not a smile. "Then you would have enjoyed this fine meal alone, Brutus, for I have no use for a man who cannot play the Game."

He took a moment to control his breathing and calm himself, dampening an arousal that was composed of equal parts ambition and desire. *He was to play the Game.* And with *this* woman? "For Artemis, goddess of the hunt and the moon, and eternal virgin, you know a great deal about the Game. Yet how can this be? The Game has no place for virgins."

"What say you? That I am not Artemis?"

"I care not who you are," he said softly, his eyes holding hers, "only that you can give me what you promised me. Only that *you* are all *I* need for the Game."

She smiled appreciatively. "You are a demanding man, Brutus. Let me say only that I doubt you shall be disappointed. And now that you have convinced me that you are the man I need, let me show you where you shall resurrect your"—*our*—"Troy. It is a great land, a magical land. Look," she said, and cast her hand in a sweeping arc over the depression filled with the goat's sacrificial blood.

The blood bubbled, slowly, as if coming to a gentle boil. Artemis cast her hand over it once again, and the blood's surface smoothed, then became opaque, and then, suddenly, became as startlingly clear as an open window on a summer's day.

It showed a gray sea, rolling in great waves toward a land of towering white cliffs.

"It lies far to the west," Artemis said very softly. "Sail south to the Altars of the Philistines, then west, west, west until you pass through the Pillars of Hercules. Then tack northwest, following the coastline, gradually easing more north-northwest, and eventually you will find this land."

She saw the lines of concern on his brow. "Your fleet will be god-favored, Brutus. The winds will follow you, and your oarsmen shall scarcely need to place hand to wood. The pirates and the sirens and the monsters of the deep will avert their faces, for they shall see on your sails my face, and know that you sail under my care. You will be safe and well."

"You bless me," Brutus said.

"I favor you," she said brusquely. "If I blessed you then you would be immortal."

"Then I await with much anticipation your eventual blessing," he murmured, and saw that she had to struggle to repress her laughter.

His mouth curved. *Gods, they were going to be good for each other!*

Once again her hand swung in an arc over the depression, and the view of the white cliffs disappeared, replaced by that of a misty landscape. The mist shifted and moved, like a cold gray ocean itself, and as it did so Brutus could see glimpses of small rounded hills, and a great expanse of marshland and river.

"The Veiled Hills," Artemis said. "This is where you will rebuild Troy."

"What is this land? Its name? Its people? Its magic? And why is this place, these Veiled Hills, so good a site to rebuild Troy?"

"The island is called Albion, and it is rich and bounteous and fair. Your people shall prosper there. The Veiled Hills lie in a river valley in a land called Llangarlia which occupies the south of the island of Albion. Nestled atop the Veiled Hills, Troia Nova will be a city like none other the world shall ever know. It shall be most exalted, Brutus, and its tentacles of power and influence will spread over all the lands and seas of this world."

Brutus could not drag his eyes from the vision set before him. Artemis' words and prophecy whispered through him, became a part of him, but in this moment, all that mattered was this vision of the misty, veiled hills.

Unnoticed by Brutus, Artemis' hand moved again, but only slightly this time.

Brutus drew in a sharp breath.

A woman walked out of the mist toward him.

She was tall, and more beautiful than he could possibly imagine. Her hair was blue-black, a heavy weight of tight-curled locks that cascaded down her back and lifted in the slight breeze that twisted the mist about her. Partway through her back tresses, twisting over her left shoulder, was a lock of russet hair that glinted in the light. Her skin was pale, her eyes the same deep blue as those of Artemis herself, her red lips slightly apart as if in anticipation. Beneath the loose woolen robe her figure was that of a mature woman who has birthed and fed several children; her gait was smooth and graceful, that of a priestess, moving to light the fires of an altar.

Her arms were bare, white, and well rounded, and Brutus drew in a deep breath at the thought of those arms wrapped about him, that body beneath him.

"She pleases me well," he said finally, very low.

"I had hoped she would," Artemis said, "for she is your destiny." *Not Cornelia*, she thought. *Not that irritating girl-child you took to your bed.*

He dragged his gaze from the vision and looked at Artemis. "She has your eyes," he said.

Artemis inclined her head, her expression saying nothing.

His eyes crinkled slightly. "She has your power."

Again Artemis merely inclined her head, as if disinterested.

"It is a long voyage to this Llangarlia," he said. "What if I should forget what awaits me?"

"Ensure that you don't," she said.

ASTERION LAUGHED, AND THE KNIFE TWIRLED madly in his hands. "One day," he said, "you are going to wish you could do nothing but forget that witch! Once I have done with her she is going to murder both you and your dreams, Brutus, one way or the other."

But that was years ahead. In the meantime, Asterion

needed some fool he could use as his knife hand, as it were.

He also needed to watch carefully for the opportunity to position himself a little closer to the action, the better to take advantage of circumstances as they arose . . . as they were created.

Asterion ran a hand over his thin ribs, feeling the pitiful fluttering of his body's weak heart. It would soon be time for him to rid himself of this fragile carcass and arrange something far more suitable.

He knew that his use of the power needed to do this would alert Genvissa, but she was lost in such delusion she would think it of no account.

Chapter Three

RUTUS AND MEMBRICUS SAT FACING each other on two of the benches for the oarsmen. They leaned their shoulders against the gently moving side of the ship, and passed between them a flask of wine.

For a very long while they did not talk.

It was late at night, the stars dazzling above them, and about them the huddled, sleeping bodies of the ship's passengers and crew. Brutus had returned to the ship at dusk, half drunk from the wine he'd consumed with the goddess and with the vision she'd granted him. He'd nodded at the people who had pressed about him, and said to their queries that they needed to sail south. When they reached the Altars of the Philistines, and the Trojans could disembark from ship to sandy shore for several days of rest, then he would speak to the assembled whole, rather than shout pieces of information from ship to ship.

For this night they would rest at anchor within the bay of the island.

Tomorrow there would be a good northerly wind, Brutus had said, and they would set sail south.

Thus he had dismissed his people's curiosity. When Cornelia had approached him, doubt in her eyes, her hands splayed across her belly as if to remind her husband of her value, Brutus had merely told her to rest in her cabin with Aethylla. He would sleep on the benches this night, and not disturb her with his tossings and turnings.

She had obviously not been pleased, nor reassured, but she had done as he asked with no protest, turning back to her cabin on the aft deck, taking Aethylla's arm for balance.

Now, as the ship slept about them, and they finished one flask of wine and broached another, Brutus finally spoke, his voice soft and intimate.

Between swallows of the full-flavored and only slightly watered wine, he told Membricus all of what had passed in the glade, all of what Artemis had told and showed him.

He hiccuped, now far more than half drunk, and grinned at the memory of his day. Then he leaned forward, partly to pass the flask to Membricus, partly to lay a hand on Membricus' warm thigh. "She showed me a beautiful woman in this land, my friend. Very, very beautiful. Breasts like globes, legs begging to be parted, a belly just waiting to be filled."

Membricus grunted, unimpressed, and brushed away Brutus' hand. "You sound like nothing more than a bragging youth, Brutus. A fit mate for Cornelia, I must say."

Angry, Brutus grabbed the flask back from Membricus—who still hadn't drunk of it—then leaned back, taking a massive swallow of the wine. "You're jealous, Membricus. You'd rather I stuck my thing in you than in a woman."

Membricus flushed. "No!"

One of the men rolled in a blanket nearby half rose, and mumbled a curse at him, and Membricus continued in a softer voice.

"No, Brutus, although you know how greatly I treasure

my memories of those days when you desired me."

Brutus snorted. "*I* desired *you?* You were the one to come creeping into my bed when I was but thirteen, if I remember aright. All sweet whispers and warm hands."

"And you as recipient as any virgin grateful to lose his untouched state!"

Brutus put down the flask of wine, his drunkenness sloughing off him like an unwanted cloak. "What is it, Membricus," he said softly. "What troubles you truly?"

Membricus took a deep breath, closed his eyes, and calmed himself. "Artemis," he said, opening his eyes back to Brutus' regard. "She has troubled me since she first graced you with her presence."

Brutus made an impatient gesture, as if he still thought this part of Membricus' jealousy.

"No, Brutus, hear me out. I say again, as I have said previously, that I cannot understand how Artemis has suddenly so much power, so much vitality, when for generations our gods have faded in power and influence. I cannot think her who she truly says she—"

"If she gives me all that she has promised me, then she is enough for me, Membricus." Brutus picked up the wine and swallowed another long draught.

Membricus watched him in silence for a long moment. "Who is she, Brutus?"

"All that I need."

Membricus repressed a sigh, deeply unhappy that Brutus did not seem to care that Artemis might not truly be the goddess at all. *I pray to whatever gods are left,* he thought, keeping his facial expression neutral, *that Brutus knows what he is doing and that he is not allowing his ambition and his pride and his damned lust do all the thinking for him.*

"There is more," he said softly.

"And why am I not surprised to hear that?" Brutus said.

"Brutus, you recognize my ability as a seer, if nothing else." He paused. "Yes?"

Brutus nodded, the movement ungracious.

"Then listen to me now. I keep seeing a knife, a great dark dangerous thing with a haft of twisted bone, as if two horns were entwined. I see blood. I see the death of dreams. I see Cornelia."

Brutus gave an exaggerated groan, and rubbed at his eyes wearily with one hand. "She does not have a twisted bone-handled knife secreted anywhere about her person, Membricus."

"She will be your death. She will be everyone's death."

"She has failed most miserably at being 'everyone's death.' She's effectively harmless, Membricus."

"No woman is ever harmless!"

Brutus shot Membricus a black look. "Is any of this true seer prophecy, or just your usual malice regarding women? You hate them all for the ability to draw men to their beds like bees to a honey pot. Membricus, I am tired of your prating about the treacheries of women. And a knife, for the gods' sakes, even one with a twisted bone handle! Can you not come up with something more dramatic? More compelling? Ah! This has nothing to do with Artemis or prophecy or vague threats of darkness and death. This is just about you and me, Membricus, and I am most *heartily* sick of it!"

"This has nothing to do with women, Brutus! It has everything to do with my abilities as a seer, with my position at your side as an adviser, and as your *friend*, Brutus. Not your once-and-forever-jealous lover, but as your friend, who cares for you."

Brutus sighed, then leaned an arm across the railing of the ship, gazing across the water to where the rest of the fleet lay at anchor. He sat there a long while, then, finally, he rose and handed the flask of wine to Membricus.

"How can you question what we do," Brutus said, "and where we go? Do you want to spend another fifteen years wandering purposeless? Another fifteen years living from hand to mouth with no pride? No, of course not. Now, perhaps I *will* cast Aethylla from her place at Cornelia's side and rest there myself."

And with that he was off, stepping between the sleepers toward the aft deck.

Membricus lowered his head into his hands, wondering how he could have allowed his warning to be so misinterpreted. These two women, Cornelia and "Artemis," had both trapped Brutus, each in their own, different ways.

After a while he lifted the flask of wine to his mouth, and drank of it deeply.

He did not sleep all night.

Chapter Four

GENVISSA WAS DELIGHTED AT HOW WELL Brutus had received and honored her, but her mind was increasingly consumed with Mag's vexatious disappearance. Mag was an irritating loose end when Genvissa wanted no loose ends at all.

Mag should not have been able to escape . . . let alone conceal herself so well.

Damn Mag!

How could she have vanished so effectively?

Genvissa was very tempted to believe that Mag was dead, that she hadn't vanished so much as winked out of existence. However seductive and comforting that theory, Genvissa knew it wasn't correct. She hadn't felt Mag's death, and had it occurred then she would have done.

No. Mag was alive somewhere. Hiding. The fact that Genvissa could not scry out the *where* of that hiding was as effective as Mag dealing her a sharp slap in the face.

Then there was the question of what Mag was doing while she had secreted herself away.

"Nothing," Genvissa whispered to herself as she sat before the central hearth in her house, sipping the broth that her middle daughter had brought her for her morning meal. "There is nothing she *can* do." There was nothing anyone could do. Asterion was too far away and hopelessly weak; Mag and Og had been crippled and Og would soon be dead (as would Mag once Genvissa got her hands on the silly witch); all the ancient gods of the Aegean were dead or so close to it that collectively they were less nuisance than a single three-legged and blind house rat.

There was nothing anyone could do to stop her now.

Nevertheless, Genvissa felt on edge. Perhaps it was that girl, Cornelia. She'd hoped that Brutus would have slit her throat once he discovered her part in the Mesopotamian revolt. But he hadn't, and Genvissa supposed that, like all men, he was hopelessly enamored of the son she was carrying.

Well, the girl couldn't hide behind her belly for the rest of her life. Once that child was born . . . then Cornelia could be disposed of.

Genvissa sighed, and rubbed at her eyes. Why was she troubled by such inconsequentials as Mag and Cornelia?

"Mother?"

Genvissa glanced up at her daughter, standing a few paces away looking puzzled. She was a lovely girl, this middle daughter, all creamy skin and gentle spirit, and Genvissa loved her dearly.

"Ah, sweet, I am but muttering away my lack of sleep. Or perhaps I have succumbed to a passing feeble-mindedness."

The girl laughed, and Genvissa smiled with her. "This broth is better than any I could have made. I thank you for it."

"My sisters have run to help the Gormagog hunt out the red-lipped mushroom for the frenzy wine, Mother. May I—"

"Of course, love. Go and catch them up. It would be best in any case, for I will need my solitude this morning."

The girl grinned, made a hasty bow of respect toward her mother, then was off out the door.

Genvissa smiled as she finished her broth, thinking dreamy thoughts of the daughters she had borne, and the one she was yet to bear, and by the time she was ready to begin her morning's labor, she was in a more cheerful frame of mind.

Her task required much thought, and some delicate spell-weaving, but once she was done Genvissa's good mood had only increased.

Time to set in motion those events that would bring Blangan home.

LOCRINIA LAY STILL AND QUIET UNDER THE clouded night sky. It was warm, and the city's citizens had left doors and windows open to catch any passing breeze that might lift off the bay or the vast seas beyond it.

That was fortunate indeed, or else far more of the sleepers would have died.

In the darkest hours of the early morning, when sleep was deepest, a faint tremor ran through the rocky foundations of the city.

Then another, a little stronger.

Then a frightful surge of energy that lifted up houses and buckled the paved streets.

Blangan had been sleeping by her husband's side. As the room lifted about her, and their bed slid sideways, Blangan grabbed at her husband, Corineus, and cried out in terror.

He half slid, half fell out of the bed, dragging Blangan with him.

"Outside!" he yelled, terror hoarsening his voice. "Now! Out! Out!"

Blangan needed no further encouragement. She grabbed at a sheet, winding it about her slim form and, Corineus' arm about her waist, struggled toward the door.

They barely made it onto the wide verandah that ran about their house before the doorway's lintel fell crashing behind them.

"What is happening?" Blangan cried.

She cried those words because she knew it was expected of her. The gentle, wise wife of the city's leading citizen was not supposed to know of the origin and meanings of earth surges and dark happenings, but despite her pretense, Blangan knew very well what was happening.

This was the work of her sister. She knew it.

"Blangan," Corineus said, taking her hand and leading her down the steps into the wide street. "Away from the building. Now. It might collapse."

But it didn't. There were no more tremors, and the only casualties were in buildings less well constructed than Corineus' house, and which had collapsed in that single destructive surge.

Corineus relaxed after it became apparent that the earth was going to confine itself to that single, if albeit frightening, tremor. He organized the people of Locrinia into open spaces for the night until their tenement buildings and houses could be examined for damage in the morning light, and walked among them, Blangan at his side, murmuring reassurances.

IN THE MORNING, HIS WORDS WERE SHOWN FOR the empty hopes that they were.

Every single building in Locrinia was cracked, so badly that it was apparent that when the heavy autumn rains arrived the mud-bricked buildings would collapse.

Come two or three months, and Locrinia would be uninhabitable.

"It is unbelievable," Corineus muttered, squatting at the foundations of one of the houses.

Behind him, Blangan, staring transfixed at the cracks, could believe it very well.

Genvissa wanted her home, and she wanted her badly.

Chapter Five

Cornelia Speaks

I DO NOT KNOW WHAT MY HUSBAND SAW ON that island, but when he came back his eyes were strange and power seeped from every pore of his body. If ever I had needed proof of the blood of Aphrodite that I knew flowed through his veins, then those eyes and that power would have been enough.

It was as much as I could do not to step back from him, nor flinch when he put his hand to my cheek.

He told me to rest, and that he would not disturb me, but late that night, when I was deep asleep, I woke to hear his voice ordering Aethylla from my side on the sleeping pallet. He lay down beside me, his breath thick with wine, and told me to sleep, and that he would not make any demands of me. Nevertheless, merely to have him there, to feel his body close to mine, and to sense the remnants of whatever power had infested him on the island, was enough to keep me sleepless until dawn broke the night.

I stirred, meaning to rise, but he held me back with a hand on my belly.

"How long?" he said, and I quailed.

"Two months, perhaps a few weeks more than that," I said, then rolled a little so I could see his face. "Brutus, I—"

But he had risen, and was gone.

WE SAILED SOUTH SOME NINE DAYS. THE WIND blew briskly at our backs and the seas rolled us gently forward. I remembered all the tales I'd heard about the black nature of this sea, how it never stayed calm longer than a day or two before it blew itself into a ship-eating gale, and how pirates patrolled its surface and monstrous marine worms its depths.

But this sea was not that of the tales and rumors. It was unnatural—even I could feel that—as if a god had passed his or her hand over its surface and calmed it for the betterment of our passage.

Brutus must clearly be god-favored, and I shivered as I wondered whether or not I could ever win enough of his affection to ensure my life.

Brutus left me well enough alone for these nine days of sail. During the day I sat with Aethylla and one or two of the other Trojan women on the aft deck, raising our faces to the sunshine, and passing stories between us of children and childbirth.

I hated it. I *loathed* it—could these women talk of nothing else but babies? They even put their hands to my belly—ugh! I felt violated—and felt the shape of the baby within, and nodded their heads sagely, and said it was bound to be a fine son for Brutus.

They said nothing to me of how this "fine son" had been got on me, or of how it bloated my body most horribly, or of the pains that shot up and down my legs and through my groin when I walked, or of its odious twisting and turning at night when I wanted to sleep, nor even of the pressure the thing put on my bladder so that I dribbled urine at the most inopportune moments. They spoke only of the fine son it was for Brutus, and how that must please me.

I smiled, and nodded, and hoped they did not see through my eyes to the fear beneath. I could laugh and gossip with the best of them when it came to saving my life.

At night Brutus came to lie beside me, but he rarely spoke to me and made no demands on my body (I was not surprised, in the past two weeks my belly had swollen most hideously, and I doubted that even the most lustful of men could climb it).

He did, nonetheless, disturb me, for when he slept he dreamed of such strange things that he tossed and turned and murmured. Among the night visions that passed through his mind was a dream of a woman. I know this because as I sat wakeful and watching, I heard him murmur to her, and reach for her, and twice I noted that his member grew hard and erect.

Then I drew back in horror, not only that I feared he might wake and use me to sate his longing for another, but that he actually dreamed of someone else.

Someone to replace me once I'd fulfilled my purpose and delivered him a son? Someone he preferred to me? Someone he . . . *liked*?

Those hours, when I sat there and watched Brutus dream of another woman, were among the blackest I'd ever known. It seemed, then, that any hope I had of gaining his regard was very slim indeed.

Sometimes I tried to remember Melanthus, but under my current trying conditions—the burdensome weight of another man's baby within me, the strangeness of shipboard life, the constant worry that Brutus would abandon or murder me once I'd given birth (an even greater fear now I knew he dreamed of another woman)—I found Melanthus' face ever more difficult to recall.

Besides, he belonged to a life long gone.

ON THE MORNING OF THE TENTH DAY AT SEA THE forward fore-looker cried out, and pointed, and between the scores of craning necks between where I sat on the aft deck and the stem of the ship, I could see a faint line of the horizon. It was an immense land, Aethylla's husband, Pelopan, told me, toward which we sailed. Vaster than could be imagined, and filled with creatures stranger than the wildest fantasy.

"Is this where Brutus leads us?" I asked, hating it that I had to ask Pelopan and so reveal my own complete ignorance of my husband's intentions. "Is this where he will build the new Troy he speaks of so often?"

"Who can know?" he said, then turned aside to his own

wife, holding her hand and smiling with obvious care at her.

I felt a sudden surge of ill will toward them. There they stood, simple untutored folk, at ease and in love with each other, while *I* . . . I, who had been bred to such luxury and such privilege, and who should have had love aplenty for the asking, was condemned to a husband I feared and a child I resented. Unbelievably, shamefully, I began to cry again, and had to stand there, enduring Aethylla's deep sighs and condescending pats on my shoulder, as I wept for all the love I'd lost.

At least Brutus was not there to witness my continuing humiliation. He spent most of the morning shouting and gesturing; doing what all men must, I suppose, when they direct a fleet so large toward a suitable anchorage point. By noon all the shouting and gesturing had paid dividends, for the entire fleet had anchored in shallow waters off a long sandy beach that appeared to extend for a lifetime to either side of our ships. Beyond the beach rose a low range of hills, covered with brush and topped at one point with two strange stone pillars. These, Pelopan informed me, were what was known as the Altars of the Philistines.

When I asked why, he shrugged, but said they were well known among sailors for the natural spring at their base.

The entire afternoon was spent in rafting people to the shore. The word was that this was, indeed, only a temporary stop. We were to camp here some days to stretch our legs, replenish our supplies both with water and with fresh game, and to hear what Brutus had in store for us.

Many of the adults and some of the older children would not wait for their place on the rafts, and jumped overboard from their ships to wade through the shallows to the beach, but I, naturally considering my dignity and my pregnancy, waited for my place on a raft.

I was surprised when Brutus came to me and indicated he would aid me to the first of the rafts.

"Will you behave yourself?" he asked me.

"Do I have much choice?" I said.

He did not smile, and he regarded me a moment with uncomfortable speculation, but then he nodded as if I'd somehow answered a question in his mind and helped me down the side of the ship to the raft with a little more consideration than the manner in which he'd bundled me aboard.

Membricus and Deimas were already waiting on the raft, and Deimas stood and aided me, stone-faced, to a clear spot. I murmured my thanks, and prayed that my plan to win Brutus might actually be having some effect.

I cheered considerably, and did not even mind when Aethylla dropped aboard so inelegantly that the raft rocked and I was splashed all down my right side with a wash of seawater.

She was the last to board, and so, waving a good-bye to Brutus who was staying aboard to supervise the loading of subsequent raft-loads, I turned to this strange new land where we were to rest for some days, at the least.

I WAS GLAD THIS WAS NOT WHERE BRUTUS MEANT us to stay permanently. Although the beach itself was pleasant enough, the wind that blew from the interior of the land was hot and dry, and carried with it the stink of hardship and toil. I walked slowly up the beach, enjoying the coolness of the water that swirled about my ankles, my hands in the small of my back, trying to ease some of the discomfort of the child. About me groups of Trojans, clearly relieved to be on dry land once again, were moving tents and cooking pots a little distance into the low hills beyond the beach to set up sheltered camps.

I stopped, and closed my eyes, and sighed in pleasure. Even the hard soil of this land would prove a more comfortable bed than that damned sleeping pallet onboard ship.

"Cornelia."

I opened my eyes and turned, a twist of discomfort in my stomach.

It was Membricus, Brutus' never far distant friend. I

feared him more than I did Brutus. I sensed that where Brutus might be swayed, Membricus was implacable.

There were no charms I could use against this man, and so I employed none.

"Yes?" I said.

"You are needed," he began, and his cold eyes slid to my belly, reminding me of *exactly* why I was needed. "Brutus has landed with the last of our people," not *my* people, "and is now asking that you join him at his side while he speaks to the assembled gathering."

My eyes widened slightly, and I smiled spontaneously. Brutus wanted me at his side while he stood and addressed his people?

And it was *Membricus* who must bring me this news, when he undoubtedly would prefer it to be he standing at Brutus' side?

Ever mindful of the precariousness of my position, I repressed my smile, nodded, and followed Membricus back to where the Trojans gathered.

"I AM GRACED WITH THE WILL OF ARTEMIS," BRU-tus said, his voice clear and strong. I stood slightly to one side of him on a small rise that faced the beach; before us were spread the assembled mass of the Trojans. Although it looked as if I had my eyes on the crowd, I was surreptitiously watching Brutus. Even though I feared him greatly, I had to admit he looked magnificent as he stood in the last rays of the afternoon. Even my father had never commanded so much authority, nor exuded so much confidence. Brutus had apparently waded or swum ashore, for his waistcloth clung to him wetly, and his skin gleamed with droplets from the sea.

About his limbs the golden bands glistened, and for no apparent reason I remembered how, when Brutus lay with me, those bands had always felt hot against my skin. I shuddered, and saw Brutus' eyes shift my way momentarily, and I dropped my eyes too quickly.

"We are to travel far to the west," he continued after a moment, "to a land of great beauty and riches. It is called Llangarlia."

Llangarlia! At the articulation of that one word it was if I were back in that strange stone hall of my vision listening to my daughter's laughter, staring through the stone of the arches into the wondrous landscape beyond.

And this is where we were going? No wonder I'd dreamed of the stone hall so often since leaving Mesopotama!

I felt a surge of excitement. That wondrous land . . . where I'd felt such a sense of "home." And it was no vision at all, but reality? It must be, surely, if that single word recalled the dream so vividly.

Llangarlia . . . I rolled it silently about my mouth, and found it wonderfully sweet.

Brutus was talking of how this Llangarlia occupied the southern part of a white-cliffed island called Albion. As he spoke I allowed myself to dream a little of this new land— my visionary land, and every time Brutus said the name of "Llangarlia" I felt another small surge of excitement. One of my hands strayed to my belly, and as Brutus' voice spoke on, my mind drifted even further, dreaming of what it might be like to stand as queen beside Brutus in Llangarlia.

I was vaguely aware that under my hand my belly was unnaturally hot, and that my fingers and palm were throbbing with that heat, but that awareness did not distract me from my train of thought. Supposing I could make him like me enough not to kill me when this child was gone from my belly, could I then endure a life with him?

Strangely, impossibly, I wondered if that might not be too difficult at all.

How odd the difference a single word could make . . .

It was only when I heard the sound of another man's voice that I blinked, and came back to the moment, dropping my hand from my belly. Brutus had apparently finished his address, and was now standing, answering some questions from the crowd.

One man asked if the people of Llangarlia would welcome the Trojans, and Brutus hesitated before answering.

"It is possible they will not do so," he said, "but we have the gods with us, and we will prevail."

There was a murmuring at that, but from what I could see most people seemed reasonably accepting of what Brutus had told them.

I was not surprised. Brutus had seemed almost godlike as he'd talked to the crowd . . . I shook my head slightly. He'd even had me dreaming of him!

Brutus must have seen my slight movement from the corner of his eye, for he turned to me and told me to make my way down to the campfires, that I should eat and rest, and not weary myself overmuch in this desert air.

I ATE SPARINGLY OF THE RAISINS AND FIGS, WASHing them down with healthy draughts of the barely watered wine; justifying the wine as an antidote to the effects of the hot wind that blew continuously from the interior of this land.

When I had done, and had drunk enough to sate my thirst, I rose, and told Aethylla to leave me be, as I needed to relieve myself at some distance among the scrubby bushes of the hills.

She subsided, nodding sympathetically and remembering, I suppose, her own numerous pregnancies.

Sometimes it helped to be a breeding woman among breeding women.

I did indeed take the opportunity of the relative privacy to relive my needs amid a thankfully dense (but scratchy) patch of shrubs but then, instead of returning to the fireside, I walked farther into the hills, drawn as if mesmerized by the hot wind that blew in my face. The wine I had drunk throbbed in my blood, and I shook out my hair from its restraints and let it blow free, relishing its freedom.

I climbed to the top of the first hill, and stopped to catch my breath. Once I would have been limber enough to run up this gentle slope and not need to pause for breath at all ... but not now. I drew in deep, grateful breaths, gazing over the hills rolling into the distance. In this evening twilight the shrubs that covered their slopes gave the hills a purple aspect, and I stood entranced by the sight, my imagination wondering what lay beyond them in this strange land.

I breathed in deep once more, and found it easy, so I walked down the far slope of this hill and toward the next, pushing my way through the shrubs, tilting back my head and letting their thorny stems catch at my hair.

It seemed like freedom, somehow.

This next hill was steeper, its footing more slippery and stony, and I took far longer to climb its height.

Yet when I did so, and stood, hands on belly, gasping in the sweet night air, the view seemed even more entrancing, the successive rolling waves of hills even more seductive.

I wondered how many people had been seduced deeper and deeper into these hills, and where their bones lay, and if they had been picked clean by strange beasts, or left, to be scrubbed white by the sun and the wind.

"Cornelia," said a voice so gently behind me, and a soft hand caught at my elbow.

I turned, but did not pull away my arm. I was somehow not surprised to find him behind me.

"I had not thought you the one to be so entranced by such wildness," he said, smiling, and I, still under the spell of the hills and the wine and that single word he had spoken hours ago, smiled back.

Brutus drew up to my side, and let go my arm, standing to look over the hills, now almost invisible in the darkening night. His own body, virtually naked save for the waistcloth, was dark and exotic, the linen of the cloth gleaming very white against the darkness of his skin.

A sensation of heat flowed down the length of my spine and I realized, without any surprise at all, that it was desire.

"Were you running away?" he asked, still looking at the hills.

"Where to?" I said. "No, Brutus, I was not running away."

Without thinking too greatly about it, I reached up a hand to the thong tying back his own heavy hair. It was a mystery to me, this hair, with its tight black curls, blued with the sheen of the herbed oil he rubbed through it every few days.

I tugged at the thong, and pulled it loose, and as his hair flew free in the wind he turned to look at me, his eyes dark and unknowable.

I reached the hand up to that flowing, snapping black cloud and ran my fingers through its mass. It was the first time I had ever done so, the first time I had freely touched his hair . . . or any part of him at all for that matter. I had seen his hair, and smelled it, and felt it brush over my skin so many nights of these past seven months. I had loathed it as it smothered my face and my body as he lay upon me, but I had never touched it as I did now, and I wondered at it, this mysterious black hair.

Any woman would have given one of her breasts to possess such magnificence.

"Is this the hair of the goddess?" I asked, wanting to know something of the god-blood that ran in him. "Is this Aphrodite's bequest to you?"

He did not answer, not with words, but he drew me in close to him, our bodies pressed hard against each other, one of his hands buried in my hair as mine was buried in his.

I found my breath short, and my throat dry.

Our hair whipped about us like a swarm of barbarous, biting bees, devouring us in its wildness until there was nothing but his warmth and the scent of his maleness and his hand hard on the back of my head and over and above all of this there were his dark fathomless eyes, centering my universe. His mouth was parted, and I could see the glint of his tongue, and smell the sweet musk of his breath.

My own breath grew even shorter, and I relaxed in his arms and against the entire length of his body.

His face drew closer, and I felt his lips brush my forehead and my cheek, and then the rough wetness of his tongue sliding along the line of my jaw.

"Sometimes you can be so sweet," he whispered. "Why not always, Cornelia? Why not always?"

As his mouth moved very close to mine, one of his hands rubbed deliciously at my breasts, tugging at the nipple through the thin linen of my gown, and I pressed myself hard into his hand.

"Brutus," I whispered, and raised my face to his.

Our mouths grazed, I felt the warm slipperiness of his tongue as it slid briefly, tantalizingly, between my lips, and I relaxed completely, utterly, and opened my mouth to his.

And almost fell to the ground as abruptly he let me go and stood back.

"What?" he said, and I quailed at the harshness in his voice. "What? You would allow me to kiss the mouth vowed only to Melanthus?"

I held out a hand. "Brutus—"

"I thought I repulsed you . . . or was it that the only reason you could bear me so close just now was because you were screaming Melanthus' name over and over in your mind?"

I sobbed. "Brutus . . . please . . ."

"You bitch," he said. "Did you think that your sudden display of wantonness would fool me?"

I was crying hard now, scared, desperate, my hands shaking. "I never meant those words, Brutus."

"Yes! Yes, you *did*! Those words must be the only truths I've ever had from your mouth. Look at you, a sniveling, cowering child. Do you think that now *I* could possibly want *you*?"

"I'm sorry," I said, so desperate I risked all by placing one of my trembling hands on his arm. His muscles tensed at my touch, but he did not throw me off, and I drew a little closer. "I'm sorry."

"Do you think I am going to kill you? Do you?"

"Yes," I sobbed.

"Good," he said, and the coldness in his tone was horrifying. "I think you can only be trusted when you are terrified."

I lifted my hand from his arm, and placed both it and its companion over my face, hiding it from him as I wept. How could I have been so stupid, so arrogant, as to taunt him in that manner?

We stood there a long time, he completely still, his eyes on me as I cried.

Then, finally, he sighed, stepped closer, pulled my hands away from my face, and with his own hands cupped gently about my cheeks, tipped it up so that he might look me in the eye.

"If you had loved Melanthus that much, and he you, then why were you still a virgin when I took you to bed?"

He waited, and I fought desperately for the right answer.

"I . . ." I said, wondering where this was leading. Was he not glad of the fact? Didn't all men desperately desire virgins? *What did he want me to say?*

"If I had been the oh-so-virile Melanthus," he said, "I would not have left you a virgin for another man's conquest."

I remembered that embarrassing fumbling in the store room, the awkwardness, the haste, the sudden, unexpected spurt of wetness against my thigh, his gasping of relief, and mine of horrid embarrassment.

"Ah," he said. "He tried, didn't he?"

I nodded, too scared to lie to him anymore.

"What happened?"

I closed my eyes one more brief, humiliated time, and told him in as few words as possible.

He gave a short bark of laughter. "He had no control at all, did he? No wonder he pissed himself when I killed him. He'd probably dribbled his way through his entire short life. And it was with *this* that you taunted me? It was with this that you *dared* to compare me?"

His hands were still about my face, but they had lost their gentleness. He lowered his own face close and said, his mouth barely above mine, his breath hot and forceful, "I will never kiss you, Cornelia. No matter how much you beg me, no matter what you say, no matter how desperately you offer yourself to me. Never. *Never!*"

Then he was gone, walking back to the camp without me, and I was left to sink to the sand and weep and mourn, but for what I did not know.

Chapter Six

*B*RUTUS KEPT HIS PEOPLE FIVE DAYS IN THE hills surrounding the Altars of the Philistines. Each day hunting parties ventured into the wild lands beyond the hills, bringing back fresh kills of stringy hare and the small antelope that fed off the shrubs.

The fresh meat was welcomed. Most of it was dried in the sun for eating once the fleet put to sea again, some of it was consumed within hours of being brought back to camp, roasted on open fires with some of the herbs and oils the Trojans had packed in their ships.

On the sixth day, at dawn, Brutus gave the order to reembark. The loading went quickly—people were now used to the rafts and loading procedures—and by late morning the fleet was under way again, sailing due west.

Artemis kept her word to Brutus, for as soon as he'd given the order to weigh anchor, a stiff easterly breeze sprang up. Ship captains raised their great square linen sails, and the oarsmen stowed their oars and reclined on their benches, enjoying the feel of their ships slicing through the blue-green waters of the great central sea.

They kept the line of the coast on their port beam, and

many a curious eye ran over the landscape that they passed. Now desert, now more verdant oasis, now hilly, now flat, many among the Trojans wondered at what lay deeper within this vast continent they sailed past. Sometimes the wind carried the howls of exotic beasts, sometimes the scents of spices strange and rare. Sometimes people appeared on the beaches, watching the massive fleet as it sailed past. They wore long, hooded, and brightly colored robes, and leaned on long crooks similar to shepherd crooks.

They never waved, nor shouted. They merely watched; praying, perhaps, that this fleet would continue onward, and not stop to ravage their lands.

Brutus kept the ships at sail for eight days and nights. His people slept as best they could among the press of other bodies, bundles of clothing and blankets, amphora of water and wine and the constantly fidgeting goats and sheep they carried with them. During the day there was little else to do save watch the passing coastline, peer over the sides of the ship into the deep clear waters of the sea in an effort to spy sea monsters, play at dice or boral stones, pass the time idly gossiping with their neighbors, or wonder at what awaited them in this new land.

Very few people had any complaints about where Brutus led them. They knew they might well be sailing into possible hardship, even conflict, but they were sailing into freedom, and in doing so they were reclaiming their proud heritage and nobility.

Brutus had made them *Trojans* again; he had handed back to them their self-respect.

BRUTUS DID NOT SPEND HIS ENTIRE TIME SHOUT-ing orders, or contemplating his future building Troia Nova. Sometimes, when he had time to rest, and sit and enjoy the sun and the sea spray that washed over the sides of the ship, Brutus followed Cornelia with his eyes, watching her. Thinking.

He'd left Aethylla to share her bed since that first night at the Altars of the Philistines, preferring to bed down with the single men and warriors.

He was still furious with her: for those hurtful, spiteful words to him in their bed, for her treachery that had caused so many deaths in Mesopotama, and, most of all, for her false seductiveness in the hills behind the Altars of the Philistines. He'd followed her into the hills because he'd wondered, despite his words to Membricus, if she had some new treachery planned, or if she thought of escape. To have her turn to him, and touch him as if she truly desired him, and press herself against him was beyond belief.

Gods! He had been aroused by her (which deepened his anger), but he'd not been fooled. She'd spent the past seven months making perfectly plain to him that she despised him, and that she preferred that immature child-boy Melanthus' fumblings to what he could offer (and he *knew* he could arouse her, he knew it!). What was she doing? What game was she playing? Was it just as Membricus had said, that she feared for her own life so much now that her treacheries had gone awry that she would play any part to save it?

Well, he would not play it with her. He would not allow himself to be fooled by her. Another waited him, a woman who could truly partner him . . . the true antithesis to Cornelia's shallow childishness.

Yet Brutus continually found his eyes drawn to Cornelia. Surreptitiously, whenever she was unaware of his regard, Brutus would watch her. Cornelia's belly was large now, ungainly, but even though she was so far into her pregnancy, she'd still found the time to continue growing herself. She'd gained a little height, and both her face and her limbs had lost much of their childish plumpness.

There was a growing grace and beauty to her movements—the tilt of her head as she laughed (pretense, undoubtedly), the languid sweep of her hand through the air as she pointed out something to Aethylla—and, perversely, that only added to Brutus' animosity. He wanted her to grow fat and ugly, so that he could truly despise her.

He hated it that in almost everything she did she only made him want her more.

He hated it that when she turned and saw him looking at her, the light faded from her face.

He hated it that whenever he thought of Membricus' prophecy that she would die in childbed, he felt a terrifying sense of loss.

ON THE ELEVENTH DAY AFTER LEAVING THE AL-tars of the Philistines the fleet approached a green and verdant land on their port beam. For the next day and a half they sailed past large towns, even cities, that appeared at regular intervals along the coast or just inland.

In midafternoon of the twelfth day a large port city appeared at the mouth of a sluggish river, and Brutus called to the captains of the fleet to lower their sails and to set the anchors.

He, accompanied by some five other men, set out in a small rowboat to the port from where he did not return until the next morning at dawn.

With him came several moderately sized sailing vessels well staffed with men who were, the Trojans were relieved to note, only lightly armed.

Brutus climbed back into his flagship, smiling at Membricus and Deimas who stood anxiously by.

Behind them Cornelia, face and body still, waited with Aethylla.

Her eyes did not once leave Brutus.

"We have made new friends," Brutus said, grinning as Membricus, then Deimas, clasped his hand and arm. "This land is called Mauritania, and it is a rich and well ordered and supplied realm."

His grin widened. "But not so rich they are not willing to part with some of their supplies for a portion of the gold and jewels I said I carried with me."

"Will we stop here?" Cornelia said, her eyes now moving past Brutus to the city about the port.

He looked at her thoughtfully, wondering at her motives for the question. "No. We stay only the length of time it takes the Mauritians to ferry out to each of our ships fresh supplies of water, grain, and fruit." He looked back to Membricus and Deimas, and the ship's captain with them. "It is too late in the summer to linger. We leave as soon as we can."

They sailed the next day in the hour after dawn.

FAR, FAR AWAY, GENVISSA STOOD BY A STILL POND, staring at the vision she could see in its mirrored waters.

A hundred black-hulled ships, sailing toward the Pillars of Hercules.

Closing her eyes, and summoning her power, Genvissa called on the sprites of the water, Mag's familiars, and stirred them into turmoil.

For all her kind words and reassurances to Brutus in her guise as Artemis, Genvissa intended to cripple this fleet long before it reached Llangarlia . . . and perhaps even finally rid herself of this mewling child Brutus had taken to wife.

Genvissa hated the way thoughts of Cornelia constantly filled Brutus' mind. It was beyond time that Cornelia died. Brutus would have to survive without his precious son.

LATE IN THE AFTERNOON, LAND MASSES TO THE north and south had closed in upon the fleet so that ahead lay only a relatively narrow strait of sea between two headlands.

Brutus—standing in the stem of his ship with the captain, Membricus, Deimas, and two other experienced sailors— looked ahead, clearly worried. Then he glanced upward toward the sky that had, in the past hour, clouded over until they were almost as crowded by low-hanging black clouds as they were by the headlands.

"So much for 'Artemis' ' pledge for calm seas," Membricus muttered, and Brutus threw him a dirty look.

"I have been through the Pillars of Hercules once before," said the captain, Aldros. "It can be a perilous journey in the best of seasons, let alone when a storm threatens to close in about us."

"How many ships abreast?" said Brutus. If he sailed the fleet through single file it would take hours to get them all to safety.

"Five, possibly six," said Aldros, his gray eyes narrowed in his weather-beaten face as he stared ahead. "But even then the captains of the ships on the outer extremities will need to be careful. There are rocks there"—he pointed—"and there, and there."

"Do we sail, or row?" said Brutus, now watching Aldros more carefully than either the sea ahead or the sky above.

"We row," said Aldros. "The Pillars of Hercules is the meeting point of two great seas, the central sea, which we leave, and the great gray infinity that stretches to the west, into which we enter. Tides and waves pull and push in every direction. If we depend on sail, we are likely to be dashed on the rocks to either side of the pillars. The oarsmen must prove their worth if we are to survive. Ye gods, Brutus, I hope you trained the new crews well in the months we waited in Mesopotama."

"Well," said Brutus, "now we will find out. Aldros, will you organize the passing of instructions between ships? We sail five abreast, and we do it before night falls. Tell the captains to stow their sails, and to tie everything down. The crews must take to their oars, and passengers must huddle as deep in the bellies of the ships as they can."

Aldros nodded, and hurried off to speak to some of his sailors.

The next moment the great sail started to come down.

"My friends," Brutus said to Membricus and Deimas,

"will you see to the people in this ship? Get them low and tightly packed."

As Membricus and Deimas moved off, Brutus picked his way toward the aft deck of the ship. Cornelia, Aethylla, and two other women were sitting in the small space beside the cabin. They stared at Brutus, and sometimes beyond him to the gray seas between the Pillars of Hercules, their faces tense and worried.

Brutus saw Cornelia finger her belly briefly, and for the first time he began to truly worry about the trial ahead. He had so many vulnerable people in this fleet . . .

He reached the women, and smiled, but because the smile did nothing to wipe the concern from his dark eyes, none of the four women smiled back.

"We have heard rumors of storms and danger ahead," said Cornelia. "Will we be safe?"

He hesitated, and then realized that because of that hesitation nothing he said would relieve the women's anxiety. He shrugged, and decided to be truthful. "I don't know. Normally a storm, even a bad one, would not concern me overmuch. But in these narrow straits, with these rocks, and with so many people packed into these ships." He paused, sighed, and said again, "I don't know."

One of the women sitting with Cornelia and Aethylla, Periopis, gave a low moan of terror.

He glanced at Cornelia: she was obviously fearful, but calm.

"You cannot stay on the aft deck," he said to the women. "It is too exposed should the sea rise and rage."

"We will huddle with the others below in the belly of the ship," said Cornelia. "Do not worry about us, Brutus. We will be well."

Brutus stared at her, surprised. He'd expected something other than this calm control. Tears, recriminations, childish temper . . . but not a composed, even discipline.

He nodded. "Wrap yourselves well in blankets—anything to keep you dry if the waves toss themselves over the side of the ship. And whatever happens, whatever you see or hear, stay where you are. There will be no greater safety anywhere else."

"We shall wrap our arms about each other and tell each other childish rhymes," Cornelia said, trying unsuccessfully to smile, "and we will not get in the way."

Brutus grudgingly admired her composure. She could have made things hard for him; instead, it appeared as if she were going out of her way to make things easier, even though she was fearful herself.

He nodded. "Thank you," he said, and then he was gone.

Cornelia watched him a moment, then she turned to the other women and began to urge them into the belly of the boat.

A half hour later, just as the first waves of ships had entered the straits between the pillars, a storm of supernatural proportion bore down on the fleet.

Chapter Seven

MANY YEARS BEFORE, WHEN HE HAD been a child, Brutus had heard the sound made by a massive block of stone falling fifteen paces onto stone pavement.

The noise that the winds made now, as they met in the center of the straits, reminded him of that, although it was ten times more powerful, and accompanied by a shrieking and raging such as no mortal ear normally heard during its lifetime.

Whipped on by the winds, the seas rose into great jagged gray-green cliffs, plunging and swirling in such a manner that the entire world about and within the ships collapsed into swirling, drenching horror.

Brutus, who had tied himself to the stem post of the ship

so that the seas would not sweep him overboard, screamed at the oarsmen—as within every one of the hundred ships in his fleet captains and officers screamed at oarsmen—to dig in and stabilize the chaotic spinning of the ships.

The oarsmen, fighting down their terror, dug in their oars into the waters in the dip-and-hold maneuver they'd practiced a thousand times on dry land. They did well, holding their oars steady against the massive pressures battering against both oars and ships, but no matter how well they managed to hold the maneuver, the ships would not stabilize.

Not in this sea, not amid this degree of rage.

Cornelia and her companions crouched as deep as they could within the belly of the ship, already drenched despite their thick covering of blankets, hardly daring to breathe in the extremity of their fear. Still alongside Cornelia and Aethylla, Periopis had begun to wail and shriek, sure that her life was near to ending.

The storm's intensity increased, and ships were driven far apart. Brutus, watching half terrified, half enraged at his post, saw one of them lifted high on an immense wave, then plummet down its face to dash against the rocks at the base of one of the pillars.

There was a brief glimpse of bodies being hurled through the air, and then the swirling waters ate the entire ship and its people and cargo.

Within seconds there was no sign the ship had ever existed.

"Cursed be you!" Brutus screamed at the waters. He bared his teeth into the storm and shook his fist at the rain that sleeted down. "Cursed be you!"

As if in answer, thunder boomed through the air, resounding horribly through the flesh of everyone who heard it, then three gigantic streaks of lightning seared through the grim sky: each one hit the mast of a ship.

All three masts exploded, sending bodies and cargo spinning helplessly into the wild seas.

Periopis, clinging to Aethylla and Cornelia, suddenly lost

all her reason. She shrieked, tearing herself from their hands, and, rising to her feet as best she could manage amid the violent motion of the ship, fought her way toward the aft deck, perhaps thinking to shelter in the cabin.

Aethylla called after her, holding out hopeless arms, but it was Cornelia who rose and, carefully, inch by inch, made her way after Periopis.

Far behind them, clinging to the stem post, Brutus saw the two women. For a moment he could not make out their identity amid the dense sea spray and foam, but then he saw the distinctive shape of the second woman, and realized who she was.

"Cornelia!" he screamed and, untying himself from his anchor, struggled toward them.

GENVISSA LIFTED HER HEAD AND SMILED. PERIOPIS *would prove such a useful tool.*

BRUTUS STRUGGLED THROUGH THE LENGTH OF the boat, tripping and falling several times as his feet caught first in those of one of the oarsmen, and then twice in the crevices between the huddled terrified bodies crouching in the belly of the ship.

Before him he could see the two women in the aft deck, struggling and swaying in the violent motion of the ship.

And, in one moment when the spray cleared for an instant, and a gap appeared in the monstrous waves that surrounded the ships, Brutus saw that behind his ship another had been caught in the raging waters, and was dashed against the rocks.

"Artemis, aid me!" he whispered, and fought his way farther aft.

"EVENTUALLY," SHE WHISPERED, "BUT NOT JUST *yet."*

*   *   *

BRUTUS MANAGED TO REACH THE STRUGGLING women, realizing that Cornelia was trying to pull Periopis back into the belly of the ship.

"Cursed bitch!" Brutus cried as he grabbed hold of Periopis.

She shrieked, trying to wrench herself away from both Cornelia and Brutus.

Brutus let go of her arm with one hand, dealing her a stinging blow to her face, hoping it was strong enough to knock her senseless.

Instead, Brutus' blow only dealt Periopis strength. She pulled away from Brutus completely, then, stunningly, grabbed Cornelia and drew her toward the edge of the craft.

"Time for you to die, you plump-thighed whore," Periopis said, almost conversationally.

Cornelia, terrified, tried to tear herself free, but Periopis suddenly seemed possessed of supernatural strength. Her hands tightened about Cornelia's wrists, and smiling calmly, all her previous terror apparently vanished, Periopis dragged Cornelia a little closer to the deck railing.

Above them a gigantic wave rose, then crashed down, washing the two women toward the very edge of their deaths, and Brutus back farther toward the relative safety of the mid-deck.

Brutus was momentarily blinded by the stinging salt water, and knocked breathless by the force of its blow. When he managed to rub the water from his eyes, and blink some focus back into his vision, he saw that Periopis had fallen over the side of the ship, dragging Cornelia, who was desperately pulling back, almost completely over the railing.

Brutus could not find the breath to shout. All he could see was Cornelia's terrified face, and her desperate cries as she tried to resist Periopis' determination to murder her.

Without thinking, Brutus threw himself at his wife, wrapping his arms about her hips, and pulling her back with all his might.

"Let her go!" he finally managed to gasp at Periopis. *"Let her go!"*

"No," whispered the demented woman, falling ever closer to the waves. "She's mine, now."

Cornelia fell forward even farther, and Brutus felt his grip on her hips sliding.

"Brutus!" Cornelia shrieked.

"Brutus!" Periopis whispered . . . and tugged at Cornelia's struggling form so that Cornelia now hung almost entirely from the ship. Only Brutus' grip on her robe kept her from going over completely.

"Brutus!" Cornelia whimpered, and horrifyingly, Brutus realized it was a form of farewell.

From somewhere came a rage and a strength he did not think he possessed. Pulling himself upright, he leaned over the ship's railing, grabbed Cornelia's sodden hair in his right hand and with his left fist dealt a fearsome blow into Periopis' face.

Her nose and cheekbones caved inward, sending a spray of blood into the wind . . . and then her hands opened, and she was gone, and Brutus was dragging Cornelia back on deck.

AS SOON AS PERIOPIS' BODY HIT THE WATER, THE storm wondrously abated. Brutus and Cornelia, kneeling on the deck, looked up, wiping the seawater from their eyes and blinking in the sudden light.

A woman stood on the deck before them, dry and serene despite the wildness of rain and wind.

"Blessed goddess!" Brutus said, and Cornelia felt something turn to ice inside her at what she heard in his voice. "Thank you! Thank you!"

"It is enough," the woman said, then turned her eyes to Cornelia, "if not altogether quite enough."

Then she was gone.

Cornelia rubbed at her eyes—they were still filmy and sore with the salt water, and she could not see very well.

"Who was that?" she whispered. "Which goddess?"

He hesitated. "Artemis," he said finally.

No, a small, ancient voice said deep within Cornelia. *That was Brutus' night lover.*

"No," said Cornelia in a tight, cold voice. "That was the woman of your dreams."

GENVISSA LAY VERY STILL, REGATHERING HER strength. She'd accomplished most of what she'd wanted— the crippling of Brutus' fleet so that it would need to seek out a port in which to shelter for repairs—but she had not managed to murder Cornelia, and that frightened her more than a little.

Brutus had tried very, very hard to save Cornelia. Far harder than Genvissa had thought he would.

Her strength had given out just as Brutus had seemed to find some extra, and the silly Periopis had not managed to pull Cornelia over the side at all.

Still, the fleet was all but crippled, and for now Genvissa must content herself with that.

"Genvissa?"

It was Aerne, and Genvissa fought back a sigh.

"I have been trying to aid Og," she whispered, "but I fear I have failed."

Chapter Eight

NONE OF THE FLEET MANAGED TO COME through the frightful storm unscathed, but only five ships in total perished. The remaining ships limped through the straits of the Pillars of Hercules in various states of damage; many completely de-masted, others trailing broken or snapped masts through the water, still others with half the ship's quota of oars washed away.

Over five hundred men, women, and children had lost their lives. Brutus ordered that the few visible floating corpses be retrieved for a suitable cremation when they could reach dry land; the others, he supposed, would spend their eternity floating at the bottom of the straits. He asked Membricus to speak prayers for them, and to cast burning herbs across the waters to still their souls, and he hoped that they would find peace, and not linger to draw others to their deaths with watery, bitter siren songs.

Night had set in quickly once the storm abated. Neither Brutus nor any of the fore-lookers could see any possible landing—and even had one been close by, Brutus would not have wanted to risk the ships on unseen rocks during a night landing. So he determined they should set anchor as best they could close to the northern shoreline, and spend a cold wet night on the ships—there was not a dry robe nor blanket among the entire fleet, and Brutus dared not allow fires to be set within the hulls of the ships.

The three ships that had sustained the least damage, however, Brutus sent sailing north-northwest, following the coastline. They were to seek a suitable bay where the fleet could anchor, the people disembark and see to their wet clothes, blankets, and their injuries, and a forest where they could cut new masts for those ships that needed them. There was still an unknown time of sailing ahead of them, and Brutus wanted to be able to take advantage of the winds while he could.

He spent many hours consulting with his officers, and clambering from ship to ship to offer support and to assess damage, and did not return to his own ship until the dawn of the next morning. His robe was still damp, his cloak a sodden, useless mess, and by the time he sat down beside Cornelia on the aft deck he was shivering uncontrollably.

She had awakened at his return—or perhaps had not slept at all—and shifted slightly to make room for him at her side. As he sat beside her, sighing gratefully as he rested his back against the side of the ship, she hesitated, then leaned in close against him, offering him her warmth.

He stiffened slightly, then relaxed. He was too tired and heartsore to push her away at the moment, and if he was truthful with himself, he did not truly want to.

"Is my son safe?" Brutus said, laying a hand on her belly.

"Aye. He is the warmest of all of us, I think."

Brutus realized he was not the only one shivering, and again after a momentary hesitation, pulled Cornelia as close to his body as he could. There were people to either side of them—Aethylla on Cornelia's right, and an oarsman called Daedeline on Brutus' left—but even as tightly packed as they were, their damp clothes and the night wind made for a miserable existence.

"What were you doing," Brutus asked very softly, lest he disturb what slumber their neighbors could manage, "to risk yourself and our child like that? Rushing to save Periopis?"

He felt Cornelia shrug. "I did not think. I thought only to save her."

"For the sake of the gods, Cornelia, she almost killed you!" Brutus truly did not know what to think about Cornelia's actions in trying to save Periopis. Had Cornelia's concern been genuine . . . or was it like her pretense at seductiveness? A ploy to win him to her so that he might not kill her or put her aside once his son was born?

"Periopis has . . . had two children, Brutus. When she ran toward the back of the ship, that's all I could think of. I heard them crying out for their mother from where they sat close to the stem . . ." She shivered again and Brutus thought it the tremor of true emotion rather than an act. "I remembered the sounds of the children dying in Mesopotama, their mothers beside them. I couldn't stand it." She shivered again. "I don't know, Brutus. I acted without thinking."

She was shivering more violently than ever now, and Brutus rubbed his hand up and down her upper arm, trying to warm her. "You should have thought of your child first, Cornelia. You risked not only yourself."

"Aye, I risked *your* son as well my body his cradle," she said, bitterness edging her voice.

Brutus let her remark go, remembering only that frightful moment when he'd seen Cornelia stumbling after the incoherent Periopis. In that moment he had not a thought for his child, but only for Cornelia. He opened his mouth to tell her so, but she spoke first.

"Who was that woman, Brutus?"

Confused by the sudden change of subject, Brutus could only say, "Who?"

"The woman." Cornelia's voice was sharp. "She who appeared before us on the deck and whom you called Artemis." She paused. "Although that I cannot believe. *I* think she is the one you have dreamed and moaned for ever since you returned from that island. Tell me, Brutus. Who is she?"

Brutus stiffened. How had she known of his dreams? Had she lain awake each night watching him, marking each movement? Planning her next treachery? Or (and Brutus would not admit even to himself that this was worse) had she lain awake dreaming of that damned piss-dampened Melanthus?

Brutus lifted his hand from Cornelia's arm, and drew away from her. The last thing he wanted after enduring that terrible storm, and witnessing the deaths of so many of his people, was to have Cornelia set on him like a harpy.

"Who is she, Brutus?" Cornelia's voice now had a hard note to it, and Brutus mentally threw up his hands and told her what she apparently wanted to know so badly. In the name of the gods, he had no reason to hide it from her! If Membricus' vision was right, then Cornelia had more things to fear than visionary women, and if Membricus was by some mischance incorrect, then Cornelia would eventually discover the truth anyway. There was no reason he should not tell her now.

"When I went to the island to sacrifice to Artemis," he

said, "the goddess showed me a vision of the land toward which we sail."

"What has this to do with the woman of whom you dream?"

Brutus forced his jaws to relax. "The woman appeared in the vision of the land, walking out of the mist. She appeared as if she were a powerful priestess, greatly favored by the gods. If that *was* she on the deck, and it was her who stopped the storm, then now I know the truth of how much the gods do favor her."

"And she makes you long for her, is that not so? God-favored yourself, you look on others similarly marked with longing. On this woman, with lust. What am I to you but a trophy of war, and a breeding vessel for your sons, Brutus? Answer me, what else will I ever be to you?"

"What in all the gods' names do you want to be, Cornelia?" He'd had enough. All the frustration and emotion of the past day suddenly threatened to bubble to the surface in a vicious, hurtful flood.

She did not reply, save for a slight stiffening of her features as she turned her face partly away from him.

Her chin tilted up, as if she thought him beneath her notice.

The bubble broke, and the viciousness poured forth from Brutus' mouth. "And why berate *me* for some dream-woman when *you* mewl constantly about that pathetic boy whose member was used for little more than spraying fear-driven piss about? Look at you! A foolish self-obsessed young girl, filled with resentment and arrogancies that deal death every time you open your spoiled, prating mouth. You're no use even as a trophy wife, Cornelia. By the gods! Who would want to display *you* about!"

She'd shrunk as far away from him as she could now, her face pale, her dark blue eyes wide and staring and brimming with tears.

All about them people had their faces carefully averted.

Those wide tear-filled eyes were too much for Brutus. Damn her!

"And if you do not bear me a healthy living son from that great belly, my dear, then I may have absolutely *no* use for you at all!"

And with that he rose to his feet, and picked his way over the legs and bodies of the people in the belly of the ship until he reached Membricus' side.

As Brutus sat down, Membricus shot Cornelia a look of sheer triumph.

Chapter Nine

Cornelia Speaks

HATE, HATE, HATE. HOW SICK I AM BOTH OF word and of emotion. All I have done in these past months is hate, and look what I have accomplished with it: the death of my father, of Tavia, of all my people.

Everything gone, sacrificed to hate.

Even my relationship with Brutus. I had bound our marriage with parameters of hatred, and if now I had come to regret it, then I could blame no one but myself.

As Brutus stalked off I sat back, closed my eyes against the contempt of all the Trojans about me, and succumbed to a fit of shivering that I could not control. I could not despise Brutus for what he had said. I suppose it was the sum of all I had said to him, and all I had done to him, over the past months. All the viciousness I had flung at him reflected back to me. Tavia would have tut-tutted and reminded me that all our words and actions will return to haunt us eventually.

The thought of Tavia threatened to make my tears flow again, but I stilled them as best I could. Ah, Hera, no wonder Brutus thought me a sniveling child! All I seemed to have done about him was weep. I had tried so hard in the past weeks to be what Brutus expected in a wife, but ob-

viously what I had said and done in Mesopotama was as
yet too great a sin for him to forgive completely.

Or even slightly, come to that. I shouldn't have asked
Brutus about the woman, but I couldn't help myself. I'd
wanted to know. I *needed* to know who my rival was.

I opened my eyes, daring to search out Brutus.

He sat with Membricus, and both men were laughing and
chatting lightly with two young women.

A nasty little knot of jealousy in my chest tightened so
painfully I could barely breathe. The two women smiled
and laughed at Brutus, and tossed their hair, and pulled
back their shoulders so that their breasts strained against
their sea-dampened robes. Although they talked with Membricus, their attention was all on Brutus.

And why not? I was patently no threat to them, and Brutus was . . . well, Brutus was a highly desirable man. He
had an aura of maturity and strength and command about
him that was almost magnetic in its pull. The sun had finally crested the horizon now, its light catching his body,
and I saw the muscles in his chest and upper arms ripple
as he stretched out in the welcome warmth of the sun.

And what was that gibe I had once thrown at Brutus?
That Melanthus was so much more athletic, so much more
desirable than he?

Gods, what overweening arrogance to have said such a
thing!

Poor dead Melanthus. He hadn't deserved to die in the
manner that he had, but his death in no way made him the
virile, athletic lover with which I'd taunted Brutus. He'd
been but a boy, naive, artless, inexperienced . . . and I'd
been a stupid, conceited girl who had imagined herself in
love with him.

I shifted uncomfortably, the baby heavy and burdensome
within me.

The two women were still laughing, their attention solely
on Brutus now. He reached out, and touched one of them
on the cheek, then ran his hand back through her hair as
he leaned forward and whispered something in her ear that

made her eyes widen and the breath catch in her throat.

I closed my eyes, trying to forget what I had just witnessed. It was too painful. I tried to turn my mind to other things . . . to concentrate on the dream of the stone hall and the daughter who waited within.

But it didn't work. Even the peace and happiness of the stone hall could not distract me from the idea that Brutus was now no doubt kissing the woman, gracing her with what he would never give me.

Perhaps he was pretending she was this woman of whom he dreamed. Perhaps she *was* the woman of whom he dreamed.

Alarmed, my eyes flew open and for an instant I could see neither Brutus nor the two women.

Then, my heart thudding in my chest, I saw that the women were stepping slowly over legs and bodies toward the back of the ship while Brutus had turned to lean over the deck railing and look out to the ocean.

My heartbeat slowly returned to normal as I confronted the startling knowledge that I was not so much concerned at losing my life when this child was born, but at losing Brutus.

Chapter Ten

FOR TWO DAYS THEY DRIFTED AT ANCHOR, spreading clothes to dry in the sun, doing what repairs they could, casting fearful eyes back to where the Pillars of Hercules lay some five thousand paces behind them lest another storm blew out of nowhere.

Brutus spent most of his time leaping between the close-anchored ships, speaking encouragement and warm words, keeping a smile on his face and the worry from his eyes.

He'd hoped that the three ships he'd sent up the coast would have returned by now with news of some shallow, mild bay with natural springs and game and tall straight trees for their succor.

But for two long days there was nothing but the silence of the fore-lookers.

He kept as far away from Cornelia as possible. He had little idea what she did, but vaguely hoped that she kept herself busy as all women did during times of such enforced inactivity. Brutus doubted she would get much sympathy from the other Trojan women. They'd spent the best part of their lives slaving and sacrificing for her and her father's comfort, and for what? To have Cornelia plot to have them slaughtered the moment they reached for their freedom.

If she sat uncomfortable amid their abhorrence, then Brutus had no sympathy for her. It was a far lighter punishment than what she'd wanted for them.

During those times he didn't worry about Cornelia, or fret over the condition of his people and ships, Brutus allowed himself to daydream about the woman who had appeared to him in the island vision.

She was no mealymouthed hag. *She* no petty, semihysterical girl. She was a priestess of great power, undoubtedly a respected and admired leader among her people, and a woman any man would be proud to have at his side.

Damn Cornelia. Damn her!

AT NOON ON THE THIRD DAY ONE OF THE FORE-lookers finally raised the alert; ships approached.

Brutus, back on his own ship, rushed to stand with the fore-looker. "Where?" he said, placing his hand on the man's shoulder.

"There." The fore-looker pointed, and Brutus squinted his eyes against the sun (and thank the gods it *was* sunny; Brutus did not think he wanted to see any more heavy seas or rain for the rest of his life).

The sunlight glinting off the water made it difficult to

focus well, but Brutus gradually made out the sails of three—no *four*!—ships sailing toward them from the north.

"Four?" he said, and shifted restlessly from foot to foot as the ships slowly came closer.

"They must be dragging their anchors behind them," Brutus grumbled as Membricus joined him.

Membricus did not reply, but concentrated on his own squinting inspection of the four ships. "Three are ours," he said.

"Yes, yes," Brutus said, annoyed that Membricus should so waste time stating the obvious.

Membricus' mouth twitched. "And the fourth is 'ours' as well," he said, then grinned at Brutus' face as he turned to stare at him.

"What? What do you mean?" Brutus turned back to study the ships. They were clearer now, their full-bellied sails filled with wind, and Brutus screwed up his eyes, trying to make out the device on the sail of the fourth ship.

Gods, but Membricus must have good vision for a man of his age.

"I can't see," he said.

"Wait," Membricus said, his smile broadening.

And then Brutus suddenly yelled in excitement. "It has a Trojan device! But how, Membricus . . . *how?*"

Membricus shrugged. "Who knows, Brutus? Trojans scattered in all directions when Troy fell. Is it so impossible that a few ships made it this far west?"

Brutus did not answer. He had shoved the fore-looker completely to one side, and had stepped right upon the stem post, wrapping one arm about it and shading his eyes with his other hand, staring ahead.

The ship was a beauty, a warrior vessel, slung low in the water and with oarsmen so magnificently skilled and smooth he could hardly make out the dip and lift of their oars in the water. The hull was daubed in the usual black pitch, but the stem of the ship had been carved into the head of a mystic serpent, and painted in blues, greens, silvers, and golds. The great linen sail had been dyed in similar colors, and in its center strained the familiar device of Troy—the spinning crown above the stylized representation of a labyrinth.

"They are brothers," he said, marveling. "They are brothers!"

He began to wave with great sweeping arcs of his arm, then, when the ships had approached close enough that their oarsmen had begun the dip-and-hold maneuver to slow them down, cast himself into the sea, swimming toward the great warrior ship of Troy.

HE REACHED ITS HULL, AND PLACED ONE HAND on its pitch-black surface as he trod water, shaking the sea from his hair and eyes.

"I have never seen a fairer mermaid," said a laughing voice, and Brutus blinked, and looked up.

A man of brown hair and fair complexion stared down at him, his open, friendly face wreathed in a huge smile. He was robed in a splendid sleeveless scarlet tunic, a scabbarded sword was belted at his hips, and gold and silver armbands ran up his arms to his muscular biceps.

"But, wait!" The man affected surprise, and stood back. "This is no mermaid! To be sure, it is a man! What do you here, man, and under what name do you pass?"

"I am come to greet you," Brutus shouted, "and, if you would be good enough to throw me a length of rope that I might climb to join you, to embrace you in friendship and brotherhood. I am Brutus, son of Silvius, son of Ascanius, son of Aeneas who was hero of Troy, and son of Aphrodite."

"Good enough," said the man, as if the progeny of gods was the least he had expected, and personally tossed Brutus a length of rope, holding it steady as Brutus climbed hand over hand up the hull of the ship.

As Brutus swung his leg over the ship's deck railing, the man caught sight of the gold bands about Brutus' arms and legs, and he audibly gasped.

"They are the kingship bands of Troy!"

"Aye," Brutus said.

"Then you are doubly welcome to my ship, Brutus, blood of heroes and goddesses," said the man, clasping Brutus first by the forearms, and then drawing him into a close embrace. "My name is Corineus, of the line of Locrinus of Troy, and I head the four clans who have descended from him."

"How came you here?" said Brutus, standing back and studying the man closely.

"Why," said Corineus, his expression lightening away from his shock and back to humor, "by ship of course!"

"I meant—"

"I know what you meant," said Corineus, his grin fading. "My great-grandfather escaped from Troy with your great-grandfather, Aeneas. They sailed together for many years, but when Aeneas decided to settle on the River Tiber, my great-grandfather decided he still had some wanderlust left in him."

"Ah, yes, I remember. Five ships of men and women continued on after Aeneas settled. And you are of those ships?"

"Aye! They established themselves on this coast, some distance north, where they built a great city and divided themselves into four clans descended from Locrinus' four sons. Come now, take this towel and dry yourself." Corineus' humor had faded completely now, and he stared past Brutus, now busily drying himself, to the fleet that lay before him. "By the gods, Brutus, something has bitten you well! And so many ships . . . how many, for the gods' sakes?"

"Seven thousand people, give or take a few hundred," said Brutus, "and ninety-five somewhat battered ships . . . we *were* one hundred grand sailing vessels until we became the victims of a supernatural-driven storm."

Supernatural storms and unnatural earth tremors, thought Corineus. What in Zeus' name was happening to their world?

"And you survived." He looked back at Brutus, and Brutus saw the sharpness in his light brown eyes, and knew that the man wore his natural humor as a mask to charm words from men who would otherwise be more careful.

Brutus suddenly felt a respect for Corineus; he would never be a man to be trifled with.

"We survived," he said, "due to the intervention of . . . a wondrous and powerful priestess. We were favored, indeed."

Corineus raised his eyebrows. "A wondrous priestess?"

"It is a long tale," Brutus said. "Should I discuss this now, or wait, perhaps, till you have guided my people to a safe harbor? We have injuries aboard, and much of our dry stores are ruined. My people are exhausted and hungry and damp."

"We attend to your people's needs first," said Corineus. "My home is not far away—a day's sail, if you can bear it, or a day and a half's row in your ships if they are too injured to raise their sails. Perhaps, if we row, we can talk tonight, over a meal?" He stopped rather abruptly, and took a step forward, peering at the ship Brutus had so precipitously leapt from. "Who is that fair lady?"

Brutus followed his eyes. Cornelia was now standing with Membricus by the stem of his ship, shading her eyes as she stared at Corineus' vessel.

"She? She is my wife."

"Your wife? Then leave her not there, anxious and curious," Corineus exclaimed. "I invite her aboard, to keep you from worrying on her behalf, and you both shall tell me your tales as we sail to my home."

Chapter Eleven

Cornelia Speaks

J WAS STUNNED INTO BREATHLESSNESS. I HAD not seen a ship so proud and so beautiful since one of the Egyptian pharaoh's vessels had docked in the bay before Mesopotama several years ago.

Then I had been a girl, and had not truly appreciated its beauty and power.

Now I was a different person entirely, and I could see that this ship was the vessel of a proud and noble man.

I could see Brutus—dripping wet—talking with a richly dressed man on board, and I overcame my revulsion of Membricus enough to stand with him in the stem of our ship so I could see the better.

"It is a Trojan ship," said Membricus, no doubt hoping to impress me. He was far too late. I was already hopelessly impressed.

The beautiful vessel had drawn very close now and I saw that the man who talked with Brutus had turned to look at me.

He smiled, wide and genuine, and it stunned me. I suppose I had vaguely supposed that Brutus' contempt of me would have already infected this man. I had not expected such open delight and even—no, that could not be possible, not in my state—frank and open admiration.

The strange warship and the vessel in which I stood were now no more than two or three arm's lengths distance and men from both ships hastened to position buffers of close-packed straw so that neither ship should stave in the other.

Before all the buffers were in place, the man leapt gracefully between the rapidly narrowing gap, landing not two paces distant from me.

"My lady Cornelia," he said, stepping closer to me. "I am pleased beyond measure that you have survived such a dreadful ordeal. Will you join me on my ship, where you may rest on silken pillows, and eat from the sweetest figs I could gather?"

I could do nothing but stare. There was not a shadow of contempt in his eyes, not a spark of hatred, not even a single measure of speculation. There was merely good-natured acceptance and curiosity and, I *still* couldn't believe it, an unabashed admiration.

I was horribly conscious of my sodden, shapeless, crinkled robe, my great belly, my hair all in oily tendrils, my bare feet. I was wearing no jewelry, no perfumes, not a single accruement of nobility.

And yet here he was, standing there with the friendly smile all about his mouth and eyes, treating me with friendliness and respect.

I grinned. Under the circumstances, with both Membricus at my side and Brutus on the deck of the stranger's ship watching me, it wasn't the most advisable thing to do, but I grinned anyway.

"You know my name," I said, studying him with as much frank admiration as he gave me. He was not a young man, older even than Brutus, and even though he wore a sword at his hip he carried about him the air of the ambassador rather than the warrior. His robes and jewelry were rich and finely made . . . but none of this mattered much to me.

All that mattered was the acceptance I saw in his mild brown eyes.

He reached out his hands, and took one of mine between them. "I am Corineus, of Locrinia," he said, "and you are most welcome to me."

Then he leaned forward and planted a polite, but very warm and very soft kiss on my mouth.

When he leaned back, all I could see was Brutus glowering at me.

I pulled my hand from Corineus' as gently as I could,

and as well bred as Corineus very obviously was, he understood the message immediately.

He turned to Membricus, exchanged greetings, then asked after the injured. "Brutus tells me you have wounded among your fleet, and your people are hungry and sore."

"Aye," said Membricus, and then the two men proceeded to discuss how best to distribute the three physicians Corineus had brought with him, as their herbs and unguents to replace those we'd lost during the storm.

I just stood there happily; in fact, I don't think I'd had a happier moment in my entire life. Everything before Brutus' arrival in Mesopotama had been so superficial, everything after so terrible (and, yes, so much of that my own fault), that this man's simple gesture of unreserved friendliness had the power to totally transform me.

I even smiled at Brutus, still staring down to where Corineus, Membricus, and I stood.

Eventually Corineus and Membricus had arranged matters to their satisfaction, and Corineus turned to me again.

"Will you join your husband aboard my vessel, princess?" he said.

I shifted my eyes doubtfully toward his ship—although the gap between his vessel and this was not overly large, the two vessels ground against each other, and anyone who fell between them would surely be crushed to death.

"Ah!" he said, perceiving my doubts. "Allow me . . ."

And in the next moment I found myself swung into his arms as he turned to the gap.

I gasped, all my joy lost in concern, and my hands tightened about Corineus' neck.

"Do not be afraid," he said softly. "I will not drop you."

With that, he began to climb into his slightly higher vessel, one arm about me, one hand on the rope, his feet braced against the outer planking of his ship: he was much stronger than I had thought him and my fear subsided somewhat.

He even made me laugh, for he thought to amuse me by singing under his breath a silly seafaring ditty about the dangers of ravenous marine worms to beautiful princesses.

We were both laughing by the time he'd hauled me to the deck railing of the ship, and there Brutus was to take me from Corineus. I breathed a sigh of relief as I felt my two feet on firm decking again, and straightened out my robe as best I might, still smiling at Corineus.

I was about to thank him when Brutus spoke.

"You are a strong man, Corineus, to carry such a load!" he said, and—oh, the insult!—patted me on my belly.

I flushed with humiliation, then caught a glint of empathy in Corineus' eyes, and managed to regain my composure.

"Do you have a maidservant, Cornelia," Corineus asked, "that I can have brought aboard to help you with your ablutions and toilet?"

"My wife has a *companion*, Aethylla," Brutus said. "Corineus, if it would not be too much to ask . . ."

"Then this Aethylla shall join your wife," said Corineus. "Please," he continued, "I have a well-appointed cabin on the aft deck. If I may escort your wife?"

I SIGHED, DEEPLY CONTENT. THIS WAS A TRULY well-furnished cabin. Tapestries and linens hung from the walls, hiding from view the wooden planking. Luxurious furs covered the floor, allowing the eye only a peek of the mosaics beneath.

And it had a bath. A *real* bath in one corner that I sank my swollen body into gratefully—only the gods knew how Corineus had caused the water to be heated, but I cared not to think on such trivialities. I luxuriated in the comfort, closed my eyes, and leaned my head back against the rim of the bath.

I heard a step.

"Could you toss in some more of the herbs, please, Aethylla," I murmured.

"These?" Brutus' voice said, and my eyes flew open. He was holding a jar, his eyebrows raised.

I nodded slowly, my joy evaporated.

"Do not worry," he said, and scattered some of the herbs

over the surface of the water, "I have no thought to join you. I need to show Corineus' physicians where they are the most needed."

Then, in part lie to his words, he sank down to sit on the side of the bath. He reached out a hand, and ran it over my belly, then raised his eyes and looked at me.

"What was that I saw?" he said.

"What?" I said, confused.

"Did you think to make me jealous?"

I sat up in the bath as far as I was able. "I do not know what you mean." His hand was still heavy on my belly, rubbing back and forth, back and forth.

"Your little display with Corineus. It shamed me."

My mouth fell open. "He was courteous to me! And I was no more than courteous in turn! What do you accuse me of?"

He did not answer, but continued to stare at me with hard eyes, his hand now very heavy on my belly.

My temper snapped. "Did I put my hand to his hair, and caress it, and whisper sweet nothings in his ear? No! *I* am not one for such things!"

"He kissed you."

"I did not ask for it!"

"Did you beg him?"

"It was a greeting only!"

"Beware, Cornelia. Do not think to use Corineus as a weapon as you have tried to use Melanthus."

And with that he gave my belly a hard, painful slap, rose, and was gone.

I burst into tears, consumed with the unfairness of his attack.

I was too young then, too inexperienced, to recognize Brutus' temper for what it was.

MUCH LATER THAT EVENING WE ATE ON THE SPA-cious aft deck of Corineus' warship. Brutus had returned, and with him he had brought his immediate command:

Membricus, who I caught watching me carefully from the corners of his sly eyes; Assaracus, Idaeus, and Hicetaon, who had kept to other ships during the voyage, and who I'd managed to virtually forget existed; Deimas and, of course, Aethylla, my "companion," twittering and blushing with pleasure at the company she found herself in.

Of course, Corineus sat with us as well, and to my delight I found myself seated on the cushion next to him. The food he caused to have spread before us was mouth-watering: fine maza and turon made of the best flour, honey, and cheese; sweet fresh figs; almonds and plump olives; sweet roasted game, both partridge and venison; salads sprinkled with mint and oregano; honeyed cakes and fresh apples and pears.

Corineus served me himself, taking the best and sweetest from every platter and lifting it to my mouth on a golden prong. I smiled agreeably, but no more than was respectful or due, and tried not to allow our eyes to meet.

Brutus watched with an unreadable expression, and from time to time I had to bury my hands in the skirt of my robe to conceal their shaking. I was both angry and fearful. All I would have liked was to enjoy the company of Corineus, but Brutus had effectively managed to ruin that simple joy with his cruel barbs.

Fortunately, Corineus made no attempt to make me the entire center of his universe during the meal. Once our group had eaten sufficiently, Corineus put down the prong with which he had fed both himself and me, and leaned toward Brutus.

"Tell me what you do with such a great fleet, and so many Trojans, Brutus," Corineus said. "By the gods, I had thought that my city held the only sizable population of Trojans left alive."

"I am here as the instrument of the gods," Brutus said, and at my side I heard Corineus breathe deeply in awe.

Brutus continued to talk, much of it new even to me (why had I never asked him this myself? I'd been dragged across oceans . . . and I had never talked to him about it).

Some of the others, Membricus, Idaeus, and Hicetaon, put in their words as well, as did Deimas and Assaracus when it came to the means by which Brutus had so horribly tricked my father and destroyed Mesopotama.

This was uncomfortable for me, and I kept very still, my head bowed, my concentration all on the empty plate before me. I did not want to live this through again.

But I was forced to. Every word that was said cut through to my heart.

Then Brutus began to talk of how he had forced Antigonus to trick the guards into opening the gates.

He described his murder of Melanthus and how he had used that murder to force Antigonus to his will. He described Melanthus' death in detail—although he never mentioned his name—and I knew that detail was meant for me, although as a warning or as a punishment I was not sure.

"The instant I had torn out the boy's throat, Antigonus capitulated," Brutus said, leaning toward Corineus and stabbing in the air with an eating prong to underscore his words, "and I had my entry unopposed into Mesopotama."

I think Corineus was about to say something but I, stupidly, opened my mouth first.

"The 'boy's' name was Melanthus," I said, "and he was my intended husband. I loved him dearly."

"But I slit his throat and took her instead," Brutus said and, I could hardly believe it, laughed.

Corineus glanced at Brutus, then took one of my hands from my lap and held it. "I am sorry for you," he said, and indeed, I could hear the sympathy in his voice, and it almost undid me. "We men rush to war, and we never think of the sorrow and heartache we cause in the homes of the dead."

"But Cornelia had her revenge," Brutus said in a hard, hateful voice.

My heart almost stopped. Oh! Why had I given him this chance? He would now tell Corineus all of my shame, how my arrogance had murdered my father and all my people, and Corineus would now regard me with the same contempt that all the other Trojans about me did . . . and I suppose I could not blame him for that.

I tried to pull my hand from his, but Corineus held it tight.

Brutus began to speak, relating in vivid detail what I had planned, what I had done, what I had, in the end, accomplished. Genocide.

I closed my eyes, waiting for Corineus to drop my hand.

Brutus finished. There was silence.

Then . . .

"Can you blame her, Brutus?" Corineus said softly. "Would you have done any different in her place?"

And he gave my hand the tiniest of squeezes.

A vast silence, this time. I could not believe what Corineus had said. That he had offered me a little understanding. My heart was thudding so heavily I felt sure that it was audible to everyone around me.

I could not imagine what Brutus would make of it.

"You do not know the half of it," Brutus said, his voice tight.

"I am sure that I do not," Corineus said, "and I apologize if I have offended, Brutus. I am only saying that we can all do foolish things in our youth and you are . . . what? How old, Cornelia?"

"Fifteen," I whispered.

"Fifteen," Corineus said, giving my hand another brief squeeze. "We all did foolish things when we were that age. I know I did, and—"

"Gods, Corineus, she murdered—"

"And I am sure," Corineus continued through Brutus' interruption, "that you also did things you may have regretted at fifteen. Yes?"

Yet more silence, this time one of deep-drawn breaths and averted eyes and suddenly, suddenly I remembered what my father had said of Brutus that first day he'd mentioned him in the megaron. *He tore his mother apart in childbirth and then, when he was a youth of fifteen, slew his father with a "misplaced" arrow.*

And Corineus, as most of the civilized world, it seemed, had heard of it also.

I removed my hand from Corineus'—he made no attempt to hang onto it this time—and raised my head to look at Brutus.

"You cannot compare an accident with what I did, Corineus," I said. "You cannot use my youth to excuse my foolishness."

Brutus was staring at me with such flinty eyes that I knew he was furious.

"I am weary," I said, despair making every one of my bones ache. Oh, what a day this had been. Anger to joy to despair. What else would it offer? "And I think my presence is troubling. Will you excuse me, Corineus? I will retire, I think."

Corineus rose and helped me to my feet and, as he gently kissed my cheek, whispered, "I will talk with him, Cornelia. *I* have made him angry, not you."

Not daring to look at Brutus, nor any of the other Trojans present, I nodded, turned, and made my way to the cabin.

Chapter Twelve

"T HAT NEEDED TO BE SPOKEN, BRUTUS," Corineus said, sitting down as Cornelia vanished into the gloom, "and it were easier said by a man who is a stranger to you than someone close. I meant no disrespect by it, not to you nor to any of yours. Cornelia has been a fool, but all of us here, *all* of us, have been fools at one time or another."

"Cornelia is a murderess!" Membricus snapped.

"She had just seen her lover murdered, and she had just been forced into a marriage with the man she could think of only as his murderer. She repaid violence with violence, and I am not excusing that, I am simply *understanding* it."

Membricus made as if to speak again, but Brutus laid a hand on his arm, and Membricus subsided.

"It was not welcome, what you said," Brutus said, looking steadily at Corineus, "but I will respect your reason for saying it."

Corineus nodded. "If my words have caused ill will and ill feeling, then do remember that they were my words, and not those of Cornelia. And remember also that what *she* said following were the words of a wise woman, not those of a silly girl."

"She has a fine champion in you," Brutus said.

"She would be better," Corineus said very softly, "in having a fine champion in *you.*"

"*I* think," Hicetaon put in, "that we have spoken enough of guilt and youth and misdemeanors for this night. Troia Nova awaits us. Can we not discuss that?"

He finished on such a plaintive note that everyone laughed, the sound breaking the tension even if the merriment was a little forced.

"Well said," Brutus remarked. "Troia Nova does await us, and all our mistakes and follies lie well behind us."

"You actually intend to rebuild Troy in this land of Llangarlia?" Corineus said.

"Aye," said Brutus. "I do."

Corineus smiled, warm and friendly. "Then hate me or not for what I said earlier, Brutus, but I am much afraid that I am your man!"

"You want to join with me?"

"Oh, aye, I do!"

Brutus was not sure how to regard this. Earlier he would have greeted it with enthusiasm. Now . . .

"But surely," said Brutus, "you are established and happy and free already, and from what you have said of your city I cannot think that any would want to leave it—"

"Ah, Brutus," Corineus said, "I have not told you all. Some weeks ago a great earth tremor struck Locrinia during the night. Some buildings collapsed, and some people died, but the true horror was not realized until the next morning. Every building within the city, *every single one*, has been cracked so badly that none will stand for much longer. Within weeks, a month or so at the most, Locrinia will crumble into the bay, and it will be as if the city never existed."

"You cannot rebuild?" Membricus said.

"Rebuild?" said Corineus. "No. The city is too badly damaged. Besides, who could want to rebuild when Brutus offers me Troy?"

He turned his attention back to Brutus. "Pray, do not allow your doubts for me make you refuse me," he said. "I can be of great aid to you. Not only can I contribute ships, wealth, supplies, and yet more Trojans to make your new Troy great, I have knowledge. Brutus, I *know* this land of which you speak."

"Tell me," Brutus said, now leaning forward himself.

"Blangan is a Llangarlian! A native! She may well be able to tell you all you need to know."

"And Blangan is . . . ?" Brutus said.

"Blangan is my wife," Corineus said, and his voice was composed of such pride and love and tenderness, that all of Brutus' doubts dropped away.

"Blangan is Llangarlian," Corineus continued. "She left when she was but fourteen, married to a merchant who died within six months, leaving her stranded in Locrinia." Corineus gave an embarrassed half shrug. "What could I do but wed her myself? Someone had to save her from destitution."

"And why am I thinking," said Brutus with a grin, his humor now fully restored, "that this poor widowed woman was probably the most desirable creature you had ever set eyes on?"

Corineus shrugged, and smiled slightly. "That *may* have had something to do with it. But to the matter at hand. While you rest in Locrinia, repairing your ships and healing your people, Blangan can teach you the ways of the Llangarlians." He laughed. "The gods drove you to me, Brutus! If the storm had not stopped you, and ripped masts from their beds in their keels, then you would have sailed past Locrinia in the dead of the night, not knowing what aid awaited you within."

Brutus looked about at his officers and friends. "Well, what say you? Should we welcome this Corineus into our midst, and take what aid and fellow Trojans he offers us?"

"Oh, we accept him," Hicetaon said, glad that Brutus had not allowed Corineus' earlier remarks to turn him against the man. "We welcome him gladly."

"YOU HAVE MADE QUITE THE CONQUEST," BRUTUS said to Cornelia when he joined her on the bed within the cabin much later that night.

He waited for an answer, but there was silence. She lay with her back to him, only the rapidity of her breathing betraying her wakefulness.

Brutus propped himself onto an elbow and, with his free hand, toyed with a strand of her long brown hair. It had become much softer with pregnancy, as slippery and fluid as honey, and with a seductive, natural scent.

"He has a wife," he said softly. "A woman called Blangan. He loves her dearly."

"And she him, I would think," Cornelia said. She rolled over. "Brutus, I had no idea that Corineus would say what he—"

He slipped his hand over her mouth, stopping her words. "Why do we hate each other so much, my little wife? Why?"

She gently pushed his hand away from her mouth. "I do not—"

"Don't dare to say to me that you do not hate me, Cornelia," he said harshly, "for I would not believe that!"

Her mouth trembled, but she said nothing.

His eyes moved from her face to her body, and his hand he lifted and rested gently on her breast.

"If only," he said. "If only . . ."

Then: "Go to sleep, Cornelia. We have all had a tiring two days."

He rolled over and, his back to Cornelia, pulled the blankets over his shoulders.

She drew in a deep breath, keeping it steady with only the most strenuous of efforts, then closed her eyes as well.

It was a long time before she slept.

BECAUSE MANY OF THE FLEET'S SHIPS WERE SO badly damaged, and the oarsmen needed longer breaks than they usually would after their ordeal during the storm, it took an extra half day longer than expected to reach Locrinia.

When they eventually approached at dusk of the fourth day after the storm, Brutus realized why Corineus had thought they'd sail straight past if it had been night—as it probably would have been if they'd sailed untouched through the Pillars of Hercules. The city was visible from the ocean, but only barely. It was tucked into the southern shore of a bay whose only opening was a narrow, rocky strait. If a fleet had sailed north along the coast late at night when the citizens of Locrinia were asleep and all lights doused, then those aboard the fleet would never have known what they passed.

And, Brutus admitted to himself, he may not even have cared very much *had* he known. He had a destination, he was eager to reach it, and he would have ignored all distractions to achieve his goal. Only injury to his people and his ships had brought him Corineus and Blangan, both of whom might well be worth their weight in gold in aid and knowledge.

LOCRINIA WAS A MEDIUM-SIZED CITY OF LOW buildings constructed in pale shades of sand and limestone and tiled in bright red and turquoise. It stretched from the southern shore of the bay halfway up the slopes of a mas-

sive mountain. At the edge of the city, neat fields ran up
the mountain to the border of a close, dark forest that covered the greater part of the peak.

The city *should* have looked prosperous and comfortable,
but here and there Brutus could see the mounds of rubble
left by the earth tremor, and in many other buildings, a
horrible list as if they were shortly to join their crumbled
fellows.

No wonder Corineus was so joyful to have Brutus appear. This city was surely doomed.

Corineus told Brutus that because of the state of the city,
most of the Trojans would have to make do as best they
could on their anchored ships. With luck, however, he
could find accommodation for enough of them that the
crowding aboard the ships would be lessened considerably.
Corineus apologized, clearly embarrassed at his inability to
house all the Trojans in accommodation ashore, but Brutus
waved away his apologies; Corineus was already doing
more than enough.

His embarrassment only mildly allayed, Corineus directed his warship in close to the stone wharf. As soon as
it had docked he jumped down to the wharf, sending mes-
sages into the city to set people to finding accommodation
as best they could for several hundred people at least, and
directions to set sailors in small rowboats into the bay to
direct the Trojan ships into suitable anchorage sites.

Then, as the gangplank was set into position, Corineus
boarded once again and escorted Cornelia and Brutus down
to the wharf.

Cornelia looked pale, and her eyes were ringed with blue
shadows as if she had not slept well, but she was composed
and polite, thanking Corineus for his assistance in aiding
her to the wharf. As soon as she had spoken, she moved
away slightly, and Corineus allowed it, knowing the reason.

For a while Corineus stood with Brutus and Membricus
watching the other Trojans disembark, then, catching sight
of Cornelia's wan face, said, "Can you leave Membricus
and Hicetaon to direct the unloading of as many people as

we can accommodate? I think it would be best if I took you, Cornelia, and Aethylla and her child and husband to my house, that the women may rest. It is but a short walk distant, and safe enough that you may all sleep well at night."

"If your Blangan won't fuss at the extra visitors," Brutus said.

"She will adore you," said Corineus, smiling, "and drive you to distraction with her chatter." He bowed slightly in Cornelia's direction. "And she will be delighted to have you to gossip with, Cornelia. I swear that before tomorrow morning has dawned, you will know all the lapses and blunders of Locrinia's most upstanding citizens. Even, I fear, some of mine!"

He was rewarded with a smile from Cornelia, probably more at his attempt to cheer her than any eager anticipation of Blangan's gossip, but it was enough for Corineus. "Come," he said gently, and led the small group forward.

One of Locrinia's wardens, a plump, cheerful man, bustled toward them, greeting Brutus and Cornelia effusively, and clapping his hands with joy at the sight of the massive fleet filling the bay. Corineus and Brutus passed a few words with him, then they were off, following Corineus up through the gently rising streets of the city.

"I have my house on this rise here," Corineus said, leading them into a wide and well-paved street. One or two of the houses had fallen, and in the others Brutus and his companions could clearly see the wide cracks spreading up the walls.

"Here we are!" Corineus said, indicating a large house standing just before them. Made of a very pale pink stone, it had been built long and low with numerous large open windows and graceful arches to allow the bay air to flow through its rooms and chambers.

It too had been cracked, and one archway had collapsed almost completely, but the walls were well propped, and the house looked solid enough, especially compared to some of its neighbors.

As they approached, a woman appeared in one of the archways. She stood there, as still as a rock pool, one hand on a pillar, her white linen robe blowing gracefully about her tall, slim form. Her hair was dark, her skin extremely pale, her features well drawn and strong.

Brutus took a step forward, a catch in his breath, then relaxed in disappointment.

This was not the woman of the vision, but by the gods, she was very much like her.

She was tall, and shapely, and with the same dark hair and blue eyes, but her face had many lines worn by care, and Brutus knew that while she was younger than Corineus, she actually looked his elder. Life had tired her, somehow.

Most telling, however, was that this Blangan had none of the god-power that had been emblazoned about the other woman. She carried about her only the power of a woman who loved and was loved, not the power of the gods that the visionary woman wielded.

She walked to meet them, holding out her hands and her cheek to Corineus to be kissed. Then she greeted Cornelia, kissing her on her cheek, then Brutus, then Aethylla and her husband standing a step behind.

"Blangan," said Corineus, "if I said to you that you might be going home to Llangarlia again, what would you say?"

Blangan's face went completely expressionless, but in that instant before the veil came down, Brutus swore he saw a peculiar mix of terror and resignation in her eyes.

THEY HAD WASHED, SETTLED IN THEIR CHAMBERS, and eaten (Membricus, Hicetaon, and Deimas having joined them), and now it was late at night, but Brutus could not go to bed before he'd had a chance to speak with Blangan.

He sat with her, Corineus, Deimas, Hicetaon, and Membricus on a sheltered portico overlooking the bay. Everyone else had gone to bed for the night—indeed, the city itself seemed lost in a languorous slumber as it spread out below them—and they finally had some quiet to talk. The warm air was very still, and the scent of a flowered climbing vine across the portico hung heavy and sweet about them.

"So," said Blangan to Brutus, a nervous, fleeting smile across her face, "you wish to build your Troia Nova in Llangarlia?"

"I do so at the goddess' wish, Blangan."

"Not the goddess of Llangarlia's wish," said Blangan. She had dropped her gaze to her lap, and she fiddled with the tassel of her belt as it lay in her lap.

"Tell me of Llangarlia," said Brutus.

"What can I say, where can I start?" Blangan took a deep breath, and lifted her eyes to stare over the bay.

Brutus did not like it that she wouldn't look at him. "Will they welcome us?"

Now she did look at him, steady and sure. "I cannot know," she said. "It has been over twenty-five years since I was last in Llangarlia. But they most certainly will not welcome *me*."

Before Brutus could ask the obvious question, Corineus, wary-eyed, broke in.

"Brutus," he said, "may I speak a little of Locrinia's relationship with Llangarlia?" At Brutus' nod he went on. "Llangarlia is not a closed country; many people trade with the Llangarlians. I and my people do, the states to the north of us do, the people of Crete even traded precious spices and gold for their tin and copper. But the Llangarlians do not encourage closeness with any outsiders."

"Yet you married an outsider, a merchant," Brutus said to Blangan.

"I was forced into the doing by my mother," Blangan said. "I admit myself glad when my merchant husband died and Corineus"—she reached out to him and took his hand—"took me into his home and his bed."

"Who is their king?" said Brutus. "What strength of swords does he command?"

"Llangarlia has no king."

"How can this be? Every land has a chief, a king, a—"

She held up her hand. "Peace. There are many tribes, or Houses, and each House has its Mother."

A *Mother*? Brutus frowned.

"But overall we defer to two people, the living representations of our gods Og and Mag. There is the Gormagog, who represents Og." Again something in Blangan's manner made Brutus study her well, but whatever discomfort the name of Gormagog caused her, she dampened it down well. "And there is the priestess of Mag, and we call her the MagaLlan."

"This priestess of Mag, the MagaLlan. Is she a powerful woman, tall and beauteous? Is there a deep russet streak through her dark hair? Does she wield the power of the gods themselves? Is she a mother, bearer of several children?" *Does she look like you?* he wanted to ask, but didn't.

"MagaLlan is always a mother," Blangan said. "It is part of her duty. But as to the rest of your questions . . . Brutus, when I left Llangarlia so many years previous, the MagaLlan was *my* mother. The woman you describe now sounds like my younger sister, Genvissa." Blangan gave a slight shiver, as if she were cold. "In Llangarlian society it is always the younger daughter who inherits the power of the Mother, or of the highest Mother, the MagaLlan. Not the son, as in Trojan society, nor even the eldest daughter."

Genvissa, thought Brutus. *I have a name for her! And this Blangan is her sister?*

"The youngest inherits?" he asked. "How can this be so?"

"Why should the eldest inherit, whether son or daughter," said Blangan, "when it is the youngest child who is the product of the mother's maturity and life-wisdom?"

Brutus thought that sounded slightly naive—all knew the firstborn was the strongest-born—but he left it alone. "And the Gormagog? Who is he? What manner of man is he?"

Blangan smiled very bitterly. "When I left Llangarlia Gormagog was an aging man," she said, "and weaker than he'd ever been when he was in his prime. I cannot know who he is now."

Brutus leaned back in his chair, and drank deeply of his wine. He was silent for many minutes, thinking of the woman of his vision, and of Blangan who seemed less than enthusiastic at the idea of going back to her homeland.

"Do you still speak the language of your birth?" he finally asked Blangan.

She bowed her head, and replied in something unintelligible.

He nodded wryly. "Will you teach it to me while my ships and people recover from the wild storm that so injured us?"

"I would be pleased. It is a simple language to master once you grasp its basic concepts. Brutus . . ." She paused, obviously uncertain whether or not to continue. "Brutus, many people have thought to conquer Llangarlia. They have marched into the mists surrounding the Veiled Hills, and they have never emerged again. Llangarlia is ancient, and unknowable . . . even to your gods. Be careful."

"You don't want go home, do you, Blangan?"

In answer, Blangan rose. "I should look in on your wife, Brutus, and make sure she is comfortable. I am sure that you and your companions have much to talk about with Corineus, despite the lateness of the hour. Enjoy my hospitality, Brutus. I give it with great pleasure."

Chapter Thirteen

AETHYLLA WAS STANDING BEHIND CORNElia, who sat on a stool, combing out the younger woman's hair.

Blangan paused in the doorway, as yet unseen, and her lips twitched at the expression on Cornelia's face.

"My dear," said Blangan to Aethylla, walking across the

room and taking the comb from her hand. "You look exhausted, and I am sure both your husband and child have need of you. Let me do that."

Aethylla handed the comb over with some relief; the silence between her and Cornelia had grown so uncomfortable that Aethylla's shoulders and neck were tense and tight. Her husband was *exactly* what she needed right now.

Blangan waited until Aethylla had left the room, then she took the woman's place behind Cornelia and began gently to run the comb through the younger woman's beautiful brown hair.

"Your husband will be hours yet," she said. "I have left him talking and drinking with his companions."

Cornelia gave a small shrug of her shoulders, as if she cared not one way or the other.

"Corineus has told me a little of you," Blangan said. As she spoke, she continued combing Cornelia's hair with long, slow strokes, more caresses than acts of grooming. "Of how Brutus forced you into marriage, and forced that child into your belly. Of how your home was destroyed, and your father killed under it."

Cornelia did not respond verbally, but Blangan could see how she'd stiffened.

"I, too," Blangan continued, very softly, "had a child forced into me when I was but a young girl, perhaps a year or two younger than you are now. I, too, was forced to leave my home. The difference between you and I, my love, was all that misery culminated in a husband who loves me dearly. I have no idea what future awaits you, Cornelia, but I do hope that joy and love will be a part of it."

There was a long silence, during which Blangan continued her long, slow combing of Cornelia's hair, then, finally, Cornelia whispered, "I do not deserve that, Blangan."

"Deserve what, my love?"

"Love and joy."

"And how is it you do not deserve such love and joy?"

"Because if my home lies in ruins, and my father under it, then that is nothing but my fault."

"Cornelia? How so?"

Hesitatingly, Cornelia told Blangan of how she'd plotted with her father to kill the Trojans as they left Mesopotama, and how it had all failed, and her city, her people, and her father had been horribly killed as a result.

"And yet if I'd left well enough alone, they would all have lived. Blangan, it was my fault!"

Blangan put down the comb and went to kneel before Cornelia, who was now crying, her face in her hands.

"Wait, Cornelia," Blangan said, pulling the girl's hands away from her face. "What of this goddess who came to you and proposed the plan. Is she not to blame?"

"Perhaps she was no goddess," Cornelia said. "Perhaps she was just my own hopes and hates assuming dream form."

Blangan frowned. "Which goddess was she? What did she look like?"

Cornelia spoke, describing the woman who had appeared before her, and as she spoke, Blangan felt a chill sweep through her body.

That was no goddess, that was Genvissa!

"Cornelia," she said urgently, "I cannot now tell you *why* I know this, but know it I do. That was no goddess appearing to you, but the greatest of Darkwitches! You were pushed into doing her own will, Cornelia. *It was not your fault!* Blame lies elsewhere."

"You try to comfort me, Blangan, and for that I thank you." Cornelia's tear-streaked face twisted ruefully. "Apart from you and your husband, not many people have tried to comfort me recently. But I must take the blame for what happened to my people. If I was a tool, then I was a willing tool."

Blangan lifted a hand and stroked the girl's cheek. Brutus, she knew, thought of Cornelia as a wayward child, untrustworthy and self-obsessed, but that was not the woman who sat weeping before her now. Most people would either have blamed others, or if they initially took the blame themselves, would then have willingly grasped an excuse to blame someone else.

"I think," said Blangan slowly, "that you will grow to be a very great woman indeed, one day."

"I cannot think my husband could ever agree with you."

"Ah, Brutus!" Blangan grinned and waved a hand dismissively. "He is but a man." She rose and, taking Cornelia's hand, led her to the bed. "This will be more comfortable for my aging bones, my love. Here, sit with me."

She cuddled Cornelia close as they sat, pulling the girl's head onto her shoulder and stroking her hair.

"In the land toward which you journey," she said softly, "Brutus will be but a man in a world where women are revered more than men."

"Women? *Revered?*" Cornelia sat up straight, her face amazed. "How can this be?"

Blangan laughed and, apologizing for her intrusion, rested her hand on Cornelia's swollen belly. "For this reason, my love. Women hold the mystical ability to grow children within their bodies. We call it the Mag within our womb, for Mag is our mother goddess, and most revered, and it is her influence within our wombs that grants to us the ability to bear children. Men are respected, and loved and adored, as the case may be, and it is their feet which tread the forests, but within the home, family, and village society, it is the women's voices which are listened to first.

"Women in Llangarlia," she added, grinning, "do not even take husbands!"

"What? Then how do they breed their children?"

"Women take whomever they want into their beds, but never make formal unions with such lovers. Children born to women always stay within their mother's house, whether daughter or son. If a woman decides to take a man as her lover and to breed from him, she lays with him either in the blessed groves of the forests or the meadows of the sun, or she allows him into her bed for a few hours at night . . . but he must be gone back to his own mother's house by morning, lest he irritate the woman's own mother with his presence."

Cornelia had her hands to her mouth as Blangan said all this, her eyes wide. "You mean, that were I Llangarlian, I could take men as it pleased *me*, and not them?"

"Aye."

Cornelia was visibly shocked. "And a woman desires daughters more than sons?"

"Always."

Cornelia fell into silence, staring incredulously at Blangan who eventually laughed, and pulled Cornelia into an embrace.

"Who knows," Blangan said softly. "Llangarlia may be the haven you seek."

"Membricus says I am carrying a son, but I hope for a daughter. Can *you* tell?"

Blangan hesitated. If Cornelia had been Llangarlian born then, yes, it would have been easy, for she would have carried the Mag within her womb, and that would have spoken to any Llangarlian woman.

But she was foreign to everything connected with Llangarlia, and there would be no possible way she could . . .

"Please," Cornelia said, looking at Blangan with yearning eyes and placing Blangan's hands on her belly. "Try. I dream of a girl . . . I am *sure* I am carrying a daughter. Membricus must be wrong."

Blangan sighed, then closed her eyes and made the effort, even though she knew it would be—

She jerked back, her eyes almost starting from her head. "By the gods, Cornelia!"

"*What?*"

Blangan swallowed. *Mag was strong within Cornelia's womb.* Stronger than Blangan had ever felt it.

"I am but surprised," Blangan said, composing herself, "for as it happens I could feel your child easily." She paused. "You carry a son, Cornelia. I am sorry."

Cornelia's face fell. "Brutus will be pleased, at least."

"But you will love him, too. You will, surely. Remember

that I, too, bore a child that was forced into me. I thought to hate him when he was born, but when I held him to my breast, it was as if all my doubts and hate had never been. I adored him."

"I cannot think so," Cornelia said, grimacing as she placed a hand on her belly. "I cannot think I could ever adore *this*."

"You will be a good mother, Cornelia," Blangan said . . . and she said it in her native tongue of Llangarlian.

"Maybe one day, perhaps," Cornelia replied, and she also spoke in Llangarlian as if she, too, had been born to it. "But not with this child, I think."

She stopped, and frowned. "What did I just say? Oh, Blangan, I must be overtired if I babble nonsense! I am sorry."

Blangan had been stunned by Cornelia's easy response in a tongue she should not have known, but hid her surprise well. "I will leave you to your rest in a moment, my love, but tell me, who was your mother? A stranger to Mesopotama's shores?"

"No. She was a Dorian Greek, as was my father."

"And her mother before her?"

"Also Greek. Blangan? Why?"

"Mag's mysteries are deeper than I thought," Blangan said. "Here, let me help you off with this robe."

As Cornelia, naked, lay back to the bed, Blangan once more laid her hand to her belly. "Sleep well," she said, and pulled the linens over Cornelia's body.

ONCE BLANGAN HAD LEFT CORNELIA AND CLOSED the door behind her, she leaned against the corridor wall, shaking, her hands to her face.

"Mag?" she whispered. "Mag?"

There was no answer.

Chapter Fourteen

Cornelia Speaks

I SLEPT BETTER THAT NIGHT THAN I HAVE FOR . . . than forever, so it seemed to me. Surely, partly it was because we were once again on dry land, and partly because I slept in a comfortable bed, and partly even because the child seemed to sleep well himself, but mostly it was because of Blangan.

I had been cross when she'd entered the room and sent Aethylla away. I was tired, and did not feel like passing pleasantries with Blangan, however agreeable she had appeared in the few short hours we'd been in Locrinia.

But Blangan surprised me. She talked to me as woman to woman, not as woman to tedious spoiled child, nor even as noble-spirited Trojan slave to hated Dorian slave-mistress.

She treated me as an equal. Just as Corineus had.

And then, atop that, I discovered that she too had been through much of what I had—the rape and forced bearing of a child, and the loss of a home. Blangan *knew* what I felt. *Knew* my loneliness, and in a few short moments I came to regard her a friend.

And this Llangarlia! I swear I must have smiled in my dreams—gods alone knew what Brutus made of it. A land where women did the choosing, and men made do as best they could with that choice.

I DREAMED, TWICE, AND BOTH DREAMS WERE most wonderful.

My first dream was of a jewel. A great emerald jewel in a gray-blue sea, with mountains and meadows, rippling streams and raging whitewater rivers, and where a magnificent white stag with blood red antlers ran wild through the forests.

This land was Llangarlia, and it was to be my future.

Then, unsurprisingly, I dreamed again of the great stone hall that stood within Llangarlia. I walked through its vast spaces, happier than I could ever imagine.

I heard the tinkle of a child's laughter, a girl, and I turned about, trying to see her.

She was there, but almost indiscernible, always just at the corner of my vision, laughing and playing. I cried out to her, calling her to me, for I knew this girl was my daughter, and the child I had always wanted.

But all she did was laugh, and slide farther out of my vision.

Then her laughter died, and I knew she had gone, but I was not bereft, for someone *else* was within the vastness of the stone hall.

A man who loved me dearly, perhaps my daughter's father, although I was not sure.

I called out a name, although it was indistinct and I could not tell *whose* name it was, and he stepped out from under the shadows of one of the arches and walked toward me.

I laughed, and ran to him and, as his arms encircled me, lifted my mouth to his and drowned in his kiss.

Chapter Fifteen

BRUTUS KEPT HIS FLEET IN THE BAY OF LO-crinia some five weeks. It was far longer than he had planned, but it took time to find the right trees to cut down for masts, and then to trim the new masts into their keel beds.

There were also several score Trojans who had serious injuries caused in the straits of the Pillars of Hercules: eight of these people died within a few days, but the others needed time to heal before they set off again on the rigors of a sea voyage.

These delays normally would have made Brutus impatient, but he found himself intrigued by what Blangan taught him of Llangarlia. The land and its people appeared wild and uncivilized, but imbued with the deep wisdom of a power so archaic that Brutus began to suspect it predated even the gods of the Greeks and Trojans.

The Llangarlian gods Og and Mag both repelled and intrigued Brutus. They were ancient—as old as the land itself; Blangan said the entire land was dotted with stone monuments built to honor Og and Mag by people who had lived so long ago that the Llangarlians had no idea what purpose the monuments originally served. When Brutus asked about their power, Blangan merely shrugged, and said that she could not believe that they would welcome Brutus' plan to build a new Troy on Llangarlia's wild shores.

Brutus was perturbed less by what she said than by the fear in Blangan's eyes every time she talked about her childhood gods. He wondered what it was that worried her, but she refused to respond to his pressing, and always turned the conversation to other things.

As Blangan had said, the Llangarlian language was relatively easy to learn once Brutus had mastered its basic structure. Brutus had spent the greater part of his life traveling about the lands of the Mediterranean, acquiring new languages as he went. To acquire one more took little effort. Within two weeks of his arrival in Locrinia Brutus had mastered the language's basic constructions, after that it was the far simpler task of acquiring new words for everyday meanings.

As Brutus learned, so too did most of his officers and those men of authority within the Trojan people. Deimas, Assaracus, Idaeus, Hicetaon, and all their immediate subordinates learned the basics of the language; Corineus already knew the tongue well enough from those bedtime conversations passed with his wife throughout their years of marriage.

Surprisingly—*stunningly*, given that she'd shown no hint of any talent save childishness and treachery to this point—Cornelia proved the most adept at learning Llangarlian. Every day she acquired more and more words, and, so Blangan said, spoke with scarcely an accent.

This troubled Brutus somewhat. Not that she was finally actually doing something useful, but the "how" of her learning. Who was she learning it from? True, she and Blangan had become fast friends, and true, they spent time together most days.

But not enough to learn so fast or so extensively.

Was she learning from Corineus? Brutus could not keep track of everyone within the household, not when there was so much to do elsewhere . . . were Cornelia and Corineus spending time together that Brutus was not aware of?

That worried him, desperately. He couldn't actually believe that Corineus was truly tempted by Cornelia—he was far too deeply in love with Blangan—but it was just that Brutus had seen the way Cornelia smiled at Corineus.

He *hated* the way Cornelia laughed when Corineus jested with her, and the way she looked at him without reserve and without fear.

Brutus bitterly regretted his vicious words to Cornelia on the morning after the storm. He shouldn't have been so cruel, but Cornelia's questioning about Genvissa had touched a raw nerve. He hadn't wanted Cornelia to be aware of her and was shocked and angered to discover that Cornelia did in fact suspect Genvissa's existence.

And yet why should that trouble him? Membricus took every opportunity to remind Brutus of his vision that showed Cornelia dying in childbirth. Cornelia had not long to live, she would not trouble him at all in Llangarlia or in whatever relationship Brutus chose to commence with Genvissa. She was carrying a son for him, an heir, and that should be all that mattered.

The trouble was that whenever Brutus looked at Cornelia, he saw not so much his son, but Cornelia herself.

He also regretted his taunting of Cornelia at dinner that first night on Corineus' ship. He didn't know what had come over him to make him behave so. Gods, how was it that one young girl could drive him to so many ill-considered barbs?

Predictably, their relationship had soured into something resembling a snowfield since their arrival at Locrinia. There was a great and cold distance between them, punctuated with the occasional sharp word. They shared a bed, but every night Cornelia humped as far away from him as she could, and sometimes, when he woke during the night, he heard her laugh softly in her sleep, and knew she dreamed of either Melanthus or Corineus.

Worse than Cornelia's sleep-laughter was the vision that had gripped Brutus himself one night. He'd gone into a deep sleep when he'd woken, startled.

He was no longer in the chamber he shared with Cornelia.

Instead he stood in a stone hall so vast that he could barely comprehend the skill required to build it. The roof soared so far above his head he could hardly see it, while to either side long aisles of perfectly rounded stone columns guarded shadowy, esoteric places.

This was a place of great mystery and power.

There was a movement in the shadows behind one of the ranks of columns, and Cornelia—utterly naked—walked out into the open space of the hall.

Brutus drew in a sharp, audible breath, but she did not acknowledge his presence, and Brutus was aware that even though they stood close, she had no idea he was present.

Cornelia looked different, and it took Brutus a long moment to work out why. She was older, perhaps by ten or fifteen years, far more mature, far, far lovelier.

Brutus realized he was holding his breath and let it out

slowly, studying her. Her body was leaner and stronger than it was now, her hips and breasts more rounded, her flanks and legs smoother and more graceful. Her face had thinned, revealing a fine bone structure, and there were lines of care and laughter about her eyes and mouth that accentuated her loveliness rather than detracted from it.

"Cornelia," Brutus said, and stretched out his hand.

She paid him no attention, wandering back and forth, first this way, then that, her eyes anxious, and Brutus understood that she was waiting for someone.

Who?

Then, suddenly, she stopped and stared straight at him.

"I thought you would not come!" she said, and Brutus almost groaned at the love in her eyes and voice.

"Cornelia!" Brutus said again, taking a step forward, his heart gladder than he could have thought possible.

And then he staggered as a man brushed past him and walked toward Cornelia.

This was the man that Cornelia had smiled at and spoken to, and he was as unaware of Brutus' presence as Cornelia was.

A deep, vile anger consumed Brutus. Who was this that she met?

The man was as naked as Cornelia, and Brutus saw that he was fully roused. Who was he? Corineus? Yes . . . *no.* Brutus had an unobstructed view of the man's face, yet could not make it out. First he was sure that he wore Corineus' fair features, then they darkened, and became those of a man unknown.

Cornelia said the man's name, her voice rich with love, and it, too, was undiscernible to Brutus' ears.

"Do you know the ways of Llangarlian love?" said the man.

"Of course," said Cornelia, and she walked directly into the man's arms, her arms slipping softly about his body, and offered her mouth to his.

They kissed, passionately, the kiss of a man and a woman well used to each other, and Brutus found his hands were clenched at his side. Then Cornelia and her lover slid to the floor, and with a sigh of complete contentment, the man mounted her.

"No!" Brutus shouted, and would have stepped forward and grabbed at the man now moving over Cornelia with long, powerful strokes save that he found himself unable to move.

He could witness, but he could not interfere.

The lovers' tempo and passion intensified, and Cornelia moaned and twisted, encouraging her lover in every way she could, and they kissed again, their bodies now so completely entwined, so completely merged, that they seemed but one.

Then the man's form changed, blurring slightly. He was grunting now, almost animalistic, and for the first time Brutus saw that Cornelia had her hands on the man's shoulders as if to push him off.

She cried out, and it was the sound of pain, not passion.

Brutus still could not move, and he watched in horror as the man's form blurred again, and became something horrible and violent.

A man, yes, with a thick, muscled body, but impossibly with the head of a bull.

The creature tipped back its head and roared, and both Cornelia and Brutus screamed at the same moment.

The creature's movements became violent, murderous, and Brutus saw that he was using his body as a weapon.

There was blood now, smearing across Cornelia's belly and flanks, and her head was tipped back, her face screwed up in agony, and her fists beat a useless tattoo across the creature's back and shoulders.

"Cornelia! Cornelia!" Brutus screamed, and for once both Cornelia and the creature heard him, and both turned their faces to him, and the creature roared once more, and Brutus knew who it was.

Asterion. Cornelia had invited evil incarnate to ride her.

He woke, violently, jerking into a sitting position in their bed, his chest heaving, his eyes wide and staring.

Beside him Cornelia had sat up as well, and was asking him what was the matter.

"Nothing," he whispered. "Nothing. Go back to sleep."

Eventually she did, but Brutus sat there the night through, awake. All he could see, all he could hear, was the sound of Cornelia's voice as she welcomed her lover.

ONE EVENING, CORNELIA ACCOSTED HIM ON THE verandah of Corineus' house. Brutus was exhausted—he'd spent the greater part of the day helping a team of men wrest a new mast into position on one of the ships, and the very last thing he felt like was a confrontation with his wife.

"Brutus?"

"Hmm?" he said, hoping the disinterest in his voice and his closed eyes as he leaned back in his chair would send her away.

"Blangan says I am within a few weeks of birth. Brutus . . . I do not want to give birth on ship. Can we not delay our departure until I've had our child?"

It was the first time he'd ever heard her refer to the child within her as "our child." It was enough to make him open his eyes and study her.

She certainly looked as if she would drop the child soon. Her belly was huge, her ankles swollen, and her face drawn with its weight.

"Blangan says," Cornelia continued, "that the baby has not moved in the womb as it should." She laid a hand on her belly, just under her ribs. "His head is here, tucked beneath my heart, and it should be—"

"I do not want to hear a midwifely discourse," he said. "It is not my concern." Despite her current condition, all Brutus could see was her face as she welcomed her dark lover, and her body as it writhed ecstatically under his.

"Is there no pity in you that you cannot grant me this small concession?" she said softly. "Blangan says it will be a difficult birth."

And so now she called on his "pity." Had she considered

his "pity" when she arranged her assignation with her lover? Brutus' small reservoir of patience ran entirely empty.

"Any other man," he said, his voice dangerously quiet, "would have had you executed after your treachery in Mesopotama. Any other man would have thrown you overboard with your sulks and petulances. Any other man"—he straightened in his chair—"would have cast you aside for your constant whining about that *pathetic* boy you think somehow better than I, or your even more pathetic chasings after Corineus. Who next, Cornelia? Who next will you lust after?"

"I do not dream of Melanthus! Nor 'chase' after Corineus!"

He leaned forward and seized her wrist. "Then of whom do you dream at night, my lovely? Not of me, for you stiffen in revulsion if I so much as breathe near you."

She blushed, and he had all the answer he needed.

"I dream of Llangarlia," she said softly.

He stared at her. "Of a stone hall in Llangarlia?"

She did not speak, but there was a faint, guilty flush in her cheeks, and Brutus had all the answer that he needed.

"Bah!" Disgusted, he let go her wrist. "Listen to me, I can no more delay the departure of this fleet than I could delay the rising of the sun. Locrinia is ready to slide into the bay, and the autumn storms already gather on the northern horizon. We *must* reach our destination before they whip the seas into something infinitely more dangerous than what we endured within the Pillars of Hercules. Frankly, my dear, I don't care where you give birth, whether it is in a rowboat or in the greatest silken bed in the known world, so long as you deliver that son to me alive and healthy."

Her face had now drained of all its color, and Brutus again felt a moment of guilt, and then a surge of renewed anger at the fact that she so constantly called that guilt into being.

"I don't care where you give birth," he said again. "I

care for that as little as I care for you. Just give me my son, for I care *nothing* for you!"

As Cornelia made her way back into the house, her hand held to her face in what Brutus thought was a truly pathetic attempt to foster his sympathy, he thought again of Membricus' vision: Cornelia would die in childbirth.

"Gods," Brutus muttered, "I hope Membricus saw aright!"

He would prefer Cornelia dead than alive and betraying him.

For a long time Brutus sat there in the dark, thinking both of the visions of death that surrounded Cornelia.

And Asterion. *Asterion!* Brutus remembered that first night he had taken Cornelia, how she had asked him, "Are you Asterion?"

Had she been expecting him, even then?

Hades' daughter. Brutus shuddered.

Chapter Sixteen

THEY SAILED ON A BRIGHT, LATE SUMMER morning three days after Brutus had spoken with Cornelia.

The citizens of Locrinia, grateful (if sad) to be leaving their condemned city, had stowed both their belongings and themselves aboard whatever vessels they could find; those several hundred who could not be fitted aboard the Locrinian fishing, merchant, and warships Brutus managed to find space for on his own vessels. It would be a crowd, but from what Corineus and other Locrinian captains told him, with luck it would only be a short voyage of under ten days to reach the island of Albion where lay Llangarlia.

It would need to be under that space of time, Brutus

thought the morning of their final departure, as the autumn storms were very close upon them.

But this day was fine. The waters of the bay, thronged with black-hulled vessels of every shape and size, glittered under the warm sun. Every ship had jewel-colored pennants fluttering from their masts and stem posts, and along every side of every hull oars lifted, waiting for the cries of the orderers. On their decks, and packed into their hulls, brightly clothed men, women, and children shouted and waved to friends and relatives in neighboring ships.

Autumn storms notwithstanding, Brutus knew they were leaving only just in time. In the past several weeks more and more of Locrinia had been collapsing: this past week alone had witnessed the final destruction of over fifty homes. They had not even needed the rains to arrive to come down. The cracks had spread farther and farther every day so that by the time the Locrinians had boarded, there remained only about half of the city habitable.

And even that, Brutus thought, would crumble into the sea within weeks of their departure.

He'd managed to put into the back of his mind the resemblance of the cracks here to those that had swept through Mesopotama. Coincidence only. Every town or city occasionally suffered the depravations of earth surges; Locrinia had just been unlucky in the strength of the one that had struck her.

"When we have gone the city will vanish," Corineus said softly at Brutus' side, and Brutus turned to stare at him.

Corineus was staring at the city, tears in his eyes. "It has been my beloved home," he said. "No matter toward what glory we might sail, Brutus, this has been my home. When it is gone the forests and grasses will creep in, and within two or three generations no one will ever know what pride and happiness existed here."

"All things must pass," Brutus said, hating the lameness of his reply.

"Aye," said Corineus, turning away. "All things must pass."

Brutus put his back to the all-but-ruined city himself, and looked at the fleet.

For the first time, Brutus truly felt the weight of responsibility settle upon his shoulders. He now commanded a fleet containing some twelve thousand souls, all of whom had placed their trust in Brutus to lead them to a better life. Not only would he need to command them through uncertain waters to their destination, but he would then need to negotiate with the Llangarlians for land on which to build Troia Nova.

None of it would be easy . . .

Cornelia's voice, murmuring to Aethylla about the ache in her back, broke across his thoughts, and Brutus sighed ruefully.

Not easy at all.

He sailed this time on Corineus' warship rather than his own. It was more commodious than his warship, fully decked above the oar benches, and had enough cabin accommodation for Corineus, Blangan, Brutus, Cornelia, and Aethylla and her husband and child, and Membricus, Hicetaon, and Deimas, who would share the smallest of the cabins.

Brutus drew in a deep breath, and nodded to Corineus, who raised his arm in a prearranged signal.

Instantly trumpets sounded from a score of ships, and a great shout rose from those who were crowded into the ships' hulls.

The orderers raised their voices and as one sang the beat, and at the sound of the beat all the oars of the one hundred and eighteen vessels in the fleet dipped into the sea.

They were on their way.

THE FLEET SAILED NORTH FOR FIVE DAYS, FOLLOWing the line of the coast to their starboard.

The weather favored them, and every dawn and dusk Brutus gave thanks to Artemis for her favor. The ships made good headway, people stayed cheerful—indeed, often the day was filled with the sound of singing as voices passed ballads and choruses between ships—and it seemed as if Poseidon himself had sent the great companies of dolphins that danced and dipped in the surging waters under the fleet's stern posts.

The peace and fair sailing lasted only a few short days. At dawn on the sixth day out from Locrinia Cornelia went into labor.

HE'D BEEN IN A DEEP SLEEP, LULLED BY THE CAressing motion of the ship into dreams of a white city rising on the banks of a noble river, when Cornelia had suddenly cried out.

Brutus leapt to his feet, clutching at his sword, before he realized he was not under attack at all, and that the cry had come from Cornelia, now sitting amid their blankets clutching at her belly.

Aethylla, who had been sleeping a few paces away, her own baby nestled safely in a cot by her side, groaned and rolled over, rubbing the sleep from her eyes.

"Aethylla?" Brutus said, hoping the woman might have some magical words to utter that might restrict Cornelia to a more dignified moaning.

Aethylla made a face and slowly rose, tugging a gown about her as she did so. She squatted down by Cornelia, and put her hands on Cornelia's belly.

She grunted. "It is the baby."

"It hurts!" Cornelia whispered, then howled as another contraction gripped her.

"It is nothing more than all women bear!" Aethylla snapped. "If you think this hurts, then wait until this evening!"

Brutus decided he'd heard enough, and snatching at the tunic and cloak he'd taken to wearing in these cooler northern climes, beat a hasty retreat to the deck.

Aethylla could cope with Cornelia.

* * *

AETHYLLA DID NOT HAVE TO BEAR THE BURDEN alone. Blangan joined her within moments of Brutus vacating the cabin, and two other women, experienced midwives, joined them shortly thereafter.

Altogether Cornelia had the care of four women who had knowledge of childbirth both personally and through aiding scores of other women give birth.

But their aid was of little use to Cornelia. She was a young girl, still growing herself, and as Blangan had realized, the baby had not moved about in the womb as it should so that it could be born headfirst. Instead, it was a breech presentation, and no matter how much Cornelia labored, the child would not shift. Caught in the terror of the unknown, gripped by horrific pain, Cornelia descended into panic. Even Blangan, who had by now long earned Cornelia's trust and regard, could do nothing to calm her. One of the midwives could have turned the baby within the womb, but Cornelia was too far lost in her panic and terror to allow any of them to touch her.

Brutus, standing as far away from the cabin as possibly he could, nevertheless heard every shriek, every groan. It tore on his nerves, driving him to distraction.

Membricus and Deimas stood with him, offering as much sympathy and support as they could; Corineus paced up and down the deck of the ship, looking alternatively between the cabin and Brutus, his expression worried.

Worried for what? Brutus thought. That he might lose Cornelia? She should be nothing but just a woman to him, there was no reason for him to evidence such concern.

"All women scream during labor," Deimas offered hopefully as Brutus continued to watch Corineus pace up and down. "It helps them to expel the baby. Cornelia will be well, have no doubt."

Brutus caught Membricus' eye, and did not answer.

"Did you not say this would be a son?" Deimas said, trying frantically to find something cheerful to say. Cornelia's wails were echoing down the entire ship, setting children to crying, and the adults to much muttering and rolling of eyes.

Soon queries were being shouted from other ships, concerned at the racket emanating from Corineus' vessel, and Brutus grew heartily tired of having to shout back that it was just his wife, giving birth.

In the midafternoon, when not only Brutus' nerves, but those of everyone else on board, had been frayed to the breaking point, Aethylla emerged from the cabin.

She caught sight of Brutus at the stem post of the ship, and marched resolutely toward him.

"Is the child born?" asked Brutus.

"I wish to the gods it were!" Aethylla said. "But it lays wrong in the womb . . . and Cornelia will not let any of us try to turn it. By the gods! I have never seen such a performance! Is this how all Dorian princesses give birth?"

Corineus had walked over. "Blangan told me that the baby sits the wrong way."

"Yes, yes," said Aethylla, "but there is no reason why it should not be born save that its mother does not cooperate."

"She is frightened," said Corineus, and Brutus saw that the man's jaw was clenched, and his eyes narrowed as he looked at Aethylla.

"Frightened!" Aethylla said, and rolled her eyes. "She has insulted us, as well you—"

"We have *all* heard," said Membricus, much enjoying himself.

"—and every god whose name she can remember. She pinches and slaps." Aethylla omitted to mention that she was the only recipient of these pinches and slaps after she'd herself dealt Cornelia a particularly stinging smack, accompanied with some harsh words about how childish Cornelia was for making so much fuss. "If this child ever manages to be born I swear to Artemis it will be born running in its effort to get away from its mother!"

She took a deep breath, during which time none of the men said anything.

"Now," Aethylla finally continued, "by the gods, now

she demands that she will not give birth unless it be on land. She says," Aethylla spat every word, "that the motion of the ship disturbs her and makes her ill and takes her mind from the task at hand. She says she will rather die than give birth aboard this ship."

Brutus swore, badly enough to make even Aethylla look at him with startled eyes. "*Is* she dying?" he asked.

Aethylla hesitated, then: "No. She is a strong, healthy girl. She should still be able to birth this baby even though it lies uncomfortably."

Corineus cursed under his breath, then turned to say something to Brutus, but Membricus spoke quickly, and in a smooth, unctuous voice, placing his hand on Brutus' arm.

"Perhaps it will be a kindness to find some peasantish hovel on the coast where she can push this child out, my friend. It might be for the best, after all. For all of us."

Brutus knew what Membricus was saying: *Let the vision fulfill its course. Let her give birth in this unknown peasant hut, and let that unknown hand slice her in two as soon as your son slides from her body. It would be for the best.*

Cornelia wailed again, then her voice broke, and descended into a heart-wrenching sobbing.

"For the gods' sakes, Brutus!" Corineus snapped. "She is your wife! Do something, anything, but remember that *she is your wife!*"

Brutus shot him an unreadable look. *My* wife, Corineus, indeed, he thought, then nodded.

"As she wants, then. As she wants." He strode down the deck, paused briefly outside its entrance, then stepped through the door into Cornelia's birthing chamber.

SHE WAS STANDING AGAINST ITS FAR WALL, HER naked body drenched in sweat, her hands clasped about her belly, her loose hair matted and damp, her eyes wild and staring, her mouth twisting into the ugliest line Brutus had ever seen.

Blangan stood with her, trying her best to offer some

comfort, but Cornelia was patently having none of it.

"What are you doing?" Brutus said, closing the distance between them in three giant strides. He pushed Blangan roughly to one side and seized Cornelia's shoulders. "Why resist those who only wish to aid you?"

Blangan tried to force Brutus' hands away from Cornelia, shouting something at him, but Brutus was in no mood for interference. He snarled at Blangan, who reeled back in shock, then shook Cornelia again. "Is there no depths to which you will not sink to get your own way?" he said.

She tried to twist out of his hands, then cried out as one of his hands dealt her a hard blow to her cheek.

Then she wailed, clutching at her belly, and started to slide down the wall to the floor.

"Brutus!" Blangan called desperately. Cornelia was behaving stupidly, yes, and she should allow one of the midwives to turn the baby, but she was also just a young girl, terrified by the pregnancy and labor forced on her by an unloving husband, and was using the birth as a means, just once, of controlling instead of being controlled. Foolish and pointless, but Blangan could understand the *why* of Cornelia's behavior.

God knows she'd wailed and wept enough when she'd been in labor with her own forced and hated pregnancy.

"Brutus," she said again, then froze as Brutus jerked his furious face toward her.

Turning back to Cornelia, Brutus sank both hands into the hair at the crown of her head and hauled her upright, ignoring the cries from Blangan and the other women present.

"Your behavior is shameful," he said, ignoring Cornelia's writhing as her contraction continued. "It dishonors my name!"

"What do *you* know of what I go through?" Cornelia managed to gasp. "Your child is tearing me apart, and all you can do is speak such revulsions to me?"

Brutus fought down the desperate desire to hit her again:

he was afraid that if he gave in to it, then he would not be able to stop.

"You are not a child," he snapped. "Stop acting like one!"

"You goatish prick," she whispered, and Brutus blanched.

"I have only to call for my sword," he said, so low that only Cornelia could hear him, "and I can relieve you of that child within two breaths. *Would you like that?*"

She whimpered, and shook her head, then, as yet another contraction struck, shrieked and just as quickly swallowed the shriek. But she could not stop the writhing of her body, and Brutus, his face disgusted, let her drop to the floor where she twisted at his feet.

"You want to give birth on land?" he said as Blangan, watching Brutus carefully, went to Cornelia's aid. "Is that your price for peace among this fleet? *Is it?*"

She managed to nod her head: once, weakly.

"And will you accept responsibility for that? For whatever consequences your demand spawns?"

Brutus turned about, glaring at the other three women and to Aethylla who had just reentered the cabin. "Will you bear witness? Will you?"

They nodded.

Brutus looked again at Cornelia, now curled in terror at his feet. "Well?"

"I will accept responsibility," she managed.

"Good," Brutus said. Whatever happened now was on her head, not his.

He turned on his heel and walked out.

Chapter Seventeen

WHERE ARE WE?" BRUTUS SAID TO CORI-
neus. "What do you know of this land?" He
waved at the coast off their starboard bow.

"I know it is a bad place to stop, Brutus. It is a fair land,
but filled with an ugly people. It is called Poiteran, and its
king is called Goffar. Brutus, are you certain that you want
to—"

"It is what *she* wants," Brutus said.

"When you say bad," Membricus said, "how bad do you
mean?" He glanced at Brutus. *Is it worth the risk to rid
ourselves of Cornelia?*

Corineus bit his lip, worried. "Goffar is a man jealous of
intruders, and greedy for the spoils of war. He will attack
first, and ask questions later . . . and even then he will not
be interested in the answer."

"*If* he were to attack, how many men might he command?" Brutus asked.

Now Corineus shrugged. "If we were to land all our warriors, he would not attack."

"But to do that we'd need a landing spot for all our
ships," Hicetaon put in.

"And you'll not find it along this coast," Corineus said.
"By dusk we should reach the mouth of a wide river. We
will be able to shelter the majority of the fleet in the mouth,
and there is landing for, oh, some four or five ships."

Brutus again exchanged a glance with Membricus, then
nodded. "The river mouth then. Pray to Artemis that Cornelia will give us some peace until we arrive, that there will
be some shelter when we land, and that Goffar will be shut
away in his long halls for the night."

"There will be both shelter and swords," Membricus said. "Prepare yourselves."

He turned, and stared down the ship toward the cabin in which Cornelia moaned.

A cold smile lit his face.

BY EVENING, AS BRUTUS' FLEET APPROACHED THE mouth of a wide and gently flowing river, a strong north-westerly wind had risen, tossing the sea into whitecapped waves that thudded cold and heavy against the hulls of the ships. The captains had ordered the sails stowed and the oarsmen to their benches to dip and hold their oars against the prevailing wind so the ships would slowly come about into the sheltered mouth of the river.

Brutus stood with Membricus, Corineus, and Hicetaon by the stem post of their ship. All were wet with spray and shivering in the wind.

"Where is it?" Brutus said, looking out to sea rather than into the dim outline of the coast around the river mouth.

"What?" Hicetaon and Corineus said together.

"Llangarlia," said Brutus. "It is close, is it not?"

Corineus nodded, hugging his shoulder with his arms in an effort to keep warm. He looked to the northwest. "There, a day's sail if the weather is good, an eternity at the bottom of the cold gray witch sea if she turns against you. If it were noon, and the weather clear and still, you might even be able to see those white cliffs."

Brutus looked at Membricus, tightening excitement in his belly. "Tomorrow then, perhaps."

"Aye," said Membricus, his teeth gleaming in the gloom, and the wind whipping his gray curls about his face, "but tonight we must collect your son."

"Cornelia." Brutus glanced at the cabin. It was heavy with silence. "Corineus, can we maneuver this ship close to shore?"

"Aye, I think so. See? There are shallow waters protected

by that headland. We can row in to a point not twenty paces from the shore, and then wade our way in."

"Do it, and signal four other ships to accompany us, and the rest to weigh anchor in the shelter of the bay. Hicetaon, arm our warriors. We will be ashore soon."

CORNELIA STARTED, AND TOOK A STEP BACK AS Brutus entered the cabin. She looked far worse than she had earlier, her hair now completely matted to her head and neck, her rib cage rising and falling in rapid, shallow breaths, her skin sallow and slick with sweat, her great belly protruding before her, red welts running across it as if Cornelia had clawed at herself in her extremity.

Her eyes were terrified and hopeless, staring at him from sunken flesh bruised with deep blue shadows.

Her limbs trembled, and she let out a moan as Brutus walked slowly over to her.

All her defiance had fled hours ago.

He stood before her, staring, then looked at Aethylla. "Well?"

"It will not be long," Aethylla said, her voice sounding almost as exhausted as Cornelia looked. "Whatever happens, it will not be long now."

Brutus took a deep breath, and Aethylla looked at him sharply, wondering why it had trembled in his throat.

"Cover her with a cloak," he said, "and yourselves as well, and bring her outside."

"I cannot walk!" Cornelia said, her voice thin and desperate.

"You have legs, and you have life," he said. "Use them both while you still can."

"I don't want Aethylla with me," Cornelia gasped. "Please."

Brutus paused on his way to the door. "You want me to risk *Blangan's* life in your foolish misadventure? No! Aethylla and one of the other midwives will accompany you. I will not risk Blangan to your stupidity."

Then he walked out.

Aethylla narrowed her eyes at Brutus' back, resentful that Brutus was willing to risk her where he was not willing to risk Blangan, then looked consideringly at Cornelia. After this dreadful day spent trying to make Cornelia cooperate, Aethylla felt that if Brutus decided to take the child by force, she would hand him the knife herself.

"No . . ." Cornelia moaned, but Aethylla had finally had enough, and she threw a cloak over Cornelia's shoulders with rough hands and together with one of the other women, propelled her out of the cabin.

If Cornelia wanted to give birth on dry land, then that is what Cornelia would do.

"You will be well, Cornelia!" Blangan called after them, tears in her eyes. Poor Cornelia. Brutalized at both the conception of the child and at its birth by a husband who had no idea of the jewel he had acquired. "Mag be with you, Cornelia," she whispered.

THERE WERE SOME THIRTY OR THIRTY-FIVE ARMED men cloaked and wrapped against the cold, standing at the side of the ship. Brutus stepped up as Aethylla and the other woman pushed Cornelia forward; the girl kept trying to fall to her knees, but Aethylla and her companion were strong, and their hands gripped tight under Cornelia's armpits, keeping her more or less upright.

It was full night now, and Brutus' body loomed large and threatening in the dark.

"Give her to me," he said, taking Cornelia in his rough hands. Then, nodding at the other men, he stepped over the side of the ship and dropped into the shallow water.

Even though Aethylla knew she, too, shortly would be up to her thighs in the freezing water herself, she could not help but smile at the sound of Cornelia's shocked cry.

Hicetaon stepped forward to help her, and Aethylla climbed down a rope ladder set against the hull, dropping the final few feet into the water.

Gods, but it was cold!

Aethylla gritted her teeth, hugged the dry portions of her cloak closer about her, and looked ahead.

Brutus, half carrying, half dragging Cornelia, was little more than a black hulk against the slightly less black night sky.

There were splashes about her as the other midwife and the warriors jumped into the water. Thirty paces distant, additional warriors dropped from several other ships, and Aethylla clenched her jaw, and set about wading toward the dim shoreline.

It was a long, hard, and viciously cold wade, and by the time Aethylla reached the shore, she hated Cornelia like she had never hated anyone before.

THEY HUDDLED TOGETHER TWENTY PACES IN from the waterline under the shelter of a group of wind-blasted and barely leaved trees.

Brutus spoke quickly, ordering the majority of the warriors, perhaps numbering one hundred and fifty, to fan out about them.

He still held tight to Cornelia, who was moaning incessantly now, her hands clenching, then releasing where they gripped Brutus' cloak. She sagged against Brutus, her almost dead weight threatening to drag him down as well.

"We must hurry," Aethylla said to Brutus, "if you do not want your child born on this beach."

Brutus began to order several of the remaining warriors to search for shelter, but Membricus, shivering so badly that Aethylla thought he looked as if he were in labor himself, interrupted him.

"It is that way," he said, pointing to a small rise some forty or fifty paces away. "On the sheltered side of the hill."

His eyes were cold, and so gray they shone almost silver in the faint light.

Brutus nodded, and walked forward, dragging the now-sobbing Cornelia at his side.

Membricus stepped forward, and grabbed Cornelia's free arm, taking some of her weight from Brutus.

The two men exchanged glances over her twisting, weeping body, and Membricus smiled, bright and eager.

For the first time, Aethylla felt a twist of unease. Beside her, Corineus murmured in concern.

The soil was sandy, soft, and hard on calves. Aethylla found herself panting within paces of starting up the slope of the hill, the sodden portions of her cloak and robe twisting about her legs so that, on several occasions, she fell over.

Every time she fell Corineus stepped forward, aiding her to rise.

At the top of the hill Aethylla looked down, and almost sobbed with relief. There *was* a small hut not thirty paces away; little more than a lean-to, it had wicker walls, branches and the tattered remnants of matting as a roof, and a bleak gap to serve as a door.

Humble as it was, the hut would keep most of the wind out, and it looked reasonably dry, and for that Aethylla thought she would offer sacrifice to the gods as soon as she was able.

Brutus and Membricus were already dragging Cornelia toward the hut, and Aethylla, calling out to the other woman who'd been lagging behind, hurried after them.

THERE WAS LITTLE IN THE HUT SAVE A COLD hearth in the center of the packed dirt floor, and a raised bed of turf and rushes against the far wall. Brutus and Membricus hoisted Cornelia onto the bed, where she instantly rolled her back to them, and drew her knees up to her belly in agony.

"There is a lamp," said Membricus, "I will light it."

Brutus motioned Aethylla and the other woman inside— they hastened immediately to where Cornelia lay curled about her belly on the bed—then walked to the door.

He hesitated just before he stepped outside. "You will

stay, and bear witness?" he said to Membricus.

Membricus' teeth gleamed in the first sputtering light of the lamp. "Oh, aye."

"There will be fighting. You know that."

Membricus nodded, then glanced at Cornelia. "It will not be long before they attack. Keep safe, Brutus."

Brutus nodded, looked one more time at Cornelia, then vanished into the night, his sword in his hand.

AETHYLLA HAD NOT LIKED THE SOUND OF THAT conversation at all. She looked at the other woman, who returned her look with wide-eyed fear, then turned back to Cornelia. By rights Cornelia should be squatting to deliver her child, but Aethylla held no hopes of being able to get Cornelia off this bed.

Well, if she wanted to give birth lying down, then she would just have to endure the additional suffering in the doing.

Without any gentleness in their hands, Aethylla and her companion grabbed Cornelia's knees, rolled her wailing onto her back, and forced her legs up and apart.

Aethylla gave a great sigh of relief. "Look, the baby's head crowns. It must have turned in the cold water."

And if I'd known cold water would help so much, Aethylla thought, *I would have dropped Cornelia overboard long before this.*

A shout from outside, then a bloodcurdling war cry, and a clash of sword against sword.

Aethylla and the midwife glanced fearfully at each other, but Membricus merely grinned. "It begins," he said, and Aethylla wondered at what she had been caught up in, and whether she would survive it at all.

The woman beside Aethylla whimpered, glancing apprehensively toward the open door. Aethylla herself was growing more and more concerned, especially remembering Brutus' reluctance to allow the nobler Blangan to come ashore, but she also knew that if they succumbed to their fear now, then it might well be the death of them. She gave her companion a sharp pinch to bring her mind back to the task at hand, then reached between Cornelia's legs to place a hand on her belly, giving the girl a reassuring pat.

"It will not be long," she said, "but now, when the pain comes, you will need to bear down with all your might."

Just then another contraction did begin, and Cornelia writhed on the bed, sobbing in her agony.

Membricus smiled.

The sound of fighting drew much closer, and Membricus tensed, looking to the door. He could see bodies silhouetted against the faint starlight outside, struggling, the blades of swords and knives flashing, sometimes clean, sometimes dulled with blood.

He swallowed, his mouth suddenly dry—not with fear, but with a sudden strange flowering of sexual excitement.

Soon . . . Soon . . .

Cornelia was screaming now, her body almost lifting off the bed with the strength of her agony, and Aethylla was shouting at her to *bear down! bear down!*

The other woman was no longer at the bedside, but had scuttled on her hands and knees to the door as if seeking escape.

The fighting drew much, much closer, and Membricus, still watching—eyes wide, mouth open, breath panting in the extremity of his own excitement—could plainly now make out the features of those who fought.

The attackers, Goffar's men, fought stark naked, their hairy bodies daubed with blue clay, their faces strangely tattooed in blue-black ink, and their bouncing genitals stained with some black substance.

As Membricus watched, only barely aware of what was happening on the bed before him, one of the Poiterans suddenly screamed, his sword dropping from nerveless fingers as the blade of a Trojan sword emerged from his belly.

At that precise moment, the baby slithered from Cornelia's body to the accompaniment of a final, brutal scream from its mother; Aethylla gave a triumphant yell; and the other woman, now terrified witless, made a dash for the door . . .

. . . where she was impaled on the sword of the gigantic Poiteran who had just stepped through the opening.

His fierce eyes fixed on Membricus, the Poiteran put his hand to the dying, screaming woman's shoulder, and pushed her off his sword.

She fell on the floor, hands to her belly, her mouth open in now-silent shrieks, convulsed, and died.

No one noticed.

Membricus gave one glance to the bed—a baby boy lay between Cornelia's bent legs, his arms and legs waving weakly, his tiny face screwed up with the injustice of his barbaric entry into the world; Aethylla, her hands held out to the baby, was nonetheless staring horrified at the Poiteran who had now taken one farther step toward Membricus; while Cornelia was trying to raise herself to reach down to the child, oblivious of everything but it.

Membricus looked back to the Poiteran who towered only a pace away.

"Kill her," he said. "Kill her now."

The Poiteran looked at the woman and the child, hefted his sword, and with a fierce cry of utter joy, buried it in Membricus' belly.

He twisted the sword, crowing with delight at the shock on Membricus' face, then jerked it to one side, then the other, opening up Membricus' entire abdomen.

Then he took a step back, grinning hugely as he dragged the sword from Membricus' flesh.

Membricus gagged, took a staggering step away from the Poiteran, and, too late, tried to stop his bowels erupting from his body.

The glistening pink ropes of his entrails steamed in the night air, so many lengths that it seemed impossible they could have been stored within one man, and slipped gently, irretrievably, from Membricus' abdomen to cover Cornelia's breasts and belly.

Membricus gave one surprised hiccup, sank to his knees,

grabbed at his entrails, and tried to stuff them back inside his ruined body.

The Poiteran, still screaming with battle-lust, lifted his sword and stepped toward Cornelia.

Chapter Eighteen

Cornelia Speaks

I THINK THAT IN EVERYONE'S LIVES THERE IS one moment, just that one single moment, where something happens that is so shocking, so profoundly extraordinary, that your life forever is changed.

For me that moment was when my son finally fought his way free of my body. After all the hatred and savageness of the past months, and most particularly of the preceding day, to have that child battle his way into life from my body was the most joyous moment of my entire life.

I loved him instantly, simply, and unconditionally. The mere fact of his existence wiped away all the pain and troubles of those long, terrible months he grew inside me.

I—*I*—had produced *this*!

How could I ever have not wanted him? How could I ever have said I loathed and resented him? At that very moment I was so full of overwhelming love that I swear that I also loved the man who had put him inside me (and at that thought I also wondered if my wits had been totally addled by the pain).

Everything Blangan had said to me was true. The instant he was born, and I could see what I had made, I adored him.

If I'd had the strength, I would have pushed damned Membricus' entrails and steaming shit off my belly and snatched him to my breast, but as it was all I could do was try and shovel what was left of Membricus off my body and reach down between my legs to touch my glorious child.

I didn't even think about why Membricus should have so suddenly and inexplicably burst apart before me, or why Aethylla was screaming at me (or was it at someone behind me?). I just wanted to touch my child.

I did, I touched his downy shoulder with one finger, and I burst into sobs of sheer joy.

Something whistled through the air where an instant before my shoulders had been, burying itself in the bed behind me, but that fact only barely penetrated my mind. I leaned farther forward, disregarding the pain it caused my body, and ran my hand over his head.

Aethylla was still screaming about something, leaning back and pointing behind me, but I didn't care.

"Shush," I murmured to the boy, and, oh, hear his cries! "Shush, my lovely, shush . . ."

Then someone grabbed my hair.

EVERYTHING CHANGED. I ABRUPTLY BECAME aware of what was happening about me: the foul smell of Membricus' spilled bowels, and the shrieks and howls that emitted from his lips; Aethylla's screams as her terrified eyes focused on someone behind me (the man who had my hair? Was it Brutus, returned to view his son?); the humped body, also curiously disemboweled, of the other woman who'd been assisting my son's birth; and then the stink of the man who had his hand so cruelly buried in my hair— a stink more foul even than that of Membricus' bowels.

I suddenly realized I was very likely about to die.

Perhaps strangely, this did not particularly perturb me. After what I'd been through, sure that I was going to be torn to pieces anyway, I was quite resigned to a death of some sort. So long as Aethylla managed to get my son to safety I wasn't particularly concerned about it.

But I twisted my face, and looked anyway.

The great naked hulk of a man loomed behind me. His

body—ugh! What a hairy gut he had!—was caked thick with blue clay. His face was a messy web of close-woven black-inked lines, his eyes wild and staring from their midst.

His genitals, wobbling on a level close with my eyes, looked as though they'd been tattooed completely black.

They smelt diseased.

I wrinkled my nose in disgust, and out of the corner of my eyes, saw him raise a blood-daubed sword on high.

His mouth parted, and his teeth gleamed.

Aethylla was screaming in the background, and something inside me just snapped.

I'd simply had enough. This day had been bad enough without this disgusting hulk trying to murder me.

I raised my hand, so recently on my son's head, and grabbed the monster's penis.

Then, infuriated with everything from Brutus' cruelty to Aethylla's insults, I yanked the repulsive member as hard as I could.

He screeched, his sword dropping from his hand. He half doubled over, his eyes popping, his mouth open and making funny gasping sounds.

I pulled again, really viciously this time, and the man toppled over, and fell directly on top of (*still* screeching, for sweet Hera's sake!) Membricus.

My attacker's face was buried in Membricus' disgusting, shredded entrails.

I put my hands to my mouth, looked at Aethylla who was now silent and staring at me, and began to giggle.

Only one semihysterical chortle managed to escape me, then suddenly the room was full of men. Brutus, shouting something; Corineus, calling my name; someone else, Hicetaon perhaps, covered in blood and lacking an ear.

Someone sank a sword into the naked man's back, and pulled him off Membricus.

There was a moment, very still, when Membricus looked at Brutus and said something—"It was *my* belly, not hers!" I think it was—and then, thankfully, he died. The moment spent, Brutus leaned over me. He spared me a glance, his face shocked, then looked at the baby.

He reached down to pick him up, but Aethylla, who had finally regained her wits, brushed his hands aside. She twisted the cord that still connected my son to my body, tied it with something to hand (a piece of Membricus' entrails, for all I know), and then bent her head down and bit it in two.

Then she tore a piece of cloth from Membricus' cloak, wrapped my baby in it, and handed him to Brutus.

"No!" I cried, reaching out, but Brutus was gone, and it was Corineus who reached down, wrapped me in my cloak as gently as Aethylla had wrapped my baby, lifted me up, and carried me outside.

THEN, SO STRANGELY, ANOTHER OF THOSE LIFE-altering moments, just when I thought I would never have another.

Men, Trojans as well as more of those blue-clayed naked savages, lay in various poses of death, limbs hacked off, bellies peeled back as Membricus' had been, throats opened to steam in the cold air.

I saw faces I knew, men who had died that I might give birth to my son.

Idaeus, his entire body torn apart by several sword strokes.

And beside his corpse, moaning quietly, was Aethylla's husband Pelopan. He would be dead soon, for there was a gaping wound in his left flank through which blood spurted, and his left arm had been severed completely below the elbow.

Poor, innocent Pelopan. He would die also, that I might sate my desire to give birth on land.

And all to what purpose? I had only insisted on giving birth on dry land because it would force Brutus to my will, and I had so hungered for a single small victory over my husband that I would have done anything to accomplish it.

But this? These men, dead and dying so that I could have one pointless, foolish victory over my husband?

Oh, Hera, had I done this? Had I learned nothing from my father's death, and that of all of Mesopotama?

"Look you at the death you have wrought," Brutus' soft voice said to one side, and I twisted my head in Corineus' arm, and saw him standing several paces away, our son curled quiet in his arms. "See the lives you have destroyed. Remember, Cornelia, what you accepted. Responsibility for all that your demands spawned."

Corineus' arms tightened about me, and ever my savior, I think, he said to Brutus, "You agreed to it, Brutus. You *rushed* to agree to it. You and Membricus. Why? Did you know this was going to happen? What did Membricus say back there . . . 'my belly, not hers'? You *knew*? Your responsibility as well, Brutus. Yours as well."

There was no reply from my husband save the cold glint of his eye on me.

And then I heard Aethylla cry out, and saw her rush to her husband's side, and I also cried out, undone.

THE TRIP BACK TO THE BOAT WAS A JOURNEY INTO Hades' hateful realm itself. Corineus carried me the entire way, as gently as he could, but as he stepped into the first of the rolling waves at the shore's edge, my belly cramped with pain again, and I twisted in his arms.

"She is expelling the afterbirth," Aethylla said. "It will not kill her."

Her eyes were hard, hateful, and I could not blame her for any particle of that hardness and hatred.

Corineus carried me, through the rising surf that drenched me, up the side of the ship, and all the time I bit my lip to keep my cries muted, hoping that the pain would overwhelm me and I could lose myself in it.

It would be better than facing my guilt.

He carried me to the cabin, and laid me on the bed, and then retired as Aethylla, hard-handed, took the afterbirth from me (Blangan, I think, was with her husband, and I thanked every god there was that he had not been killed as well; Blangan's grief I could not have faced). Once my afterbirth was gone, Aethylla fetched a bowl of water, and cloths, and washed and attended me, and all the time I wept, and cried out, "I'm sorry, I'm sorry, I'm sorry," but I think that she never heard me.

When she was done, and I dry and well blanketed again, she went outside, and when she returned she brought with her Brutus, still carrying our son.

"He will need to feed," Aethylla said and Brutus leaned down and handed the baby to me.

I could not look at my husband's face.

I concentrated on my baby, folding back a corner of the blanket, and lifting his dear face to the nipple of my breast.

He grabbed hold of it, his mouth strong, and I gasped in delight.

He suckled, then again, hard and demanding, and then he let go my breast and wailed.

I tried again, pushing the nipple into his mouth.

Again he suckled, and then once more let go, and wailed his disappointment.

Aethylla leaned down and snatched him from my arms. "She has no milk," she said, and with that single condemnation, lifted aside the bodice of her robe and put my son to her breast.

He suckled, and was instantly contented. All the happiness of his birth vanished, and I was left a husk, a failed mother, and a woman who trailed death behind her at every turn.

Hades' daughter, hadn't Brutus once called me?

Hades' daughter, indeed.

VERY MUCH LATER, WELL AFTER DAWN, BRUTUS came to see me.

I had my son back from Aethylla then, and I was weeping that the smell of milk from his mouth was not the smell of *my* milk.

I raised my head as I heard his step in the door.

"You're still awake," he said.

"Yes."

"Aethylla?"

"She has gone, perhaps to mourn her husband." My voice trembled as I said that last, and Brutus walked over to the bed.

He stood a long moment, then pulled up a stool and sat, leaning forward, his elbows on his knees, his hands dangling between his legs.

His face was haggard.

I thought I was surely dead, and I thought also that I deserved it.

And what need had he of me? Aethylla could feed his son.

Brutus reached out a hand, and touched the baby's face. "It has been a hard night," he said.

"Brutus—"

"Say nothing. I do not need to hear what you have to say."

He paused, and his hand strayed from his son's face to mine. He lifted my chin so he could the better look me in the face, then he dropped his hand away from me.

"We are doomed to each other," he said. "By the gods, I think. It was you who should have died in that hut. Membricus had seen it."

"No wonder you were so willing to allow me ashore," I said, a little surprised there was no bitterness in my voice.

"Cornelia, Corineus spoke truly outside that hut. I *knew* from Membricus' vision what would happen, and *I* ordered those men to accompany us, not to protect you, but to ensure that you died. *I* ordered them to their deaths, for a foul reason. In all of this, you were as much the victim as the instigator. I have just come from talking with Aethylla, and I have told her what I have just told you. If her husband lies dead, then his death lies on my soul, not yours."

I closed my eyes, almost unable to bear what he confessed to me. *I ordered those men to accompany us, not to protect you, but to ensure that you died.* Strangely, that degree of honesty comforted me. It did not hurt.

And to admit that he was as wrong as I . . . was I to be allowed to breathe, and to take pleasure in life? My arms tightened about my son, and I looked once more at my husband.

"We are doomed to each other," he said again. His face became ever more drawn and exhausted with each word. "The gods will have it no other way. Cornelia, I need to know, do you dream of another man? I could not bear being married to a woman who—"

"No!" I said. "If I taunted you with Melanthus, that was to be cruel, to punish you for his death. And Corineus . . . you accuse me of lusting after Corineus, and I do not. If I smile at him, it is merely because he has been kind to me."

"And your dreams? Why do you laugh in your dreams?"

"I *do* dream of this land toward which we sail. Not of a man, but of green meadows and secret places. And also of this great stone hall that you mentioned. There is a child who plays there, and I think she is our daughter. Brutus, how did you know of this hall? Did you also dream of it?"

"Aye." His eyes were veiled now, and I wondered at his thoughts. "But I do not see this child."

"If we both dream of this hall, then it must be."

"Perhaps," he said, and his tone was cooler than ever. Then he sighed, and his face relaxed a little. "If we can trust each other, Cornelia, perhaps . . ."

"Yes," I said, so relieved I swear my eyes were brimming all over with tears again. "Yes."

We stared at each other a long time, then he forced a smile to his mouth, and looked once more at the baby. "Aethylla said that after all your weeping and wailing and cursing, the instant you laid eyes on our son you changed. She said she saw it."

"Aye. I loved him, even though I had hated him ever since I first knew he was growing inside me. I could not believe that I"—my eyes flew to his—"that we had made this between us, between all our hatred. I could not believe it, and yet there he lay."

He sighed, then stood. "Make your peace with Aethylla, Cornelia. We cannot afford to war with each other."

He walked to the door, and then turned back once more. "The child, is there a name you wish to call him?"

Would I never stop weeping? I did not realize a single woman could have so many tears inside her, or that she could ebb between despair and joy so many times in a single night. "You choose," I said. "He will be a king in your steps."

He stared at me a long time. Then . . . "We shall name him Achates."

"It is a good name," I said, and he nodded, and left.

"Achates," I whispered, and kissed my son's head.

PART FOUR

LONDON, MARCH 1939

"Does Asterion have Cornelia?" said Stella. "Ah, my love, I cannot answer that. You know it. I may not speak of him."

Skelton regarded her bitterly, wishing he could step back three thousand years and do everything so differently. Wishing he could have forced the truth from her then. Wishing he could do so now.

Something in her face shifted, and Skelton saw the yearning deep within her.

"The remaining kingship bands?" she said. "Are they safe?"

"Is it you who asks, or Asterion?" he said.

Her eyes filled with tears, and she dropped her gaze.

"This is the last opportunity we will have. The last Gathering," Skelton said softly. "What chance do we have, Stella?"

"There is always hope," she whispered, still not looking at him.

"Do you think I find comfort in cliches?" Skelton said. "Look!" He took the newspaper he'd kept folded under his arm and shook it out. "Look!"

Despite herself, and even knowing what it revealed, she

glanced down at The Times. "Munich Betrayed!" *screamed the headline.*

"Hitler has invaded Czechoslovakia," Skelton said. "The Rhineland, Austria, and the Sudentenland have all gone. Now Czechoslovakia. Asterion is behind this. I can smell it."

She said nothing.

"This is a bleak tide indeed sweeping down upon us," he said. "Aimed at you . . . at me . . . at that." He jerked the newspaper towards St. Paul's. "This time he is going to destroy the Game completely, and you and me and Cornelia with it. The world with it, Stella. Everything."

Now Stella looked further down the Thames to where the Houses of Parliament rose in the distance. "Perhaps—"

"Them? They are merely the tired sons of a long line of tired aristocrats. They can do nothing against what Asterion is going to throw at London this time. Ye gods, Stella, have you not thought of what weaponry Asterion can use now? Have you not thought of what he can do with it?"

"Brutus—"

"Don't call me that! Brutus died a long time ago, a sad, broken, hateful man. I stand here now."

He drew in a deep breath. "What I need to know, Stella my dear, is whether I stand alone. Are you with me? Can you do what is needed?"

Stella turned aside her face as answer, and Skelton's expression hardened.

"Tell Asterion," he hissed, "that if he wants the remaining kingship bands, then he is going to have to kill me to get them!"

And then he was gone, his footsteps ringing out into the night.

"He is going to kill us all," Stella whispered. "You should know that by now, Brutus."

Chapter One

LLANGARLIA

SHE ROSE FROM HER BED, AND WALKED naked from the house to greet the dawn.

They had survived, and had they not, Genvissa would have hunted through this world and the next to tear the senseless Cornelia apart.

To expose Brutus to such danger!

Genvissa drew in a very deep breath, more angry than she'd ever been in her life . . . and yet, puzzled also, for through all of this she had felt Mag much closer than she'd felt her for many long months.

Did it have something to do with Blangan?

Suddenly all of Genvissa's ill-humor dissolved, and a small smile curved her lips.

Blangan was with Brutus' fleet. And when Brutus' fleet drew close . . . suddenly Mag felt much closer than she had for months.

Blangan. Of course.

Mag had fled to Blangan. Genvissa should have thought of it before.

Well, wasn't Mag the senseless one as well? Now she was as trapped as poor, almost-dead Blangan.

A slow grin lifted her mouth. *Bad place to hide, Mag.*

Cheered, Genvissa walked back inside to wash and robe for the day.

Some good had come of the day, after all. Not only had she realized where Mag had secreted herself, but Cornelia's petulant adventure had resulted in Membricus' death. Genvissa splashed cold water over her face, singing under her breath. Membricus had been a nasty, horrid little man. A nuisance with too much hold over Brutus.

Now he was gone, and there was no one, *no one*, to stand between Genvissa and Brutus.

Not now she knew where Mag was.

ASTERION SHIVERED, SEEMING FOR THE FIRST TIME *to be aware of his surroundings. He looked up, staring at the alps soaring to either side of him, feeling the murderous intensity of the wind.*

It was, finally, time to leave this place and this body, time to arrange his rebirth in circumstances infinitely more suited to his plan.

An image of Brutus' golden kingship bands flashed into Asterion's mind, and his tongue flickered over his lips. How he wanted those bands!

Asterion picked up the twisted bone-handled knife, running a finger along its edge to test its mettle.

The blade sliced open his finger with only the slightest of pressures, and Asterion grinned.

"I wonder," he said, "if Genvissa knows of that vow Ariadne made to me when I taught her the darkcraft? That if she reneged on her word, then she became my creature entirely. I wonder if Genvissa possibly knows the implications of that? No, I think not, for if she did then she would be beside herself with terror."

He laughed, soft and joyous. "How shall it be, Genvissa, when I stand before you and demand what is mine? How deeply shall you cringe before me, Genvissa?"

Then, even as he continued to laugh, Asterion put the blade to that vulnerable flesh at the juncture of neck and shoulder and without hesitation pushed it in to the hilt of the twisted bone haft.

Instantly blood pumped from his neck, and while he still had the strength, Asterion tore the knife downwards, further opening the tear in his flesh.

Blood poured down his chest, pooling between his still-

crossed legs, then expanding out to fill the heart of the labyrinth Asterion had drawn in the earth.

Asterion continued laughing, but the sound was wet and horrible now, and bloodied froth bubbled out of his mouth. He maintained both laughter and posture as long as he was able but, as the blood emptied out of him, his laughter came to an end, and his dying body pitched forward.

As his face hit the earth, Asterion whispered a single word. "Resurgam!"

His eyes fluttered closed, but his heart, even as weak as it was, continued to beat spasmodically for some minutes further, pumping more and more blood out of the rent in Asterion's neck.

It collected in the heart of the labyrinth, then, when it could be contained no longer, seeped along the pathways of the labyrinth until, finally, it trickled out the entrance.

At the precise moment his blood escaped the labyrinth, Asterion's heart fell still.

Chapter Two

LLANGARLIA

HE WOKE, SUDDENLY AND COMPLETELY, THE dream still vivid in his mind.

He trembled, the anger that had consumed him in the dream even stronger now he was awake.

The girl beside him murmured and shifted, and Loth eased himself away from her, untangling their limbs, and sliding out of the bed.

He waited a moment, willing her back into sleep, and she quieted, pulling the wraps tighter about her, forgetting his presence.

Loth lifted a piece of beautifully woven green and red cloth from the end of the bed, deftly tying it low on his hips, slipped his feet into his leather sandals, and took from a bench a short cloak of a similar but heavier material than that of his hip wrap.

As he tried to throw it about his shoulders, the cloak caught for an instant on one of the protuberances on his skull, and Loth gave it an impatient tug to settle it where he wanted.

He smoothed down his hair where the cloak had disturbed it, then moved, not toward the door of the large circular dwelling, but to another sleeping niche on the far side.

There the Mother of the House lay awake.

As he approached the Mother stood, not bothering to hide her nakedness from this man. She was an old woman, her breasts scrawny and low, her belly lost in many folds, her long pubic hair gray and straggly.

"I must go, Mother Mais," Loth said very quietly as he reached her. She held out her hands, and he took them in his. "For your food and shelter and warmth this night, I do thank you."

"There is trouble," she said.

"There is trouble," he agreed. "Great trouble."

The woman took a deep breath, but she knew, *they had all known*, this was coming. She looked past Loth to the bed he had left.

"Has she conceived of her daughter?" she said.

Loth smiled, and nodded. "She will be a strong and healthy child."

"I thank you! You honor my House."

He leaned his malformed head forward and kissed her gently on the brow. "I increase the herd," he said. "It is my duty, and it is my privilege."

THE SIX ROUND HOUSES WERE GROUPED TO-gether at the edge of the great northern forest. Loth paused as he left Mother Mais' house, looking at the trees.

Normally Loth would have found the pull of the trees almost irresistible, but tonight his concern drowned out even his need for the forest and its mysteries.

He turned to the open fen land before him, striding forward.

Within moments he broke into an easy jog, his long legs covering the soft ground with the grace and economy of movement of a forest deer.

It was still dark when he left Mother Mais' house, but by the time Loth reached the small rise that overlooked the valley floor and the sacred mounds, the sun had crested the horizon, tingeing the Llan's marsh mists a soft gold.

Loth paused, his breath easy despite the distance he had covered, his face reverential. Slowly he dropped to his knees, bending his forehead to the ground in obeisance to the valley of the Veiled Hills, the sacred heart of the land.

Then, rising, Loth skirted the northern perimeter of the Veiled Hills, jogging across gently undulating ground thick with late summer flowers and grasses.

There were hares and birds and badgers out in this early morning: they all raised their heads to study the strange half man half beast that ran among them, then, unconcerned, resumed their morning feeding.

The sun had fully crested the horizon by the time Loth reached his destination—Genvissa's strange stone house.

SHE WAS WAITING, AS HE KNEW SHE WOULD BE.

"Loth," she said, calmly. "Have you seen?"

"Yes. Where is the Gormagog?"

"Your father is asleep. He is old, and weary, and not given to early risings anymore."

"Genvissa . . . does he realize how many there are? By Great Og himself! I saw countless score after score of those black-hulled ships! And they were packed with people."

"Loth—"

"Tens of thousands! You never mentioned tens of

thousands! And they are only just across the Narrow Seas! They can be here within a day!"

"Loth—"

"They will *swarm* over us!"

She reached out and grabbed his elbow, giving it a little shake. "For mercy's sake, Loth! Will you listen?"

He subsided, and Genvissa let out a relieved sigh. "There are not tens of thousands, a little over ten thousand, yes, but not *tens* of thousands," she said. "And they will not swarm. They want to settle here, and they, and their leader, are intelligent enough not to swarm like damned hares!"

She forced a smile back to her face. "Besides, you know as well as I that we may not need them."

"My mother."

Genvissa almost smiled at the vengeful hunger on his face. "Aye, Blangan. She is with them. Did you not see her amid all your *tens* of thousands?"

Loth shook his head. If truth be told, his sight had been unusually attracted to the woman who gave birth. Every time he'd tried to drag his mind's vision closer to the occupants of the many score black-hulled ships, it had been dragged back to the hovel where the young woman had almost died.

It was rare that Loth was granted such power of vision, and to have it drawn constantly to the young woman when he could have scried out his mother . . .

"Well," Genvissa continued, "Blangan *is* with them. She is our chance, Loth."

He nodded, his eyes aglow at the thought of Og's restoration at her death. "Where?"

"Mag's Dance."

"Mag's Dance? Why there?"

Genvissa shrugged. "Trust me, Loth. It will be best there." *The best place to take both Og and Mag in one economical swoop.*

"But their ships are just across the seas. They will sail straight to the mouth of the Llan."

She shook her head. "There will be a wind awaiting them once they gather themselves enough to set to sea again. It will drive them south, far south. They will land close to the Dart. Loth, can you speak to Coel? Ask him to move south to meet them. He can then lead a small party of Trojans north to meet with myself and the Gormagog. A small party that shall include Blangan, of course."

Loth grinned. "And their path shall pass straight by Mag's Dance."

"Exactly. Send Coel today. It will take him a week or more to get to the Dart."

"Should we not consult with my father?"

"I speak for both of us, Loth. Your father needs his sleep. Leave him be."

Then she stepped forward, put her hands on Loth's shoulders, and kissed him softly on the mouth. "When Blangan is dead, and Og's power is returned . . ."

He seized her, stricken with longing, and for a moment or two Genvissa allowed him to rub against her breasts and belly, and to kiss her mouth.

Then she pushed him back. "Not yet, Loth. Not yet . . ."

He growled, and made as if to snatch at her again, but she spoke sharply. *"Not yet!"*

He turned away, breathing heavily, bringing himself back under control, hating himself for his yearning and lack of control.

When he finally looked back to Genvissa his face was neutral. "And if we take Blangan, and all goes well?"

"Then you may take this Brutus," she said, "and do what you will with him. I shall have no need for him."

"And the ten thousand?"

"They will be back at the Dart," Genvissa said, then she laughed. "Where they will be surrounded by half a country's worth of forest!"

"And the forest can take them?"

"Whatever you wish, beloved," she whispered, a hand to his cheek. "Whatever you wish."

Chapter Three

MAG STOOD TO ONE SIDE OF THE LABY-
rinth in the center of the stone hall. Her head
was down, her hands folded before her.

She waited.

Before her, in the heart of the labyrinth, the flat stone
with the word *resurgam* inscribed on it moved slightly. It
appeared as if it floated on a pool of black, bubbling blood.

Mag prayed, seeking within herself the courage for what
she now had to do. Oh, Og! This was such a loathsome
alliance, but it was the only way Genvissa could be stopped
and, eventually, Llangarlia freed of all her darkcraft. Mag
could not do it by herself. She needed help.

"Poor Cornelia," Mag whispered to herself. "I am sorry
to be the one to set you down such a path."

There was a step in the great distance within the hall.

Mag raised her head. Her expression was calm.

Another step and then, in the shadows at the distant eastern end of the hall, a man stepped forward.

He was of a haunting dark beauty.

ASTERION WALKED SLOWLY. HE HAD EXPECTED THIS
invitation, but he kept an expression of mild surprise on his
face, as if both circumstance and stone hall were curious
to him.

The hall stank of the girl he had seen giving birth beneath the Poiteran's sword. Cornelia. Asterion almost nodded to himself. Yes, Cornelia was going to be as useful as
he had hoped.

He caught sight of the small, dark, and undoubtedly fey

woman standing by the labyrinth carved into the floor of the hall. He smiled, and stepped confidently towards her. He was not even going to have to work for Cornelia.

The poor innocent was about to be handed to him on a plate.

MAG WATCHED HIM APPROACH, WATCHED HIM smile malevolently when he saw the word that was carved into the heart of the labyrinth.

"This is a place of great power," he said, now standing at the edge of the labyrinth, opposite from Mag. Very slowly he began to walk about the outer rim of the labyrinth, playing ignorance to perfection. "Who are you?"

"I am Mother Mag, the mother goddess of a realm called Llangarlia where Genvissa, fifth daughter-heir from Ariadne, now seeks to build this." She nodded at the labyrinth.

"Why am I here?" Asterion said. He was three parts of the way about the labyrinth now, every step deliberate, his unblinking dark eyes never once leaving Mag.

"You are here so that I may offer an alliance," Mag said.

"You know who I am?" He had almost reached Mag now.

"Yes."

Suddenly he was upon her, and he allowed his heavy hand to fall on her shoulder.

She jumped under his touch.

"You are terrified," he said, leaning down so he could whisper the words in her ear.

"I am filled with terror, yes, but I am not afraid of you."

He drew in a sharp, affected breath, as if it were he who was afraid. "Have I met my match?"

She twisted away from his touch. "Do not make fun of me, Asterion. We both want the same thing, yet we are weak singly."

Her face was averted from him, and she did not see the gleam of amusement in his eyes at her words.

"If we ally," she continued, *"then we will be powerful enough to stop Genvissa."*

"But why is it," Asterion walked a few paces away, wagging a finger as if he deliberated a mighty problem in his mind, *"that I feel that once you were allied with Ariadne."*

"I welcomed her into my land. I thought her magnificent. I thought she was what I had been seeking. But she betrayed me, and she betrays my land with her Game. If she constructs this Game you will be trapped forever and my land will be turned into a dustbowl. We were both once allied with Ariadne, Asterion. Once we both loved her. Now we suffer for it."

He had turned back to her now, all affectation dropped. *"And your proposal is . . . ?"*

She nodded about her at the stone hall. *"That we use Cornelia to work our will for us."*

"The girl who just gave birth."

"You know of her already?"

"Her screams drew my vision to the place where she gave birth. The land of the Poiterans. They shall prove useful, I think."

"You will be reborn among the Poiterans?"

"They seem a kindly enough race for my liking."

"It will take you years to act on your own."

Of course, you stupid bitch, Asterion thought, keeping his face neutral. This will not ever be over with a single sweep of the knife. What I plan is going to take far longer than just "years". *"I know this."*

Again Asterion walked away, as if considering the matter. In truth, there wasn't much to be considered at all. He needed a tool, a knife-hand, and Cornelia would do as well—better—as any other. It also did no harm to allow Mag to think that he was indeed weak, and that he needed this alliance as much as she did.

Asterion stopped, his back to Mag, allowing his triumph a momentary release across his face. He knew very well what Hera had told Mag, and what Mag now planned.

Fool! *She had no idea of what power she was toying with.*

"*Very well!*" *he said, turning about on his heel. He offered Mag his hand, and she took it.* "*The bargain is made!*" *He grinned.* "*Shall we cement the bargain with the sweat of our bodies?*"

"*Don't patronize me. Besides, you have no time. See? Goffar of the Poiterans is already arranging your rebirth.*"

KING GOFFAR OF POITERAN, FURIOUS HIS MEN had been driven back, stormed into his long house. He threw to one side his sword, and tore the cloak from his shoulders.

Beneath the cloak his body was naked, although glistening with sweat and the blue clay that had been carefully daubed into intricate blue designs across his belly and thighs.

His wife came to meet him, concern in her eyes.

He hit her, his rage finding an acceptable outlet in the person of his long-suffering mate.

She fell to the floor, a shocked gasp escaping her lips.

Goffar leaned down, seized her by the hair, and, as she shrieked, dragged her to the bed pile by the fire.

IN HER BED GENVISSA WOKE, WIDE-EYED AND staring, her heart thudding.

She sat up, staring about her, but could not discern the reason for her fear.

Then, just as she'd convinced herself that it had been a mere nightmare, and she lay down to sleep once more, she realized what it was.

Asterion was no more. He was dead.

Genvissa drew a deep breath and held it. What did this mean? Should she fear?

What if Asterion was about to reincarnate again?

Then Genvissa smiled, and laughed softly.

And what if he did? Brutus would be here soon, and they would build the Game into its full power within six months, a year at the outside.

There was nothing a mewling babe could do about that. Nothing at all.

Genvissa slept.

Chapter Four

THE NARROW SEAS

IN THE EVENT, THE CROSSING OF THE SEA BEtween the land of Poiteran, where Cornelia had given birth, and the island of Albion took two days. A stiff north-northwesterly wind sprung up as they turned west, and combined with a strong tide, the fleet was pushed a little farther south and west than Brutus had originally wanted. Nevertheless, when one of Hicetaon's men woke Brutus at dawn, Brutus knew why.

The fore-looker had sighted land.

Leaving Cornelia sleeping, the baby safely wrapped and held tight in her arms, Brutus threw on a tunic against the cool wind and hurried forward.

Hicetaon, a bloodstained bandage wrapped about his head where once his left ear had been, was standing by the stem post of the ship.

Before them, just visible in the dawn's faint lightening, rose a line of green-swathed cliffs. In several places the face of the cliffs had crumbled, sending the trees and under-vegetation tumbling into the sea, and in these gashes white chalk glowed eerily.

Hicetaon nodded to the line of cliffs. "Is this it, Brutus?

Is this what we've been sailing and fighting toward all these past months?"

Brutus stared at the coastline before them, a tight knot of excitement in his gut. "Aye. This is the island of Albion, and here the realm of Llangarlia. I know it. I *feel* it."

Hicetaon, nodded, and Brutus suddenly noticed the shadows under his eyes, and the lines etched into his face. "You have not slept."

"No. My head aches abominably, and the wound still drains."

"The physician . . ."

"Has seen it, and mutters darkly about the blade that sliced into me." Hicetaon stood straight, and shrugged. "It is a wound, no more, Brutus. I am fit enough to continue."

"Have you sent a man to rouse Corineus?"

"Aye, and Deimas as well," Hicetaon replied. He hesitated, his gaze returning to the cliffs. "I pray to all gods that be, Brutus, that this land finally brings the Trojans luck. That here, at last, we can rest in the favor of the gods." He paused. "Surely . . . *surely* there can be no more ill luck left in this world that we have not already endured?"

Brutus shifted uneasily, his mind filled with the image of the great Minotaur Asterion atop Cornelia's body.

"We have left ill luck well behind us," he said finally. "Of this I am certain."

WITHIN HALF AN HOUR, JUST AS THE SHIPS WERE turning into the wind to tack north along the coast, Corineus, Blangan, Deimas, and Cornelia, who had insisted on joining them, stood with Brutus and Hicetaon on the small deck by the stem post. Cornelia walked carefully, her post-birth discomfort still obvious, but she looked healthy and her color was good (and her eyes unusually bright as she stared at the distant coast); Aethylla had privately remarked to Brutus as she'd taken the infant Achates away for his morning feed that Cornelia was recovering well from the birth.

Blangan had caused a platter of fruits, bowls of maza, and some well-watered wine to be brought to the group, and they sat cross-legged on the deck, sharing food, and watching the cliffs to the port bow of the ship. The ships were close enough to the cliffs now that they could hear the sound of the surf breaking at their base, and see the shape of the trees and the richness and variety of the undergrowth.

"It is a good land," Deimas noted, and none present could mistake the relief in his voice.

"It is so . . . green," Cornelia said, and Brutus found himself agreeing with her. He'd rarely seen a land with such abundant vegetation—and the mere fact of that abundance augured well for their future life here. Game would abound, and the soil was obviously fertile beyond anything he could have imagined.

It would be a fine place in which to raise both flocks and children.

"Blangan," Brutus said, laying aside his empty bowl and taking a fig from the platter. "Is this Llangarlia? Is this your home?"

Blangan had hardly eaten since she'd joined the group at the stem post. Her eyes were weary, the gray shadows underneath suggesting she'd slept even less than Hicetaon, and her thin fingers toyed ceaselessly with the dangling tassel of her waistband.

She'd scarcely taken her eyes off the cliffs rising to their port.

"Blangan?" Brutus said again, after she'd failed to answer.

Corineus, sitting beside his wife, looked at her worriedly, and took one of her hands in his.

Her other hand jerked, suddenly bereft of its companion in fidgeting.

"Yes," she said, very low, finally looking away from the cliffs and back to Brutus. "This is Llangarlia. But do not call this my home. My true home I have left far behind me."

Irritated, Brutus ignored the second part of her answer. "Do you know this coastline? How far does it stretch? How many people live along here? And is there a place where we may safely land, and continue in safety once we are on land?"

"So many questions," Blangan said. Then she sighed. "The coastline of the southeastern portion of Llangarlia is much like this for its entire length. It has many entrances to bays and rivers where you might land . . . but where we are exactly I cannot tell you. It has been so very many years since I was last here."

"There is a great river to which we must travel," said Brutus. "It is surrounded by marshland and is grouped about by low rounded hills—the Veiled Hills. It is here that we are bound. Are we close?"

"To the Veiled Hills?" Blangan responded. "No. We are far to the south. The wind"—*Genvissa*, she thought, wondering why Genvissa wanted them this far south—"has pushed us well away from the Veiled Hills."

"How far?" Brutus said.

"The River Llan is much farther to the north. Perhaps two or three days' sail, or more, if you must tack against this wind."

"Thank you." Brutus leaned back, suddenly realized he still held the fig in his hand, and took a bite out of it as he looked at the others. He thought for a moment, then spoke to Blangan again.

"Where is the main population of Llangarlia grouped? In these hills to our west, or in the lands about the Llan, and the Veiled Hills?"

"In the lands about the Veiled Hills to the north," Blangan said. "The land is far richer there—"

Richer than this? thought every Trojan, as well as Cornelia. *Richer than this sweet land of rolling wooded hills?*

"—and the climate milder. Also, most people like to live not too far distant from the Veiled Hills, which is a place of great mystery and sacredness and . . . power." She smiled a little, but it was sad. "We are a lazy people, and do not like to walk longer than two or three days to reach the site where most of our festivals are held."

"Your advice?" Brutus said, now looking to the others. "Should we sail straight north for the Llan and the Veiled Hills, or look for a landing spot along this coastline?"

"We seek a landing spot as soon as possible," said Hicetaon. "For two reasons. One, we need to replenish our fresh water and meat, and secondly, we are truly unsure of our reception among the Llangarlians. I, for one, do not fancy sailing directly into their lair around these Veiled Hills, even if we do number twelve thousand. But our numbers *will* serve us well this far south where the population is less and likely to be scattered. An isolated village of thirty or forty people will give this fleet no problems. The larger and stronger communities to the north may."

At that moment Aethylla returned with Achates who she handed to Cornelia, who smiled and took her son eagerly.

"I admit myself intrigued by these Veiled Hills," said Cornelia, cuddling her son close to her breast. "But I should be grateful to sleep on dry and firm land as soon as I might." Then she added, "I want to see this land, my new home. Can we land now? Today?"

"There are many who would add their plea to that of Cornelia," Deimas said. "Cornelia is not the only woman among us who has recently given birth, nor the only one who feels tired, dispirited, or ill. The ships are crowded, the people are tired, and I think I speak for most when I say my desire is to land as soon as possible, and as safely as possible. If the risk to us is lesser in these southern regions of Llangarlia, then I say we land here. Soon."

Brutus grinned at the eagerness in Deimas' voice. "If we find a suitable landing spot today then we will eventually have to reboard to move farther north—if negotiations with this Gormagog and MagaLlan go well. If we land today, then how ready will people be to reboard in a few weeks' time?"

"For a few more days' sailing only?" Deimas said. "They

will not be unwilling. And if it brings us rest and comparative safety, then I say that we land now."

Blangan lowered her head at Deimas' "comparative safety," but she made no comment.

Brutus laughed, and held up his hand to stop Deimas. "I submit! And I agree, too. It is best that we find a congenial landing spot as soon as we can, and rest our people."

He rose. "Hicetaon, where did you put that fore-looker? We will need him, as all other fore-lookers in the fleet, to keep their eyes wide for possible bays, or river mouths. I do not want this fleet trying to offload in ocean swells."

Chapter Five

Cornelia Speaks

I THINK THAT IF I HAD NOT HAD THE DISTRACtion of my love for my new son, I would have thrown myself overboard if I'd thought I might reach this land the faster.

It was the land of my dream, the land beyond the stone hall. If I had thought it when Brutus had first mentioned the name "Llangarlia" during his speech at the Altars of the Philistines, then I *knew* it now. I caught sight of those cliffs, and the thick green woods atop them, and such a burst of emotion boiled up from my belly I thought I would cry.

It was the most extraordinary sensation of relief, and of homecoming, and it was so beautiful, so comforting, that I did not even think to question it.

All I know is that when I emerged from the cabin, and walked (slowly and stiffly, for my lower parts felt heavy and bruised and more sore than I had thought possible) to the deck rail, and stood there with my hands upon it, and saw that line of cliffs, I knew I had come home.

Home.

I drew in a very deep, very emotional breath. This new land of Llangarlia represented so much. I looked at the line of cliffs and the green swath that topped them and I saw a new life and a new beginning. It had appeared—very literally—on the horizon at the same time as two other great discoveries: the totally unexpected love for my son, and the realization that Brutus and I might have a future together that was defined not by hate and mistrust, but by liking and respect.

Since that night when Brutus had talked to me and taken on his own shoulders a part of the blame for the debacle surrounding Achates' birth, we had managed a respectful and an almost friendly dialogue (although that very friendliness created difficulties, for we had no understanding of *how* to be friends to each other). We had a shared love—Achates—and a new understanding. It was as he'd said, we were doomed each to the other, so perhaps we ought to make the best of it.

Thinking of that stone hall, remembering how I had turned from the laughter of my daughter toward a man I loved beyond life, I wondered if I might dare to hope that the "best" I could hope for for Brutus and myself might also, one day, include love.

I shook myself, a wry grin on my face. A few days ago I had been sure he was about to kill me; now I was daydreaming about him as a lover. Perhaps that was the sight of the distant cliffs talking, perhaps all the unresolved emotion of birth, perhaps just the foolish thoughts of the young girl I was desperate to leave well behind.

Respect was enough to hope for now, and even that might be asking far too much.

Blangan eventually joined me at the deck railing. She put her arm about me, and we leaned in close to each other, and I knew, somehow, that she was indescribably sad. Over the past weeks we had talked of many things, but apart from that first night when she'd offered me so much comfort, she had rarely mentioned her homeland, or the child she had lost.

"Blangan?" I said, and she somehow knew to what I referred.

"I will not be welcomed here," she said, and then her arm squeezed my (newly refound!) waist. "But I think that somehow you will find yourself a true home. But beware, Cornelia. There will be those who will seek to harm you."

That man Hera warned me against? I thought. Gods! I hadn't thought about Hera's warning for months!

And what was his name? Birth must truly have muddled my wits to have forgotten that . . . there was something she'd said . . . some description . . .

"The Horned One?" I said, relieved that something had finally come to me, but Blangan frowned.

"Loth?" she said. "I would not have thought so. I admit, he was only a baby when I held him, but surely I would have felt any malevolence—"

"No. Not Loth. Another name . . . I'm sorry. It was so long ago. I can't recall. I was warned against him. A long time ago. Ah, do not worry about it, Blangan. I am sure it is nothing."

"Well . . ." Blangan faced me fully, and pulled me yet closer, and kissed my cheek and then my mouth, almost as a lover would. "Whatever happens to me," she said, very low, "keep safe, Cornelia. Keep safe."

I opened my mouth to ask her why she should think *she* was in danger, but she had turned and was gone, and I was left staring foolishly after her with a profound sense of loss and sorrow that was as unknown, and as unsettling, as was my strange reaction to this new land.

Chapter Six

WITHIN THE HOUR BRUTUS HEARD THE combined shouts of several of the fore-lookers. Already standing close to the stem of the ship, he raced forward, Hicetaon and Corineus at his side, to see at what they shouted.

On their port bow the cliffs had drawn back into what appeared to be a wide bay, or perhaps the mouth of a river, flanked on both sides by high headlands. As they drew close to the opening, Brutus could see that the bay stretched back as far as his eye could see. It was so big it could easily hold five hundred vessels; his fleet would almost be lost within its vastness.

He turned to Hicetaon and Corineus. "Well?"

"We take five ships and sail in," said Hicetaon without hesitation. "If this is as good as it appears, then the rest can follow at our signal."

Brutus looked at Deimas who had joined them. He nodded his agreement.

"Good," Brutus said. "We take this ship, and those of Assaracus, Aganus, Peleus, and Serses. Signal them, Corineus."

Brutus stepped up to the stem post, the fore-looker moving aside for him.

"I can hardly believe such a land exists," the fore-looker said with the reverence of a man who had hitherto been used to the thinner soils and harder climate of western Greece.

"Aye," said Brutus. He leaned over the stem post, hanging on with one arm, and shaded his eyes against the now bright sun. "I see no smoke, nor no sign of habitation. You?"

The fore-looker strained his eyes, then shook his head. "It is a paradise, waiting for us."

"Aye," said Brutus. "Waiting for us."

OARSMEN RAN TO THEIR BENCHES AND SLIPPED their oars in the five ships Brutus had selected, their captains ordered the sails lowered and stowed.

Within minutes the ships had come to, navigating through the wide opening between the headlands.

"Order the men to keep close lookout," Brutus said softly although there seemed no sign of danger, or even of further watching eyes, in the wide bay. Formed by the great mouth of a river estuary, the bay was flanked on either side by steep wooded hills that rolled away into the distance.

There were no smoke trails, no sign of habitation, no tracks that led from the woods to the foreshore, no fishing boats drawn up on the occasional sandy beach.

On the other hand, there were numerous water birds, the flash of fish schools within the water, and the mouths of several creeks that emptied into the bay.

The river estuary itself stretched wide and deep, and wound into the hills in a general northwesterly direction.

"Even if there are archers hiding in those hills," Hicetaon said, "the estuary is wide enough to allow the entire fleet entry without danger."

Brutus took a deep breath, considering. The five ships were now deep into the bay, the river stretching invitingly before them, and they could see nothing, nor had their presence elicited any reaction from the close woods.

It could be a trap . . . but . . .

"Signal the other ships to follow us in," Brutus said, "but signal also that the archers are to stand ready, should we have need of them. We need to land somewhere, at some time . . . and I can see no sweeter place than this. We have to risk it."

"Do we land here, on one of these sandy beaches?" Hicetaon said.

"I think not. None of them are large enough to allow for the size of our fleet, nor for the numbers of our peoples. There is no place here to establish an easy camp for twelve thousand; besides, this bay is still too open to the sea. If a storm should blow in then the ships would be dashed against the rocks. We follow the river, and see what we may see."

SLOWLY, SINGLE FILE, THE BLACK-HULLED SHIPS of the Trojan fleet sailed into the mouth of the estuary and up the river. On either side reared the steep wooded hills; now and again among the trees close to the waterline the Trojans caught a glimpse of deer or hare, and even once of several slow-blinking wild sows standing at the water with their piglets, watching the gradual progression of oared ship after oared ship pass up the channel.

Corineus' vessel led the file, Brutus standing alert close to the stem post. His eyes continually moved between the two shorelines, looking for signs of human habitation—or human ambush.

Once they'd left the wide bay at the mouth of the estuary, and moved into the river, Cornelia came to stand with him.

"Achates?" Brutus said, glancing at her.

"Aethylla is feeding him," Cornelia said, her eyes on the passing hills.

Brutus opened his mouth to say something, thought better of it, and merely nodded instead.

"This is a mysterious land," Cornelia said after a few minutes.

"You said it was green earlier."

She shrugged. "It is green *and* mysterious. What lives in those woods, do you think, Brutus?"

"Deer, hare, birds, wild boar. All the creatures woods harbor."

"But what *else*? There is surely something else in these woods . . ."

Brutus looked at her curiously. "What do you mean?"

Cornelia took a moment to reply, staring into the forested slopes to either side of the river as if she looked for something . . . or someone.

Eventually she shrugged, giving a small embarrassed smile. "I don't know. Maybe my thoughts remain muddled from Achates' birth. Forgive me, Brutus."

He smiled himself, very gently. "I will allow you a few muddled thoughts in return for the gift of Achates. It is not a heavy price."

He reached out a hand, and after a small hesitation, she took it. "I have been impossibly foolish, Brutus, and my thoughts and hopes mired in the past. We have a marriage to make, you and I, and I think . . . I *know* I would very much like to make the best of it that I can." Tears glinted in her eyes. "As you said, perhaps we should make the best of our doom. Perhaps . . ."

"Perhaps," he said, making the effort to respond to her effort, "we can even make something good of it."

One of her tears spilled over, and he lifted his other hand and wiped it away with his thumb, gently, almost caressingly.

"We have wasted too much time," he said softly.

FOR TWO TURNS OF THE RIVER THE LANDSCAPE RE-mained unchanging; steep rolling and closely wooded hills, sometimes plunging to the water's edge in cliffs, sometimes easing down more gently to small sandy beaches.

Nowhere, thus far, was there a good place to land such a large fleet.

As the leading ship rounded the third turn, Brutus suddenly swore, and let go Cornelia's hand, pushing her none too gently away from the stem post.

Cornelia, who'd been about to protest, scrambled even

farther back when she saw what it was that had grabbed Brutus' attention.

On the north side of the river there was a small valley created by a merrily tumbling stream, and at the point where the valley flattened out to join the river stood a moderately sized village surrounded by well-cultivated fields and orchards. The village was unwalled or fortified—which surprised Brutus—and made of some twenty or twenty-five circular huts made of logs, stone, daub, and thatch.

People were running from the huts, standing to stare at the ship as it came about the bend, then turning on their heels to race deeper into the village where a much larger and well-fortified round house stood on higher ground.

Corineus and Hicetaon had joined Brutus. Behind them the Trojans crammed into the ship muttered and pointed as the villagers continued to rush for the safety of the large round house.

"What do we do?" asked Corineus.

"Nothing," said Brutus. "They will see soon enough that we have an army of ships following . . . they will not risk an attack."

"And if they warn others of our presence?"

Brutus shrugged. "There is not much we can do about that save protect and fortify our eventual camp as best we can. We will have to meet this people sooner or later, Corineus. We can't hide forever."

"They are well clothed," remarked Hicetaon. "Even from this distance I can see their tunics and robes are woven with fine patterns. And look—they have herds of sheep and goats."

"Only a few of them carry weapons of any note," said Brutus. "These are not an aggressive people."

From among the scurrying villagers walked forth one woman. She was old, but not ancient, with long graying brown hair and a thin, weary face that was enlivened with very bright, very intelligent eyes. She wore no mark of leadership, but somehow exuded an aura of power that made her stand out from her villagers as no torc or golden band could.

As she watched them, standing close to the shoreline, she laid a hand to her belly and looked directly at Brutus, as if she knew who he was, then her eyes slid momentarily to where Cornelia stood several paces away from Brutus.

When her eyes came back to him, Brutus raised a hand over his head and very slowly waved it back and forth several times, then pointed upriver.

We greet you, and mean you no harm. We continue forward.

The woman stared, then, very slowly, lifted one open-palmed hand to shoulder height, acknowledging the message.

"I wonder how many more villages we will pass?" Corineus murmured.

TWO MORE, AS IT TURNED OUT, BEFORE THEY AP-proached a site Brutus thought suitable for landing.

In similar fashion to the first village, the people of the next two villages tended to panic at first sight of the ships, then they would slow to stare as they—and their headwoman—realized the foreigners meant no harm.

Not yet, at least.

None of them moved to attack, and Brutus dared to hope that his Trojans would remain unmolested.

At noon the leading Trojan ship moved about a bend in the river—although still wide, the main channel of the river was now growing considerably shallower, and Brutus knew they'd need to find a suitable site before long—and found the landscape flattening to flowery meadows on either side of the riverbanks, the woods sparser, and, on the northern bank, a very large and relatively clear meadow surrounded by marshes and tidal mudflats.

Behind the clear area rose a steep-sided hill topped with a rocky outcrop. The riverside flank had a gradual incline, but on every other side the hill fell away steeply.

It would be a good defensive location: with all the Trojan men to hand, and all the wood surrounding them, Brutus knew he could build a wooden palisade within a week. It wouldn't be large enough to contain all the Trojan campsites . . . but with luck it would be large enough for them to huddle within should there be need for protection.

He turned about slowly on the deck, studying the surrounding landscape.

It was good. The site itself was large, relatively level, high enough to escape any tidal fluctuations in the river level, and with a covering vegetation that would soon be cleared away for a campsite. There was a stream . . . no, three streams emptying into the river at a close distance. The woods in the nearby hills were full of game. There *were* too many trees too close to where Brutus wanted camp set up, a potential concealing place for attackers, but again the thousands of able-bodied men could clear those within a day or two.

And the riverbank at the foot of the clearing was wide and broad enough for a score of ships to unload at the same time.

It was unlikely that he could find a better spot in time for them to disembark before nightfall.

He nodded, smiled at Corineus and Hicetaon. "This is the place," he said.

Chapter Seven

ISEMBARKATION TOOK MANY HOURS, AND it was not completed until very late that night. Oarsmen maneuvered ship after ship to the beach where strong men waited with ropes to haul its stem partway onto the sand. They were helped by a good high tide, and by a sharp drop away into the river so that the ships found it easy to move to the beach. Part weary, part wary, shipload after shipload of people clambered down to the dry land, hauling out their possessions, carrying struggling sheep and goats and children, and standing, once landed, to stare about at this land to which Brutus had brought them.

Brutus' first task was to establish a secure perimeter about the landing area and the hill that rose behind it. The first several hundred people to disembark were warriors, swords drawn, fanning out to scout the woods that not only surrounded the landing site and the hill, but the bank on the other side of the river as well.

Brutus wanted no surprises.

Once he was certain the immediate area was secure, Brutus and his immediate subcommanders—Corineus, Hicetaon, Assaracus, and Deimas set about establishing a camp for the night: no easy task for some twelve thousand people. At best they could hope for campfires and enough space to allow everyone to stretch out; over the next few days everyone would have to work as hard as possible to build temporary shelters.

As people milled, bustled, shouted, laughed, and occasionally wept in the doing of their tasks, Brutus climbed to the top of the hill while it was still light. It was a large hill, very high, its almost-level crown large enough for a moderate-sized fortress, and it commanded a good view of the surrounding countryside.

From the river the landscape had seemed to be composed of almost-endless undulated and densely wooded hills; from his vantage point atop the hill Brutus could see that the wooded hills extended for many miles in every direction. There were small patches of open land where diseased trees had fallen, but generally the forests looked almost impenetrable. In the very far west, however, Brutus saw that the hills leveled out into flat and mostly unwooded plains. Looking back toward the coast he could see a few twists of smoke rising from the riverside villages they'd passed, but there were no smoke trails rising from anywhere farther inland. Brutus guessed that unless word had spread about his fleet and fires had been doused, the only villages in the immediate area were on the river itself where transport was possible.

There were very obviously no large towns or fortresses within several days' march at the least.

For the time being they were relatively safe.

Hicetaon joined him on the hilltop, puffing a bit after the steep climb, and for a few minutes they studied the landscape together, discussing what they would need to accomplish in order to build a secure campsite for the Trojans.

"And if this is not to be Troia Nova," Hicetaon said, "what shall it be, then? What name will you give to this first Trojan settlement in the new land?"

Brutus gave a short laugh, caught by surprise. He thought a moment, then grabbed a knife from his belt and leaned down to a patch of damp moss-covered rock. He scraped industriously for a few minutes, then stood back to admire his handiwork:

here i stand and here i rest.
this place shall be called totnes.

"Totnes?" Hicetaon said.

Brutus grinned. "When I was a toddler and still suckling at the breast of my nurse, she used to sing over me that I would be a great king and go to lands far distant. 'Tis only fair I name this first landing spot after her—Totnes. Besides, the shape of this hill reminds me most particularly of her full breasts."

Hicetaon roared with laughter, then sobered as he looked back to where another group of black-hulled ships were drawing up one by one to the landing beach. "All these years I traveled and fought with you, Brutus, I have never doubted that you were a capable and great man. But to see this, to see our fellow Trojans—so many thousands of them—brought out of misery and slavery and to a new land to rebuild their pride . . . well . . . I have never realized how great you truly were."

"The fighting is not yet done, my friend. If the Llangarlians refuse to accept us, then the worst battle of all may yet be before us."

Yet even as he said the words, Brutus was certain they were not true. *She* would have prepared the ground for their arrival.

BY THE TIME FIRES WERE LIT AND HAD ROARED back to cooking coals, and bands of hunters had returned with carcass after carcass of plump deer from the woods, it was near midnight, and people had only enough energy left to huddle by the nearest fire and eat what was handed out to them.

Brutus made sure that the ring of surrounding warriors were fed, and that others would relieve them after a few hours, before he sank down beside Cornelia, Aethylla— nursing both her own son and Brutus' on different breasts— and Corineus who sat among a group of some thirty people about one of the fires. Everyone looked exhausted, and much of the food lay uneaten. Already over half of the people about the fire were asleep.

Cornelia reached out a hand and briefly touched Achates' soft downy cheek, then looked to her husband who was finally managing to eat some food.

"What do we do?" she said, then waved a hand vaguely about. "Is this where we stay?"

"For the time being," Brutus said about a mouthful of barely cooked venison, "but not permanently. We stay here, we rest, we regain our strength, and while we do that I seek out this MagaLlan, and negotiate with her our permanent settlement."

"And the Gormagog," Corineus said, yawning. "Don't forget Blangan said that the various Houses of Llangarlia deferred to two people, the Gormagog and the MagaLlan."

"Where *is* Blangan?" Brutus said, suddenly realizing she

wasn't in the group of people about this fire, nor about any of the nearby fires.

Corineus nodded at the hill. "She said she wanted to see more of her homeland than just the nearby trees."

Brutus put down what remained of his hunk of venison, and sighed. "I need to speak with her," he said, and rose, his tired muscles and joints audibly creaking.

"You're exhausted!" Cornelia said, seizing his hand. "Rest first, surely!"

He gave her hand a squeeze, then let it go. "No. Blangan knows more than anyone the inherent dangers of this land. I need to speak with her before I sleep . . . or else I shall *not* sleep."

SHE TURNED AS HE APPROACHED, AND HE SAW that she had been weeping.

"We need to speak candidly, Blangan," Brutus said as he came to a halt by her side. "I have twelve thousand people to protect, and I have known since I first saw you that you are terrified of returning to Llangarlia. What is wrong? Why are you not overjoyed at coming back to your homeland?"

He dropped down to sit at her side. "Blangan, no more evasions. Answer my question. Should *I* fear, too?"

She turned her face away from him, back to the rolling forested hills. "Not as much as I." She paused, thinking, then came to a decision. "I have been brought home to be killed, Brutus."

"*What?*"

"Let me tell you in my own way, and to fill in some of the gaps in my story. What did Corineus tell you about me . . . that I left this land when I was fourteen, then married to a merchant who died within six months, leaving me stranded in Locrinia where Corineus, the beloved man, offered me marriage?"

"Aye. And you told me later that you were forced into leaving this land. Why, Blangan? Why did they force you to leave?"

She sighed. "Because it suited them—"

"Who are these 'them'?"

"My mother, Herron, who was the MagaLlan twenty-five years ago, and my father Aerne, who was the Gormagog. Maybe just my mother . . . I am not sure.

"I come from the most powerful House within Llangarlia, Brutus. The House of Mag. My mother was the MagaLlan, and I was conceived as her eldest daughter during the midsummer fertility rites. My father was the Gormagog. I was not my mother's heir, for that role would belong to my youngest sister . . ." She glanced at Brutus, wondering if he would remember what she'd told him of Llangarlian society during his time staying in her house in Locrinia.

"I understand. The heir of the Mother of any house is her youngest daughter, born of the wisdom of her maturity rather than the naivety and thoughtlessness of her youth. The younger is always considered the more capable and powerful child." He paused. "Your youngest sister, your mother Herron's heir, is Genvissa."

"Ah, yes, Genvissa. She was only some eight or nine years old when my son was born, and while I can accuse her of much, I cannot accuse her of any complicity in my downfall. No, wait, Brutus, do not interrupt just here. I will talk more on Genvissa later."

Blangan paused to take a deep breath, then continued.

"When I reached womanhood at thirteen I already had two younger sisters, so I knew I would never be my mother's heir. But as her first daughter to reach womanhood, I nevertheless had certain responsibilities. The most important of those was to conceive a child within my thirteenth year. This did not trouble me, I longed for my own child, and as I had been bleeding at the change of the moon for the previous eight moons, I knew I was physically capable of conceiving. It was just that . . . it was just that my mother, Herron, the MagaLlan, overrode my own choice of father for that child. She determined that I should conceive of a child by the Gormagog himself."

"Your own *father*? That is allowed?"

"Under normal circumstances, no. But between the Gormagog and a daughter of the MagaLlan's?" She shrugged again. "I protested, but my protests were ignored. Both MagaLlan and Gormagog were insistent. They said my child would be special. Powerful." She hesitated. "The Gormagog came to my bed one night, and there, despite my protests, he lay with me."

She closed her eyes for a moment at the memory, and her shoulders stiffened. "I tried to fight him off, and then to close my womb to his seed, but whatever power I had was useless that night. Brutus . . . I don't know, but there was *something* there that night that was so powerful that nothing could have stopped my father getting a child on me.

"And, oh, how tragic that was."

"How so?"

Blangan told him of how, at that moment when she'd felt her father's seed spill into her womb, the Gormagog's Og power had split in two, divided between the Gormagog himself and the son he had just conceived on his own daughter.

"This land depends on the combined power of Og and Mag, the union of the male and female, to remain in health. At that moment when Gormagog's power split in twain, Og's power was virtually destroyed. This land might look rich and green to you, Brutus, coming as you do from an area less endowed, but it has been touched by blight."

Brutus remembered what he'd seen earlier in the day, the patches within the forest where diseased trees had fallen.

"I understand," he said. "With the union disrupted, the land dies?"

"It sickens, certainly. And I was, and shall always be, blamed for it. Og's power had split, and even as my father lifted himself off my body, my mother the MagaLlan rushed into the chamber moaning and shrieking and tearing at her hair"—Blangan's face twisted bitterly—"and shouting that I had cast a spell of darkcraft over both Og and this land. It was a disaster. There I was, weeping in pain and humiliation, there was my mother, shrieking that I'd laid a dark enchantment on the land, and there was my father, jiggling naked up and down beside the bed and wringing his hands and staring open- and dribble-mouthed at me as if I were darkness incarnate."

Her voice softened into a whisper. "And all I was, Brutus, was a terrified thirteen-year-old girl, having just been raped by her father and with no more ability to weave darkcraft than I could command the tide to retreat. *Someone* had cast that darkcraft, but it was not me."

"Who?" Brutus said, very softly.

"My mother, I think. No one else would have had the power."

"Why?"

"I don't know, Brutus. In the end, I can't think why a MagaLlan, dedicated to the care of the land and to maintaining the union between Mag and Og so that the land would prosper, would do something so horrific.

"Whatever the who and the why, soon my name was being spoken with revulsion by every Llangarlian. My mother kept me close while my belly swelled, not even letting me outside her house during those long, long months; she was terrified I might do something to lose the child, and that she would not allow. When my time came to give birth . . . by Mag herself, Brutus, it was terrible. Worse than what Cornelia went through. No one helped me, but my mother, and my very youngest sister, Genvissa, stood there for all those long hours, watching silently. I tore apart as I gave birth—because of that I have been unable to give Corineus children—"

Her voice broke on a sob, and she had to take some time to compose herself.

Brutus laid a hand on her shoulder, knowing that she would accept no more than that small gesture of sympathy.

"I tore apart with the birth, and as soon as my son was born, and I put him to my breast, my mother leaned down and took him without a word or a look to me. The next day, still bleeding, I was delivered to the merchant who wived and bedded me within the day, and who bore me from Llangarlia."

"Oh, gods, Blangan . . ."

"Now that I am back," Blangan continued as if Brutus had not spoken, "my name will be blacker than ever. I will be the evil Darkwitch who destroyed the land's well-being, and who decimated Og's power. At some point, I will be taken and killed. The MagaLlan cannot afford for me to have my say."

"I will protect you—"

"I doubt very much if you will be able to protect me. Not here. Not in Llangarlia."

"I *will*—"

"No, shush." Blangan put her fingers on his mouth. "Make no promises you cannot keep. I am at peace with this. If I had wanted to escape death, Brutus, I would not have come with you."

"Corineus . . ."

"Do not tell Corineus. There is no point. And do not tell Cornelia."

Why not Cornelia? wondered Brutus. *What has she to do with all this?* And suddenly that nasty worm of suspicion flowered again within his belly. Corineus . . . widowed . . . and Cornelia. But then Blangan was speaking again, and Brutus tore his mind away from Cornelia and Corineus.

"There is more I must say, and if you have found the previous difficult to accept, then I fear that what I say now will make you angry. But say it I must."

"Genvissa," he said, his voice low.

"Aye. Genvissa. My younger sister and undoubtedly MagaLlan by now. That day you first met me you described her to me, Brutus, and Cornelia tells me you have dreamed of a strange woman."

Damn Cornelia, Brutus thought. *Has she told you how thick my erect member is? How many times I prefer to move my bowels every week? How golden my stream of piss is in the morning as compared to the evening?*

"Cornelia has needed a friend, Brutus. If she has told me that you have dreamed of this woman, then do not begrudge her this."

"She has dreamed of—"

"Not of her young lover who you murdered, Brutus. Yes, she has told me of that as well . . . but are you aware that Genvissa has also appeared to her in a dream? Cornelia does not yet know the identity of the woman who appeared to her . . . but she described her to me, and it was Genvissa."

"What? When? She has not told me . . ."

"She would not think to have told you, Brutus, because she blames herself for what happened, not the woman—the goddess, Cornelia thinks her—who appeared to her . . . and told her in precise detail how to plan and organize the Dorian uprising in Mesopotama!"

Brutus was so shocked that he could only stare at Blangan, openmouthed.

"Cornelia has also told me of the manner in which Mesopotama died, Brutus. She told me of the cracks that spread up the walls of buildings. Cracks, Brutus, that sound very much like those that appeared in Locrinia."

"You can't think—"

"I *think,* Brutus, that Genvissa's hand is everywhere in your life for the past year. Cornelia may have been a thoughtless young girl, but not everything she has done has been on her initiative only.

"Genvissa has brought you here for a reason. I have no idea what that reason is, but I fear it is dangerous, both to you and to the Llangarlians."

"I cannot think her that cruel. That manipulative."

Blangan sat back, a cold hard smile on her face. "No, of course you can't."

And with that she despaired, for she could see in Brutus' hesitation that Genvissa had already caught him within her darkcraft.

How I wish, she thought in a sudden rush of cold horror, *that I had not told him as much as I did.*

Poor Cornelia. She will never be a queen in this land. Genvissa will see to that.

IT WAS VERY LATE AT NIGHT WHEN BRUTUS LAY down beside a deeply asleep Cornelia. He was exhausted, but with all Blangan had told him, he did not think he would be able to sleep for hours, if at all.

Cornelia was curled up under her blanket, a bundled shape held tightly against her breast, and Brutus lay his head against her shoulders, thoughtful.

Had Genvissa manipulated all of them?

Was that terrible revolt, and all the subsequent death, Cornelia's fault entirely, or should the fault be shared? He reached an arm over Cornelia, and touched his son.

Cornelia did not stir, and Brutus did not wake her. He left his arm lying across her body, his fingertips lightly touching his son, and despite thinking he would never sleep, slipped quickly into an exhausted slumber.

WHEN HE DREAMED, IT WAS NOT OF CORNELIA, BUT *of the dark-haired, laughing woman with the streak of russet through her hair.*

Genvissa.

She was standing before him laughing, naked, her hands splayed over her round pregnant belly. As he stood staring, lust stirring in him even though she was pregnant, her belly swelled, as if months passed instead of moments, then Genvissa dropped to the ground, moaning.

She writhed once or twice in agony, then lay on her back and spread and lifted her legs, and strained to give birth.

Brutus moved, looking between her thighs.

Genvissa screamed, arching her back, and something slithered from her birth canal and lay between her legs.

It was not a baby at all, but a city.

It was the city he had seen on the wall in Assaracus' house. Beautiful, extraordinary, white-walled, many-

turreted, gleaming in the sunlight. A city such as the world had never seen before.

Genvissa raised herself on her elbows, and looked over her now flaccid belly to what lay between her legs. She smiled, and Brutus thought her face lovelier even than the city.

"See what we have made between us, lover," she said. "The greatest city the world will ever know."

He dropped to his knees beside her shoulder, and leaned down and kissed her deeply.

As he raised his face from hers, she said, "Other women may give you sons, Brutus, but only I can give you immortality."

Only I can give you immortality . . .

WHEN BRUTUS WOKE IN THE MORNING, IT WAS TO find that he'd rolled far away from Cornelia and Achates, and that, as he recalled what Blangan had said to him the previous night, it was to dismiss it as the addled meanderings of a woman grief-stricken and bitter at her inability to bear her husband children.

Chapter Eight

THEY RODE THROUGH THE FOREST, THREE men on low, sturdy, shaggy-haired dun horses. Under their light cloaks they wore finely woven woolen tunics, richly patterned and colored, over similarly fine woolen leggings. Knives were slipped under their belts, and at their hips swung swords of elegant craftsmanship.

One man, of some thirty years, was set apart from the other two by the fine bronze and gold jewelry he wore in his ears and at his neck and wrists. He had very pale skin, dark hair and eyes, and a sensitive, thin, and clean-shaven face with light grooves running from nose to mouth. When he chose, and that was often under normal circumstances, he also had a brilliant smile.

Atop his physical comeliness, the man wore an air of moodiness about him, and a certain degree of mysticism, that, while complementing his sensitive face, seemed at odds with his warrior bearing and the hardness of his hands.

His name was Coel, a proud younger son of the House of Erith, and while he came here at the behest of the MagaLlan (and through her, the Gormagog), his true allegiance was to Loth, with whom he had played as a boy, watched over as a youth, and confided in as a man.

His mission was twofold, to escort the leader of this vast fleet north to the Veiled Hills, where he might meet with the MagaLlan and the Gormagog, but also to lead Loth's mother, Blangan, to her death.

Unbeknown to the MagaLlan and the Gormagog, there was a third part to Coel's mission, something Loth had confided in him, and something Coel did *only* for Loth.

Apparently there was a woman among these strangers, a woman as any other, but who Loth said intrigued him. Loth had told Coel of his vision of the great fleet that was sailing toward Llangarlia, and he had also told Coel that his vision as constantly pulled back to watch this woman—girl, really—giving birth.

"She intrigues me," said Loth. "Something about her kept pulling my vision back to her when I had no mind for anything but for the size of the fleet. Coel, my friend, find out for me what she has about her."

Coel had laughed, and made a ribald comment, but Loth had hardly even grinned.

"There is something strange about her, Coel. Find out for mc what that is."

COEL PULLED HIS EXHAUSTED HORSE TO A HALT, stared for a long moment at the hill rising in the distance, then slid from the beast's back, giving it a well-earned pat on its neck. He and his two companions, Jago, a young and smooth-cheeked man, and Bladud, a much weightier and grim-visaged warrior who had a scar neatly bisecting the beard on his chin, had taken almost a week to ride this far. They'd changed their horses twice and sometimes three times a day at villages along their route, invoking the Gormagog's and the MagaLlan's names as security against the horses' eventual return.

Five days out they'd begun to hear rumors, and then firm reports, of a massive fleet of black ships that had entered the Dart River far to the south.

Terror was spreading among the tiny villages of southern Llangarlia, and Coel did all he could to reassure the frightened people: these newcomers were no threat, Gormagog and MagaLlan knew of them, and knew how to control them.

At least, Coel fervently hoped so.

He thanked Og and Mag that there were no reports of fighting: these strange people had arrived, but were apparently content to hunt for food, and to establish a basic camp, and had not embarked on a rampage of terror through the forests surrounding the Dart.

This seventh day since their departure from the Veiled Hills had brought Coel and his two companions to the very edge of the Dart River. Before him, although still some distance away, rose a great hill. Here, so Coel had heard from reports and now could hear with his own ears, the foreigners had established their camp.

He turned to Jago and Bladud, Jago's face clearly showing his nervousness while Bladud's remained inscrutable, and nodded that they should also dismount.

"We'll walk from here," he said. "These black ship people will have warriors in the woods surrounding their camp, and doubtless we will be intercepted before long. If we are on foot, then we will the more clearly be seen as emissaries rather than attackers."

"I fear them," said Jago.

"We all do," Coel said, "but it weakens us to voice such fear."

Jago's cheek reddened, but he bowed his head, accepting Coel's rebuke.

"Gormagog and MagaLlan will direct them to our purpose," Coel continued, now feeling a little sorry for Jago, "rather than allow them to work against us."

Jago raised his head, about to say something, when all three men jerked to a halt, their horses shying, and stared at the five men who had appeared silently on the forest path before them. Like the Llangarlians, they were dressed in tunics that came to midthigh, but they wore no breeches or leggings, and the material of their tunics was of fine linen rather than wool.

They were well armed with both lances and swords—the like of which Coel had never seen before—and had hardened leather circular shields, a curious device in their center, held on their left forearms by straps.

Their faces were strange, their skin swarthy, and their hair and eyes were very dark—a darkness Coel had only ever seen in one other family before.

Coel risked a single step forward, spreading his hands well away from his sides to show his peaceful intent.

"I have come to speak with your leader," he said, hoping the warriors would understand his intent rather than his words. "I mean you no harm."

The lead warrior grunted, as if he had understood what Coel had said, then nodded, and beckoned the three men forward. Seven other warriors stepped silently out of the woods—Coel had not even realized they were there—relieving the three Llangarlians of their swords and knives, and then the party set off, walking steadily toward the hill.

COEL, JAGO, AND BLADUD WERE ESCORTED TO A clearing on the edge of the Dart. Here they were stopped while several among their escort went forward into the greatest mass of people Coel had ever seen.

They were everywhere—the dark-haired, exotic-featured people of the black ships; Coel had no means of estimating their numbers. The people swarmed the open spaces and the gently sloping side of the hill, while scores of ships crowded at anchor in the calmer sections of the river. In the days since their arrival they had managed to set up a basic camp—wooden shelters covered with rushes or branches, hundreds of campfires over which pots bubbled and meat smoked, women crouched at water's edge washing clothes and minding children, while herds of goats and sheep—even more exotic to Coel's eyes than the people themselves—were corralled at the edges of the woods.

He was still gaping when he realized that the warriors were returning, and with them walked a man who Coel instantly realized was not only this people's leader, but a man who wielded great god-power.

Coel stiffened a little, and he felt both Bladud and Jago shuffle in their discomfort.

The man continued to walk toward them, his face devoid of any expression. He moved with the strength and grace of a hardened warrior, and the gleaming bands of gold about his legs and arms gave him an almost supernatural glow; if nothing else, they told Coel that the man was a king of some standing. He had very long curly black hair tied at the base of his neck, and wore a fine linen tunic of ivory belted about his waist with a belt of woven gold and silver threads.

He was unarmed, not wearing even a knife for his food. The man came to a halt two paces away from Coel, regarding him with as much care and curiosity as Coel knew he studied him.

"You have a fine cloak to hang over your equally fine tunic," said the man in quite reasonable if highly accentuated Llangarlian, and Coel jumped in surprise—he had expected to communicate with this stranger by means of hand signals and significant looks.

One among Coel's escort of warriors handed Coel's

sword to this man, and he turned it over in his hands slowly as he examined it.

"And your sword," the man continued, "is far better crafted than any I have ever wielded. Are you the Gormagog himself, come to greet me?"

He turned slightly, handing the sword back to one of his men.

Despite all his caution, Coel's face dropped in shock. *He knew of Gormagog?* Great Og, what else did he know?

Clearly amused at Coel's reaction, the man raised a black eyebrow, waiting for a response.

Then the man said, smiling as Coel continued answerless, "I, as you see"—he held his arms out—"have come unarmed."

"Save for your knowledge," said Coel, and stepped forward, holding out both his hands. "I am Coel, son of Erith. I am not the Gormagog, although I am here at the behest of both he and the MagaLlan, and with their authority."

Brutus took Coel's hands in his and gripped them tightly. "I am Brutus, son of Silvius, son of Ascanius, son of Aeneas, son of Aphrodite."

They dropped their hands, the ritual greeting done, and it was apparent that Coel was clearly unimpressed with Brutus' lineage. "You come from a line of *men*?" He patently did not know—or was underawed—that Brutus had dropped in the name of a powerful goddess as the founder of his line.

Brutus tried not to smile. No doubt this man, who let his House Mother nag him at his hearth, found the idea of a house of men astounding. He nodded. "In my heritage," he said, "a family's name and honor is handed from father to son."

Coel shook his head, then said, "My companions are Bladud and Jago," adding their House affiliations, "and we have brought with us flasks of our honey wine, that we might greet you properly. Is there . . ."

"Somewhere to rest, and to sit and talk among all this crowd?" said Brutus. "Aye, I think I can find somewhere."

He turned to his men, and continued to speak in Llangarlian, telling Coel that not only he but all his warriors spoke his language. "Hand back to our visitors their swords, and take their horses and water and feed them well."

The men nodded, and after Coel, Jago, and Bladud had retrieved their swords and the flasks of wine that had hung behind their saddles, Brutus led them toward the hill.

AFTER THEY HAD REACHED ITS ROCKY SUMMIT, Coel and his companions spent a long moment studying the crowds below them, and the infinity of black ships that were either moored in the shallows of the river or drawn up on the foreshore.

When he finally turned to Brutus, Coel's eyes were bleak. "What do you here, with so many women and children and flocks of animals?" he said. He knew very well why the Trojans were here, but he wondered if Brutus would prevaricate.

"I will not lie to you," Brutus said, standing easy with one foot resting on a small rock before him. "We come here to make a home. We are Trojans, vagabonds for these past ninety-eight years. Now we will make our home here."

"Why here?" Coel's voice had a hard edge to it, and Brutus could not blame him for that.

"The great Artemis, goddess of the hunt, has directed us here."

"This is the land of Og and Mag," Coel said, both voice and eyes now flat. "Your 'huntress' will have no place within our forests and fens."

"Is that what your MagaLlan and Gormagog told you to tell me?" Brutus said softly, holding Coel's stare.

Coel held Brutus' gaze for a few more heartbeats, then dropped his eyes to the flask he held in his hand, and managed a small and not altogether unnatural smile. "We have brought the welcoming wine," he said. "Will you sit, and share it with us, while I pass on the message I have for you?"

Slowly, infinitely slowly, he raised his dark, deep eyes back to Brutus.

For no reason at all, Coel's movement and expression made Brutus recall Blangan's words about her undoubted death.

There was something here, a power, that was unknown to him, and Brutus knew that wariness and temperance would do more for his cause than any untoward display of arrogance and incaution. There was something *behind* Coel, something powerful, and Brutus knew better than to tempt it forth now.

He needed to win for himself a kingdom among these people, and he would do it the more easily by listening than by shouting.

He nodded. "The sun is warm here, and I fancy that your wine will be more than welcome." He glanced to his left as footsteps sounded, and Hicetaon and Corineus joined the group of four men atop the hill.

Coel instinctively tensed, then relaxed as he saw that the two older men wore no weapons apart from small eating knives. The older man, bald and muscular and with a deep wound scabbed on one side of his head, was clearly a warrior, while the thinner-faced man looked more the intellectual than the soldier.

Brutus introduced them to Coel, Bladud, and Jago, and motioned everyone to sit down.

Coel unstoppered his flask of wine and took a long draught himself (*See, this wine is not poisoned*) before passing it to Brutus.

"Drink," Coel said, "of the welcoming wine, and as you do, I will speak the words I have carried so far south with me."

Brutus drank, managing to swallow without grimacing. The flask contained a rich, honeyed liquid, far sweeter than the wines Brutus was used to, and he gave Corineus a warning glance as he handed it to him.

Brutus hoped this land was warm enough to grow vines,

because he didn't think he wanted to get too used to this syrupy draught.

Coel cleared his throat, and when he began to speak, it was with the melodious rhythmic voice of a poet, so beautiful that Brutus had no doubt he could win any woman he wanted into his bed.

"Greetings, Brutus, heir of Troy," he said. "We wish you health and life, and we also wish you to know that we understand why you are here, and for what purpose: to rebuild Troy, on these our meadows and forests."

Brutus' face remained impassive, but those words confirmed what he had suspected for weeks: Artemis had never once come to him. Only Genvissa, in a guise he would trust.

By the gods, he thought, *she has so much power!*

"We know your longing for a home," Coel continued, "and for Troy so long dead, but we also need you to understand that your purpose causes our people and our gods great dismay. But rather than dismiss you, and ask you to leave—"

Despite himself, Brutus couldn't resist a smile at that. "Dismiss him," indeed! Genvissa had a fine sense of humor to complement her power.

"—we ask instead that you and a small band of your companions travel to the heartland of Llangarlia there to meet with us, and to see if our mutual fears and needs cannot be mutually accommodated." Coel's voice slipped back to normal. "These are the words of the MagaLlan and the Gormagog combined, united as the living representatives of the gods, and the unified voice of the people."

"They want me to travel to the Veiled Hills?" Brutus said, and saw Coel's composure slip at the mention of Llangarlia's sacred heartland.

"Yes," said Coel, reasoning that most of Brutus' knowledge must have come from Blangan, the traitorous bitch. He looked weary now, as if his delivery of the message had come at the expense of his own strength.

"Just myself and a small band of my companions? What

reassurance do I have that we will not be killed?"

Coel, in his turn, managed a wry smile. "What guarantee do we have that you will not set your tens of thousands against us?"

All humor dropped from Brutus' face. "We have a mere few thousand warriors," he said. "The rest of my people are wives and children, the elderly, and untrained youth. As an 'invading force' we are severely hampered by those we need to protect. We defend, we do not attack. And we are not 'tens of thousands.' "

"You are more than we could ever hope to assemble in one place," said Coel softly.

There was a cold silence as both groups of men stared at each other.

"Perhaps I may suggest a compromise?" Corineus said eventually.

Eyes swiveled in his direction.

"If Brutus and his companions travel into Llangarlia's heartland, not knowing what they may find, or how they will be received," Corineus said, "then perhaps a small band of Llangarlians, of similar standing, enjoy our Trojan hospitality here within Totnes camp."

"Reciprocal hostages," said Hicetaon, always blunt and to the point.

Brutus raised his eyebrows at Coel. "Your younger companion, Jago, can surely escort us to the Veiled Hills. Will you stay here, with Bladud?"

"You will need me to escort you through the territories between here and the Veiled Hills," Coel responded. "Only my name and word can get you through. But your companion Corineus has suggested a good compromise. Although I cannot offer my family to dwell among you—they also dwell close to the Veiled Hills, and it would take weeks to send word and then for them to travel down to the Dart River—may I suggest asking the three Mothers of the three villages close to this location? As Mothers of their Houses and villages, they are greatly revered. No one would ever risk their lives, most certainly not either Gormagog or MagaLlan. If these three Mothers agree, then, Brutus, will you and your immediate companions, as well your wives and children, accompany me back to the Veiled Hills? If we both risk our most valued and honored, then both surely will rest assured that peace will be maintained."

Brutus exchanged glances with Corineus and Hicetaon, then nodded. "I agree."

Chapter Nine

Cornelia Speaks

J CONTINUED TO BE ENTHRALLED BY THIS NEW land. I, who once had never thought to be enthralled by anything save a new jacket or a bauble thrown my way by my father! Yet here I was, with an infant in my arms I had once thought to loathe, a husband I had once thought was little more than a brutish goat, not a single remaining remnant of my Mesopotamian finery, living in an overcrowded camp that was growing muddier by the day—and I was so enjoying myself anyone would have thought me born in a meadow.

Achates was a great joy, but I must admit that lying next to Brutus at night made me wonder when I would heal enough to make love with him again. Once the thought of bedding with my husband had caused me physical revulsion and mental torture; now I found myself daydreaming about it as I had once daydreamed about Melanthus. Over the past few weeks I had become more and more aware of his . . . well, of his desirability. It had begun that night at the Altars of the Philistines where I had run my hands through his hair, felt his tongue graze mine, and had continued ever since. I had noticed how other women watched him as well, had noticed his magnetism, had realized that they looked at me with envy underlining their contempt.

And, of course, there was the dream of the stone hall with the sweeping green hills and silver river of Llangarlia beyond, the sense of waiting for a great love to arrive, the daughter I could see playing from the corner of my eye. It came upon me with ever-increasing frequency now, and each night that it came, it was more vivid, more real.

So I daydreamed of him, constantly, through the hustle and bustle of the river camp. In this state of mind I no longer resented Aethylla for her ability to feed Achates where I could not; instead, I was relieved that Achates' hungry mouth did not prevent the rapid firming of both my breasts and belly back to a gentle roundness.

I could barely wait for my body to heal completely.

So, with my baby in my arms, my body springing back to a much appreciated slenderness, and my eyes occasionally wandering after my husband as he undertook the governance of this bustling camp, I turned my curiosity to this land.

It was so beautiful (*just like my vision from the stone hall*) that sometimes contemplation of it left me in silent tears. The country was not only unusual in its greenness, and the very exuberance of that green, but also in its soft light and comforting coolness. My own land, my girlhood home, had been clear and bright and harsh, the foliages more gray, the sun bolder. Here, tiny flowers that could never have survived Mesopotama's hard light thrived in shallow crevices of rock and flowered in great ebullient carpets where the soil was deeper. The trees had the thickest of canopies, stunningly clothed in the reds and golds and russets of their autumn canopies: I spent many an hour while Achates slept in my arms watching their seductive dancing against the sky.

Thus it was that when Brutus announced that I would accompany himself, Corineus, Blangan, Hicetaon, and several others on a journey north to the Veiled Hills, I was filled with excitement. The fact that I was being taken as a virtual hostage against the Trojans' misbehavior, as Corineus explained to me, did not concern me in the least. There was travel and excitement ahead, a chance to perhaps draw a little closer to Brutus, and Aethylla to look after Achates' needs.

WE LEFT ON OUR JOURNEY NORTH SOME FOUR days after the Llangarlian Coel and his companions had arrived to speak with Brutus. As we stood about, waiting for the small, shaggy Llangarlian horses to be brought forward, I felt my spirits rise even higher than they had been. The sun was shining, partly negating the cool touch of the southerly breeze, and I was wearing a becoming robe that Blangan had given me, a pale blue and black patterned woolen garment that flattered my coloring. I had managed to belt this robe quite tightly, which success made my mind wander to the coming night, our first away from the Trojan camp . . . and the first where I would be allowed to cuddle up close to Brutus without the overwhelming companionship of twelve thousand people snoring and breaking wind within my immediate vicinity.

Our party that, with Coel and his two companions, Brutus, myself, Corineus and Blangan, Aethylla (looking grumpy with both Achates and her own son slung across her back), Hicetaon and two other Trojan warriors, numbered only eleven seemed positively diminutive by comparison.

So I was happy. Not only would I have a chance to explore further this wondrous land, but the journey ahead promised to further cement the growing bond between Brutus and myself.

Only one thing bothered me: the Llangarlians' reaction to Blangan.

They completely ignored her, almost as if she didn't exist. I thought it rude, and went to comfort Blangan, but she waved me away, and said it was of no concern to her. I said I would speak to Coel or the other two, but then her voice grew sharp, and she told me to leave well enough alone, and somewhat hurt, I wandered away.

*   *   *

OUR PARTY WAS FINALLY READY TO DEPART AT midmorning, and Coel aided me to mount my horse, a little dun mare with a thick black mane and tail. The opportunity gave him a chance to send me several admiring glances that I found faintly disturbing. I worried that he might take advantage of me as he lifted me to the mare's back, but he was most respectful, and his hands lingered no more than was fitting for the task.

"You are unused to riding on a horse's back?" he asked me as I shifted uncomfortably.

"Yes. In my country women of my status did not ride. If I needed to go somewhere in style, then my father would order a chariot and charioteer to see to my needs."

I realized that sounded a little pompous, so I added, "The chariots were bumpy, and dusty, so I rarely used them."

He was taking his time fiddling with my horse's halter, and eight or nine paces away I saw Brutus glance at us impatiently.

"You came from a large city, I have heard. All stone ramparts and walls."

"Yes." I regretted the shortness of my answer, but Brutus' regard made me think that perhaps I shouldn't extend this conversation any more than I could help.

Something on the halter suddenly clipped into place, and Coel gave my mare's neck a pat to reward her for her patience. "You miss your home," he said. "Your stone ramparts and encircling walls."

"I used to miss my home greatly," I said, Brutus forgotten. "But now"—I looked about at the nearby forest and the hills rising away into the distance—"not at all. This land is too beautiful for me to linger over memories of the city where I was bred." I smiled, and was going to say something more to compliment Coel on his homeland, but then Brutus rode up, and I dampened my smile.

"Is there a delay?" Brutus said, looking between Coel and myself.

"Only in my clumsiness," I said. "Coel was reassuring

me that this fine mare will not toss me the moment we set off."

"Perhaps," Coel said, "I could lead your wife's mare? She is not experienced in the ways of riding, and—"

"Yes, yes," Brutus said, losing interest. "Whatever is best."

He turned his horse, and began shouting at the rest of the group to move out.

I thought this a little inappropriate, as it was Coel who was supposed to be our guide and leader on this ride north, but when I looked back to Coel in some embarrassment, he merely lowered one of his eyelids in what might actually have been a wink, then took the halter rope of my mare, vaulted gracefully onto his own horse, and led me forward to join up with Brutus' well-herded group.

I GASPED AS THE HORSE MOVED UNDER ME—IT felt as if the earth itself was tilting this way and that, and despite being not far from the ground, every one of the little mare's strides seemed to take an aeon to stretch itself out.

Worse, as discomfort flared through my lower body, was the sudden realization that I was going to end this day's ride very sore indeed.

"Everyone takes time to get used to a horse's stride," Coel said to me, having turned to make sure I was still on my horse. "In a few days your body will have settled to your mare's pace and rhythm, and your joints will have loosened, and riding will become a greater comfort"—he paused, and I could see the tip of his tongue glistening behind his very white, strong teeth—"than you could have thought possible."

I nodded a thanks to him, concentrating mainly on burying my hands deep in my mare's coarse black mane, when my face flamed.

Something, I have no idea what, made me wonder if in fact Coel had been talking about two things: the riding of a horse, and the riding of a woman by a man.

I glanced back to him, to see what was on his face, but he had turned about, and kicked his horse forward to the front of the column, my own mare following obediently. For many hours after that he did not speak to me but for the occasional passing comment, but merely led me into wonder.

ALTHOUGH FOR THIS FIRST PART OF OUR RIDE WE passed through forest, the trees were not so close that I couldn't see through them, nor so dense that they blocked out the sun. This forest was not imprisoning, but liberating. We rode through the most delightful dappled light, and in glades and among the trees the most lovely of flowers blossomed. Above us warbled birds, the like of which I'd never heard before, and butterflies and great, brightly colored dragonflies that dashed from plant to plant, and high into the trees. If I half closed my eyes then the dappled light and the brightly colored insects darting this way and that combined into a wonderful kaleidoscope that lulled me into a state of such tranquillity that I could almost believe that nothing bad had ever, or would ever, touch me.

Then the lurching of the horse would disturb my dreams, and my body would complain loudly, and I would grit my teeth and study Coel's straight, graceful back to distract myself from the discomfort. He always seemed to sense whenever I felt my muscles ache, for he would always pull his horse back until we rode side by side, and engage me in pleasant conversation until my aches were forgotten.

SO WE CONTINUED.

For several days we journeyed through wooded country in a northeasterly direction. It was not always as beautiful as that first day's ride, for sometimes we rode through patches of woodland where the trees had died, and the grasses turned to mildewed mush. On these occasions, if I happened to see Coel's face, I noticed that it was grim, and his usually laughing mouth closed in a thin line.

Usually, as we rode through these dark patches, he would swivel about on his horse, his eyes seeking out Blangan, and send her a glance of such malevolence that it left me breathless.

It was the only time that Coel ever acknowledged Blangan's presence.

The weather continued amenable, although it was cold at night, and I was glad for Brutus' warmth against my back and the roaring fires that either Jago or Bladud or one of the Trojan warriors tended throughout the night.

The horse's rocking gait and its slip-sliding spine continued very painful for the first two days, but after that I grew more used to my conveyance, and my muscles slowly ceased their grumbling.

Like a virgin who grows used to a man's intrusions . . . as Coel had intimated.

For this period of traveling Achates continued mostly in Aethylla's care. After all, it was her breasts he fed from. Besides, she had a broader back than mine, and it was better he traveled bound tight against her than against my teetering form. But at night when we dismounted, and in the morning, I was glad to hold him and caress him, and sing to him the songs that my nurse Tavia had sung above my own cradle.

After three days the landscape changed. The woods fell back until we traveled over gently undulating meadowland, filled with flowers and birds and the most heady, sweet scent that rolled down from the highlands to our west. Now we rode into the land of people, for every day we encountered at least one collection of round houses atop a small hill or mound, often surrounded by a palisade of wood, and always with a patchwork of fields encircling the village compound.

The villagers were unsettled by us, and whenever we approached, Coel would hand my mare's halter rope over to either Bladud or Jago and ride into the village. There he would reassure the villagers—I could always see their shoulders relax and their faces lighten as Coel spoke to them—and he would request from them some provisions, which they always seemed to provide willingly.

As we waited for Coel to return to our party, I would glance about at the village. All the houses were circular, their walls made either of stone or, more usually, wood or mud-packed wickerwork, with a single, low door for egress. They had no windows, and I thought that inside they must be smoky indeed, as the houses' thatched conical roofs had no opening for their occupants' cooking fires.

There were always flocks of sheep and goats and pens of massive, blotched, and ill-tempered tusked pigs. Often some of the beasts looked sickly, and I wondered what ailed them.

One day, I saw a sheep attempting to suckle a lamb with five legs, and I felt sick to my stomach, and grateful that Achates was such a beautiful and healthy child.

TWO DAYS INTO THE MEADOWLANDS, WE CAMPED for the night a little distance from a clutch of tumbled rocks that held within their midst a hot spring.

I could hardly believe my luck. After five days of riding, even though the pace had been easy and we rarely moved the horses out of a walk, I felt filthy with sweat—not only mine, but my mare's as well, for she was much given to lathering and foaming. Brutus took one look at my face as I stared at the steaming pool some twenty or thirty paces distant, and laughed, and told me that I had time enough for a good soaking before our meal was ready.

It was bliss. I swear I almost tore off my robe in my haste to jump into the water—which jumping I instantly regretted as the overly hot water bit into my flesh. But within minutes I relaxed and closed my eyes, sighing with delight as I heard the distant sounds of people talking and working to set up our night's camp.

When I opened my eyes again, I saw that Coel—completely naked—was sitting at the edge of the pool, about to slip in himself.

His nakedness—or mine, for that matter—did not perturb me in itself. Nakedness was never frowned upon in Mesopotama, and most of the court had spent their time in a state of near, and even complete, nakedness.

And on the voyage to this land, there had been little opportunity for privacy on board those crowded vessels. Every time I moved about the ship I stepped over naked men and women trying to wash themselves, or changing their garments, or simply enjoying the feel of the sea air on their exposed flesh.

Neither was it unusual to have to move over or about men and women coupling: every part of life had to be lived amid the crowd.

A naked body, whether a man's or woman's, simply did not bother me.

But Coel's unclothed body made me very, very uneasy.

"Am I intruding?" he said.

"No," I said, meaning "Yes!" and then stared at him as he ignored my unspoken discomfort and slid slowly down into the water, closing his eyes in exquisite discomfort as the hot water crawled up his body.

I couldn't take my eyes off him. He was like this land, almost an extension of it: powerful, mysterious, beautiful, haunting.

He slid under the water completely, his black hair floating momentarily over the spot where he had disappeared, then it vanished as well.

I felt a tingle of apprehension, and glanced about, hoping Brutus was close, and yet, at the same time, hoping he was far away.

His voice sounded, and I jumped, but it was indeed very far away.

And then I jumped again, even more so, for Coel surfaced in a foam of bubbles directly before me.

I slipped on the rock on which I had sat myself, and Coel grabbed at me, steadying me in the water.

His hands were about my waist, and we were suddenly very, very close.

"Do you know," he said, "that in Llangarlia women do not take husbands? That there is no one to guard women's beds in sustained and outraged jealousy?"

"I had heard that," I stuttered.

"Instead, women take men as men appeal to them. There is no jealousy, no bad feeling. Merely"—his hands moved, running up my body to my breasts—"the seduction of freedom."

"Coel," I said. "Don't."

"You want to," he replied, his dark eyes reading mine with a disconcerting accuracy.

"I—" I began.

"Your mind has barely strayed from the pleasures of the bed since we set out," he said, my ever-deepening flush all the confirmation he needed.

"I was thinking of Brutus."

"Really?" he said. "And now?"

I hoped to every god I could think of that Coel could not read the images that filled my mind at this moment.

He smiled, very slightly, and I knew that he could.

Something clenched, deep within my belly; a tightness that I could hardly bear.

"The water is freedom," he said, running his thumbs over my nipples. "Can you feel it?"

"Yes," I whispered, closing my eyes. *Damn him!* I wanted to resist—it would be my death (or at least the death of my hopes) if Brutus found us together like this—but there was something in him that called to me as powerfully, as irresistibly, as did this land.

Was he the man I waited for in the stone hall?

No . . . no. That was Brutus. I was sure of it.

"Can you feel the power of the water?" he whispered.

Indeed, I could feel it. Come to that, I could feel the power that was in him.

"If you allow me entry to your body, if you allow me to

slide deep inside you in this pool, then it will not be a betrayal of your husband, but merely a prayer to Mag herself. A confirmation of your own womanhood and the power of your womb."

I could feel his breath fanning over my face, feel his words—*a prayer to Mag herself*—vibrate through my body and touch something very deep inside me. Without thinking about it, without considering the consequences, I leaned forward, and let him kiss me.

And he kissed me as Brutus had never kissed me.

Oh, gods, his mouth tasted wonderful, his tongue as strong as his hands and as sweet as honey, and as he slid his hands behind my back and pressed my breasts against his chest I moaned, and gave myself up completely to the pressure of his mouth.

His hands, now on my hips, lifted me a little so that I floated up in the water, and then he brought them close to him, and my legs parted as if of their own accord, and wrapped themselves about his body and I felt the tip of his penis just, just *barely*, enter me.

I let my hips relax, and allowed him to thrust deep inside me.

Brutus' voice sounded, a little closer.

I panicked, hardly believing I had allowed this to progress so far, and pressing my hands against Coel's chest, pushed him away with all my might, hating the feel of him leaving me, but knowing there was nothing else I could do.

Coel's face was stunned, but it was not because of my abrupt rejection of him at a moment that would normally have driven any man into a grim, frustrated anger.

He stared at me, treading water a few paces distant. "By Mag and Og," he whispered. "Who are you, Cornelia? What was it that I felt just then?"

I clambered from the pool, drew on my filthy clothes directly over my dripping body, and ran back to camp and my husband.

When we sat down to our meal, Coel now rejoined us,

and as calm as if nothing had happened, I drank a little more liberally of the honey and meadowsweet wine than I usually did.

LATER THAT NIGHT I FOUND MYSELF OPPOSITE the fire from Coel. Brutus was sitting next to me, and with the coldness of the night a suitable excuse, I pressed myself close to him, and was rewarded with a smile and the pressure of his arm.

But I could not look away from Coel, nor forget the feel of his hands about my breasts or his tongue in my mouth.

I could see him through the flickering flames, see his eyes on me, and I remembered even more intimately how it had felt to have him kiss me in the pool, and how our bodies had felt so good together, how we had fitted together so perfectly . . .

I still couldn't believe I'd let him do what he had. Hera, had Brutus discovered us . . .

He would have discarded me utterly. Then and there. A few choice, harsh words, some flung recriminations, and then he would have turned his back and walked away and I would have lost the chance forever to have him hold me, and love me, and place me by his side as his equal.

I would have lost Achates, for my son had no need for my body—Aethylla fed him, and would no doubt have been pleased to see Brutus discard me as a piece of whorish trash.

I would have lost it all. Brutus, his love and regard. My son.

All for a moment's pleasure with Coel.

Perhaps I *was* nothing but a piece of whorish trash!

I snuggled closer to Brutus, but still I could not tear my eyes away from Coel. Suddenly the gloom of the night swept over me and that was not Coel sitting across the fire from me at all, but a strange, terrible man with a head so repulsive, so deformed, he could not possibly . . . he could not possibly . . . *I* could not possibly . . . his eyes burned into mine . . . and, oh, Hera—

Brutus spoke, and broke the spell, and I finally managed to wrench my eyes away from Coel.

THAT NIGHT, WHEN WE HAD ALL EATEN AND BED-ded down for the night, I turned to Brutus, and placed his hand on my breast. Surprised, both that I should want to make love so soon after childbed *and* that I should be the one wanting in the first instance, he nevertheless responded, and I know that our grunts and breathless, muffled cries must have entertained our huddled fireside companions.

It was uncomfortable at first, this lovemaking (even though those brief moments with Coel had held no discomfort at all), but I soon forgot my soreness, and gave myself entirely to the pleasure that Brutus offered.

At the last moment, when reason had all but deserted me, the fingers of my hands tangled themselves in Brutus' wild hair. But they did not encounter his wiry curls, rather the soft velvet of antlers . . .

Or the hard rasp of a bull's horn, perhaps. I was not sure.

I WAS VERY QUIET IN THE MORNING, SUBDUED, and I would not meet Coel's eyes.

Chapter Ten

THE GROUP WAS QUIET AS THEY PREPARED TO break camp and move out, and Brutus wondered whether it was because he and Cornelia had made love so conspicuously the night before, or if the dampness of the mist had laid its heavy pall over everyone's spirits.

Brutus himself felt edgy, and irritated with that edginess. Cornelia's responses last night had surprised him, yet they had also made him wonder. There had been something about their lovemaking . . . something he could not recognize.

Something unknowable, and somehow dark.

And Brutus had hardly failed to notice the intense looks passed between Coel and Cornelia as they'd sat about their hearth fire. They'd been *so* intense he'd spent part of the evening wondering if Coel had been the face on the man in his vision of the stone hall . . .

Well, if he was edgy, then Corineus was in a completely foul mood. Brutus heard him snapping at Coel regarding the way the three Llangarlian men were ignoring Blangan. Coel just shrugged and walked away which made Corineus curse foully—something Brutus had never heard him do previously.

And why was Corineus in such a foul mood? Just for Blangan's sake—or because Corineus was jealous of Brutus' lovemaking with Cornelia last night . . . or even of Cornelia's heated glances to Coel?

Ah! Brutus shook off his unease. No one could wake into this thick, clinging fog, knowing they would have to spend the day trudging their way through it, and remain cheerful.

"How long now?" Brutus asked Coel as he slung a cloak across his shoulders, drawing it tight about his neck against the water droplets in the air. Behind him his horse snorted, then shivered, and Brutus felt it shift closer to him.

"Until we reach the Veiled Hills?" Coel asked, and Brutus nodded.

"Another seven days' ride," Coel said, then glanced at Jago and Bladud, standing silent by their horses' heads, and then to Blangan who already sat her horse a little distance away.

Coel looked back to Brutus, then suddenly bent and

scooped a small amount of loamy earth in his hand. "But in a sense, Brutus, we are here already."

Brutus frowned.

"We are now within the circle of the hills' influence," Coel said, a strange half smile playing about his lips. "This land, this soil, is a part of the Veiled Hills. Feel the throb of the hills, albeit soft at this distance."

Cornelia had now come to stand at Brutus' shoulder, leaning against him as did his horse, seeking either warmth or reassurance. He hesitated slightly, seeing another glance pass between Cornelia and Coel, then slid a possessive arm under her cloak and about her waist, pulling her very close.

"This land is like a body," Coel said, his eyes now resting on Cornelia, and Brutus felt her shiver under his arm, "and the Veiled Hills its sacred heart. At a vast distance you cannot even feel the beat of that heart, but here, closer, we can feel its throb. All of us." Now Coel's eyes slid to Blangan who looked quickly away.

"This is all very well," said Aethylla, who was sitting her own horse on the other side of Blangan, and so thickly wrapped with blankets about her and the two babies she had slung across her back that she looked like a gray tree stump tied to her horse's back, "but I am cold, whatever heartbeat *you* feel. I would prefer moving to this standing about talking of throbbing dirt. Perhaps we can stay the night in a village for a change. My cold bones fancy a hospitable house with a broad and well-lit hearth."

Brutus laughed, gave Cornelia's waist one last squeeze, and the group mounted and set off.

THE FOG LIFTED AS THEY PROGRESSED, AND BY midmorning Coel had led them onto a well-traveled trackway that wound northeasterly. Their way was easier-going here, the road packed gravel, and the horses picked up both their ears and their stride as if they, too, sensed that heartbeat Coel had talked about. The land continued green and verdant, wildflowers spread in great blossoming drifts up the sides of the low hills. Here and there Brutus could see the thin trails of smoke in the air, and knew that within the hills lay villages or scattered farming communities.

Just before midday, as the weak sun had finally managed to warm both riders and horses, they rode about the curve of a small hill. Before them the land flattened out a little, although it once again rose toward a mound some hundred paces distant.

A family group of aurochs—a bull, five or six cows and their young—grazed on the mound's slopes, but even the sight of these huge black and tan horned creatures could not distract the groups' eyes from what sat on the summit of the mound.

A circle of gray stones, twice the height of a man, and capped by lintel stones about the entire circle. On the eastern side of the mound there was an avenue of small standing and lintel stones that led into the stone circle.

Behind him, Brutus thought he heard Blangan murmur something—a prayer, perhaps.

He was about to turn to her when Coel spoke. "Behold," he said, indicating the mound. "That mound and its stones is a deeply sacred place."

"How so?" said Brutus, forgetting Blangan.

"These circle of stones are called Stone Dances," said Coel, but before he could add any more, Cornelia spoke.

"They are places deeply sacred to women."

Everyone twisted about on their horses to look at her, their expressions ranging from puzzled to stunned.

"How did you know that, Cornelia?" said Coel.

She had her hand resting lightly on her own belly, and she dropped it away under Coel's intent gaze.

"It is obvious," she said. "Look, that avenue of stones leading into the circle. It depicts a woman's birth canal leading into her womb."

Coel nodded, more intrigued with her than ever. He felt Brutus' eyes on him, and he let his own gaze drift away from Cornelia and back to her husband. "The Stone Dances have been used for hundreds of generations as potent places for fertility rites," he said.

"It is where the stag comes to mate," Blangan said, making everyone look at her as they had previously looked at Cornelia. This time the looks ranged from the interested to the coldly antagonistic.

She ignored most of them, and smiled at Cornelia. "It is shame, perhaps, that you will not witness any of these."

"The Stone Dances are rarely used?" Brutus said, trying to deflect some of Coel's and his two companions' hostility away from Blangan. From what Brutus could see of the circle of stones, the Stone Dance, it was not only well built, but an imposing site that dominated the entire surrounding landscape. He could imagine people, many thousands of people, perhaps with torches in the deep mystery of the night, moving up the hill toward the Stone Dance, and a shiver ran up his spine at the image.

"There are certain ceremonies that are still held within the Stone Dances," Coel said, "and people who live close by them continue to use them throughout the year. But the most sacred of our ceremonies, our most sincere rites to Og and Mag, are now conducted within the Veiled Hills."

Then Cornelia spoke again, and what she said sent a jolt of fear deep into Brutus' belly.

"Is that where the stone hall is?" she said to Coel.

He frowned. "The stone hall?"

"A hall built of stone, ten times the height of the stones in the Dance beyond, great arches for walls, and a domed golden roof. Is it in these Veiled Hills?"

Brutus' mouth thinned at the eagerness in her voice.

"We have no such hall," Coel said, his voice soft and puzzled. "There is an Assembly House made of stone, but is it not so large as you describe, and has no arches, nor a golden domed roof."

Brutus let out a soft breath, allowing himself to relax. It was just a dream, nothing more, and perhaps merely something he'd caught from Cornelia because of their proximity in bed. It didn't exist.

"Cornelia," he said. "Do not trouble Coel with your childish fancies. We have better things to do than listen to your dreams."

"I never tire of listening to dreams," Coel said softly, looking Brutus in the eye. "I find they add beauty to what is otherwise unbearable."

It was Brutus who looked away first.

FOR TWO MORE DAYS THEY TRAVELED, PASSING sereral more Stone Dances on their way, and on the third day they came in the evening to a village that rested some five hundred paces away from the largest and most imposing of the Stone Dances they had yet encountered.

Looking at it, Blangan lost what little color remained in her face.

She knew why they'd come here.

Chapter Eleven

THIS TIME THE VILLAGE HEADWOMAN—THE mother of this particular clan—agreed to Coel's request that he and his companions might stay in her village for the night. The Mother's name was Ecub, a woman in her late middle age, her face worn, her body slightly stooped with the hardness of her life, and with a flintiness in her sharp brown eyes that made it difficult to believe she could ever unbend enough to love.

She greeted the group politely, moving from one to the other, taking the person's hands in hers and briefly laying her cheek to theirs. She had greeted Coel first, her hands squeezing his slightly harder than they squeezed anyone else's, then moved to Brutus, who she studied with marked speculation, then Cornelia, who caused her a puzzled frown.

As she drew back from laying her cheek to Cornelia's, Ecub said, "You have given birth recently?"

"Yes," Cornelia responded. "A few weeks ago. See, my son nestles at Aethylla's back."

Ecub completely ignored Aethylla and Achates. She had not yet let go of Cornelia's hands, and she tightened them momentarily. "Yes. You have just given birth. That must be it."

Then she dropped Cornelia's hands and moved on before either Cornelia or Brutus could say anything.

Ecub moved through the group, greeting each in turn, until she finally reached Blangan.

"You have caused us the world of trouble, girl," Ecub said in a flat voice. "Have you not seen the blight on this land as you passed through it?"

"It was not I, Mother Ecub," Blangan said.

Ecub's mouth twisted disdainfully. "You are not your mother's daughter."

Surprisingly, Blangan managed a smile at that. "No," she said, "I think that may be safely assumed."

VARIOUS MEMBERS OF THE GROUP WERE BEDDED in several of the circular stone-walled houses in Ecub's village—Coel, Brutus and Cornelia, and Corineus and Blangan were to sleep in Ecub's personal house—but everyone met in Ecub's house for the evening meal.

This was the first time the Trojans had been inside an Llangarlian house, and they looked about them curiously.

The circular stone walls, only shoulder height from the outside, were sunk into the ground so that the internal floor of hard-packed earth and stone flagging was several steps lower than ground level. Combined with the high, conical thatched roof, that meant that the house was much roomier inside than external appearances indicated.

The low door opened onto several steps that led down

to the floor that was dominated by a large central hearth. Here a huge pile of coals glowed, serving both as a cooking fire and a means to heat the house. Several earthenware cooking pots sat in the coals, the steam rising from their lids making everyone's mouth water.

Bedding niches had been built into the walls, all piled high with animal skins, furs, and woven woolen blankets and covers over the straw and woolen bedding, while tools and other farming implements hung from the walls and roofing rafters, along with dried vegetables and smoked meats and baskets of preserved eggs and fish. In one part of the floor were tightly woven wicker lids that hid deep food and grain storage pits sunk into the earth.

The house smelled of smoke, of the spice of the dried foods and of those cooking in the coals, and of the stale musk of human bodies packed into a relatively small space.

Ecub, her brothers and sons, as well as her daughters and their children, lived in this house; some twenty people all crowded into a circular space some twenty-five feet across.

Benches and stools had been set about the hearth, and to these Ecub's daughters—two women of mature childbearing years—directed their guests.

With Ecub's immediate family, and the eleven members of the traveling band, it would be a tight fit indeed.

But fit they did, and once everyone was seated Ecub's daughters and granddaughters handed about a rich stew that they ladled into semi-hollowed out portions of heavy grained bread. Salad herbs and cooked vegetables lay on plates about the hearth, and after Ecub had said a blessing to Og and Mag for the bounty of the food, everyone fell to.

Ecub also handed about flasks of wine, and this was wine such as the Trojans had not yet tasted. It was honey wine, but without much of the cloying sweetness, and with an undertaste of herbs and flowers that lent it a complexity that made many among the Trojans reach again and again for the flask.

Ecub caught Coel's eyes, and smiled secretly.

Once the food had gone—but with the flasks of wine still being passed about—Ecub said a word to one of her sons, and he picked up a small drum and began to play upon it a complex, throbbing beat.

Shoulders dipped and swayed, and eyes half closed as people gave themselves to the power of the music.

Again Ecub said a word, and her two daughters rose, loosened their hair and the belts that held their robes close to their bodies, and began to dance.

Like the throb of the drum, it was a slow, sensual dance. They moved separately about the outer circle of benches and stools, but nevertheless danced to each other as if there was no one else present. It was a dance of lovers, and even though both the daughters were mothers themselves, and one was some five or six months gone with her next child, it was as though they were virgins, moving ever closer to that moment of their first bedding.

They twined about behind the people seated on the benches, their hips or hands or bellies occasionally brushing someone's shoulder or back, but always Ecub's daughters kept their eyes firmly fixed between themselves, acknowledging no one but the other, demonstrating desire for no one but the other.

Whenever they passed in their intricate orbits about the benches, their hands and lips would graze that of the other woman in abandoned promise.

Brutus was stirred by the women's dance as he had never before been moved. Part of it was sexual desire—the way these women moved their bodies, the patent sexual intent of their rhythmic motion, combined with the throb of the drum, meant that no one in the house could fail to be aroused—but the larger part was a sense that the dancers led him into a far deeper plane, an ancient mystical realm where strode gods and powers he could never hope to understand.

He drank heavily of the wine every time the flask came by him, and soon the wine throbbed inside his veins with the same beat of the drum, and every time one of the dancers passed behind him, and brushed him with hip or belly, he moaned, his hands clenching into fists where they lay on his thighs.

The Llangarlians, women and men, had closed their eyes to sight, and let themselves drown in the sound of the drum and the touch of the dancers. They seemed to know whenever the flask was being passed their way, for they put out their hands at precisely the right moment, grasped the flask, drank of it, and passed it on without ever opening their eyes or interrupting the swaying movements of their bodies.

The Trojans, too, although more inhibited, gave themselves to wine and music and dance, and soon everyone was half mad with drink and sensuality, and the dancers' rhythm increased until they were twirling about the circular rim of benches, their colorful robes a blur of brilliance, their hair and hands flying, and soon there was nothing but madness and pleasure, and people took partners as they pleased.

LATER, MUCH LATER WHEN THE NIGHT WAS STILL and cold, Ecub rose from her sleeping niche, leaving Coel fast in sleep behind her, and walked naked to where Blangan lay with Corineus.

She reached out a hand, but Blangan's eyes flew open before Ecub touched her.

"Is it time?" Blangan whispered.

Ecub nodded, and stepped back.

Blangan slowly rose, careful not to wake Corineus, then stood next to the bed, gazing down at her husband.

"How I have loved him," she said, then, her face composed but her eyes desperate, she followed Ecub out the door.

Chapter Twelve

Cornelia Speaks

J ROLLED OVER, AWAY FROM BRUTUS' WARMTH, and peered from under the thick wrapping that lay heavy and comforting over me.

I was rigid with foreboding, yet I could remember no dream, nor think of any reason why this should be.

Then I saw two naked female figures briefly highlighted in the open door.

It closed, but I'd only needed that brief glimpse to know who they had been: Ecub and Blangan.

Hera! What was going on? What were they doing to set out unclothed into the frigid night?

The deep, horrible sense of foreboding increased, and I felt as though my stomach was turning over and over in its panic. I'd begun to sweat, as though I were consumed with fear, and I felt my heart racing.

And yet there was nothing to fear . . . was there?

Unable to lie still, I slipped quietly from the bed, slid my feet into my leather shoes lying close by, and grabbed a cloak.

Pausing to make sure that everyone else slept on, I opened the door and followed Blangan and Ecub into the night.

I COULD NOT SEE THEM, BUT THAT DID NOT DIS-turb me. I was certain I knew where they were going.

The night was almost freezing, and I shivered, and pulled the cloak tight about me as I hurried through the few cir-cular houses of the village, past the pens where the village goats and sheep slumbered the night away, and onto the path that led through the harvested fields toward the plain in the distance.

Once I was on the track I saw Blangan and Ecub walking side by side, now well ahead of me. How could they walk so calmly? They must be frozen!

They were almost to the embankment that encircled the Stone Dance, and they had shifted from the path I was on to a broad raised pathway clearly defined by ditches on either side.

Something made them stop, and turn to look behind them.

They saw me instantly: in this treeless landscape they could hardly have missed me.

Blangan became excited, turning to Ecub and grabbing at her arm with one hand, pointing to me with the other.

Ecub shook her off, and said a few words.

Blangan subsided, but her entire body language projected misery.

I wondered why she didn't want me to come to the Dance. I suppose I should have taken note of Blangan's fear, her wish that I not follow, but my foreboding had grown stronger with every step toward that Dance that I took, and there was nothing that could stop me now.

What was wrong?

All I knew was that my foreboding somehow involved Blangan, and for love of her I kept on going.

As I continued to walk forward, my breath frosting about me, Ecub lifted a hand, pointed it at me, then slowly moved it about until it pointed at the raised path on which they stood.

The message was clear: *You may join us, but to do so you must walk this path.*

I nodded, and cut across the turf between their path and mine. The going was difficult, and I stumbled several times, once almost falling.

I was wondering why on earth I was out here in the freezing night, and had started to think that the wise and sensible thing would be to return to my warm bed and husband, when the raised pathway suddenly loomed before me. I climbed down into the ditch, then scrambled up to the path's surface using my hands for purchase.

Blangan and Ecub had gone, presumably inside the Stone Dance where the great dark monoliths, topped with their oppressive lintel stones, were now wreathed in thick garlands of a faintly yellowed fog.

When I had left the smaller pathway to cross to this raised one, the night had been frosty and clear.

It still was, where I stood, but not where the Stone Dance rose.

There, mystery gathered.

Suddenly Ecub appeared, standing alone, dwarfed by the stones towering over her. She saw me, and beckoned again.

I took a step toward her, hesitated, then took another, then another, and before I knew why I was walking swiftly toward the Stone Dance.

Ecub held up a hand just before I reached the circle of stone—twin circles, I could see now, as there was an inner ring of smaller stones.

"Stop," Ecub said. "Why have you come?"

I licked my lips, then spoke the truth. "Because I fear for Blangan."

"How did you wake?" Ecub said, ignoring my remark about Blangan. "The wine was drugged so most would sleep insensible."

Most? Hera, who else was going to join us?

"Fear woke me," I said, my eye sliding past her beyond the stones. "Fear for Blangan."

"Blangan is not deserving of such care," Ecub said, her voice hard.

"To me she is," I said quietly. "I love her dearly."

Ecub was unmoved by my words. "Only Mag herself knows why you are here," she said. "Only she could have woken you."

"Then Mag must care for Blangan, too."

Ecub's face flushed—with anger, I think. "Mag has no care for Blangan at all!" she said. "Now, as you are here, and I must assume there is a reason for it, then you may enter. But stay with me, and do only as I tell you.

"And divest yourself of your clothes. Mag's Dance will only accept you naked."

I hesitated, unnerved not so much by any thought of modesty but because of the frigid air. How could Ecub stand so calmly, so still, when her flesh must be screaming for warmth?

"You will be warm enough," Ecub said, and so I shrugged off my cloak and kicked my shoes to one side.

Ecub looked at the faint lines of pregnancy still visible on my belly, and nodded. "Your fertility blesses you," she said. "Enter."

And with that she turned, and walked into the stones.

With no more hesitation, but with my unknown sense of fear growing every moment, I, too, stepped into Mag's Dance.

WE STOOD WITHIN THE OUTER CIRCLE OF MONO-liths, halfway between it and the inner, smaller circle.

"This is the greatest Stone Dance of them all," Ecub's soft voice said. "This is Mag's Dance, her Dance, her womb."

She led me to the very center of the Dance through the inner circle of smaller and uncapped stones to where five great stone arches stood in a "U" shape.

"The cup of the womb," said Ecub, and reached down to the foot of one of the arches. She lifted up a flask. "Drink," she said, and handed it to me.

I hesitated, and looked at Ecub.

The woman's eyes glinted at me, daring me. "Are you afraid?" she said.

Yes, I wanted to answer. "No," I said, raising the flask to my lips, drank deeply of the warm, pungent liquid within.

It bit into my throat, then into my stomach, and I gagged,

spilling some of the liquid from my mouth as I all but dropped the flask.

"Careful," said Ecub, tut-tutting as if she was, indeed, my mother. "Do not drink too much."

"Who would want to?" I murmured, and she smiled, and took the flask and drank deeply of it herself.

She saw me staring as she finally lowered the flask. "I am used to it," she said, her words lightly slurred, and I found that when I opened my mouth to comment my mouth, too, did not work well.

My tongue and throat felt thick, as if they were coated with rotten honey, and I gagged once more, and would have retched had not Ecub grabbed my arm and put a hand to my forehead.

"Be still," she said, and some of the rotten taste and thickness in my mouth and throat faded, and I felt easier again.

I relaxed a little, and Ecub must have felt it under her hands. She smiled, and I saw that her face was beautiful— far more beautiful than I had previously thought.

Was it the starlight? I wondered.

"You are a mother," she whispered, the hand on my arm now sliding over my breasts, oh, so slowly, and my belly. "You are beautiful in Mag's eyes. Whatever happens here tonight, Cornelia, Mag will protect and nurture you. She is strong here tonight, stronger than I have felt her in many, many years." Ecub's voice, oddly, sounded rather surprised. "I think you bring a blessing to this Dance, strange Cornelia."

"I had no thought to," I said. "Where is Blangan? Should she not also drink?"

"No," said Ecub. "I have asked Blangan to wait at the outer circle. She does not know of the frenzy wine."

Frenzy wine? I thought, and then realized that Ecub must have put this wine here earlier as she had very obviously carried nothing to the Dance on her way here with Blangan.

This night was planned long before we arrived.

"Mag has brought you here," whispered Ecub, and I

thought her voice sounded as if it came from a distance greater than that of the stars. "But not through fear for Blangan, I think. She wants you to witness something, Cornelia."

"What . . ." I mumbled. The frenzy wine was coursing through my blood, and I could not think in a straight line. The stones about me blurred, melding one into the other until it seemed as if I were enclosed within a solid wall of stone.

"You are within Mag's womb," Ecub whispered. "See . . ."

She spread her hand out before me.

Figures suddenly emerged from the stone. Men. Women. Beasts. A donkey, draped in ribbons and baubles. A stunningly beautiful white mare. An auroch, flowers festooning its horns. A wiry sheep, bleating pitifully.

"Here, in this circle," Ecub whispered, "in Mag's womb, came men and women to celebrate the gift of life, and to offer dance and frenzy to Mag and Og in thanks for their fertility and life. See."

And I saw the men and women, dancing and writhing, copulating on the ground and in the spaces between the stones.

One naked, muscular man stood out, for on his head he wore the bloodied antlers of a stag. He seized a woman, and rode her as a bull rides a cow, then let her go when she started to shriek. He took another woman, then another, then yet one more, and all shrieked, although whether in fear or joy I could not tell.

The circles of stone blurred, and I felt faint, and only the pressure of Ecub's hand on my arm kept me upright.

"This is not now," she whispered. "This is what is past. Do you understand?"

"Yes," I said, my eyes still on the man who wore the stag antlers. He had just left a woman, and stood not five paces from me.

Our eyes met, and held.

I moaned, wondering if he would take me, for I found

myself wanting him more than anything I had ever previously lusted for in life.

The donkey wandered between us, and the man seized it.

I cried out, but both the man and Ecub laughed. The man grabbed the donkey's hindquarters in his strong hands, and drew her toward him.

He mounted her, thrusting strongly, and the donkey and I shrieked at exactly the same time, and . . .

. . . then everything vanished, and I stood again amid the circles of stone, Ecub by my side.

The writhing, copulating couples had gone; the stag man had gone; the donkey had gone, as had all the other beasts.

Now Blangan walked toward us, summoned by a soft word from Ecub, her naked skin gleaming soft ivory in the starlight.

I had always thought Blangan somewhat plain, but here, now, within these magical circles and with the frenzy wine throbbing through my veins, I thought her beautiful. Her limbs were perfectly formed, her hips and belly, like mine, rounded through motherhood. Her breasts were small globes, like firm apples, and her nipples were likewise girlishly small and pale pink.

I jumped. Beside me Ecub had begun to clap a haunting rhythm with her hands; much like what her daughters had danced to, this beat was nonetheless far stronger and more potent.

It throbbed, as the frenzy wine throbbed, and both Blangan and I moaned.

"Dance!" said Ecub, and Blangan began a hauntingly slow, beautiful dance.

Her movements looked first like a sapling bending in a breeze, then like a field of grain, waving in the wind. Her movement quickened, and although she never danced as wildly or as quickly as Ecub's daughters had done, her dance nevertheless seemed far more powerful, and far more secret. Her feet blurred, their movements intricate, tapping out the rhythm of Ecub's hands, and she swayed this way and that, weaving a pattern through the twin circles of stones, and the arches within the center.

She looked like one possessed, and yet at the same time everything she did, every movement, every tap of her foot and arch of an arm, was clearly part of a deliberate pattern of movement.

Her passage through and between the circles of stone was labyrinthlike, beautiful, demanding, complex. How could anyone learn these steps?

My own body yearned to sway and dip as did Blangan's.

"She remembers what Mag taught her as a girl," Ecub said over the beat of her clapping hands. "This is Mag's Nuptial Dance, Cornelia. Her mating dance."

"Mates with whom?" I whispered, yet knowing the answer.

The stag man, the wild beast of the forest.

I gave in to my impulses, and began to sway back and forth with the rhythm of Ecub's hands.

"Only initiates into Mag's ways can dance this—" Ecub began, and then she stopped, or I failed to hear the rest of what she said, for the frenzy wine was soaring through my blood, and I found my feet moving, and my arms, and then I was in among the stones as well, dancing with Blangan.

Behind me I very faintly heard Ecub cry out something in surprise, or warning, but I did not care. I found that this dance seemed to rise from the very pit of my womb, as if I had known it all my life, and all my unborn life before that.

Blangan saw me, and her face suffused with joy. We laughed at each other, then rather like Ecub's daughters, we effortlessly joined our dances into the one. We danced in counterpoint, each one mirroring the other's movements through different quadrants of the circles.

My chest tightened, my breath harshened, my feet blistered with the agony of the dance, my breasts and belly burned with the liquid tempo of my body.

Thoughts of the man with the stag antlers filled my mind,

and I wished he could see me as now, wished he could see my dance.

The stones about me blurred, the stars in the sky became one blinding searing light, and I thought I must be near death . . .

. . . and then everything stopped.

I opened my eyes. I stood, breathing deeply but not heavily, under one of the lintels in the outer circle of stone. Blangan stood directly opposite me across the twin circles, under her own lintel.

Ecub stood between us, her hands fallen still, and I realized we had stopped dancing the instant she had stopped her clapping.

I gazed about me.

The mist that had been drifting between the stones when first I'd approached Mag's Dance had now thickened. The stones themselves still loomed through the mist, but the surrounding countryside had gone.

The stars had vanished overhead, and all the noises of the night—the wind, the rustling of grasses and shrubs, the sleep movements and chirpings of birds—had stilled.

I looked again at Ecub—her hands folded before her, her face lowered—and then at Blangan who was staring at me with such profound love on her face that my breath caught in my throat.

"Oh, thank you, Cornelia," she said, her soft voice reaching me even though a vast distance separated us. "Thank you for so blessing me tonight."

I gulped, not so much at what she said, but because she looked lovelier than I had ever seen any woman. Her face was alight, her eyes shining, her mouth slightly parted to show the tips of her white teeth.

And then the foreboding roared through me more vicious that it had heretofore been. For no other reason, I think, than the fear that gripped me, I remembered Hera's warning: *Beware of the Horned One. The Bull. The Enemy. Asterion.*

"Blangan!" I cried, and would have moved to her save that she held up a hand to halt me.

"Fear not for me, for I have seen what you are, and it comforts me. I am not sad, but blessed. Be still, Mag, for I am content in your love."

I think I saw Ecub lift her head slightly at that last, and stare between Blangan and myself, but I paid her no mind. The inner core of foreboding, that terrible distress, had suddenly ebbed, but my own fear and love for Blangan kept me tense and afraid.

"Be still," Blangan said again.

Then I heard footsteps.

Behind me.

I turned toward the sound, my heart thudding, and Hera's warning suddenly very much to the forefront of my mind.

The footfalls approached steadily—yet with a deliberate slowness—from that part of the fog that overlay the raised pathway leading to Mag's Dance. The archway under which I stood was the entrance archway into Mag's Dance, and I should have been afraid, I should have been *terrified*, because whoever (*whatever*) made those footsteps would enter via this archway.

But someone spoke to me, I suppose it was either Ecub or Blangan, and said, *Be still, Cornelia. This is not the Bull, not Asterion. Be still.*

My hand hovered over my womb, and I felt a sense of safety so consuming I relaxed, and let my fears slide away.

Not the Bull. Not Asterion.

I straightened my shoulders, and lifted my chin, and waited.

WHEN HE—IT—WALKED OUT OF THE MIST I WAS NOT surprised.

It was the stag man I had seen copulating with the women and the donkey, and yet it was not. The man I had seen had antlers tied to his head with thongs, he had been a representation (*of Og*, something whispered in my mind) only.

This man had no antlers tied to his head; rather, he had four or five horned spurs growing from his skull. White protuberances that glistened with exposed blood vessels and bone . . . and yet that looked velvety smooth to the touch.

He was monstrous, his entire skull and forehead deformed into something that should not, could not, have been allowed to live. Everything bulged as if he had uncontrollable tumors within his brain that demanded an escape; in places his scalp had burst to allow those horns egress, in other places scant, thin brown hair covered other protrusions that threatened to break through at any moment.

He stopped beside me, so close I could feel the heat from his naked body. Apart from his head he was as any man: hard-muscled, generously proportioned, brown-skinned from the sun.

But that head . . . and that distended face beneath it . . . Oh, Hera, he was ugly.

He reached out, and touched my breast, gently at first, and then cupping it in his strong hand.

Then he ran his hand over my belly. "Mag is powerful with you," he said, and I was stunned to hear such a melodious voice exit from such ugliness. "Yet how can that be in a stranger to this land? You draw me to you . . ." He sighed, and his entire body trembled. "If this had been another night, *any* other night, and you had danced for me, then I would have come, and together we should have protected and increased the herd."

I understood little of what he said, yet I felt the same powerful pull that he spoke of. My body trembled, and my flesh broke into a sweat.

"Perhaps—" I whispered, but he dropped his hand from me, and a hardness came over his face.

"Not tonight," he said. "Tonight is Og's night only. His resurrection amid the witch's death."

And suddenly, horribly, I knew why he was here.

Why Blangan was here.

He snarled, unexpectedly, viciously, and I jumped, breaking the contact between him and me.

He did not notice. In a flurry of movement, so fast his form blurred, the stag man closed the distance between himself and Blangan.

I jerked, and cried out, and would have moved to aid Blangan, but just then I heard yet *another* footfall behind me, and there was Coel, and he had wrapped his arms tightly about me so that I could not move.

"Leave it alone," he whispered harshly in my ear. "This does not concern you."

I wailed, horrified for Blangan, but Coel was too strong, and he raised one hand and clamped it over my mouth so that I could not even scream my horror.

All I could do was witness.

The stag man had grabbed Blangan's hair in one hand, and twisted it back so that her throat was exposed.

"Darkwitch!" he hissed, and I gasped, for I somehow realized that *this* was Blangan's son.

"I loved you, Loth," she whispered, her voice strained but nevertheless calm. "I love you still."

"Yet you destroyed the land!"

He dipped his head, and suckled at one of her breasts.

Blangan moaned. "It was not I," she whispered, and I could see that she was finally afraid, and that she fought with herself not to struggle.

"It is time," this Loth-thing said, raising his mouth slightly from his mother's breast, "to break the enchantment of your darkcraft and restore to Og his potency!"

His stance changed, and where one moment he had been suckling, the next he was biting, the muscles in his neck and shoulders bulging.

Blangan screamed, a thin high wail of absolute fear and torment.

Her son raised his head for an instant, and I caught a glimpse both of his blood-covered face, and of Blangan's left breast, now hanging from her rib cage by only a thin rope of flesh.

I gagged beneath Coel's hand, but I could not look away.

"It is time your evil died, Blangan."

And then he plunged his fist into her chest, shattering her ribs asunder.

THE WHITE STAG, ALREADY SKELETAL WITH LOSS OF power, writhed in its death agony as the hunter leaned down and tore out its heart.

It lay against the pure white of the stag's coat, beating and throbbing in its extremity, and then it lay still.

With the stag's last breath, Og's crippled power vanished completely from the land.

BLANGAN'S DEAD BODY FLOPPED TO THE ground, her still heart lying exposed on her belly.

Loth staggered back, his face a mask of terror and disbelief. "No! No!" he cried, Ecub's cries intermingling with his.

"What have I done?" Loth screamed, and I heard Coel cry out behind me.

"What have you done? What have you done?"

There was a long, long silence, where I could do nothing but stare at Blangan's corpse, and I could feel nothing but the viselike grip of Coel's arms about me.

Then Ecub said, in a very small voice, "This was not supposed to happen, Loth. You were supposed to kill Blangan, not Og with her."

NOT QUITE DEAD YET, SAID MAG WITHIN HER STONE hall. Then, before it was too late and using most of the power remaining to her, she cast a spell-weaving over the corpse of the poor half-starved stag lying on the forest floor, and its heart gave a single faint beat—so faint it was barely a tremor—as it would beat just once a year from henceforth until . . .

Until all has come to pass, Mag said, and then fainted in her own extremity.

SOMEONE ELSE SAID SOMETHING, I KNOW NOT what, for I felt a terrible loss within me, and I fainted.

Chapter Thirteen

CRADLED IN SLEEP, WRAPPED IN GENVISSA'S arms, watched by her appraising eyes, Aerne, Gormagog of Llangarlia and living representative of Og, suddenly screamed into wakefulness, hot torment coursing through his chest and brain.

He jerked upright, his hands clutching into the graying hair on his chest, his eyes staring almost out of their sockets, his mouth gaping in a rictus of agony.

"Aerne?" Genvissa cried, pressing herself against him. "Aerne?"

He expelled a wheezing breath, his fingers still scrabbling in his chest hair, jerked in another breath, then howled in both pain and loss.

"Aerne?" Genvissa cried again.

"Og is gone!" Aerne managed to say. "Something terrible has happened!"

"What? Where? How?"

"I can not tell—" Aerne was about to say more, but then he howled in pain again, and his entire body stiffened and then jerked.

He lay a long time, breathless, gray-skinned, sweating, as Genvissa whispered endearments and comforts to him, then, just before dawn, he whispered, "I am dying, Genvissa. All the life has been pulled from me. Maybe not today, or even next week, but death is close now."

"What can I do? Oh, dear Aerne! What can I do?"

He tried to smile for her, his beloved Genvissa, and lifted his hand and grasped hers in a weak grip. "You have already done what was needed, beloved. Bringing to Llangarlia's shores the Trojan magic. I will soon be gone, and Og's power is all lost. Loth cannot replace me, or be what it is that this land needs. If Llangarlia is to survive it will need the Trojan magic. Genvissa, I have doubted you, but now I can see that what you have done is truly for the best."

She smiled. "Of course it is, Aerne. Of course it is. Sleep now. Rest."

When he finally did sleep, Genvissa lay back beside him and closed her eyes.

Inside, she seethed, both with triumph and with frustration.

Og was dead, as Genvissa knew he would be when Loth murdered his mother—it was the final weaving in the darkcraft her mother Herron had cast.

But where was Mag? Genvissa had been *certain* she was lurking deep within Blangan's womb. While there had been a sudden drop in Mag's power as Og died, there had been no cessation of it, as there surely should have been had Mag been caught within Blangan's dying body.

Thus Mag must still be alive somewhere *else*, albeit weakened beyond measure.

Genvissa sighed, putting the problem aside. In the end it was of little matter. Mag was essentially powerless without Og, and could do little to stop Genvissa now.

Alive or dead, Mag was nothing.

COEL GRUNTED AS CORNELIA'S BODY FELL SLACK in his arms, and he lowered her carefully to the ground.

"In Og's name," he said, staring at Loth who was standing, white and shaking. "What has happened here?"

Loth did not answer him. He did not look as if he had even heard.

Coel turned to Ecub. "Ecub? What has happened? Has Og's power been restored?"

She swallowed, and shook her head.

Her skin was almost as pale and as clammy as Loth's.

She opened her mouth as if to answer, but before she could speak, Loth moaned pitifully, and fell to his knees beside Blangan's corpse. He grabbed at her still, blood-clotted heart and tried with shaking hands to shove it back inside her chest.

"What has happened?" Coel shouted, Loth's and Ecub's obvious distress terrifying him.

"Og was destroyed when Loth killed Blangan," Ecub whispered.

"I didn't know!" Loth cried out. "I had no idea!"

"But Og's power was supposed to be restored when Loth killed Blangan!" Coel said, his heart thudding painfully in his chest. Og's power could not have been *destroyed*. It could *not* have been! "Blangan's death was supposed to have shattered the darkcraft which had split Og's power. It was supposed to have—"

"Be quiet!" Loth screamed, twisting about to face Coel. He was holding his bloodied, trembling hands at chest height, his fingers curled into claws. "*Be quiet!*"

"Loth," Ecub said firmly. "You were not to know. Genvissa had told you . . ."

There was a long, horrified silence.

Loth managed to get to his feet, his hand still held before his chest. "Genvissa," he said. "I must speak with Genvissa . . ."

Swift as a striking adder, Ecub grabbed one of his wrists. "This was her doing, Loth."

"No, no, it could not be . . ."

"*This was her doing!* She had no need of Og! She has her Brutus now; her Trojan magic. This was her doing, Loth. Believe it."

"I must talk to her . . . there must be some reason . . ." Now it was Loth's voice that drifted off. "Oh, Ecub, what have I *done*?"

"Listen to me, Loth, Coel." Ecub's eyes flitted between the two. "We can do nothing until we find out exactly what has happened, and what caused it. We watch and we learn. For the moment that can be our only course of action."

"Og is *dead*!" Loth said, his face a tragic mix of pain and horror. *"I killed him!"*

"You were the weapon which killed him," Ecub said, *"but you were not the hand that wielded it!"*

"I have killed Og," Loth said, the trembling of his hands now far worse.

Ecub slapped him across the face, hard enough that Loth rocked on his feet.

He stared at her with pitiable eyes, but Ecub had no time for pity.

"You go back to the Veiled Hills," she said. "Find out what you can, but tread lightly, Loth, for Mag's sake if for no one else's! We must find out what is happening!"

He nodded. "I . . . I must wash my hands."

"Then do so in a stream as you travel north. Waste no more time here. Get to the Veiled Hills before Coel and Brutus arrive. *Find out what is happening!*"

Ecub's words finally filtered through Loth's numbed mind. "Yes. Yes, I will." He looked to Cornelia, lying senseless on the ground. "What do we do about her?"

"Coel and I will take care of her. Go, Loth. *Go!*"

WHEN HE'D GONE, ECUB TURNED TO COEL WHO BY now was looking almost as wretched as Loth had done.

"Take Cornelia and put her back to bed with Brutus. She's had many draughts of frenzy wine . . . if any god-favor is still with us then she will remember nothing when she wakes."

For a long minute they stared down at Cornelia's immobile, naked form.

"I thought she had some connection to Mag," said Coel eventually. "She drew me to her with such strength . . . and when I entered her . . . I felt such . . . such . . . ah, I must have dreamed it. She is so powerless now. Just an ordinary woman." He lifted his face to Ecub. "Did you feel anything from her?"

"I felt something—but maybe it was just a passing phantasm. So much is wrong in our world that I think nothing can be trusted, not even our senses."

Some of what Coel had said finally made some sense in Ecub's mind. "You *lay* with her?"

He shrugged. "Briefly. I entered her, but she drew away almost immediately."

Ecub looked down at Cornelia, still senseless, breathing quietly. "And what did you feel?" she said.

"I thought I felt Mag. But I must have been mistaken. There is nothing about her now that calls so powerfully to me."

"Yet she danced Mag's Nuptial Dance," Ecub said, still studying Cornelia.

"What? I did not see that."

"Well, she did. Although I suppose Blangan could have taught it to her."

"Perhaps," Coel said, but neither of them sounded convinced by the argument.

Ecub sighed, exhausted by the events of the night. "I suppose she shall have to remain a mystery to us for the moment, Coel. But watch her as you travel north. Sensible or senseless, she is still a puzzle. Take her back to her bed, Coel. Do it now. First light is not far distant."

He nodded, and bent down to Cornelia.

Chapter Fourteen

"BLANGAN! BLANGAN IS GONE!"

Brutus lurched out of his sleep, his mind confused with dream and weariness. Beside him Cornelia had sat up, the bedcovers clutched to her breasts, her eyes wide and disoriented.

Corineus stood by the central hearth of the house, his hair mussed, his chin stubbled, his entire stance taut with worry. "Blangan is gone!"

"She has likely gone to the privy pit," Brutus murmured, yawning and rubbing at his eyes with one hand.

"She is not there! I looked. She is *nowhere* in the village."

Brutus' hand stilled, and he looked at Corineus with a peculiar kind of intensity, as if the possibilities contained within the fact of Blangan's disappearance were only now occurring to him.

"Move over," he said to Cornelia, who drew up her knees and swiveled to one side so he could climb past her. The covers tangled in Brutus' legs as he tried to slide out of the bed, and he cursed and tugged hard enough at the blankets that he pulled them completely from the bed, leaving Cornelia naked and shivering in the sudden cold.

Brutus tossed Cornelia her robe, and pulled his own tunic quickly over his head, belting it as he slid on his shoes. He grabbed his cloak, and looked about the house.

Everyone was accounted for: Coel and his companions, Hicetaon—now also out of bed and dressing—and Aethylla and the babies, the two Trojan warriors who accompanied them, and Ecub and the members of her household.

"Coel?" said Brutus, buckling his scabbard belt to his hips.

Coel, sliding from Ecub's bed himself, shrugged. "I have no idea," he said.

Brutus looked at the Mother. "Ecub?"

She also shrugged. "How would I know? The woman hardly spoke to me. She is a stranger. I cannot tell her mind."

Brutus studied her, hating her words. If Blangan did not speak, then it was because she had been made to feel wholly unwelcome within Ecub's house.

He was also vaguely disturbed by Ecub's lack of care.

She seemed completely unperturbed about Blangan's disappearance when on two counts she should have been at least mildly worried: firstly, her ability as a Mother would be seriously called into question if a guest of hers had come to harm under her roof (but would that truly matter if the guest in question was the hated Blangan?), and secondly, as the head of her household and the village, Ecub should at the very least be slightly anxious that a stranger was wandering around unsupervised.

Especially if that stranger was the hated Blangan.

"We will need to search for her," Brutus said, finally taking his eyes off Ecub. "Hicetaon, take our men and search the village. Corineus, you and I will take Jago and Bladud and search the surrounding fields. Coel." Brutus paused, and gave Coel a hard glance as well; the man had such a bland face on him that Brutus wondered if he was hiding something. "Coel, you come with me."

"We should try the Stone Dance," Corineus said. He was shifting from foot to foot, almost twitching with impatience and dread. "Blangan talked of it yesterday. Perhaps she was drawn there last night."

"Perhaps," said Brutus, sending Ecub one more speculative look, then he motioned to the other men, and they left the house.

As soon as the last man had gone, Ecub looked over to Cornelia.

Cornelia blanched, and stepped back against the bed, almost tripping over the blankets Brutus had left tangled on the floor.

Ecub's mouth hardened into a thin line.

THEY FOUND HER ALMOST IMMEDIATELY. THERE was little to search in the village that Corineus had not already checked, and so Hicetaon and the two other Trojans rejoined Brutus, Corineus, and Coel just as they approached the Stone Dance.

They knew even before they entered the circles: crows

and ravens were heaped in a squawking, heaving mass of feathers, wings, and flashing beaks on the far side of the Dance.

Corineus gave a ghastly cry, and ran toward the birds before Brutus could stop him.

As soon as he arrived to within two paces of the shuffling mass of birds, Corineus threw himself at them, shouting madly.

They erupted in a dusty, foul-smelling cloud of black feathers and flew off, screeching in disgust at the interruption.

As they lifted away, Corineus gave one long, despairing cry and sank to his knees, his hands to his face.

When Brutus reached his side, he took one look, then turned aside his head, swallowing.

Even his battle experience had not prepared him for this.

What was left of Blangan lay by one of the stone uprights; it was a hideous, twisted mess of blood and flesh. The birds' feeding had damaged her, but even so it was clear enough what had been done to her before the ravens had descended.

Her left breast had been ripped almost from her body, its flesh mangled as if it had been chewed.

Her heart lay exposed, half out of her chest . . . and in the clotted blood that covered it Brutus could clearly see the finger marks of her murderer.

Corineus was keening, thin and high, one hand now patting at the air above Blangan's corpse as if he wanted to touch her, but did not dare.

Hicetaon, glancing at Brutus who stood staring at Blangan with anger so deep it seemed quite possible that he'd take his sword to the stone as a revenge for Blangan's murder, squatted down by Corineus, and put his arms about him. He hugged Corineus tight, murmuring words of comfort.

Brutus took a very deep breath, then looked at Coel who had stopped a little distance away.

His face had not altered from its carefully composed

blandness. "Who did this to her? *Who*, Coel? No one hated Blangan this much save for your people!"

"Take your hand from your sword," Coel said. "*No one* from among my men or this village did this to her! If Blangan died here, and in this manner, then it was the work of gods, not of man."

"Do gods have murdering fingers?" Brutus shouted, jabbing his hand at the marks about Blangan's heart. "Damn you and your dark gods, Coel! Blangan was a woman innocent of *any* wrongdoing! Do not blame *her* for the split in Og's power, for she was a victim as much as this blighted land of yours!"

Coel's face had lost some of its composure, but the fact that Brutus could still see no sympathy or understanding there drove him even deeper into anger. "Do you know what she told me, Coel? Do you? She said that she was a terrified thirteen-year-old girl, raped by her father and with no more ability to weave darkcraft than she could command the tide to retreat. *Someone* had cast that darkcraft, Coel, but it was not *her*." Brutus flung his hand at Blangan's corpse again.

Something shifted in Coel's eyes, an uncertainty perhaps, but it did not reflect in his voice. "She had no right talking to you of matters that did not—"

"She had every right, Coel! *Every* right! She was terrified . . . she knew she had come home to die. All she wanted, Coel"—Brutus' voice dropped, now soft in its disgust—"was for someone to believe in her."

He turned away, and dropped down by Corineus, leaving Coel staring at him in sudden horror.

THEY CARRIED BLANGAN'S CORPSE BACK TO THE village, a silent line of men wrapped either in thought or in grief, and into Ecub's house.

Ecub hurried to meet them, exchanging a quick, knowing look with Coel, then taking charge.

"Cornelia, Aethylla, my daughters, and I will wash and

tend her," Ecub said, "while you men build a funerary pyre. Go now, and leave women to tend to women."

Brutus nodded, grateful to hand the horrible corpse over to Ecub, then he saw Cornelia's pale and frightened face. "Cornelia? Are you well?"

"How can I be well, Brutus, when I loved Blangan so dearly. Go now, please, leave us alone."

As Brutus turned away, Coel caught Cornelia's eyes, and saw the fright within them.

Frenzy wine or not, Cornelia remembered.

THE WOMEN TOOK THE ENTIRE MORNING TO WASH Blangan clean, stitch her wounds, and wind her in her shroud. Their work was done in silence, save for the odd query regarding their hideous handiwork.

Ecub shot Cornelia many a reflective look, but Cornelia refused to catch her eye, and Ecub could not talk to the woman with Aethylla or her daughters present.

At noon, Blangan's body tended, they called in two of the men to carry her out to the funerary pyre.

THE FLAMES CAUGHT, SNAPPING AND TWISTING at the base of the huge pile of wood and brush on which Blangan lay. Corineus knelt in the dirt a few paces distant, his face twisted into tearless grief, his hands held out, keening soft and desolate. Everyone else—Ecub and her family, the villagers, the Trojans, and Coel, Bladud, and Jago—stood about in a circle. After a word with Coel, Ecub had seen to it that Cornelia stood distant from Brutus or any other Trojan, and that Coel stood next to her.

"Cornelia," Coel said softly, his eyes remaining steady on the now-flaming pyre.

She did not answer.

"Cornelia," he said again. "I am sorry that you are fearful."

"You stopped me from aiding her." Her voice was flat,

toneless, yet carried many layers of accusation within it.

"If you had gone to her then you, too, would have died."

"I wish I had, Coel. I loved Blangan. I cannot believe that you could have abetted such a cruel death." Her voice became harsh, horrible. "I cannot believe that I let you touch me and hold me in that—"

"Cornelia!" Coel hissed. "Keep your voice down! Do you think that Brutus will thank you *now* if he finds out you witnessed Blangan's death? What will he think if he knows you kept a silent tongue in your head for all this long morning?"

Cornelia said nothing, but from the corner of his eye Coel saw that she flickered an uncertain glance Brutus' way.

"Blangan knew she came home to her death," he continued, his own voice calmer now. "She knew it, and I think that you knew it, too, even if she had not put her knowledge into words for you. There is . . . there is a treachery going on about us, Cornelia. Blangan's death was a part of that treachery."

"And yet you allowed it to happen!"

"Then I did not know what I do now. Cornelia, there are things you need to see, and words you need to hear, but I am not the one to—"

"Not that Loth, surely!"

She had turned to face him now, her wide eyes furious and frightened all in one, and Coel cursed silently, knowing that her movement had made Brutus turn his eyes their way.

"You need to know why Blangan died," he said, staring fixedly at the fire and talking through lips that barely moved. "You need to know who killed her."

"Loth killed her!"

"No," Coel said. "Loth did not kill her at all."

Cornelia looked at him, then looked at Brutus, still watching them, then she lowered her eyes, and said no more.

*   *   *

WHEN THE PYRE HAD BURNED COMPLETELY, AND Corineus, weeping, gathered the ashes into an urn, Coel moved to speak with Ecub.

"I do not think Cornelia will talk, not to Brutus. She is too frightened."

"Watch her. I do not know what to make of her. I still do not truly know why she came to Mag's Dance in the first instance, nor how she knew how to dance Mag's Nuptial Dance with Blangan. She is a mystery, and in these dark blighted days I find that mysteries unnerve me."

Coel could see that Brutus, at Corineus' side, was *still* watching him, and he knew he could not afford to spend too long whispering with Ecub.

"Mother Ecub, there is something I think you should know."

"Yes?"

"Brutus said something to me that made me think. Ecub, I cannot explain it, nor justify what I am about to say, but I think that Genvissa, or more probably her mother, was the one to cast that darkcraft over Og. Blangan was blameless, a victim, just as Og himself has been."

"Coel—"

"I have stood here all through this afternoon, watching Blangan's body burn, and thought about it. Ecub, we have no time to talk of this now, but think on this: you said last night that Loth's manipulation and Og's death was Genvissa's doing. I think you're right. Moreover, I think that all the darkcraft which binds us is of her, and her line's, working. MagaLlan? Nay, I think not, Darkwitches indeed, all of them."

Ecub's face had gone white, but Coel was striding away before she could speak, and despite all her efforts, there was no opportunity to talk privately with him again before his party left the next morning.

Chapter Fifteen

YOU KNEW THAT KILLING BLANGAN WOULD draw Og to his final death!"

Genvissa raised her eyebrows, not looking at Loth, as if disinterested. They were walking—rather, Genvissa was walking with smooth graceful strides and a haggard-faced and patently furious Loth was progressing in a jerky gait at her side—through the meadowland that divided two of the Veiled Hills—Pen Hill and the Llandin. Loth had only just arrived from Mag's Dance, his body and his hip wrap stinking of travel-sweat, and had accosted Genvissa on her daily walk among the sacred hills.

"You told me that in murdering my mother Og's power would be restored!"

"Did I?"

"You said—"

She stopped, and rounded on him, irritated with his naive stupidity. "And you listened, you fool! The only thought you had was for power and the only tool you used to think with was *this*!"

She grabbed at Loth's genitals through the soft material of his wrap, and he jerked back before she could bruise him too badly.

"You knew what would happen?" He had accused her, but had not thought she would admit to it.

"Yes." Genvissa resumed walking.

He stared after her, then ran to catch up. "By Og, Genvissa, why? *Why?*"

"Because Og was useless. He needed to be replaced."

"With *Brutus*?"

"With what Brutus can offer, yes."

"How long have you planned this? What *else* have you done?"

"Enough, Loth. Now stop whining. I can ensure you a good enough place in—"

"No! No! I will go before the Assembly of the Mothers, Genvissa, and tell them what you have done!"

She turned on her heel and grabbed his chin in one strong hand. "You will not do so, Loth. If you open your whining mouth to anyone else I will personally tell not only your father, but the entire Assembly and through them all Llangarlia that *you* were the one who killed Og." Her upper lip curled. "Like mother, like son. They will believe me, Loth. Not you."

"I was only the weapon," he said, wrenching his chin free. "Not the hand of the murderer."

Genvissa laughed softly. "How sweet, Loth. Who gave you those words, then? Ecub, I assume, as I can't imagine you coming up with that concept by yourself."

He flushed, humiliated. "Then why not kill me, too?"

"Because, my dear boy"—she patted him on the cheek—"I may yet have a use for you."

"Darkwitch!"

Genvissa finally lost her temper. "And what of it? What I do, I do for this land! Mag and Og were old, useless, and this land was failing by degrees anyway. If I replace them, then I replace them with *strength* so that this land may flower in the sun again!"

She paused, her breasts heaving with emotion. "I love this land and its people as much as you do, Loth. Believe that! What I do, I do for Llangarlia."

"What you do," Loth hissed, "you do for your own gain only."

He backed away a step, then another, his mouth—his entire face—snarling. "I will destroy you!"

"You are too late," she said. "There is no weapon left."

PART FIVE

LONDON, MARCH 1939

I saw that satchel you gripped so closely when you left *Waterloo, Major Skelton,*" said the voice, whispering out of the darkness. "*Were the remaining kingship bands in it, then? Are they back at Frank Bentley's cheerful establishment, unguarded, waiting for me?*"

"*Asterion,*" Skelton said, stopping and looking into the dark doorway from where had issued the voice. "*Are you so afraid to reveal yourself that you must speak from the shadows?*"

Asterion stepped forth into the dim street lighting. He had taken his true form, his naked, muscular man's body topped with the blue-black head of the bull.

Skelton glanced up and down New Bridge Street, but it was deserted. As always, Asterion had chosen the moment well.

"*You were right,*" *Asterion said,* "*when you told my pretty Stella that this would be the last time, the last Gathering. I've grown tired, impatient. It is more than time that the Game was finalized.*"

He walked further forward yet, close enough that he could reach up a hand and grasp Skelton's chin. "This stupidity has gone on long enough. Give me the rest of the kingship bands."

Skelton wrenched his face free. "I'll see you in hell first."

Asterion laughed, low and sweet. "How, Brutus? The Game is all but over. There is no point in trying to fight on. No point in trying to deny me. Hand over the bands and—"

"And . . . what? You will treat me 'mercifully'?" Skelton turned his back to Asterion, and began to walk away.

"You cannot finish the Game, Skelton. You know that. You cannot finish what you and Genvissa started!"

Skelton halted, then spoke to Asterion over his shoulder. "Then I will safeguard what I may. I will not let you destroy the Game, Asterion. I will not let you destroy this." His chin tilted, and with its movement took in all the sprawling vastness of London.

"Walk away then, fool," Asterion said. "Walk away. There is nothing you can do to stop me now. Nothing. You lost a long, long time ago. Walk away."

Skelton whipped about, stung into fury, but Asterion had gone, vanished into the drifting London frost.

Chapter One

ON THE MORNING OF THE SIXTH DAY AFTER they'd left Ecub's village Coel led his party into a wide valley, that, even despite the occasional evidence of blight, seemed rich and fertile. Here fields and droveways stretched in every direction, their boundaries marked with ditches and well-tended hedges. Even now, in the early autumn, it was easy to see that this was a fruitful land: there were numerous flocks of sheep, cattle, pigs, and goats as well as great gaggles of geese and poultry feeding along the stream and river meadows. In some fields there were still men and women harvesting late grain crops; again, while blight had left some coarse and thin patches within the crops, in most of the crops the stalks crowded thick and tall, their grain heads heavy and generous. Here, unlike the relatively sparse lands they passed through from the River Dart, villages and farming communities were dotted at regular intervals, surrounded with their own intricate web of fields and droveways. There were orchards and well-tended herb gardens, as also carefully managed coppices and lightly wooded areas where wild boar and deer roamed.

Roads wove their sinuous way through all this abundance, their surfaces carefully leveled and graveled for wheeled traffic.

It was a countryside richer than Brutus could ever have imagined. In the lands in which he'd been born and spent his life hitherto, the thinness of the soils meant sparse fields and even sparser crops. He had never seen such an intensity of agriculture, nor such an easy wealth of food. Gods, if this land was not at its best, then how remarkable must it be when it was whole!

He rode his horse up level with Coel's, and nodded at the surrounding countryside. "This is a good place."

Coel and he had ridden in silence for two days after leaving Ecub's village, and had then come to a silent agreement to clothe their disagreements with politeness. Since then their relationship had been cool but not hostile.

Despite the thawing in his personal relationship with the man, Brutus kept a close and somewhat suspicious watch over Coel's dealings with Cornelia. That they were none—Coel kept a great distance between himself and Cornelia—only increased Brutus' suspicions. For the first part of the journey Cornelia and Coel had chatted as if they were old friends. Now they would have nothing to do with each other.

Something had happened, and Brutus wished he knew what it was.

"A good place?" Coel said, glancing at Brutus, then smiling to himself as he recognized Brutus' admiration of the countryside. "This is the valley of the Llan," he said, nodding forward to where Brutus could see a very faint wide expanse of silver, "but it is only the beginning of Llangarlia's wealth. From here to the north, and to the southeast, stretches some of the most wondrous land in this island. Mag and . . . and Og have blessed us indeed."

"The Llan is close?"

"We will reach it this evening."

"And the Veiled Hills?"

"Are on the northern bank of the Llan. Whether you see them or not depends on the MagaLlan and Gormagog's goodwill."

"When will I see them?"

"When you are settled this evening, I will send word. Then you will wait."

Brutus nodded, lapsing back into silence as he thought of the MagaLlan—Genvissa. He'd had little time to think of her in the past two weeks: the journey, Blangan's death,

and then his suspicions about Coel and Cornelia had filled
his mind.

But now . . . now she was so close. What she had promised him was so close . . .

The Game.

Power—beyond anything he'd dared dream of.

Immortality.

IN THE LATE AFTERNOON THEY WOUND THEIR WAY
northeast along a road that ran parallel with the southern
bank of the River Llan. The dwellings, granaries, and barns
were becoming ever more frequent, and Brutus noted that
they were among the best constructed buildings he'd seen
since he'd begun his journey through Llangarlia.

Farther south the houses had been made largely of
wooden frames filled in with clay-daubed wickerwork walls
and with thatched or turf roofs. Here the houses, while still
predominantly circular, had walls of stone, and sometimes
even roofs of slate. Many of them had walls and roofs high
enough to suggest several levels inside. Some of the buildings had even been constructed in the wide marshes and
tidal flats that formed the southern boundary of the Llan.
Here solidly assembled wooden walkways ran out to the
buildings that sat on thick stilts above the waterline.

Boats, some quite large, were either tied to posts within
the river or were pulled up on the mudflats, and Brutus
guessed that they were used both for fishing and trade.

"How far are we from the sea here?" he asked Coel.

"A day's sail, or row, if your men are strong," he answered. "And the river remains navigable many days to the
west. For so many generations we have been blessed.
Now?" He shrugged, and Brutus shot him a dark look at
even this oblique reference to Blangan.

THE RIVER BENT NORTHWARD, THE ROAD THEY
were traveling with it, leading into a large bustling town con-

structed just east of the mudflats and marshes that lined the river.

Coel waved the party to a halt. He pointed to the river to their left, and indicated a small, hilled island at the mouth of a smaller river that emptied into the Llan on its western bank.

"That is Thorney Island," he said, "and it marks the spot where the Ty River meets the Llan. Thorney Island also marks the first fording spot across the Llan above its mouth. Several of the coastal roads merge at this point to cross the ford; once across the Llan they again divide up, heading north, west, and south to the very edges of the land."

Brutus nodded, understanding why the settlement was so large. Here all trade routes converged on the ford across the Llan at Thorney Island. And the Veiled Hills were close.

As if reading Brutus' thoughts, Coel now pointed to the north. "Above the town, which we name Llanbank for the river, the Llan curves to the east. It is on the northern bank of the east–west stretch of the river that the Veiled Hills sit."

He looked again at Thorney Island. "On the island rises Tot Hill, and that hill marks the very southwestern point of the Veiled Hills."

"It is sacred?" asked Hicetaon, who had ridden up on Coel's other side.

"Oh, yes," Coel responded. "Tot Hill is sacred. Now, come, I shall show you to your house." He grinned, looking over his shoulder to where Cornelia sat her horse. "Which we shall call Cornelia's House, as it is the custom of this land to name a household after the senior woman."

He was rewarded with a polite smile, although it never reached Cornelia's eyes.

THE HOUSE TO WHICH COEL LED THEM WAS LARGE and substantial. Constructed of gray stone walls a pace thick and reaching well above their heads, it had a towering conical roof twice as high as the walls and densely thatched with new, sweet reeds. When they entered the single doorway it was to find that the floor was paved, and that there was a second level that could be used for extra sleeping space or for storage.

There were sleeping bays cut into the walls, with storage platforms above them and privacy drapes before them, and a bright fire burned in the central hearth, a pot already bubbling in its coals.

"You will be comfortable here," said Coel. "In the morning, I will come for you."

With that he was gone, and Brutus was left staring at the doorway, realizing that not only was it their only way out of this substantial building, but that the long shadows outside revealed the presence of guards.

He doubted any of them would be allowed the freedom of Llanbank this night. He caught Hicetaon's eye, and both men shrugged—they had expected little less.

Then one of the babies cried, and Brutus sighed, and turned to help the women settle before they tasted of the pot.

Chapter Two

BRUTUS WOKE EARLY, AND PREPARED HIMself as best he could. He washed thoroughly with water he heated at the fire, and oiled his hair so that it shone and snapped into tight black curls, then tied it securely behind his neck with a new thong. His body likewise he rubbed with oil until his skin gleamed and the engraved bands of kingship about his arms and legs sparkled. He scraped his teeth with a stick, then rubbed them with astringent herbs, finally rinsing out his mouth with fresh cold water.

He wanted to look his best. He wanted to be his finest.

Today he would meet with Genvissa, the MagaLlan.

And the Gormagog, of course, but frankly Aerne was not the one raising the excitement in his belly to the point where he was unable to break his fast for fear of retching the food straight up again.

He rose from the fire, its light catching the warm hues of his naked body, and wrapped a fresh loincloth about his hips.

Then, from the small pack he'd brought all the way from Totnes camp, Brutus lifted a fine closely woven white tunic. It was sleeveless and came only to midthigh, so that his bands of kingship would not be hidden. About his waist Brutus belted a leather strap studded with gold-leaf insets, and to that he attached his sheathed knife.

He would not wear a sword to his meeting.

About his neck Brutus clipped a wide torc of gold that had been finely inlaid with mother-of-pearl, and on his feet he slid a new and finely crafted pair of shoes.

When he was done, he looked up and saw that Cornelia, Aethylla, Hicetaon, and the two warriors were all awake, and variously propped up on elbows or sitting in their bed spaces, watching him.

"Will you win us a land today, Brutus?" Hicetaon asked. Beside him lay Aethylla, who had quietly taken to sharing Hicetaon's blankets on the final leg of the journey north. She had a baby to each of her breasts, and watched Brutus with wide, appreciative eyes.

"This land is already ours," Brutus said. "It is only that the Llangarlians have yet to realize it."

Then, with a nod for Cornelia, Brutus grabbed his cloak and strode through the door.

COEL WAS WAITING OUTSIDE FOR HIM.

"You think to dazzle the MagaLlan and Gormagog with that finery?" he said.

"I merely think to show myself as I am," Brutus said, making Coel bark with laughter.

"You are a fine king, to be sure," he said. "All a-glittering and a-gleaming."

Brutus' face stilled, then he pushed past Coel and mounted his horse.

COEL LED THE WAY ON HIS HORSE, GUIDING BRU-tus through Llanbank's wide streets toward the ford on the Llan. The morning was sweet and soft, people only just stirring, and what noise and movement there was came from the waterbirds on the riverside marshes, rising to begin their day's feasting amid the river's bounty.

Coel led Brutus along a raised and well-graded trackway that wound through the wide mudflats and marshes abutting the river. There were deep ditches on either side to drain away the marsh water, and Brutus wondered at the effort that must have gone into constructing such a causeway.

After some minutes the causeway led to the river itself, and here Brutus could see that the work had continued into and across the river, for the ford was a wide-graveled path under water that would reach to a man's knees.

"We can only cross at low tide," Coel explained as their horses splashed into the ford. "At high tide the Llan is the province of ships and fishes only."

"And when the river floods?" Brutus asked. Most of the surrounding land was so low that he imagined it was at severe risk of flooding.

In answer, Coel grimaced. "We pray to Mag and Og to keep the river peaceful," he said.

"And do they listen to your prayers?"

"Some years," Coel said, and pushed his horse forward so that further conversation was impossible.

Brutus turned his attention to the far bank of the Llan, still some distance away. He could clearly see Thorney Island, rosy in the dawn light. It sat squarely in the mouth of the River Ty that had to split into two in order to flow around the island and into the Llan.

Thorney Island was not particularly large, rising from its spot at the junction of the two rivers to a central mound some eighty paces high. Much of the island, particularly about its shoreline, was thick with thornbushes and beds of reeds, and Brutus grinned to himself as he imagined the first men who dared to climb the island trying to push their way through that natural barrier—no wonder the name.

The central mound, Tot Hill, was clear of any shrubs and trees, and it boasted a large rectangular stone building on its southern slope that looked over the river and ford. At the very summit stood what appeared to be either an altar or the base of a pyre . . . or perhaps both.

Brutus had caught up with Coel now, and he nodded at the buildings. "The MagaLlan and Gormagog live there?"

"No," said Coel. "They live elsewhere. This is merely where they have chosen to meet with you."

"But that building is very well constructed, and very large," said Brutus. "It must be important."

Coel sighed. "The island is used as a place of Assembly," he said. "The building houses a great meeting chamber."

Brutus nodded; this must be the Assembly House Coel had mentioned on their journey north. He assumed that he would met with the MagaLlan and the Gormagog in this building, but when Coel led the way from the river onto the island—fortunately through a path cut through the thornbushes and reeds—he bypassed the turnoff toward the great stone building, and instead rode for the very summit itself.

Coel pulled his horse to a halt some twenty paces from the top, then slid to the ground, indicating Brutus should do the same.

"I will hold your horse," he said to Brutus. "You are to go to the summit. Meet me below once you're done."

WHEN BRUTUS REACHED THE SUMMIT THERE WAS no one nor thing there save the large raised platform of stone. He climbed onto the platform—the stones were creamy and pitted with age but still fitted together closely enough to form a completely flat surface—and looked about the surrounding countryside.

Llanbank spread out directly to his east across the river. Thick twists of smoke rose from the dwellings as fires were rekindled, children darted out from doorways and between the legs of those adults already out and geese cackled and flapped their wings as they rose from their slumber and contemplated what mischief they might make during the day.

To the south, across the great bend in the river as the Llan turned westward, fields spread as far as Brutus could see. Along one droveway close to the Llan's marshes a shepherd drove a flock of wiry pale brown sheep toward their morning's grazing, a small black and tan dog barking at their heels.

To the west much of the same, marshes and fields, the riches of Llangarlia spreading on either side of the great silvery expanse of the Llan. Where the ford across the Llan joined the western riverbank of the Llan three roads forked out, each to their separate destinations. One wound to the north, one to the south, and one to the southwest.

Finally, Brutus turned to the north and northeast, the northern banks of the Llan, where stretched the Veiled Hills.

Nothing. Nothing save mist and mystery. Where the Llan was bathed in clear early morning light elsewhere, in its northern and northeastern reaches it was lost in dense, ivory fog.

"The Veiled Hills," said a voice behind Brutus, and he sprung about, angry that he'd been surprised.

"And not for you. Not now," the man finished. "Yet, even so, I welcome you to my land, Brutus, great-great-grandson of Aphrodite."

"You are the Gormagog," Brutus said, staring unabashedly. "Aerne."

"Oh, aye, I am the Gormagog," Aerne said, his mouth

twisting at Brutus' uncomfortably frank inspection.

Brutus was not in the least intimidated, and certainly not overawed, by the man standing before him. The Gormagog was an old man who had, perhaps, once had a commanding presence, but who had lost that presence many, many years previously. He was tall, but stooped, his shoulders and back bowed, his limbs now almost too thin to be able to support the weight of his overheavy bones. His body, near naked save for a plain leather loin wrap, was thin and stringy, with the slack skin and the sagging belly of age. Across his chest, still visible among the wrinkles and the sagging pouches of flesh, were the faint outlines of an ancient tattoo of a full spread of stag antlers.

His huge hands, hanging with a slight tremble at the end of arms, reminding Brutus of the spades that farmers used to clean out piss heaps and pigpens.

Overall, Aerne the Gormagog gave the impression of a man who may once have been powerful and impressive, but who was now a pitiful shadow of his former self.

He also carried about him the gray miasma of a man dying: it was discernible in the milkiness of his once hazel eyes, in the tremble of his gray lips, and in the rapid, shallow thudding of a weary heart pounding at the confines of his rib cage.

Brutus felt disgust rise in his gorge. This was a man who had raped his own daughter. "Where is Genvissa?" he said.

"I am here to greet you, Brutus. Am I not enough?"

"No, you are not. Your power is gone, you failed many years ago. Genvissa needs *me* to save this land. Why am I here talking to *you*?" He made a gesture of impatience. "By the gods, why is she toying with me like this? I *must* see her, speak with her. If she is not what *I* need, and what the *Game* needs, then all this prattling is useless."

"Then we will cease with the useless prattling," said a soft voice behind Brutus, "and speak of the you and I, Brutus."

He turned about, taking deliberate ease in doing so, angry that she should have sent Aerne to waste time.

Standing several paces away from him on the platform was Artemis herself, draped in her hunting costume, her hunting bow over her shoulder.

"Genvissa," Brutus said, in a curiously flat voice.

Artemis laughed, soft and musical, and then she appeared to waver, as if a waterfall of light had cascaded over her, and then Artemis was gone, and standing in her place was the woman of Brutus' vision.

Tall and straight, her figure rounded by motherhood, her black curling hair cascading down her back with its peculiar russet lock gleaming in the morning light, she stood proud and beautiful, sure both of Brutus and of her world.

Genvissa. The woman with whom he would play the Game. His partner in immortality.

"Finally," he said. Stepping forward, Brutus took her face between his hands and, without hesitation, laid his mouth on hers.

Chapter Three

AERNE, WHO HAD LOVED GENVISSA FOR ALL the years of her life, turned his head aside, shocked that this inevitable moment could cause him so much misery.

Eventually, Brutus lifted his mouth away from Genvissa's, but only barely, and only very reluctantly.

"I am Genvissa, MagaLlan of Llangarlia," she whispered. "And it was *my* foremother Ariadne who stole the Game from your world and brought it here. It was *I*, her fifth daughter-heir in direct line, who appeared to you and set your steps on the path for Llangarlia, not Artemis. She lingers cobwebbed with all your other gods. I have the Game now, and all I needed to activate it was you."

His thumbs rubbed slowly over her soft cheeks. "Then why the pretense of Artemis?"

"You know why. Because you would have believed her over a strange woman."

"Genvissa," he said, "if you had appeared to me as you stand here now, in my hands, and offered me the same promises as Artemis, then I would have walked barefoot over burning charcoal fields to have reached you. I would have brought you the sun itself, if that is what you had demanded." He paused. "But toy with me no longer. If indeed you have the Game—"

"I do."

"And if Ariadne was indeed your foremother—"

"She was."

His fingers tightened fractionally around her face. "Then that must mean, it *must* mean, that you are—"

"You know what I am. You can feel it through your hands. I am the Mistress of the Labyrinth."

Genvissa laughed as she saw the flare of hunger in his eyes, heard the sharp indrawn breath of jubilation. She pulled herself free, taking a half step back, her eyes shining, her chin tilted up very slightly. "But this is no place to speak. Not of that. It is too cool and windy, and far too open for what I have to say. Will you join me in the meeting house? I have food spread out, and we shall be more comfortable there."

Walking past Brutus, her hip and shoulder brushing his, she caught and held Aerne's gaze for a brief moment, then she led the two men down the hill toward the stone Assembly House, Aerne hobbling with the pain in his stiff muscles and joints, Brutus never once taking his eyes off the supple sway of Genvissa's body as she walked several paces in front of him.

She trailed power behind her like a scent, and Brutus knew he would never be able to breathe enough of it.

THIS ASSEMBLY HOUSE WAS A BUILDING SUCH AS Brutus had yet to see in Llangarlia, although he'd seen sim-

ilar buildings regularly in his travels about the Aegean and
Ionian Seas. The house was rectangular, its stone courses
well laid out although its walls were only barely higher than
the head of a tall man, and with a slate roof. It had windows, somewhat poorly constructed as if someone had
known what windows were but had not been truly able to
pass the concept on successfully to the builders, but the
openings were nevertheless windows, and Brutus had not
seen them in any other Llangarlian construction.

The building faced east–west, and on the eastern, shorter
wall there was a large arched doorway, flanked by two
(slightly cracked) columns that supported a (sagging) porch.

The wooden door stood open.

Genvissa led Aerne through, then, hesitating only
slightly, Brutus followed.

The interior of the building was composed of a single
space. Running parallel to, and two paces inside, the long
walls were twin rows of wooden posts supporting the heavy
roof. Apart from those wooden posts the space was virtually
empty save for a waist-high stone platform halfway down
the hall that Brutus supposed could serve either as table or
altar.

There were three high stools pulled up to this platform,
on which was spread an array of platters containing food.

Table today, then, not altar.

Genvissa aided Aerne onto one of the stools, then took
one herself, while Brutus settled himself on the remaining
stool, looking at the table. It contained four or five platters
containing a selection of herbs and salads, cooked vegetables, and cold meats and sauces.

Brutus hesitated, deciding, then took one of the small
joints of meat and bit into it.

"Tell me of Ariadne," he said to Genvissa.

She took a large leaf from one of the platters of herbs,
and wrapped a slice of meat in it, biting into it delicately.

Swallowing her mouthful, Genvissa said, "My fifth foremother came to this land a stranger, Brutus. She was
brought here by a merchant who found her and her girl-

child on an all but barren island north of Crete. He had thought to sell her as a slave, but the then MagaLlan, who had lost all her daughters to a fever—a sudden and most unexplainable tragedy—recognized that this stranger woman had the aura of power about her, and adopted her as her daughter-heir, training her in the ways of Mag.

"Ariadne began a new life here with her daughter," Genvissa continued, "bred on her by her betrayer lover Theseus. She took over the duties of MagaLlan when her adopted mother passed through to the Far World, accepting Mag into her life and Llangarlia as her home. She did this willingly, for both Mag and Llangarlia had accepted her when her own world and its gods had cast her aside."

"Her own world and its gods had 'cast her aside'?" Brutus said, watching Genvissa carefully. "That is not the tale I heard."

"Ariadne was a scorned woman, and there is little more dangerous, Brutus, than a scorned woman." She half smiled. "That is always good to remember. Ariadne, determined to not only have her revenge on her own lover and world, but to reward the gods and the land which had given her love and succor, determined to steal the Game away to Llangarlia."

Now Genvissa's smile blossomed, and her eyes snapped merrily. "She succeeded! And what happened, Brutus, what happened?"

Brutus knew that Genvissa didn't truly want an answer to her question, but he gave it anyway. "Irrelevance. Decay. Death. Catastrophe. My world was torn to pieces, Genvissa. And did Ariadne feel the better for it? Did she?"

Genvissa leaned very slightly toward him, her eyes locked in to his. "Would you have me undo it, Brutus? Knowing what loss that would thereby bring to your life? Your ambitions?"

To one side, a silent but watchful Aerne poured out barley beer into three beakers and slid two across the table to Genvissa and Brutus.

Both ignored them.

"Well?" Genvissa said, very softly. "Could you bear to reject what I offer you?"

"You cannot afford to have me reject you . . . can you?"

She laughed, leaning back, and, breaking eye contact with him, took her beaker of barley beer and drank of it deeply. "I need a Kingman," she said, placing her beaker down. "You are he."

He lifted his arms, the golden bands of kingship glinting. "For the sake of everyone and everything murdered and destroyed by Ariadne," he said softly, "am I the only one left?"

"Yes. You are the only one left. All the others, their lines, their heritage, their powers, lie dead in the rubble of the Catastrophe."

"Was that merely ill luck, Genvissa, or design?"

"You are the one I need," she said.

Unbidden, Brutus suddenly thought of his father Silvius' death. Gods, was that *his* hand that had driven the arrow deep into his father's brain . . . or . . .

Genvissa's eyes crinkled, just very slightly. "You needed to be able to dare the dark heart of the labyrinth, Brutus."

Brutus dropped his gaze from her, and studied the platters of food.

A long silence ensued.

Eventually he looked back at her, and when he spoke, his voice was even, nonjudgmental, as if he had come to an acceptance within himself.

"Is it true," he said, "what I have heard, *and* seen evidence of, that this land is failing? Rain and cloud has closed in? Livestock dropped from the womb deformed? Children and trees dying to unknown diseases?"

"Yes," Genvissa said.

"So you ask that I and my people rebuild Troy here in this land"—he glanced about at the building they sat in, realizing that someone, Ariadne perhaps, had tried to get the less-skilled Llangarlians to build her something of what she'd known in Knossos—"and that we use the Game—"

"The 'Troy Game,' " she said, nodding at his Trojan kingship bands.

"—to tie city and land together in a magical association to protect both. You want us to use the Troy Game to strengthen this land against the evil that blights it."

"Yes," she said. "Both land and city will be the most wondrous the world has ever, or will ever, know."

"You must know, Genvissa, how dangerous the Game is."

"We will be able to endure it," she said, favoring him with a smile.

"It will take many months to re-create the Game," he said. "And we will *both* need to live through those months, otherwise we will destroy both ourselves and this land." Brutus knew he had to emphasize that point. Gods, if either of them died before the Game was completed . . .

"We are both young and strong. We can live a few more months, I expect." *No need*, she thought, *to mention Asterion*. He could do nothing to stop them. "Imagine the power," she said, very softly. "Imagine, Brutus. You and I, tied forever together in the stones of Troia Nova."

He took a deep breath, seduced both by her sexuality and by the power she offered. Immortality. They would live forever in the stones of the city.

Brutus dragged his thoughts back to the present and looked at Aerne.

"Your people?" he said. "The Game is foreign and powerful magic. Will they accept it?"

"If it means security for their lives and life for their children and livestock, then, yes, they will accept it in the same manner I have."

Brutus frowned slightly. Aerne's voice had not been as certain as he would have liked. "There will be some opposition?" he said.

Genvissa shrugged slightly. "No doubt some people will raise their voice against it. But they will be few." *And easily silenced*. "Brutus," she said, leaning far enough over the table that she could place her hand over his. "We have talked enough for today. I will come for you tomorrow, and show to you the Veiled Hills. Show to you the site where we will build our fabulous city. For the moment, go back to your house—you are comfortable enough?—and rest, and tell your companions that your journeying is done."

They rose, making superficial comments about the food, the fine weather, the beauty of the view from the porch of the Assembly House, then, as they were about to go their separate ways, Genvissa turned one last time to Brutus. Best to dispose of Cornelia now.

"Your wife? She is well? It is just that I heard she has recently had a child . . ."

For some reason Brutus thought of that night under the stars on their journey north when Cornelia had turned to him with such wild abandon. He smiled crookedly, the memory showing in his eyes.

"Oh, yes, she is well," he said.

Something in Genvissa's face froze, then she smiled easily. "I heard you had some trouble at Mag's Dance, Brutus. Do ask Cornelia about it. I believe she witnessed it all."

And with that she took Aerne's arm and led him away.

Brutus stared at their retreating backs, and he did not think at all of the fact that Genvissa had referred to her older sister's death only as "some trouble."

All he could think about was that Cornelia had lied to him.

Again.

AS AERNE AND GENVISSA WATCHED BRUTUS stride down the hill to where Coel waited with the horses, Aerne said, "What did you mean when you said to Brutus that he had some trouble at Mag's Dance? What happened at Mag's Dance?"

"A trifling incident only," Genvissa said, and kissed Aerne's cheek. "Do not fret about it. It need only concern Brutus and his wife." There was no need for Aerne to know that Mag's Dance was where Og had met his death.

Chapter Four

COEL SHOT BRUTUS A LOOK AS THEY RE-mounted and headed back across the ford—their horses had to struggle through almost chest-high water now that the tide had begun to rise—and wisely decided to make no comment. He wondered what had happened on Tot mount to have made Brutus this dark with anger.

As their horses clambered up the eastern bank of the Llan Coel's eyes drifted to the north, to where the Veiled Hills sat behind their protecting cloak of mist.

He could feel Loth there, standing on the northern bank, staring out toward Llanbank with his strange, angry eyes.

Waiting.

They had to speak. Soon.

But not before Coel discovered what had happened on Tot Hill.

BRUTUS JUMPED DOWN FROM HIS HORSE, AND strode into the house without so much as a word or a glance for Coel.

Inside, Corineus and Hicetaon jumped up from their stools about the hearth.

"Well?" said Hicetaon.

"Have they agreed?" said Corineus.

"Yes," Brutus said, then proceeded to ignore them both. He strode over to where Cornelia sat, cuddling Achates. He bent down, ignored the apprehension on her face, took his son, and handed him to Aethylla who, having taken one look at his face, retreated as far away within the circular house as she could.

"Why do I pretend that I can trust you," Brutus said, standing before Cornelia with straddled legs and hands half clenched at his sides, "when time and time again you show me how little you can be trusted?"

"Brutus . . ." Corineus said, taking a careful pace toward him.

Brutus half raised a hand, and Corineus stopped dead. "Do not think to speak for her, Corineus, when she has kept her pretty mouth closed all this time about your wife's death."

Cornelia blanched, and shrank back. Now all eyes in the house were on her.

"Cornelia?" Corineus said, half in question, half in confusion.

"Did you witness Blangan's death?" Brutus said to Cornelia.

She did not answer, her eyes huge and round, now flitting about the interior of the house as if someone might save her.

"Did you witness Blangan's death?" Brutus said again.

She looked back to him, straightening her back and regaining a little composure. "Yes."

"What?" cried Hicetaon and Corineus together, although Corineus' cry was distressed where Hicetaon's was merely confounded.

"Yes," Brutus said softly, his gaze still riveted on Cornelia's face. "And yet she has never thought to remark on the fact to any of us. Did you plan it, Cornelia? Is that why you have kept so silent? Did you aid in the doing, is that why you have kept your knowledge to yourself? Or is it just your vicious, duplicitous nature not to remark on an event which has caused Corineus—"

Cornelia flinched.

"—so much grief and which"—Brutus' voice rose to a shout—"the MagaLlan Genvissa has just thrown in my face? *She* knew—why didn't I?"

One of his hands shot out, grabbed Cornelia by the arm, and hauled her to her feet. With the other he grabbed his knife from his belt, tossed it so that he held it by the blade, and thrust the hilt in Cornelia's face. "Take this cursed knife now, and thrust it into my belly. No need to toy about behind my back."

"I was scared," she said softly. "As I am now."

"Brutus," Hicetaon said quietly, coming to stand by Brutus and Cornelia and taking the knife from Brutus' hand. "We should hear what she has to say before we judge her harshly."

"The fact she has not spoken before now is her judgment," Brutus said bitterly, but he let go Cornelia's arm and stood back a pace.

Cornelia took a deep breath, glanced at Corineus, flushed, then looked back to Brutus.

"That night Blangan disappeared, I woke, and saw her leave the house. I was curious, and followed. No, do not ask what bred that curiosity, for I do not know . . . perhaps the god who destroyed Blangan."

"What 'god'?" Brutus spat.

Cornelia licked her lips, her hands clasping and unclasping before her. "I followed Blangan to the Stone Dance where I hid behind one of the great stones. She did not see me. I watched for some minutes—"

"What was she doing?" Corineus asked, his voice breaking.

Cornelia's eyes flickered to him, and her flush deepened. "She was walking about, tracing her hands about the stones. She looked . . . she looked as though she were remembering. I don't know. How can I have known her mind?"

Her voice cracked on that last, and Brutus made a gesture of angered impatience.

"Go on," said Hicetaon.

"I waited a long time, and I grew cold, and thought I should return to my bed. But before I could move, I heard Blangan cry out, and I saw . . . I saw . . ."

"What?" cried Corineus. He had come close now, staring at Cornelia as if he could drag the words from her.

"I saw a monstrous man enter the Stone Dance," Cornelia

said. "He was young, and muscular, and completely naked. If it had not been for his head I would have thought him most well made and pleasing."

"Cornelia . . ." said Brutus, and she hurried on.

"He had bones growing from his head in four or five places. Like horns of a beast of the forest. His entire head and face was distended, as if the underlying bones bulged unnaturally. He . . . he stank of musk, and exuded an aura of such power and such bestiality that I cannot think him anything but a god, or an imp of some degree."

Corineus made a strangled sound, but Cornelia swallowed, and continued, taking care not to look at him. "The man rushed to Blangan, and grabbed her. He snarled, and then . . . then . . . oh, Hera, then he began to *eat* her! I could not stay, I was terrified he would murder me as well, and I ran back to the house and crawled into bed. I did not speak of it afterward, for the terror continued. I thought if I spoke, then he would come for me, and bite into my breast, and tear me apart as well."

There was a long silence. Corineus put his hands over his face, and his entire body shuddered.

Hicetaon laid a gentle hand on the man's shoulders, then wrapped him in a tight embrace.

"He stank of musk?" said Brutus softly, his gaze still unrelenting on Cornelia. "How close was he if you could smell his stink? Why should I believe this?"

Then . . . "Was Coel there?"

"No!" she said, perhaps too quickly, for Brutus' eyes narrowed suspiciously.

"No!" she said, more forcefully, meeting his eyes, and this time Brutus accepted it.

"How can I ever trust you again," he said, "when you kept this from me? I thought we had agreed to build a marriage, you and I. Then . . . *this*. What else will you do to me, Cornelia? What other dagger can I expect in my back?"

She was weeping now. "None, I swear, Brutus! I am sorry, I was scared."

"What have I done to deserve a wife such as you?" he said softly, and turned his back on her.

As he walked away from Cornelia, Hicetaon rose from Corineus' side. "It *is* 'yes'?" he said quietly to Brutus. "We *can* stay?"

Despite his anger and frustration with Cornelia, Brutus managed a small smile. "Aye, my friend. And . . . and I am to rebuild the Troy Game."

"*The Troy Game?* But how can that be? To rebuild the Game, surely, you would need . . . need—"

"Stop rattling on so, Hicetaon. Yes, to build the Game I need the Mistress of the Labyrinth. And I have her, my friend. I have her. The MagaLlan *is* the Mistress of the Labyrinth."

Chapter Five

COEL STRAIGHTENED UP FROM HIS POSITION crouched against the point where the thatched roof met the outer walls, his expression thoughtful.

The "Game"? This was the Trojan magic Genvissa had brought to Llangarlia? And Genvissa was this "Mistress of the Labyrinth"?

This he must tell Loth, and soon.

But . . . Cornelia. Coel couldn't believe that she'd kept so much silent. She'd protected him, she'd protected Ecub, she'd protected Mag in that she had not told Brutus of the Dance or of some of the mysteries she had been privy to.

I do not deserve such a wife as you, Brutus had said, and Coel agreed wholeheartedly with him. Brutus most certainly did *not* deserve a wife such as Cornelia.

All Coel's curiosity regarding Cornelia resurfaced a hundredfold. Yes, she'd told Brutus about Loth, but that was to be expected. Genvissa had placed Cornelia at the scene, and Cornelia had to tell *some* of the truth or risk further discovery.

Loth had to hear all of this. *Now*.

Besides, Coel was desperate to tell Loth that he believed Blangan innocent of the original darkcraft, and to learn what, if anything, had happened between Genvissa and Loth.

Coel looked about. Bladud was lazing about in the mid-morning sun at the door of a house some distance away. If anything else interesting was going to happen inside this house, then Bladud could just as easily spy as Coel.

Coel jogged toward him, whistling softly to catch Bladud's attention as he drew close.

"I have a task for you," he said as Bladud rose. ·

ONCE AGAIN ASTRIDE HIS STOCKY, SHAGGY horse, Coel rode eastward through Llanbank until he reached the outer market area and livestock pens of the town. Here the main road from the southeast coast joined the north-south road, and here, three times a year, the major trading and market fairs of Llangarlia were held. Livestock traded hands, shepherds won themselves work for the next year, tin and copper from the mines in the far west were traded for gold and silver and fabric from the foreign merchants who had sailed up the Llan from the coast, eager for the metals to take back to their homelands.

Coel turned his horse along the northern road that twisted through the mudflats and tidal marshes of the Llan as it flowed east toward the coast. There was no place to ford the river here, the water was too deep, but a sturdy ferry operated to transport the traffic to the northern road where it continued at the far bank.

He was in luck, the ferry was waiting on the southern bank, the ferryman looking pleased to see someone to distract him from the boredom of his morning.

"Few people on the road today?" Coel said as he led his horse into the flat-bottomed boat.

The ferryman nodded toward the deep bank of fog on the northern shoreline of the Llan. "It makes people think twice," he said, "even though the road skirts the dangerous places."

"Well, that's as it should be," Coel said, and the ferryman nodded, now too busy with his oars (and with shouting at the two other oarsmen to put their backs into it) to answer.

Besides, he knew Coel, and he knew Coel had no reason to be afraid of the mist.

ON THE FAR SIDE, COEL THANKED THE FERRYMAN and his assistants, saying that he would sacrifice metal on their behalf.

Pleased, the ferryman bobbed his head, and grinned contentedly. "Will you be wanting transport back to the southern shore?" he asked.

Coel nodded. "Wait for me. I should not be long."

FROM THE FERRY, COEL RODE NORTHWARD FOR A time along the road. It led through the eastern sector of the Veiled Hills—most of the holy mounds rose to the northwest, but two of the most sacred mounds were directly to his east—but was safe enough for the ordinary traveler so long as he or she did not leave the road.

But Coel was not especially ordinary, and he knew Loth would give him protection, so when he'd ridden only some four or five hundred paces he turned his horse off the road toward the northeast where, a short ride away, lay the edge of the great sacred forest.

Where ran Loth.

Normally Coel would find Loth waiting for him among the outer trees of the forest, but today Loth met him halfway across the grassland, emerging out of the mist a few paces ahead of Coel's horse, making the beast snort in star-tlement.

Loth smiled gently as he walked up and placed a hand on the horse's forehead; it quieted instantly.

Then Loth raised his eyes, still and hard, to Coel. "There is more doing here than we ever realized."

Coel slid from his horse. "I know," he said. "Will you speak first, or shall I?"

"I," said Loth. He closed his eyes briefly, and drew in a deep breath, humiliated to have to confess this. "I was used. Used by Genvissa. She tempted me with power and lust, then sent me to murder Blangan in order to finally destroy Og."

"I thought as much," Coel said softly. He could hardly bear Loth's pain, and moved close enough to him that he could rest his hand on Loth's shoulder.

"She has me trapped," Loth continued. "If I try to move against her then she will say *I* murdered Og in my own maddened quest for power . . . and maybe that's the truth, Coel. Maybe it is."

"Do not be so harsh on yourself, Loth. Genvissa is not alone in this . . . she has the help and support and work of the five damned foremothers before her. This has been planned far longer than I think you realize."

Coel told Loth what he'd surmised—that Blangan had never been the one to wield the darkcraft that had split Og's power—and what he'd heard—that Genvissa was also what she called the Mistress of the Labyrinth, and that the Trojan magic she'd brought to Llangarlia with Brutus involved something called the Troy Game and the building of a mighty city.

"What is this 'Game'?" Loth said. "Of what manner of power does it consist? And what meaning this reference to the labyrinth? By all the gods in every land, Coel, *what is going to happen?*"

Coel shrugged his shoulders unhappily. "Perhaps at the Assembly we can—"

"Genvissa controls great power, Coel. What we *know* is

not what the Mothers will *see*. If Genvissa tells the Mothers that she has a means, even through a strange magic, to counter the downfall of Og and ensure that their daughters will not die in childbirth again, then they will do whatever she says, even if it means they must lie down with dogs."

"And your father . . ."

"Has been Genvissa's willing tool for too many years to change now." He paused. "Genvissa told me there was nothing I could do, that there was no weapon left. *Bitch!* What if she is right, Loth? What if she is right?"

"Loth, listen to me. I need to speak to you of Cornelia."

"What of her? She had little—"

"Loth, *listen*." Coel summarized what he knew of her: Cornelia's strange attraction to the land; her unexplained knowledge of the Stone Dances; the feel of Mag within her womb that was so strong when Coel had entered her in the rock pool; her uninvited appearance at Mag's Dance *and* her intimate knowledge of Mag's Nuptial Dance.

"Moreover, Loth," Coel continued, "she remembered all that had happened. Neither the drugged wine she'd drunk in Ecub's house nor the frenzy wine she'd imbibed in Mag's Dance hid the memory."

"But later," Loth said, "when Blangan was dead, there was no power left in her. I, too, had thought there was *something*, but . . ."

"She'd fainted, Loth. Might that not explain it?"

"I don't know . . ."

"There's something else you need to know, Loth. Genvissa told Brutus to ask Cornelia how Blangan had died."

Loth went very still, and the mist rushed in close about them.

"Brutus was furious that she had kept this secret from him. He threatened her, with his voice and his fists."

Loth lifted his lips in a silent snarl, and the mist trembled.

"Yet even so threatened, Cornelia only told him of you, and of the manner in which you killed your mother."

"She did not mention Ecub, or what happened in Mag's

Dance before I arrived? She did not mention *you*?"

"No."

"She did not mention the Nuptial Dance that she had made with Blangan?"

"No."

Loth frowned. Cornelia had *no* reason to protect Mag (or, indeed, anyone who had been within Mag's Dance). None. Unless . . .

Loth finally looked at Coel from out of his hideously deformed face. "This woman is very enigmatic," he said. "Very much so. Not only that she has protected so much when Brutus, as you say, threatened to beat it from her . . . but that Genvissa was so careful to set Brutus against her. Why would Genvissa feel threatened by Cornelia?"

"Because she is Brutus' wife, when Genvissa wants him in her bed, as she surely does?"

Loth shook his head. "A wife here or there would not bother Genvissa. A wife would just be something to be ignored. No, she is somehow disturbed by Cornelia, and that makes *me* more than curious to discover why."

He considered, looking away into the mist as if he could find hope there.

When he finally looked back to Coel, his friend thought that maybe he had.

"I think that you are going to find Cornelia's company a compelling thing over the next few weeks," he said. "I think you are going to become a very great friend to her."

Coel smiled, very gently, very warmly. "And *I* think that your suggestion will not be a hard thing, Loth. *I* think that I will not find it an arduous task at all."

Chapter Six

Cornelia Speaks

SOMETIMES I FIND MYSELF WISHING I COULD bite my tongue, and take back unthinking words, and sometimes I find myself wondering why it is that I have remained silent.

Why did I not tell Brutus in the first instance about the manner of Blangan's death and then, in the second instance, hold back so much when I *was* forced to tell him?

That night spent in Mag's Dance remains with me so clearly. The dense mystery of the yellow mist, the sensuality of Blangan's dance, the power of Ecub and her frenzy wine . . . that monstrous man, and the touch of his fingers on my breast and belly.

How could I tell Brutus that, and expect him to understand the beauty of it?

Yet holding back that part that was *not* beautiful—Blangan's death—destroyed that which was growing between myself and Brutus. We had existed so long in mutual hatred that the slow and desperately fragile growing together after Achates' birth had been the sweeter for what had preceded it.

Then that single omission, that simple silence, and Brutus' angry face and the hilt of his dagger thrust into my face.

Aethylla, of course, made things no easier for me. She chided me for my stupidity, for my naivety, and my *unthinkingness*. Worse, she scolded me while nursing my son, ensuring I had to endure the double burden of my stupidity as a woman and my failure as a mother.

And all this she did while Brutus stood and watched.

I could have wept. I *did* weep, once Brutus, Corineus

(shooting me a half-sympathetic, half-accusatory glance), and Hicetaon wandered off somewhere to discuss whatever Brutus had been told that morning, and I was left to my own devices.

Left to consider my failings.

And so I did, for Brutus' departing face left no doubt in my mind that he considered me less than the dustiest, flea-ridden cur. I spent the first part of the morning sitting inside that round, stumpy stone house, alternatively weeping and cursing myself silently as I rocked a sleeping Achates (Aethylla having generously allowed me to hold him) to and fro in my arms.

Later, when I managed to calm a little, and Aethylla had fed Achates once more, I noticed that it was a wonderfully clear morning. I ventured outside, Achates in my arms, wondering if the Llangarlian guards beyond the door would allow me to walk about the town.

The only guard, as such, was Coel, leaning against the outer wall of the house, idly chewing a twig, and looking for all the world as if he had been waiting for me to appear.

"Cornelia," he said, spitting away the twig and standing straight. "I would like to make amends for creating this distance between us. Can we talk?"

Tears sprang unbidden to my already red and swollen eyes. I was so desperate for a moment's kindness, a kindness from anyone, that I didn't even consider that it was Coel who had begged me to remain silent in the first instance.

"I thought," he continued, "that I might be your escort for the day. What say you? Would you like to see some of this land and its people?"

And then he lifted his hand, and with the gentlest of fingers, wiped away one of the tears that had escaped down my cheek.

He nearly undid me, as he had undone me in that rock pool. No one, save Blangan or Corineus, had ever been this kind to me, or treated me as a respected equal.

I opened my mouth, unsure what to do (what if Brutus

discovered it?), but before I made any sound I heard Aethylla calling my name, and her voice was hard, and spoke of further judgment.

"Yes," I said in a rush. "Thank you."

He nodded, his eyes twinkling at my obvious desire to escape Aethylla.

We walked away down a street toward what Coel said was the market area of the town. "Many of the local hamlets and farmsteads are herding their cattle and sheep to the pens here for the autumn sale," he said. "It is one of the busiest times of the year for Llanbank."

I could not have cared less about any market, but thought it impolite to say so. I nodded, and tried to look interested.

Coel laughed. "What am I doing?" he said. "Marketing is a man's world and of no interest to you. Besides, the ground grows muddier toward the market, and your shoes are too fine to ruin. If we go this way, along this path toward the fen lands, we will come to some pleasant meadows, where we can sit and talk."

Reluctantly (I truly did not want to spend a morning talking with Coel in some wild grassland when it might provide Brutus with yet more fodder for cruelty) I followed him along the path. The houses soon fell back, allowing sweet meadowlands to take their place. Coel led me to a spot underneath a stand of young ash trees, and we sat among the periwinkles and columbines that grew there.

"This is a very beautiful land," I said, made uncomfortable not only by the silence, but by the warmth and gentleness of this man beside me.

"For a stranger," Coel said, "you have a deep regard for Llangarlia, don't you? A bond, almost."

"It is very beautiful," I said again, briefly closing my eyes in agonized disbelief that I could be so incapable of a coherent conversation.

Coel drew up one knee, resting his extended arm on it. He looked out at the meadowlands, and the glint of the Llan lying just beyond.

"Brutus has been cruel to you," he said.

Oh, Hera, if he continued on with this then I was going to cry again!

"Yet you did not tell him about Ecub, nor of Mag's Nuptial Dance, nor of anything else save Blangan's death. That was so well done, Cornelia."

I still could not speak.

"And you did not tell Brutus of me." Now his voice was very soft.

He turned and looked at me. "I thank you for that, from the depth of my being. And Loth thanks you as well."

"Loth!"

"Yes, Loth. There is no need to be afraid," Coel said. "Not of Loth, anyway. He is no danger to you."

"He killed Blangan."

"He was the one who tore her apart, yes, but—"

"How can you defend *that*?"

"—he was sent there, Cornelia, sent by Blangan's *sister* who wanted her dead more than anything."

I was silent.

"Blangan has—had—a younger sister called Genvissa, who is now the MagaLlan of Llangarlia. She is the woman who Brutus went to see this morning."

I frowned, thinking there was some connection that I should be making.

"Loth did wrong, Cornelia, and no one is more aware, and more regretful, of that than Loth himself. But Genvissa sent him there saying that if he killed his mother then he would restore Og's power to this land."

"Og's power?" I had no idea what Coel was talking about.

Coel talked for many minutes then, telling what I did *not* know about Blangan, the conception and birth of her son, the splitting of this power of Og, and of how Blangan had been blamed for what was probably the darkcraft of this Genvissa's mother.

Now Genvissa, the MagaLlan, had apparently taken up the same darkcraft with as much success as Herron.

Coel was sitting very close to me now, our bodies touching at hip and thigh. "Cornelia, Loth is not the one you should fear. Genvissa is."

"But . . . why?"

"Genvissa wants Brutus, Cornelia. She will make sure, one way or the other, that you are set aside."

"No!" But it was true, for as Coel spoke my mind had suddenly, belatedly, made that connection it should have made minutes ago.

Was *Genvissa* the woman of whom Brutus dreamed? And then I wondered how I could have forgotten all about this dream woman—had I been so desperate to believe Brutus and I had a viable future together?

"No, surely not," I whispered, hoping the denial would ensure the fact.

"Genvissa," Coel said, "was the one who told Brutus that you had been in Mag's Dance. *She* told him to ask you what had happened."

Of course, I remember Brutus mentioning her in those horrifying moments when he had accosted me.

"Genvissa," Coel went on, cruelly driving home into my mind the name of my rival, "feels threatened by you, Cornelia. Why is that?"

"I am Brutus' wife, of course! She wants Brutus and yet here I am! She is jealous."

He gave a small, sad smile. "No. No wife would ever stand in Genvissa's way . . . and it is hardly as if Brutus loves you, Cornelia, is it?"

Oh, how could he be so heartless? I was crying now, for I knew that Brutus indeed did not love me. He reviled me.

And all I wanted . . . all I wanted was for him to love me.

"Cornelia," Coel whispered, and again wiped away the tears from my cheek.

I would have been completely undone then, I think, save that Achates stirred in my arms, and whimpered. I looked down, rocking him, glad of the interruption. "I will have to go. Achates needs to be nursed, and—"

"I saw that on the journey north you gave Achates to

Aethylla to nurse. You did not wish to feed him yourself?"

I found myself flushing, not at the talk of nursing, but with shame. "I cannot. I have no milk. I need to give him to Aethylla to suckle."

Again Coel reached out with his thumb, this time gently touching my cheek. "You feel shame at your lack . . . and you should not, Cornelia. But I still do not understand. Many women give birth and find their milk does not come for several days. The child spends that time whimpering, or at the breast of a temporary nurse, but always a mother's milk comes and she can suckle her own infant. Your milk never came?"

I found myself blinking, unable to believe I could be having this conversation with a man. "I . . . I tried to nurse him on the day he was born, but I had no milk. Aethylla took him from me, and fed him."

And I remembered how my breasts had ached for a week afterward . . .

"And she never gave him back?" His voice was angry, unbelieving.

"No."

Achates' whimpering was rising to a fully fledged wail now, and Coel, giving me one more disbelieving look, rose effortlessly to his feet and walked a little distance into the surrounding meadowland. He spent a few minutes looking at the plants about him, then suddenly bent, pulled an entire plant out of the ground, and tore off its fleshy root.

He walked slowly back to me, using his teeth to strip the root of its hard, outer skin, then he bit it in two, and handed me the smaller portion as again he sat down beside me. "Give it to your son to suck. It will sate him for the time being, although he will be wanting the breast again before midafternoon."

I took the root from him, and tentatively held it to Achates' lips.

The baby suckled at it, whimpered one more time, then fell to the root with a vengeance, suckling madly as if it were better than any breast milk.

Coel laughed at the expression on my face. "We call it the milk root," he said. "For obvious reasons. Many mothers use it to soothe their babies."

"And you *know* this?"

He looked surprised. "Why not?"

I gave a small shake of my head, trying to imagine Brutus, or Corineus, or Hicetaon, possessing such female knowledge, then gave up.

"Thank you," I said.

In answer he only smiled once more, his beautiful face close to mine, and then he leaned that remaining distance between us and kissed me.

I had known he would do it, and I should have stopped him, but I did not. Brutus had sent my soul plunging into the depths of Hades' Underworld this morning, and to have this man, this stunning combination of care and sexuality, put his mouth to mine was what I desperately needed to somehow manage the rise back into the warmth and sunshine.

I kissed him back, hard, and leaned even farther into him as he put his hand to my breast.

Oh, Hera, this man was sweet! Every part of me throbbed, my belly felt as though it had exploded in fire, and—

Achates moved against me, and I came to my senses.

"No!" I said, pulling my head back and jerking my breast out of his hand.

"Oh, gods, Cornelia!" he groaned.

"No," I said, hating myself.

He gave a short, humorless laugh. "Are all Dorian princesses taught how to torment a man to that point where he can hardly draw back, and then say 'no!'?"

I began to cry all over again at the censure in his voice, and the guilt in my own heart, and he was instantly contrite.

"It is alright, Cornelia," he said. "Forget your guilt. Remember, my would-be-lover, that all women in Llangarlia can choose as they will." He smiled, genuinely now. "And

they always have that right to say no. I just wish you'd
said it a few minutes earlier."

"I'm sorry," I said, knowing that if this had been Brutus
he would never have heard that "no." He would not even
have let my lips frame the word . . .

"Have you had many lovers?" I blurted, trying to change
the subject and, as always, only making it worse.

"Yes. Many women have asked me to their beds."

"And do you have children?"

"Two daughters, both with the same woman, and a son."

"And your lovers, the women who have had your children, would not be jealous that you are here now? With
me?"

"No." He touched my face again, but it was merely the
lightest of caresses, and not demanding. "They would be
pleased for me, *and* for you. They would hope that you
bore a child."

I was suddenly very, very glad I'd brought the proceed-
ings to a halt. Brutus would kill me if he thought my belly
was full of another man's child.

"Who are you, Cornelia? How can you make me yearn
for you so deeply?" Coel said softly, and to that I had no
answer.

WE SAT THERE FOR A LITTLE WHILE LONGER,
hardly speaking, enjoying the sunshine and the insects as
they buzzed about the late flowers. Then, as even the milk
root failed to please Achates, Coel led me back to the house
(*my* house, he called it, Cornelia's house) and back to the
less than tender care of Aethylla who by now, having
searched for me all morning, had yet one more reason to
chide me.

Brutus, Hicetaon, and Corineus came back to the house
after several hours, sitting about the hearth with Aethylla
and myself and eating a simple meal.

Brutus ignored me, and although I expected it, I could
hardly bear his pointed dismissal. I rebuked myself yet

again for being so stupid in destroying that fragile harmony that had grown between us since Achates' birth . . . right at the point where Brutus' dream woman had become a living, breathing reality.

Hera! I doubted *she* would be so stupid as to alienate Brutus with ill-considered stupidities!

Later, when we'd retired to our beds, Brutus turned to me as we settled down, and I tensed, hardly believing he could be this kind, after all.

But he just stared at me—I could see the flat, irritated gleam of his eyes in the light of the oil lamp left burning by the door—and then turned away, rolling over to sleep with a disinterested grunt.

Unsurprised, hurt beyond knowing, I eventually managed to slide into sleep myself.

I WOKE VERY LATE IN THE NIGHT, SUDDENLY REalizing there was someone standing by our bed.

"Shush," said a woman's voice, and I blinked, my eyes adjusting to the dim light cast by the glowing coals in the hearth.

A woman stood by our bed, black-haired and beautiful, and I gasped, suddenly knowing who she must be.

Genvissa, the MagaLlan, she who wanted me gone from Brutus' side and of whom Brutus dreamed.

But I also *recognized* her. This was the "goddess" who had come to me and pushed me into precipitating the Mesopotamian rebellion!

That was no goddess appearing to you, but the greatest of Darkwitches! Blangan had said.

"Go back to sleep, girl," the Darkwitch said, and her voice was an ice field. "I have come only for your husband."

Brutus was awake now, and he sat up in our bed.

"Genvissa," he said, and his voice was a seething, vast hunger.

Chapter Seven

$\mathscr{G}$ENVISSA DREW BACK FROM THE BED, AL-
lowing Brutus space to stand and dress himself. She
drew her cloak tighter about her, the cold of the autumn night biting deep, and saw that Brutus' child-wife
stared at her with wide, apprehensive eyes.

Her distress pleased Genvissa. Gods, she could not understand what Brutus saw in her! She was so young, and
unbelievably irritating in that youth. She was cringing back
in the bed like a baby who didn't know whether to sulk or
weep in fright, and Genvissa could not for an instant imagine how Brutus had roused himself enough to get a child
off her.

Well, son or not, Cornelia would never hold Brutus.

Genvissa lowered her lids and sent ill will coursing Cornelia's way, wishing that Brutus had knocked the life out
of her when he'd discovered she'd kept secrets about Blangan's death.

And what was the girl doing there in the first instance?

Cornelia was still regarding Genvissa with those huge
childlike eyes, and Genvissa felt a moment of doubt, almost
of trepidation. She shivered. *Damn this girl.*

"Why are you here so early?" Brutus said, finally slipping on his shoes and reaching for his cloak.

Genvissa gave Cornelia one final, baleful glare, then
searched out Brutus' eyes in the gloom. "We have a long
way to go before dawn," she said, then brushed past him
and left the house.

Brutus saw Hicetaon sitting up in his bed, Aethylla looking over his shoulder with nervous eyes.

He nodded at Hicetaon, then he, too, left the house.

There was a silence, then Hicetaon sighed and snuggled down, pulling Aethylla down with him.

Across the chamber, in the sleeping bay Brutus had left, Cornelia curled into a ball and wept silently.

WHEN BRUTUS EMERGED FROM THE HOUSE HE saw that Genvissa sat on a horse several paces away.

She reached behind her and patted the horse's rump. "Come."

He looked at her face, then smiled and vaulted onto its back behind Genvissa.

It shifted, not liking the double weight, and Brutus needed no more excuse than that to grab at Genvissa's waist to steady himself.

Her flesh was firm underneath the layers of material, and the shifting of her body with the movement of the horse made the breath catch in his throat.

He dropped his hands to his thighs, rebalancing himself, and he thought he saw her smile as her face turned slightly toward him.

"Steady?" she said.

"Yes," he replied, roughly.

She took the halter rope of the horse in her right hand, gripping its shaggy mane in her left, and touched her heels to its flanks, guiding it toward the ford over the Llan at Thorney Isle.

"We go to the Veiled Hills?" Brutus said.

Again she shifted slightly so that her face was half turned to him. "Indeed. I want to show you where we shall rebuild Troy."

She turned even more, and Brutus' body tightened as her body moved against his. "I want to show you," she said, "where we will play the Game."

He wanted to kiss her then, very hard, and he thought he would have done save that she turned back to the front, and he was left with nothing but the flowing blackness of her hair, and the scent of her warm flesh rising through her cloak.

He lifted his hands, hesitated, then rested them lightly on her hips.

She did not react, but neither did she object.

Thus they rode, swaying in harmony with the horse's movements, their bodies lightly touching with every jolt, both thinking of the Game, and of the power and the dance they would make together.

GENVISSA GUIDED THE HORSE ACROSS THE FORD, then stopped at the base of Tot Hill on Thorney Isle.

"Within the circle of a day's ride," she said softly, "there are many holy hills and mounds. But there is a gathering of six of them, the most sacred of all, and it is these six which form the Veiled Hills. This"—she nodded at Tot Hill looming dark above them—"is the first of them. It guards this ford, and the roads that converge at this point from all corners of Llangarlia. It forms one point in the circle of light we make during our most important yearly rituals, and is also the Assembly hill, where the Mothers of all Houses meet once every year at the time of the Slaughter Festival to settle disputes and discuss those issues needed to keep our society living in harmony. This year, this Assembly, I will talk to the Mothers of you, and of the Game."

"*Will* they agree?" said Brutus softly into her hair. "And when? How long must we wait for this approval?"

He felt rather than saw her smile. "The Slaughter Festival is in a week's time, Brutus. I will talk with the Mothers then. And yes, I will give them no choice."

"How can you be sure, Genvissa?"

"Aerne is dying, Brutus. You saw this, surely."

"Yes."

"And his god Og is dead. The Mothers will have no alternative but to accept you. They need you, and me, and the Game, if this land is to survive."

"Og is *dead*?"

"Aye." She shrugged. "He had been dying a long time. Now shush," she said, and he felt her body move under his hands, "and still your worries. They can wait until we reach our destination. It won't be long. Wait."

She urged the horse forward, and Brutus leaned in against her back, feeling her warmth, and put his concerns away as he enjoyed the swaying of her body.

They skirted the shoreline of Thorney Isle, moving about its southern aspect, then turned north to cross another, and much shallower ford, through the northern arm of the Ty River.

North of the Ty stretched extensive marshlands, but there was a raised road that wound through them, its perimeters clearly marked with pale stone. Genvissa pushed the horse into a trot.

"This is one of the roads that lead into the central heartlands of the island," she said. "Within three days' ride it leaves Llangarlia, entering the wild tribal areas of the central and western regions of Albion."

"It is a well-constructed road," Brutus said, meaning the compliment. He'd rarely seen a road so well graded, graveled, and clearly marked. "And it leads straight into wild tribal lands?" He chuckled softly. "No wonder you think Llangarlia needs the protection of the Game."

"In our defense," Genvissa said, "the central and western regions of Albion were not always as wild as they are now. Once they were stable, gentle farming communities, as we are, and the road was needed to trade with them. But over the past two generations dark tribes from the wild island to the west have overrun much of Albion, and now threaten us."

They rode a farther distance in silence, Genvissa eventually turning the horse northeast off the main road as it left the marshes. The ground very gradually began to rise.

Once they were on the trackway leading northeast, Genvissa dropped the halter rope of the horse, allowing it to continue forward unguided. "She knows her way now," she said, and pointed ahead.

Brutus peered through the faint moonlight—it was close to the full moon, but the sky was heavily clouded—and saw a hill rising in the distance. It was a good size, girded about its base by several stands of trees, its slopes steep but smooth, its summit flattened.

He suddenly realized that for the first time since he'd arrived this area north of the Llan was completely free of mist or fog.

"The Llandin," she said softly, and Brutus could hear the awe in her voice. "It is a place of immense power and holiness," Genvissa continued. "It is the greatest of the Veiled Hills.

"See"—again she pointed, this time to a vast tree standing at the base of the southern slope of the Llandin—"the Holy Oak, and beside it a spring-fed rock pool with water so clear and still that when you pour it into a bowl, and say the right words, you can see into the Far World."

"And do you do that often, Genvissa?"

"Whenever I need to consult with my foremothers," she said. "Yes."

They'd reached the oak tree now, and Genvissa indicated they should dismount.

Brutus jumped to the ground, then reached up to help Genvissa down.

She rested her hands on his shoulders as she slid down, and smiled her thanks, then took his hand in hers, and led him to the foot of the tree, deep beneath its gnarled, twisting branches.

There was a faint, strange light here, and Brutus shivered.

Feeling it, Genvissa tightened the grip on his hand, and led him several paces away to where, amid several large, moss-covered rocks, a small stream bubbled out from deep underground into a waist-deep pool. It steamed in the night air: the waters were warm.

It was from the water that the light emanated.

Again Genvissa's hand tightened, and she drew Brutus close to her. "For many generations, countless generations, Llangarlia's mother goddess Mag lived in the waters of the land. This spring was her favorite haunt. Sometimes"—she drew in a deep breath, resting her free hand on her belly—"when a woman wanted to conceive, she came here and prayed to Mag to gift her child a soul great in power and mystery. She washed these waters over her breasts, so that when she suckled her newborn, it would be nourished with the wisdom of the earth."

Brutus studied Genvissa's face. Her eyes were downcast in reverie, settled on the bubbling water. A great gentleness had settled over her features, an emotion Brutus had hitherto not thought her capable of, and without thinking, he lifted his hand and touched her cheek.

"Did you come here," said Brutus, "before you conceived your children?"

She looked at him, startled, then smiled. "Yes. I came here before I conceived each of my three daughters. But Mag is weak now"—*gone, where I cannot find her*—"and these waters pretty but ineffectual, and I doubt I will come here before I conceive my daughter-heir. There will be far more power in her making than these waters can give."

There was a message in her eyes, and Brutus understood it very well. "Your daughter-heir . . . will her conception form part of the Game?" he said.

"Partly," she said, "but mostly her conception shall be part of that smaller, but no less holy game that is played between a man and a woman. The game between"—she paused—"you and I."

He stared at her, not able to speak, feeling as if his entire body were frozen with a combination of longing and fear—fear that somehow this *was* all a dream, a phantasm sent by a malicious god who used hope to destroy.

Then, for no reason at all, Brutus remembered that night he and Cornelia had made love under the stars by the rock pools, and remembered how gentle she had been then, and willing, and sweet.

"I have a wife, Genvissa. I cannot just cast her aside."

"Does she matter to you that much? Would a Kingman

allow a *wife* to keep him from the Game, and the Mistress of the Labyrinth?"

He was silent, and the fact that he did not immediately agree with her infuriated Genvissa. But she hid her rage well, and all she did was smile, and lay her hand lightly on his chest. "If you had known of me and what I was before you married Cornelia, would you still have married her?"

"No," he said. "I wouldn't, but you chose to appear to me as Artemis. If perhaps you'd chosen your true form, and your true state, then I might not have been so ready to take a wife when I did. Then *you* could have been my wife."

"Neither MagaLlans nor Mistresses of the Labyrinth are ever *wives*, Brutus."

He grinned slightly. "Then how can you object to Cornelia?"

Genvissa drew in a long, deep breath. Brutus saw that she used it to calm herself. He was amused by her jealousy, and also gratified by it. That she was jealous of Cornelia gave him some much-needed leverage over her.

"She can never compare to you, Genvissa," he said softly. "What is Cornelia, but a girl, and a too-predictably tiresome one at that?"

Genvissa relaxed and gave him a brilliant smile. "As you say. We are lovers destined to power and immortality, and she is but a wife."

He kissed her again, enjoying her taste, her softness, and all the promise of her.

Eventually, reluctantly, she pulled back, and laughed.

"Climb with me," she said. "Climb the Llandin with me."

Chapter Eight

THEY STOOD, BREATHING HEAVILY FROM the climb, on the summit of the Llandin. Genvissa still held Brutus by the hand, their fingers entwined, and she drew him to the southern rim of the summit.

"Behold," she said simply, and the clouds parted, and silvery moonlight spilled over the land spread out before them.

The first thing Brutus saw was the great stretch of the Llan running east–west several thousand paces distant directly in front of him. Wetlands—tidal mudflats and marshlands—stretched on either side of it, making its shoreline indistinct, and giving great swaths of land a shimmering, mystical aspect in the moonlight.

He looked slightly to the west, and saw where the Llan turned south, and the Ty River flowed to meet it, its two arms enclosing about Thorney Isle in close embrace. On the other side of the Llan from Thorney Isle, Llanbank slumbered dark and unknowing, only a few trails of smoke marking the existence of the sleepers within.

Genvissa had followed the direction of his gaze, and now she drew his attention to the east, to a hill rising halfway between the Llandin and the Llan.

It was a little smaller than the Llandin, but had a Stone Dance atop its summit.

"The Pen," Genvissa said. "See"—Brutus followed her finger—"it also has a stand of trees at its base, and under those trees, as here at the Llandin, there is a sacred well. There, unlike where we stood, there is a small entrance into the hill, and if a man or a woman is brave, and has no misdeeds to mar their soul, they can follow the twists and turns of the rock tunnel to a great cave, whose roof is made up of great crystals. When you stand beneath this dome of crystal, and raise your torch, it is said that the light is brilliant enough to hurt your eyes."

"You have not been?"

She shook her head. "It is not important to me. Ah, Brutus, can you see, beyond the Pen, there, to the east, on the bank of the Llan, do you see those three smaller mounds?"

Forgetting the cave beneath the Pen, Brutus looked where she indicated. There, in the southeast, sitting virtually on the northern bank of the Llan, were three mounds only some twenty paces high. Two streams—the western one almost a small river—flanked the nearest of them. The wetlands had retreated here, and Brutus saw that the land on which these three mounds stood, and through which flowed the two streams, was solid and good.

Something flickered in his belly, and he knew what Genvissa would say next.

"That is where we will build our Troia Nova," she said softly, squeezing his hand, "encompassing those three mounds. The farthest from us, and the one closest to the Llan, is called the White Mount, and it, like the Llandin and the Pen, has a sacred well beneath it. The next mound, sandwiched in the middle, is Mag's Hill, and the last, closest to us, is Og's Hill. You can see where the ferry crosses the Llan, connecting the great northern road to the road leading to the coast. It is a good place, Brutus, commanding both the river and the roads, and taking as its base three of the Veiled Hills."

Brutus drew in a deep breath. Here. Troia Nova.

"By the gods," he said. "This is an auspicious location. But"—he looked at Genvissa—"this site also encompasses deep troubles. I am a stranger, bringing with me many thousands of strangers, trampling into the most sacred site of your people to build—with a powerful foreign magic—a city such as Llangarlia and its people have never seen before . . . never even *conceived* of before. Are you enough to ensure that all opposition is quelled? By the gods, Genvissa, surely there will be *some* opposition."

She let go his hand, and he was not unaware of the significance of that action, then sighed.

"What must I say to convince you, Brutus? The Mothers will not oppose me, and the people of Llangarlia will do whatever the Mothers advise them. The Slaughter Festival is in a week's time."

"And the goddess Mag. What will she think?"

"Mag is irrelevant!" Genvissa snapped.

"Well, then, what of that monster that Cornelia told me of? That creature who devoured Blangan? Your *sister*?"

"Do you think I have not mourned her loss, Brutus?" She drew in a deep breath. "Blangan talked to you of her role in the splitting of Og's power."

It was not a question.

"Yes. She told me of her rape, of the birth of her son, of how her—*your*—mother forced her to leave this land."

"All true, Brutus. I deny none of it. But what I did, and what my mother did, was all done for this land. Og was weak anyway, as was Mag. They could no longer protect this land which I, as all my foremothers including Ariadne, loved so much. We *knew* how to protect it—rebuild the Game here—and, yes, we took steps to ensure that both Game and land would flower. When you were fifteen, Brutus, you took steps to ensure your future. I, and all my foremothers, merely did the same thing."

He nodded, his eyes moving past her to wander once more over the enchanted landscape that spread beyond the Llandin. "There will be no other opposition?"

"No. Of course not. Who could there be?"

He looked back at her, his eyes now unreadable. "There will be no trouble from Asterion?"

ASTERION WAS BARELY MORE THAN A MASS OF *unrecognisable tissue clinging relentlessly to the wall of the womb of Goffar's wife, yet was nonetheless fully aware and wielding all the power of which he was capable. His simple body mass quivered in delight at Brutus' words.*

There will be trouble a-plenty, *he thought*, but you will never see it coming until it has torn your entire world apart.

PROFOUNDLY SHOCKED, GENVISSA ACTUALLY took a step back. *"What?"*

"Asterion. You know he walked free once Ariadne destroyed the Game in the Aegean, spreading evil and malevolence everywhere. *He* cannot be pleased at the idea the Game is to recommence—he cannot wish to be trapped again. Have you thought of Asterion, Genvissa? Will he come to tear out our throats while we sleep sated with love?"

"Why do you ask me of Asterion?"

Brutus nodded very slightly, looking at her. *So. Asterion was a threat.* "Cornelia mentioned him. The first night I took her, she asked me if I was Asterion, as if she were expecting him."

Genvissa hissed, but Brutus continued.

"And I dreamed of she and him, in a great stone hall. She had invited him to lie with her, and he repaid her with death."

Genvissa closed the distance between them and grabbed Brutus' wrist. "She is his tool! Brutus, she must die!"

"Tell me of Asterion, Genvissa."

"Cornelia must—"

"Tell me of Asterion! Damn you, Genvissa, I am your Kingman. I need to know. Don't think that the pretty sway of your hips and the swell of your breasts have addled my wits completely!"

She drew in a deep breath, then let it out slowly and visibly relaxed her shoulders. "Asterion has lived many lives since Ariadne destroyed the Game and freed him."

"Stop there. What no one has ever understood, Genvissa, is why Asterion should be free anyway. Was he not destroyed by Theseus?"

"Ariadne made a pact with his shade. She needed power to enact her revenge, Asterion gave her that power in return for her destroying the Game and giving him rebirth into life."

Brutus threw up his hands and walked away a few paces. "Gods, Genvissa. He is going to come after you—*us*—with every particle of his malignant humor!"

"No! No. Brutus . . ." Genvissa walked over to him and put a hand on his arm. "He is no threat. None whatsoever, thus I have not mentioned him to you."

Brutus shot her a cynical look. He was "no threat," yet she still wanted Cornelia dead just in case Asterion used her as his tool?

"My mother, Herron," Genvissa continued, "cast a great enchantment—one so great it killed her in the doing. Asterion was due to be reborn, and she made sure that he was not only born into a weak and crippled body, one that gave him very little power, but was born in a place so far away that ten years' travel would never broach the distance between here and there. He would know that the Game was being resurrected, but there would be nothing he could do about it."

"So Asterion lives, crippled, a lifetime away."

She hesitated, and Brutus seized both her hands. "Asterion lives, crippled, a lifetime away? *Yes?*"

"He killed himself," Genvissa said, very low. "Very recently. He is preparing for rebirth."

"I can't believe you did not think this important enough to mention to me, Genvissa. For all the gods' sakes, *I am your Kingman!* I needed to know!"

"And what threat do you think a mewling infant is going to be, Brutus? Tell me that! We can rebuild the Game within six months . . . a year at the outside. He won't even be toddling before he is again trapped. *Asterion is no threat!*"

Finally, Brutus nodded. "Don't ever keep such a thing from me again, Genvissa."

"Of course not." She leaned forward and kissed him.

"And don't," he said, drawing back infinitesimally from her, "hurt Cornelia."

Genvissa's lips drew back, revealing her teeth, but whether in a smile or a grimace, Brutus could not tell.

Chapter Nine

Cornelia Speaks

WEPT, FOR MY OWN FOOLISHNESS MORE THAN anything else. How could I have left it until that moment when my rival stood before me to realize that I loved Brutus, and wanted him more than anything else in my life, even Achates?

Are other women this foolish, or did I invent the condition?

Oh, Hera, this Genvissa . . . I had never imagined a woman so beautiful, so powerful, so *sure* of herself and of Brutus.

I remembered Coel's words to me: *Genvissa wants Brutus, Cornelia. She will make sure, one way or the other, that you will be set aside.*

No! No, surely I could do something . . .

After all, Cornelia, it is hardly as if Brutus loves you, is it.

I wept. Who was I compared to *her*? A foolish girl who had surely destroyed any chance she ever had to make Brutus love her. Maybe Brutus would set me aside, maybe not. But even if he did not, I doubted I would be anything more than an irritating and gratefully occasional distraction.

I would be the butt of everyone's jests, and pity.

I remembered Brutus once saying that he would make me queen of this new land to which we sailed, and I wept yet more. I would be an empty husk of a queen, sitting forgotten to one side while the *real* queen, Genvissa, basked in the adoration both of my husband and of legend.

I was nothing, and it had taken me all this time to realize it.

BRUTUS CAME BACK SEVERAL HOURS AFTER dawn, brimming with excitement. He spared me a glance, dismissive and cold, then clapped Hicetaon and Corineus on the shoulders and drew into discussion.

I heard *her* name mentioned, many times, and with that same hunger and admiration he'd used when she'd come for him during the night.

In the end, driven to distraction by Brutus' mutterings with Hicetaon and Corineus, and by Aethylla's barely concealed amused glances in my direction (did she revel in the knowledge of Genvissa, then?), and not able to hear my husband say Genvissa's name one more time, I wrapped myself and Achates warmly against the cool gray of the day, and escaped the house.

Would Genvissa take Achates, too, when she took my husband?

I suppose at some level I knew where I was going, who I was going to. I had only one friend, one person I could talk to, and that was Coel: Corineus had become ever more distant with me since he'd realized I'd witnessed his beloved Blangan's death and not said anything. In the end, I did not have to find Coel at all, for, as always it seemed, he waited for me in the shadows of a house some twenty paces distant.

"So," he said, "you have met Genvissa."

I said nothing.

"You must not judge us all by one woman," he said, and I looked away, determined not to succumb to weeping again. What must this man think of me?

"Have you eaten this morning?" he asked.

I shook my head. "I am not hungry."

He tsked softly, but did not comment further on the subject of food. "Would you like to meet my family?" he asked. "My mothers and sisters and aunts and their children?"

Some part of me knew what he was doing—offering me an antidote to Genvissa. "Thank you," I said, and he smiled and, a hand gently on my elbow, guided me through Llanbank.

LLANBANK WAS LARGER THAN I THOUGHT, AND I said as much.

Coel explained that Llanbank was the largest settlement in Llangarlia, catering as it did both to the trade routes that crisscrossed Llangarlia and to the proximity of the Veiled Hills, the sacred heart of the land. He explained a little about the Veiled Hills, pausing briefly at a crossroads within Llanbank so we could look north across the Llan to where the hills rose in the distance.

"Where is the mist?" I said. "Every day that I have been here thus far the hills have been veiled in fog."

"Sometimes they wish to hide themselves, sometimes to reveal themselves," he said. "Perhaps, because we are close to the Slaughter Festival, they have decided to—"

"The *what*?"

He grinned at the expression on my face. "The Slaughter Festival," he repeated. "That most sacred festival of the year when we seize all strangers within our midst and sacrifice them to the great gods Og and Mag . . ."

He saw the horror on my face and burst out laughing. "I jest only, Cornelia. The Slaughter Festival is the autumn festival where we give thanks to Og and Mag for the harvests of spring and summer, and also slaughter the stock we cannot keep over winter. Despite its name, it is a celebration of great joy, and much good-hearted mischief. Ah, I am sorry, Cornelia, I did not mean to scare you."

To my shame, the tears were now flowing freely down my face (I cannot *believe* I was spending all this time weeping in Coel's company!). It was not his ill-timed jest as such, but that the scare it had given me had brought to the surface all my fears about Genvissa.

"Did she frighten you that much?" he said, very soft. Then, very slowly, very gently, he gathered myself and Achates in his arms, and held us tight. He rested his chin on my head and, as I sobbed the harder, rocked me tenderly back and forth, as if I were the baby and not Achates.

"Genvissa is not greatly loved by many among my people," he said eventually, once my sobs had quieted somewhat. "You are not the only one she terrifies."

He tipped my face up to his, and kissed me—without lust, or passion, or even love, but deep with reassurance and comfort, those two things I needed most.

Again he grinned. "I would not have done that if I had known I would have made you weep again," he said, and I managed to wipe away my tears and return his smile.

"Now," he said, "my mother's house is not far from here, and I can feel you shivering from both cold and hunger, so it is to my mother that I must take you."

As he led me down the road, I realized we were in the heart of Llanbank, and that we'd been standing there, close together, embracing, while about us people walked and gossiped. The circular, stone-walled houses were everywhere about us, crowding on either side of the roadway, and while some people were idling about, gossiping over outdoor cooking fires, others were making the way down the street with baskets of produce or herding small flocks of sheep or goats.

I blushed, for shame at what Coel and I had been doing, and then realized that no one had taken much note. Many people called out greetings to Coel, or stopped him for a word or two, but there was no derision or mockery in anyone's voices, and only a simple curiosity expressed about my presence.

To everyone who stopped, Coel introduced me as "Mother Cornelia," the head of my household, and that made me smile at the thought of Brutus being relegated to the status of the breeding stallion who was kept in his stall most months of the year, and only allowed out when he was needed for mating purposes. People smiled at me, and said welcoming words, and blessed Achates, and treated me as one among many . . . as one of them, which the Trojans had never done.

As we progressed (now somewhat slowly) down the road toward Coel's house, I began to cheer up considerably.

Coel's home was as most other houses—a circular, thick stone-walled house with a conical roof of thatch. There was a woman standing outside, watching our progress down the road toward her, waiting patiently for our arrival.

I glanced surreptitiously at her the closer we came, curious, and somewhat nervous, at what she would make of me . . . and of her son bringing me into her house.

But I need not have worried. Coel's mother, Erith, was a tiny woman, almost birdlike in her manners and movements, and possessed of such a mischievous sense of humor that every third remark made me grin. She was much older than I, and I thought that Coel must have been a child of her later years, but she was possessed of so much life that I wondered, despite her lines, if she was still producing children even now.

She welcomed me at the door of her house with a hug and a laugh, gently chiding Coel for taking so long to bring me to her, then led me inside.

I stopped the instant I stepped inside the house, stunned by its beauty.

The house that Coel had given us on the outskirts of Llanbank had been bare inside, save for the necessary furnishings and blankets needed for our comfort, and with the experience of the isolated and functional hamlets we'd stayed at on our travels from Totnes to Llanbank, I'd thought that all houses must be the same.

But this interior, this was a miracle of color and life and movement. Like our house, there was a second level, a wooden platform resting on the inner circle of wooden posts that supported the top of the conical roof. From this platform were a series of woven banners and ribbons, in every hue of nature, that moved on every breath of air. Among the banners and ribbons hung pieces of carved antler and bone, as well as tiny pieces of quartz hung on slivers of almost invisible gut, pieces of hide and fur, carved seashells, and what I thought was probably dyed seaweed. All these strange things had been hung so cunningly, and with such understanding, that even though the effect should have been that of an overcrowding of completely incompatible objects, they all merged to create instead a sense of grace and light and movement.

It was as though Erith and her family had managed to hang all that was most beautiful and wondrous in the world of nature from the central raised wooden platform.

Erith saw my face and, in what I was realizing was her normal reaction to most things, laughed. "This is our living house," she said, a soft hand in the small of my back guiding me toward the central hearth. "We have a smaller house at the back of this one in which we cook and weave and do all the snarling at each other that all families need to do." She grinned. "No one dares snarl in this our living house."

There was a bench of stone built about the hearth, and I sat down, still staring about me. The house was much larger than the one I shared with Brutus and our companions, with sleeping niches for at least fifteen people, and room for far more about the hearth.

Indeed, there were already some eight other women and two men seated about who, as Erith introduced me, all came up to me, took my hands between theirs, and kissed me a welcome on my cheek. Most of their names fled my head as soon as they were spoken, I was still so overcome with wonder at both Erith and her house, but I retained enough wit to understand that they comprised two of Erith's elder sisters (and if I'd thought Erith tiny and birdlike in her age, then these two women looked as if the merest breath of wind might shatter their fragile bones), three of her daughters (two of whom were noticeably pregnant, and one of whom—a woman named Tuenna—had two toddlers playing at a safe distance from the hearth), one a cousin visiting from the north, and the final two were grown grand-daughters. The men, both older than Coel, were his broth-ers, and I was given to understand that there was another brother as well as two uncles who, in the Llangarlian man-ner, still lived in the house of their maternity, but who currently were out minding the family's flocks of sheep and goats.

One of Erith's daughters, the one farthest forward in her pregnancy, brought me a bowl of broth that, despite what I'd told Coel earlier, made my mouth water with hunger. Erith took Achates from me—I found I did not mind in the least her presumption—and bade me eat.

And as I did so, the warmth and laughter of Erith's fam-ily flowed over and about me, warming me through as the fire and the food never could, as they chatted about family matters and the gossip of the town.

The entire mood and sense of the house were unarguably feminine, yet neither Coel nor his two brothers seemed out of place nor even uncomfortable. They melded perfectly into the discussion, much of which was about Coel's two sisters' pregnancies, as if conversing about such things was as natural to them as arguing about the strength and sharp-ness of a sword.

I was fascinated. I'd known of the matriarchal nature of Llangarlian society, but this was the first time I'd been so exposed to it: Ecub's house had been too riven with un-derlying tensions for me to feel as much at home as I did here.

Eventually I realized that the family was discussing the two sisters' yet-to-be-born children as if they already knew the sex and even the personality of the babies the women carried.

Intrigued, I put aside my now-empty bowl (thanking Er-ith and her family as I did so), and waded my way into the conversation.

"How is it," I asked, leaning forward, "that you know the sex and character of your unborn children?"

Erith, handing Achates to Coel, took my hand, and held it between hers. "It is Mag's gift to women," she said, and explained—as Blangan had once explained—how Mag graced the women of Llangarlia with the knowledge of the sex and character of the child they carried.

"All Llangarlian women feel Mag in our wombs," Erith went on. "It is where she lives . . . although in the past year her presence has been but a whisper." Her voice was indescribably sad, and for a moment she paused, as if collecting herself.

Then Erith glanced at Coel, and when she looked back to me one of her hands shifted, and rested on my belly. "Do you feel her within you, Cornelia?"

I opened my mouth to deny it, for how could I if I were not Llangarlian born? But then I remembered that night I'd spent in Mag's Dance, and the dance that I had done without ever being taught, and I was no longer so sure of myself.

"I don't know," I said.

Erith lifted her hand from my belly to my face. Her own face was puzzled, all her humor momentarily gone. "You *do* have the feel of her about you," she said. "How odd, for a stranger . . ."

And again her eyes met Coel's.

I was now feeling most uncomfortable, as if my flesh were being assessed for market, but then Erith laughed, and my uneasiness subsided.

"But then you are a mother who loves her child," Erith said, "and perhaps that is what I feel."

We talked then of many things: a strange spring where women could beg Mag's aid in choosing a caring soul for their child; the meaning behind the dangling decorations above our heads; the blight that had struck Llangarlia in the past generation; Coel's children, and those of his sisters and brothers; the men whom Erith had taken to her bed in order to get her own brood of wonderful children; Erith's mother, who had been one of the strongest Mothers in Llangarlia when it came to weaving Mag's magic.

At this last subject the mood grew somber.

"I doubt any Mother will ever again know Mag in the same manner and depth that my mother did," Erith said. "Mag has faded away in this past year. Her power has all but gone. Perhaps as her lover Og's power waned, so did hers. No one knows. But no Mother has been able to use Mag magic to any great degree since last autumn. We can still touch her, barely, but not as once we could."

"Many of us," Tuenna put in, "wonder if that is Genvissa's doing."

There was a silence, and I knew a line had been crossed.

I also realized, if I hadn't previously, that I had been accepted completely into this community of Erith's house. This talk was not meant for untrustworthy ears.

"Genvissa?" I said softly. *You are not the only one she terrifies*, Coel had said.

"Who else could have harmed Mag, *and* Og, so easily?" said Erith. "And who else would it benefit so much as Genvissa? Yes, Genvissa, Cornelia. Our MagaLlan. The woman who is supposed to protect our gods and our land before all else."

"She is a Darkwitch," I said, remembering what Blangan had said. Then, from nowhere, came more words. "Her foremother Ariadne destroyed an entire civilization. Genvissa will do the same here."

There was a silence, and I knew everyone was watching me.

"I wish . . ." I said, and did not know how to finish the sentence; I felt as though something was tearing apart deep inside me.

"I know," Coel said very softly, and gathered me into his arms.

Chapter Ten

THE RECTANGULAR STONE BUILDING ON the slopes of Tot Hill was filled with women. They milled about its internal space, their quiet talk a low hum, their movements deliberate, tempered, courteous, their faces gentle, whatever may have been on their minds.

They were the Mothers of Llangarlia, the women who headed each household, who spoke for each family, who gathered here today as they did once a year to discuss how what they had learned from the past would lead them into the future. The oldest of them was a wizened ancient, her back so curved she had to deliberately lift her face upward to avoid continuously studying her feet, her facial features so drooped both her nose and her mouth had collapsed to rest on her chin. The youngest was a woman only barely into her twenties, her belly rounded in pregnancy, her eyes and demeanor respectful of all the experience and wisdom that walked about her.

Every one of them felt the weight of not only her own responsibility in leading and advising her own House, but of her part in their collective responsibility.

Every one of them had heard of the arrival of the Trojans—of their *numbers*, by Mag!—and on their wish to settle in Llangarlia.

Every one of them had lost sleep in worry over the situation, and yet every one of them here today presented a calm and ordered face to the world, for there was no benefit in panic, and no possible need to push their troubled peoples even further into worry.

Three women had grouped into a corner, their faces as

calm as everyone else's, their eyes as watchful as they studied the other women milling about them.

Ecub, only very recently arrived from her journey from her home next to Mag's Dance, looked particularly weary. Her face was pale, her eyes dulled with lack of sleep. Nevertheless, her hair was carefully dressed, her wool robe neatly arranged, her shoulders straight, and she held herself tall, her hands folded before her.

Beside her Erith looked even tinier than usual, although in no way diminished.

Their companion was Mais, Mother of one of the Houses closely associated with the forests above the Veiled Hills, one of Loth's strongest allies, and mother of a daughter who had only recently conceived of her own daughter by Loth.

"What can we do?" Mais said. "She will destroy us!" Coel had earlier spoken with them, telling them of what he and Loth now knew.

"She will most certainly destroy us if we speak publicly against her," Erith said. "Our respect and our loyalty should be to the MagaLlan."

"Our respect and our loyalty *was* to the MagaLlan," Ecub said, her voice low to disguise its bitterness, "before that Darkwitch from Crete corrupted that once-remarkable line." She was dressed in a robe of very deep red wool, and for an instant the red of her robe reflected in her eyes, and Erith shuddered.

"We cannot speak publicly against her," she said. "Not yet. This Assembly's loyalty will still hold with Genvissa, even if what she presents us with today will tear out the heart of Llangarlia."

"You would have us smile, and nod, and *agree* with her?" Ecub hissed.

Erith fought the urge to grind her teeth, smiling and nodding at another of the Mothers who momentarily passed close by.

"I am saying that there may be better ways to deal with

her, and her wicked witchery, than making victims of ourselves by speaking out in this assembly."

"Yes?" said Ecub. "How might that be then?"

Erith, who'd had her hands folded before her in the Mother's traditional posture of calm authority, now dropped them to her side, taking a hand of each of the women beside her. "I think Genvissa has an enemy she may not recognize until it is too late," Erith said, so very, very softly Mais and Ecub had to lean close to her to hear.

There was a silence, a great stillness.

"Cornelia?" Ecub whispered. "I had wondered about her, too, but . . ."

"Yes," Erith said. "Cornelia. Whatever happened at Mag's Dance, I think Mag's power is still with Cornelia. I felt it a bare few days ago."

"Who is this Cornelia?" Mais said. "I have not heard of her."

"She is the wife," Erith said, and all three women's faces assumed pained expressions at that most horrid and foreign of offices, "of the leader of the Trojans, Brutus. She is young, naive, foolish, ignorant . . . and yet . . ."

"Yet she came to Mag's Dance unannounced," said Ecub. "And she danced Mag's Nuptial Dance!"

Mais exclaimed softly, while Erith, who had known this from Coel, merely nodded consideringly.

"She is a natural mother," Erith continued, "and when I laid a hand to her womb I swear that I felt Mag . . . in a *Greek* woman! My son Coel tells me he sees magic in her, and felt it on a brief occasion when Cornelia permitted him brief penetration. He thought to loathe these Trojans, these invaders, and yet for Cornelia he feels only respect. Warmth. An urge to protect. Love."

"He wants to sleep with her," Mais said, and laughed.

Erith giggled, making her seem momentarily girlish. "Oh, yes, that too. But Cornelia *is* intriguing. The fact that she came unannounced to Mag's Dance, *and* then took a part in the Nuptial Dance as though she had been born to it . . . well, that's astounding. And hopeful."

"When Loth came to her there," Ecub went on, "he did not roar at her, but handled her gently, and spoke well to her."

There was another silence, the three women's eyes on the Mothers moving about the room, not looking at each other.

"We need to speak to Loth," Mais said. "Tonight. Before tomorrow's ceremony."

"Aye," said the other two. "We will speak with Loth."

"MOTHERS!" GENVISSA CALLED, AND STEPPED forth into the center of the room.

As one, all the Mothers present turned to her with bodies and eyes, their movement as choreographed as the most careful dance.

"Our Assembly this year comes at the most opportune time." Genvissa looked about her, ensuring she was the center of attention.

She was dressed in a very white linen robe that left her rounded, strong arms bare, and which was sashed tightly about her waist with a scarlet band, highlighting the sweep of hip and breast. Her raven hair was, as usual, left to tumble carelessly about her shoulders and back, its russet lock marking her as god-favored. Her hands folded before her in the traditional gesture of humility, but above them her eyes flashed, negating any of the humility she may have wished to convey.

She lifted one of her hands, and smiled, warm and gracious. "Please, seat yourselves."

The women lowered themselves to the floor, today covered with soft, warm matting. The younger among them moved swiftly to aid the elder to the few available cushions, and soon all were seated, their eyes centered on Genvissa who had remained standing.

"I come today on a most important and urgent matter," Genvissa said, turning slowly within the circle of Mothers, her eyes making contact with each one in turn. "I come to seek your counsel and guidance."

Ecub grunted, and Erith shot her a warning glance.

"You know of the Trojans," Genvissa continued, "of their arrival, of their numbers, of their wish to settle within Llangarlia. I see no reason to deny them their wish."

The Mothers were too gentle, too restrained to break into an uproar, but they did nevertheless stir, and a great murmuring rose among them.

Genvissa held up her hands. "Mothers, please, hear me out! I speak plainly and swiftly, for events demand no less. You *know* of the troubles which have beset us over the past generation—"

"Ever since your witch mother Herron worked her darkcraft," Ecub muttered, very, very low.

Erith laid a restraining hand on the woman's arm.

"How many of your Houses have lost children to unexplained fevers?" Genvissa cried, her arms now outstretched in supplication. "How many have watched your daughters writhe to their deaths in childbirth where before they dropped their children with the same ease that apple trees drop their fruit in autumn? Our livestock increasingly succumb to malignant diseases, our crops wither in the fields, the ice and the rain and the snow sleet down from the north and turn the thatch of our houses into sodden, moldy useless caps and the flesh between our toes to mildewed horror."

Her voice dropped, and she lowered her arms and her eyes, as if grieving. "And our beloved Gormagog is dying. You know of this. You know"—her voice broke on an almost sob—"you know that Og has finally deserted us."

"And in answer to this you threaten us with an invasion of Trojans?" Ecub could keep her peace no longer, and Erith's fingers dug into the flesh of the woman's forearm.

Ecub ignored the pain. "Who needs these Trojans, MagaLlan. *Us?* Why? Why?"

A murmuring again arose among the Mothers, and Genvissa held up a hand to silence them.

"Mother Ecub speaks only what many of you must think," Genvissa said mildly, although her jaw and shoulders had noticeably tensed. "But I say to you, these Trojans will not harm us; rather, they can protect us. Furthermore, their leader, Brutus, controls a great magic that can restore to us our prosperity and health."

Erith's fingers by now had dug so deep into Ecub's arm that the woman's flesh had turned a deep crimson.

"We *need* his magic, sisters, to fill that void that Og's failure has created. Without him Llangarlia will fail. With him it will regain its strength."

Ecub muttered something uncomplimentary, but to Erith's and Mais' relief she did not raise her voice.

"I have spoken to this Brutus," Genvissa said, her voice once more quiet, compelling. "He will settle among us, become one with us, and in return he will build a great city, powerful with magic, that will guide our return into abundance and happiness."

"Where will he build this 'great city'?" asked a Mother on the far side of the room, and Erith sighed in relief that someone else had managed to deflect Genvissa's attention from herself and her two companions.

Genvissa took a deep breath before answering. "In the Veiled Hills," she said quietly. "Atop the White Mount, Og's Hill, and Mag's Hill."

There was instant uproar, and Genvissa allowed it to continue for several minutes before she again held up her hands for silence.

"Og is dead," she said, "he will not suffer at the loss of Og's Hill. His replacement magic, the Trojan magic, will need to combine with what is left of Mag's power and those strange spirits who live under the White Mount in order to be most effective."

Then, as the muttering continued, she turned to the door, left standing open, and held out her hand.

Aerne, dressed in nothing more than a scarlet hip cloth, entered the chamber, leaning on a great staff. He walked with considerable stiffness and shortness of breath to Genvissa's side, and glared implacably about at the Gathering of Mothers.

"It is necessary," he said.

"Or else?" Ecub shouted, and Erith groaned.

"Or else we will perish," said the Gormagog and, taking Genvissa's hand in his, waved the staff in the space before him.

A vision appeared, and it was one of dread. Naked warriors, daubed in blue clay, swarmed over their land, raping and slaughtering and burning, and howling with laughter all the while.

"They mass to the east," the Gormagog whispered through the horror, "and undoubtedly one day they will launch themselves at us. We have not the strength to defend ourselves. We will vanish, as surely as the autumn leaves are swept into oblivion by the winter winds."

"Mag?" someone cried out, helplessly.

"You know she cannot help against such as this," Aerne said, waving his staff so that the vision folded in upon itself and then disappeared. "Not only is her power weak, but the art of protecting us against swords and fury is alien to her. She is the fertile mother goddess, not the stag-god."

Again, silence, as the Mothers contemplated this.

Everyone knew of Mag's horrifying and deepening weakness. Everyone had felt it.

If she is weak, Ecub thought, her face creased in a savage frown, *it is only through witchery!*

"If we conduct an alliance with the Trojans," continued the Gormagog, "merge their magic with ours, then *this* is what awaits us."

Again his staff waved, and again vision filled the air.

Now a mighty city rose on the banks of the Llan, covering the three sacred mounds, encircled by a high white wall. Its gates stood open, and people were free to move in and out of the city as they willed. In the meadows surrounding the city children played, watched by strong healthy women with big, swollen bellies. Men walked the roads, driving heavily laden grain carts into the city, or hefting the tools of their trades over their shoulders, singing songs, or swapping jests.

The Mothers were silent. They had never seen anything like it—nor had they ever *thought* to see anything like it. How did this pile of stone—this artifice—protect and nurture the *land*?

"This city itself will be the magic," Genvissa said, seeing the expressions in the women's eyes. "It will be as a talisman to us, protecting us for an eternity against all evil and ill favor, and using an ancient magic called the Game."

"Tell us of this 'Game,' " Erith said.

Genvissa cast a glance Erith's way, but was satisfied by the curiosity she saw there. "The Game is used at the foundation of new cities, played first when the initial course of the city walls are laid down, then again when the walls have risen to their full height and are gated. It is a powerful spell-weaving that binds the city to this land as its protector, but," she stressed, as a few Mothers murmured again, "its most potent benefit is that it attracts and then traps all evil besieging a country. Who can deny that evil and blight spreads over this land and through our families?"

Genvissa paused, and when she resumed her voice was low but powerful. "The Game will absorb that evil, trap it, and the blight that has plagued us will vanish as if it had never been. Llangarlia will be strong again, stronger than previously."

"How does it work?" asked a Mother called Lilleth.

Genvissa smiled. She knew she would have them with this next. "It is danced," she said, watching delighted surprise light up many faces. "A labyrinthine dance, very much like Mother Mag's Nuptial Dance, that uses the power of the male and the female to bind and empower the spell-weaving. There are two dances, the first is performed when the foundations of the city walls are laid, and this is called the Dance of the Torches. This first dance raises the evil and blight from the land and traps it in the labyrinthine enchantment of the Game. Then, when the walls are completed, comes the second and last dance, the Dance of the

Flowers, and this will trap the evil forever by erecting a gate of great beauty and sorcery at the entrance to the labyrinth."

"And who will dance?" cried one of the Mothers.

"Myself, and Brutus," said Genvissa. "I need a *strong* partner"—she looked sadly to Aerne, who, humiliated, turned his face aside—"who can withstand the forces of evil the Game shall attract.

"Brutus, the Kingman of the Game, and I will be the male and female force that weaves the Game and ties it to this land. Mothers, I know you distrust strangers, but within a few generations we will all merge into the one people. Look how easily I and my foremothers assimilated into your society!"

Ecub opened her mouth to say something, and Erith clamped a hand on the woman's arm and sent her a warning glance.

"The Trojans *are* our only hope," Aerne said. "They *are* the only thing that stands between us and total annihilation. If we refuse them entry, if we turn them away, then we risk two fates. One, the Trojans will not accept our denial, and will attack us as enemies, seizing our land. Second, even worse, is that they will sail away, taking their magic with them, and our grandchildren or great-grandchildren will suffer and die under the swords of the blue-faced invaders. Without them, Llangarlia is doomed. With them, it will survive into glory."

Aerne and Genvissa continued to speak, arguing persuasively that the Mothers needed to make this great step for the future of their peoples. It was a difficult decision, it was a decision that went against everything they'd ever thought right and proper, but it was the decision they *must* make, and it was a decision that they, the Gormagog and the MagaLlan, *knew* the Mothers were *courageous* enough to make.

"Do you think that this has been easy for *me*?" Aerne said. "First watching as the Blangan Darkwitch stripped me of my power, and then as Og failed into death? Watching this land succumb to blight and pain and knowing there was nothing I could do about it? You cannot imagine what a bitter blow it has been to me that my long struggle to ease Llangarlia's plight has been in vain; what a bitter blow it is that now I say to you that I, and Og, are useless. Accept this Trojan magic, accept their Game and their Kingman, or die."

It was enough.

When Genvissa asked if there were any dissenting voices, the Mothers gave her only silence.

"THEY CAPITULATED?" LOTH SAID, HIS EYES BLAZing.

"Aye," said Mais.

"And you added their voices to theirs?" Loth said, looking at Mais, Ecub, and Erith individually.

"We had little choice, Loth," said Erith. Then at his frown, she continued. "If we had spoken out we would have been dead by dawn. As it is, Genvissa will undoubtedly suspect us."

They were standing on the northern bank of the Llan, slightly to the east of the White Mount. It was deep night, long after the Mothers had agreed in Assembly to MagaLlan and the Gormagog's plan to allow the Trojans to not only settle within Llangarlia, but to allow them to build over three of their sacred hills. Ecub, Erith, and Mais had been circumspect in meeting Loth, leaving it until late at night when most others were well in bed and gathering in sleep the strength they would need for tomorrow's Slaughter Festival.

"She may not be confronted directly, Loth," Erith continued. "You must know that."

He snarled, more in frustration than anger, and turned away.

"What is this Trojan magic Genvissa speaks of?" Loth eventually said over his shoulder. "What is this 'Game'?"

They told him what they knew, and at the end of it Loth was even unhappier.

"Evil? This Game will attract and then trap evil? What if it goes awry? What if it attracts . . . but doesn't trap? I do *not* like this!"

Erith shrugged. "The Game will take the evil *from* this land, Loth. No Mother was going to argue against any means of doing that."

"Not even you," Loth said bitterly.

"What do you *want*, Loth?" Erith said, her nerves strung so taut that she was prepared to confront a man she normally only showed total deference to. "For Mag's and Og's dear sakes, what do you *want*?"

"I want this land to shake off the Darkwitch's power! I want this land to lie blessed under the benefice of Og and Mag, our Father and Mother, not some stone monstrosity that sits atop trapped evil! Is that so wrong, Erith? Is that so damned, cursed wrong?"

She hung her head, and it was Ecub who spoke next.

"She has taunted you with having no weapon, Loth. There is nothing left with which to fight her, not you, not your dying father, not even Mag, who none of us can touch anymore. The Mothers have agreed, the Game will be played. There is no weapon we can use against Genvissa."

Loth was silent, then he looked up, his green eyes alight. "Yes, there is!"

"Cornelia," said Erith.

"Yes!" said Loth. "Cornelia is the weapon. I don't know how, or why, but even Genvissa is instinctively afraid of her as *I* am instinctively drawn to her. *Cornelia* is the weapon. All we need to do is learn how to wield her."

"What can we do?" Erith said.

He grinned. "Tomorrow is the Slaughter Festival," he said. "There will be power about, as weak as it might be. I will ask Coel to bring Cornelia to the summit of Pen, but I will need you there as well."

"We will be there," Erith said.

Chapter Eleven

T HEY AGREED," GENVISSA TOLD BRUTUS AS soon as she met him at her house that evening, and he visibly relaxed.

"Good," he said. "Tomorrow I can send Corineus south to arrange the passage of the rest of my people north." He'd chuckled at that. "I hope they have not settled in too happily while waiting for word from me."

Genvissa smiled, content at the light in his eyes, and, taking him by the hand, led him into her house.

Now Brutus sat with Genvissa by the fire, replete with the tasty meal her three daughters had prepared for their mother and Brutus.

"They are lovely girls, Genvissa," Brutus said, watching lazily as the three girls sat gossiping and laughing over their spindles at the far end of Genvissa's house.

Genvissa smiled, and leaned against Brutus. Apart from her daughters, she and Brutus were alone: Aerne, ill and weak, had elected to stay at one of the houses in Llanbank.

For the moment, almost dozing with the effects of the meal, Brutus was content to watch the girls. He almost grinned, remembering the performance they'd put on in the serving of the food. The three girls had been all wit and smiles and (perhaps) unconsciously provocative movements as they laid dishes before him. In feature they looked much like Genvissa herself, save that they were slightly shorter, and much slimmer and more girlish.

The eldest one, Llana, touched Brutus particularly. She had an air of sadness and loss about her eyes, and she was far less a child than the other two. Keeping his voice low, Brutus asked Genvissa about her.

"She still grieves for the child she lost a year ago," Genvissa said, very low. "She conceived him when she was thirteen, bore him when she was fourteen, and lost him the same year."

"How did he die?"

"A fever." Genvissa shrugged. "Poor Llana. Still, she will no doubt bear more children."

"I had thought your own daughters would be protected against this blight."

Genvissa looked at him strangely. "My family must be seen to suffer, as does every other," she said.

Poor Llana, indeed, thought Brutus and then, before he could follow that thought through with anything close to a judgment, Genvissa leaned more firmly against him, and he felt the heaviness of her breast against his arm.

His breath caught in his throat . . . and then he leaned back a little from her. "And you are sure about Asterion?"

"There is no need to talk of Asterion," Genvissa said and, taking one of his hands in hers, put it to her breast.

He glanced toward Genvissa's daughters, and as he saw that they still had their heads bent low about their spinning, ran his hand softly over her breast.

"We can't do this," he said, very low. "If we lie together now it will ruin the order of the dances."

Genvissa's mouth twisted ruefully as Brutus dropped his hand from her.

"When I sailed toward this land," Brutus continued in his low voice, "I dreamed of you all night, thought of you all day. Now you are so close, *this* close, the waiting is torture."

"And yet," Genvissa breathed, moving close to him again, and putting her mouth to his ear, then to the back of his neck, then to his throat, "the Kingman and the Mistress of the Labyrinth may come together for the first time only on the night of the Dance of the Torches. And that night must wait until the foundations are ready. Months and months."

He pulled her face about to his, and kissed her. "You

don't need to remind me." Then he pulled away completely. "Don't do this to me now, Genvissa. You're teasing me, for no purpose, for I am yours."

"And yet you took a wife."

"I did not know of you then. Do not worry about Cornelia. She is nothing to me."

"Then put her aside. Renounce her. Give her to . . . to Corineus, perhaps."

Brutus' face hardened the moment she spoke, and something severe and uncompromising came into his eyes. "I will *not* give her to Corineus!"

Genvissa fought down a moment of panic. "Brutus—"

"If you are denied me for months to come," said Brutus, "then I have need of a wife."

"You cannot truly mean to lie with her."

"Why does she upset you so much, Genvissa?"

"You know why! How many times has she betrayed you? Kept things from you? And Asterion . . . you have said yourself how she mentioned his name as if she expected him, and you saw her lying with him in vision—"

"But Asterion is no threat. This you keep saying. Should I think different?"

"Asterion *is* no threat." Inwardly seething, Genvissa forced a pleasant look to her face. "I am jealous, Brutus. That is all. If I sought to alleviate my desire for you in some other man's bed, would you not also be dismayed?"

"Aerne . . ."

"He is an old man. I have not shared his bed for years."

Brutus smiled, and the gesture was so gentle and so beautiful it brought tears to Genvissa's eyes. "I can wait for you," he said. "Cornelia does not tempt me."

"If you find the waiting hard," she said, touching his cheek with soft fingers, "and you need relief, then you may take one of my girls—"

Brutus rose, suddenly, leaving Genvissa sitting awkwardly with her hand extended into empty air.

"You are surely the woman toward whom I have been moving all my life," Brutus said, his voice flat, "but you must know that I am not a man who enjoys violating children."

Before she could respond, Brutus was gone, and Genvissa was left staring incredulously after him.

Then where were your principles when you bore Cornelia down to bed? Genvissa thought. *She was no older than my Llana!*

"Mother?"

It was Llana, come to see what ailed Genvissa.

"It is nothing, Llana. Be a good girl, now, and see your sisters to bed."

As her daughters moved softly about the house, Genvissa went to stand outside, staring into the blackness toward the distant Llanbank.

"Who are you, girl?" Genvissa whispered, unconsciously echoing what Coel had once said. "What are you? And what *danger* are you?"

Why had she been at Mag's Dance when Blangan had died?

Why did she mention Asterion's name, and feature in visions beneath his body?

Why, in the name of all that was honest, did Brutus demur about putting her away?

Why had he not killed her when he'd learned she'd deceived him about Blangan's death? Or even after Cornelia's treacherous instigation of the Mesopotamian rebellion?

Why, why; why?

"Cornelia?" Genvissa said, narrowing her eyes. *Don't touch her*, Brutus had said.

Ah! He was bewitched only by her youth. If she died, then he would not really miss her . . .

But best not to move until she had Brutus completely. The night of the Dance of the Torches.

Cornelia, she thought, her mouth twisting viciously. *Cornelia is as good as dead.*

Chapter Twelve

EVERY YEAR AS MANY PEOPLE AS POSSIBLE from the tribes and houses of Llangarlia traveled to the Veiled Hills for the Slaughter Festival. They brought with them those goods they had made at their hearths over the past year to sell in the markets, they herded before them their spare livestock that they might barter them at the livestock fairs (as well as one fat beast upon which they would feast), and they carried wrapped in cloth their finest bronze pieces—swords, knives, arrow heads, pins, or brooches—that they might offer them to their gods in thanks for their lives and for the food and children that had graced their households over the past year.

If perhaps the food had not been so plentiful this past year, or their children not so hearty, then the family would bring more than perhaps they could afford to offer Og and Mag, desperate for a turn in their fortunes.

The sudden influx of people on Llanbank and the surrounding area created mayhem—but it was a happy, genial mayhem, for the Slaughter Festival was the most eagerly anticipated social occasion as well as religious rite of the year. All the homes within Llanbank took in as many people as they could; the overflow encamped in the areas to the south and east of the town, their children running about, laughing and playing, their beasts baying and bleating in confusion at the throngs of people and their own crowded kind packed into pens and runs.

Of all homes within Llanbank, Cornelia's house was the only one that was not overflowing with guests, its internal quiet a strange counterpoint to the bustle and noise everywhere else.

On the evening of the Slaughter Festival, Cornelia took herself off to the northern bank of the Llan. Aethylla remained within the house: her own son was slightly ill with a fever—probably caused by his teething—and of necessity she had to remain behind to tend him. That meant Cornelia could safely leave Achates behind as well, and although she adored her son, she thought that perhaps this was one night where he would be better off left behind in the warmth and security of the house and Aethylla's care.

Hicetaon escorted her; Brutus was long gone—off somewhere with Genvissa probably—and Corineus had headed south in the morning, armed with the news that the Gathering of Mothers had agreed to Genvissa's plan to settle the Trojans in the Veiled Hills. He would bring the Trojans north by ship, and no one expected them for several weeks.

It would take at least that long to arrange space and accommodation for them, and Hicetaon, who was in charge of arranging such space, knew he would have his work cut out.

The crowds pressed uncomfortably, and Hicetaon moved close to Cornelia, trying to keep her free of the press. She was dressed very beautifully, in the Llangarlian manner rather than the Trojan, and Hicetaon wondered from where she had found her sleeveless robe. Its full skirt hung to only just below her knees, leaving her strong brown calves and ankles bare above her fine leather shoes. The material was a finely woven wool and patterned about its low-scalloped neck and hem with a twisted design that Hicetaon realized only after several minutes of surreptitious observation was of entwined antlers. Cornelia wore a matching cloak on her back, its weave slightly denser than that of the robe but even then light enough to flow back from her body with every movement she made.

In counterpoint to her Llangarlian clothes, Cornelia wore her dark hair in full Greek fashion, twisted and arranged to fall in carefully controlled cascades from the crown of her head. It became her, Hicetaon thought, and wryly observed that many others thought so as well, judging by the number of admiring glances sent her way.

They walked toward the riverbank, the crowds drawing ever closer, and Hicetaon had to fight to make room for them. Cornelia was becoming agitated, her cheeks flushed, her eyes bright, and just as Hicetaon had begun to wonder if it might not be safer after all to escort her back to the safety of their house, a voice spoke, and warm hands took hold of both Hicetaon's and Cornelia's elbows.

"I have just the place for us to view," Coel said, and Hicetaon frowned at the sudden smile on Cornelia's face.

"I don't think—" Hicetaon said, and then stopped, realizing that the pressure on his elbow was gone.

Cornelia and Coel had vanished . . . they had simply melted back into the crowds pressed about him.

Hicetaon bellowed Cornelia's name, furious both with her and with Coel, straining on the tips of his toes to see above the heads surrounding him.

But to no avail. They were gone, and Hicetaon was left to be carried along with the flow of the crowds toward the Llan.

Brutus will be furious, Hicetaon thought, and then wondered if he had the nerve to tell him.

"MY SISTER'S ROBE LOOKS WELL ON YOU," COEL said, holding Cornelia close before him. They were standing on a small raised knoll on the northern bank of the river partway between the White Mount and Mag's Hill.

Cornelia smiled, apparently not uncomfortable with his closeness. He had swept her through the crowd with effortless ease, conveying her to the small ferry on the Llan's southern bank, and persuading the ferryman with charm and a curiously carved seashell to convey them to the northern bank.

Here, on the northern bank, the crowds were far less as the people about generally consisted only of those taking part in the ceremonies. Coel had led Cornelia to a spot where they would not only be able to have a good view of the rituals about to be enacted, but at the same time not be in anyone's way.

"Thank Tuenna again for me," said Cornelia. "I cannot believe she would gift me such a treasure."

"She liked you," Coel said, very slightly increasing the pressure of his arms where they wound about her body below her breasts. "My entire family liked you."

Cornelia colored very faintly. "You say too many kind things about me," she said. "Others might not be so generous."

Coel resisted the urge to grind his teeth at her reference to Brutus, but let it pass. "You deserve all my kind words, and more," he said. "I am your friend, and your guide through tonight's mysteries," he said, his voice filled with laughter. "I adore you." His arms tightened again, but in a manner that was somehow mischievous and teasing, and not in any manner demanding.

She laughed, and relaxed against him, pleasing Coel. Perhaps one day, perhaps soon, she might overcome her inhibitions and accept him as her lover. He *knew* she desired him, but he feared that Cornelia was too trapped by Brutus, and by fear, guilt, and love to ever take that step away from her husband.

Coel repressed a sigh. Whatever happened, if ever Cornelia consented to lie with him, it wouldn't be tonight. Loth had asked him to bring Cornelia to the Stone Dance atop Pen once the main rituals were done. Please Og, Coel prayed silently, closing his eyes for a moment, let Loth discover the "why" of Cornelia. Let him discover *how* to use her to restore balance and health *and* Llangarlia's true gods to this land.

He shuddered, and she felt it, half turning against him until he could see the curve of her cheek in the starlight.

"The cold," he said. "There will be a heavy frost at dawn, I think." He lifted his hands and pushed her cloak over her shoulders, wrapping her the more tightly in its warmth.

"We should be well abed by then," she said, and he grunted, able to make no other reply to her.

Then he felt her start, her head moving back to the river again. "What is happening?" she said, and Coel heard the strain in her voice.

On the banks of the Llan below them, several hundred women had gathered. They were cloaked, but as Cornelia and Coel watched, they allowed the cloaks to drop to the ground, leaving the women naked.

"They are Mothers," Coel said quietly against Cornelia's hair. "Not all of them, but a representative grouping of them. They are here to offer sacrifice to Og and Mag." In desperation, thought Coel, for they know very well that Og is dead and Mag too weak to respond.

Perhaps this was just a formality, done for the comfort it gave rather than in any expectation of actual aid.

"Sacrifice?" Cornelia said.

He smiled, and she felt the movement in her hair. "Metal, Cornelia. Not blood. The most precious metal objects we have. Given to the river as thanks and offering."

"Why the river . . . and why such a waste of such precious objects? Hera! Each of those bronze axes might well feed a small community throughout an entire winter!"

One of his hands lifted away from her, extending toward the wide river. "See the stillness of the waters? The gleam of its surface? Is that not the most mysterious thing you have ever seen? Water is the gateway between this world and the Far World, the mirror that reflects both worlds, and what we offer to the river is taken in thanks by the gods on the other side . . . in the other world. Any why such precious objects? Because they *are* such precious things to us. See . . . the Mothers take up their offerings."

"They're breaking them!"

Indeed, each of the women, no matter what she held, was now ritually breaking the objects—bending, twisting, mutilating, and shattering, if able.

"They do that to show the gods to what lengths they will go to honor them. These objects are precious, and it is in honor of the gods that we break them before offering them."

The beat of a drum began, and then the thin, almost-frightening wail of a pipe.

"There," Coel said, and pointed toward Mag's Hill.

Figures stood on its summit, and Cornelia and Coel were close enough to see.

Genvissa—there could be no mistaking her statuesque figure nor her wild dark hair. Brutus was with her, wearing nothing but a white loin wrap and the gleaming bands of kingship about his arms and legs. His hair, too, was left free for the wind to tug and caress. Three women—no, girls—stood behind Genvissa and Brutus, and as Cornelia watched, Brutus turned and laughed with them about something, touching the cheek of the eldest girl who was, Cornelia saw, about her own age.

Coel felt Cornelia tense at that simple display of affection. Poor Cornelia, what she would not do to have Brutus touch her cheek just once with that tenderness.

Coel felt a tightening in his gut, and he knew it was jealousy.

"They are Genvissa's daughters," he said softly. "Fathered on her by the Gormagog during rituals such as these."

Cornelia said nothing, staring at the tableau above her.

"Why do you love him so deeply when he treats you so badly?" Coel said, truly wanting to know. "How can you want to please *him* so much?"

"He is everything to me," she said, and Coel's arms tightened about her in agony.

"Everything awaits you, Cornelia, and it is not in that man."

Above them, Brutus turned to Genvissa, and kissed her; far below in Coel's arms, Cornelia gave a low moan of distress.

"If you were one of us," Coel said, his eyes fixed on Brutus and Genvissa, "you would discard any man who so maltreated you. How could you want such a man as the father of your children?"

"You don't understand," Cornelia said. "I have been so foolish, done so many wicked things, hurt so many people."

"You? What?"

"My father . . ." Cornelia began, then shuddered and said no more.

Below them, the Mothers had walked far into the waters of the Llan so that the waves of the great river lapped at their breasts.

As one, and to the accompaniment of a surging of the pipes and drums and the ululations of the watchers on the far riverbank, the Mothers threw their offerings of precious metal far into the river.

"I know some of the circumstances in which Brutus took you to be his wife," Coel said, his voice low and hard. "By Og and Mag, Cornelia, in our land he would have been slaughtered for what he did to you!"

Gigantic bone-fires now roared into life on the summits of all the sacred hills and mounds, and as they did so, black figures began to twist and turn about them in wild dance.

She pulled out of his arms, and turned to face him. Her cheeks were streaked with tears, her eyes pools of distress.

"I have lied to him and plotted against him," she said. "I have destroyed lives—I destroyed my father, my home, and all who lived in it! Idaeus is dead because of my actions, as also Aethylla's husband! Is it any wonder he turns to Genvissa? Look at her! He wants a queen by his side, Coel . . . why should he want *me*?"

"You are a greater—"

"Don't patronize me!" she shouted. "I don't *want* to be a little girl who people think to ease with lies and platitudes!"

And with that she was gone, running into the night.

Chapter Thirteen

S THE GREAT BONE-FIRES ROARED INTO LIFE, the Slaughter Festival moved from formal rite to popular revelry. Flasks of honeyed mead were produced and consumed, the carcasses of pigs and cattle were spitted and roasted, and the wail and throb of pipes and drums worked their sinuous magic among the crowds.

Atop Mag's Hill, Brutus and Genvissa and her three daughters made their way down to the river, then across to the southern bank to partake themselves of the revelry and merrymaking, as did those Mothers who had cast their metal into the river.

Coel initially made after Cornelia, but she was younger and fleeter of foot than he, and she easily outran him in the dark.

In the end, he slowed to a halt after only a short chase. Cornelia may have outrun him, but Coel had also seen the direction in which she had unwittingly run, and knew that something other than her grief was guiding Cornelia's footsteps this night.

CORNELIA FLED, SEEING ONLY BRUTUS LEANING toward Genvissa, seeing only his hand lifting to her cheek as he had laid his mouth to hers.

In the first minutes of her flight Cornelia had seen other people—dark shapes moving slowly through the night—but once she'd moved a little distance from the river the shapes drew back and Cornelia was left alone in the night.

She stopped, eventually, her chest rising and falling in agony, her legs quivering and weak. She bent over, resting her hands on her thighs as she tried to regain both breath and composure.

After a few minutes she straightened, and looked about her, suddenly realizing not only how far she had come, but how isolated she was in this strange landscape in the middle of the night. She twisted about, trying to get her bearings.

To the north and west fires flickered on hills. She turned the way she had come—there, the faint outline of the river, marked with further fires and smoky torches and the dancing, twisting shapes of thousands of merrymakers.

The dull sound of distant music and laughter reached her, and Cornelia's face creased as she again fought back tears.

What was she doing here?

"Cornelia."

She gasped, twisting about so violently toward the voice that she tripped and sprawled in the turf.

"Cornelia."

A figure emerged out of the night, and Cornelia drew in one terrified breath, then froze, sure she was about to be murdered.

"Cornelia," said Loth yet one more time, strolling completely out of the darkness to stand above Cornelia's sprawled form.

Her eyes were wide, terrified, her breast heaving, her unblinking eyes unable to move from Loth's terrible head.

"If I did not kill you in Mag's Dance," he said, his voice soft, "why should I do so now?"

He stretched down a hand to her, holding it there, waiting.

Her eyes flickered from his face to the outstretched hand, back to his face, then finally settled on the hand.

Very slowly she lifted her own hand, hesitated just as she was about to take his, then, holding her breath, slid her palm against his.

He grasped it tight, then leaned back, pulling her to her feet.

"I am Loth," he said. "The Horns of Llangarlia—as useless a title as can be, now. You are Cornelia, and everyone has yet to discover who *you* truly are, and whether you encompass usefulness . . . or uselessness."

His eyes narrowed, studying her, and even though she pulled against his hand, he would not allow her freedom.

"Who are you, Cornelia?" he whispered, and he was so close she blinked as the warmth of his breath played over her face. "Do you, a stranger, carry Mag in the pit of your belly?"

His pressure on her hand increased, and despite herself, Cornelia found herself being pulled closer.

"Do I frighten you?" he said. "Do you think me dangerous?"

"Yes," she whispered, and he laughed, soft and gentle.

"Good," he said so low his voice sounded like part of the night. "Very good."

Then his grip on her hand changed, and he moved forward, and Cornelia found herself being pulled along by his side as he walked farther into the night. She tried to balk, to pull away from him, but again he was too strong for her, and he gave her hand such a strong tug that she almost tripped again as she stumbled after him.

"We are going to dance for Mag," he said.

He stopped abruptly, surprising Cornelia so that she inadvertently stumbled against the warmth of his near-naked body.

"You did not tell Brutus of that night," he said. "Not all of it. Why?"

"I don't know," she said, drawing back as much as she was able.

He lifted their intertwined hands, pulling her close yet once more. "You do not like Genvissa. Why?"

"Because she is so much better than I," she whispered, frightened not so much by his appearance and power now as by his nearness and warmth. "And because of that, because of her power and wit and magic, my husband wants her and not me. I am but a child. She is a woman."

He snarled, his teeth glinting wetly in the faint moonlight. "You are very young if you think Genvissa is better than you," he said, then resumed walking again, tugging her after him, "and your husband is but a foolish man whose lusts for flesh and power have trapped him."

As they did me, he thought.

"Where is Coel?" Cornelia said, trying to look over her shoulder. "I was with him and—"

"Coel is not wanted now," Loth said, "Not tonight. Not where we are going."

"Where are we going? Please, let me go. I want to go home, back to my son . . ."

His only answer was a tightening of his grip on her hand.

Cornelia almost cried out with the pain, then *did* begin to cry with her anxiety. "I am frightened," she said.

"We all are," he snapped. "But it would help if you walked *with* me, and do not try to pull me back. Cornelia, I will *not* hurt you, I am not *interested* in hurting you, and what I will show you tonight few of our people, let alone strangers, are allowed to witness. Now, *will you walk with me?*"

Her only answer was a very slight nod, and a lessening of the pressure she was exerting on his hand and arm, but it was enough, and he relaxed and smiled, then laughed out loud at the stunned expression on her face.

"Yes, even I can be comely enough when I am happy, Cornelia. Walk with me now."

Chapter Fourteen

Cornelia Speaks

T HE CHANGE THAT CAME OVER HIM WHEN he smiled shocked me so thoroughly I think I followed him throughout the rest of that long night in the simple hope of seeing him smile again.

His great, misshapen, monstrous head became as nothing

when he smiled, for the light and warmth in his eyes and mouth negated everything else about him. All that the watcher saw was a joy so great that it had the potential to extinguish all the darkness and horror that collected in everyone's life. I wondered at this, that a man who, quite literally, carried a weight so great on his shoulders that its very oppressiveness must have dampened every piece of gladness in him should still be able to laugh with such merriment, such lack of care, that he thereby took away from his listener every care that they, too, carried.

I followed him, ran to keep up with his long strides, merely so that he would turn to me again, and smile.

HE LED ME TO A HILL ON WHICH STOOD A STONE dance. The Dance was much smaller than the great Mag's Dance, but it had an elegance to it that Mag's Dance lacked.

"Where is this?" I said, a little breathless.

"This hill is named Pen," Loth replied, stopping so we could gaze up at the Dance. "Its cap of stone hides its greatest secret—"

"Which is?" I was no longer afraid of him, and risked even teasing him.

I was rewarded with another of his smiles, and I felt myself smile back. I suddenly realized, in a bolt of understanding, that this man had the ability to make the entire world laugh with him, if only he had the *will* to laugh.

"A hole," he said. "A great light hole."

I frowned, and would have asked more, but Loth started to climb the hill, and pulled me after him.

He may have been joy incarnate when he smiled, but I was truly getting sick of all this pulling and tugging.

"I will follow by myself," I said, and pulled my hand in his once more.

This time, he let it go. "Your feet are on the hill," he said. "I have no need to lead you."

*   *   *

ALL MY BREATHLESSNESS HAD RETURNED BY THE
time we reached the top of Pen, and for a few long minutes
I did nothing but haul in deep painful breaths. Loth had
walked inside the Stone Dance, but I turned back to look
at the view spreading below me.

I could see the river, stretching out all silver and mystery
in the deep of the night, its waters at the southern shoreline
reflecting the light and movement of the Slaughter Festival
revelry.

I wondered for a moment where Brutus was . . . what he
and Genvissa were doing (*were they lying together? Coupling to the frenzy of the music?*) and I felt a great cold fist
clutch all the entrails in my belly into one twisting, jealous
mass.

I hated her so much . . .

I wanted to be like her so much . . .

"Cornelia."

I turned about, back to where the Stone Dance rose behind me.

Ecub stood under one of the great stone arches, completely naked, and I was not surprised.

"Join us," she said, and without prompting I slipped the
shoes from my feet, and the cloak and robe from my body,
and walked into the circle of the Stone Dance.

The cold and frost of the night did not touch me, nor did
the sudden roar of flames within the Dance perturb me.

ERITH WAS INSIDE THE DANCE AS WELL, AND AN-
other woman I did not know and who was introduced to me
as Mais. Loth joined us, as naked as were we three women.

Fire was everywhere. I think the flames came from the
stones of the Dance themselves, but they did not touch me,
nor did their heat sear me.

As the quiet introduction finished, Loth drew me to one
side, and the three Mothers—Erith, Ecub, and Mais—began a dance. It was like, yet unlike, the dance that Blangan
had drawn me into inside Mag's Dance. It had the same

sensuality, but not its sexuality. It had the same sinuosity, but not its complexity. They danced in a circle, weaving their way about each other, their outstretched hands brushing each time they passed.

Their heads they kept bowed, as if in homage.

It was a dance, I thought, that only women with the wisdom of maturity and experience could execute: a younger woman would only have blundered the steps.

I blinked, for suddenly their forms appeared indistinct to me. They were still there, I knew that, for something within me could sense not only their presence, but their continued dance, but as heartbeat succeeded heartbeat their forms vanished completely, and all I could see was the center of the circle about which the Mothers danced.

It was filled with vision.

A pond, crystal clear yet with unknowable depths.

A grassy verge, verdant with health and life.

A white stag with blood red antlers, skeletal and dying, his eyes frantic, his breath heaving in agony from his bloodied, foamed, gaping mouth.

His heart, torn from his breast, and hanging by a tendon.

It beat. I could not see it, but I knew it. That heart continued to beat, but so slowly that its measure had to be counted in aeons, not in moments.

Beside me Loth muttered something, his voice tight with excitement, but I paid him no attention.

All I could see, all I knew, was that pitiful stag crawling on its belly toward the pond, dying—literally—for a draught of its healing waters.

I cried, and held out my arms to the stag, and would have gone to it, save that Loth held me back.

And then the waters of the pond stirred, and an arm rose from its depths. It was an arm of no natural creature, for it was composed of the water itself, and it glittered with the shards of firelight leaping about the Stone Dance.

It reached for the stag, but in vain, for the pitiful creature was as yet too far from the edge of the water.

The arm moved in a gentle circle, as if waving, or summoning.

Cornelia, whispered a desperate, dying voice, so strangled and breathless it was barely audible, let alone understandable. *Cornelia . . . Cornelia . . .*

And then the vision was gone, and everyone—Loth and the Mothers—was staring at me.

I CRIED OUT, I THINK, AND ERITH HURRIED FORTH, holding my clothes. She assisted me to dress, wrapping my cloak warmly about me, and all the time she sent Loth wondering glances.

I knew that whatever she and her companions had *thought* would happen tonight within the Stone Dance, what *had* happened was not it at all.

Loth had garbed himself quickly in his hip wrap, and had built a fire in a cold ring of stones in the center of the circle. He beckoned myself and the three now-clothed Mothers in close, and we sat about the growing flames, grateful for its warmth and comfort.

"Og is *alive*," Loth said eventually, his voice wondering and relieved and mystified in equal amounts. "Og is alive."

"Barely," said Ecub, always the one to see the dour side of things, but even her voice was rich with relief.

"But alive," said Erith. "Alive, and that is all we need for hope."

"And Mag called Cornelia's name," said Mais.

"Aye," said Loth. "She has picked Cornelia to help her. That is clear."

Then, as one, Loth and the Mothers looked at me. "Mag needs you to help her," Erith said.

"Against *Genvissa*?" I said.

"Of course," said Loth. "Against everything she and Brutus plan."

"No," I said.

"How can you say 'no'—" Mais began, but Erith silenced her with a raised hand.

"Why do you say 'no,' Cornelia?" she said.

"Because if I did this, if I set out against Brutus, then I would lose him forever."

"Do you not love this land, Cornelia?" Loth asked.

"Not so much that I would lose Brutus for it!"

"You *must* aid Mag!" Ecub said. "You *must*! She *named* you, she—"

I shook my head, slowly, forcefully, side to side. "No. I will *not*!"

"Cornelia," Loth said, "if you help us against Genvissa, if you help destroy the Game, then you *will* have Brutus back!"

"No. No. He will destroy me if I plot against him again. I will not do it." I could feel my voice rising, and I could not stop it, nor did I want to. How dare these four try to set me on a course that would destroy *any* regard that Brutus had left for me (and Hera alone knew how little that was)? "I . . . will . . . not . . . do . . . it."

"Cornelia," Loth began, his voice hard and heavy, but Erith forestalled whatever he was going to say.

"Cornelia is tired, and cold, and shocked by what she saw—as are we all. This is no time for us to argue, nor to persuade Cornelia to a course she fears. Loth, be gentle now. Walk Cornelia back to the ferry."

I sent Erith a glancing smile, grateful to her, and was even more grateful when Loth's face relaxed and he gave a nod.

"Yes," he said. "Perhaps that would be best. Come, Cornelia. I will walk you back to the Llan."

WE WALKED IN SILENCE FOR A LONG TIME, AND finally it grew so uncomfortable that I blurted out the first thing I thought of.

"How is it your head grew like that?" I said. "Were you born with those great bony spikes?"

I wished to snatch back the words as soon as they had left my mouth, but Loth did not seem perturbed by them.

Presumably he'd faced similar questions all his life.

"I was born as any other child," he said, "and grew as did any other child. But when I was six or seven, I was stricken with aches in my head so painful, so agonizing, I could barely move. I could not stand light, and I was racked with nausea so bad that whenever I retched my head exploded in pain infinitely greater than what I already experienced."

"And that was the growth of these horns?"

"No. I endured these pains and spasms for many months, with barely a single pain-free day in all that time. I would not eat, and lost so much weight my father and aunts thought I would die.

"Eventually, driven to desperate measures, they asked in an old man with a cruel skill. He was a head borer, a lifter of evil spirits."

He stopped, not only talking but walking as well, and I could see his face twist with the memory.

I wanted to tell him to stop, that I did not want to know, but somehow the words would not come out.

"They thought that if they released the evil spirits from my head then I would be well again," he said. "And so one day they caused me to drink great quantities of honeyed mead—I retched most of it up again, but enough stayed down to blot out much of my consciousness—and held me down. And this old man took to my head the tools of his trade."

I gaped at him, appalled.

"He had a drill made of hardened bone, and this he drilled into my skull."

Without thinking I took his hand, feeling the shudder that shivered his flesh.

"They say"—his voice had dropped—"that when he drilled into my skull, great black matter bubbled its way free . . ." He took a deep breath. "They bound up my head, and waited. For some days it seemed as if the hole had indeed let escape the vile spirits that had plagued me . . . but then one day the headache struck again, infinitely worse than usual, and in a different part of my head."

"Oh, Loth . . ."

"And so the old man came back, and he drilled again. And then again the next week when still the pain did not abate. And each week for seven weeks after that until I swear my skull was nothing but searing holes that leaked black vileness. Eventually the pain in my head *did* abate . . . and the old man packed up his bone drills and let me be . . . but as my skull regrew about the holes he'd drilled into its bone, so it grew in strange humps and lumps, and thus . . ."

His free hand waved vaguely at his head. "Thus I am marked. But . . . but in a strange way I did not mind all that pain and despair . . . for amid the worst of it Og came to me, and held me and comforted me. He said I had shown strength and endurance, and that this strength and endurance, bolstered with his love, would see me throughout my life."

He looked at me, a peculiar light in his eyes. "I thought to have lost his love and support, Cornelia. I thought Og was dead. But tonight I find I have hope again."

I was still holding his hand, and now I let it go and backed away again, fearing Loth would try once more to persuade me to plot against Genvissa.

But Loth's face suddenly clouded over, and all the hope and light in his eyes dimmed.

"My father," he said in a hoarse voice. "My father. He is dying."

Chapter Fifteen

 ENVISSA LOWERED HER HEAD OVER AERNE'S struggling chest, her eyes dutifully moist. Behind her stood her three daughters, Brutus, and some fifteen or sixteen Mothers all crowded into the house.

Witnesses.

This was a terrifying moment for most of the Mothers. With Aerne's death, they were launched totally into the unknown. Always there had been a Gormagog and a MagaLlan, guiding and directing them in the love and care of Og and Mag. Now Og was dead, and his final representative, Aerne, was dying also.

Aerne's final breath would herald a new age, frightening for its unknowability.

For Genvissa and Brutus, contrariwise, it was merely another step toward their ultimate goal.

Nevertheless, Genvissa appeared truly saddened at Aerne's dying. She wiped his brow, and brushed back his hair with a soft hand. She leaned and kissed his cheek, and smiled so that his final sight would be pleasing.

"I have let you down," Aerne whispered. "Everyone. If only I hadn't lain with Blangan—"

"Hush," said Genvissa, "you were not to know she was such a Darkwitch."

"I tried so hard to make matters well again," Aerne continued. "You cannot know what a bitter blow this has been to me that I have failed."

"There was nothing any more or any different that you could have done," Genvissa whispered, stroking Aerne's brow. "May all the gods in the Far World bless you and defend you."

"If only Loth . . . if only Loth . . ." Arne said, weeping.

"Loth is here," said a gentle, loving voice, "and Loth shall do all he can to take your regrets and rectify them."

Brutus turned about, very slowly, and looked at the man—the deformed monster—who was now walking calmly through the throng of Mothers to Aerne's bedside.

Gods, no wonder Cornelia was so terrified of him!

"What do you here?" Genvissa's voice was flat, and very cold.

"I come to farewell my father," Loth said. "He may have regretted my mother, but I have never regretted him."

"Go away, Loth," Genvissa said, but Loth ignored her, and sat down on Aerne's bed, taking his father's hand.

"There is no hope, save for Genvissa," Aerne said.

"There is always hope, and in the strangest places," Loth said.

"Promise me you will aid her," Aerne said. His eyes were watering, his lip trembling with the effort of speaking.

"I will do everything I can for this land," Loth said, wiping away one of his father's tears. "And if the only way to do that is aiding Genvissa, then that is what I will do."

Genvissa gave a hard, triumphant smile, and Loth looked at her.

"I will do *everything* I must in order to protect this land," he said softly, and Genvissa's smile slipped.

For some time no one spoke, all eyes back on Aerne. The old man's eyes were now closed, although tears still trickled from under their lids, his skin was gray, his breathing was becoming ever more erratic. Genvissa laid her hand on his brow, and Loth's hold on his father's hand tightened.

Softly, regretfully, weeping, Aerne died, and one among the Mothers wailed.

Loth raised his face, tears streaking down his cheeks. "I am my father's heir," he said, looking between Genvissa and Brutus. "Never, *never* forget that!"

Then he rose, and was gone.

Genvissa's eyes locked in to Brutus', and they knew they had a bitter enemy.

NOT SO FAR DISTANT, A MATTER OF SEVERAL DAYS' *journeying only, King Goffar of Poiteran stood and stared* *unbelievingly at his wife.*

She stood before him, trembling, her head bowed, her *hands splayed over her stomach.*

She had just told him that after so many years of bar-

renness, she was now some five or six weeks gone with child.

Goffar burst into laughter. "I shall have a son!" he roared. "A son!"

Chapter Sixteen

*G*ENVISSA BENT HER HEAD BACK AND LET THE late autumn sunshine wash over her face. Winter was rushing upon them—the nights were heavily frosted now and the days bitter with northerly winds and miserable flurries of icy rain. This hour or two of sunshine was to be treasured, a gift perhaps from her foremothers watching over her from the Far World, wishing her love and wellness in these days leading to the final accomplishment of their dream.

To reconstruct the Game, to build a citadel of power, to ensure that they could never ever again be thwarted: to cement their power in the walls of this city and the labyrinthine enchantments of the Game.

It had taken so long . . . but Ariadne's dream would shortly be realized.

Genvissa tipped her head forward again and looked about her. She stood on Og's Hill, the Llan and Llanbank spread before her, Pen and Llandin at her back. Brutus, her partner in her dream, was conferring with Hicetaon a few paces away, talking of walls and foundations and water levels. Their faces were animated, their voices excited—now raised in frustration at the complications of an errant stream across the proposed line of the city wall, now energized with purpose as they discussed the local rock, a gray sandstone, and whether it would be strong enough to carry not only the weight of the proposed walls, but the weight of the years and expectations it would of necessity have to bear.

Genvissa smiled, content. Whatever Loth had rambled about at his father's deathbed, Og and Mag were gone, or so enfeebled as to be of no threat whatsoever.

Asterion . . . well . . . not even he could darken Genvissa's happiness. She knew he had been conceived by Goffar . . . but it was too late, far too late, to stop her.

There was just her and Brutus now, and this land.

Soon no one would remember Og's and Mag's names; all would celebrate hers and Brutus'.

As if her thoughts had communicated themselves to him, Brutus looked up, and smiled at her.

Ah, but how she adored him! He was everything to her; so strong and virile (and how she looked forward to their first bedding, that magical moment when she would bind him to her entirely, and when he would sire her daughter-heir), he was the one who would turn her dreams, and all the dreams and hopes of her foremothers, into a reality.

The great reality: Troia Nova, citadel of dreams, keeper of the Game, their road to immortality.

His smile deepened, and she wondered if he, too, were thinking of that moment when they could allow their lust free rein. If they had just been man and woman, then they would undoubtedly have already consummated their passion.

But they were not just man and woman. They were the Mistress and the Kingman of the Labyrinth, and that meant their physical desires must be played out to the steps of the Game so that both it, and they, would be the stronger for it.

They would be wedded to each other *and* to the Game, for there could be no other possible existence for them.

"We will enclose these three mounds," Brutus said, his eyes still locked in to Genvissa's. "The southern wall of the city will run along the Llan, making full use of the cliff faces of its northern bank. Then"—his eyes moved away from Genvissa, to the north, and he gestured with his hand—"the wall will curve in a flattened semicircle above the Llan, enclosing the White Mount, and Mag's and Og's Hills. This will be a good city, strong and easily defended, and sitting atop these mounds, it will command the entire Llan Valley."

She walked down to join him and Hicetaon. "Will it have grand bastions and walkways, Brutus? Will the wall shine in the sun, dazzling all who gaze upon it?"

Brutus laughed, sharing a glance with Hicetaon. "If we can make the foundations strong and deep enough, then, yes, Genvissa, it will be a dazzling city, surrounded by the mightiest wall in the world."

"We can entirely enclose the Wal," Hicetaon said enthusiastically, referring to the wide stream that flowed between Og's Hill and Mag's Hill into the Llan. "Troia Nova will have a permanent and secure water supply. No one shall ever be able to lay successful siege to it."

"Llangarlia will be strong," said Genvissa.

"Indeed," said Hicetaon, then forgot what else he was going to say as his eyes shifted. "Ah, here comes Cornelia. You have not yet shown her the site, have you, Brutus? Perhaps you can point out where you shall build you and her a palace."

He was looking at Cornelia as he spoke, and he missed entirely the furtive glance shared between Brutus and Genvissa.

Genvissa sighed and straightened, moving away from Brutus to look down the hill.

Her face tightened, irritated beyond measure. Cornelia was indeed making her way up the slope, a somewhat forced smile on her face and a sway to her hips that the silly thing undoubtedly thought was attractive.

Then, stunningly, Genvissa felt a moment's queasiness in her stomach, as if a darkened fate walked up that slope rather than Cornelia, and she kept her face expressionless only with great effort.

Why was Asterion's name so allied with this girl? Why?

Why? Genvissa sent a short, but fervent prayer to whichever gods were listening that Brutus would rid himself of this girl. Soon. Permanently.

And if he did not . . . Genvissa nodded slowly to herself, her dark, hard eyes not once moving from Cornelia. If Brutus did not, then Genvissa would.

Soon. The night of the Dance of the Torches.

She almost smiled. How . . . balanced. A conception and a death, and the Game would be safe forever.

Cornelia threw Genvissa another glance, even more apprehensive now she saw the cruelty in the older woman's eyes, and walked to Brutus' side.

"Cornelia," Brutus said, and Genvissa's determination increased as she sought, but failed, to detect any discernible irritation in Brutus' tone.

Cornelia spent a moment studying the view, apparently riveted by its beauty, then turned to her husband. "Are you planning out your city?" Cornelia said. "Will you show me?"

Genvissa rolled her eyes, knowing Cornelia could see her, and turned away, hoping that Brutus would dismiss Cornelia.

But he didn't. He merely sighed. "I had not thought you to be interested," he said. "Will you not be bored with talk of masonry and footings?"

"I have not come all this way to be bored," she said, trying too hard to appear relaxed. "I want to know. Please, will you show me?"

Brutus looked at her, wondering if this was coquettishness on her part (when had Cornelia ever been interested in what he planned?), but seeing only genuine interest, he began to feel a little guilty. Since his arrival at the Veiled Hills he'd made no secret of his alliance with, and deep attraction to, Genvissa. Cornelia must surely be certain they were already lovers, and yet she had said nothing to him. Indeed, she had made no complaint, acceded to his every request and demand without hesitation or question, and had been compliant and submissive.

Almost as if her spirit had been broken.

Feeling guiltier than ever, Brutus gave her a small smile. "Well," he said, "I would have shown you before if I'd known of your interest."

He put a hand on Cornelia's waist, hesitated, then drew her in close to his body, and began to point out the course of the walls.

Genvissa watched, unbelieving.

"The city will be astounding!" Cornelia said, as Brutus finished.

"Three times the size of Mesopotama," Brutus said, his voice rich with good humor at Cornelia's reaction. "But it will not all be built over. There shall be gardens and orchards, light and shade."

"Space enough for me to play with our children," Cornelia said, smiling again as she looked into Brutus' eyes. She was glowing at his attention and favor. "Space enough for them to grow."

Genvissa had endured enough. "Children?" she said, arching one of her eyebrows, and walking close to Brutus herself. "I thought you only had one." She made that "one" sound like a desperate failing. "Not all women are as blessed as I in their fertility."

She rested one of her hands on Brutus' shoulder, and leaned close . . . too close, if the sudden flush in Cornelia's cheeks were any indication.

Genvissa smiled.

"Not every woman," Cornelia said, with a surprising quiet dignity, "has had the numerous opportunities *you* have taken to catch with child."

Now Genvissa flushed, and her hand tightened on Brutus' shoulder.

"Cornelia," Brutus said with some slight remonstration, but his eyes sparkled, and he moved away from Genvissa.

"Ahem," Hicetaon put in, almost as red and flushed as the two women were. "Perhaps you can show Cornelia where the main buildings will be, Brutus? I confess some curiosity myself, lest this dazzling city of yours is to be all wall and no buildings."

Genvissa made a dismissive sound, and turned away.

Brutus bit the inside of his lip, trying to keep the grin from his face. "There," he said, pointing to the White Mount. "I have a great desire to build a palace atop that mound, Cornelia. Shall you enjoy the view, do you think?"

"It will be most agreeable," Cornelia said.

"And there"—he pointed to the top of Mag's Hill—"a great market, commanded by a civic hall."

"And on this hill?" said Cornelia. "On Og's Hill?"

"Here?" Brutus looked at Genvissa. "Here we will play the Game, Genvissa and I. Here we will construct the labyrinth, and there"—he pointed to the western slope of the hill that sloped down toward the Magyl River—"will be the main gate of the city."

Cornelia's face had fallen at Brutus' easy coupling of his name with Genvissa's. "A labyrinth?" she said. "On this hill? But I thought—"

"A labyrinth—" Brutus began to say, but was interrupted by Genvissa, staring with baleful iciness at Cornelia.

"We will make this city between us," she said, making no effort to hide the triumph in her voice, "Brutus and *I*."

THEY LAY IN THEIR BED THAT NIGHT, CLOSE, THEIR skin filmed with sweat, their breathing slowly returning to calmness. This had been the first time since their arrival that Brutus had lain with Cornelia, and he wished he hadn't left it so long. She'd pleased him today with her interest in the city he planned, and he also had to admit he'd enjoyed the spat between her and Genvissa.

Brutus ran a hand very slowly down Cornelia's back, feeling and caressing every nub of her spine. She had been sweet and pliable, eager even, and Brutus was well pleased with her.

She trembled against him, and he smiled against her forehead, reveling in the manner in which she made him feel so strong, knowing it would be a long time yet before he allowed her to sleep.

"I love you," she whispered, and Brutus cradled her face in his hands, and wondered if, finally, he should lay his mouth to hers. Kiss her, at last, as he should have done that first night.

He smiled, and his head moved forward, and then, suddenly, his mind was filled with a memory:

Genvissa, standing before him, her hands splayed across her huge belly.

"Only I can give you immortality," she whispered. "Only I."

Brutus let Cornelia's head drop back to the pillow. "Sleep," he said, "for we are both tired."

Then he sighed, and rolled away, and Cornelia was left staring at his back.

Chapter Seventeen

"YOU LAY WITH HER."

Genvissa's voice was harsh, her stance stiff and unyielding.

They were walking along the northern line of the walls, inspecting the trenches and foundations.

"She is my wife."

Genvissa was silent.

"You have no need to be jealous of her," Brutus said. "She is nothing compared to you."

"You almost kissed her," said Genvissa, not knowing *why* that would have been catastrophic, but knowing it nevertheless.

"What is a kiss?" said Brutus, laughing at the thunder of

Genvissa's face. "There are more intimate things between a husband and a wife."

They walked in silence a few more paces.

"Perhaps you should live with me in my house," Genvissa said. "There is space enough for you."

"In your bed?"

Genvissa almost cried in frustration. "You know that cannot be, Brutus! Not yet!"

"Then I shall stay where I am." He stopped, and took Genvissa's face in his hands as he had Cornelia's the previous night. This time he did not hesitate when he leaned forward, lay his mouth to that of the woman he held. "Gods, Genvissa, there is *nothing* for you to fear. When we start the Game, then nothing will undo us. We will be together, bound, tied, and conjoined as few men and women ever are. Nothing will separate us. Nothing."

Genvissa relaxed. Those were words he'd never spoken, nor would ever speak, to Cornelia. They kissed again, deeper, passionately, and eventually Brutus stepped back, laughing shortly.

"Enough!" he said. "I cannot stand more!"

"Imagine it, my love. The Night of the Torches, the Game begun, you and I, together, at last."

"I am imagining it right *now*," he said hoarsely, and Genvissa laughed, delighted.

"Good! So tell me, will there be enough warriors and virgins among your Trojans to use as dancers?"

"Yes, warriors certainly, and virgins, too, even if I have to sew them back together myself."

Genvissa's mood sobered, Brutus' comment making her think, for no apparent reason, of Asterion growing in the womb of Goffar's wife in Poiteran. There was nothing to worry about, surely, but . . . but this *was* something she should tell Brutus. She dare not alienate him when so much was at stake. "Brutus, Asterion has entered rebirth."

He stilled. "Where?"

"In the womb of the wife of Goffar, king of the Poiterans."

"So close? And a Poiteran? Genvissa . . ."

"There is nothing to worry about, my love. He is a bare few weeks old in the womb. He shall only be a grizzling, toothless infant when we complete the Game, and then it will be too late for him. The labyrinth shall trap him."

"But reborn as a Poiteran, Genvissa. I cannot just ignore that."

"We will be strong enough, Brutus. But . . ." Her voice drifted off, and she cast down her eyes and bit her lip. "But just in case, surely, it would be best if Cornelia—"

"Genvissa . . ."

"If Cornelia were to be sent away, perhaps, my love. It cannot do any harm."

Brutus hesitated. It would not do any harm, but all he could think of was her sweetness this past night. "I will keep a close watch on her," he said finally.

Genvissa's mouth hardened into a thin line, but vanished almost instantly as she laughed, and drew Brutus against her.

"I have waited for you forever," she said, and kissed him. *And nothing will keep you apart from me. Nothing.*

Chapter Eighteen

SIX WEEKS LATER

BLACK-HULLED SHIPS, ALMOST A HUNDRED of them, crowded the banks of the Llan. They'd arrived a month earlier, bearing within them the joyous faces of the Trojans, their journey of almost one hundred years since the fall of Troy finally done.

Almost a thousand of the Trojans, headed by Assaracus, had elected to remain at the original settlement that Brutus had somewhat jokingly named Totnes, and which was now firmly fixed as the developing town's name. It was a good site, and in the weeks they'd spent awaiting word from Brutus, many of the Trojans had decided that Totnes would be an excellent place to live, and raise their children. They'd grown to good terms with the small villages dotted along the Dart River, helped in no small degree with the acquaintance, and then deep friendship, with the three Mothers who'd resided within the Trojan camp as "hostages."

Brutus was not unhappy about the decision of Assaracus and the thousand others to remain in Totnes. It was a pleasant site indeed, and having another Trojan settlement within Llangarlia would certainly be no bad thing.

And it made one thousand less people to have to fit into the area surrounding Llanbank.

An influx of eleven thousand people into any area was bound to cause problems; the fact that these eleven thousand were foreigners merely deepened the problems. Brutus was keenly aware of the need not to alienate the people of Llanbank in the first instance, and the wider population of Llangarlia in the second instance, and so he took several measures to ensure the influx of Trojans was as painless as possible.

It helped that the majority of the Trojans themselves were acutely aware of the need not to estrange the Llangarlians. Many of the spoils of Mesopotama—the gold and jewels, and the silks and linens that had survived the sea journey—were now exchanged with the Llangarlians in thanks for the tracts of land that stretched east from Llanbank, where the Trojans would make temporary settlement until Troia Nova was built north of the river. None of the Trojans intruded upon Llanbank unless they were asked, and they took care not to trample the meadowlands where grazed Llanbank's flocks of sheep and goats, and where roamed their pigs and cattle.

If the Trojans needed meat or grain, then they paid for it. If they wanted company and conversation, then they invited families of Llangarlians into their temporary shelters, and were grateful when and if they themselves were invited into one of Llanbank's houses in order to share warmth, food, and companionship. Most of the Trojans had taken the trouble to have, at the very least, a rudimentary understanding of the Llangarlian language, and the people of Llanbank returned the favor by acquiring words of the Greek that the Trojans spoke.

Within weeks the conversations between the Trojans and those of Llanbank were a chattering mixture of Greek and the native language.

Soon, both peoples were exchanging ideas along with tales of adventures and gods. The Trojans, back in Mesopotama, had used a plow that the Llangarlians thought would work well in the soils about the Llan; on their part, the Llangarlians shared their local knowledge of fishing and hunting to aid the Trojans in their search for meat.

No one, however, hunted in the sacred forests north of the Llan.

Brutus gave the Trojans one week in which to unpack their ships and to erect suitable shelters against the oncoming winter (which were chilly and damp, so the Llangarlians told their new neighbors, but not as frigid as the winters in the north of the island), then he set the men to work on the foundations of the walls of Troia Nova. He needed to work quickly—Genvissa had told him that the best time to work the first Dance of the Game, work the first enchantment, would be the winter solstice, and that was only two months' distant.

By then, the foundations needed to be complete and the gate marked out.

Evil needed to know where the entrance to the city was in order for it to be trapped.

So the Trojans set to work. The walls were to be huge— the height of five men, and half as thick at its base. That meant the foundations had to be dug at least the height of a man into the ground, and preferably the height of one and a half men. The ground was generally easy to dig—

beneath the surface soil and loam lay well-packed gravel whose discovery made Brutus exultant . . . this land was *made* for the support of walls. In most areas the foundations of flint packed into clay could be laid down directly, but in those few parts where the ground was soft and water-logged the builders would need to drive in wooden piles for extra support. The Wal would be diverted via stone culverts under the walls in the north, and then under a low stone gateway where it emerged into the Llan.

All in all, to Brutus' delight, there would be few problems apart from time—and that could be defeated with good planning and willing backs.

By the winter solstice he had every expectation of being ready to begin the Game.

CORNELIA STOOD ON THE SOUTHERN BANK OF Llan, watching the activity across the river. The site surrounding the three holy mounds swarmed with men—digging, carting, excavating.

She shuddered, and drew her cloak tightly about her.

"Cornelia," said a voice. "How pleasant to see you here."

Cornelia jumped, swiveling about, her face white, her eyes wide, and stared at Genvissa.

Genvissa walked to her side, and looked across the river herself. "All goes well, does it not? Brutus assures me we will be ready for the Game by the night of the winter solstice." She turned slightly, so she could see Cornelia out of the corner of her eye. "You only have a few weeks, Cornelia."

"A few weeks?" Cornelia's voice cracked slightly, and Genvissa had to suppress a smile.

"Surely Brutus has told you about the Game, and his and my role in it?"

Cornelia flushed, the color moving up her neck to mottle her cheeks. "What do you mean, 'a few weeks'?"

Genvissa sighed. "The Game requires myself as Mistress of the Labyrinth, and Brutus, as Kingman of the Labyrinth, to unite as one in order to ensure the success of the Game. You *do* know what I mean, don't you, my dear?"

Cornelia stared at her, white now, her eyes unblinking.

"I'm sure you've been worried that Brutus and I have become lovers," Genvissa said. "But we haven't. Not yet."

She glanced slyly at Cornelia again before continuing. "We're waiting only for the first Dance in the Game, little girl, then Brutus and I will be far more 'married' than you and he ever were. Wedded together in such power you will become nothing more than an irritating insignificance. If I were you, Cornelia, I'd allow Brutus as much use of your body as he can tolerate between now and the winter solstice."

She paused. "I doubt he'll make much use of you after it."

Then she reached out a hand and put her palm against Cornelia's cold cheek. "Poor girl. You've always been too much the simpleton to keep Brutus occupied in any meaningful way. You've had a pair of legs that can be parted, you've a body that can be penetrated, but you're not much else, are you?"

Cornelia drew in one deep, shocked breath, then with all the strength she could muster, she hit Genvissa across the cheek.

Genvissa's eyes flared, but she made no move to retaliate . . . at least, not physically.

"You've nothing to make Brutus love you," she said, her voice now as cold as the frosty air about them. "Nothing."

ERITH LOOKED UP, STARTLED BY CORNELIA'S SUD-den entrance into her house. She had been expecting the girl, but not this early . . . and not in this state.

"Cornelia?" she said, rising from her bench by the hearth. "What is wrong?"

"Forgive me my entrance," Cornelia said, paused, then began to cry.

Erith shot a significant look at Loth, who sat deep in the

shadows of the far side of the house, then put her arm about Cornelia and drew her close to the fire.

"Genvissa," Loth said, his voice deep with anger.

"Undoubtedly," Erith agreed, "for she has been as cock-sure as the sun these past weeks. Cornelia?"

Cornelia sniffed, wiped her hand across her eyes, and made an effort to compose herself. "I apologize, Erith. And yes, Loth"—she nodded at him in greeting—"is right. I have just been bested by Genvissa . . . again. She told me that the Game will begin on the night of the winter solstice—"

Loth rose very quietly and came to sit at Cornelia's other side.

"—and that . . . that it will cement she and Brutus in a partnership closer than he and I could ever share. Wedded together in such power, she said, that I would become an insignificance in his life."

"And still you do not wish to aid us, aid *Mag* against Genvissa?" Several times in the past weeks Loth had approached Cornelia, and asked her if she would aid him and Erith and their allies against Genvissa, but every time she had refused.

To do so would only be to alienate Brutus, and that she would not risk. Cornelia had even taken to avoiding Coel, as if that would keep her determination intact.

Cornelia turned aside her face, as she had every time Loth approached her to aid him, and there was a long silence.

Finally, Erith sighed, and took Cornelia's hand. "Girl, we wish you to help us, for we think you are the only one who *can* help us, but we will not force you."

"Would it help," Cornelia said very softly, "if Brutus were to renounce Genvissa?"

Erith and Loth exchanged glances.

"What do you mean?" Erith said.

"If Brutus renounces Genvissa for me, completely, then he will not begin this Game with her, would he?"

"Perhaps," said Loth, wondering what manner of plan

Cornelia had dreamed up to make Brutus turn completely from Genvissa. It would have to involve the counterturning of both the sun and moon, for he did not think anything less would manage it.

"If I were pregnant again," Cornelia said, "surely he would renounce Genvissa?"

Loth fought the impulse to roll his eyes, contenting himself with yet another glance at Erith. "Cornelia . . ."

"Erith," Cornelia turned to the House Mother, turning her back to Loth and speaking rapidly before he had a chance to interrupt her. "You once told me about the spring at the foot of the Llandin where a woman can go to beg Mag's mercy in conceiving, and to win for her child a soul most worthy. Is it true? Will you show me?"

"But we don't think Mag's power is there anymore," Erith started to say, but Cornelia hurried on, her hope so desperate it would brook no counterargument.

"It is my only hope, Erith. If I caught with child again . . . I just know Brutus would stay with me! When I was carrying Achates he kept me with him even though he hated me!"

"I don't think this would be the same—"

"If Mag aided me to conceive, if she helped me to choose a bright soul for my daughter, then . . . then . . ."

"I don't see why we shouldn't aid you," Loth said smoothly, ignoring Erith's startled glance. "It just might work."

LATER, WHEN CORNELIA HAD GONE, ERITH turned to Loth with wide, questioning eyes.

"She is naive, yes," Loth said. "A bellyful of six squirming children is going to do nothing to break Genvissa's hold over Brutus. But taking her to Mag's spring . . . maybe we can learn more about how she can aid Mag. Whether Mag is there or not, Erith, those are magical waters. They might show us the 'truth' of Cornelia."

Erith shrugged. "It won't do any harm, I suppose," she said.

Chapter Nineteen

Cornelia Speaks

*J*WAS DESPERATE FOR BRUTUS, AND DESPERate for a child, a *daughter*. This desire was not only because I was sure that should I have a belly on me again then Brutus would be sure to abandon his questing after Genvissa, but because of my continuing dreams of the stone hall. Always, it seemed, my daughter was there, playing just beyond the field of my vision, her laughter like music. Always I was happy there.

I knew that this daughter was fated. When Coel had told me that Llangarlia had no great stone hall I'd been bewildered. Perhaps it had been but a dream, after all. But then, on that day I'd climbed Og's Hill, and Brutus had put his arm about my waist and explained his plans, I'd known it to be no dream, but a truth.

The view from the top of Og's Hill was *exactly* the view from the stone hall in my vision. It might not be built yet, but it would be soon, and then Brutus and I would reign from there, and watch our daughter play among the great hall's shadowy aisles. Brutus had dreamed of this stone hall, too. He must have seen what I had. Once he knew I was with child again, and with a daughter, then he would forget Genvissa and whatever hold she had over him.

Then he would love me.

I also would have a baby to mother. Aethylla was increasingly becoming Achates' mother. He cried whenever I lifted him from Aethylla's arms, he yearned for Aethylla's breast, he played in her lap, he slept in her bed.

This time, I was going to have a child that loved *me*, not Aethylla and her damned milk-engorged breasts. This time, *my* breasts would feed my child.

No one would take this child from me.

I think that, in a tiny part of me somewhere, I thought that if I *did* lose Brutus, if he did leave me for that witch, then I would always have his daughter, I would always have a bond with him.

But, oh . . . Genvissa.

You've had a pair of legs that can be parted, you've a body that can be penetrated, but you're not much else, are you?

Had she fed that particular bit of nastiness to Brutus as well? Had they laughed about it, laughed at me?

That evening, while Brutus was still occupied at the building site (and no doubt laughing with Genvissa over yet another of my failings), and Achates suckled contentedly at Aethylla's breast, Erith took me to the Llandin spring.

IT WAS SO COLD MY NOSE FELT AS THOUGH IT HAD frozen and would drop away from my face at any moment, and I partly wished that I had not asked Erith to bring me.

But I was determined to conceive of a child that would bind Brutus to me; if this did not win him back to my side then nothing would.

I'd been here several weeks previously when Coel (careful never to touch me, nor to push me) had taken me on a tour of the Veiled Hills. The hills made me feel much as I had at the first sight of Llangarlia: breathless, excited, overwhelmed, and strangely loved. This land, and these sacred hills particularly, made me feel as I imagined it would feel to be held safe and warm in a mother's arms.

The spring with its delightful charm had made me laugh—and Coel had then laughed to see my joy—and now I was happy to be coming back. To beg of its waters, and of this Mag, a daughter that I would love and who would love me and who would bind Brutus to me forever and ever and ever.

When we arrived at the great gnarled oak that guarded

the approaches to the Llandin, I was annoyed to find Loth waiting for us. I shot him a dark look. No matter what he pleaded, I would not aid him, nor Erith either, if it meant antagonizing Brutus.

"Cornelia," said Erith's gentle voice as we stopped at the edge of the streaming pool of water under the rocks from where the spring bubbled. "You will need to disrobe."

I dropped my cloak and slid the robe over my shoulders. "What now?" I said, shivering in the cold air.

"When you enter the pool," Loth said, "you will experience a vision. This will be your vision alone. Neither Erith nor myself will see what you do. Whatever happens, Cornelia, you must endure by yourself. Are you prepared for that?"

"Yes. Please, what do I do?"

"I have told you of the Mag that Llangarlian women feel in their wombs," Erith said to me.

"Yes, Blangan told me of it."

"If you want Mag's aid," Erith said, "then you will need to feel the Mag within your womb. *Do* you feel Mag within your womb, Cornelia of Mesopotama?"

My eyes had strayed to Loth, and now I jerked them back to her, and I flushed a little. "Yes," I said, spreading my hands over my belly. "Yes, I feel her."

And indeed, I think that I did. There was a tingling deep within me, a warmth. It was nothing like the growing heat of sexual passion, but as if my womb contained a roughened ball slowly turning within its confines, rubbing against its walls.

A hand, perhaps, slowly turning deep within me.

I shuddered. "Yes, I feel her."

As I was speaking Erith had crooked an eyebrow at Loth, but all she said to me was to ask me to walk to the pool and step in until the waters reached my waist.

I did as she said, sliding my feet one by one carefully into the water in case the footing was slippery, my hands now at my side, outstretched for balance.

I shivered in delight at the warmth of the water, and as

the footing proved soft but not uncertain, I moved easily into the center of the pool, then turned and looked back at Erith and Loth, now both standing at the edge of the waters.

"Close your eyes," said Loth, his voice very soft.

I did as he asked.

"Can you feel your womb?" said Erith.

I nodded.

"Can you imagine it, squirming with child?" said Loth.

I smiled, and nodded. My belly felt suddenly full, distended, my womb stretched with the child it carried.

A girl, I could almost *see* her curled up within me, dreaming of the day when she would be born and free. Plump and healthy, with tight black curls plastered to her scalp by the waters that cushioned her and strong healthy limbs that she moved languidly about within my womb, pushing against its confines.

"Yes," I whispered. "She is lovely . . . my daughter."

"What would you like her to be?" said Erith. "What kind of woman do you want your daughter to grow to?"

I felt as if I would melt with happiness. "She will be strong and beautiful, and lucky in every way. She will choose her own path in life, spending all her days in love and laughter." My hands were again wrapped about my belly, but where it had been only gently rounded when I had stepped into the waters, now it was huge, distended, roiling with the life it contained.

Loth said something, I could not catch the words, and then Erith repeated his words.

"Open your eyes, Cornelia," Loth said, "but say and do nothing, whatever strangeness your eyes encounter."

I did as he asked, then only barely managed to restrain my gasp, and to hold myself still in the waters.

A small woman stood in the water before me. Dark and fey, with very bright eyes, she was the woman I'd seen with Hera in the stone hall.

"Mag?" I whispered.

She lifted a hand from the water and placed it over one of mine on my belly.

"I can give you all you want in your daughter," she said, "although it will do you no good now. It will be many years, Cornelia, before you hold your daughter in your arms. Many years and many tears . . ."

Her voice drifted off, and then the pressure of her hand on mine increased, and suddenly I saw a vision of such horror that I gasped.

Fire, so consuming that everything before it crumbled to ash.

Invaders, clay-daubed like those that attacked Brutus and his men that night Achates was born, only infinitely more frightening, more murderous.

Fire and invaders, together, dropping from the sky, and a presence so evil behind them that I cried out, and tried to twist away from the woman's hand.

"Cornelia, Cornelia," she said, and I saw that she was crying, as if this vision terrified her as much as it did me. "Only you, Cornelia. Only *you*, Cornelia."

"No!"

"Tread down the steps, Cornelia, through fire and death, into the darkness, into the heart, around and about, mouth to mouth, soul to soul, 'mid deafening bells, through sirens' call, 'twixt thunderous roar and shattering wall. Face the evil, turn it about, dance with your lover, *and seal the gate!*"

There was a silence, reverberating with her frightful words.

"And then, Cornelia," she whispered, and her other hand was at my cheek, wiping away the tears, "then you will have your daughter."

"No!" I cried. "I want my daughter now! Now!"

"And surely you shall have her now, but never in your arms, never in your arms . . ."

Then she seemed to relent, for she smiled, and said, "Bathe your breasts in these waters, and you shall have the daughter you desire."

And she was gone, and I stood in that pool, scooping water over my breasts, putting everything she had said to

me out of my mind, save that I would have my daughter
. . . I would have my daughter . . .

I calmed, breathing deeply, thinking only of the girl I
would conceive tonight, and then . . .

I SAW GENVISSA, STANDING OUTSIDE HER HOUSE,
staring wildly at Brutus, who rode away into the night.

"Come back!" she cried, holding out her rounded white
arms in appeal. "Come back . . . do not go to her, not to-
night! Not tonight!"

But she was too late, Brutus had already gone.

Genvissa turned, and saw me somehow, and her face
twisted into a mask of spite.

"Your belly is meaningless, girl," she said. "It is mine
that shall count, mine that shall birth the most beautiful
girl the world will ever see. Mine, my daughter. Not yours,
Mag."

I GASPED, AND FOUND MYSELF SINKING AS IF A
great weight had grabbed my legs. I screamed, flailing in the
water, then there was a great splash, and Loth was beside me,
holding me up, and guiding me to the edge of the pool.

"What happened?" I heard Erith say, and then I knew no
more for I fainted.

Chapter Twenty

S SHE BREATHING?" ERITH SAID, TRYING TO
roll Cornelia over onto her back.

"Yes," Loth said. Then he looked up at Erith.
"Gods, Erith, *what happened?*"

She shrugged. "I don't know—neither of us shared her vision. Quick, grab her clothes . . . she's wet through, and in this cold . . ."

Loth grabbed at Cornelia's robe, somehow managing to slip it over her head and arms and drag it down her wet body.

"Did it work?" Erith said.

Loth, in the process of pulling Cornelia's robe down over her hips, stopped and slid his hand over her belly.

"Yes," he said. "If she lies with Brutus tonight she will conceive of this daughter she wants so badly."

FAR DISTANT, IN HER HOUSE NORTH OF THE veiled hills, Genvissa leaned in the open door and watched Brutus ride into the night.

Back to Llanbank.

Back to Cornelia.

Back to plant within her a daughter.

As MagaLlan Genvissa had a powerful connection with Mag's Pond, and she'd understood where Mag had got to the instant Cornelia sank beneath the pond's waters. *Mag had hidden within Cornelia!* No wonder she'd felt so uncertain about Cornelia, no wonder there were so many shadows hanging about her. It was not just that she shared Brutus' bed; it was not just that she'd once mouthed the name of Asterion, or that Brutus had seen Asterion riding her; it was that Mag, the poisonous bitch-goddess, had secreted herself within Cornelia's womb!

And now Mag was going to give Cornelia a daughter. Genvissa's mouth curled. That was one daughter-heir that was never going to draw breath. It could not, Genvissa *dared* not allow it.

Only one daughter-heir could live, and Genvissa was determined—*obsessed*—that it would be hers.

Genvissa drew in a breath, not surprised to find it shaking.

"You spiteful, plotting bitch, Mag," she whispered. "For

this deception you can die along with Cornelia's brat."

For a long time Genvissa waited in the door of her house, sensing what was happening, then, finally, walked back into her house, and lay down on her bed, knowing she would never sleep.

CORNELIA GAVE A HEAVE, RETCHED, THEN VOM- ited forth a little water. She lurched upward, her arms flying about, hitting Loth a stinging blow across his face.

"Cornelia! Cornelia!" Erith shouted. "You are safe!" She tried to grab Cornelia's arms, but it took both her and Loth to manage to subdue the struggling girl.

"The fire!" Cornelia finally managed to splutter. "The fire, oh, Hera! The fire!"

"What fire?" Loth said evenly.

"The fire, from the sky, evil, so bad, the heart, the soul, the pit, the blackness . . ."

Cornelia was rambling, and Erith and Loth exchanged looks.

"I saw Genvissa!" Cornelia said. "Genvissa! She *saw* me!"

Both Erith and Loth stilled, their eyes locking.

"Genvissa was in the pool?" Loth said very quietly.

"I saw evil and destruction, and heard things that must have come from Hades' realm," Cornelia whispered, her eyes staring.

Again, Erith and Loth locked eyes. *What had happened?*

"Cornelia," Loth began to say, then stopped. He was still looking at Erith.

We cannot allow her to conceive of this child, he said in Erith's mind. *Fire? Destruction? And Genvissa? Evil? No, no, this child must not be conceived.*

Erith held his glance a heartbeat, then nodded. "Corne- lia," she said. "It would be best if you slept at my house tonight. You've had a shock, and have swallowed some water into your lungs. It is best that—"

"No!" Cornelia said, struggling to her feet, and tugging

her damp gown straight about her body. "No. I must go to my own home tonight. You understand that. I must—"

"*Not* conceive this child," Loth said, and stepped up to Cornelia, taking her arm. "You *must not conceive this child!*"

"No!" Cornelia said, struggling with him. "What are you saying? You bring me here, and now you say I can't conceive this child? *Nothing* is going to stop me conceiving my daughter! Nothing!"

"What you spoke of in the water is an aberration! And Genvissa was there? No, you must not conceive of this child," Erith said, her voice frantic.

"What are you trying to do to me?" Cornelia said. "I don't understand. Let me go . . . let me *go!*" She started to cry, sobbing wretchedly, and slapping ineffectually at Loth's strong grip about her wrist. "Let me go . . ."

"You will come with me tonight," Loth said. "I'm sorry, Cornelia, but I—"

"What are you doing? Let her go, you monstrosity! *Let her go!*"

There was a flurry of hooves, and the heat of a horse's body as it pushed into the little struggling group.

Taken by surprise, Loth lost his grip on Cornelia's arm and fell to the ground as the horse careered into him.

Brutus reached down and grabbed at Cornelia, who had raised her arms to him. He lifted her behind him on the horse, then turned it about in a tight circle, making both Erith and Loth, who had managed to regain his feet, scurry backward.

"Leave . . . her . . . alone!" Brutus said very slowly, very menacingly, his eyes furious. Cornelia had wrapped her arms about him, and melded her body to his back, sobbing even harder than she had been previously.

And then Brutus twisted the horse's head about, and they were gone, and Erith and Loth were left staring helplessly after them.

"Damn her," Loth whispered, then flung out his arms and screamed into the night. *"Damn her!"*

*   *   *

FAR AWAY, IN HER NEST, GENVISSA SNARLED.
"Damn him," she whispered.

CORNELIA CRIED OUT, ARCHING HER BACK AND
pressing her body as hard against Brutus' as she could.

He drove into her, again and again, possessed by her
wildness, crazed by lust as he had never been before. Her
fingers were scratching at his back, digging into his buttocks, her teeth were deep in his shoulder, drawing blood.

He had only barely dragged her off the horse outside
their house, meaning to ask her what she'd been doing out
there at the Llandin so late at night with Erith and Loth,
when she'd thrown herself at him, tearing at her clothes
and his before they've even stumbled in the door.

They'd barely made the bed before she'd grabbed at him
and pushed him inside her.

Now he was as wild as she, his weariness forgotten, *everything* forgotten but the scent and the feel and the tightness and the movement of the woman beneath him.

When he finally fell, spent and exhausted, across her
body, she continued to move under him, as if intent on
dragging forth from him every last drop of essence that she
could.

Eventually Cornelia stilled, her eyes closed, a smile on
her face.

Deep within her, her womb burned.

LOTH AND ERITH WERE STILL AT THE EDGE OF THE
pool under the oak. Loth sat, his head in his hands, slowly
shaking it back and forth in denial.

"What can we do?" he whispered.

"Nothing for the moment," Erith said. She shivered. "The
child is conceived. I can feel it. Loth . . ."

He looked up, his entire face haggard.

"We can kill the child before it is born. It would be easy enough to—"

"No!" Loth leapt to his feet. "How can you suggest that? No one takes the life of a child, no matter how much they fear it!"

He sighed, the breath shaky. "We need her, Erith. We can't threaten her child . . . that would turn her away from us completely."

"As if what we did to her tonight won't," Erith muttered.

"We have to destroy the Game. We can't let Genvissa continue on with it. I don't know how, Erith, or when, but we have to destroy the Game . . . or watch it annihilate everything we hold dear. And"—he hesitated, the uncertainty sitting uneasily on his normally sure face—"we will have to use Cornelia to do it. That much, at least, Mag has made clear to us. Cornelia must be our weapon."

"The ways of Mag are wondrously muddled," Erith said sarcastically. "Rely on Cornelia to help you destroy the Game? You might as well wish the stars themselves from the sky to aid you."

Chapter Twenty-One

Cornelia Speaks

J THINK I CONCEIVED THAT NIGHT . . . BUT I WAS not sure. I desperately *wanted* to have conceived that night . . . but I didn't want my desperate wish to mislead me. I wanted to be able to tell Brutus I had conceived of another child, this time a daughter who would be most wondrous . . . but I thought that if I told him, and was then proved to be mistaken, it would be the end of whatever regard he had left for me.

I had made so many mistakes of judgment, I didn't want to curse myself completely with another one.

Besides, two weeks after that passionate, wild night, I began to bleed. Not much, just a faint smudging, nothing like my regular monthly courses . . . but it was in itself enough to make me hesitate yet further. My breasts were tender, as if in pregnancy, but my womb seemed uncertain, and no matter how much I rubbed my belly, and closed my eyes and concentrated on my womb, all I felt was a continuance of unsurety and confusion.

And all my dreams of the stone hall had ceased completely.

So, for weeks, many weeks, I did not take Brutus' hand, and lay it on my belly, and smile, and say we had made another child between us.

He still slept at my side at night, so I felt relatively safe. Genvissa had not yet taken him to her bed, so it would be *my* womb to quicken with his child, not hers. It must, it *must*.

Yet even if he slept at my side, he made no further attempt to use me sexually. I tried to rouse him, I ran my hands over his body and spoke sweetly and softly in his ear, but he brushed aside my hand, and turned aside his head, and said that he felt weary, the building work was draining, and he would prefer to sleep.

One night, six weeks after I'd bathed in the pool under the Llandin, I made particular effort. I took his hands and rubbed them across my naked breasts. I pressed my body against his, and reached down my hand to his member, that I might rouse him to use me.

This time he did more than just turn aside claiming weariness.

"I may not, Cornelia," he said roughly, as if my initiative irritated him. "The ceremony to bless the city and begin the Game is only two weeks distant, and I must keep myself unsullied."

"*I* would sully you?" I said, trying somewhat unsuccessfully to keep my voice down in the house that Hicetaon and Aethylla still shared with us. "You did not use *that* excuse the night you so roughly took my virginity, as I remember."

"It was different then."

"Oh, yes, it was different then. *Then* you merely took what you wanted; now, when I want, I am cruelly brushed aside. Brutus, you said to me the day after Achates was born that we should make the best of the marriage we were doomed to. I have tried . . . have you?"

"Cornelia, there are great matters that you cannot understand—"

"There is only one 'great matter,' " I said, truly angry now, "and her name is Genvissa."

"You cannot possibly understand," he said, his voice cold and dismissive. "You are but a girl."

And with that he rolled over, presented his back to me, and feigned sleep.

I lay awake the rest of the night and seethed, and in the morning, when he was gone, I went to see Erith.

I HAD AVOIDED HER SINCE THAT NIGHT AT THE spring. In part because she had tried to keep me from Brutus' bed that night (why, I have no idea, for had she not aided me in my quest to conceive?), but mostly because I felt slightly ashamed. I had behaved badly—*again*—and I did not wish to see the gentle censure in her eyes.

But I need not have worried. Erith greeted me kindly, did not remark on how long it was since I had been to see her, and hastened me inside from the wintry weather into the warmth and comfort of her house.

Coel was there, his clothes mud-stained as if he had only recently arrived himself, and he, too, greeted me warmly, bending to brush my cheek with his. I had not seen him much recently, and I felt a surge of guilt. Coel had been as good a friend to me as ever I could want, and—again—I had treated him poorly.

I peered over his shoulder into the depths of the house, and was glad to note that Loth was not present.

"Erith," I said. "I cannot stay long . . . but I need your aid."

Something came over her face then—a hesitation, perhaps.

"I need . . . I need to know if I am with child."

She frowned. "Did you not lie with Brutus that night after your visit to the spring?"

"Yes, but—"

"Then you are with child. Here." She drew me to her, and laid a hand firmly over my belly.

She let it lie there a moment, then she raised her eyes, now curiously flat and dead, back to my face. "You have the daughter you wished for, Cornelia. Can you not know this?"

"I was confused. I—"

"You didn't feel Mag within your womb, telling you it was so?"

I blushed, although I did not know why. "I was confused, Erith."

Erith shared a glance with her son, and I felt as though I had been judged at that moment.

She let me go, stepping back. "You are with child, Cornelia. Is that not what you wished for?"

I sighed in relief. "Yes. Yes, it is Erith. Thank you."

I turned to share my joy with Coel, and found him looking at me with a great sadness.

It stunned me, and momentarily drained away all my own happiness—had he wanted me that much?—but then I tossed my head, put the smile back on my face, thanked Erith once more, and left the house.

I would find Brutus, and tell him, and all would be well.

Chapter Twenty-Two

ERITH LOOKED AT HER SON WHO WAS STILL staring at the door where Cornelia had disappeared. "Oh, Coel, be careful. I feel doom in my bones, and cannot but help think you are somehow caught up in it."

He pulled his gaze reluctantly from the door, and smiled gently at his mother. "There is doom abroad for all of us, Mother. The day of the Game draws near . . . and what can we do?"

"Nothing," she said, very low, her expression defeated. "Genvissa holds our people enthralled, no one will move against her."

"Cornelia?" Coel said, but his voice was hopeless.

"She cannot see past Brutus," Erith said.

She gave a low, bitter, hopeless laugh, and sank down to one of the benches before the hearth. "How can it be that Mag has chosen Cornelia as her weapon against Genvissa? If this is truly so, then we are surely lost, as is Mag."

CORNELIA HASTENED BACK TO HER HOUSE, COLlected a warm cloak against the cold and slipped her feet into a pair of sturdy clogs against the mud, and then hurried out again, walking through Llanbank and then the Trojan settlement to the ferry crossing.

People were everywhere, despite the cold. Many of the Trojans still worked on fortifying their winter settlements—houses within the city walls would not be available for at least a year. Women worked at their household tasks, weaving and baking, minding children, drawing water.

The road that led north through the settlement was now virtually impassable—so many bullocks and carts had drawn building materials from the southern quarries northward toward the ferry over the Llan that the graveled surface had been trodden into ankle-deep mud—so Cornelia stepped carefully on its verges, mindful of the need to avoid slipping.

As she neared the Llan, she stopped, tightened her cloak about her, and raised her face to the northern bank.

It was a hive of activity. Where six weeks earlier had been three gentle grassed mounds, divided by the stream of the Wal and bounded on their southern edge by the clay cliffs above the Llan, were now three humps, their grass mostly trampled into the earth beneath, covered with teams of laborers, groups of engineers, piles of gravel, wooden piles, rough-cut stone sections that stone masons were hewing into neatly edged building blocks, and intermittent heaps of soil that had been dug out of the wall's foundation trenches.

Cornelia had been to the site two or three times in the past weeks, but had not stayed long. She had felt in the way among all the scurrying and purposeful workers, and when she'd managed to talk to Brutus, he'd been distant, distracted, and had turned aside as soon as he could.

She held her breath, nervousness fluttering in her stomach. Where was he? What was he doing? Surely he would not be distant with her when he heard she was carrying his child . . . would he?

Cornelia's eyes traveled over the site, but she was too far distant to be able to see many details. With a sigh, and yet a further tightening of the cloak about her body, she set off to the ferry.

THE FERRY LANDED ON THE NORTHERN BANK OF the Llan at the midpoint of the southern wall. Cornelia accepted the ferryman's assistance in stepping from ferry to muddied foreshore, thanking him, then turned and studied the immediate area.

The foundations of this southern wall seemed all but done. The trenches had been dug, and were now filled with a mixture of gravel, flint, and clay. Already stonemasons were laying the founding course of stones for the wall. Cornelia stopped by the first group of men she came to, and asked where Brutus was.

The foreman stopped, straightened, stretched his back, and then wiped his sweating face.

"You're like as not to find yourself knee deep in mud, my lady," he said, eyeing her cloak and footwear. "This is no pleasure garden."

"I need to see my husband," Cornelia said, as firmly as she could manage.

"He's up on the White Mount," the foreman said, nodding in the direction of the easternmost mound. "Surveying the site of his palace."

Cornelia smiled, her eyes alight. "He is beginning on the palace?"

"Aye," the man said. Several other of the men in his work squad had now put down their tools and were studying Cornelia silently.

Cornelia's smile had now widened until it lit her entire face. "For me?"

The man smiled, but it was brittle, false. "A palace fit for a king and his queen, my lady."

"He hadn't told me!"

And with that she was gone, moving as quickly as she could through the gangs of workers and piles of building materials.

The men watched her go.

"Fool," said one.

The foreman watched Cornelia pick her way toward the White Mount. "Not for much longer," he said. "Not when she finds there's no chamber in that palace for her."

*   *   *

THE WHITE MOUNT ROSE AT THE APEX OF THE southern and eastern walls. It was smaller than either Og's or Mag's Hill, but still commanded a good view of the river and the surrounding countryside. As Cornelia drew nearer, she could see that the wall's eastern foundations were as advanced as those of the southern wall. Brutus will be pleased, she thought, and then shivered with pleasure at how much more pleased he would be when she told him their news.

When Cornelia reached the foot of the White Mount she looked up, pausing to catch her breath for the climb, and could clearly see that there was, indeed, building work going on atop the mound. She began to climb the slope with strong, confident strides, avoiding as much mud as she could, and finding several remaining grassy tussocks to speed her on her way.

When she was but ten or twelve paces from the top, and had the low rising walls of the building in sight, she heard Brutus' voice floating down to her.

It was light, and laughing, and made Cornelia laugh herself in anticipation.

She scrambled the final few paces, breathing heavily, and paused to catch her bearings. The top of the mount had been covered with the foundations of a large building—the palace. It was much smaller than the Mesopotamian palace Cornelia had been raised in, but the very fact of its existence, and that Brutus thought enough of her to build her a fine palace atop an airy hill, made Cornelia forget all her fears.

If he had not made love to her in weeks, then it was only because he had been weary.

If he had appeared callous and uncaring, then that was because he was weighed down with the cares of construction.

All the time, *this* had been rising.

Cornelia halted, then jumped slightly.

Brutus, a faint shadow, had moved through a half-completed doorway into a chamber that was surely meant to be the megaron. The walls of this chamber were almost complete, and already wooden beams stretched across its roof space.

It would be finished within weeks.

Smiling, Cornelia ran through the building, disregarding the mud or the curses of the builders she jostled. The chamber Brutus had vanished into lay just ahead of her and, when the doorway loomed before her, Cornelia ran straight through it, looking only at Brutus standing at the far end.

"Brutus!" She stopped halfway down the chamber, and raised her hand.

He jumped, then turned to stare at Cornelia, a frown marring his features.

Cornelia's smile faltered a little, and she dropped her hand, but then, recomposed, she picked her way across the stone floor toward him. "Brutus," she said, coming to a halt before him.

"What do you here?" he said.

"I . . . I came to bring you good tidings." Cornelia took the final step that closed the distance between them, took his hand, and placed it on her belly. "I am with child again. A daughter."

"A child?"

"Yes! Are you not happy?"

"It is well enough, I suppose."

"Well enough? Do you not care?" Her smile had gone now, and her shoulders had tensed.

He pulled his hand away from her. "Cornelia. I am tired. If I am not as enthusiastic as you wish, well, then I am sorry for that. But this"—he glanced at her belly—"this is a bad time for you to conceive, and—"

"This is not something I did alone!"

His expression hardened. "Did *I* have much say in that night?"

"I carry our *daughter*, Brutus."

Brutus had no idea why she kept stressing the sex of the child. Did she expect him to do a dance of pleasure at the idea of a daughter? "What use have I for daughters, Cornelia? I need sons." His voice hardened into overt annoyance. "And what do you here? This is no place for a woman. Go back to the house, where you will not be in the way."

Tears glistened in Cornelia's eyes. "Do you not want to show me my palace while I am here?"

"*Your* palace? Cornelia . . . it is possible . . . that you won't . . . that this won't be . . ."

"You're going to share this with *Genvissa*?"

"Cornelia, listen to me. I am a Kingman and my future rests with the Mistress of the Labyrinth, not with you. I'm sorry. I shall build you a house close—"

"I am your *wife*! What is all this talk of Kingmen and Mistresses? *I am your wife!*"

He took her shoulders between his hands, and his face finally gentled. "Cornelia, I should have spoken of this to you long before, and for that I apologize. You and I are patently not a good match, we—"

"You said that we should make what we could of our marriage! You said that we would try—"

"Then I did not know of Genvissa. Cornelia." Brutus paused, wondering how he could put this gently, and then deciding there was no possible means of doing that. "What Genvissa and I are is fated, together we are much more than you and I could ever be. Ours will be a union of power and sexuality and majesty. You and I were never . . . could never . . . oh, Cornelia, I should never have taken you as wife in your father's megaron. Never."

Brutus meant to say more, that he would look after Cornelia, that she would enjoy status and privilege in the new city, that their children would have everything they could possibly need or desire, but the look in her eyes stopped him. He lifted his hands from her shoulders and took a step back, hating the guilt that coursed through him.

She put a hand to her mouth, the tears finally breaking free to run down her cheeks. They locked eyes, each unable to speak, then she turned on her heel, stumbled, caught herself, and ran from the building site.

As she went, Genvissa stepped out from beyond the wall just behind Brutus.

"She says she is with child," he said.

Genvissa's eyes followed the distant figure of Cornelia making her way down the mound. "It does not matter," she said, then turned her stunning face to Brutus. "Besides," she said, her expression sorrowful, "perhaps the child is not yours."

"What?"

She gave a small, indifferent shrug. "Take no meaning from my words, Brutus." She smiled, leaned close, and laid her mouth to his, knowing she spoke Cornelia's death. "I am but a jealous woman. I am sure I speak but a silly rumor. Forget I said the words."

He kissed her, hard, but when she snuggled into him, kissing his neck and ear, he turned his face, and watched as Cornelia disappeared from sight.

LATER THAT NIGHT, SITTING ON THE AS-YET-unfinished steps leading into the palace, Brutus sat and regretted again the brutality of his words to Cornelia. But what else could he have done? The news of the child had truly shocked him—although he couldn't quite pinpoint the "why" of that shock, Brutus assumed it was merely the surprise. He just hadn't expected another child from a woman he had, if he was honest with himself, been distancing himself from ever since he'd arrived at Llanbank and met, finally, Genvissa.

He sighed, rubbing a hand over his eyes. Thank the gods that Genvissa had been so understanding. He hadn't expected it, and the fact of it had made him stunningly grateful.

At least Genvissa didn't stamp her foot and sob whenever life didn't turn out quite the way she'd hoped.

Brutus looked over the building site, watching several guards pick their way carefully through the rubble and chaos.

What had Genvissa meant, that the child might not be his?

He drew in a deep breath, remembering the dream, thinking that he'd barely seen Cornelia for days on end, *weeks* on end sometimes, during the past months.

There'd been too much to do.

What had she been doing during that time? Perhaps he should ask Aethylla . . .

If the child was not his, then *whose*?

Brutus sat there, the stars spinning slowly above him, not noticing the cold, remembering.

Not Corineus. Corineus had either been traveling down to Totnes, or constantly with Brutus. Besides, Corineus had ceased to be Cornelia's champion that terrible moment he'd realized she'd known of the manner of Blangan's death and not told him.

Who, then?

Coel. It could be no one but Coel.

Images and memories tumbled over in Brutus' mind.

The way Coel looked at Cornelia. The longing in his eyes for all to see.

The way Cornelia had looked over the fire at Coel that night traveling north.

That long space of time they'd both been missing when Cornelia was bathing in the rock pool.

And the numbers of times that Cornelia and Coel had opportunity to be together, alone, since their arrival in Llanbank.

No . . . surely not. She wouldn't do that to him . . . would she? Not after everything else she'd done to him, kept from him, said to him.

Would she *dare*?

The answer his mind fed him gave Brutus no relief. He wrapped himself in his cloak, and sat all through the night, staring unseeing into the distance, thinking of Cornelia and Coel, yet not ever considering that one solution that would have occurred to anyone else: Cornelia would be better with Coel than with himself.

That was a concept Brutus' mind refused to encompass.

Chapter Twenty-Three

$\mathcal{J}$T WAS EVENING, AND VERY COLD, BUT, THANK-fully, clear. Genvissa stood atop Og's Hill watching the preparations about her and communing, very gently, very softly, with the shadowy spirits of the five foremothers who had helped her to this point. Now it was her turn, and her time. Her mother had split Og's power, rendering him useless, as well as casting Asterion into a crippled and weakened life far, far away: she had managed to contain Mag (well, she would once Cornelia was dead, and that death was now a foregone conclusion) and had brought to this land the magic she needed to resurrect the Game in all its power: Brutus, heir of Troy, Kingman of the Labyrinth, soon-to-be mate of the Mistress of the Labyrinth.

Genvissa stood at the southern edge of the plateau of Og's Hill. The slopes of the hill were clear, both of people and of the mud that had thickened and dirtied the hill during the construction of the city wall foundation. Now the foundations were done, the first course of stonework laid, and the gate opening to the west of Og's Hill defined.

It was time for the first Dance of the Game.

Everyone intimately concerned with the Dance—Genvissa, Brutus, and the two hundred young Trojan men and women of the dancing corps, as well all the people needed for the physical preparations—had spent these past ten days in feverish activity. The two hundred dancers had been carefully rehearsed, and their dancing garments sewn. Og's Hill and its immediate surrounds had been cleared of building debris, and its slopes regrassed with turf.

Its summit had undergone a transformation.

Genvissa smiled, and turned.

Where once had been a grassy knoll now stretched a carefully leveled plateau. In its center lay an enormous floor of cream and brown stones, intricately laid so that the brown stones delineated a unicursal labyrinth: the seven-circuit Cretan labyrinth.

The Dancing Floor.

Genvissa took a great breath, closing her eyes, feeling her foremothers swirling around her. They were with her, strong, and Ariadne was the strongest of all. Tonight they would restart the Game, take the biggest, most dangerous step . . . and once this night was done they need wait only for the completion of the walls when they could conclude and seal the Game for all time with the Dance of the Flowers.

Tonight.

Genvissa opened her eyes. She would have to leave soon. Prepare herself. Spend time in seclusion and prayer, muttering over and over the spells and incantations that she'd need to make this night a success.

She looked over to the palace. The central megaron and living quarters were complete now, their walls rising smooth and creamy in the evening air, their roofs covered with slate. Brutus would be in there, also alone, beginning his preparation.

Concentrating on his task . . . even more dangerous than Genvissa's.

"Please, all gods in creation who can hear me," she prayed softly, "let there be no disruption to the Game. Let it all flow smoothly. Let nothing stand in our way, nor darken the time between this night and the Day of the Flowers. Let Cornelia and Asterion both be confounded and contained."

The prayer eased her mind, and Genvissa relaxed. All would be well. Brutus would triumph. He was a strong man, unafraid, sure of himself. He would need to be all that tonight . . . but he *would* be all that tonight. He was the heir of Troy, he wore the bands of kingship, he knew the steps, he was the Kingman, her man, her light and her life.

Genvissa had not thought to love him so deeply. She had lusted for him, and wanted him. She had spent years plotting to get him, and trap him back into the Game.

She had not thought to love him.

Her smile faded, her eyes became distant. Tonight they would lie together for the first time. It was part of the Game, a step in the dance, but it was also something that Genvissa now wanted so badly she trembled whenever she thought on it.

Tonight she would lie with Brutus. She felt weak-kneed as if she were a young girl again, and Genvissa treasured the feeling. Tonight she would lie with Brutus and conceive from him her daughter-heir.

And tonight Cornelia would die.

And that bitch-goddess who thought to hide within her!

"Tonight," she said, and looked over the river to where thousands had already journeyed to the shoreline, waiting for that moment when they could cross the Llan and surround the hill. All the Mothers were there, together with their daughter-heirs. This would be a great moment in Llangarlia, and they would need to witness.

"Tonight," Genvissa whispered again, then she gathered her cloak about her, and walked down the hill into her destiny.

THE MOTHERS GATHERED ON OG'S HILL ONCE night had fallen. They stood at the northern edge of the plateau, distant enough from the central labyrinth so that the dancers could have room but close enough that they could witness.

Most were apprehensive, but gladly so. Tonight the MagaLlan would lead the dancers and this Trojan king Brutus in the first of two great dances that would celebrate the birth of a new city, the birth of a great king, *and* which would lay down the founding enchantment that would protect both city and land and would bring prosperity and health back to the Llangarlians forever and evermore.

Once this dance was done, and the final Dance of the Flowers completed when the walls were finished, then Llangarlia would be secure. After all the bitterness and blight of this past generation, Llangarlia and her daughters and sons would finally be safe.

Among the Mothers, however, were several who were considerably more apprehensive than the others. Erith, Ecub, and Mais again stood together, again welded into a triumvirate of useless opposition to Genvissa. They could do nothing but watch, and fear.

To the side stood Coel and Loth, both men dark-visaged. Loth's hands were clenched, and his angry, frustrated eyes flickered between the labyrinth and Cornelia, standing a little distance away with Hicetaon and Corineus—who returned Loth's regard with a dark and forbidding stare—and several other Trojan men that he did not immediately recognize.

Cornelia looked pale, her face drawn, her hands held before her in a loose agony of movement this way and that. Loth knew she had told Brutus of her pregnancy, and that Brutus' reaction had not been all she had hoped.

In fact, it had been nothing like what she had hoped.

Loth had thought that Brutus' disinterest would finally bring Cornelia to her senses. She would never have Brutus' love, she could never compete with the mystery and seductive power of Genvissa. Her time would be better spent working with Loth against Genvissa and Brutus . . . but, no, she would not do it. She didn't want to alienate Brutus, she wanted to be his wife, she wanted his respect, she wanted his love . . .

Loth could have wept—indeed, he *had* spent many nights weeping as he walked the forests. Cornelia was a fool, a silly naive girl who still believed, after all the humiliations Brutus had heaped on her, that his love was the best thing she could ever hope for and the greatest thing she could ever work toward.

By every god that had ever walked this land, what did Mag see in her? Why chose her as her champion?

Cornelia was useless, she would always be useless, and Loth would have torn out her throat if he thought it would have done the least bit of good.

So there Cornelia stood, looking as if she would snivel at any moment, wringing her hands futilely, helpless and hopeless in the face of Genvissa's triumph.

Loth finally gave vent to his anger and frustration and *did* snarl, making everyone within ten paces of him jump in fright.

Coel put a hand on Loth's shoulder. "We can but watch and wait," he said quietly, "and hope for some glimmer of an opening."

To Loth's other side, Ecub took his hand.

"If I kill Genvissa, will it help?" Loth said, very low, his eyes very bright.

"It may tear this land apart," Ecub said softly, intently. "We do not know the how and the why of her trickery, Loth. If we kill her—do we destroy her trickery . . . or do we make it the stronger?"

"I want—" Loth began, but both Coel and Ecub tightened their hands upon him.

"We know," Ecub, said. "We know . . . and we want, too."

THE CEREMONY BEGAN ONCE FULL NIGHT HAD DE-scended. Tens of thousands, both Trojans and Llangarlians, had crossed the Llan to surround Og's Hill. They carried no torches, made no sound. They were simply a dark silent mass of gently shifting bodies, come to witness.

Suddenly, without warning, the heady throb of a drum began, and then, far distant, the sound of voices raised in an eerie, tuneless song.

Atop the hill, people jumped, and heads craned.

"Look!" whispered Erith.

From east and west danced two lines of light; one line came from the White Mount, one from the banks of the Magyl River to the west of Og's Hill. As the lines drew closer—the crowds surrounding Og's Hill parted to give them egress to the hill—the watchers could clearly see that they were composed of barefoot dancers, each line being constituted of alternating young men and women dressed identically in short white linen skirts that flared in tiny pleats from their hips. The dancers' chests were left naked, the men's torsos strong and muscular, the women's breasts firm and high. The women held in their right hands a torch, while their left hands held lightly to a thick woven scarlet ribbon; the men held the torches in their left hands, their right holding the ribbon that snaked between the dancers, binding them in a line of mystery, enchantment, and seductive movement.

At the head of the western line, which had emerged from the Magyl, danced Genvissa, bare-breasted, garbed similarly to all the other dancers save that her white, pleated linen skirt hung to her ankles.

She held nothing in her hands, clasping them lightly to her waist, so that her every movement, her every step, made her hips and breasts sway in provocative invitation.

The scarlet ribbon was tied lightly to her left wrist, and with it she led her dancers toward Og's Hill.

Brutus, the Kingman, led the other line that had emerged from his palace atop the White Mount.

In contrast to every other dancer, and to Genvissa, he was completely naked save for his gleaming bands of kingship on his legs and arms and for a circlet of gold about his brow. His hair, newly washed and oiled, was bound in a tight braid and then clubbed under at the back of his neck with a thin scarlet ribbon.

It glowed in the torchlight and with his movements like a black pool reflecting the light of the stars.

The ribbon that bound his line was tied, as lightly as was Genvissa's, to his right wrist.

In his left hand he carried something round and as black as his hair. It was a ball of pitch.

The twin lines danced, slowly, sinuously, their dancers singing the ancient hymn of the labyrinth, wending their way to Og's Hill through the great crowd that surrounded it.

They reached its foot, and, very slowly, as if they hardly dared, began to climb the hill, each line taking an opposite slope and line of ascent.

As they mounted, their voices growing louder and their movements more confident, the two lines of dancers intertwined and twisted, dancers raising and lowering their arms in arches so that the other line might dance under or over them.

It was an intricate dance, a dance of great beauty and mystery, and everyone watching atop the hill found themselves caught up in its enchantment, no matter whether they wished the dancers death or life.

Loth risked a glance at Cornelia.

She stood, her hands tightly clenched and unmoving before her, tears streaming down her face.

Then there was a shout, a cry of victory, and Loth turned his gaze back to the dancers.

The two lines had emerged on top of the hill, Brutus and Genvissa still leading them. Now the lines danced toward each other, moving close enough to the watchers that they could see the sweat trickling down the dancers' bodies, and see the brightness in their eyes.

Brutus and Genvissa led their lines in opposing circles about the labyrinth, in one, two . . . seven circuits.

At the completion of the seventh circuit, Brutus and Genvissa unbound the ribbon from about their wrists and tied their two lines together.

The lines began to move about the labyrinth again, but now in a very different pattern.

The dancers still formed two lines, but they did not use the lines to form two complete circles. Instead, the two lines—in reality one line doubled—danced in the shape of an almost-closed U about the labyrinth, the opening of the U marking the opening into the labyrinth itself. The outer line danced sunwise, the inner line countersunwise, the dancers moving from one direction to another when they moved from outer line to inner line at the open mouth of the U.

They danced, Erith realized with a jolt, in the shape of a woman's womb.

Mag! she thought. *What are they going to birth from that womb?*

Brutus and Genvissa stood at the mouth of both womb and labyrinth, hand in hand, looking into the labyrinth itself. They remained still for long moments, staring, perhaps praying, then Genvissa stepped back from Brutus, and walked to the edge of the hill.

She raised her arms above her head, her breasts lifting high, and spoke in a ritualized, chanting voice that carried over the watching crowd.

"Behold!" she cried. "The Kingman stands before the labyrinth! Here, tonight, in this land of magic and mystery and power, he will risk his life to guarantee yours! Here, tonight, in this land of magic and mystery and power, he will lift from this land the evil which has beset it, and best it, and trap it, so that you will live your lives long and happy. Here, tonight, we will witness the birth of a new city, a new age, and we will consecrate the talisman which will protect us from all evil and harm forevermore!"

She lowered her arms, and turned to face Brutus.

As she did so, the dancers lowered their torches, holding them down and away from their bodies, and turned their faces away from the labyrinth. They kept moving, but their movements were very slow now, very deliberate, as if they danced the measure of Death itself.

"Behold," whispered Genvissa in a voice that, while very low, nevertheless traveled to every ear, "the Kingman!"

And Brutus began to dance, moving into the paths of the labyrinth.

He lifted his left hand so that he held the ball of pitch high above his head, and his right he held out before him, his arm slightly curved, as if he held a woman within its bounds.

His body moved sensuously, very slowly, displaying its

beauty. With each dance step one of his legs lifted, its foot turned slightly outward, held, then lowered, moving the dance forward with measured deliberation.

With each dance step, his left hand, high above his head, moved a little, twisting the ball of pitch this way and that, his head moving slowly, deliberately, contrariwise below his hand.

Each step took him farther into the labyrinth, each step marking a seductive, measured invitation to follow.

Everyone felt his pull, felt the urge to follow him into the labyrinth, but no one moved.

As seductive and compelling as Brutus' dance was, and as much as all the watchers felt that urge to dance after him, all also realized that this was a dance and an invitation meant for one person only.

Or for one *thing* only.

Genvissa, standing at the mouth to the labyrinth, lowered her head, and stepped to one side.

Brutus moved deeper into the labyrinth, twisting and turning within its coils, the ball of pitch slowly turning this way and that over his head.

A beacon of, and to, darkness.

Loth gasped, the next instant feeling all about him stiffen in shock and horror.

Something had slithered up to the mouth of the labyrinth, coming to rest only paces away from Genvissa who was carefully keeping her gaze on her feet.

It was a mass of darkness, a writhing malaise of evil and ill feeling and bad doing.

Everything, Loth realized, his heart thudding, that had afflicted Llangarlia this past generation.

ACROSS THE GRAY WATERS OF THE NARROW SEAS, the nascent infant Asterion stirred in his mother's womb. Protected by its walls, the magic of Brutus' dance did not affect him, nor did the ball of pitch tempt him.

For the moment he was safe.

*   *   *

GENVISSA STOOD AS STILL AS DEATH, GIVING THE writhing mass so close to her no recognition at all.

Brutus, although he must also have seen it, continued on with his deliberate, sensual dance through the labyrinth.

The mass of evil quivered uncertainly at the mouth of the labyrinth, then it sent forth a tentative sliver of darkness.

Finding no pain, no concern, the mass slithered to catch up with its leading tentacle, then humped even farther into the labyrinth.

Brutus danced on, and by slow degrees, the corrupt mass humped after him, stopping occasionally as if to sniff out any potential trap, then gathering its energy and following the ball of pitch ever deeper into the labyrinth.

Loth's mouth had gone completely dry.

This was to lie buried at the heart of the new city? At the heart of Llangarlia? *This* obscenity?

Loth looked to Brutus, now approaching the heart of the labyrinth. His movements were strained now, more restricted, as the coils grew ever tighter as they led him to the center.

Gods, what would Brutus do when the horror caught up with him at the center of the labyrinth?

Loth looked back to Genvissa, expecting to see her still standing, face lowered, at one side of the labyrinth's entrance.

But she had moved. Now she stood just inside the entrance, her face up, her eyes shining, a gentle smile curving her mouth.

Brutus reached the center of the labyrinth, and stood, as Genvissa had been, his head down.

But he still held the ball of pitch aloft.

The darkness writhed closer and closer, picking up speed as it approached its goal. It was muttering now, a horrid hum of angry whisperings, as if it couldn't wait to feed.

One more turn, one more slither forward, and it, too, had reached the heart of the labyrinth.

The outer lines of dancers stopped, heads down, torches pointing to the earth, as still as death.

Brutus turned, and faced the evil.

Faced the evil within himself.

BRUTUS FITTED AN ARROW TO THE BOW, AND LIFTED *it to his shoulder. He could hear crashing in the shrubs just to his left, could see the flash of the stag's antlers above the greenery, could hear the beast's terrified breath.*

Excitement flared in his chest, and he let fly the arrow.

There was a silence, then a shout of horror from beyond the path.

"Our king! Our king! He has been struck!"

And the excitement in Brutus' chest collapsed into dread, and he knew what he had done.

He darted behind the greenery, fighting his way through, and came to a small glade.

In its center sat his father Silvius.

He was contorted in agony, both his hands wrapped about the shaft of the arrow that had pierced his eye.

Brutus moaned, and walked over to stand a pace before his father.

Silvius, blood streaming in a thick rich river down his cheek and neck, gradually became aware of him. He dropped his hands from the shaft of the arrow, and held them out in appeal to Brutus.

"What have you done?" he said, his voice a groan. "What have you done?"

Brutus looked at his father for a long moment. There had been pity on his face, but now it had metamorphosed into something else . . . speculation, perhaps.

"I am taking my heritage," he said, and he leaned down and took the arrow in one hand and a handful of his father's hair in the other.

Steadying himself, and firming his grip on his father's head, Brutus said, "It is time your kingship bands adorned my limbs."

*"No, no," said Silvius. "How can you base your reign
on the corruption of your own father's murder? Everything
you do, everything you touch from this time on will be corrupt! Brutus, I beg you, do not murder me. Take this arrow
from my eye, do not thrust it farther!"*

*"I can accept your murder," Brutus said, and Silvius felt
his son's hand firm on the arrow, the head of the weapon
slice infinitesimally farther through his flesh.*

*"I have raised you, and loved you, how can you do this
to me?"*

"Easily," and the arrow slid farther.

*Silvius shrieked in agony. "You would found your city
on this? On my murder? On the destruction of everything
that has loved you?"*

*"I feel no guilt," said Brutus. "Not you, nor anyone else,
can use it to hurt or bind me. This act has made me the
stronger man, and it has marked me a king."*

*The agony was unbearable now, but still Silvius found
the courage to scream one last warning. "This is not how
the Game should be played! It is not what I taught you! If
you found the Game on corruption, then—"*

*"I was ever sick of your words as a child, Silvius, and I
find them even more tiresome now. I shall play the Game
as I wish!"*

*And then, as Silvius shrieked and writhed, Brutus thrust
the arrow brutally deep into his father's brain.*

"I SHALL PLAY THE GAME AS *I* WISH," SAID BRUTUS
to the evil before him and, lifting the ball of pitch, tossed
it forward and high into the air.

The gathered darkness shrieked, and surged upward as if
to catch the ball, but it had gone too high and sailed too
far forward, and the mass fell back upon itself, howling in
frustration.

The ball of pitch burst into flames, disintegrating midair.

Genvissa muttered a spell, weaving the pattern with her
hands, and as the flaming pieces of pitch fell to the laby-

rinth they marked out the path Brutus must follow to escape.

Brutus stepped around the mass of darkness as it writhed about looking for the ball of pitch.

It did not see him, so horrified was it at losing the pitch.

Slowly, yet with far more eagerness in his movements than before, Brutus began to dance his way out of the labyrinth. He kept his hands clasped before him, and his eyes on Genvissa, who had her own hands held out to him.

He danced the path marked by the burning pitch, and as he passed, so the pitch fell into ashes, and the path went dark.

Behind him the darkness twisted, and howled, seeking a way out of the labyrinth, always missing the path, confused by the twists and turns of the circuits of the labyrinth. It hunched about and about the central chamber of the labyrinth, becoming ever more frantic, its cries ever more desperate.

"He's trapped it!" Coel said in an undertone. "He's trapped evil at the heart of the labyrinth!"

"And that is good?" muttered Loth. "How can it be good to found a city on a bed of evil?"

Brutus was now very close to the outer entrance of the labyrinth. The dancers around the outer wall of the labyrinth had now lifted their torches again, and were singing joyously, and Genvissa stood, her arms outstretched, her brilliant eyes locked in to Brutus', willing him ever forward away from the trapped evil.

Finally he stepped forth, and a great shout went up as, in the center of the labyrinth, the mass of darkness fell to the ground and, in the blink of an eye, vanished.

As Brutus stepped forth, so Genvissa stepped to meet him, and they fell into each other's arms, Brutus picking her up and spinning her joyously about.

Then, suddenly, extraordinarily, they disappeared, and Og's Hill was left bathed in light and joy and the celebrations of the thousands about it.

ASTERION WAS GROWING WITH EVERY BEAT OF HIS mother's heart, and his body mass was large enough by this stage that when he twisted and kicked she would put her hands on her belly, and pale.

He twisted and kicked now, partaking in the celebrations atop Og's Hill. *The Game had begun!*

Once Asterion would have been enraged by this knowledge, for the Game's completion would mean his reimprisonment within its black heart, unable to find his way out into freedom.

Now? Now he was overjoyed. He was certain that he could seize control of the Game—rather than it seize him—and use it for his own ends. Not just yet, but soon . . . soon enough.

He knew also that Brutus and Genvissa were together now, indulging their success in the pleasures of the flesh. They thought they had begun a triumph; instead they had embarked upon an agony so vast it would take them aeons to comprehend it.

Many years and many tears, *Mag had said to Cornelia. Many years, indeed. And more tears than anyone could possibly imagine.*

Best enjoy your celebration while you may, *the Minotaur thought and wriggled some more for the sheer joy in bringing his mother discomfort.*

PART SIX

LONDON, MARCH 1939

*T*he cathedral stood open, waiting, and Jack Skelton entered through the great west doors. He walked along the empty nave until he stood under the massive dome, its heights lost in shadows, staring at the marble flooring, remembering that terrible night long ago when vision had become reality.

Although he could not visibly see it, he could feel the word "Resurgam" burning up through the marble.

There was a sound of footsteps behind him, and the soft scrape of crutches, but Skelton did not move.

"You're back, then."

"Aye." Skelton finally turned about, looking at the man leaning on crutches before him. He wore dark vestments, the collar of a cleric, and the thin, lined face of a man who lived with constant pain.

"I am scarcely prettier than you remember," the man said, then held out his hand. "But at least this time I have no horns to my head. I am Walter Herne, an apt enough name, don't you think?"

Skelton shook Herne's hand, introducing himself. "I have seen Genvissa, and Asterion. But not Cornelia. Do you know where she is?"

"You think that Cornelia would make any haste to meet you? Never!"

"We are Gathered, Herne. Asterion has called us all back for his final play. She must be about, surely. She has to be!"

"Is that desperation I hear in your voice, Skelton?" Herne said.

Jack Skelton narrowed his eyes, studying Herne, thinking. *"Is Coel here?"* he asked suddenly.

"If he is," Herne said, *"do you think Cornelia will be with him?"*

Skelton's face sagged, and for a moment Herne thought the man might actually weep.

"I am afraid that Asterion has her," Skelton said. *"After what happened last time we were Gathered . . . I am afraid. . . ."* He paused, pinching the bridge of his nose between a thumb and forefinger, and when his hand dropped away Herne saw that Skelton's eyes were indeed wet. *"By God, Herne, I would prefer it that she were with Coel than still trapped by that monster."*

"You have changed," Herne said. *"It is a shame you could not have spoken those words three thousand years ago: 'It is better she be with Coel than still trapped with that monster.'"*

"I? The monster? Aye, I suppose I was."

There was a silence, Herne studying Skelton, Skelton staring at the floor.

"Is the way open?" Skelton finally said, raising his head.

Herne nodded. *"It will be difficult, but there is a way down."*

Skelton sighed, and looked about the cathedral. *"Does no one know what lies beneath, Herne? Do they come in here every day, and worship, and not know?"*

"They are not part of the Game, Skelton."

Skelton's mouth twisted. *"No, they are merely its victims."* He paused. *"Asterion is going to take us out this time, my friend, and I do not think there is anything any of us can do to stop him."*

Chapter One

Cornelia Speaks

"THUS IS BORN TROIA NOVA," SCREAMED A voice, "and the greatest Kingman among the living!"

Stunned even beyond what had shocked me during the dance, I cried out, and jumped to one side.

It was Hicetaon, only half a pace from me, his voice thunderous.

He strode forward, his arms held high above his head, his fists punching into the night sky.

"Thus is born Troia Nova!" he screamed again, circling atop the hill, dancers scattering about him, laughing and jumping, their torches thrust as high as his fists.

Thus is born Troia Nova and the greatest Kingman among the living!

I was still shocked, too shocked to move, even as the celebrations erupted about me. The people who had been watching from the ground below now swarmed up the hill; fires roared into life from hitherto cold pyres; voices lifted in song and triumph; people danced, bodies pressing each against the other; flasks of frenzy wine—by the strange glazed eyes and the slack wet mouths of those who drank of it—were handed about; clothes were stripped off and flesh left to glint naked among the flickering light of fire and torch.

I stood there, unmoving, hardly seeing.

All I could remember was the stunning sight of Brutus and Genvissa dancing at the head of the lines of dancers, the power of their movement, the way they had danced together, wove enchantment together.

Wedded together in such power that I had become nothing more than an irritating insignificance.

And where were they now?

I spun about, half moving of my own volition, half being pushed by a group of dancers who had staggered against me.

Where were they now?

What were they doing?

Ah, but I knew what they were doing, didn't I? They were consummating their marriage of power, this Kingman and Mistress of the Labyrinth. And with each thrust, with each moan, with each grasping clutch, I was becoming an ever greater triviality in Brutus' life.

A nothing.

An insignificance.

Not even a body with legs to be parted. Not now.

I sobbed, consumed with panic.

Where were they? Where were they?

If I could stop them somehow, if I could take this one final chance to tear Brutus away from Genvissa . . . if . . . if . . . if . . .

I turned about again, knowing where they would be, seeking a way down from this damned hill. But just as I took a step forward, Loth grabbed at my arm and spun me about.

His face was twisted, furious, his green eyes dark and glassy, reflecting the writhing light of the fires and the dancing bodies about us.

"What have they done?" he hissed.

"They have destroyed my life!" I cried, trying to twist my arm free. "Let me go! Let me go!"

"Damn your precious life and your little-girl dreams! They are as *nothing* in the enormity of what they have visited on this land! They have crippled Og, and devastated Mag. Doomed us with that creeping evil they have invited into our midst!"

His free hand waved at the labyrinth, now lost under the sea of undulating bodies and wild, drunken laughter.

"They have saved you," said Hicetaon, emerging out of the chaos about us. "Trapped evil forever so that this city will grow in peace and prosperity. Could you do that for your land and your people, useless lump-head?"

My mouth dropped open, then my eyes flew back to Loth. Useless *lump-head*?

He was staring at Hicetaon himself, shaken not so much by what Hicetaon had said, but by the utter contempt in which it had been mouthed.

His hand loosened about my arm, and I tore it free, and without even waiting to see what transpired between the two men, I turned and fled.

I RAN AS QUICKLY AS I DARED DOWN THE HILL, pushing my way through the throngs of celebrating people. There were Trojans and Llangarlians both, intermixed with happiness and relief—

Genvissa and Brutus had saved them, and woven for them safety and prosperity with the power of their combined magic.

—dancing and singing, sharing from mouth to straining mouth the flasks of frenzy wine—

Gods, what would happen this night? What darkness would transpire?

—bodies pressed undulating with dance and want against their neighbors.

Everywhere happiness. Everywhere lust. Everywhere the release that came with the sudden realization that darkness had been vanquished and only days of light and good harvest lay ahead.

Sudden nausea gripped me, and I bent over and retched.

Someone grabbed me, and for a heartbeat I thought it was to help, but then hands snatched at my breasts, and wine-thick breath washed over my face.

Another hand burrowed under my cloak, and dug in between my legs.

I threw my arms out, catching one man with my elbow

in a sickening crunch, another in the corner of an eye with the nail of my thumb.

They let me go, and I fled, now not even trying to measure my progress, desperate to get out of the crowds and to find . . .

Them.

I reached the bottom of the hill, and moved eastward, the crowds thankfully thinning the farther I moved away from the revelry atop Og's Hill.

By the time I'd splashed across the Wal and passed Mag's Hill, barren save for five people dancing in a ring at its base, there were few people about, and I could lift my skirts and run as fast as my breath would allow me.

The White Mount. Brutus' palace (*not* my *palace*).

They would be there. Genvissa would *ensure* they were there, because that would make my humiliation complete.

I reached the mount, paused, then stared upward to the black bulk of the unlit palace, felt my stomach turn over in my belly, then, very slowly, infinitely slowly, began to climb.

The mount was still a building site—only the central portion of the palace had been completed, and once near the top I had to pick my way carefully about stacks of timber, empty mortar pails, and jumbled, careless stone blocks awaiting the attention of masons.

Every step was a nightmare.

Every step was a step too late.

Every step was another thrust against me.

And with every step I reviewed in my mind, in that peculiar clarity that comes with either death or the death of hope, every step in the path I'd taken to losing Brutus. Every whine, every moan, every treachery, whether small or immense, every death that littered my obsessive self-absorption.

When I reached the doorway of the megaron, standing open, I stopped, closed my eyes briefly in an attempt to gather my courage, then walked through.

The megaron was empty, but there was a flicker of light

at its far end, in the archway that led to Brutus' private apartments.

I walked slowly through the megaron, remembering that other megaron where Brutus had made me his wife, and wondered if I now walked through this one to the death of that marriage.

I paused again at the archway, then walked through.

They were lying in a pool of torchlight in a tangle of furs on the floor.

Genvissa, naked, on her back, her body sprawled beneath Brutus.

He, lifting himself first up on his hands, then away from her body, kneeling upright between her bent legs, his still-rigid member glistening with the fluids of their lovemaking, smiling at her.

She, her hands splaying across her belly, saying: *We have made a daughter between us, Brutus. A daughter-heir.*

He, leaning down to kiss her, saying: *You have blessed me.*

Her daughter was a *blessing*, when all he could summon for the daughter we had made together was *irritation*?

I wanted to kill them then, the both of them, but I did not know how. I had no weapon to hand, no knife, even no rock with which to beat them.

Genvissa saw me, and she whispered something to Brutus. He looked at her, then laughed.

He laughed.

I threw myself at him, screaming, terrified, knowing I had lost him, tearing at his face with my nails, trying to kick him with my heels, succeeding only in further humiliating myself as he caught my arms easily and threw me away.

"Cornelia," he said. "Go away. This does not concern you, and this is not your place."

"No!" I screamed, stabbing a finger at Genvissa. "*That* is my place! There, beneath you!"

Genvissa laughed, tilting her head back, the sound rich and husky in her throat. She was not in the least perturbed, having me find her naked under my husband's body.

My husband? Or hers, now?

"Go away, Cornelia," Brutus said, more gently now, and there was in his eyes something even more humiliating than his anger.

Pity. He pitied me.

Poor Cornelia, too young, too girlish to understand.

I stepped forward, leaned down, and hit him as hard as I could.

Then, sobbing and wretched, I turned and fled.

Chapter Two

ENVISSA SIGHED, AS IF IN PITY. SHE LIFTED A hand, and touched Brutus' cheek where Cornelia's hand had slapped him.

"Poor girl," she said.

"I should go to her," he said.

"Yes, but wait a moment, wait a while . . . wait a while."

She pulled him back to her body, and kissed him, and roused him to lust once more, and pulled him back into the deep warmth of her body.

She needed to give Cornelia just the right amount of time to damn herself, then she would send Brutus after her.

To kill her, the silly, irritating, useless, deathly dangerous girl.

Who Brutus thought of too often . . .

Brutus thrust inside her, and Genvissa tilted back her lovely head and laughed once more for the joy and success she had already made here this night, and all that was yet to come.

Chapter Three

Cornelia Speaks

I KNEW WHAT I WOULD FIND. I *KNEW* BRUTUS would take Genvissa as a lover. I knew that after all I had done, every mistake I had made, Brutus had little respect for me.

And none of it made any difference to how I felt. The *knowing* never takes away the pain.

I stumbled away from that palace, my eyes blinded by grief and pain, and I somehow made my way to the ferry crossing and from there through the Trojan settlement and Llanbank toward my house.

At least I could have Achates to comfort me. I didn't care if he was asleep, or if Aethylla growled at me, I just needed my son in my arms. I just needed to know that *someone* loved me.

Thus it was that when I entered the house, wiping the tears from my face lest they scare my son, and found it completely empty, my world collapsed entirely.

I stopped by the central hearth: there was a single lamp left burning, enough light for me to see that all Aethylla's and Hicetaon's belongings were gone.

Achates, and all his baby paraphernalia, were gone.

All Brutus' clothes and gear were gone.

Everything of mine remained.

I started to tremble, my mind accepting what my eyes told it, yet not accepting the actuality of it.

Everyone had moved out, leaving me behind.

I sank to my haunches, my hands trembling so badly I had difficulty in lifting them to my face.

There could be only one reason for this: *They had moved to the palace*.

There could be only one person behind this: *Genvissa*.

My shoulders began to shake in sympathy with my hands, but my throat was so tight I could not manage a sound. I hunched by the fire, my hands to my face, my entire body shaking, staring at Aethylla's empty sleeping niche, unable to accept how splendidly, how bitterly splendidly, Genvissa had outmaneuvered me.

She had everything of mine: my husband, my son, my place as queen.

Everything.

"Cornelia? Ah, Cornelia, I am sorry. I had thought to be here before you."

I rose, but slipped over in the doing, sprawling inelegantly to the floor.

It was Coel, reaching down to me, murmuring soothing words, wrapping me in his arms, rocking me to and fro.

"You knew?" I managed.

"I saw Hicetaon come for Aethylla and the babies," he said. "I knew then. I wanted to be here for you when you returned. I am so sorry. I came as quickly as I could."

I clung to him, my weeping increasing, and Coel rocked me back and forth.

"Cornelia," he whispered, "don't cry, please don't cry."

I tried to stop, but I couldn't. My nose was running, my eyes were so swollen with tears I could hardly see out of them, and my chest kept wracking out sobs from so deep within me I thought I might actually bring up my stomach with the strength of them.

"Cornelia," Coel said, running one hand through my hair and using the other to wipe my nose with a corner of his cloak. "Don't cry, please. You are so beautiful, so lovely, I can't bear to see you so unhappy."

My only answer was yet another sob.

He gathered me to him, holding me close, then he swore softly under his breath, tipped back my face, and stifled my sobs with his mouth.

It was as though we were back in that rock pool, yet this time he was not offering me sheer physical pleasure, but a depth of comfort and loving I had always yearned for, but never found.

His mouth was so sweet, his arms so soothing, and *he* was the beautiful one, not merely in body, but in nature as well.

"Cornelia . . ." he said, and I heard the longing in his voice, and this time I was not predisposed to refuse him. After all, there was nothing left for me to lose, was there?

And some small, petty part of me whispered that it would be a sweet revenge for Brutus' infidelity. It would salvage a part of my pride if, like Brutus, I took for myself a lover.

Perhaps this way Genvissa would not win.

Not completely.

"Yes," I said.

Somewhere an unknown voice screamed not to do this, to think, to not let passion and hate and revenge rule my head, but I refused to listen to it. No doubt Brutus and Genvissa lay in their furs, laughing at the thought of me weeping alone.

Well, I was not alone. *Damn them! Damn them!*

"Yes," I whispered again.

Coel smiled, so happy my tears almost flowed anew, and aided me to my feet, and slipped away my clothes, and then his. We stood there for a while, barely touching save for his fingers that wiped away the last of my tears.

And then we went to my bed.

Oh, Hera, he was so slow, so gentle, and his smile . . . he made me laugh with his silly, comforting words, and but a short while ago I would have thought laughter impossible. We kissed, and touched, and lay beside each other. I ran my hands over his body, marveling, for he was so lovely—clean-skinned and lean and so unlike Brutus in every respect.

I was almost happy, for I was taking my life in my own hands with this action. I did not love Coel, although one part of me thought that I was foolish not to, but I was immensely grateful to him . . . and immensely attracted to him.

The light touch of his fingertips, the warm caress of his breath as he ran his mouth down my body . . . eventually I could wait no longer, and pulled him into me, and sighed with bliss as he began to move so gently, so slowly, within me.

If only Brutus could treat me with this much gentleness, this much respect.

I closed my eyes, lifted my body against his, and imagined that this was Brutus, this voice in my ear was his, saying he loved me, this mouth that laid itself so sweetly on mine was Brutus' mouth.

This the act that had made my daughter within me, not that animalistic grabbing and coupling.

"Cornelia," he said, his movements now more urgent.

I moaned, curving my hands about his buttocks, pushing him deeper inside me. "Brutus," I whispered.

He cried out, a noise both of passion and of frustration.

"Damn you!" he whispered as he collapsed across my body. "*Damn* you, Cornelia!"

"No!" I opened my eyes, aghast at what I had done, and clasped his face between my hands. "Coel, I—"

And then his face was torn from my hands by a great black shadow that loomed over us, and I saw a glint of metal that swept in a vicious arc across Coel's throat, then his body, still deep within mine, convulsed, and I screamed, and blood spurted over me in a hot, sticky flood.

Brutus took a firmer grip on Coel's hair, then he tore him from me, tearing him painfully out from me, and all I could do was cry, "No! No! Oh, gods, Brutus, no! *Not Coel!*"

Not Coel, who had always comforted me, and whose only crime had been to love me too much.

Not Coel, for if Coel died, then it would be my fault, as so many other deaths had been my fault . . . but this one, Coel's death, would be the worst of all, it would be a catastrophe, and if Coel died because of me then I thought I would lose my mind.

I scrambled to the edge of the bed, one tiny part of my mind knowing it was far too late, but the larger part desperately believing that I could still make a difference . . . I scrambled to the edge of the bed just in time to see Brutus dash Coel to the floor and bury his blade in his belly.

It was a fruitless gesture, for by that time Coel was already dead.

"NO, BRUTUS," I KEPT SAYING. "PLEASE, NO . . . no . . . not Coel . . . not Coel."

He turned to me, raging. "Whore! I have *always* known this!"

I could not take my eyes from Coel, and I tried to scramble down to the floor to try to close that gaping wound in his throat, to hold together his belly, to close his sweet, loving eyes, but Brutus hit me, and I fell backward so violently my head cracked against the stone wall.

"I have had *enough* of you and your treacherous, whorish ways!" he screamed at me—gods, I could feel his spittle fleck my face. "Enough! I renounce you. You are no wife to me, no fit mother for my son, no fit mother for that bastard child in your belly!"

"No, she is your daughter! She—"

"You have never been a wife to me," he continued, not acknowledging what I'd said. "You were a whore in your father's court, and—"

"I was a virgin when you took me, you know that!"

He hit me again. "Whore's tricks, for all I know. Who else have you taken behind my back? Hicetaon? Corineus? Is Achates *mine*, or a hybrid of all the men you've had crawl between your legs?"

I was screaming now as well; incoherent, shrill shrieks designed to shut out his loathsome words.

Oh, Hera, what had I done? Killed Coel and ruined in

a single moment any chance I ever had to make Brutus love me?

At that moment I wanted to die, and I think I would have provoked Brutus into a greater rage so that he would mercifully batter me to death had not at that moment the entire house exploded into a worse disaster than that which already gripped it.

Loth burst into the house, absorbed in a single appalled glance all that had happened and that was still happening, then roared.

Or screamed. I am not sure. Perhaps he did both, but all I can remember of that instant is a shrieking, thundering sound that reverberated about the room, shocking me into silence and making Brutus sink momentarily to his haunches before he recovered enough to swing about to face the attack.

But it never came. Not in the manner that Brutus—nor I, for that matter—expected.

Instead, Loth took a step farther into the house, stared for several long heartbeats at Coel's body on the floor, raised his head, sent me a look of utter contempt, then looked steadily at Brutus.

"This is enough," he said, his voice very carefully controlled. "I have had enough. I have had enough of you, Brutus, of your Trojans, and of your damn whore-mistress Genvissa. I have had enough of that monstrosity you are building atop Og's and Mag's sacred hills. I have had enough of your Trojan magic and your *cursed* Troy Game!"

His voice suddenly rose, and he took a step forward. "What evil have you invited into your world? What evil is that atop Og's Hill?"

"I have trapped evil," Brutus said in a very even voice. He held Loth's furious gaze easily, but I saw his grip alter fractionally about the hilt of his sword. "I have made your land safe for you. I, and Genvissa."

"She is the blackest witch alive," Loth said. "Be wary in your association with her."

"She has acted where you have failed."

Loth turned his head and spat. "She has enslaved our gods to her own purpose. I have had enough," he said again. "Far and well enough."

"There is nothing you can do," said Brutus. "Take your friend's body and get out of here."

"There is everything I can do," Loth said very quietly. "I stand here to represent my gods, Brutus. Og and Mag." For an instant his eyes slipped my way, as if he expected (wanted?) me to object to his representation of Mag. "I challenge your right to settle here, Brutus. I challenge your right to assume the place of Kingman. I challenge your right to live."

"What?"

"I challenge you on behalf of Og and Mag, who are so crippled they cannot speak for themselves. They want you gone, Brutus, as do I. Will you meet me?"

"Are you challenging me to a combat?"

Loth's mouth trembled very slightly, as if he were shaken by Brutus' incredulity. "Yes. Tomorrow at dawn. On Og's Hill."

"You cannot be serious."

"Whoever wins will have indisputable right to this land."

"Ye gods," Brutus muttered, "it might be worth it just to get your glowering face out of my life."

"No!" I cried, belatedly realizing I still lay naked atop the tumbled bed. I pulled a wrap about me, and slid out of the bed to my feet. "Loth, no! He will kill you!"

Brutus whipped about to me. "You speak on Loth's behalf?"

I knew what he was thinking—I'd had Loth as well. At that moment I wished that I actually had, because then I could have thrown it back in Brutus' face.

"Have *you* ever spoken on my behalf?" I said quietly.

And then, as I suppose it must have been fated, Genvissa walked calmly and serenely into the house.

Her serenity lasted as long as it took her to spot Coel's body.

"Brutus?" she whispered, raising her eyes to him. "You killed *Coel*?"

My stomach turned over as I realized the extent of her manipulations. All this had been planned. Every last bit of it, but for *my* death, not Coel's.

Brutus, the fool, missed the implications of his lover's words. "And look what I have received for it," he said, waving his bloodied sword toward Loth. "He wishes to fight me in combat for my right to sit as Kingman by your side. Very well then. Tomorrow." He paused, his chilling gaze riveted to Loth's face. "In the labyrinth atop Og's Hill."

Genvissa stared at him, then turned to look at Loth, still glowering at Brutus.

Then, very, very softly, she began to laugh.

Chapter Four

LOTH SAT IN HIS FOREST, CHILLED AND numbed and angry and heartsore, mourning his friend and pledging revenge.

But how? Loth was not trained as a warrior; Brutus would slaughter him in a moment.

Loth had no power, or very little of it. There was no Og magic to throw at Brutus, and slow his sword arm.

And Brutus had Genvissa. Genvissa would give him everything she had, and Loth had to admit that was a great deal.

He'd thrown out the challenge to Brutus in that first, terrible moment of anger and grief and frustration, without thinking about it, without thinking through the implications.

Now Coel was dead (and, oh, by Og! Loth had not even gone to Erith to comfort her!) and Loth soon would be, and then there would be no one left to counter Genvissa and her damned evil-lodestone of a Game.

Not Cornelia. Never Cornelia.

"What can I do?" he whispered. "What can I do?"

He had not expected an answer, but he was shocked to receive one.

There was a step in the forest, a slight sound, but nevertheless a step, and Loth sprang to his feet.

For the first time in his life, he felt afraid of the forest.

"Who goes there?" he cried.

"It is only I," said a soft, sad voice, and a man stepped out from behind a tree.

Yet not a man at all, but a shade, for both shadows and a stray moth passed straight through him.

Loth did not recognize him. The stranger was a tall man, strong and muscular, and dressed in the clothes and armor of a Trojan. He was of middle age, handsome enough if you liked the Trojan bluntness of feature, and with long, curly black hair tied with a thong at the base of his neck.

At his hip hung a sword, and in his hand he held a bloodied arrow.

His left eye was a mass of congealed blood.

"Who are you?" said Loth.

"My name is Silvius," said the shade, "and I am the fool that fathered Brutus." He started to moan, as if in agony, saying, "Oh, I was seer-warned when I had barely planted Brutus in his mother's body, but I did not listen. I should have pummeled my son from his mother's womb before she gave him birth! Then she would be alive, and I also."

The shade of Silvius wept—horrible thick blood tears from his ruined eye—and handed the arrow to Loth. "Take this into the labyrinth tomorrow, Loth, and it will be your guide. Draw Brutus in, and *I* will take up the fight for you."

A vision appeared before Loth, passing quickly in flickering images before his eyes.

The hunt.

The forest.

Brutus aiming his arrow into the bushes.

Silvius, crippled on the ground.

Brutus, seizing the opportunity and taking his father's hair in one hand and the arrow in the other, and driving it deep into Silvius' brain.

"I should never have fathered him," Silvius said. "Brutus is my responsibility. What happens to the Game he has started is my responsibility. Thus *I* will deal him death."

And then, suddenly, horrifically, all hesitation and sadness were gone from Silvius, and he drew out his sword and roared, stabbing the sword toward the sky. "Brutus!" he screamed...

... and then was gone.

Loth stared at the place where he had been, then slowly lifted his hand and looked at the arrow. It was fouled with old, crusted blood, and Loth swallowed, momentarily sickened.

Then Loth jerked in shock with another and vastly more frightening surprise.

Coel's voice, whispering through the forest. *Think not that Brutus will allow Silvius to best him, my friend.*

"Coel! Coel!" Loth spun about, but could not see his friend.

Brutus has never allowed Silvius to best him, and I doubt he will on the morrow. Loth, be silent and listen to me: whatever happens, Loth, let no harm come to Cornelia. Let no one harm Cornelia. She is far more than she appears, and only she holds the key, only she knows the steps to the dance, only she can close the gate. Let no harm come to Cornelia!

And then Coel too was gone, and Loth was left alone, weeping for all that had been lost to Brutus' vile sword.

"TELL ME," SAID GENVISSA, STROKING BRUTUS' hair as they lay side by side on the furs in his palace, "what form did the evil challenge you in the heart of the labyrinth yesterday?"

Brutus hesitated, then told her—all of it, the manner of his father's death, and his own part in it.

"Then that is what Loth will use against you tomorrow," said Genvissa. "He will use what is there already."

"How—"

"Shush," she said, kissing him. "We will kill two birds with one sword tomorrow." She grinned. "This is what you will do."

Genvissa whispered to him, long and sweetly, and eventually Brutus laughed, and placed his hands on her breasts.

"I am blessed with your care," he said, kneading at her flesh, but thinking only of Cornelia, and the terrible sight of Coel atop her.

"Aye," she said. "You are. I will allow *nothing* to threaten the Game. Not Loth. Not Cornelia. Nothing."

Chapter Five

HE DAY WAS COLD, HEAVILY OVERCAST, WITH a distant curtain of rain approaching from the northeast. For the group surrounding the labyrinth on top of Og's Hill, the weather seemed only an outward manifestation of their own dispiritedness, their sense that somewhere, somehow, unwittingly (or even wittingly, which was even worse) someone had made a hideous decision that now no one could escape.

Loth's challenge to Brutus was merely an outcome of that decision, not the decision itself. It was almost as if all of Llangarlia had lurched into a great darkness at some point in the past, and that darkness was only now revealing itself.

But what to do? Loth's anger, or the anger he represented, needed an outlet. If not now, then later, when the outcome might be even more tragic.

The Trojan witnesses, Hicetaon, Corineus, Deimas, and a score of others, did not seem so badly affected by the blanket of gloom that overlay the Llangarlian witnesses. The Trojans were used to war, to challenges, to sieges, to tragedy. Brutus, their leader, representative, and increasingly their demigod, would not fail them. He stood to one side of the entrance to the labyrinth, wearing only his bands of kingship and a pristine white hip wrap, an unsheathed sword in his hands, an expression of calm determination on his face.

Loth stood the other side of the entrance, a pace or two away from Brutus. Save for the bands of kingship, he was garbed similarly, but today he had shaved and oiled his head so that the great bony protuberances of his skull gleamed gleefully as if pleased they had finally won their freedom from the surrounding mat of hair.

His face was not so calm as Brutus'. He looked nervous and unsure, and he clasped nothing but a blood-encrusted arrow.

It was at this arrow that Genvissa stared, and which caused her, eventually, to look at Brutus with a small smile of victory.

If Genvissa looked certain of herself, and of Brutus, the rest of the Llangarlians present, mainly Mothers, looked wan and desperately worried. The Mothers had met very early that morning to discuss Coel's death. Both the manner of his death and the reason behind it—Brutus' jealousy— were abhorrent to them. Cornelia had freely chosen to lie with Coel—how could Brutus wreak any kind of revenge at all when no wrong had been committed? Despite their allegiance to Genvissa, the Mothers may well have chosen to act against Brutus save that Loth had already acted for them. Fate would decide today who was right and who was wrong.

While all the Mothers looked pallid and anxious, Erith looked the most ashen and distressed. Her worry for Loth and the outcome of this challenge was superseded only with grief for her son. Very late the previous night she had been woken from her slumber by a neighbor, who had begged her to hurry to Cornelia's house.

There she'd found her son dead, and a distraught and barely coherent Cornelia smeared with his blood.

Erith had no time for Cornelia; not then, not when her beloved Coel lay slaughtered on the floor. She and her two other sons, Hoel and Cador, had carried Coel's corpse back to his house where Erith and her daughters washed and tended it. He would be cremated and his ashes cast into the Llan later today, after this farce was over, when there might well be another corpse to weep and mourn over.

Erith may have ignored Cornelia last night, but she was sorry for the fact now. Cornelia had not been responsible for Coel's death, not in any significant manner. She'd only accepted what Coel had been offering for months; and if her husband had then descended on the coupling pair with his revenging sword, then Erith thought that had more to do with Genvissa than anyone else.

Coel himself had to bear some responsibility for what had happened. He had known of the marriage contracts and beliefs of the Trojans, had known that if he lay with Cornelia he would call Brutus' wrath down upon his head, and yet he had still allowed his lust to get the better of him.

Erith sighed, and looked to where Cornelia was standing by herself, isolated in her own patch of misery in a spot apart from both the Trojans and the Llangarlians. She had washed herself of what remained of Coel, but had taken little more care. Her robe was haphazardly pulled about her body, and Erith could see that its normally creamy wool was gray with dirt and sweat. Her hair hung lank and uncombed; her face was almost as gray as her robe, and almost as lifeless as poor Coel lying wrapped in his shroud in Erith's house.

Glancing at Loth and Brutus, Erith walked over to Cornelia, stood by her side, then took her hand, giving it a slight squeeze. Cornelia shuddered, and momentarily leaned close to Erith, making the older woman even sorrier about her seeming rejection of the girl last night.

"Get it over and done with," Genvissa said in a cold, harsh voice, making most of the spectators jump. "Get this farce done before the rain arrives."

Brutus looked at Loth, raised his sword, and pointed into the labyrinth.

Loth nodded, once, and stepped inside.

Brutus waited until Loth had walked ten or twelve paces into the labyrinth and then he, too, entered.

And everyone standing about gasped, because at the moment Brutus had stepped fully into the labyrinth, both he and Loth vanished.

AS HE KNEW HE WOULD, BRUTUS FOUND HIMSELF in a close, oppressive forest. Everything about him—Og's Hill, the witnesses, the bleak wintry landscape spreading out beyond—had vanished.

There had never been a forest such as this. The trees were huge—oaks and elms—kings of the forest, but denuded of any leaves, their trunks and branches black and harsh.

Yet they were still draped in greenery, for over every tree hung great swaths of holly and ivy, so lading the branches that Brutus could hear them creak under the weight.

The dead trees pressed in close, the sky was obliterated by the holly and ivy, and the way to either side of the path on which Brutus stood was choked with their tangles.

There was only one way, and that was the path forward.

Brutus, his chest tight with vigilance, stepped forward.

A noise sounded to his left, and Brutus jumped into a defensive stance, his sword raised.

Silence.

He relaxed, and after a moment continued on his way. He knew what was happening.

The noise came again, much louder this time, and to his right.

Brutus crouched low again, his sword up, his eyes narrowed and watchful.

Silence.

Then a flash of color on the path ahead of him, and yet another movement.

A man, a Trojan, dressed in hunting attire.

Silvius.

Brutus moved forward, very careful, one hand spread to balance himself, one clutching the sword before him, ready to strike the instant the opportunity presented itself.

The path wound through the tortuous forest. Swags of holly and ivy reached out and grazed his flesh, cool to the touch, yet vibrantly alive. Their touch was assessing, draining, and Brutus found himself slashing at the tendrils, hating their abhorrent caresses.

"Silvius," said Brutus. "Stand and fight me, if you dare."

"I am your conscience, Brutus," the impassive-faced Silvius said. "I am your conscience, I am this land, and I am the Game. Turn back now. The Game can be ended. You know that."

And he stepped back and vanished into the shadows of the trees.

Brutus walked forward, angry at Silvius' words. The path twisted and turned in an exact replica of the twists and turns of the labyrinth. Silvius was leading him into the heart of the labyrinth—into a final confrontation.

Brutus hurried now, determined to finish what had begun fifteen years previously. He stepped into the heart of the labyrinth and there, facing him, was his father Silvius and, to one side, Loth.

"You are unfit to wear those armbands," Loth said. "Unfit to be Kingman of this land or of this Game. You murdered your own father before his time in your own lust for power. You are walking corruption. If I allow you to complete the Game, you will marry this land to corruption forevermore."

Brutus laughed. "And so you have called back my father's shade to kill me, Loth? Are you too afraid to do so yourself? Are you so powerless yourself?"

"If you are not challenged," Loth said, unperturbed by Brutus' sarcasm, "you shall make *this* the heart of this land."

And he threw the arrow into the space between Brutus and his father.

Silvius attacked the instant the arrow hit the ground. Here, in the labyrinth, he was all flesh and blood and bone, taller even than Brutus, as strong, with no fear of death, and with absolutely nothing to lose. Wielding the sword in both hands, sweeping it down in an arc from over his left shoulder, Silvius leapt with all the full power of his revenge, determined to cut down his son.

Brutus stepped forward to meet him, sword clashing against sword, face set and grim, muscles straining.

They were matched, this father and son, and for long minutes they traded blows, their sweat spattering over their opponent, their eyes hard and cold and flat, never leaving those of the man they sought to best. Loth watched from the side, his hands clenched at his sides, his own eyes wide and staring, willing Silvius on with all his might.

Silvius feinted to his left, fooling Brutus, then cut his son deep across his right hip.

Brutus hardly noticed the wound. He bore down on his father with a flurry of strokes and, as Silvius stumbled for the first time, struck his father a glancing blow across his right biceps.

Silvius' flesh opened, but no blood flowed.

"I am enjoying this," said Silvius, and Brutus laughed.

"I will kill you again," he said. "What was once done cannot be undone."

And again they fell to with monstrous, hurting blows, blade shrieking off blade, muscles bunched and glowing with hate and heat.

"Where," gasped Brutus, after a particularly heavy exchange of blows, "is an arrow when you need it?"

Where nothing else had touched Silvius, this particular piece of cruelty undid him.

His sword arm fell still, and he gaped at his son.

And Brutus lifted his sword, and sent it hurtling toward his father's head.

At the very last moment he turned the weapon so that the flat of the blade slammed into Silvius' skull, sending him senseless to the ground.

Brutus leaned down, panting with the effort of the fight, and seized his father's hair in his hand hauling him half upright, and putting his sword to his throat.

"Your choice, monster," he hissed to Loth. "Either I will kill him all over again, or I kill you!"

"Kill him," said Loth, desperate with disappointment, "for then you will merely confirm your corruption."

Brutus grinned, and his grip in Silvius' hair changed slightly.

OUTSIDE THE LABYRINTH, STARING DEEP INTO ITS apparently empty circuits, Genvissa muttered a spell-weaving, moving her left hand slightly as she did so.

Then Erith cried out, for suddenly Cornelia was gone from her grasp.

"YOUR CHOICE, MONSTER!" BRUTUS HISSED TO A now staring and stunned Loth. "Her life or yours."

In his hands he held a terrified Cornelia, his sword to her throat.

Let no one harm Cornelia, Coel had said.

Let no harm come to Cornelia.

Brutus laughed, delighted at the horror on Loth's face. "Do not think I won't do it," Brutus said. "She is a whore, a traitress, a threat to the Game, and a complication I will be more than glad to get rid of."

"She carries your child!"

"Oh, nay, I think not. Your child, or Coel's, or one of a dozen men, perhaps, but not mine."

The sword moved, and the blade cut, and blood flowed from Cornelia's neck.

"At least you haven't pissed yourself, like your boy-lover," said Brutus conversationally.

Loth screamed, and leapt forward. "Take me! Take me!"

Brutus dropped Cornelia, who instantly grabbed at her neck, and stepped the one pace distance between himself and Loth, raised his sword, and struck at the man's neck.

And then something moved, something from the forest, something skeletal and barely alive, its white pelt thick with its own blood, and it knocked both Loth and Brutus, so that one fell and one stumbled, and so that when the sword flashed down . . .

It cut deep into the fallen Loth's spine, just above his buttocks, and Loth screamed, and writhed, and Brutus leaned down with all his weight and strength on that sword.

EVERYONE STANDING ABOUT THE LABYRINTH SUD-denly jumped or cried out, or both.

Loth and Brutus had reappeared in the heart of the labyrinth; Loth sprawled on the ground, his face pressed against the stone flooring, blood pouring from a great wound in the small of his back.

Brutus standing over him, a triumphant smile on his face as he raised his head and sought out Genvissa's eyes.

Cornelia, small and tragic, curled into a ball in the heart of the labyrinth, her hands to her throat, blood seeping out from between her fingers.

Erith moved instantly. As she ran into the labyrinth she tore from her waist her wide cloth belt, and as soon as she reached Cornelia she wrapped it about the girl's throat, thanking all gods that ever were that Brutus had cut open a vein and not an artery.

Then she knelt by Loth, and looked, and lowered her head into her hands and wept.

Brutus tossed aside the bloodied sword, staring at Genvissa. "I have won," he said, then pumped his fists on high. "I have won my right as Kingman!"

None disputed him.

SAVE THE WHISPERS IN THE HEART OF THE GAME.

There sat the shade of Silvius, gray and weary and heartsick at his continual failure.

He should have put a stop to Brutus as an unborn baby.

He should have put a stop to Brutus here in the heart of the Game.

He sighed, and his entire form trembled.

Beside him, the all-but-dead white stag sighed also, and Silvius lay down so his cheek rested on the shoulder of the stag, and together they slept.

Waiting.

BEHIND THEM, YET ANOTHER SHADE, BARELY VISIble, but also caught through murder into the twisting of the Game.

Coel.

Silent.

Watching.

Waiting.

Chapter Six

Cornelia Speaks

 ADOR AND HOEL, ERITH'S SONS, CARRIED Loth from that bloodied hilltop, while Erith and her daughter Tuenna aided me. We stumbled our way to the ferry and then back to my lonely, deserted house in Llanbank.

I was out of immediate danger, Erith's cloth belt having stanched the flow of blood, but Loth . . . Loth was alive, but only just, and existing in such a state of agony that I thought I would have to scream myself, if only to vent some of my own horror.

Was this my fault, too?

Erith took charge as soon as we'd reached the house. She set Tuenna to stitching my neck back together, while she directed her sons to lay Loth on what had once been Aethylla and Hicetaon's bed.

Once Tuenna was done, I looked to Loth. Erith and her sons had been busy while her daughter had attended me. Loth was quieter now, and I saw that Erith had given him some frenzy wine that she'd caused to have brought from her house.

I stumbled forward, desperate to see.

Loth lay on his side, facing into the center of the house. A dribble of wine ran down his chin and his eyes lacked focus. Nevertheless, he saw enough to know I was there, and he held out a hand for me.

"Cornelia," he croaked.

His hand trembled.

I walked forward some more, close to the bed, feeling Erith's and her children's eyes on me, and slowly lifted my hand to take his.

"I'm sorry," I whispered.

"Don't be," he said, and laughed a little.

It was a horrible guttural sound, and I must have flinched, because he cut it off midchortle as he regarded me.

"Don't be sorry," he said. "There's still you."

"No!"

"There is still you," he said again, and that thought apparently gave him some comfort, for he smiled very slightly, then lapsed into unconsciousness, so that Erith and her kin could work whatever aid they could on his body.

*   *   *

IN THE END IT WAS NOT MUCH. THEY SAVED LOTH'S
life, but they could do little else.

What Brutus had done to Loth's back would never heal.
Not completely.

The sword had cut deep, severing Loth's spine just above
the swell of his buttocks. Bone, muscle, and tendon had
been shattered, and no matter how carefully Erith and
Tuenna picked and probed, they could not remove all the
fragments of bone from Loth's flesh.

Neither could they restore his spine. Loth lost all movement from his waist down, as well as control over his muscles. He became as a great baby, save with the bitterness
and hatred of a man, soiling and wetting his bedclothes
several times each day, needing either myself or Erith or
one of her children to roll him over and clean and dry him
and change his bedding.

Erith's two sons, Cador and Hoel, became his constant
companions. Loth was a dead weight, and it needed men
to help shift him. And, as the weeks passed and his wound
closed over—his physical wound, at least—then Hoel and
Cador would lift him from the bed, wrap him well in blankets and furs, and carry him outside, and sometimes down
as far as the river.

I think I existed in a state of constant misery as an accompaniment to Loth's constant pain. My throat hardly
troubled me, for Tuenna had done an excellent job, and I
was left with barely a scar, but I was now completely isolated from the Trojan community, and most particularly
from Brutus, and my son Achates. Brutus lived in the rapidly expanding palace in Troia Nova now, rarely leaving
the just as rapidly growing city walls. Aethylla and Hicetaon lived with him, and Achates, my son.

And Genvissa.

I had lost my husband. I had lost my son. I had lost all
to that witch-woman who was even now carrying Brutus'
child.

As was I, although Brutus refused to acknowledge her.

My growing pregnancy was the only thing that kept me from throwing myself into the Llan. At night, listening to Loth muttering and twisting in his sleep, or to Hoel's or Cador's ever-present snores, I would wrap my hands about my small, hard round belly and feel my daughter inside.

I longed for the day when she would be born, when I could hold her in my arms, and feed her—*no one would take this child from me!*—and we could laugh at and love each other. Then perhaps the hurt at losing Brutus would dull.

Then I would cry, as silently as I could, and still always Loth would hear me, and he would sigh, and call my name softly.

Sometimes, not always, but sometimes I would rise from my bed and lie down beside him, careful of his injury.

He would put an arm about me, and hold me as I cried some more, and always he would say, "Genvissa. Genvissa has done this to you, as she has ruined this land. What will you do about it, Cornelia? What will you do?"

Over and over, his voice a bitter repetition, until his words were as close to me as the child growing in my womb.

Will you aid us now, Cornelia? Will you?

Chapter Seven

WINTER LENGTHENED AND TURNED TO an equally hard spring, the frost growing thick and bright on the ground each morning at dawn. It was cold, but not overly wet, and work on the walls progressed apace. By the turn of the year they had grown to the height of a man. The wall itself was composed almost of three walls. On the outer and inner faces heavy, pale dressed stone blocks rose smooth and unclimbable. Into the internal spaces of the wall, supporting the outer and inner faces of stone, men poured rubble and clay and flint, pressing it down as hard as they could. At twenty-score-pace intervals semicircular bastions protruded from the wall like the swelling bellies of pregnant women. Eventually these would be topped with guardhouses and filled with watchful eyes and hands filled with lances and bows, human defenders standing atop stone where once only the goodwill and care of Mag and Og had shielded the land and its people.

The wall was broken in four places. The great gate, called Og's Gate by Trojan and Llangarlian alike, pierced the wall on its western aspect just beyond the foot of Og's Hill itself. In the northern wall was a very low arch—barely rising from ground level—which allowed the Wal egress into the city, as well as a small and heavily fortified gate that allowed the northern road exit from the city. Finally, on the southern aspect, which ran atop the cliffs along the northern bank of the Llan, there were two openings: one very wide but equally low arch that allowed the Wal exit into the Llan, and a small gate at the Llan ferry's northern dock where travelers would need to access the great northern road that would, for its first part, run through the growing city of Troia Nova itself.

Inside the walls the city of Troia Nova was emerging from what was once free meadowland. There were still great patches of open ground—their green often buried beneath the hoar—where gardens and orchards would prosper in the spring and summers, but now graveled roads and streets crisscrossed the entire enclosed area, and to either side of these roads and streets rose the emerging skeletons of houses and public buildings.

Many of the public buildings were of stone, but most of the houses were built in the Llangarlian manner: circular configurations, their walls of ill-dressed stone or of wattle and daub, topped with conical roofs of thatch or, in a few cases, slate. The Llangarlian houses were easy and quick to build—by summer most of the Trojans hoped to be able to move themselves and their goods inside the walls. Eventually the Trojans expected to replace the Llangarlian structures with the houses they remembered from their Aegean towns and cities, rectangular solid stone or brick houses. For now, however, the native style of building would suffice.

Brutus' palace grew to cover the entire top of the White Mount. It was a beautiful structure, many towered and windowed, with deep eaves and balconies and airy rooms, hung currently with thick woolen tapestries and draperies against the Llangarlian winter and warmed with hot fires built in the huge central hearths of the main chambers.

Genvissa moved herself and her three daughters into the palace: no one opposed her, no one thought to. Genvissa's power was complete: the blight that had afflicted the land had lifted, women and livestock gave birth easily, plants and landscape recovered from the malaise that had afflicted them. It might still be winter, but the change for the better was noticeable.

The Llangarlians whispered Genvissa's name, as Brutus', almost as that of a god. She and her Kingman had saved the land, and even if the strangeness of a city now covered half of the sacred hills, and if there was no Gormagog to watch over them (or, as was increasingly rumored, no Og), then that was of no matter, for there was Genvissa, and there was Brutus.

Cornelia, if she was remembered at all by the majority of the population (now an easy comingling of Llangarlians and Trojans), was regarded only with contempt. As Brutus's former whorish wife and, it was said, a traitress who had caused the deaths of tens of thousands in her home city of Mesopotama (and of Coel, for if Coel had died then that was Cornelia's fault as well), Cornelia's company was rarely sought out.

Loth likewise. People still regarded him with some affection, even some respect, but his powerlessness—*and* his foolishness in trying to challenge Genvissa and Brutus, the pair who had led Llangarlia back into the sunlight—as well as his reclusiveness (Loth rarely left the immediate surrounds of Cornelia's house) made the majority of people forget him.

For Llangarlia, life blossomed, and day by day the labyrinth drew more and more of the evil that had once afflicted the land deeper into its heart.

Its influence extended even beyond the shores of Llangarlia, but Asterion, safe in his mother's womb, chose to disregard it. This time he would win, and the Game lose.

OFTEN, AT NIGHT, WHEN BRUTUS WAS ASLEEP, Genvissa would rise from his side, throw a heavy cloak about her naked shoulders, and walk to the balcony which adjoined their sleeping chamber. There she would stand for hours, immune to the frost, staring across the Llan and over the muddied and jumbled Trojan settlement to Llanbank to where Cornelia shared her house with the crippled Loth.

Genvissa would stand, very, very still, one hand resting inside her cloak on her own swelling belly, thinking about Cornelia's child.

Genvissa was not concerned about Achates. All men desired a son at some point, especially someone like Brutus who had been raised in a society where heirdom was passed down the male line. It wouldn't happen here, of course, for Genvissa was determined that Brutus' heir (and Genvissa's heir, and heir of this entire, powerful city and of the Troy Game, the only Game in existence and therefore the only Game that would ever be) would be their daughter, but Genvissa did not begrudge Brutus his son.

Time enough to do something about him in later years if Brutus' attachment grew too strong.

But Cornelia. Genvissa could hardly believe that once *again* Cornelia had escaped Brutus' deadly wrath. Dear gods, why would he not finally kill her? It made Genvissa doubt what Brutus said about Cornelia—that he did not care for her, that he regarded her only with disdain, that he would never again touch her or caress her or lie with her—because no matter how Genvissa arranged it, when it came to that killing blow, Brutus always hesitated.

Cornelia was not going to live, and this time Genvissa would do the deed herself. No mistakes. Not this time. Cornelia (*and* that damned daughter of hers!) would not see the summer.

Whatever the Llangarlians and the Trojans thought, the Game was still vulnerable. It had yet to be closed, and if anything happened to either her or Brutus before it was . . .

Every time that thought darkened Genvissa's mind, her face twisted, she looked over the darkened landscape to Llanbank, and she plotted murder.

One night, darker and wetter and colder than most, something else caught Genvissa's attention.

ACROSS THE NARROW SEAS, IN THE LONG HOUSE that was the residence of the king of Poiteran, King Goffar's wife struggled in the agony of birth.

She had been in labor now over two full days, and she was growing weak.

King Goffar stood by her side, looking at the great mound of her belly. He raised his eyes and stared at the two midwives standing on the other side of the bed.

They shook their heads slowly.

Goffar looked back to his wife, ignoring her pleading eyes, then his eyes slid to a table that stood to one side.

In its center lay a twisted bone-handled knife that Goffar had come upon by chance in the forest five days ago. Admiring it, he'd taken it for his own.

Now it lay awaiting his will, its blade glinting in the torchlight.

Another movement caught Goffar's attention. The baby, struggling for life within his wife's belly.

He reached for the knife.

Two minutes later, amid his wife's frightful shrieks, Gof-

far pulled a perfectly formed male child from the ruins of her belly.

"A son!" he cried. "A strong, lusty son!"

The child wailed, the sound announcing the truth of Goffar's words, and one of its waving hands fell against the hilt of the knife still in Goffar's hands, and the boy grasped it tight.

If Membricus, Brutus' friend and onetime lover, had still been alive and witness to this scene, he would have recognized it for the vision he had wrongly attributed to the birth of Achates and the death of Cornelia.

SHE SAT BOLT UPRIGHT IN BED, HER HANDS ON her belly, breathing in harsh, heavy breaths.

"What is it?" Brutus said, rousing to wakefulness at the sound of Genvissa's distress.

"Asterion," she whispered. "He is reborn."

"In Poiteran?"

"Aye. Son to Goffar."

He lay one of his hands over hers. "We are almost there," he said. "The walls are almost ready. He cannot touch us."

Very slowly she relaxed. "Yes. Of course. You are right. He is too late." She smiled, and leaned over to kiss Brutus. "He's too late."

FAR AWAY, GOFFAR LOOKED TO WHERE HE'D LAID *the knife.*

It was gone.

ONE COLD, WET NIGHT, WHEN WINTER HAD GIVEN way to an equally cold and brutal spring, Genvissa left Brutus' sleeping side and went, completely naked, not even a cloak about her, to stand on the balcony. She stared over the Llan and the Trojan settlement (now rapidly emptying as Trojans moved inside the city walls) to Llanbank, where Cornelia slept in her house.

Save for the crippled, useless Loth, Cornelia was alone. Genvissa knew that this night, unusually, Cador and Hoel had gone back to their mother's house after settling Loth. There would be no one to summon help.

No one, save Loth, to hear Cornelia's screams.

Genvissa smiled, sure of herself and her power. She rested her hands on her swollen belly (she was five months gone with this daughter, and it was time, finally, to remove any threat to herself, her daughter, and the Game), and began the first of the incantations that would see both Cornelia and her daughter die in agony.

Genvissa *could* have done it quickly and cleanly, but that was not in her nature.

Genvissa's hand tightened on her belly, then she tipped back her head, closed her eyes, and pushed down with all her might.

Chapter Eight

Cornelia Speaks

I WOKE BARELY AN HOUR OR TWO AFTER I HAD lain down, the horrifying pain ripping through my entire body. I grunted, curling about myself, protecting my belly, refusing to believe what the pain told me.

My daughter was being born.

It was far too early. She needed to grow another two months at least in my womb!

Panicked, grunting with the pain—the contractions were coming so fast, and yet they had barely started—I sat on the bed, gathering my breath and my strength, and then stood up.

I should have to summon help.

Damn it! That this should happen on one of the few nights that Cador and Hoel were not here! I had gone to bed grateful to have a night spent without their constant rumbling, now I would have given anything to be able to merely reach across the hearth and shake one of them awake, asking him to fetch his mother.

"What is it?" Loth's sleepy voice said from across the darkened house.

"The baby."

"But—"

"I know! I know!" I tried to keep the panic out of my voice, but couldn't manage it. It was too early . . . even with the benefit of a skilled midwife like Erith, it was way too early.

Far too early.

"Genvissa," whispered Loth.

"No!"

"She will not want your daughter to threaten hers, Cornelia."

"No!" But at the same time I remembered what Mag had said to me: *I can give you all you want in your daughter, although it will do you no good now. It will be many years, Cornelia, before you hold your daughter in your arms. Many years, many tears . . .*

"Yes! Ah, curse my legs! Cornelia, you must get help. Fast! If Erith or Tuenna can come, and bring their pouch of remedies, they may be able to stop the contractions. Cornelia, you must get—"

"I know it!" I struggled to my feet, then screeched as a jolt of pure agony swept through my body.

Achates' birth had been bad enough, but it had never been like this.

"Gods, Loth, I cannot—"

Yet another pain, this tenfold worse than the last, and I screamed, and fell to the floor, clutching my belly. The baby had shifted brutally, almost as if she were being pushed into her birth journey by a vicious hand.

She was tearing me apart internally. My body wasn't

ready to give birth, my pelvis hadn't relaxed, my birth canal was still closed . . . and yet something—*Genvissa!*—was pushing this baby down with such force that—

I screamed again, writhing in agony.

No, no, gods, no, not my daughter! Please, please . . . Mag, anyone, save my daughter . . .

She was all I had left.

Something ripped apart within me, and I felt hot, thick blood gush from between my legs.

Then a thump, and some part of me realized Loth had pushed himself from his bed and was crawling toward me.

More blood, more agony.

I think my womb had ruptured.

I was incapable of speech, incapable of releasing my fetal crouch about my belly. I think I thought that if I curled myself tight enough about my daughter, then somehow I could save her.

Loth reached me, grabbed at me.

I shrieked, and hit out at him—more in my agony, I think, than in any sensible thought of keeping him at bay.

"Cornelia," he said, and I heard that his voice was breaking. "Cornelia . . ."

And at that moment that black-hearted witch pushed with all her might, and my daughter and womb both were torn from the walls of my belly and expelled from my body.

There was a moment when I lost all sense, and when they returned to me all I could feel was the continuing agony in my belly, and Loth's hand scrabbling between my legs, trying, I think, to aid my daughter in any way that he could.

It was hopeless. I knew that. There was a cold rock that had once been my heart, and it told me that Genvissa had murdered my daughter and probably me as well, for I could feel the hot blood pumping out from between my legs.

Loth was shouting, at what and at who I do not know, and I cared not.

My daughter was dead, and I was dying. There was no point to life. Not anymore.

The next moment I lost all my senses, and I knew no more.

I died.

I WALKED THROUGH THE STONE HALL, COMFORTED that I should have come here in death.

The small, dark woman I had seen with Hera in this hall so long ago was here again now, and she folded me in her arms, and hugged me, and loved me.

It was Mag. She'd been with me all this time, and I'd not known it.

"Hush," she said, leaning back and taking my face in her hands. "Do not succumb to that dreadful guilt of yours again."

"My daughter . . ."

"Your daughter lives still, in this stone hall. Do you see her?"

Mag's hands fell from my face, and I looked about. Ah! There she was, playing with some dolls in the shadows of the aisles. I made as if to go to her, but Mag stopped me.

"Not yet," she said, and I wept.

"There is something yet for you to do," Mag said, and she took my hand and led me to the very center of the hall where, to my disbelief and dismay, lay carved into the floor the very same labyrinth that Brutus had caused to be constructed on Og's Hill.

"This is your future," said Mag.

"No."

"This is you."

"It can't be."

"Sweet Cornelia." Mag kissed me, and then she spoke, very low, very fast, for a very long time.

When she had done, and I was more numb than I thought possible, she said, "Will you do this?"

"It is such a long way," I whispered.

She was silent, regarding me.

I sighed, and looked to where my daughter still played.

She was far away, but nevertheless my daughter felt my eyes upon her, and she looked up from the dolls in her hand, and saw me, and cried a most strange word: "Mummy!"

Although I did not understand that word, it nonetheless brought joy and comfort to my heart.

"Yes," I said. "Yes, I will do it."

Mag had my hand in hers, and she gave it a squeeze. "Look," she said, and pointed into the heart of the labyrinth.

There lay a knife with a curiously twisted bone handle.

Chapter Nine

LOTH SOBBED WITH FEAR AND SHOCK AND hatred. He should have foreseen this, he should have *known* that Genvissa would murder Cornelia and her baby. Genvissa could not afford to let Cornelia live; even if she was not precisely aware of the "why," Genvissa *knew* that Cornelia must die.

The house was dark, the oil lamp usually left burning through the night was dead, and Loth wondered if somehow this was part of Genvissa's plan as well. After all, what was the murdering of an oil lamp flame when she could accomplish the death of a woman and her child with so much ease?

He patted at Cornelia's body, trying to discover if there was anything left he could do.

There was a steaming, bloodied mess between her legs—what was left of the baby, as well as Cornelia's womb and, for all he knew, half of her other pelvic organs as well. Loth lifted his hands away in horror, wiping some of the thick blood that coated them away on his bare chest. Then he felt up Cornelia's body to her chest.

She was not breathing.

"Cornelia!" he cried out. "Cornelia!" Absurdly furious with her that she should have died so easily, Loth grabbed at her shoulders and shook them as hard as he could.

He felt her head flop about, but there was no response.

There was, however, the faintest echo of a laugh in his head, and Loth knew that it was Genvissa, returning satisfied to Brutus' bed.

"Cornelia," he whispered, feeling in her cooling, dead flesh the final loss of everything he had tried to save: Mag and Og, Llangarlia itself.

Everything gone, lost to Genvissa's Game.

"Is there warmth left yet in her womb? There must be, for I can yet speak."

Loth's head, which had dropped to Cornelia's breast, jerked upright.

There was the faintest of luminescences rising on the other side of Cornelia's body. As Loth watched, it resolved itself into the faint outlines of a small, dark woman.

Mag, but a Mag so weakened she was almost gone.

"Is there warmth left in her womb?" Mag whispered, her every word an agony of effort.

Loth stared, then fumbled a hand back to the mess between Cornelia's legs. He could feel the womb, hard taut muscle, still stretched with the baby it contained.

It was warm, but only just.

"Yes," he said. "There is a little warmth left."

"If there is warmth left, there is life," Mag said, her voice fading in and out so that Loth had to strain to hear her. "It must be returned to Cornelia's body. It is my, our, only hope."

"How? How can I put it back inside?" Loth's voice broke in horror.

"The baby is lost for this time; poor Cornelia, I had tried to tell her. We can do no more for the baby. But Cornelia we must save. Tear the baby from the womb, Loth, my son, and then take the womb in your hand and slide it back inside Cornelia. You must do this."

Appalled, Loth stared at the apparition. Even now it faded, almost gone, and Loth knew that if he didn't act *now*, then not only Cornelia but Mag would be lost as well.

Hauling himself into an upright sitting position, carefully balancing his weight on his dead hips and legs, Loth put both his hands about the solidness of womb and baby. "Tear her out?" he said. "*Tear* her out? I will destroy the womb if I do that."

"What can be torn can be mended. *Do it!*"

Taking a deep breath, and closing his eyes even though he couldn't see what he was doing anyway, Loth dug his fingernails into the walls of Cornelia's womb, and began to tear.

It was brutal, horrible work. The womb was strong, banded with muscles that not only bore the weight of Cornelia's child-baby, but had the strength to then push that baby out when it was time for it to be born. Loth had to use every ounce of strength he had in his arm and shoulder muscles, and the feel of his fingers tearing deeper and deeper into the smooth muscles of the womb made him retch, once so violently that he had to momentarily stop what he was doing.

But in the end it was done, and he had made an opening large enough to pull the baby through into his hands.

"Is there nothing we can do—"

"There is nothing we can do to save the baby," Mag said, now barely visible, "but everything we can do to save Cornelia and this land. Put it back! Now!"

Loth laid the limp baby gently to one side, his heart breaking for the loss of its life, then collected the now-flaccid weight of the womb in his hand. He paused, his face muscles clenched against what he had to do, then pushed the mass back inside Cornelia's body. He pushed hard, poking at the mass with insistent fingers, but the womb seemed intent on bulging back out again every time he thought he'd managed to push it just that little bit farther inside Cornelia.

Eventually, his eyes now screwed shut, he took the womb in his fist and, murmuring prayers against darkness and hurt, thrust the horrid mess as deep inside Cornelia's body as he could.

He was glad she was insensible (*dead*) for he knew that had she been conscious, then he would not have been able to do it.

But eventually it *was* done, and the lips of Cornelia's torn vulva closed in upon themselves again.

Loth pulled his trembling hand away from Cornelia's body, and held it to his chest.

He opened his eyes again, and stared at Mag's apparition. For a moment it flared strongly, and Mag smiled. "Thank you!" she whispered.

Then, in a voice that strengthened even as the apparition faded back to nothingness, Mag said, "Genvissa must be stopped, Loth, stopped until we have the strength to fight against her. Cornelia will know what to do. Poor Cornelia . . ."

There was a sense of great sadness, then Mag vanished, and before Loth even had time to move, the door to the house opened, and Erith and Tuenna, Cador and Hoel directly behind them, walked in.

"By Mag herself!" Erith breathed as one of her sons held up a lamp. *"What has happened?"*

SHE'D BEEN WOKEN WITH A DEEP DREAD PRE-monition of death, Erith explained as her sons first lifted Cornelia to her bed, then Loth back to his.

She'd come as soon as she could, and in explaining this, Loth realized that the events that had seen Cornelia wake with her first pain to that moment when he'd forced her torn womb back inside her body had taken only the shortest spaces of time.

Genvissa's magic had been potent, indeed.

But then, so had Mag's. Loth had not realized that the goddess had retained enough power to do what she had . . .

and it made him further realize just *why* Cornelia was so important.

Cornelia did not simply hold Mag in her womb in the accepted sense that all Llangarlian women understood it—that she held a tiny piece of Mag's power in her womb—but she literally held *Mag* within her womb.

No wonder Genvissa so feared Cornelia.

Cornelia was her nemesis. She carried within her the single power that might finally defeat Genvissa and the Game.

Loth lay back on his bed, accepting Cador's ministrations in washing his body free of Cornelia's blood, and listened to Erith and Tuenna fussing over Cornelia's body across the way. The way forward was clear to him now. It was frightening, not only in the darkness of the path they would all have to tread, but in the length of that path and in the horrors he suspected they would all endure along the way.

He began to laugh, weakly, and more from fright and dismay at the thought of the road ahead of them than out of any sense of mirth, keeping it up until finally Erith snapped at him to stop.

"Has Cornelia come back to life yet?" he said, sobering.

"Come *back* to life?" Erith said. "She is bitterly torn, Loth, but she still clings to life. Now be quiet, for Tuenna and I have much work that needs to be done before morning."

"Nay," Loth whispered so that no one else heard him. "I think the work will take much, much longer than this night, Mother Erith. Much longer."

Chapter Ten

ERITH CAME TO SIT ON LOTH'S BED IN THE hour after dawn. Her face was wan, the delicate skin under her eyes a translucent blue with weariness.

"Cornelia should be dead," she said. "Why is she not dead, Loth?"

He said nothing, but his eyes glinted.

"When first I attended her," Erith continued, "when Cador and Hoel lifted her to her bed, I saw that pieces—*pieces*, Loth—of her womb bulged from her body. I did what I could, thinking that fever and death would inevitably take her within the next few days. Yet just now, when I checked, I find that her womb has moved back to its normal place within her belly *and* it is apparently whole. All her bleeding has stopped, her tears have fused, her skin is cool and dry."

"She *was* dead," Loth said. "Genvissa's darkness had torn both her child and her womb from her. Cornelia had bled to death before you arrived."

He paused, and Erith waited.

"Mag came—"

Erith's eyes widened, and she drew in a shocked breath and held it.

"—sick and tired and barely visible, and told me to push Cornelia's womb back within her. She said it was her and our only hope."

Erith frowned. "Why?"

Loth laughed, soft and somehow mirthless. "Can't you see what Mag has done, Erith? How Mag has avoided Genvissa?"

Again Erith's eyes widened, but now with understanding.

"Mag is in Cornelia's womb, Erith. Mag herself *lives* in Cornelia's womb. It is where she hides from Genvissa."

Erith stared at Loth, then turned to look at Cornelia. It made sense, but . . . "But . . ."

"What can we do?"

Erith nodded, and Loth's head fell back on the pillow. "We give Mag the time she needs to regain her strength, Erith."

"And she can do that in time to prevent Genvissa and Brutus completing the Game?"

"No."

"But—"

"What Genvissa and her five Darkwitch foremothers have done, Erith, cannot be undone in a few weeks. Nor in a single lifetime."

Erith shuddered, horrified at the implications of what Loth had said.

"What will we do?" she whispered. "How can we survive that long?"

"We must," Loth said, simply.

LATER THAT DAY, WHEN CORNELIA HAD WOKEN and eaten a little, Loth asked Hoel to carry him over to Cornelia's bed, and set him on its edge. Balancing himself with his arms, Loth nodded at Erith, who brought over a small, blanket-wrapped bundle and placed it on Cornelia's abdomen.

"Your daughter," Loth said softly.

Cornelia lifted her hand, hesitated, then slowly unfolded the blankets.

Underneath them lay the body of a tiny, perfectly formed baby girl.

Cornelia gently rested a hand on the girl's cold body. She shivered, and tears slid from her eyes.

"Genvissa did this," Loth whispered. "Genvissa did this to you last night. She tore the baby from you and killed it in the doing. Genvissa did this to you and to your daughter."

The tears trickled down Cornelia's face. "I know, Loth," she whispered. "I know."

"Cornelia, you have to—"

She lifted a hand to his mouth. "I *know*, Loth. You do not have to persuade me. Not anymore. I have seen what lies ahead."

There was a long silence. Loth bowed his head, then pressed Cornelia's hand more firmly against his mouth and kissed it before he let it go.

"I need to do something," Cornelia said eventually. "After all the death I have caused—"

"You have caused *no* death! You have only been the receptacle for other people's guilts!"

"After all the deaths I have caused," Cornelia said again, her voice very weary, "all I can do now is help. Mag grant me the strength I need."

Loth felt tears sting his eyes, and balancing himself carefully on his hands, he leaned down and kissed Cornelia softly on the mouth.

"You *are* Llangarlia," he said, very soft, his lips still touching hers. "You *are* this land. There is a winter ahead such as I think we cannot imagine, but remember that spring always follows winter. And remember that whatever the deceitful promises of this false spring that Genvissa and Brutus have given us, *you* will be the one to bring this land back into sunlight again, Cornelia. *You*."

"Mag said to me," she said, "that it would be many years, and many tears, but that it would happen."

"It will happen," Loth said, now almost unable to speak through his tears. "It *will* happen."

"So many years," Cornelia whispered, then raised her hand to Loth's face, and laid her palm against his cheek.

Chapter Eleven

SEVEN WEEKS PASSED. SPRING PASSED INTO summer, and the skies passed from clouded to open and blue and warm. The sheep and cattle and goats dropped their young, and all were born healthy. A score of women within the Llangarlian and Trojan camps also gave birth, and mothers and infants grew hearty and strong. The crops in the fields and the fruits of the trees and vines waxed fat and hearty: this year's harvest would be the best in a generation.

On the northern bank of the Llan the walls grew to their full height, the gates for the main entrance to the city were built and hung, although not closed, and the preparations for the final dance of the Game neared completion.

Genvissa's belly swelled toward her daughter's birth, and the Mistress of the Labyrinth spent much time in laughter and joy as she toured the city with her partner in power, Brutus.

Across the river, in her darkened, lonely house in Llanbank, Cornelia grew stronger. She made a complete physical recovery from her daughter's tragic birth, and an emotional one, too, for to many a person's amazement, Cornelia often seemed almost cheerful.

They did not know that late at night when Hoel and Cador slept, Loth and Cornelia talked quietly for many, many hours.

If there were dark circles under Cornelia's eyes, it was not through pain or loss, but through mere lack of sleep.

The weeks turned, the walls had their final cap stones put in place, Llangarlia basked in the warm summer days, and, finally, the eve of the summer solstice arrived, and it was time for the final dance of the Game.

The Day of the Flowers.

THE FINAL DANCE OF THE GAME, THE DANCE OF the Flowers, was held at dawn on the day of the summer solstice. The initial Dance of the Torches had been held at night, symbolic of the evil it was to trap. The Flower Dance was held at dawn, symbolizing the dawn of a new age of prosperity and happiness for the city the Game protected.

Evil would be trapped forever by the great sorcery of the flower gate that Brutus and Genvissa would erect at the entrance to the labyrinth.

In the hour before dawn people gathered on Og's Hill. The labyrinth still lay open to the sky—after this dance was done Brutus would cause a temple to be built over it, sealing it forever against those who would unravel the Game and ensuring the city's integrity against all attack.

The dancers were there, in one line this time, and still in alternating ranks of young men and women. Now, however, they bore flowers rather than torches. They wore the flowers in garlands about their heads, and carried them in their hands, and where they had once held a ribbon to bind them, now they held a chain made of flowers. They encircled the labyrinth in a complete circle, but at a distance of some three or four paces, leaving a wide pathway between their line and the outer ring of the labyrinth.

They stood still, awaiting the first light of the dawn.

Brutus and Genvissa, both robed in luminescent white linen, stood in the space inside the circle of dancers and outside the outer wall of the labyrinth. Each stood a quarter circle away from the entrance, one on either side of the labyrinth.

As before, there was an assembly of witnesses. Many of the Mothers were there, although not as many as had witnessed the initial dance as the need for as many hands as possible to bring in the summer harvest had kept most Mothers close to their homes.

Of those Mothers that were in attendance, Erith, Mais, and Ecub were the only ones whose faces looked as though they were there to witness a catastrophe rather than a triumph.

Hicetaon, Corineus, and Aethylla were there, together with Deimas and some two score of Trojan elders. They were joined by a similar number of Llangarlians, daughter-heirs of the Mothers in attendance, and some of the elder brothers and sons.

Cornelia was there, standing slightly apart from everyone else, as she had lived slightly apart from everyone else these past months. Her gown was drab, her long, free-flowing hair slightly unkempt, her face very thin and pale . . . but her eyes were calm and steady.

Loth, watching from ten or twelve paces away, thought that her weight loss and the slightly emaciated lines of her face suited her. She'd lost entirely her girlish demeanor and, while she could not compete with Genvissa's fertile beauty, still managed a dignity in her lingering sadness that Genvissa could not match.

Cornelia, finally, had grown up.

It would be enough. Cornelia, as Mag had said, knew what had to be done.

"Loth?" whispered Hoel at his side. Hoel had carried Loth from the house to this hill without so much as a puff of breathlessness. Now he leaned down anxiously to where Loth sat on a broad stool, blankets wrapped about him and under the stool so that he could the more easily maintain his balance.

Loth waved a hand dismissively. "I am well enough," he said. "Now, we should be quiet. Look, they are about to begin."

The first rays of dawn had lit the hill, and the circle of dancers began to move. They danced sunwise about the labyrinth with slow, sensual movements, dipping and swaying, and holding out their flowers as if in offering to the strengthening rays of the sun.

They sang as they danced, a soft, rhythmic hymn that was accompanied by the aching, haunting beat of several drummers sitting to one side.

Inside their circle, Genvissa and Brutus also began their dance.

If the outer circle of dancers was sensual, then Genvissa's and Brutus' movements were the height of sexuality without ever descending into coarseness or lechery. Genvissa was stunning. Heavily pregnant, she nevertheless still moved with a grace and a fluidity that even the most nubile of young virgins would have envied. Her arms extended full and round, her legs, where they emerged from the thigh-length slits in her robe, were long and deliciously limber. Her hair hung free, slipping with raven silky suppleness over her shoulders and back and arms, her face was serene and beautiful, her eyes closed as she danced to the rhythm of drums and song.

Brutus, likewise, danced with the full strength of his confidence and sexuality. His movements were stronger than Genvissa's, more powerful, but even so, nonetheless subtle and haunting. The armbands of his kingship glinted with every slow, deliberate movement of his limbs.

His eyes never left Genvissa's beautiful form.

The circle of dancers now increased the rhythm and tempo of their movements. As the circle passed toward the entrance to their labyrinth, its line dipped inward, and as each dancer passed the opening, she or he tossed down the flower they carried in a graceful arc.

The flowers, although apparently tossed without concern as to how they fell, did not pile up haphazardly at the labyrinth's entrance. Instead each one moved slightly as it fell, so that the gradually accumulating flowers formed a pattern, a weave, at the entrance.

Loth, watching, saw that it was the movements of Genvissa and Brutus that controlled the flowers.

They were weaving them into a gate, or a door, that

would permanently seal the labyrinth and the evil within it.

And Brutus to Genvissa, Loth realized. If they completed this dance, no one would ever best them.

He caught Cornelia looking at him, and she inclined her head, softly, sadly.

She took a step forward.

Loth grimaced, both fearing and embracing what approached.

Cornelia took another step forward, no one seeing her, their eyes fixed on Brutus and Genvissa, and her right hand crept toward her robe, toward the deep pocket that ran down its right seam.

Then, as Brutus and Genvissa moved to within two paces of each other, their hands outstretched to clasp over the strange weave of flowers that hovered over the entrance, Cornelia ran forward.

She ran lightly, as if she had suddenly cast aside all her doubts and cares.

She ran quickly, too quickly for anyone to react, even Brutus who could see her approaching behind Genvissa's back.

She ran surely, truly, and Genvissa never even knew she was there.

As she ran, Cornelia drew from the deep pockets of her robe a knife, wickedly sharp, with a curiously twisted bone handle.

"Mag!" she cried as, with one final, long stride, she slapped her free hand on Genvissa's shoulder, and as the woman's head whipped about, her eyes both wild and startled, with her knife hand Cornelia sank Asterion's malignant blade to its hilt into the base of Genvissa's neck.

EVERYTHING STOPPED: THE BREATHING OF THE watchers; the very movement of the dawn stars; the rising of the sun; the running of the deer in the forests above the Veiled Hills.

Then movement resumed. Cornelia, her face and eyes

relieved and anxious all at once, took a pace back, as if to avoid the sudden, vicious spurting of blood from Genvissa's neck. Genvissa, twisting as she sank to the ground so that her eyes, her wild, vicious eyes, never left Cornelia's face. Brutus, crying out, reaching for Genvissa.

The mysterious weave of flowers, collapsing into an untidy heap at the entrance of the labyrinth.

Loth, laughing, the sound soft but joyful.

People, moving.

But none moved as fast or as maliciously as did Genvissa.

She reached to the hilt protruding from the junction of her neck and shoulder and gripped it with both her hands.

"Witch!" she hissed at Cornelia, now standing two or three paces away.

Brutus was at Genvissa's side, distraught, no eyes for anyone but his stricken lover.

He grabbed at her shoulders, and she turned her face back to his.

Blood was now bubbling from her mouth, and her chest was heaving in her desperate effort to breathe.

"You should have killed her," she whispered. "See this knife? It is Asterion's knife, and *she* his tool. You should have killed her."

Before anyone could react or say any more, her hands tightened about the hilt of the knife, and with a shriek of pure fury she pulled it forth.

Blood spouted from the wound in her neck, and Brutus tried to stanch its flow with his fingers, as if his touch could somehow stave off her death.

"Save the Game," Genvissa said, her voice now horribly liquid. "Hide it, for Asterion is surely on his way." Then, with one frantic, desperate look into Brutus' eyes, she pushed him away with her remaining strength.

Brutus fell back, and Genvissa, stunningly, managed to struggle to her feet.

She swayed, her life blood pumping out of her, then caught her balance one final time.

Long enough to do what she needed.

"Think not to have bested me," she bubbled to Cornelia, her eyes sliding also to Loth. "Think not to have destroyed the Game. Not when *I* control it!"

And with that she tossed the knife high in the air.

Its blade was thick with blood, and as it flew so heavy globules of blood also flew, spattering Brutus, Cornelia, and as the knife descended, Loth also.

As the hot blood hit them, they flinched as if burned.

The knife fell to the ground with a clatter, sliding several paces until it came to a stop just before Corineus.

He had been staring, as appalled and shocked at everyone else, at the desperate trio of Brutus, Genvissa, and Cornelia.

Now his eyes slid down to the knife, paused, and then, very slowly, turned to Loth.

Genvissa swayed, and would have fallen had not Brutus risen and grabbed at her.

"Listen all you marked with blood," she said, her voice now heavy and barely intelligible, yet nevertheless deep with power and malevolence and with the measured beat of witch-speak. Her hands moved, slow, coarse with death, in a spell-weaving of such force and intent she did not take a single breath throughout its uttering. "Dance with me through deadly vale through birth again until the day .we stand afresh at this gate, the dance to end, the Game to play, the flowers to grow, the walls to hold 'gainst fear and flame. Dance with me, dance with me, never shake me free." Her voice was lowering, made horribly incoherent by the blood that filled her throat and lungs. "Dance with me, dance with me, never shake me free," she bubbled, and with a horrid, frightful grimace on her face, she fell to the ground and died.

Brutus moaned, bending to his knees and burying his face in her breasts, and then again against the mound of her belly.

Unremarked, Corineus leaned down and took Asterion's knife in his hand.

Brutus raised his face and stared at the circle of people

still standing at a distance; his features were obscured by Genvissa's blood.

"You *witch*!" he shouted hoarsely at Cornelia, laying Genvissa down gently and standing up. "True Hades' daughter! Do you know what you have done? *Do you know what you have done?*"

"Yes," she said.

"You willingly conspired with evil? With Asterion?"

"Yes." Cornelia's voice was very soft, and her eyes were deep with pain.

"At the cost of this?" Brutus flung a hand out, indicating the city and the land surrounding it. "The Game has not been completed, you have left the way open for Asterion! You have brought Catastrophe to this fair land!"

"No, I have saved it," she whispered, but he did not hear it.

"Have you no idea of what you have done, bitch?" It was all, now, that Brutus seemed able to say. "Genvissa is *dead*! *Dead!*"

"I'm sorry, Brutus. I know you loved her."

That was too much for him. He stepped forward and hit her a great blow across the jaw, snapping her head back and sending her tumbling to the ground with a cry of pain.

"What we had begun," Brutus screamed at her sprawled body, "we had to complete together. *Together!* Now? Now we—"

"Now?" Loth interrupted in a strong voice. "Nothing has changed much, Brutus, save the length of time between the first dance and the last. Did you not hear Genvissa? We'll all be back again someday, bound by Genvissa's hatred and Mag's need, bound in the struggle with and against her. At least, I can pray that when I come back my legs will be strong once more."

"Then start praying," said Corineus. He had Asterion's knife in his hand, and now he stepped forward and, as Cornelia had done to Genvissa, sank the blade into the juncture of Loth's neck and shoulder with a sickening crunch. "This I do for Blangan, your mother. I hope, you monstrous bastard, she hunts you down through all eternity."

Loth was staring at Corineus with eyes filled with pain and, curiously, joy. Blood bubbled out of his mouth, but like Genvissa, he made a last supreme effort to speak. "I will greet her in death with love, Corineus, as I should have done in life."

Corineus' face twisted, and he would have said more, but then Loth collapsed, and died, and Hoel shoved him to one side to bend over Loth's body, grieving.

Brutus stared at Corineus for a long moment, then he sank back to Genvissa and cradled her body in his arms. He looked across to Cornelia, struggling into a sitting position, wiping blood from her mouth. "Bitch daughter of Hades," he said in a voice flat with hatred. "I wish I had never seen your face."

ACROSS THE NARROW SEAS IN THE LONG HOUSE OF poiteran, the dark-haired baby boy lay waving his arms and legs before the fire.

He was overwhelmingly joyous in his youth and his strength and in the devastation of Genvissa's and Brutus' plans.

The Game was begun but not completed. It would sit and wait, wait for Genvissa's and Brutus' rebirths, wait for the Mistress of the Labyrinth and the Kingman to return and finish what they had commenced.

Return Genvissa and Brutus would—but not under their terms. Oh no . . . never that. He would seize control of their rebirth, he would dictate the terms under which Genvissa and Brutus drew breath again. A time and a place of Asterion's choosing, not their's. A Gathering of all those who had a place in the Game.

Of course, the Gathering would be a little more crowded than Asterion had anticipated. He hadn't expected Genvissa's dying curse, the scattering of her thick blood that would pull back with her and Brutus all that it had touched, but that was of no matter. Cornelia and Loth, and whoever else had been stained by Genvissa's blood, were of no consequence and had no role to play in what Asterion planned. They would merely be incidental, witnesses to Asterion's ultimate victory.

The baby lay, waving his limbs back and forth, admiring their sheen in the firelight. Now all he needed was to grow into adulthood, seize the kingship bands either from Brutus' aged limbs or the younger and less experienced ones of his son, arrange the Gathering at a time of his pleasing, twist Genvissa to his will (did she realize in death what she had forgot in life? That in restarting the Game she must become Asterion's creature entirely?) and take control of the Game, using its power to his will, and his will alone.

Dark, vicious joy surged through Asterion. In time, the power of the Game would be his and, through that, all of the world he cared to take.

Chapter Twelve

T HAT EVENING, WITH GENVISSA'S NOW-dried blood still caking his face, Brutus burned her on a great pyre atop Og's Hill.

When she was nothing but ashes, Brutus took those ashes, and buried them at the entrance to the labyrinth.

There he stood for many hours, entirely still, grieving, feeling such loss that he thought he could not bear it.

Then, in that still, dark hour before dawn, Brutus raised his head and looked east towards the Narrow Seas.

Two or three days' journey, nothing more, and there sat Asterion. Waiting. Evil personified. A baby of no more than a few months old who had infinite patience and infinite time on his side.

There was little he could do, but what he could, Brutus

did. He took from his limbs the golden Kingman bands, for if Asterion was going to seize the Game, he would need these. Then, using a combination of his power and that of the Game's, Brutus cloaked his actions against Asterion and buried the bands at strategic points within and about Troia Nova, murmuring incantations as he did so.

There. Let Asterion find those, if he could. Amid all his grief and his anger, Brutus found a dull satisfaction in knowing that Asterion would have never expected him to relinquish the kingship bands in order to hide them.

Gods, *he'd* never expected to voluntarily take those golden bands from his limbs, either.

When he was done, and the bands hidden away and protected as best he could manage, Brutus raised his head and looked about him as the first of dawn's light stained the sky. His beautiful city, Troia Nova, would not last for many years beyond his death. Asterion would destroy it in his desperation for the bands . . . but better that than allow Asterion the bands themselves.

"Damn you," he whispered, thinking of Cornelia, rather than of Asterion.

Then he roused himself, and dampened both his grief and his anger, and went in search of his engineers, for there was one more thing he could do to ensure that when he and Genvissa were reborn, they would be able to complete the Game.

He needed to keep the labyrinth safe from Asterion.

WITHIN THE WEEK CONSTRUCTION BEGAN ON A magnificent temple on Og's Hill. Its beautiful stone flooring completely covered the labyrinth, and to its walls Brutus tied the concealment magic of the kingship bands; once it was fully constructed then the magic of the labyrinth would combine with the magic of the bands (*the labyrinth would continue to listen to the instructions of its Kingman*) and would turn Asterion's eye from the site. He would know the labyrinth existed, but he would never be able to find it.

Not without the kingship bands. It was the best he could do to keep the labyrinth safe until he and Genvissa, returned, could retrieve the Kingman bands and once again raise the magic of the labyrinth.

He hoped.

Once the temple was completed, Brutus dedicated it to Artemis in honor of Genvissa.

He thought she would have laughed at that.

It was all he lived for now, to hear Genvissa's laugh again . . . and to hear it, he would need to die.

Until then, there was only revenge.

Chapter Thirteen

TWENTY-SEVEN YEARS LATER

Cornelia Speaks

E TOOK ME BACK TO WIFE, AS UNBELIEVABLE as that sounds, although it took more than three years (three years I spent in confinement, never allowed to see the sun, nor feel the soft breath of Llangarlia on my face), and even though in the rest of our lives together he never said a word to me. He ordered me to his empty palace from that cold prison, demanded my presence in his bed, and thought there to punish me with his coldness and hatred. He believed to torture me with his lack of love, with his constant remembrance of Genvissa, with his constant sure hope of meeting and loving her again in that future life to which she had damned us all.

When the dance and the Game would be completed.

Although we could wash the redness of her blood from our skin, its stain never left our souls. Brutus and I might have left Og's Hill that dreadful day still breathing, but we were in many ways walking corpses, waiting only for death, and the battle to be renewed in a later life.

The years passed, cold and lifeless. The city grew, as yet unsoured by the incompletion of the Game. Brutus continued as its king (no longer Kingman, for his golden bands had mysteriously disappeared), apparently joyous and content in his power and the stunning beauty of Troia Nova, inwardly cold and dying, yearning and angry, using the years left to him in this life only to punish me.

We had two more sons. Two years after Brutus had commanded me back to his bed I discovered myself again with child. I could not believe it for several months, until the hard swelling of my belly left me in no doubt, for I thought my womb had been entirely destroyed when Genvissa had murdered my daughter.

But then I had Mag, didn't I. I smiled, and put a hand over my womb.

She lived there still, sad, sorrowing as much as me, but with eyes for the future, and the struggles that lay before us.

Brutus considered my unexpected pregnancy a triumph, a further mark of his conquest of my spirit, and when another son followed two years after that, he could hardly contain his malicious glee.

I could not love either child very much. I did not hate them, nor resent them, but rather I regarded them with nothing but indifference. Besides, as sons, and as happened with Achates, they were absorbed completely into Brutus' world, removed from mine almost as soon as they were born, for Brutus would not allow me to suckle them.

"I shall not have them imbibe her hate and malevolence," he remarked to the midwives who attended me. "Take them from her as soon as they leave the womb, for I will have my sons have no dealings with the witch that bore them."

Oh, to call me a witch, when it was his sorceress lover who had set out on the path of destruction.

He had other children, daughters as well as sons, with women he took as concubines. Their laughter rang up and down the corridors of the palace, their every footstep and joyful shout a stab wound in my heart.

I missed my daughter, my beloved daughter, with every beat of my heart and with every breath I drew for so long as I lived. She had been my only hope for love.

The *only* hope . . . in this life, at least. Twenty-seven years after that dreadful day, Brutus lay dying on his bed as a cancer ate out his throat. He had lived out his time, and none were truly sad, save, I think, for me. I still loved him, in a sad, terrible way, and I sorrowed for him, and for me, and for Coel and Loth and all that might have been.

Achates would take Brutus' place as king, his younger brothers supporting him. He knew nothing of the Game. Brutus had told him nothing, had taught him nothing, remarking to the air one morning as he rose from our cold, hateful bed (he would not speak to me, but he was much given to speaking to the air as if it were a beloved companion) that there was little point. There was no Mistress of the Labyrinth, no hope of completing the Game save when Genvissa's magic (her malevolence, more like) could pull us all together again to finish what I had interrupted.

"My son will be the lesser man," he said, fastening his belt and striding from the chamber, "for the evil that walks as his mother."

And yet still I could not hate him. I cannot truly say why, given the cruelty with which he treated me, but still I could not find it in myself to revile him. I often recalled that day we'd stood above the hill behind the Altars of the Philistines, and the love that had almost blossomed then. I remember how he had bent his face to mine, his hair blowing about me like a swarm of wild bees, his mouth and tongue tracing lines of desire across my flesh . . . and yet never laying that warm, wonderful mouth to mine. Teasing me with its closeness, its wantonness, but never laying it against mine.

Never had he laid his mouth against mine.

Apart from my daughter's death, this was the greatest regret of my life—that I had been so filled with folly and pride to swear before him on our wedding night when all vows and words were binding that I would never allow his mouth to touch mine.

What would have changed had I allowed him that? What folly and murder and madness would have been avoided had I allowed him to kiss me? Would we have been real lovers before we ever set foot in Llangarlia, too close even for Genvissa's ambition and magic to tear us apart . . . or was this only wishful thinking, had she sunk her claws into him long before we ever reached Llangarlia's shores? When I had wasted so much time in childish hatred of Brutus, had she been even then comforting him, tempting him, offering him a woman, where I had offered him only a girl?

When Brutus lay dying, he called out for Genvissa.

I knew she lurked just the other side of death's door, waiting for him. I had no doubt whatsoever that my husband sank the quicker into death in his haste to meet her.

When he did die, drawing his last rattling breath, I cried for all that could have been. I bent down to him, saddened beyond reason, and laid my mouth on his.

But his lips were cold and stiff, and all that issued from his mouth was the stink of death.

And, as my sons (Brutus' sons, really, they had never been *mine*) gathered about the bed, and the court pressed close, paying their final respects, I rose from the bed and backed away, walking from the room, walking to that small chamber where I spent my days sewing and listening to the gossip of Brutus' concubines.

There, in a box hidden under layers of colorful linen thread, was the knife with which I had murdered Genvissa.

Asterion's dagger. Oh, yes, I knew who it belonged to, and I knew of the dark alliance between him and Mag. I also knew what Mag had planned for that alliance.

It made me weep, knowing what lay ahead.

I lifted the knife from its hiding place, the bright threads tumbling about my feet.

"Brutus," I said on a sob, and desolate, wretched, more lonely than I think anyone has ever been or will ever be, I put the knife to my throat in that same place where I had sunk it into Genvissa's neck, and thrust it through my skin and flesh with all the strength I could muster.

The pain . . . the pain was dreadful and yet, somehow, merciful . . .

Chapter Fourteen

THEY TOOK THEM, THE WASHED AND CARE-fully bundled corpses of Brutus and his hated wife Cornelia, to the well that sunk deep into the White Mount from the basements of the palace. There they were lowered, and placed into a chamber that had been hollowed out in the heart of the mound.

Their mourners thought that the gods would take Brutus and Cornelia into their care, but instead they were taken by the Troy Game, and it was not into care at all. Drawn through death, trapped by Genvissa's curse and the desperateness of love and ambition and the need of a great city both trapped and blessed by the enchantment that had birthed it, the Game played on.

SIX MONTHS LATER A MAN LED AN INVASION force across the Narrow Seas. He stood in the prow of the ship, uncaring of the sea spray that drenched him, staring at the faint smudge of the white cliffs in the distance before him.

Naked, and daubed with intricate swirling patterns made with blue clay, he was a young man of uncommon dark beauty, and a man who radiated strength and power and purpose.

In the belly of his ship, and in the scores of ships that

surged in his wake, crouched thousands of weaponed men who would lay down their lives for him without an instant's hesitation.

Their king. Goffar's son, Amorian.

Asterion reborn.

THEY ATTACKED TROIA NOVA WITHIN TWO DAYS OF landing on Llangarlia's shores.

Achates and his brothers put up a brave defense, for Brutus had warned them that such attack was likely, but nothing had prepared them for the viciousness and madness of the Poiteran attack.

These crazed, naked, blue-daubed warriors feared nothing, and it was as if they were protected by some dark enchantment, for whenever a Trojan or Llangarlian sword aimed directly for Poiteran flesh, something turned it away at the last moment, and instead it was the Poiteran blades that sank successfully into their destination.

The Poiterans initially attacked the main western gate, and Achates concentrated his defenses there, but unbeknown to him Amorian knew of the low, hidden arch in the northern wall of the city which allowed the River Wal entry into Troia Nova. Through this arch Amorian led a band of some several hundred Poiterans, and they attacked Achates from behind, surprising him so greatly that it took only the work of an hour to open the gates of the city to the main Poiteran force.

The remnants of the Trojan and Llangarlian force fought their attackers for an entire day through the streets of Troia Nova, the Poiterans slowly driving Achates and his men back towards Brutus' palace atop the White Mount. In the evening, when the defenders were exhausted and the Poiterans, unbelievably, appeared as fresh as when they had first launched their attack, Amorian himself cornered Achates in Brutus' megaron.

He laughed in joy when he saw what Achates carried in his hand: the twisted bone-handled knife. A simple feint, a distracting scream, and the knife was back in Amorian's hand.

Amorian killed Achates with it, slowly, that he might feed from the power of Achates' life force seeping from his body.

And then Amorian raged, unbelieving, for when he cut away Achates' clothes, he saw that the man's limbs were bare.

Brutus was dead, Achates should wear the kingship bands! Where were they? Where were they?

What had Brutus done with them?

A shiver of fear ran through Amorian. How was it he hadn't known that Brutus had not passed on the bands to his son? Where had Brutus put them? Where?

Infuriated, blind with hatred, Amorian allowed his men free triumph through the city. The slaughter was terrible: infants were thrown to the flames or tossed from blade to blade amid Poiteran laughter; women were raped, the prettiest kept for later amusement, the older or the very young used eight or nine times before having their throats cut; men and boys were savaged, slowly and terribly, and left to die in gutters.

Amorian left the corpse of Achates and walked through the butchery. His mind was consumed with thoughts of the kingship bands, but his outward demeanor was that of the victor. His body glistened with sweat and blue clay and blood, his head was thrown back, eyes laughing, mouth screaming encouragement to his men. Sometimes he paused to take his turn with a woman, sometimes he delayed to murder a child, or its father, and drink of the blood that pumped from the death wound.

As Amorian walked, so evil followed unhindered in his footsteps.

When dawn came, Amorian began a systematic search for the golden bands of Troy. It surely would be no trouble to scry out their location, nor, come to it, that of the labyrinth.

Brutus did not have that much power, surely.

And yet the niggling memory that Brutus was powerful. Had Amorian not once thought of Brutus as a "fine adversary"?

Too fine an adversary, as it turned out. Once Amorian started searching, it did not take him long to realize that both the bands and the labyrinth had been disguised in such a cunning fashion that they repelled any enchantment he used to discover them. Every time he sent out his power it was reflected—*repulsed*—back to him. Where were they? By the gate to the city? Under the palace? On one of the hills enclosed by the city's walls? Where? Where? *Where?*

Nowhere that Amorian could discern.

And yet the golden bands, as the labyrinth, *were* here. Amorian could feel them in his gut . . . but whatever Brutus had done to disguise them had been so cunning that nothing Amorian could do could discover them.

Finally, enraged, Amorian screamed at his men to destroy the city, to raze it stone by stone, to tear it apart.

Then, surely, he would find the bands and the labyrinth.

They could not be far away.

But, over the next few weeks as his men carried out his will, and Troia Nova fell to the hands and muscles of the Poiterans and the darkcraft that Amorian used to speed their work, Amorian finally, grudgingly admitted to himself that Brutus had woven such an extraordinary disguising about both bands and labyrinth that he would not find them.

Not on his own.

It would have to wait until the Gathering, until both Genvissa and Brutus were reborn and cowering before him.

Then the blood would flow as it never had before . . .

"Well," Amorian said one morning as he walked over the rubble covering the most westerly hill within the city, "I admit you have outfoxed me for this moment. But this is a temporary reprieve only. When I bring you back, when I convene the Gathering, you shall grovel before me and you *will* tell me where you have hid the kingship bands and the labyrinth. You will. You *will*!"

He turned about, and surveyed the destruction about him.

The entire city was now nothing more than massive piles of masonry, stained here and there with blood, softened elsewhere with the thin smoke of the fires that still burned in buried chambers under the rubble.

Over all hung the stench of well-rotted corpses.

"No one will ever be safe," he whispered, "not until I have those bands."

Epilogue

London's streets were cold and bitter, a mortar and brick echo of Jack Skelton's heart. He strode towards St. Paul's Underground station, a small, disinterested part of his mind hoping there would still be a late train to get him back to Bentley's house.

Mostly, however, he thought of Cornelia and of the Game. How he'd betrayed both of them, one way or the other. How he'd allowed his stupidity and his pride to dictate his actions when he should have listened to his reason and to his heart.

He reached the station, and saw that it was closed. He would have to find a cab to take him back to Highbury.

Skelton turned back to the street. He crossed his arms, as if against the cold, but his hands moved to his biceps as if he sought those ancient golden bands that had once adorned them.

Asterion had four of them. The other two . . .

"Cornelia," Skelton whispered, "where are you?"

"Gone!" whispered Asterion, rising out of the shadows behind Skelton. "Gone!"

Glossary

ACHATES: first-born son of CORNELIA and BRUTUS.

ACHERON, RIVER: a river of the western coast of Greece, the Acheron rises from HADES' Underworld, then flows underground for many miles, emptying into the IONIAN SEA close to the city of MESOPOTAMA.

AEGEAN SEA: the sea that lies between the eastern coast of Greece and the western coast of present-day Turkey (ancient ANATOLIA).

AEGEAN WORLD, the: a term that refers to the ancient lands and civilizations grouped about the AEGEAN SEA; principally the Greek (or MYCENAEAN) civilization, the Cretan (MINOAN) civilization, and the Trojan civilization.

AENEAS: a hero of the Trojan war against the Greeks and beloved of the gods, Aeneas was the son of a goddess, APHRODITE, and a mortal man, Anchises. Aeneas fled the destruction of TROY to Alba on the River Tiber in Italy. He is the great-grandfather of BRUTUS. Aeneas is dead at the time of *Hades' Daughter*.

AERNE: the GORMAGOG (living representative of the stag-god OG) of LLANGARLIA. His son by BLANGAN is LOTH. With GENVISSA he has three daughters.

AETHYLLA: a Trojan woman from MELOTAPA, companion to CORNELIA.

ALBION: an ancient name for the main island in the British Islands.

ALDROS: captain of BRUTUS' warship.

AMORIAN: son of GOFFAR and king of POITERAN.

ANATOLIA: now known as Turkey. On its west coast stood TROY, as well as many other magnificent cities.

ANDRON: the dining room of a Greek house. Generally the room where men gathered to talk.

ANTIGONUS: brother of PANDRASUS, father of MELANTHUS, Peleus, and Andronus.

APHRODITE: goddess of love, mother of AENEAS and great-great-grandmother of BRUTUS.

ARIADNE: Mistress (or High Priestess) of the LABYRINTH on Crete. Ariadne is the daughter of King Minos and half sister to the Minotaur ASTERION. Her lover is THESEUS, and her sister is Phaedre.

ARIADNE'S DANCING FLOOR: the labyrinth as laid out in a pattern in a stone dancing floor. See also LABYRINTH.

ARTEMIS: Greek virgin goddess of the moon and of the hunt, sister to Apollo.

ASSARACUS: a Dorian Greek of the city of MELOTAPA. Born of a Trojan mother, Assaracus is allied with BRUTUS.

ASTERION: the name of the Minotaur at the heart of the Cretan labyrinth, son of King Minos' wife and a white bull, and thus half brother to ARIADNE, the MISTRESS OF THE LABYRINTH.

AUROCHS: massive prehistoric cattle.

BLADUD: a Llangarlian warrior.

BLANGAN: daughter of HERRON and AERNE, sister to GENVISSA, wife to CORINEUS, mother of LOTH.

BRUTUS: son of SILVIUS, great-grandson of AENEAS. An exiled Trojan.

CADOR: son of ERITH.

CATASTROPHE, the: In the late Bronze Age the cities and civilizations of the MINOANS (CRETE), the MYCENAEANS (Greece), and the Anatolians (Turkey) suffered a catastrophe so severe it destroyed most cities and ended higher civilization: for instance, Greeks lost the art of reading and writing for almost a thousand years. Some of the cities destroyed during the Catastrophe were TROY (the most famous of all), Knossos, Tarsus, Pylos, Iolkos, Thebes, Midea, and Nichoria. Although there are many theories, no one truly knows what precipitated this Catastrophe.

COEL: a Llangarlian warrior and nobleman, son of ERITH.

CORINEUS: a Trojan of the line of Locrinus, husband of BLANGAN, the leading citizen of the city of LOCRINIA.

CORNELIA: a Dorian Greek woman, daughter of PANDRA-SUS, princess of MELOTAPA.

CRETE: large island in the central eastern Mediterranean. It is the center of the MINOAN civilization and the home of the LABYRINTH, and its capital is Knossos.

DANCE OF THE FLOWERS: one of two dances involved in creating the GAME, the Dance of the Flowers is performed at the end of the ceremonies and enchantments used to establish the GAME.

DANCE OF THE TORCHES: the magical dance used to commence the GAME.

DEIMAS: leader of the Trojans enslaved in MELOTAPA.

ECUB: MOTHER of a village near MAG'S DANCE.

ERITH: mother of COEL, and MOTHER of a LLANGARLIAN House.

GAME, the: In the ancient world most major cities were protected by a mysterious rite called the Game. The Game was based on the secrets of the LABYRINTH, originating within the Cretan labyrinth before its secrets were shared among the Bronze Age Greek and Anatolian worlds. The Game is controlled by a KINGMAN and the MISTRESS OF THE LABYRINTH. For each city there is a slightly different version of the Game, thus the Game used to protect Troy is known as the Troy Game. The Mistress of the Labyrinth and the Kingman work the magic of the labyrinth mainly through the performance of two dances, the DANCE OF THE TORCHES and the DANCE OF THE FLOWERS.

GENVISSA: daughter of HERRON, and the current MAGALLAN (female representative of the goddess MAG) of LLANGAR-LIA.

GEOFFREY OF MONMOUTH: the twelfth-century chronicler who detailed the Trojan founding of London.

GOFFAR: king of POITERAN.

GORMAGOG: living representative of the god OG, called the

Giant of Madog. The current Gormagog is Aerne father of LOTH.

HADES: god of the Underworld.

HERA: wife of Zeus, queen of Olympus, first among all the goddesses, and patron of CORNELIA, princess of MELO-TAPA.

HERNE, WALTER "BRAINS": deputy headmaster at Maze Hill School, Greenwich, just to the east of London.

HERRON: GENVISSA'S and BLANGAN'S mother, and a former MAGALLAN.

HICETAON: one of BRUTUS' commanders.

HOEL: son of ERITH.

IDAEUS: one of BRUTUS' commanders.

JAGO: a young Llangarlian warrior.

KINGMAN, the: Kingmen were the princes of the ancient world who were trained in the skills of the GAME. They knew the dances and the paths of the LABYRINTH, and were trained to combat whatever it was they encountered in the heart of the LABYRINTH.

LABYRINTH: The symbol of the labyrinth occurs throughout the ancient world, never more so than in the MINOAN civilization of CRETE where it was deeply associated with both political and religious cultures. The ancient labyrinth is a unicursal labyrinth, not a maze. There is a single pathway leading into the heart, with no dead ends or false turns. When the labyrinth is laid out as a stone pattern in a floor it is called (and used as) a "dancing floor," thus in *Hades' Daughter* the labyrinth on Og's Hill (see THE VEILED HILLS) is occasionally referred to as ARIADNE'S DANCING FLOOR.

LEVANT, the: the Holy Lands, specifically what is now Israel and Lebanon.

LLAN: the great river of LLANGARLIA. Now called the Thames.

LLANA: the eldest of GENVISSA'S daughters.

LLANBANK: the market town on the eastern shores of the LLAN across the river from Thorney Island.

LLANGARLIA: the prosperous country in the southeast of

what is now England, encompassing the southeastern counties and centered on the Thames (or LLAN) Valley. It is a matriarchal society, governed by the MOTHERS of each House, or tribe. Llangarlia is a pre-Celtic society; the Celts did not begin to infiltrate the British Islands until some six hundred years after the events of *Hades' Daughter*.

LOCRINIA: a Trojan city on the west coast of the Iberian Peninsula.

LOTH: sometimes called the Llangarlian Bull, son of AERNE and BLANGAN, heir to the title and position of GORMA-GOG.

MAG: The great mother goddess worshiped by the Llangarlians, Mag is particularly associated with the waters, with birth, and with growth. She is the mate of OG, the forest stag-god of LLANGARLIA. Mag's High Priestess among the Llangarlians is known as the MAGALLAN.

MAGALLAN: the High Priestess of MAG in LLANGARLIA. The current MagaLlan is GENVISSA.

MAG'S DANCE: Stonehenge in Wiltshire.

MAIS: MOTHER of a Llangarlian House, allied with LOTH.

MAURITANIA: a land in North Africa, close to what is now Morocco.

MAZA: a porridge made of flour, honey, salt, oil, and water. One of the staples of Bronze Age Greek diet.

MEGARON: the throne room of a Greek palace.

MELANTHUS: son of ANTIGONUS, nephew of PANDRASUS. Melanthus is the erstwhile lover of CORNELIA.

MEMBRICUS: companion and former tutor to BRUTUS, Membricus is a visionary and a seer.

MERIAM: a midwife on the island of NAXOS.

MESOPOTAMA: Dorian city on the River ACHERON on the west coast of Greece. Ruled by PANDRASUS.

MINOANS: people of the Minoan culture on CRETE, centering on the city of Knossos.

MISTRESS OF THE LABYRINTH: the High Priestess of the LABYRINTH, keeper of its secrets.

MOTHERS, the: LLANGARLIA is a matriarchal society. Each

tribe, or House, is led by its senior Mother. Each year at the time of the SLAUGHTER FESTIVAL, the Mothers attend an Assembly on Tot Hill within the VEILED HILLS to discuss any problems that affect Llangarlian society.

MYCENAEANS: Greeks of the proud Mycenaean culture belonging to the east coast and Peloponnese of the Greek mainland. The culture centered on the city of Mycenae and reached its height just before the CATASTROPHE of the late Bronze Age.

NAXOS: island 175 km (108 miles) to the north of CRETE in the eastern Mediterranean, and 40 km (25 miles) to the north of THERA.

NICHORIA: a city on the western coast of the Greek Peloponnese. It is ruled by PODARCES.

OENO: a Trojan woman.

OG: the great forest stag-god of LLANGARLIA, mate of MAG. In later ages he was known as Cernunnos, later still as Herne, and in medieval times as the Green Man.

PANDRASUS: king of the Dorians in MELOTAPA. Father of CORNELIA.

PELOPAN: husband to AETHYLLA.

PERIOPIS: a Trojan woman.

PHILISTINES, ALTARS OF THE: two strange stone pillars on the coast of North Africa.

PILLARS OF HERCULES: now called the Straits of Gibraltar.

PODARCES: king of NICHORIA.

POITERAN: a kingdom in the west of France, led by GOFFAR.

SARPEDON: a counselor to PANDRASUS.

SILVIUS: father to BRUTUS. Silvius died in a hunting accident when, according to gossip, BRUTUS mistakenly shot an arrow into his father's eye.

SLAUGHTER FESTIVAL: the great autumn festival of LLANGARLIA. It is a trading and festive occasion, although it also marks the annual Assembly of MOTHERS on Tot Hill. The name derives from the fact that in premodern times most livestock was slaughtered in autumn to prepare for the coming winter.

STONE DANCES: circles of standing stones—stone henges.

TAVIA: nurse and companion to CORNELIA.

THERA: tiny volcanic island some 120 km (75 miles) north of CRETE (almost halfway between CRETE and NAXOS) that exploded in the late Bronze Age, devastating the AEGEAN WORLD by shock blast, tsunamis, acid rain, ash, and gases that obliterated the skies around the globe, and related earthquakes about the Aegean and eastern Mediterranean shorelines. The eruption on Thera was roughly four or five times the intensity of the eruption of Krakatoa in 1883.

THESEUS: son and heir of the Athenian king, he was sent as tribute and sacrifice to CRETE where he was to be fed to the Minotaur ASTERION. But Theseus, aided by his lover ARIADNE, managed to defeat the Minotaur and escape from Crete. Later in life he was the first lover of Helen, whose abduction precipitated the eventual destruction of TROY.

THYMBRAECEUS: father of ASSARACUS.

TOTNES: name of BRUTUS' nurse and also the name given to BRUTUS' first landing site on the River Dart in Britain.

TROIA NOVA: literally "New Troy."

TROY: the fabulous city of Troy sat on the western shores of ANATOLIA (modern-day Turkey). Paris, son of the Trojan king Priam, stole away Helen from her husband, Menelaus, king of Sparta, precipitating the Trojan war in which the city-states of Greece united against Troy. Although it survived a long Greek siege, Troy was eventually destroyed due to a combination of hubris, the betrayal of the gods, and Greek cunning. Those Trojans who survived the destruction scattered about the lands of the Mediterranean, either as refugees or slaves.

TUENNA: daughter of ERITH.

TURON: a porridge compounded of flour, cheese gratings, eggs, and honey. One of the staples of Bronze Age Greek diet.

VEILED HILLS, the: the six sacred hills of LLANGARLIA, clustered above the LLAN RIVER in the area now known as London. The six hills are: Tot Hill (where now stands

Westminster); the Llandin, the most sacred of the hills (now called Parliament Hill); Pen Hill; Og's Hill (Ludgate Hill); Mag's Hill (Cornhill); and the White Mount (Tower Hill). The hills are intersected by three small rivers that flow into the mighty LLAN: the Magyl (now called the Fleet), the Ty (now the Tyburn), and the Wal (now the Walbrook).

ZEUS: leader of the immortals, first among the Olympian gods.

Forthcoming from Sara Douglass
and Tor Books . . .

THRESHOLD

Now available in hardcover!

Turn the page for a preview

Chapter One

VILAND IS A COLD, BRUTAL PLACE, YET I grew there and loved it as much as it would allow. Cruel seas batter rocky harbours through winters that last a good nine months of the year, months, when all crowd about fires amid the cheerful belchings of onion and ale fumes, and tell endless stories of adventure at the end of the harpoon. In the brief flowering of summer, the Vilanders hurriedly eke out their living from the whales that throng the icy coastal waters, selling the great fish's meat, oil, hide and bones to any who care to pay for it. Not many, some years. Yet in those years when the whale sold well, my father gained enough in commissions to keep us through the leaner seasons.

But there wasn't much to spare, as we came to discover to our sorrow.

Despite the ice and the ever-threatening poverty, my father and I were happy, content. Until the day my father's thoughtlessness and poorly buried heartache matured into the sour fruit that destroyed us both.

Mam had died young, before I was two. Rather than hire a nursemaid, my father took me into his workshop, and my earliest memories are of the fascinating world encompassed by the shadowed spares beneath my father's work table. Here I played blithely all day amid the shavings of glass and globs of discarded enamel, scraping the bright shards into piles and sifting them through hands too small and fat to be of practical use to my father. The table protected me from the worst of the furnace heat and from most of the problems of the outside world, and when the workday was over my father lifted me into his strong arms and carried me back to our cold, motherless home.

Always I yearned for the morning, and the warmth of the workshop.

When I was five, and too curious to fit comfortably beneath the table, my father decided to teach me his craft. Along with the techniques of mixing, firing and working the glass, I had to learn the common trading tongue of nations, as well as several other languages. All craft workers needed to converse with those merchants who might bring them the one commission to keep starvation at bay for another month or two.

I was young and quick-witted, and I learned the languages and the craft easily. By the age of ten, my hands were slim and capable enough to take on some of the fine work my father increasingly found too difficult, and my tongue was sufficiently agile to chatter to the occasional merchant from Geshardi or Alaric who passed by the workshop. I did not mind spending my days at the work table, learning a trade, when I could have been imbibing the raucous street games of my contemporaries. My father and the glass formed the boundaries of the only world I needed, and if my father was more often silent than talkative, then I found all the conversation and company I desired in the shifting colours of the glass.

The glass told me many things.

When I was eighteen my father often left me working on the final engraving of a goblet or, more and more frequently, the finishing work for cage lace, while he wandered the streets in search of old friends with whom to pass an hour or two. At least, that's what I thought until the bailiffs came. I did not know that my father's long festering grief for my mother had found outlet in the quest for luck at fate. But luck deserted him as completely as my mother had. My thoughtless, loving father lost our freedom on the spin of a coin and the sorry futility of a fighting cock with a broken wing.

I was at the table in the workshop when they came.

The vase I had in my hands was the result of four

weeks' tireless work and it was at last approaching its final beauty. My father had fashioned the mould, mixed the glass, and added the deft flurries of base metals and gold which produced the exquisite marbled walls that were the mark of the master craftsman. Then he had sat over the kiln as the fires patiently birthed his creation. It was his finest effort for six months, and he could hardly bear to pass it over to me to cage.

But caging would produce a work guaranteed to feed us for the next year, and his hands could no longer be trusted with the delicate touch.

It was one of our best works. I had caged to create one of the Vilanders' favourite myths—Gorenfer escaping the maddened jungles of Bustian-Halle.

The workroom door burst in and I spun around on my stool, the vase in my hands.

My father stumbled in, followed by five men I knew by sight and reputation. Instantly, intuitively, I understood the reason for this ungracious entrance.

One of the debt-collectors shouted my name, his face red and sweaty, his hand outstretched and demanding.

Shocked, and frightened beyond any fear I'd experienced before, I dropped the vase—its death cry adding to the terror about me.

That vase could have saved us, it could have paid my father's debts, but I let it shatter on the floor.

After that I could blame my father for nothing. If he had temporarily impoverished us, then he had also created the beauty that would have saved us.

But I dropped it . . . and condemned us to slavery.

NEITHER MY FATHER'S ENTREATIES, NOR MY TEARS, could move these five hard-souled men. There were debts, and they must be paid. Now. Nothing in our poor house (save the once beautiful vase scattered in useless shards at my feet) could be sold to pay recompense—except us.

We were handed directly to the local slaver who dusted

us down, inspected us from head to toe, and stood back, considering.

I had learned my father's craft well. For that reason the slaver kept us together, even though, at nineteen and fair enough, I would have fetched a reasonable price hawked to some tired bureaucrat or lordling bored with his wife. So I was saved from the bed of some paunch-bellied magnate, and my father kept his tools and the last living reminder of his wife. After our initial tears and protests, we resigned ourselves to our fate. It was regrettable but not unknown; over past years I had seen three other craftsmen sell themselves and their families to escape starvation. We would still practise our craft, if to the dictates of a master rather than to the satisfactions of free choice.

And we would still be together.

WE DID NOT STAY IN VILAND LONG. THE SLAVER, Skarp-Hedin, decided we'd fetch the best price in the strange, hot realms to the south.

"They have fine sand a-plenty for you to melt," he said, "and the nobility to buy what you craft of it. You'll fetch five times what you will here in this sorry land."

My father bowed his head, but I stared indignantly at the slaver. "But Viland is our—"

"You *have* no home!" the man shouted. "And no country, save that of the market place!"

Within the day we were bundled into the belly of a whaler for cheap transport south. For six weeks we rolled and pitched in that loathsome cavern, my father clutching his tools, I retching over whatever stale food the crew provided us. We were chained, he and I, although where anyone thought we would escape to in the glassy grey waters of the northern seas I do not know, and the chains ate at our ankles until they festered and screamed. The pain drowned out the soft whisperings of the metal links.

Finally, gratefully, the whaler docked. My father and I sat in the hold, trying to ignore the bright pain of our ankles, listening to the muted sounds of a bustling port. Over the past ten days the weather had warmed until the interior of the hold sweltered day and night. The whale meat stank with putrefaction, and I wondered to what possible use it could now be put. After an hour the crew swarmed into the hold to begin the disagreeable task of forking the meat into cargo nets to be off-loaded. On the fourth load one of them remembered we were confined somewhere in the dim hold as well; he soon caused us to be netted along with the rotting meat, and we were unceremoniously swung ashore.

Outside the intense sunlight seared my eyes. I cried out in pain, and my father tried to comfort me, but his mumblings did nothing to ease my terror. I felt the net swing high in the air, and I almost vomited, clutching at the rough rope, trying to gain any handhold that might help save me should the net break. Beside me I heard the bag of tools rattle as my father clutched it closer to his chest.

The next instant there was a sickening jolt as the net landed on the wharf. I lost my grip, and my father and I slid down the pile of sweating whale meat to land in a tangle of chains and rope and greasy, rotting fish flesh on the splintery boards of the pier.

"*Kusl.* Is this what you have brought me, you godcursed whale-man? Look at them!" The man spoke in the common trading tongue of nations.

He was bending down, a robe of shimmering green weave drifting free and cool about him. His hand grasped the net and shook it free as men hurried to unhook the loading chains. Then he caught my upper arm and hauled me to my feet.

I stumbled, my ankle chains snagging amid the rope and fish.

The man breathed in sharply, then he helped my father to his feet.

"Strike these chains from their ankles. Now!" And men hurried to do his bidding.

I wept as those hateful metal bars and links fell free.

Our rescuer was a man of middle age, dark-haired and

ebony-eyed, with swarthy skin stretched tight over a strong-boned face. His robe was of good linen, loose-fitting and hanging unbelted to his sandalled feet. He looked clean and cool and very sure of himself. I had been none of those things for a long time.

He inspected my hands carefully, then those of my father.

"Well, at least your hands are undamaged, and that is all that counts." He caught my chin with his fingers. "And you have a pleasing face under that grime and stinking oil." Now his fingers lifted one of the lank strands of my hair. "Blond, I'll wager, to go with your blue eyes."

His voice was softer now, thoughtful, and I could see him sifting the possibilities in his mind. "Skarp-Hedin sent word that you work glass. Is that true?"

"I have been a master craftsman for over twenty years," my father said, "and my daughter has more talent than I." He hesitated. "None can mix the colours as I, nor carve the moulds or blow the glass. And my daughter cages as though blessed by the gods."

The man's eyes were very sharp now, and they swung back my way. "You are too young," he said.

"I have been working at my father's side since I was five," I replied. How much longer would he keep us standing in this frightful sun? "And caging since I was ten."

"Well," he said, "you have come from Skarp-Hedin, and I have never received anything but the best from him previously. I will trust him on this as well. See that cart?" He inclined his head to the side. "Then get in."

He turned and left us to clamber in.

As his driver slapped the mules into action, the man told us his name was Hadone, and he worked in occasional partnership with the Vilander slaver who'd sent us south. They would share the proceeds of our sale, but Hadone had no intention of presenting us to the market in our current state. From the wharf, we drove to quarters deep in the town—Adab, Hadone informed me as I peered over the rim of the cart, too unnerved to sit upright.

"And this is the realm of En-Dor." Again he ran his eyes over my face and hair as he twisted about on the seat next to the driver. "Although glassworkers sell well here, I wonder if I might get yet a better price for you in Ashdod."

My father noticed Hadone's tone and the direction of his eyes. "Skarp-Hedin said we'd be sold together. That's how we work. A team."

"Of course," Hadone said, swinging back to face the street before him. "That's how I intend to sell you. As a team."

My father and I exchanged a glance, then turned our eyes back to the strange sights around us.

The dirt-packed streets were crowded with men and women dressed much as Hadone was—in brightly coloured robes that swung loose to their feet. Many had lengths of fine white cloth wrapped about their heads, the tasselled ends drifting lazily about their shoulders.

We were surrounded by blocks of mud-brick shops and houses, plastered either in white or pale pink, with flat roofs and canvas awnings that hung out into the street and shaded those passing by.

Among all the people wound donkeys bearing loads on their backs or pulling carts like ours. An occasional rider on a finely boned horse, always grey, pushed through the crowds; both horse and rider were invariably richly draped with silks and ropes of jewels.

About all hung the dust of thousands of scuffling feet, and a rich, heady odour of spices and fragrance that did nothing to soothe my stomach.

It was so strange, so unlike what I'd known in Viland, and every minute the sun beat down with increasing fierceness. I crept as close to the walls of the cart as I could, trying to escape both the sun and the strangeness. Opposite me, my father huddled miserably about his sack of tools.

"We'll be there soon," Hadone said, and I closed my eyes and hid my face in my arms, almost undone by the kindness in his voice.

Within minutes we'd turned into a shaded side alley,

and then into a cool courtyard. I heard Hadone jump down from the cart, and I sat up, looking about. The spacious courtyard was bounded on two sides by what looked like Hadone's residence, and on the other two sides by stables, score houses and a slavery large enough for several dozen inmates. The buildings were all clean and in good repair, and the courtyard itself was paved and swept clean of any dung or dust.

Hadone's man—I never knew his name—helped us down from the cart, then Hadone handed us over to a man and a woman who escorted myself and my father to the separate men's and women's slave quarters.

I watched my father being led away with some nervousness, for I was loath to be parted from him, but I let the woman, Omarni, guide me to a cool room. There she bathed me, tended the festering sores about my ankles, and persuaded me to eat some fruits and drink some milk.

Despite my fears, I slept better that night than I had in weeks, and my sleep was dreamless.

For eight days we were left in peace while our sores closed over, our ankles thickened with scar tissue, and our faces plumped out from their gauntness. But on the evening of the ninth day Hadone sent for me.

His man escorted me to Hadone's residence, where he stood looking me up and down, and fingering my now clean and shining hair. "In a week or so I will take you and your father to market," he said, "and for the remaining nights you will spend an hour or two in my quarters. You will be sold for your talents at glass making, not for your virginity."

And so he proceeded to divest me of it.

He was vigorous and painful but not intentionally unkind and, to be frank, I had known that sooner or later rape would be an inevitability of my enslavement. Well, I should not have dropped that vase. For all pain, there comes pain repaid.

When it was done he sent me back to the slavery, and Omarni gave me a cup of a steaming thick herbal to drink.

"It will save your belly from swelling with child," she said practically, and I realised she must have served this brew to a score of slaves before me.

It was bitter, and it made my stomach churn, but I drank it gratefully. The last thing I wanted was to walk into a lifetime of servitude encumbered with the squalling brat of a slaver.

A WEEK LATER WE WERE TAKEN TO MARKET—I WITH a little more experience and a few more skills than I'd had when I landed amid the pile of stinking whale meat on the wharf.

Who would buy us? Would he be a kind man, or a harsh taskmaster? And, I wondered further, would he be a satisfied husband, or a man seeking diversion amid the trapped delights of his slavery?

Neither, as it turned out.

The market was crowded with vendors selling fruits, cloths, plate and lives. One corner was devoted exclusively to the trade in human flesh, and there Hadone directed us and three other men in he intended to sell this day. We were guarded, but only lightly. None of us had anywhere to run.

The guards took the three men directly to the open slave lines, where prospective buyers could prod the merchandise and inspect their teeth, but Hadone took my father and me to a stall at the back of the lines.

There a tall and painfully thin man, as dark as Hadone, unravelled himself from a stool and bowed slightly. His eyes were as sharp as his face was thin, and I decided instantly that I did not like him.

Hadone returned the bow with far greater obeisance than he had been afforded. When he spoke, he kept his hands clasped over his heart and his eyes fixed on the dirt. "Kamish. May your sons win renown and your daughters rich husbands."

Kamish's thin mouth twisted cynically. "I have no children, Hadone. You know that."

"I was merely trying to be polite," Hadone said, finally rising, and I realised he did not like Kamish very much either.

"These are the two you wrote me about?"

"Indeed," Hadone said. "The man has won renown over many nations with his skill at mixing and moulding, and his daughter," he paused slightly, "has been trained well. Among her many skills, she can also cage."

"She cages?" The gleam in Kamish's eyes increased. "My masters—"

"Would surely pay well for the skills these two carry. I believe your masters are scouring all living lands for such as these."

"And she cages," Kamish repeated. I waited for the inevitable "She's too young", but it never came.

"Cages," he said yet again.

Hadone's mouth drooped in imitation woe. "And with such skills, Kamish, I regret that I must ask a price to match."

Kamish had given too much of his eagerness away, and his bargaining power was severely curtailed. Within minutes, as my father and I stood by while our lives were haggled away, Hadone had won a price for himself and Skarp-Hedin that would not only pay our debts but leave the two slavers rich men.

As Kamish bustled about, shouting for his men, Hadone turned to my father and myself. "I wish you well," he said, and his eyes met mine.

I was astounded to see a trace of regret there.

But then he jingled the coins in his purse, and the regret faded and he turned away.

I never saw him again.